HAIL THE CONQUERING HERO

By
Frank Yerby

THE FOXES OF HARROW

THE VIXENS

THE GOLDEN HAWK

PRIDE'S CASTLE

FLOODTIDE

A WOMAN CALLED FANCY

THE SARACEN BLADE

THE DEVIL'S LAUGHTER

BENTON'S ROW

THE TREASURE OF PLEASANT VALLEY

CAPTAIN REBEL

FAIROAKS

THE SERPENT AND THE STAFF

JARRETT'S JADE

GILLIAN

THE GARFIELD HONOR

GRIFFIN'S WAY

THE OLD GODS LAUGH

AN ODOR OF SANCTITY

GOAT SONG

JUDAS, MY BROTHER

SPEAK NOW

THE DAHOMEAN

THE GIRL FROM STORYVILLE

THE VOYAGE UNPLANNED

TOBIAS AND THE ANGEL

A ROSE FOR ANA MARÍA

HAIL THE CONQUERING HERO

A NOVEL BY *Frank Yerby*

The Dial Press ❧ *New York*

Published by
The Dial Press
1 Dag Hammarskjold Plaza
New York, New York 10017

Manufactured in the United States of America

First printing

Library of Congress Cataloging in Publication Data

Yerby, Frank, 1916–
Hail the conquering hero.

I. Title.
PZ3.Y415Hai [PS3547.E65]   E813'5'4   77-12530
ISBN 0-8037-3417-4

A Note
to the Reader

This novel is—more or less—a sequel to an earlier novel of the writer's called *The Old Gods Laugh*. It takes place in the same location, the imaginary, and hence entirely real, Caribbean Republica de Costa Verde, and the major characters of the first novel—or at least those who survived until the end of it!—reappear as minor characters in the second.

Its themes are human valor, the nature of love, and man's sickening inhumanity to man. As a subtheme of this last, the disquieting question of the use of torture as a routine method of police procedure and political indoctrination and/or repression is raised. The reader is hereby assured that in this regard—most unfortunately!—the writer has invented nothing. The methods of breaking the human spirit, of degrading people to a degree unheard of since the fall of the Third Reich, herein described, are in everyday use all over today's world, the most flagrant examples being the Empire of the so very charming Shah of Iran; in Africa, the White Republics of Southern Rhodesia and South Africa, and the Black Dictatorships of the Central African Republic, Uganda, and Equatorial Guinea; and in the Western Hemisphere, Chile, Equador, Brazil, and Argentina.

Beyond that the writer would like to add the cautionary note that the social mores, the psychological and sexual behavior patterns attributed to some of his characters, are characteristic of only a very small segment of the Latin American public, the great mass of Spanish-speaking people continuing—*¡A Dios gracias!*—to go their quiet, sober, devout, and timeless ways.

Frank Yerby
Madrid, Spain
January, 1977

HAIL THE CONQUERING HERO

CHAPTER

1

When the receptionist—not half bad, Jim Rush decided, as Washington receptionists go—ushered him into the Assistant Secretary's office, after a wait calculated to the second to put on record the Assistant Secretary's importance, Jim realized at once that he was in for trouble. He had spent time enough in the State Department by then—mostly as Vice Consul, and finally as Consul, in various Latin American countries—to have grown the necessary antennae in his ganglia, in his raw and bleeding (the qualifying adjectives were his ex-wife, Virginia's, not his own) nerve ends, to pick the signs out of thin air.

He saw the Assistant Secretary's fingers rise suddenly to toy with the knot of a tie just wide enough to be fashionable, with colors and a pattern sufficiently strident to announce that the Assistant Secretary wasn't old hat; caught the fleeting expression of pure, unalloyed dismay, quickly repressed, to be replaced by one of dignified severity, aristocratic *hauteur,* that crossed the Assistant Secretary's face as he weighed, measured, estimated his visitor's quality; and, as people usually did, got it all wrong.

Jim didn't say anything. He stood there, repressing the efforts of his admittedly oversensitive nerves to make him tremble. He was good at it by then. When you'd been posted to as many of the Western Hemisphere's most abysmal ratholes, at their absolutely worst moments, as he had, you soon learned at least the basic minima of self-control. He stood there quietly, achieving so convincing a counterfeit of perfect ease, that he won that particular round of the Diplomatic Corps' perpetual game of one-upmanship by a comfortable margin. The Assistant Secretary's hand shifted away from his tie, and patted a lock of his exquisitely coiffured, fashionably long, greying hair back into place.

Jim stood there, estimating what that haircut had cost the Assistant Secretary. And what it said about him.

'Twenty-five bucks a throw,' he decided, 'every time he visits his barber—correction! his hair stylist—and the hallmark of a phony. Probably even a closet queen.'

"Mr. Rush, I believe?" the Assistant Secretary said. He made no effort to rise from his high backed, leather upholstered, Danish-modern desk chair, or offer to shake hands. He sat there, waiting.

'Your round,' Jim conceded. 'So the game's to go on. Defined your limits, haven't you? Established the territorial imperative. So now I know which side of that sandalwood and teak desk is which. Let me see—better win some ground back before we go into why ever the hell you sent for me . . .'

He looked quickly at the triangular-shaped glass nameplate with the gold letters cut into it that rested upon one corner of the Assistant Secretary's desk. It wasn't an ordinary nameplate. It had weight, presence. The crystal was smoky, and of the very finest quality. "Mr. Franchot Townley," it read.

'All right, I'll present my credentials,' Jim thought wearily. 'The only ones that characters like you will respect or can understand. A brief demonstration that you and I belong to the same world. To the *old* State Department, that you got into, not because you had brains, ability, or simple guts, but because your great-great-grandfather—give or take a great or two—swam across ahead of the *Mayflower* and was on hand to greet the Pilgrim Fathers when they arrived. With a turkey in one hand and Pocahontas in the other—I hope!'

"Georg Jensen's?" he said, nodding his head towards the nameplate.

The Assistant Secretary loosed a purring little laugh. Baritone. Musical. Grave. Amused. Mundane.

'And practiced before your shaving mirror every goddamned morning,' Jim added in his mind.

"I can see you know crystal, Mr. Rush," the Assistant Secretary said.

"My mother used to collect it," Jim said. "Inherited a houseful of it when she died. Used to drive my wife straight up the nearest wall. We really hadn't room in our place for so many pieces—plus all the Dresden, Meissen, Limoges, both porcelain and bone china, she'd already showered down upon us over the years—and it was much too good to throw out . . ."

"Your wife?" Townley said. "So there *is* a Mrs. Rush? I've been having a glance at your records, but—"

Jim measured Mr. Assistant Secretary Townley with his eyes. His gaze had hoarfrost in it, suddenly.

"Say—there *was,*" he said quietly.

"Divorced?" Townley persisted. He was well within his rights to ask that question, Jim knew. The State Department was much more vulnerable to the side effects of public scandal on the part of even its minor hirelings than most government agencies were. The wonder was that he didn't *know* the answer to it, already. But Jim Rush's finely tuned ear told him that the question hadn't been rhetorical. By some miracle or another, Franchot Townley didn't know his—or more to the point, Virginia's—personal history.

"Dead," Jim said. He didn't add that both qualifications applied. Divorced first, then dead. By her own hand, after the boy fifteen years her junior whom she had gone away with had left her.

"I see," Townley said. "And I'm sorry. But, even so, it's strange that—"

"There's no mention of her in my service records? No, it isn't, Sir. I married her on one of the two occasions I was—voluntarily—out of the State Department. She died during the second. In neither case did my private life appear to me to be, well, a matter that warranted the State Department's attention. It touched upon no sensitive areas, and was tranquil enough, so—"

"Hmmmmn—let's say you have something of a point, there. Your last statement, anyhow. You've been with us long enough to know that any unsavory episodes in a diplomat's life can cost the whole Department dearly. And he needn't even be the guilty party. Anything—an indiscretion on the part of a close relative—or on his wife's—"

He paused, giving Jim time to wonder whether he hadn't italicized those last four words on the office's refrigerated, dehumidified, and filtered air. Then he went on, smoothly:

"—that can give our enemies the opportunity to blackmail him for classified information could, conceivably—"

Jim shrugged.

"Don't think I was ever within ten miles of anything that the Russians hadn't already read in the newspapers," he said; "so you needn't worry about that, Sir."

"Only now, you're going to be. Though I must say that in those areas your record's remarkably clean. Not a hint of scandal. No little secretary's accused you—even falsely—of having chased her around the desk, or such like—"

"Haven't the knack," Jim said dryly. "With women, my score is zero–minus. They don't even look at me and grin. Instead, they yawn. Forgetting even to cover their pretty little gaping mouths with the backs of their dainty hands. So, if you'll permit me the frankness, Mr. Secretary, if the reason you called me in was to post me to some area where your man is supposed to display glamour, sex appeal, turn on the charm, you'd might as well forget it. My abilities in those directions are nil."

Franchot Townley smiled.

"No. As a matter of fact, we have a much more serious mission for you, Mr. Rush; one that calls for the qualities of discretion, caution, coolness of head, decision making; qualities you seem to have in abundant measure, at least according to the sub-departmental heads who recommended you. But sit down, will you? And forgive me my inquisitiveness. I like to form my own opinion of a man before I send him out. Get a sort of quick psychological profile of him, as it were. It has saved me trouble in the past, by at least limiting the gravity of the errors I've made. For instance, is this particular failure you mention a *thing* with you? You've been married—and widowed—so you must have scored at least once—"

Jim slid into the chair. As he'd known it would be, it was a damned uncomfortable chair. 'The Inquisitory Seat,' he thought. He shrugged.

"In Spanish we say, '*Hay un roto para cada descosida.*' You know what that means, of course."

" 'There's a broken man for every undone woman'? Yes. Naturally. More or less the theme of the well-known motion picture *Marty* of some years back. But I seem to detect something in your remarks that goes beyond a gentlemanly modesty. A—well—hint of bitterness, shall we say?"

Jim Rush stared at the Assistant Secretary.

"Well, it hasn't made my life a bed of roses," he said, dryly. "But I've got to a state of resignation about it. It's not important—at least not anymore."

"Good. The next thing is something you've already mentioned, but I'd like to go into it a little: those two longish gaps in your records. You mentioned they were voluntary. Mind telling me why?"

"Not at all. Wanted to see if I could make it in the world, the real world, which, to put it bluntly, the State Department isn't. You see, Mr. Secretary, I'm a diplomat's son. The first Jim Rush, about whom departmental wags coined the slogan, 'Rush just doesn't rush,' was my father. He was rather overpowering, if you get what I mean. So I was more or less dragooned into a diplomatic career my first year out of Harvard—"

"I'd noticed the accent," Townley said, with a smile.

"Did you? Been trying to get rid of it for years. Anyhow, in case you don't know, my father was, at one time or another, Ambassador to every major country in Central and South America, and finally to Spain. After which he retired, bringing me home a stepmother ten years younger than I am. So, naturally enough, I fought against following in the old man's footsteps. When you've spent your childhood being dragged from one unlikely place to another, the glamour of a diplomatic career—escapes you, shall we say?"

"I quite agree. Children need stability," Townley said gravely. "Hmmmn—accounts for the Spanish on your record. Any other languages?"

"Portuguese," Jim said; "some French; some German; neither of the latter very good. The old man seems to have got stuck in Latin America . . ."

"And so have you, from the records," Townley said; "but then, the languages themselves would account for that, wouldn't they?"

"Probably. Which is why I've been taking crash courses in three more."

"Which are?" Mr. Assistant Secretary Townley said.

"Arabic, Russian, and Chinese," Jim said quietly.

Again that purring baritone chord floated across the air-conditioned air.

"Your way of informing me you don't like Latin America?" Townley said.

Jim shrugged.

"Wouldn't put it so strongly," he said. "Some of the countries down there I like very much. Others give me a pain where I sit. But the main trouble with Latin America is that a place you love can change overnight into a place you hate—with all your friends dead in bloody heaps on the sidewalks, or screaming their guts up in some bemedalled and beribboned little monster's torture chambers . . ."

"Then I'm afraid that what I called you in for isn't going to seem good news to you," Townley said. "But before we go into that, satisfy my curiosity about your second voluntary absence from the Department. Surely you were too old by then to attribute it to—well—adolescent rebellion against the father figure?"

"My late wife didn't like travel. Nor foreign countries. Which is, incidentally, another reason she doesn't appear in departmental records, since I never had to apply for a travel allowance for her. But it made for prolonged separations at times. She felt—rightly, I believe—that a husband should stay at home. I tried it for several years. But I don't seem to be much good at anything else. So I drifted back. She died while I was in Panama . . ."

"I see. Well, Mr. Rush, I hope you won't be too disappointed. You're being sent to South America again; but as Ambassador this time"—he paused long enough for that to sink in—"to the Republic of Costa Verde. . . ."

Jim sat there. Then he said:

"Oh, Jesus!"

"I take it that you know that country, then?"

"I've been there. Briefly. Passing through. But I've friends who've lived there, two of them married to Costa Verdian women. Their theory is that it's the original site of hell, and that the Devil moved out, to find a place with a better climate and subjects with better manners. Their wives agree with them—"

"I see. Then you want to refuse the appointment?" Townley said quietly.

"D'you know how long it would take me to make Ambassador's rank again if I did?" Jim said. The question was rhetorical, and they both knew it.

"I do," Townley said, "but do you?"

"Yes. The answer's forever, six months, and one day," Jim said. "And meanwhile I get sent out as Assistant Vice Consul to Uganda."

"Well?" Mr. Assistant Secretary Townley said.

"Oh, hell, I'll take it. If I survive, I can buck for a decent post: Madrid, Rome, Paris. When do I have to leave?"

"How much time do you need to set your personal affairs in order?"

"If getting them in order includes taking intensive courses in judo, karate, and small arms marksmanship, say—three weeks," Jim said.

"Oh, come now, Rush! Costa Verde isn't all that bad . . ."

"It's the worst. The very worst. The place where they torture the women relatives—wives, daughters, sisters, mothers—of suspected guerrillas in order to get said guerrillas to surrender. And when they do surrender—"

"When the Tupamaros, Montoneros, and other assorted *Red* terrorists surrender, then what?" Mr. Franchot Townley said pointedly.

"They hang them. In *la Plaza de la Liberación.* By their balls. Using barbed wire as a noose," Jim Rush said.

"Then you approve of Costa Verde's going Red?" the Assistant Secretary said. "Again?"

"Don't believe in the Domino Theory. Besides, the Costa Verdians, being the quintessential *Latinos,* will fuck up, no matter what color they turn."

He saw Townley wince at his language, and enjoyed it. He went on:

"The friends I mentioned—both newspapermen, both stout anti-Communists—were down there during the 1962–63 Red takeover. They barely escaped with their lives. Both of their names were high on the Reds' list of people to be 'wasted' as soon as it could be conveniently managed. But they both agree that Costa Verde was a hell of a lot better off during the three years, 1963 through 1965, when the Communists were in power—after which, of course, with the reglementary rumors of CIA assistance, the next Rightist dictator appeared and executed the Reds in carload lots—than it has ever been before or since. Not that that's saying much . . ."

"What are your personal political leanings, Mr. Rush?" Mr. Townley said, very, very softly.

"Haven't any. Politics, in any of its variants, is a system for deluding the masses into believing that they have what the masses in no country in the world have *ever* had, or ever could have, which is actual power. So call me a pragmatist. I'm for what works least painfully wherever I happen to be at any given moment."

"A nice theory. But what if what happens to work where you are also happens to run counter to the best interests of your own country, the one, whom, as Ambassador, you are pledged to serve?"

"If the issue's clear-cut, I defend my country tooth and nail. I think that's clear from my record, Mr. Townley. But I should like to be allowed to decide from my vantage point close to the local situation what my country's interests actually are. They don't necessarily coincide with ITT's or Exxon's, you know. And I'll accept the post only with the understanding that the CIA is to be kept the hell out of my hair. No staged coups to put into power people you think won't expropriate North American concerns. In the first place, the few who won't will ruin the companies in question by the size and the frequency of the payoffs said companies will have to fork over to keep them happy, and all the rest will expropriate regardless of their political coloration. In the second, anyone who invests in a country like Costa Verde needs his head examined. One of my friends quoted Lincoln's phrase, 'Shoveling fleas in a barnyard,' to describe what it amounts to—"

"Then you haven't been told that oil has been discovered off Costa Verde's shores, well within its territorial waters? A pool that experts believe will have provable reserves at least as great as Saudi Arabia's?" Townley said. "Nor that an outside influence—whose word carries considerable weight here in Washington—has quietly let word fall into receptive ears that he should be vastly pleased if you did receive the ambassadorship?"

Jim sat there.

"Crowley," he whispered. "Wildcat Crowley. President of Worldwide Petroleum. Am I right?"

"For whom you once worked—in a public relations capacity—during the second of your two absences from the Department," Townley said. "Well, what do you say to that?"

"Oh Jesus. Oh double Jesus, twice crucified," Jim said.

"It's up to you. You have the appointment if you want it. Do you?" Townley said.

A slow grin crawled across Jim Rush's homely face.

It had a glint of triumph in it, Townley thought.

"I want it. Oh, how I want it, Mr. Secretary!" he said.

CHAPTER

2

*W*hen the big jet banked, sliding into the radar-controlled landing pattern while still high up and far out over the ocean, Jim Rush could see the lights of Logan International Airport, and, beyond them, in a fan-shaped, semicircular spray, those of Boston itself. He could feel some of the tension ease out of him. He wasn't a brave man, and though he had long since mastered the abject terror he had suffered on the first five or six of the flights that his diplomatic career all too frequently obliged him to make, a certain irreducible residue of that fear remained even yet, buried layers deep in his subconscious. On the rare occasions he was aware of it, it was one of the many aspects of his personality that he was ashamed of, but he was intelligent enough to realize that he was himself, and that the human adult psyche is at least as immutable as the primordial stone.

By the time the plane had slanted down towards the night-stabbing brilliance of its own landing lights, racing yards high between the twin blue glares of the long succession of flight-strip marker beacons, sinking, sinking, until finally it lurched and bumped and set its tortured gear-train tires screeching, all that kind of tension had left him; and another had taken its place. A kind he hated even more. For now he had to do the thing that called all his acknowledged inadequacies and accepted inferiority feelings to the fore; he had to look up the two men who, more than any others he had ever known, easily, without even meaning to, made him feel an ineffectual fool.

'I'll call Tim first,' he thought. 'Maybe he can brief me well enough about present conditions in Costa Verde so that I won't need to see Peter at all . . .'

And sat back in his seat, staring at the still lighted seat-belt warning and no smoking signs, rigid with shock and shame.

'This is—unpardonable,' he told himself; 'after all Peter has done for you from the time you were at Finch together, right down the years, and now you—'

The warning lights flickered out. Jim unfastened his seat belt, dragged his inflight bag from beneath the seat ahead of his own, stood up, and joined the stream of passengers who were moving towards the exit door—open now, with the black rubber cushioning of the covered deplaning ramp pressed firmly around it—and saying their quite mean-ingless good-byes to the two brightly smiling female cybernetic robots that all airline stewardesses seem to be. And he, nodding absently in their direction, managing a brief upward flicker of lip corners, was think-ing: 'I've had no better friend in all my life. I know of no man more worth of admiration and respect than Peter. So why—?'

But he knew why. Peter was completely free of the vice—and the solace—of self-delusion.

'Envy is the one totally indefensible emotion,' he told himself bit-terly. 'But there it is. And you're stuck with it. As far as Peter Reynolds is concerned, you've always been . . .'

He went on walking down those long colorless and characterless corri-dors that make every major airport on the face of earth almost the exact duplicate of every other, until he came to the baggage counter. Stood there. Waited for his luggage to come bumping down the conveyer belt. Took his suit hanger bag, his overnight case. Looked around for a phone booth. Found one. And called Peter Reynolds first.

It was a sort of penitence.

"Why Chubby Rush!" Peter's deep, musical baritone came over the wire, warm with unfeigned pleasure. "Where *are* you, Boy? Boston! Great! Where're you staying?"

"I haven't a hotel yet, Peter," Jim said; "I'm calling from the airport. Just got in. You see, I wanted to make sure I could catch you—and Tim, if possible—for lunch tomorrow. I need some straight dope—poli-tical, social, financial, and so forth—on an area you both know, and that I don't. I've had the usual departmental briefing; but you know State Department briefings are worth . . ."

"About as much as what the mule leaves behind him in the road," Peter chuckled. "Now listen, Chub. You march your little fat tail right into the airport bar and sit tight. I'm coming after you. We've a two-hundred-thirty-odd-year-old barn—built with *pegs,* Boy, because nails cost too much in those days—and the only thing it's got more of than rooms is drafts. A hotel's *out.* With all the catching up we've got to do, I won't hear of it! So just you possess your overstuffed soul with patience and—"

"Peter," Jim said; "as I remember, you live all the way out near Concord. And—"

"And nothing. You know how I drive. Be seeing you, Chub!"

"Peter, wait! I—I've been married, too, you know. You simply cannot bring a guy you haven't seen in years, and whom your wife's *never* seen, home unexpectedly this way! It's not fair to Alicia and—"

"*You* couldn't, maybe," Peter said with cool amusement; "I can. Picked mine carefully, and broke her in right. Seriously, Chub, Alicia'll be delighted. She's been hearing me talk about you for years—"

"Oh, God!" Jim said.

"Oh, I edited my version of your life. Laundered it where necessary. Give me an hour. No—make that an hour and a half . . ."

"Peter, let's compromise. There's a U-Drive It desk right across from this phone. I'll rent a car and drive out there. Save time that way. Maybe I can even get there before your kids' bedtime. I'm longing to see what kind of production you were capable of—"

"The best," Peter said; "absolutely the best. With Alicia, how could I miss? Okay, Chub, pick up a heap and drive in. I'm only letting you do it because I am a little bushed. The years don't pass in vain, you know." He said that last sentence in Spanish, so it sounded considerably less stilted than it does in English. Spanish is a formal, even a stately language, so you could get away with things like that in it, Jim reflected. 'And cuss in it even better,' he added wryly, 'which is exactly what I feel like doing now, for letting myself get roped into this!'

"Be seeing you, Peter," he said, and hung up the phone.

He hadn't needed to ask Peter where his house was, because with that almost male-spinsterish meticulousness that was another of the many things he disliked about himself, he always carried an alphabetically listed and indexed address book with him, containing the name and address of every single person he might one day conceivably have need to get in touch with. Some of them jotted down and forgotten more than twenty years before. Peter's house—still called the Old Stuyvesant House after the long deceased family who had rebuilt it in 1746, from the original structure that dated back to at least 1680—was on the Old Bedford Road, some miles outside of Concord. It was one of the few demonstrably authentic pre-Revolutionary War houses still in use as a residence, and was as Jim remembered it, quietly beautiful. 'Wish I had a house like that one,' he thought, 'with those rough adzed beams and those huge fieldstone fireplaces and—and the kind of a life that would permit me to stay in it. Without moving. Until they buried me under that big oak in the yard . . .'

But that was too much to ask of mocking, malicious, indifferent fate, and he knew it. Sighing, he crossed the corridor to the car rental desk.

When he drove up to the house, all the lights were on, and Peter was out in the yard, standing by the swinging gate.

"Jesus, Chub!" he said. "You had me worried! What the hell took you so long?"

"I'm a cautious driver, Peter," Jim said, and put out his hand to him; "you should know that. . . ."

But Peter ignored the outstretched hand and gathered Jim into a rib-crushing bearhug, while pounding him on the back at the same time, the kind of embrace that Spanish-speaking people call *el abrazo*. This wasn't at all surprising because Peter Reynolds, in pursuit of his own career as war correspondent and reporter, had spent almost as many years in Latin America as Jim had. But it brought all Jim's feeling of shame back in a rush. There was no doubt of Peter's fondness for him; what was doubtful was his own ability to reciprocate—in spite, or perhaps even because, of the many things that Peter, with unthinking generosity, with that *largesse* characteristic of people who have every reason to be sure of themselves, had done for him over the years.

"C'mon, Chub, meet the Missus and the kids," Peter said. "Tim and Marisol are down in New York; but you'll see them tomorrow. I phoned them at their hotel and told them you were here. So Tim's cutting short their weekend on the town just to see you. Evidence of your greatest talent: winning friends and influencing people. They live right down the road, and—"

He stopped short. Stood there, staring at Jim. Said, measuring the syllables out on the night air: "Je–ho–si–phat!"

Jim Rush smiled at him, shyly.

"Why 'Jehosiphat,' Peter?" he said.

"Chub, you've lost all of forty pounds, haven't you?" Peter said accusingly. "So I can't call you 'Chub' anymore—and getting used to saying 'Jim' is going to cost me. How'd you manage it, Boy?"

"You know that saying, 'There's a thin man inside of every fat man, screaming to get out'? Well, I got out, finally. Actually it was Ed Crowley's fault—"

"Old 'Wildcat' Crowley? That's right, you did work for him once, didn't you? What'd he do? Lock you up on bread and water? He was quite capable of it, the old pirate!"

"No. All he did was to growl at me: 'Y'know, Rush, I'd give you a better job with the organization if you wasn't so damned fat. Shows a lack of will power. Fellow who's a slave to his belly is likely to be weak in other ways, too . . .' It hit me right down where I live. Because it came to me that he was dead right, Peter. Of course I had already realized that my gluttony—to call it by its right name—was a compensatory behavior reflex, to make up for all my other lacks . . ."

"The trouble with you, Chub—I mean Jim—is that you were born without a skin. Being as introspective as you are never did anyone any good. But speaking of Old Crowley, it's a pity about his daughter, Jenny, isn't it? You knew her, didn't you?"

"Yes, I did know her; and it *is* a pity, a very great pity," Jim said.

Peter stared at him, as though surprised at the noticeable pain in his voice. He started to say something, and must have thought better of it, for all he did say was: "C'mon, Chub, give me the car keys so I can get your bags out of the trunk . . ."

"Oh, no, you don't, Peter!" Jim said sharply, glancing at Peter's sadly withered left arm.

"Souvenir of my wife's charming fellow countrymen," Peter said with a grin. "They play rough down there. Don't worry; I shan't lug your bags in. I can't. My kid will do that." He lifted his head, called: "Mario!"

"Yeah, Pops?" a boy's voice said. "Coming!"

The boy, Jim saw, was his father's image. Tall, lanky, graceful at an age (he was about twelve, Jim knew) when most boys are falling all over their own hands and feet. He reopened the deepest of Jim Rush's many wounds and made it bleed—his longing, even his need, for a son of his own. But Virginia had been opposed, and—

"Mario," Peter said; "this is my oldest and best friend, Jim Rush. Jim, this is my son, Mario—first off the production line . . ."

"And your masterpiece," Jim said sadly, and put out his hand to the boy.

"Glad to know you, Mr. Rush," Mario said, and shook hands, gripping firmly, without shyness or self-consciousness. As he started lifting the bags out of the trunk of the car, Jim saw suddenly all the ways he was *not* like his father. There was something—highborn, princely— about him, although the words Jim Rush thought of in Spanish, '*hidalguez, estirpe de principes,*' don't literally mean that, but rather something more. The strange thing was that while Mario was his father's exact physical image, he didn't look North American. He had a Latin look that Peter Reynolds didn't have in spite of the fact that his hair, eyes, and complexion were all quite as dark as those of his son. Mario's *Latino* aspect surely was a heritage from his mother, Jim thought.

But once in the hall, seeing Alicia Reynolds coming towards them, Jim was shocked. She was an ugly, skinny little thing, with a big mouth, and greying black hair cropped into a Peck's bad boy haircut of twenty years before.

Then she smiled at him, and his breath stopped. Because he knew he'd been wrong, all wrong. For Alicia Villalonga de Reynolds was one of the most beautiful women he'd seen in all his life. Only her beauty was so—different. So strange, exotic—and *erotic,* he groaned in his lonely and deserted heart—that you didn't see it at first. But when she smiled, it was there: a felt presence, a warmth, a glory.

"Alicia," Peter said happily, "This is my oldest friend, Chubby Rush—Oh, hell; there I go again! I mean Jim Rush—"

"At your feet, Madame," Jim said in Spanish; "your secure servant." Which was another of the rolling, sonorous formal phrases you could say in Spanish without sounding like a fool.

"Enchanted," Alicia said in her native tongue, at which not only Mario, but the two little girls Jim hadn't even seen before set up a chorus of groans.

"Oh, no!" Mario said; "don't tell me we're going to have to speak *Spanish* tonight, Mama!"

"For me, no," Jim laughed; "I can manage English if I try real hard!"

"This is—strange," Alicia said. "You do have a slight accent, Mr. Rush; but in English, not in Spanish. Very, very slight, but one hears it. Why is this, may I ask?"

"Because I spoke Spanish first," Jim said. "Which is why I sympathize with your children, Mrs. Reynolds. I was born in Colombia, Bogotá to be exact, and I fought like blazes against learning English. Never did learn it really until my father shipped me back here to attend Finch Academy. Since all my childhood friends were Spanish—or rather *Latinos*—I didn't want to be an oddball, I suppose. That's it, isn't it, Mario?"

"Right, Mr. Rush!" Mario said fervently. "*Nobody* around here speaks Spanish but *us,* and when Mama and Papa talk to us in it, and the other kids hear us answer, they look at us like we'd just escaped from the zoo!"

"Would take an awfully big zoo to hold us all," Jim said, "since there're about three hundred million Spanish-speaking people in this world, Mario. So these are your daughters, Peter? What little beauties! What's your name, my dear?"

"Two," the eight-year-old said; "*dos.*"

"Her name is Alicia, the same as mine," Alicia said; "but we've got into the habit of calling her Number Two to avoid confusion, so I'm afraid she forgets what her name is, most of the time. . . ."

"No, I don't!" Alicia II said. "It's 'Licia. 'Licia *Numero Dos.*"

"Now, don't you go'n start it, you dumb bunny! Say 'two,' not '*dos*'!" Mario said.

"And yours, darling?" Jim said to the smaller girl, an angel sprite who seemed to be practically buried under tons of jet black hair, her tiny face almost eclipsed by her enormous, equally black eyes.

"Mari," the six-year-old piped.

"Mary?" Jim said.

"Marisol, after Tim's better half," Peter said. "C'mon, sit down. Still a Scotch drinker, Chub?"

"Why do you call him 'Chub,' Peter?" Alicia said. "He is not at all fat. In fact, he is rather too thin—like me."

"Because I used to be, up until about five years ago, Mrs. Reynolds," Jim began; but Alicia stopped him with a lifted hand.

"Please call me Alicia," she said, "and I shall call you Jim. You see, I like you."

"Why Lord love us all!" Peter laughed. "And me thinking I had a *faithful* wife! Now don't you go and break up my happy home, Chub-Boy!"

"Give him a drink, Peter," Alicia said, "while I put the girls to bed. Mario, you may stay up until eleven; but in your room, watching the tele, if you like, so that your father and Mr. Rush may talk in peace. Come now, Son—"

"Aw, Mama!" Mario said.

"Don't be obstreperous, Mario," Alicia said.

She used words like obstreperous with perfect naturalness, probably because she had obtained her university education in England, a fact that Jim knew through the infrequent correspondence he had maintained with Peter over the years. As a result, her English was both effortlessly fluent and grammatically perfect. But, like everyone who has not been bilingual from earliest childhood, her pronunciation betrayed her national origins in slight, small ways. Like most Latins, she couldn't quite manage the short English "i," so that "it" came out "eet" and "Jim," "Jeem," which made everything she said curiously charming.

"What we have to talk about would bore the pants off you, son," Peter said. Listening to him, Jim was thinking sadly how unusual it was in this day and age to encounter a boy who *wanted* to stay with his father and his father's guests, and about what that meant: that Peter Reynolds had managed marriage and fatherhood as well and as gracefully as he had always managed everything; while he, Jim Rush, had been a miserable failure as a husband, and had never achieved fatherhood at all.

"How d'you know it would, Pops?" Mario said challengingly.

"Because we've got to talk about Central and South American affairs, my boy," Peter said with perfect gravity, although Jim, who had known him since boyhood, sensed the amusement in his voice. "And you've made it abundantly clear how much you love *that* subject!"

"You can say that again, Pops!" Mario groaned. "Whose turn it is to revolt this week! Plus which nice, sweet, innocent lamb d'you think it is the CIA is going to knock off next! Lead me to the nearest exit! Goodnight, Mr. Rush. 'Night, Pops."

Then suddenly, shyly, he bent and kissed his father's cheek, a thing Jim had never seen any North American boy do, and marched out of there. Shepherding the two little girls, Alicia followed him up the magnificent curving stair that was perhaps the very best feature of the Old Stuyvesant House.

"You're a lucky man, Peter," Jim said; "I'd give my right arm up to the shoulder to have a family like yours."

"You should try again, Chub. What are you—forty-six, right? That's not too old."

"No," Jim said; "I've had it, Peter."

"You're too thin-skinned, Boy. Hell, you haven't even got a skin. Look at me. I'd been down for the nine count *twice* when I met Alicia . . ."

"Twice?" Jim said. "Then Alicia's your *third* wife? I didn't know that. Constance, I knew; but the second one, who was she?"

"No; 'Licia's my second wife, legally, anyhow; but between Connie and her, on a long-term basis, without benefit of clergy, of course, there was Judith Lovell, Chub."

"The movie star?" Jim said, staring at Peter. "My God! You do have your depths, don't you? That absolutely gorgeous creature!"

"That absolutely gorgeous creature who made me see more hell than most men do in forty lifetimes," Peter said dryly. "Cured me of blondes for life. Which accounts for 'Licia, maybe."

"I won't buy that one," Jim said. "What accounts for Alicia is Alicia, herself. She's truly stunning, Peter. I say, what *is* she? Oh, I know she's Costa Verdian; but she—she's *Mestiza,* isn't she?"

"Right. Spanish and Tluscolan. With a flick or two of the old Tarbrush to judge from her lips. Shocked, Chub?"

"Good Lord, Peter; you know me better than that! The only thing I want to know is whether she doesn't have a sister, preferably a *twin* sister down there in Villalonga City—"

"A twin, no; but a sister? Could be, Chub. Half sister, anyhow. And more than one, likely. Don't ask me to explain that; it's 'Licia's family history, and it wouldn't be fair to her to flap that much soiled ancestral linen in the breeze. Let me freshen up that drink, will you?"

"All right," Jim said, "but make it light, Peter. I've never developed a head for the stuff—and, unfortunately, this visit's more than half business . . ."

Peter stared at Jim. His gaze was suddenly sober and troubled.

"Chub," he said, "you're being sent to Costa Verde, aren't you?"

"Yes," Jim said. "How'd you know?"

"Figures. What other country do both Tim and I know well enough to brief you on it? And our better halves, even better, having had the misfortune to have been born there. But, before 'Licia comes back downstairs, can I put my oar in? As a friend, Chub. I may be way out of line, but—"

"You're never out of line with me, Peter," Jim said; "but, before you say it, I've got to tell you I won't take this particular piece of advice—which is to refuse the assignment, right?"

"Right," Peter said. "And you're well within your rights, Jim. There! I've got it! Mainly because you don't even *sound* like old Chub anymore. Mind telling me why you won't refuse the appointment? Believe me, it's the world's worst."

"Hard to say, Peter. I'm not even sure I know why. I could say it's because this will be my first shot at an ambassadorship, but that's a half truth at best. Let's say it's something in my makeup: all odds and ends, concurrent contradictions loosely sewed or glued together to make—"

"One hell of a tough, brave little guy," Peter said.

"Brave? Lord God, Peter! You know damned well—"

"Brave. Why the hell d'you think I stuck up for you at Finch's? Because of that. There you were: a fat, moonfaced, pimply little kid, with a trick accent, thick glasses on your pudgy nose that made you look like a bemused owl, clumsy as all get out, not strong enough to fight your way out of a wet paper bag, scared shitless three-quarters of the time—"

"Correction," Jim said bitterly, "scared shitless *all* the damned time—"

"Right. But who the hell ever saw you run or quit? You took on the school's meanest, roughest customers and—"

"Got my ass kicked from hell to breakfast, never won a fight, never—"

"Who does?" Peter said. "Who ever wins more than a round or two in this life, Chub—Jim? By the time I pitched in and helped you out, you'd cut Finch's Corps of Upper Form Sadists down to manageable size. It wasn't because you'd licked 'em, but because you'd made the ones who weren't quite Grade A, simon pure, unmitigated bastards enough ashamed of themselves to quit picking on you, leaving a Bullies' Cadre small enough for me to handle. Besides, you've got your definitions screwed up. A brave man's not a guy who's never afraid. The only term that fits that one is idiot—or moron, maybe. A brave man is the type who maybe is crapping his pants from fear, but who doesn't panic; who doesn't quit. And thereby survives—"

"You call *that* a virtue? Mere survival, I mean?"

"Yes. At least when it's a person of your quality who's surviving, Chub. Rats do it by sheer instinct. Human beings have to learn how. And we can't leave the future to rats, Jim. Somebody's got to defend the continuity of history—of civilization. Jesus! What a sententious line! End of sermon for tonight—"

"There's more to survival than that," Jim said; "or at least more to continuity. You've managed it; I haven't. You've already projected your qualities—your authentic qualities—into the future, Peter. While I—in spite of your sterling efforts to get me through Finch's Fag Factory with my heterosexual inclinations reasonably intact—have failed to—"

"What is this—a Fag Factory?" Alicia said, and came into the living room bearing a tray full of canapés.

"Finch's training school for *mariquitas, maricas, y maricons,* 'Licia," Peter said, using the Spanish words for the three kinds, or at least degrees, of homosexuals. Then turning to Jim, he went on: "Okay—so I arranged for you to get into Sadie Stubbin's flour-sacking bloomers. Big deal! But it did help, didn't it?"

"Right," Jim said; "the rites of spring! My passage into manhood. A trifle unwashed. Noticeably smelly—but, to quote you that time I asked you why, it did confirm my uncertain heterosexuality, for all the good that's ever done me—"

"Then you have never married?" Alicia said. "It seems to me that Peter once told me—"

"That I was married. Yes. Some time ago. But my wife—died."

"How sad!" Alicia said. "Of what did she die, Jim?"

Jim looked at her, and his eyes were stark naked, suddenly.

"Of twenty-seven sleeping pills," he said.

"Oh!" Alicia gasped, and put her hand on Jim's arm. "Do forgive me, Jim! It was not my wish to cause you pain."

"I know," Jim whispered; "it's just that I can't shake the feeling that her death was my fault. If I had been a different kind of a man, maybe—more like Peter is, say—she'd never have gone away with—"

"A little jerk fifteen years her junior?" Peter said. "Oh, yes, she would have. People do what they do because they are who, or rather *what,* they are. You're forgetting Constance left *me* in exactly the same fashion. And wound up just as dead, because *her* jerk, whom she'd divorced me to marry, and to whom she'd given three kids, had her murdered so he could take off with his secretary . . ."

"Peter—are you *sure* that's what happened?" Alicia said in a troubled voice. "I have never been convinced that it was not perhaps Luis, after all, who—"

"Luis?" Jim said.

"My half brother, Luis Sinnombre. He's dead now. But in those days he was head of the Costa Verdian secret police. And he had reasons to—but, has not Peter told you about my family?"

"No," Peter said; "and don't you start it, 'Licia! That tribe of howling savages you sprang from—a good long way, thank God!—is best forgot, it seems to me."

"I agree," Alicia said sadly; "but I should prefer that our friend Jim heard the story from me—or from you. For if we do not tell him, he is sure to hear it from someone who would make it more horrible than it is, if that is possible. You said that you thought that Jim might have been assigned to Costa Verde, because what other country do both you and Tim know well enough for him to consult you both about conditions there?"

"He has been," Peter said grimly.

"Jim," Alicia said, "you must not go! My country is—horrible. I am sorry that this is so; but it is. There are dozens of organizations, most of them Leftist—*far* Leftist—to whom any *diplomatico norteamericano* is fair game—"

"I know that," Jim said; "but I don't mean to expose myself unnecessarily, Alicia. And there's a chance—slight, but still a chance—that the presence of an American Ambassador on the scene might curb at least some of the worst abuses, by submitting them to the world press with proof of what goes on down there, give them the kind of publicity that even the Reds don't want and—"

"*¡Mierda!*" Peter swore. "American diplomats are clay pigeons in most of Latin America. In Costa Verde, you'll be target for tonight, every night. Hell, Jim, if any part of your problem's financial, Tim and I can definitely help out. You know that little political and economic news sheet we started when we both got out of the roving reporters' racket? Well, it's doing great, much to our surprise. And we could really use a guy with your know-how, so—"

"Peter," Alicia said quietly, "look at his clothes."

Peter looked at Jim. From head to foot. Slowly.

"Jehosiphat!" he said. "Raw shot silk suit. Italian. Three hundred bucks. No, four. Handmade shoes. Alligator—no, snakeskin. Discreetly black so they don't knock your eyes out. Another one-fifty. You've been holding out on me. Found yourself a *rich* Sadie, Chub?"

"No," Jim sighed. "The truth's simpler—and sadder." Then he told them about his father's death. About the trusts.

"Then I'll reword my question," Peter said. "Why in hellfire do you

20

even stay in the State Department, much less taking an appointment to the jade green asshole of the Western Hemisphere?"

"I was trying to explain that to you before. Say I'm proving things to myself again. That I can make it to the top—which an ambassadorship, even to Costa Verde, definitely is—on my own steam. That I can handle a difficult assignment—an understatement for Costa Verde, I gather— and bring it off. I do mean to quit the Department, Peter; but on the day they offer me a decent assignment, not before. So they'll know I can tell them just where to shove any assignment, a point that can only be proved by my refusing the best, not the worst."

"Chub, don't be a fool!" Peter began; but Alicia cut him off.

"Peter, no," she said softly. "A *man* always does what he must. You, more than most men, should know that."

Hearing what had got into her voice then—that atavistic, bone deep, womb deep, purely female note of admiration and warmth—Jim Rush had to count up to ten, to thirty, and finally to fifty before he could answer her. He said:

"You're right, Alicia. But do you know what the *first* thing I must do is?"

"No. What is it, Jim?" she said.

"Find myself a girl down there who looks *exactly* like you!"

She laughed then. But there was a little tremolo in her laughter, Jim Rush thought.

"A project of enormous facility!" she said. "Most Tluscolan girls look much like me."

"No, they don't," Peter said.

"Oh, yes they do, *me amor*! But even if it is a much closer resemblance that our friend Jim demands, the matter can be accomplished with a more disgusting ease, considering what all my male relatives were like. Stand on any street corner in Ciudad Villalonga for half an hour, Jim. Or better still, visit the Blue Moon, and—"

"Alicia!" Peter said.

"Sorry. Do forgive me, *Cielo*. But, of a verity, Jim, my father was— very busy in his youth, shall we say? Not to mention my brother—my brothers. So doubtless I have dozens of half sisters and not a few nieces who—"

"I'm not joking, Alicia," Jim said.

"Nor am I. I can even tell you how to accomplish it. There is a man who works at the American Embassy, as majordomo. Peter got him the job—"

"Tomás," Peter said. "True. And 'Licia's probably right. You tell him you're looking for 'Licia's double, and he'll trot you in fifty reasonable facsimiles before night. He knew 'Licia well. Hell, he helped us escape from that Monkey's Paradise. I'll write him a letter—in self-defense. Get you tied down so you can't wreck my happy home—"

"Oh, come off that one, Peter!" Jim said. "You know damned well that I couldn't—"

"Do not be too sure of that," Alicia said with mischievous solemnity. "Even Peter gets to be tiresome at times! Ah, but I talk too much! Would you like some canapés, Jim?"

"No, thank you," Jim said; then, a trifle too quickly: "Peter, brief me, will you? This new Dictator. General Manuel García Herredia, better known as *el Carnecero*—the Butcher. What's he like?"

"One moment, Jim!" Alicia interrupted. "You are determined, then, to accept the post of Ambassador to *la Republica de Costa Verde*?"

"Yes, Alicia," Jim said; "I'm afraid I must . . ."

"*De acuerdo.* Then there is a favor that you can do for me down there—"

"Now, Alicia!" Peter said.

"It is a favor of the most honorable kind, *Cielo,*" Alicia said; "though a trifle delicate for a man, I'll admit . . ."

"What is it?" Jim said.

"I wish you to buy me four Geri Pyle dresses—each of a different color—and send them to me by your diplomatic pouch. Peter will, of course, pay you back for them. But unless you send them by diplomatic courier I shall *never* receive them; and, oh, I do want them so very much!"

"Done," Jim said at once. "But just who is Jerry Peel?" He pronounced the name the way Alicia had.

" 'Licia, you're the limit!" Peter said with real exasperation. "Jim, you're under no obligation at all to—"

"I know I'm not. Only think of what a ball I'm going to have trying them on Alicia's double once I find her . . ."

"Not to mention stripping them off her again," Alicia said sweetly. "I only hope you do not tear them in your haste! That is, if she will consent to part with them. Most women won't. Geri is a genius, and his clothes look so very nice on *morenas*—brunettes—like me. Most designers seem to have tall blondes—like Peter's eternally wept for Judith Lovell—in mind when they pick up their sketch pads."

" 'Licia, I'm going to *hit* you in a minute!" Peter said.

"Whereupon I shall run away with Jim here who is not *un brutote* like you and is also very nice, thus saving him the trouble of having to search for my double," Alicia said.

Jim threw back his head and laughed aloud.

"Go on, Peter! Belt her one!" he said.

"Afraid to take the chance," Peter said solemnly. "With 'Licia, you can never tell. She just might mean it. Come to think of it, you should know Geri. He ran the most expensive dress shop in Santiago during the time you were Vice Consul at our Embassy in Chile. Put the *haut* in *haut couture* down there, I'm told. But when Allende got his, Pinochet and company made it too rough for poor old Geri. Wasn't political. It was simply that Geri was the most unsuccessful closet queen in human history. Limpest wrist you ever saw. And that hip swing! I've heard that the current Madame of the Blue Moon sends the girls over to him to learn how to walk."

Jim sat there. Then he said, the words a groan:

"Not old *Siete Machos*! Good God! That's all I need!"

"The same," Peter said. "Though why he thought Costa Verde would be any less chauvinistic than Chile, I'll be damned if I can see. Gays have a rough time anywhere in Latin America, but Costa Verde! Hell, you could get rich down there manufacturing toupees for them to glue to their chests—"

"*¿Siete Machos?*" Alicia said. "Seven Male Ones? But Geri is, as you have said, a little *efeminado,* so I do not see—"

"Good Lord, 'Licia! That's how *Latino* humor works. In reverse. You ought to know that. Ever see a type called '*el flacucho,*' the skinny one, who didn't weigh three hundred pounds? So Geri, naturally, is The Seven Male Ones, and down there he'll catch it from those types—"

"No, he won't," Alicia said. "Their wives will protect him. And their mistresses. So Geri, who is very charming and also a genius of *la moda feminina,* will be perfectly safe. You will do this for me, will you not, Jim?"

"Of course. It will be a pleasure. Anything else you want?"

"No, nothing more, thank you. And I have ceased to interrupt. Go Peter, tell him about *el Carnecero*—"

"The name's an understatement, if anything," Peter said. "He invented the tactic of putting the wives, sisters, girl friends of known or suspected Leftist guerrillas under what he calls 'protective custody' so they won't, he piously claims, fall victims to the 'just but misplaced wrath of the people . . .' "

"I've heard that one," Jim said. "The idea being, I'm told, to induce the guerrillas to surrender in order to save their women from abuse by his soldiers—"

"Abuse?" Peter said. "Jesus, Chub—how d'you spell torture? The occasion *starts* with a gang bang, participated in by all members of the arresting police squad. This gentle courtesy is repeated nightly by the prison guards until one of four things happens: the guerrilla in question surrenders; the poor girl under 'protective custody' goes insane; or commits suicide; or dies of pure shame and horror. The last is not at all infrequent, since a goodly number of the guerrillas are university students, and their women are from gently bred, upper-middle-class families. Later on, if the type they're after delays too long in giving himself up, she is simply tortured to death. Or 'beer bottled' as they put it down there—"

"My brother's trained assassins invented that one," Alicia whispered, her eyes brilliant with sudden tears.

"Oh, I say!" Jim said then. "Let's change this subject! We're distressing Alicia and—"

"No," she said. "Please continue, Jim. You *have* to know."

"All right," Jim sighed; "why 'beer bottled,' Peter?"

Peter glanced quickly at Alicia; said:

"Let's save that beer bottle bit for later, Chub. That would distress 'Licia, I'm afraid . . ."

"Then *I* will tell him!" Alicia flared. "For I too witnessed it! There is in my poor martyred country a fabricator of beer called Green Cross Beer. The beer is excellent, and sold throughout South America—"

"I know it," Jim said; "it's damned good."

"Then you know the bottle it comes in. Long and slim. Of green glass. Slim enough to be pushed up between a woman's legs and—and into her body without too much difficulty. Once inserted they—they hit you—here. With the fist. So hard the bottle breaks, and—"

"Jesus!" Jim said.

"It is not a pleasant way to die," Alicia said slowly. "It takes a long time. And the pain—is enormous. Sometimes it is the bleeding that kills one. And they—those who bleed to death—are the fortunate ones. For after that—it is the gangrene. And the smell—is of a horror unimaginable. Some—kill themselves. Those who can. And some die of heart attacks—having burst their lungs with screaming. And some few—are saved. At least my Peter saved some when he took the Women's Detention Camp at Chizenaya, by providing them with medical attention at the hands of our trained Sanitary Corpsmen. Only they—they were all—"

"What?" Jim whispered.

"Insane by then. Some of them—girls of eighteen, twenty, twenty-two—had snow white hair, and looked seventy. Others were bald. Most had lost the use of speech. They howled and grunted and barked—like animals. When Peter and I left Costa Verde—escaped that enormous Green Hell my country is—they were all in the State Insane Asylum. Ninety percent of them died there. The rest remain there still . . ."

"But surely now," Jim said, "things have improved. At least somewhat, haven't they? After all, the three of you got out of Costa Verde in 1963, as I remember, and—"

"They've gotten worse," Peter said. "For the Reds, having learned that to surrender only meant to exchange their lives for the lives of their women—broken women by then—started to fight fire with fire. So now they kidnap upper-class women from Rightist families to hold as hostages to insure the safety of their own. Doesn't work. García refuses to deal with Reds no matter whom they kidnap. He has no daughter, and his wife is accompanied by armed guards even *inside* the ladies' room, so it's a standoff. The Reds are a trifle nicer to their female captives. They allow a ten-day grace period before mass rape starts . . ."

"I can safely take it that Women's Lib hasn't caught on very well down there?" Jim said.

"You may *not* take it so, Jim!" Alicia said sharply. "Dozens of young women are in the jungle fighting shoulder to shoulder with their men. The nieces and daughters of friends of mine—and of Marisol's—but please continue, Jim; ask all you need to know—"

"One thing does puzzle me," Jim said. "The CIA has been pretty badly battered by all the investigations over the last few years. How then does it dare back García?"

"It doesn't," Peter said; "it simply does what it is told. And it's no better or no worse than any other Intelligence service. It simply has the misfortune to have to operate on behalf of a nation that has never outgrown its infantile puritanism, and which is collectively too stupid to realize the inadvisability of washing its own dirty linen in public."

"Then you *approve* of the CIA, Peter?" Jim said.

"I don't approve of *any* spy organization. I reluctantly accept the necessity of its existence in a somewhat less than perfect world, Chub. And unless you actually believe in going that second mile and turning the other cheek work, you've got to let our trained paranoiacs fight at least as dirty as the other guy's. The main trouble is that spy organizations by their very nature attract sick types. But don't let me get wound up on *that* subject, for God's sake! So, to backtrack a bit: Washington's wilting liberals were rallying round to force the Government to withdraw all aid to García, just as their predecessors pulled the same stunt in the case of my sweet, lovable, late brother-in-law, Miguel Villalonga—"

"Thanks to your dispatches, *Cielo*!" Alicia said, too sweetly.

"All right. Maybe so. Who knows? And what difference does it make? Perhaps García ultimately would have been forced out, or liquidated; but then another element entered the picture: oil."

"I knew that," Jim said.

"Oh, I don't mean the old, inland oil fields that were never anything much, and which Zopocomapetl put completely out of business with its last major eruption, but the new offshore oil that Worldwide Petroleum's prospectors found, drilling down into the seabed from those floating platform rigs—another coup for your dearly beloved ex-boss, Crowley . . ."

"I also knew *that,*" Jim said.

Peter stared at him.

"Jesus, Chub, how could you? Tim and I have the best inside men in Washington feeding us information for our little political sheet—which, if I may boast, has become required reading for a good many government agencies, and the political analyst for the *Wall Street Journal*—and it took some doing to get our hands on that pay dirt, so how in hellfire could you—"

"It was leaked to me, deliberately. But before I go into the why's and wherefore's—which will surely sidetrack us from the issue at hand—what effect is the oil going to have besides making García and Company filthy rich, I mean?"

"Gives him one hell of a political clout. He's promised to stay out of the OPEC, and to keep the price of *his* crude down to a measly eight dollars a barrel in exchange for the most sophisticated military hardware we've got. To give you an idea: What he wants delivered first are 'people detectors,' those heat-sensitive devices that pick out a lone man by his mere body temperature although he's hiding in the jungle two miles away; sniper rifles mounted with those new electronic telescopic sights that concentrate the faintest available light, and, to the eye that's looking through them at least, turn midnight into day; chemicals to defoliate the jungle—the whole antiguerrilla bit we developed in Viet Nam—tanks, jet fighters, ground to ground, ground to air, air to air, and medium-range ballistic missiles. Not so medium at that. Range enough to drop them on Havana and singe Fidel's curly whiskers for him—"

"And we're going to give him all *that?*" Jim said.

"That and the President's lace trimmed scanties if Crowley and the Oil Lobby have anything to say about it. Now it's my turn: How in hellfire did you find out about that damned oil?"

"Not yet. One other item, Peter: Is there anyone—anyone at all down there I can trust? I may need help damned badly, you know. If there's even one chap I can rely on to get a message out without going through channels, say, and—"

"You're in luck, Chub. In fact, we've already mentioned him: Tomás—the Embassy majordomo. Complete name: Tomás Martinez Galán. My ex-guide down there. He got into trouble because of Alicia and me. He was supposed to have been our right hand man in that comic opera some friends of ours, mostly Shocking Pink University types, staged, and that Zopocomapetl won for us . . ."

"The volcano?"

"Yes. Pulled a *deus ex machina*. Blew its top at just the right moment. But our Pinko friends were overthrown by the real Reds who came next, and started staging purges and show trials under the expert direction of one Ernesto 'Rubles' Ramirez, a Moscow trained Agit-Prop Pro from Cuba—"

"I've seen a CIA confidential on him," Jim said. "Real name's Grünwald, isn't it? Ernst Grünwald. A Czech and an ugly customer. Where is he now?"

"In Spain, lousing up the deal for the Spanish. But, where was I? Oh, yes. 'Rubles' and Company wanted to shoot poor Tomás on the charge of having aided such terrible fascist spies and hirelings of the capitalistic press as Tim, Alicia, and me to escape the country—"

"But not Tim's wife?" Jim said.

"Marisol? No. She was already in New York. Alicia had got her out before then—"

"Shall I tell him *how*, Peter, *Cielo?*" Alicia said mischievously.

"Goddamnit no! And if the two of you don't stop interrupting me, I'll never get this briefing over. Anyhow Tomás got away by the skin of his teeth and took refuge in the American Embassy. Of course our Ambassador and his wife were both dead by then—murdered—but the Chargé d'Affaires, one Donald Filton, was there. And he was a friend of my father's—and of yours, Chub—"

"That old school tie!" Jim quipped.

"It helps sometimes," Peter said soberly. "Anyhow, he queried me in New York—using the diplomatic pouch to do it—and I gave Tomás a clean bill of health. So Filton, who had his lean, aristocratic guts, despite his look of a blind and greying turkey buzzard, kept Tomás safe. Then the Right—with the usual rumors of CIA assistance—staged the *next* revolution. And Tomás, as a refugee from Red persecution, became an automatic hero . . ."

"And?" Jim said.

"Tomás was too smart to depend upon such uncertain laurels. He asked for, and got, the job of majordomo, head butler, at our embassy, when Filton was elevated to Ambassador's rank. He's been there ever since. And every Ambassador we've sent down there swears by him. You can take my word for it, Chub; you can rely on Tomás . . ."

"Peter," Alicia said quickly, "you are forgetting two more; both of them much more important than Tomás is . . ."

"Such as?" Peter said.

"Doctor Gomez—and the Archbishop."

"More important, how?" Peter said. "Socially, 'Licia? I grant you that. But both of them much less well placed to do Chub—Jim here—any real good if the going gets rough. As the going sure as hell will. But all right—add them to your list, Jim. There! I'm getting the hang of it! Doctor Vicente Gomez Almagro. Harvard Med School grad; one of the damn-finest surgeons anywhere, Jim, which could come in handy if those types ventilate you, as they did me. Vince saved my life that time—with a powerful assist from 'Licia's and Padre Pío's prayers. Which brings me to his Grace, the Archbishop. Name: José María Zaratieguí Istúriz, but known throughout his long and devoted service as Father Pious for the simple reason that nobody but another Basque can pronounce Basque names. Must be close to eighty by now, but as spry as a spring chicken, and as full of hell and ginger as ever. The one truly good human being I've ever known. Religion does that—when you can believe it. The only problem is that García's got Padre Pío bottled up in the Ecclesiastical Palace and won't let him out. Afraid of that sweet, simpleminded old coot. The one man in Costa Verde García dares not kill. The one man he can neither intimidate, bend, nor break. That one poor, eighty-year-old saintly fool who—"

"Is magnificent!" Alicia said. "And a hero. And a Saint. May God bless him eternally!"

"Amen!" Peter said. "Agreed—on all counts, 'Licia. But, granting you all your points, Vince Gomez can only do Jim some good if Jim's brought to him on a stretcher. And Padre Pío is virtually a prisoner, so—"

"Perhaps," Alicia said, "he will again perform a miracle—on Jim's behalf. I must write to him and recommend Jim very specially, so that he will pray for him, and—"

"I thank you for that, Alicia," Jim said solemnly. "I probably need someone to pray for me, sinner that I am! Good—I guess that about winds it up. Lord, it's late! I had no idea—"

"No you don't Chub! You're going to tell us how you found out about an oil discovery that the State Department has moved heaven and earth to keep secret—with the willing help of Wildcat and Buddies—so they can spring it on our kaffiyeh-wearing friends at the next bargaining session at Geneva and use it to club crude prices down from the absolutely outrageous to the merely ruinous," Peter said.

"It was leaked to me. By my departmental head—a *very* Assistant Secretary of State. To pull me down a peg or two. I guess I had been a little high-handed with him. Money does give you that kind of security . . ."

"Riddles," Peter said. "And in pure Attic Greek, at that!"

"No. He wanted me to know that Ed Crowley was largely responsible for my getting the post. That he'd pulled a considerable number of wires to make sure I would get it . . ."

Peter and Alicia both stared at Jim. Then Peter said:

"You've just answered the question I hadn't dared asked you, Jim. Never did believe there was any truth in that story, anyhow—"

"*What* story, *Cielo?*" Alicia said.

"Off the record, 'Licia. It's a part of Jim's past—and private—life. Which he's entitled to *keep* private, *Muñeca.* One of the few inalienable rights remaining, it seems to me . . ."

"I thank you for that, Peter," Jim said solemnly. "But you have my leave to repeat it to Alicia. Later on. In bed. Pillow talk is one of the indisputable advantages of matrimony. I won't even enter a plea in my own defense . . ."

"Now I am intrigued!" Alicia said. "Were you a *very* naughty boy, Jim?"

Jim smiled. It was a smile of almost infinite sadness.

"Let's say I was in there trying, Alicia," he said.

CHAPTER

3

On Monday, Jim Rush took a midmorning flight back
to New York. In his State Department records, that
city was listed as his "place of residence," a much more accurate way of
putting it, in one sense, Jim conceded, than to say he lived there. He
owned—since the death of his father—a townhouse in the East Seventies. It had come to him as a legacy, along with the income from the
quite respectable trusts that had been accumulated by several generations
of Rushes, all of them so hedged about with prudent codicils, added as
financial circumstances changed, that they nearly always passed from one
Rush to the next with their basic capital not only intact, but actually
increased.

But now, he reflected sadly, both house and trusts would have to go
to some worthy charity when he died, because he was the very last Rush,
and divorced, widowed, and wifeless at close to fifty, the likelihood was
that his line would end with him.

He took aboard the plan an attaché case filled with notes of the long,
detailed briefings both Tim O'Rourke and Peter Reynolds had given
him. This was more out of a seasoned traveler's bitter experience with
the airlines' maddening habit of forwarding one's most valuable piece of
luggage to Shanghai, than from any intention of even glancing at those
notes. They were full of the biographical data of the current dictator,
General Manuel García Herredia, his principal supporters, his chief

enemies, and a whole alphabetical soup of far Left and far Right subversive and/or terrorist organizations, but, as was usual for Latin America, absolutely no moderates at all.

Of course, on a jet that would scream and whistle him down from Boston to New York in a matter of minutes, so that the taxi rides out to Logan and in from La Guardia would, he knew, cost him far more time than the actual flight, opening the attaché case and making an attempt to go over those notes simply wasn't worth the bother. What he did do, once settled in his seat, was to take out the Polaroid picture that Tim had taken of him standing between Alicia and Marisol with his arms around both of them, and study Alicia's remarkable heathen idol's face with great care. Of course, Tim had taken many other pictures that Sunday morning and had given Jim his choice. And though Jim, out of diplomacy and politeness, had chosen—or, he admitted to himself wryly, pretended to choose—several of them, the only one that interested him truly was this one.

'Why?' he asked himself. 'You're not going to sell yourself the absolutely profitless proposition that you've fallen in love with your best friend's wife, are you? Developed a healthy yen for her—of course! Who wouldn't? Lord Jesus! She turns those slanting, night black, jungle eyes of hers on you and—hold it, Jim! Heavy string of adjectives to hang on to a pair of eyes that are simply—Indian. Tluscolan, Peter said. You've seen their like ten thousand times.'

But he hadn't, and he knew it. Never before. Nor anything remotely resembling the curiously contradictory quality of her mouth. Sensual. That was right, so say it. Sensual. And yet—tender. Achingly tender. Defenseless, somehow. More adjectives. And he had had far too much experience as a writer, both in college and in his public relations and advertising jobs not to know what overindulgence in their use did to the necessary economy of English prose. But there they were and he was stuck with them. Maybe because they're so damned accurate, he thought.

He didn't really know why he had asked Tim to take that particular picture. He had joked that he was going to show it to all and sundry and boast that Alicia and Marisol were his *"queridas,"* a word whose accepted meaning among all Spanish-speaking peoples is "mistresses" instead of the "sweethearts" or beloved ones that the dictionary gives. But that wasn't the reason. He knew what the reason was. He also knew damned well that said reason was insane—or close to it. Because he was almost surely going to take that picture down to Villalonga City, show it to the majordomo at the American Embassy there and say:

"Look, Tomás, go find me a girl who looks exactly like this one."

And with some chances of success from what both Peter and Alicia had said. For it was abundantly clear that Alicia's father had been a *"mujeriego,"* a Spanish expression literally translated by its British equivalent "womanizer," though perhaps more accurately by the slangy American "skirt chaser." Conditions in Latin America—especially the Roman Catholic Church's iron grip on questions of sexual morality, which made at least the logistics of effective contraception very close to an actual impossibility—the probabilities were that he had fathered numerous illegitimate offspring in addition to his legitimate children. These were, Jim had gathered indirectly during his weekend visit to the Reynolds' home, only Alicia herself and her late brother, the Dictator Miguel Villalonga, assassinated by the Communists during the revolt of 1963. Jim could no longer recall how many times he had heard the reply that *Latinos* make to the question, "How many children do you have?" said reply being, *"¿En que calle?"* "In which street?"

So that supposition being granted, and even all but confirmed by Alicia's own words, an actual probability that in Ciudad Villalonga—named after Alicia's murdered brother, or, more likely, in view of any *Latino*'s gift for self-glorification, named *by* Miguel Villalonga in honor of himself!—that he, Jim Rush, could, if he gave the matter so much as a halfway serious try, meet one of Alicia's half sisters, or one of her nieces, enough like her to make him overcome his almost morbid timidity and risk another humiliation of the women had constantly inflicted upon him throughout his life. And with his absolute command of Spanish to aid him, he stood at least a fair chance of ending his loneliness for good.

'Better than fair,' he admitted to himself, slowly. 'You know *Latinas.* They're the most realistic women on the face of earth. It's the *norteamericanas* and other *nordicas* who are hopelessly romantic—one of the reasons for the appalling divorce rates in any country where blondeness prevails. How many absolutely stunning Latin girls have you seen married to men old enough to be their fathers—or to young men close to being physically repulsive—because the men in question were highly placed socially and well off financially? Hundreds. And you, yourself—you retarded adolescent fool!—could have married any of a dozen at least attractive women since Virginia's death, if you hadn't held back, waiting for the miraculous appearance of your dream girl, who'd come to you with her eyes aglow with true and tender love. Horse droppings! What's love got to do with any really workable marriage, anyhow? Damned little. I'd say that liking, mutual respect, and above all resignation to each other's irritating quirks, bad habits, and small madnesses are the factors that make the whole proposition even remotely acceptable. If it ever is. If there's even any such thing as a good marriage . . .

'Good, perhaps not. Good was maybe too much to ask for. But workable, yes. Workable in the sense of being serene, comfortable, stable—that was the word! How he longed for continuity, stability; he who had had neither, never in his life.'

And, he had to admit, among the people he had met in Latin America—nearly all of them upper class—marriages were usually stable. There was, of course, a fairish amount of playing around on the part of the husbands in that small group rich enough to afford it. But among the wives—almost never.

'Or maybe,' he thought, 'Latin women being as clever as they are, they manage not to get caught. Would you also accept *that*—on the sound basis of what you don't know can't hurt you? Yes,' he answered his own rhetorical question bleakly; 'as things stand now, I probably would . . .'

He remembered then how honest Virginia had been. How chillingly, cripplingly, castratingly honest about admitting her adulteries. Virginia who, because of his frequent, unavoidable, and prolonged absences—with the added aggravation that their separations were wholly due to the fact that she flatly refused to share his professionally necessary exiles—had had every conceivable means at her disposal for easily and completely concealing her utter faithlessness.

But Virginia had been a romantic—'An approach to life that should be prohibited by law!'—and was constitutionally incapable of indulging in a simple, physically satisfying affair unless she were convinced that the man in question was her—belatedly encountered!—perfect mate; and that the affair in question was going to go on forever. 'And since,' Jim mused sadly, 'both concepts rank high on the list of total illusions, she was always being disappointed. So then she'd try again, gradually lowering her standards as she grew older. I suppose that that last time the truth must finally have hit her: that there is no perfect mate and no love whatsoever that lasts beyond life's midsummer season—and she couldn't take it. She must have looked in the mirror and saw herself as she was—a thin, faded, never too attractive woman, with a deep vein of sensuality in her that she couldn't accept unless it were prettied up with offstage music, hearts and flowers!—and realized that she had very little to offer anymore, that—cruel thought!—perhaps she never had. Because it was always her lovers who tired first, always she who was left, not the other way around—the sole exception being one Jim Rush! And faced with the proposition of spending the rest of her life with the dull, pokey, placid man she despised—largely because he had never reared up on his hind legs and beaten the living hell out of her as she knew damned well she deserved!—she preferred, and chose—to die.

'And now here you are, with *that* behind you—with the sure knowledge that at least one woman decided she'd rather be dead than to have to go on living with you—thinking, almost planning, to stick your neck out again . . .'

He seized the photograph between his two hands and started to tear it across. But he couldn't. He literally couldn't. He sat there staring at the image of Alicia's face, caught forever at one glorious instant of time in the light-darkened silver slats and colored dyes of the photo, and his hands started to shake. Slowly he put it back into his inside jacket pocket.

Then, perhaps because she had seen the gesture, accurately estimated the degree of pure despair it contained, was professionally oriented towards the avoidance of emotional outbreaks, suicidal impulses, madness, anything at all that might upset the even tenor of the flight, one of the stewardesses was bending over him, saying, too brightly:

"Would you like a drink, Sir? Or something to read? Oh, dear! That's or/and, of course! You can have both, if you like . . ."

Jim glared at her. Then he sighed, relaxed.

"The drink, no thanks," he said; "but a paper—a New York morning paper, if you have one; I shouldn't mind—"

"Can do!" she said. Or maybe it was "Roger!" or something else equally as inane. He wasn't quite sure and it didn't matter. She was back in seconds with the paper. Jim thanked her; took it. And one more episode from that long, slow, dull, but achingly anguished drama his whole life had been, rose up and hit him between the eyes.

"Jenny Crowley Believed in South America!" those headlines screamed at him; "Missing Oil Heiress, Wanted by the FBI in connection with the Satan Cult Child Murders, Sighted in Venezuela, Witness Claims!"

There was more: columns and columns of pure, unsupported speculation, plus a rehash of the whole case. But Jim didn't read them. The speculations interested him not at all, and the case, in all its nauseating details, he already knew. Instead, he thought about Jenny Crowley. Recreated in his mind her sweet, childish, but endlessly stubborn face. "Jenny, with the light brown hair," he had called her, after the old folksong, though her hair, actually, had been dark blonde instead of brown, and—come to think of it!—it was "Jeanie" not "Jenny" that the song said. He reached again the conclusion he had come to long before, a conclusion indistinguishable from conviction, really: He didn't give a good goddamn how many eyewitness accounts placed her in one of the two cars along with Jeremy Whittle and his Coven of Junior Grade Witches on the night they raided the Catholic orphanage, leaving the two good Sisters on night duty gagged and bound, and bearing away with them the two little girls whose dismembered bodies had been found on the high altar of their "Temple," apparently having been offered up as a blood sacrifice to their Satanic Lord. Jenny Crowley, the Jenny he had known, was capable of only one reaction to a child: She'd gather it—Black, White, Oriental, or Chicano, unwashed, in rags, stinking to high heaven—as he had seen her do a dozen times, in her starved and longing arms, and almost smother it with kisses.

'Excretia!' he snorted. 'Bovine and equine, both! Why wasn't she captured along with the rest of those insane and murderous young swine? Jeremy and twelve girls—she, herself, supposedly made up the reglementary thirteenth of a Witches' Coven!—most of them stark naked and smeared with those poor babies' blood, were still on the scene, asleep, or apathetic from narcotics—'Stoned right out of their skulls,' Jenny would have put it!—except that Black boy, Ronald Spearman, found shot to death in one of the cars outside. The car with Jenny's fingerprints all over the rolled up window. A pack of marijuana cigarettes beside him on the seat. Smoked-out butts, some of them lipstick stained, in the ashtrays and on the floor. So Jenny is charged with his murder, and suspected of participating in the "Satan Cult Orgy Child Murders!" to quote the chaste and simple language of the daily press.'

He shuddered a little, thinking about those stories. They hadn't been pretty. The papers had had themselves a picnic speculating over the precise nature of Jenny's relations with Spearman, and her motives for killing him.

'They hinted as broadly as they dared that she and that poor devil were lovers,' Jim remembered sadly. ' "Her Favorite Partner in Cult Gropes?" was the way they put it. Which I can believe, because, by then, Jenny would have gone to any lengths to get even with her father, revenge herself for a lifetime of neglect and bad tempered abuse, alternating with overpampering. Out of simple fairness, I have to admit that when Ed was in one of his generous moods, she could have anything that money can buy. Only it never seems to have occurred to the old pirate that what she needed was one of the few things it *can't* buy. So little Jenny struck back with a real shocker: flagrant miscegenation. Knew just how and where to hit him, didn't she? Nothing, not even her becoming the star performer in that Las Vegas whorehouse he practically owns by now—having bought it by installments!—could have outraged Ed Crowley more than that. Hell, on a gut deep, emotional level, it outrages me; and I call myself a liberal! To which the highminded, chivalrous, and considerate members of the Fourth Estate added that the motives for the crime were perhaps "a bad trip" or a drugged and drunken lovers' quarrel.

'Bad guesses, both. Because Jenny Crowley, the Jenny who used to call me "Uncle Chub" and cry upon my willing and available shoulder was, is, and always will be, incapable of killing anything or anybody. And on that I'd stake my life!'

But he had no more time for thinking about anything, because by then the plane had slid down a long, long blue and white and golden slant of sky, and was screeching its tires against the landing strip.

He went through the dull and weary business of deplaning, wondering idly what the hell—besides poring over those notes with a drink at his elbow—he was going to do with the rest of the day. About the night, he didn't even speculate. All his nights were beyond speculation. He'd do battle with his loneliness, his aching need—though by now far more for human warmth, company, affection, love, than for mere sex—until sleep, usually induced by a pill or two, called a merciful, if temporary truce . . .

He was reaching forward to grab his suit bag from where it wobbled and swayed on the luggage conveyer belt when a hand shot past his and snatched it off. He whirled, more in astonishment than anger, and stared up into the square jawed face of one of those impeccably groomed, flawlessly dressed, but always tremendously muscular young giants that Ed Crowley usually had surrounding him. And had a definite need of, he figured. Ed's Gorillas, he'd called them, during the years when he, too, had been at the oilman's beck and call.

"Just who the devil are you?" he said.

"The handle's Mike Harper," this one said; "and I guess you could say I'm a member of Mr. Crowley's personal staff, Mr. Ambassador. Let me take your flight bag and that case, will you, please? The car's just outside Exit Thirteen. Mr. Crowley said you'd come in today; but since he didn't know which flight, he's had us take turns at meeting them all—"

"And why on earth did he do that?" Jim said.

"Damned if I know," Harper said. "Mr. Crowley doesn't give explanations to his hired help—or to anybody else for that matter, as you probably know, since you worked for him once; didn't you, Mr. Ambassador?"

"Oh, for God's sake, call me by my name!" Jim said, with real exasperation.

"You're the boss, Mr. Rush!" Mike Harper said. "By the way, if you've a hotel reservation, better let me have it so I can cancel it for you. Mr. Crowley said to tell you he'd be putting you up. You'll have the whole guest suite in Crowley Towers."

"I haven't a reservation," Jim said dryly. "But then, I don't need one. I have a house—a townhouse at 268 East Seventy-second Street. You can drop me off there, if you care to. Or you can call me a taxi—preferably the latter. And tell your boss no thanks. I've had enough of his brand of hospitality to last me a lifetime."

He saw, astonishingly, that Mike Harper's forceful young face was truly stricken. Part of it was amazement that anyone dared refuse Ed Crowley anything whatsoever; but the rest of it was perplexity at being confronted with a situation that couldn't be resolved by a variety of karate chops, judo holds, a blackjack, a knife, or a gun. 'Probably silencer equipped, that last item,' Jim thought mockingly.

"Look, Mr. Rush," Mike Harper, the—'What was it that Ed Crowley called the members of his goon squad? Oh, yes! the Confidential Aide'— said slowly "let's compromise, will you? I don't bring you to the Towers, and the Boss will have my hide—my job, too—a thing I can't afford. What d'you say you ride in with me to the office, and you, yourself, tell Mr. Crowley you don't want to stay? That way the whole thing will be off my back, and—"

Jim thought about that. Realized that Ed Crowley's muscular young flunky was telling the truth. Wildcat's reaction to being crossed was notorious.

"All right," he said; "I shouldn't like to cost you your job, Michael. Besides," he grinned suddenly, "it will be a pleasure to read Ed the lesson for today."

"The lesson for today?" Harper said, "I don't get you, Mr. Rush . . ."

"Yes. That a good many people can't be bought. And that as far as he's concerned, I head the list. Now come on. Lead me to the car. What's it this time, a Rolls?"

"No, Sir—a Mercedes 450 SE," the Confidential Aide said. "Just as good a car for my money. Hell, it's better. And it doesn't attract as much attention . . ."

"Go to the head of the class. I can see Wildcat's trained you well. Now lead on," Jim said.

CHAPTER

4

*I*t is an indisputable fact, though, curiously enough, Jim Rush had never realized it before, that one of the things that money *can* buy is taste, with the inescapable reservation, of course, that the possessor of the money must be intelligent enough to accept and respect the advice of the possessor of the taste. And though Ed Crowley had been called—with much justification!—every unprintable epithet in most of the languages of the Western world, the one thing no one, not even his worst enemies, had ever called him was a fool.

For those offices in Crowley Towers were a marvel; and in precisely the way and the sense that Jim had expected them *not* to be. That is, they were quiet, restrained; following that canon of flawless elegance that Jim's London tailor—Savile Row, of course, and his services inherited from Jim Rush, Senior, like so many good and pleasant things in his present life—had impressed upon Jim when his father had taken him, as a callow youth, to have his first really good suit made: "A well-dressed man, young Mister Rush, is that man whom, afterwards, you remember as having been well dressed, without being able to recall a single detail of his clothing . . . ."

That, suitably adjusted, applied to Ed Crowley's outer offices. They were not, as Jim had been sure they were going to be, breathtaking. What they were, was perfect. Sparse, simple, spare—as really good things always were. On the walls, paintings that reached out and held him with quiet force. Here—a Cézanne. *Mont Sainte-Victoire,* of course; a late, late version of the scene Cézanne had painted thirty times. Dating from his last period, when he had constructed his paintings from solid masses of color. *"Cauchemardesque!"* "Nightmarish!" the critics had screamed. Monet, a London scene, painted during the years when that most French of painters had wandered as far north as Norway, seeking a subtler play of light and shadow than was to be found in his native Argenteuil. Had anyone ever painted mist and fog better than Monet? Well—Turner, perhaps. But only perhaps. Hell, you could feel it, breathe it in! Renoir—a rosy nude, with a degree of *embonpoint* and ripe peach-colored flesh that made even glancing at the signature unnecessary. *Two* Degas—possibly because their themes struck chords of resonance, of memory, even in Ed Crowley's flinty soul: a ballet dancer, and a horse race, subjects no one had ever come even close to equaling Degas at painting. A Toulouse Lautrec poster—a prancing music hall *comedienne,* her face a ghoulish horror. On very small Van Gogh—a bridge near Arles, aflame with golden sunlight. That was all. But how many national museums could have matched this collection? This tiny collection of softly glowing, absolute perfection?

'Or could have raked up the millions they cost the old pirate?' Jim thought sardonically. 'Nothing but the Impressionists, and nothing but their very best, except—'

Except, unobtrusively, in a little niche, a T'ang horse. An authentic, honest to god T'ang horse and rider, some twelve inches high, and thirteen hundred years old, that Jim would have given a reasonable facsimile of his own immortal soul to own.

Even the receptionist—English, from her accent—fitted into all this quiet perfection. A real beauty—Ed Crowley had never permitted an ugly female job applicant, or a plain one, for that matter, to remain in his irate presence seven consecutive seconds—she still wasn't the type whom, some years back at least, Jim would have found gracing Ed Crowley's reception desk. That is, her contours were not obviously designed to unseat a visitor's reason the exact second he entered the door, to make him, upon the spur of that same instant, fall prey to the pitifully facile dominance that certain mindless little glands—confronted with the proper stimulae, of course!—have over the at best uncertain cerebral function in the male of the human species. She was neither astonishingly top-heavy—Ed's Cantilever Jobs, Jim used to call them—platinum blonde, nor noticeably sensual. Not at all the kind of a girl that Ed would look at twice. 'Perhaps he doesn't look at her,' Jim thought mockingly. 'Probably bought her to match the office decor!'

She had brought him into this little waiting room, explaining that

Mister Crowley was in conference but would be available shortly, offered him a drink from the all but invisible mahogany sheathed refrigerator built into the wainscoting, and had been discreetly surprised at his reply, which was:

"No, thank you, my dear. Since I plan to say 'Hell, no!' to every single thing your horny-handed old scoundrel of a boss asks me to do, I shall need my wits about me. But if you know how to make tea the way they make it in Devonshire, I should very much like a cup or two. Especially if you'll join me . . ."

"Why—" she faltered; then she smiled. Her smile was dazzling. "I should be delighted to have a cup with you, Mr. Ambassador! Wait a sec. I'll see what can be arranged . . ."

And now, almost too quickly, she was back; but, Jim saw with real disappointment, without the tea.

"Your tea is served, Mr. Ambassador!" she said cheerfully. "But in Mrs. Niven's office. She's Head of Personnel, y'know. She asked me to have it served there, and requests you to join her. Mr. Crowley will be tied up for at least an hour; and, besides, Mrs. Nivens is most anxious to have a chat with you."

"Why?" Jim said glumly. "I'm not looking for a job. And if I were, Worldwide would be the last place on earth I'd apply. I honestly believe I'd starve first."

"Oh, Mrs. Nivens is perfectly aware of that, Sir!" the receptionist said. "She wants to talk to you about quite another matter—"

"Which is?" Jim said.

"I don't know," the receptionist said, and glanced uneasily at the door.

"You *do* know," Jim said dryly; "and I should be most grateful if you'd tell me."

"Can't. Beyond the fact that I don't *really* know, Sir; so that anything I could tell you would be a supposition, at best."

"A damned shrewd supposition," Jim said. "A guess bordering upon certainty."

She faced him, then.

"Mr. Rush—Mr. Ambassador—I *like* working here. This is the very best job I've had in all my life. I should prefer—keeping it, if you don't mind."

He smiled at her then, said:

"Sorry! I'm way out of line, aren't I? I apologize. I know what you're up against. I once worked for Mr. Crowley, myself . . ."

"I also knew that. Mrs. Nivens told me. So I know what *you're* up against, Sir! Now, if you'll come with me—"

"Not until you tell me I'm forgiven," Jim said.

"I took no offense, Mr. Rush," she said gently; "and, if I may be so bold, I'd venture that people—especially women—seldom do with you . . ."

She saw his face tighten; burst out:

"Oh, I say! I am sorry! I didn't mean that the way it sounded—"

"Doesn't matter. The truth is that I'm an inoffensive soul, and inoffensiveness is a reasonable synonym for—dullness, isn't it? Don't answer that. The question's rhetorical. Are you going to have tea with Mrs. Nivens and me?"

"One cup. Can't leave my desk unattended too long, y'know. Now, if you'll be so kind—"

"Kindness has nothing to do with it, my dear," Jim said sadly. "Call it, rather, resignation. Lead on! I confess I'm curious. For Ed to have given a woman the job of Head of his Personnel Department, she must be—extraordinary, shall we say?"

"She *is*," the receptionist said; and, saying that, pronouncing those two words, her voice was suddenly fervent, warm.

Jim stared at her. She saw that stare.

"In my opinion, Mr. Ambassador," she said, almost defiantly, "for whatever that opinion is, or may be, worth, Grace Nivens is the kindest, sweetest person I have ever been privileged to know. And the best. Oh, quite!"

"Hardly qualities one would expect to find in the Head of the Personnel Department of Worldwide," Jim said.

"True," she said slowly. "But then she is also efficient. Most efficient. Good at her job. And the—qualities I mentioned help. She can even sack people and keep their friendship. Their admiration, as well. Because, you see, Sir, she is never, never unfair."

"Quite a trick," Jim said; "especially working for Ed. She's English, then; like you? Nivens has a very British sounding ring to it, somehow . . ."

"No. Grace is American. What Mr. Nivens was, I really don't know. She's never so much as mentioned him to me. Deuced odd, come to think of it! She simply doesn't talk about herself. Her private life is just that—private. A closed book, even to her best friends. And yet, there's not the smallest detail of my life—even episodes I jolly well should have kept my mouth firmly closed about!—that she doesn't know. Don't get me wrong, Sir! She doesn't pry. She simply inspires confidence. You find yourself telling her things you wouldn't tell your own mother—or more accurately, your own sister; for there's a ruddy lot one couldn't tell one's mother these days! Well, here we are . . ."

She pushed open the door. Stood aside to let him enter. At once Grace Nivens came forward, smiling, her hand outstretched.

"Good afternoon, Mr. Rush!" she said in a pleasant alto voice. "I am delighted to meet you. You see, I've wanted to, for years!"

The way she said that, it sounded as though she meant every blessed word of it. Which wasn't the reaction Jim Rush had come to expect from women. Especially not from women like this one.

He stared at her, taking in all the details. She was tall. *Very* tall. The kind of a girl who would have a hell of a time finding a dancing partner. Whom men made bad jokes to, asking how the weather was up there. *Much* taller than he was, even taking into consideration the really quite sensible heels she wore. He was surprised to find that her height didn't bother him. Not at all. In fact, he rather liked it. It was one of the things, he supposed, that made her uniquely herself. He was suddenly almost deliriously glad that it didn't bother him when so many other, less noticeable, less striking, things about the people he came into contact with did. But it didn't. All her willowy, soaring verticality did was to remind him of a verse from the *Song of Songs:* "Thy stature is like unto a palm tree, thy breasts its clusters of dates . . . . Lo! I will go up that palm tree; I will take hold of the clusters thereof; and the smell of thy mouth will be as of apples; thy breath, the sweetest of wines!"

He went on looking at her, lost, bemused. She was slender, but not thin. A good figure. A damned good figure. She had on heavy dark-rimmed glasses that, oddly enough, became her. Her hair ("Thy head is held high as Carmel; and its plaits are as dark as purple!") was dark, too; though plentifully—and honestly, he added in his mind—streaked with silver. But her eyes, in almost startling contrast to her rather Mediterranean coloring, were blue. Not dark blue, but clear blue, like a blonde's.

She was still smiling at him, a little quizzically now; and her big, wide-lipped, wryly humorous mouth was, he decided then and there, a joy forever. What was it the receptionist had said? Oh, yes: "What Mr. Nivens *was,* I really don't know—" Was. Past tense. Blessedly past.

'Slow down, Jim Rush, you poor starved and horny bastard, you!' he snarled at himself inside his mind. 'Remember that you *never* get anywhere with women. Especially not with this kind. Pure class. A thoroughbred. Lines, breeding, intelligence, looks—the works. So once again, Lord High Mayor of Dullsville, slow down!'

He took her hand, deciding as he did so that she was close to forty. Perhaps even past it. Which was all to the good, as far as he was concerned.

"The pleasure's all mine, Mrs. Nivens," he said; "but satisfy the one honest emotion I have left—which is curiosity. Why—accepting for the moment your much too flattering remarks at face value—have you wanted to meet me for years?"

"Because," she said simply, and with so obvious a sincerity that not even he could doubt it, "I've heard so much about you—all of it paeans of almost worshipful praise!—that I literally *had* to meet you. Paragons of all the virtues—especially, if you'll pardon my frankness, Mr. Ambassador Rush, among the male half of humanity—aren't exactly in oversupply, you know. Besides, my profession has made a skeptic of me. I like to form my own judgments. So, to repeat, I am delighted to meet you at long, long last, Mr. Rush!"

"And now that you have, I've my job cut out for me," Jim said, trying to keep the bitterness out of his tone.

She peered at him through those glasses. Her eyes—what *did* her eyes do? 'Her eyes,' Jim mused, 'make midsummer lightnings in a dark and golden sky. A line of truly sophomoric sentimentality, if I ever heard one! And godawful poetry. But that's just what they do, so I'm stuck with it!'

"Your job?" she said, questioningly.

"Yes—to limit your disappointment to at least reasonable proportions," he said.

"Only I'm not disappointed," she said quietly. "Quite the contrary. You're not at all what I expected, Mr. Rush. But sit down, will you? The tea's getting cold. Oh, no, Meg, darling—I'll pour. You were not hired to wait on me, you know . . ."

"But I *like* waiting on you, Grace," the receptionist said; "I only wish it were part of my job—and that what I was hired to do were half as pleasant."

"Thank you, Meg. You are a dear, you know. Well, Mr. Rush, which do you prefer: milk or lemon?"

"Lemon," Jim said. "Would it be too much of a chore for you to call me Jim? I'd like you to. Very much, in fact."

"I was going to. In the very next breath, likely. In return for which, you must call me Grace."

"Suits you," he said. "A remarkably apt and fitting name, come to think of it. Not only are you physically graceful, but you have grace. The quality, I mean. And that's very rare—"

"Thank you," she said, a little stiffly; "but you really don't have to pay me compliments, Mr. Rush."

"Jim," he insisted.

"Jim. The fact is, I don't like them. They're a hangover from a stage in the relationship between men and women that we should have outgrown by now . . ."

"*I* haven't," Jim said, and grinned at her. "You have my leave to pay me all the compliments you want to. I'll sit here contentedly and lap them up!"

She laughed at that. Relaxed a little. Said:

"Then you'll be disappointed, Jim. On the other hand, I'll offer you something more valuable: the truth. Put as diplomatically as I can manage, of course. Oh, dear! Meg, must you leave us so soon?"

"I really must, Grace," Meg said; "if Mr. Crowley comes storming out of his office and finds my desk unoccupied, I shall be reading the want ads tomorrow morning! Good afternoon, Mr. Rush. It has been a pleasure—"

"All mine," Jim said, and stood up.

She smiled at him, made an impish face.

"I doubt that—*now,*" she said solemnly.

"Why do you doubt it, *now?*" he asked, emphasizing the element of time, just as she had done.

"Because now you've met Grace," she laughed. "Which is the exact point at which the majority of men—and all the really attractive ones— lose interest in me. And you, my dear Grace, had better take care! Mr. Ambassador Rush is a bit on the smooth side, wouldn't you think?"

"He is; and I mean to," Grace said, smiling. "Now get out of here, Meg, baby! This chat *is* private, after all . . ."

After Meg had left the room, with a delightful little swish and sway that convinced Jim Rush, again, that British reserve and apparent coolness were evidences of their exact opposites held valiantly in check, Grace turned to him with a sigh.

"Meg *is* a dear," she said; "but I'm afraid I'll have to rein her in a bit. She's never been out of England before, and the greater freedom of our manners—"

"And our behavior," Jim said, dryly.

"That, too, I sadly fear—have gone to her head just a trifle. But since she's basically sound, I'm not too worried about her. More tea, Mr. Rush? And something to accompany it?"

It was a high tea, complete with scones, crumpets, buns, pound cake, a huge pile of butter, and three kinds of jam besides the traditional bitter orange marmalade. But, Jim found with quiet pleasure, he wasn't even tempted. Food, at least—and at long, long last!—was an emotional crutch he no longer needed.

"No, thank you," he said; "tea is quite enough at the moment."

She smiled at him, a little mockingly.

"Are you a weight watcher, Jim?" she asked. "I was told you'd be on the plumpish side; and you aren't. Not at all."

"You were told that I'd be grossly fat," Jim said bluntly, "which means you were briefed by someone who hasn't seen me in quite some time. At least five years to be exact. Would it be an indiscretion on my part, Grace, to ask who your informant was?"

"Not at all. It was Jenny. Jenny Crowley—who was also the source of those paeans of praise I mentioned. She was quite dreadfully in love with you, Jim. Don't tell me you didn't know that!"

He stared at her, anger rising in him. But he controlled it.

"You're a very intelligent woman, Grace," he said quietly, "not to mention a damned good-looking one. So let's get to the point, shall we? Nothing about you inclines me to the idea that you invited me in here to play games."

"Oh, dear!" she sighed; "I've really shoved my size nines in among my bridgework, haven't I? Do forgive me, Jim!"

She leaned forward, laid her hand on his arm.

"Jim, I'm trying—rather desperately—to help Jenny, if and when she's found. Beyond my professional interest in her as my patient—"

"Your patient!" Jim said.

"Yes." She nodded with brusque, angular grace towards the wall behind her desk. It was literally covered with diplomas. B.S. and M.S., Columbia University; Ph.D. in Psychology, the University of California at Berkley; M.D., the University of California's Medical School; Doctor of Psychiatric Medicine, the University of Vienna; Certificate from the State Medical Board licensing her to practice as a Physician and Surgeon in the State of New York; another, granting her the same rights and privileges as a Psychiatrist; certificates of honors and awards from a score of learned societies both in the States and abroad . . . The works.

'And too damned much!' Jim thought grimly. He didn't doubt her intelligence; but just what the hell was she trying to prove with this exhibition? It was rather plebeian, somehow. In the circles to which he had been born, one never mentioned one's qualifications unnecessarily; not to mention placing them on display. Her State Certificate licensing her to practice psychiatry, and that only in the office in which she practiced it, would have been enough. But here in an office where her professional skills were not directly connected with her work . . . He thought, 'I guess I'm a damned snob, after all!' He said, with a little laugh:

"You surely don't hide your light under a bushel, do you, my dear?"

She stared at him. Then, very slowly, she smiled.

"Meaning that all this is horrendously vulgar ostentation, Jim? It is. I agree with you. But Ed—Mr. Crowley—insists upon it. And you know just how far I'd get trying to teach him a little taste at this late date!"

It wasn't what she said; rather it was the way she said it—that too quick correction from "Ed" to "Mister Crowley" uttered with an amused little purr—that caused suspicion, fully armed, to poke an obscene finger into his gut. 'You have no right,' he snarled at himself, 'no right at all . . .' But, all the same, gone beyond his will, he heard his own voice—'Giving vent to your nasty, little emotional cripple's spleen!' he thought sadly, angrily, bitterly; but unable to stop himself, totally unable—saying dryly:

"Somebody has. These new offices are a marvel. And, when I worked for him, he wouldn't have chosen your little friend Meg as a receptionist. Nor you, I firmly believe, for anything whatsoever. So, as soon as I figure out just where and to what degree you fit into the Crowley pattern, I'll be able to judge how much his taste has improved—"

Her heavy brows, completely natural, untouched as they were by either tweezer or razor, shot upward. Her blue eyes flashed and flared storm signals in her deeply tanned face. But her voice, speaking, was very quiet. And matchlessly serene.

"Jim," she said; "I was beginning to—to like you. Even—on the basis of too little evidence, perhaps!— to concede that Jenny's estimation of your—your character—was correct. Now you've disappointed me. And I don't like disappointments. Had too many of them, I suppose."

"Then I apologize," he said evenly, the bile of thwarted hope, of a disappointment greater and more bitter than any she could know still driving him on. "Do forgive me, Grace. But, unfortunately it has been my sad, and perhaps even cynical, experience that even the most exquisite—orchids—can be bought, if the price is high enough."

She said: "Oh, God!" Bowed her head. Looked up again, having mastered herself in that brief interval.

"You really are quite something, aren't you, Jim?" she said. "To combine your implications with—well, call it flattery, anyhow. Though it is, isn't it? Well-turned flattery, polished to a high gloss! All right. Let's have this out. I am *not* Ed Crowley's mistress, which is obviously what you wanted to know. And though I fail to see what concern it is of yours, I doubt that I appeal to him at all, in the physical sense. I *know* he doesn't to me. The truth is I feel rather sorry for him. Jenny's—flight—has all but wrecked him. He has become my patient, too. This job was his not very subtle way of getting me away from my practice so that he could have my services—my professional services, Jim Rush!—exclusively for poor Jen, at first; then later, for himself. I accepted—I *was* bought; but my price wasn't money, Jim. Say it was—love, and pity. Both feelings as far as Jenny was concerned, pity alone for Ed. I have accepted as my salary not one penny more than I was already making in private practice; I have refused all his subsequent offers of raises. And that salary, for your information, is paid me for my brains and skill—I'm damned good at aptitude testing, y'know; and I've saved Worldwide Petroleum a sizable fortune by weeding out emotional misfits before they could be hired, as well as standing as a buffer between talented, sensitive employees, and Ed Crowley—not for my abilities, if any, as a bedmate!"

He grinned at her then; said:

"By the way, how are they?"

"Men!" she said in a tone of pure exasperation. Then she added, mockingly: "Let's say they're a good deal more than *you're* prepared to handle, Jim Rush!"

He said then, flatly, quietly, the pain in his voice naked:

"I shouldn't doubt that. I've always been lousy in the hay."

She stared at him and slowly, but quite visibly, her hostility began to melt. He could see it drain out of her, the rigidity of her pose softening, her wide-lipped, generous mouth losing its tautness, her pale blue eyes taking on a hint of a glow—

'Of pure pity!' Jim snarled inside his mind.

"D'you know, Jim," she said; "you're the first man I've ever known to admit that—spontaneously, I mean? A good many of my male patients—nearly all of them, in fact—have admitted it finally. But it had to be dragged out of them with fish hooks, thus delaying curing that particular aspect of their problems by months. If it's any comfort to you, the condition—conditions, really, since it takes many forms—are, one, far from rare; two, practically always psychological; and, three, curable ninety-seven percent of the time. It's a pity you're leaving the country so soon—"

He said, slowly:

"Why? I could never bring myself to talk about my love life—my quite nonexistent love life!—to *you*, Grace. To some other psychiatrist, perhaps; but to *you*, never!"

She stared at him. Said:

"Why not, Jim?"

"That business about transference," he said; "you know far better than I do that it's accepted Freudian doctrine that the patient will, sooner or later, transfer his feelings—his frustrations, his love, his hate—to the psychiatrist, making the psychiatrist a love object, or a hate object—or both."

She went on looking at him. Said, quietly:

"So?"

"I'd never get past the first, or to the second—though women, including dear little Jenny! have given me abundant reason to hate them, God knows! And in neither case would I even want to," he said. "Which would make matters more than a little burdensome for you, I'm afraid."

She peered at him through those glasses; said, her voice somber with real pity:

"Have you no vanity at all, Jim Rush?"

"No," he said grimly; "not a goddamned bit!"

"And I thought that she—Jenny—was wrong about you, as she generally was about most people. Only she wasn't. I can even see why she loved you so—"

He said, angrily:

"How can you see that, since she *didn't*? No woman ever has, really; but Jenny least of all. I was only an available shoulder for her to cry on. Her fat, jolly 'Uncle Chub' who—"

"Whom she loved. Even sexually—"

He stopped her with a lifted hand. Said:

"You've made your position clear, Grace. So allow me to make mine even clearer: The story that Crowley fired me because he caught me in bed with his darling daughter is quite true. But also inexact. It was the other way around, since both the bed and the room, in that overpowering Wild West Hunting Lodge cum Mansion of Ed's in Colorado, were mine. But we *were* in bed together. Fully clothed. And little Jenny was crying on Uncle Chubby Jim's shoulder because Ed was demanding that she have an abortion, get rid of the package from heaven that some other and far speedier type than I'll ever be, had left her with. Which is the exact truth of the matter, Grace. You can believe it, or not believe it, as you like; but that's the way it was!"

"I do believe it. Not only because you've already convinced me that you don't lie; but because Jenny, herself, told me the same thing. When I said 'sexually,' that wasn't what I meant."

He stared at her.

"Then what in God's name *did* you?" he said.

"Only that she didn't know it at the time," Grace said serenely. "I dug that detail out of her subconscious, made her see it. Unfortunately, she was a victim of Anglo Saxon puritanism, with its emphasis on moral dichotomies, shall we say? She compartmentalized people. You, she loved, respected, fixed all her repressed Electra complex upon—so that having sexual relations with you became a kind of an incest tabu. You follow me, don't you?"

"Of course. But I don't believe a word of it!"

"You needn't, especially if you find the idea offensive. I have no reason to convince you; not now, at any rate. A pity. If you had had an affair with Jenny, you'd have probably ended up married to her—"

"With, or without benefit of Ed's shotgun?" Jim said.

She laughed.

"*With* probably! But the detail's unimportant, Jim. Even irrelevant from my point of view. What's more to the point is that I'm sure you would have made her happy. And vice versa, likely. For talking to you has let me see how right you two were for each other. You're both such gentle people, though I must say you do have a fine, healthy streak of bastardy in you, don't you?"

"More than a streak. And being one of what you call the 'gentle people' is no damned fun, Grace!"

"I know it isn't. If I had time, I'd teach you a few defensive tactics. And offensive ones as well, since to go on the offensive is often the very best defense possible . . ."

"All right. Then allow me to enter one small defense plea, Doctor! When I said that about figuring just where and to what degree *you* might fit into the Crowley pattern, I wasn't—at least not intentionally!—trying to be nasty. That slipped out, Grace. You see, the idea that Ed Crowley might conceivably have added you to his collection—hurt. I resented his having acquired that Cézanne, that Monet, the Renoir, the two Degas, the Toulouse Lautrec, the Van Gogh, and, above all, that miraculous little T'ang horse—because, knowing Ed, I'm sure he seldom even looks at them; and when he does, he hasn't the faintest notion of what the hell he's looking at. Beauty—on that level, on that exquisite level—should belong to, or at least be shared with, people who can appreciate it . . ."

She sat there, looking at him. Really looking at him. Inside him, that tattered village idiot, that forlorn clown called hope, stirred, cut a weary caper, tried a listless grimace, whistled out of tune . . .

"So?" she said.

"The same thing goes for you, Grace. Only more so. Raised to the tenth power, at the very least."

"Then," she all but whispered—and her voice, his much too acute ear told him to his dismay, had frost and flint in it again; that, and something else, something he did not realize then was bitter hurt—"you consider me an *objet d'art,* Jim? I'm to be flattered at the idea that—a *connoisseur*—would consider adding me to his collection? List me among his *possessions?*"

"You'd head the list," he said then. "Head any true connoisseur's list of the absolutely priceless, Grace. But you'll grant me that I corrected that particular—and instinctively male!—*gaucherie* almost as soon as I'd let it out. I also said: 'Or at least be shared,' remember? And all sharing is voluntary, or it isn't even sharing. Good Lord! Any man who ever even dreamed he could own you, or even that he could bring to the—the partnership; all right?—anything remotely approaching your—no, not value! Sounds too damned commercial, doesn't it?—anything remotely approaching your quality, say, should be certified and committed. And I'd personally chip in to buy him a deluxe model straightjacket, and a padded cell to howl in!"

She smiled at him—wryly, he thought.

"You're as slippery as an eel, aren't you, Jim Rush?" she said. "A real escape artist—with words, anyhow. But I'm not inclined to let you off so easily! For if we're ever to have a civilized world, men have simply got to stop thinking of women as objects—however priceless!—or even as qualities to be shared. We're—people, too, you know. Quirky, subjective, often unpleasant, difficult to deal with, never *objets d'art* in any sense—"

"Not even God's?" he said. "Perhaps even—his masterpiece?"

"I don't believe in God," she said, and her voice was bitter, suddenly. "In my life I've seen no evidences of a kindly, guiding hand. Besides, as an art object, how would *you* catalogue me? A Renoir? No, thank you! I could never make the weight. Manet? Absolutely not! I'd cause instant indigestion in any man planning a *Déjeuner sur l'herbe*. Degas? Can you picture me as *une petite rat de l'Opéra*? One of his horses, perhaps? I am a big horse, aren't I? So, let's settle for that, shall we? A Degas cum T'ang dynasty horse, with a Toulouse Lautrec type face! That's what I usually look like early in the morning. One of his absinthe drinkers at her absolutely worst moment, and—"

She stopped short, caught and held by the astonishment in his eyes. And the pain.

"Oh, dear!" she sighed. "I should have warned you! My nightshade sense of humor takes some getting used to, I'm afraid."

He went on looking at her. Quietly. Speculatively. Studying her, actually.

"It isn't—humor," he said.

"Oh!" she whispered; then: "Oh, Jesus! 'Out of the mouths of babes and sucklings—' "

"Meaning?" he said.

"Jenny. She was right. You—you're quite as perceptive as she said you were. An uncomfortable trait in a man, Jim! Plays havoc with a woman's defenses. I know! I know! The next line is: 'Physician, heal thyself!' Only I—can't. I wish I could; but I simply can't. Now, what are you thinking?"

"That he should be shot. Dead. Buried in a dung heap. And no prayers said for his miserable soul."

She sat there. He saw her breath stop, caught and held at the base of her throat. It was a full half minute before she let it out.

"*Who* should be shot, Jim?" she whispered.

His voice speaking was very quiet, but unmistakably freighted with his anger, pity, pain.

"The bastard who did *this* to you, Grace," he said.

She bowed her head. Looked up again. Said:

"What about the woman who—"

"Used that gelding knife on me?" He shrugged, went on, calmly. "Her name was legion. But the main one is—out of it now."

"Out of your life?" she said; and he had the sudden, warming feeling that the question wasn't idle. But he repressed that feeling sternly. Emotions of that sort, hopeful assumptions, really, had cost him too much pain too many times for him to give them houseroom now. He said, his voice ashes, sand:

"Yes. And out of her own. Twenty-seven sleeping pills. In a motel room. The one her—latest lover—had left her in. Hell of a place—and a way—to die, wasn't it?"

She stared at him. Said: "Jim, I—" Then: "Oh, Christ! I knew it!"

For sharply, clearly, they both heard that knocking on the door.

"Come in, Meg!" Grace called.

Meg pushed the door open, stuck her tousled auburn head through the gap, chirped cheerfully:

"Mr. Crowley's ready to see you now, Mr. Ambassador—"

"Meg, baby," Grace said, the exasperation in her voice unfeigned, "do you think that you, or I, or anybody, could teach Ed Crowley how to spell?"

"To spell?" Meg said.

"Yes. Starting with inopportune!"

Meg stared at her.

"Good heavens!" she laughed. "Don't tell me I interrupted something—exciting, Grace!"

"Well, say—interesting. I was enjoying my conversation with Mr. Rush. Especially—the last part of it."

"Then, let's continue it, later," Jim said. "May I take you out to dinner tonight?"

"No," Grace said; "You may *not*, Jim Rush!"

He frowned. Said shortly: "Sorry!"

"Don't be," Grace said gaily; "for now it's my turn. May *I* take *you* out to dinner tonight, Mr. Ambassador Rush?"

Jim stood there. Very slowly, he smiled:

"Women's Lib in action, Grace? Very well. I accept—gladly. And, if it ever comes to that, you may even keep me in the style I'm not accustomed to. Told you a while back I have no pride!"

Grace laughed then. Freely, joyously. So joyously that Meg stared at her in sudden wonder.

"Oh, get out of here, Jim Rush!" she said.

CHAPTER

5

Meg led Jim Rush to the door of Ed Crowley's private office and stood there a long moment, frozen into an absurdly charming study of arrested motion, her tousled head bent forward, intently listening, her hand raised and poised to knock. But the oilman's voice came through the massive mahogany panels, reduced to a steady drone by their thickness. Meg waited, evidently listening for a break in the flow of what was surely dictation before announcing his visitor to her employer. But none came. Ed's lazy Texan's voice droned on and on.

Meg turned to Jim, whispered:

"Oh dear! I don't know what to do! Sometimes he rips one's head completely off if he's interrupted, and—"

Jim grinned at her; said:

"Don't interrupt him. I'll just sneak up on the old scoundrel. I want to see what his latest girl Friday is like, anyhow. The last one I knew looked like an ad for that condensed milk company. You know: 'Are you sure it's from Contented Cows?'"

Meg clapped a slim hand over her own mouth to stifle a burst of appreciative laughter.

"This one, too?" Jim said.

"I'm always expecting her to topple over forward when she stands up!" Meg giggled. " 'Bye now. Have fun!"

When she had gone, Jim put his hand on the doorknob and turned it very slowly. Pushed the door open even more slowly. Stepped inside. Stopped. Stood there without moving. Smiled to himself with wry amusement. That Ed Crowley was still unaware of his presence was clear.

Jim stared at the secretary and his grin widened. 'One of the Cantilever Jobs, all right,' he thought. He studied the extravagantly decorative and—at least from his own rather restrained point of view—excessively nubile blonde with some care. She was the same type as all Ed Crowley's women, tailored to the exact measure of the oilman's preferences, not only physically, but intellectually as well, to judge from her frantic struggles to keep up with Ed's slow Texas drawl in the penciled hieroglyphics of an obviously unpracticed shorthand.

Quietly, trying all the time not to indulge the swift surge of relief and elation that was warming him all along the surface of his skin, Jim Rush considered what her presence in Ed Crowley's office meant. Item one, he granted that the oilman was very far from being a fool, and certainly not the goddamned one he'd have to be to flaunt such bargain basement—and obviously shopworn!—goods as this in Grace Nivens's face, if there were any kind of amorous relations between him and the newly hired Head of his Personnel Department. The longer he studied the blonde, the surer Jim became of that. He kept reducing his estimation of her pitilessly downward, arriving finally at the weary conclusion that she probably hadn't even been a pro, but one more poor dumb cluck of a part-timer Ed had recruited some bleak morning from Times Square's Dawn Patrol, and had given a job here in the Towers under the contemptuously transparent camouflage of a secretarial position—a position not even really designed to hide the fact that she, like all her predecessors, had been explicitly hired for his private pleasure, rather than for whatever hypothetical and almost surely nonexistent typing and shorthand skills she may have laid claim to.

Item two, therefore, was that Grace had been telling the truth when she'd sworn that no relations at all, except professional ones, existed between her and her employer—and very likely not even exaggerating when she'd added that the only emotion Ed awoke in her was pity.

Item three was a little harder to get to, but once reached, it was, to a man as prone to self-doubt as Jim Rush, the most comforting of them all. He struggled against it with angry astonishment, but at long last and reluctantly had to concede that, given the crass vulgarity of Ed Crowley's tastes, Grace could even be right in her unlikely contention that Ed, in his turn, didn't find her especially attractive either.

Having got that far, Jim Rush surrendered to his feeling of relief, let it invade him, completely. But then he stopped that. Stopped it so fast that the reasons for not giving houseroom to either relief or hope only came to him after his automatic defense mechanisms, the conditioning built into his reflexes with a rigor beyond anything Pavlov ever dreamed of, had already done their work; had stilled the lark song at dawning; murdered the dream.

'Fat lot of good her not being hung up on Ed or his money will do *you*, Great Lover!' he snarled at himself, and moved towards the desk.

The blonde saw him first and jumped up. Meg had been right; that she didn't topple forward meant that her sense of equilibrium was at least as well developed as her physique. 'She,' Jim surmised with bemused and sardonic wonder, 'must have spent the better part of all her recent paychecks on silicone injections to have achieved *that* pectoral formation. Means she's dreaming of becoming the third—or is it the fourth?—Mrs. Edward Crowley. Forlorn hope! Honey, I've got news for you: Only the ones who have fought him off have got their dainty little hooks into this old bastard. Ed *never* marries his easy lays . . .'

Ed Crowley turned then, saw Jim, growled to the blonde:

"Git outa heah. This is more important. Call you back later, Babs—" and unrolled his endless length up out of the big chair.

Jim was shocked at his appearance. Ed Crowley had always projected a perfect image of the lean, sunbrowned, roughhewn son of the Old West, oozing homebrewed charm from every pore. That image was ninety-nine and ninety-nine one-hundredths percent faked, Jim had long since learned to his own sorrow; but Ed Crowley practiced it so assiduously, polished every facet of it with such constant, loving care that, even knowing his former employer as he did, Jim occasionally found himself almost believing it. But now that image was gone. The man who stood there wasn't even a relic of his former self. 'Say, rather—a ghost,' Jim thought with real pity, seeing how mist grey that old face was, how painfully thin that once fine body, how the out-thrust hand visibly trembled.

"Glad to see you, Son," Ed said in a croaking whisper, and shook hands. His grip was noticeably feeble. "Had lunch, Boy?"

"No," Jim said; "but it's early yet. We can talk better here than in some restaurant . . ."

"Wasn't planning to take you out. Got myself a first class chef right here in th' Towers. So if you're hungry—"

He still retained his Texas accent. That "hungry"came out "hongry."

"I'm not," Jim said. "My stomach's suffering from semipermanent jet lag. I've been on the move a lot, lately . . ."

" 'N you're as thin as a snakebit hound dog. Took my advice, didn't you? Better like that. Only thing lard is good for is to grease buckboard axles. You're looking great, Boy."

"You're not," Jim said flatly. "In fact, you look like hell, Ed."

"I know. Kind o' troubles I've been having here of late don't help my appetite. Grace says I just gotta quit worrying. But talk is mighty cheap 'n easy. Doing it takes a sight more managing. You met Grace yet? She's my shrink. Hell of a note, ain't it? A lady psychiatrist. Never thought I'd need that kind o' foolishness, but—"

"But now that you do, it's a bit more comfortable to have a female doctor hold your hand, eh, Ed? Especially one who looks like Mrs. Nivens . . ."

"So you've already met her? Great girl, Grace. Planning to make her my Missus. Could do worse, now couldn't I?"

'Damned right you could!' Jim thought. Aloud, he said: "Then what becomes of all the Cantilever Jobs?"

"The what?" Ed said; then he got it. After all, he was a first class practical engineer; and he'd even got around to taking his degree in that discipline some years back. Not that he'd needed to; but merely to show "all them pointy-headed young fellas" on his engineering staff that he could. He cackled mirthlessly at the joke.

"Got my number, ain't you, Boy?" he said. "Always purely did admire a gal with something you can grab a hold onto. 'N here I am planning to marry one who's got th' smallest little ol' titties you ever did see. Not flat—but they don't exactly poke yore eyes out, do they, Jim?"

Jim grinned at his ex-boss. He was completely at ease, now.

"I liked them," he said; "but then, tastes differ. By the way, Ed; when's the wedding?"

"Damned if I know," Ed said sadly. "That there Grace is th' hardest headed she-critter I ever run up against. Says I ain't up to gettin' hitched. Now what d'you think o' that?"

"That you ought to appreciate her point of view," Jim said. "At least it shows she's in no hurry to become the world's richest widow."

"Ain't got that much dough," Ed said automatically. "But what burns me up is that she ain't even in a hurry to get her hooks into me alive. 'N it's my *money* she objects to. Took me a long time to believe that, but now I do. That there little girl actually don't want to be *rich*. Says, given her druthers, she'd druther be happy—"

"I fail to see that money's any obstacle to the pursuit of happiness," Jim said dryly; "quite the contrary, it seems to me."

"Just what I told Grace. But then she give me a rundown on what happens to folks who've got too much. The real rich, she swears, plain can't be happy. Things come too easy to 'em, so they spoil just as easy. She's right, Jim. She's dead, damned right!"

"Then," Jim said, "why are you diving headfirst into Costa Verde's offshore oil, Ed? Why'd you pull every wire in the books to get me appointed Ambassador to that screwed up Monkey's Paradise? Ed, you've been down there—several times, in fact. You *know* what Costa Verde's like. And I worked for you long enough to learn the one thing you're not, is stupid. So now you've got me puzzled. Did you actually believe that I'd be so dazzled by a full ambassadorship that I'd be grateful to you for it, even though it includes being sent to *the* most miserable tropical hole in the Western Hemisphere?"

Ed glared at him. It was the glare of a sadly moth-eaten old eagle. Or a turkey buzzard, Jim thought.

"You took th' appointment, didn't you?" he said.

"Yes. But only as a stepping stone to something else. Something better. My greatest ambition, in case you're even slightly interested, is to get out of Latin America, permanently. Of course, you may not have known that; but, even so, the whole thing makes no sense. You ought to remember that the way we parted company wasn't exactly friendly, and that's understating the case. That fact alone being considered, the hypothesis that I'd be grateful enough to you for the appointment to become your 'boy' again, do your dirty work down there, win friends and influence people on Worldwide's behalf, simply doesn't stand up to rational examination. I won't even argue that you know what my ethics are, because you might be banking on my cowardice—"

"You ain't yellow, Jim," Ed said.

"Oh, yes, I am. I'm a coward. Always have been, always will be. The fact that I worked for *you* all of three years proves that. But, in this case, even my yellow streak would mitigate against you. Since I want to go up in my career, the thing I'd have to fear *most* would be having my name associated with yours. Let one paper print—as they *all* will if they can get their hands on the information—that I'm Worldwide's Ambassador to Costa Verde instead of the State Department's, and I'm finished, Ed. Since Watergate, since the hachet job they did on the CIA, since all the bribery scandals involving multinational corporations like yours, the press is riding high. And they'd love to get their hooks into you. If they have to squash me like a bug to get you, then consider me squashed. Flat. And they'll take turns poking around in the resulting goo. That being so, two consecutive minutes' thought ought to have demonstrated to you that I *can't* do you any good down there, which is why I don't see—"

Ed Crowley sat there. Then he said, very slowly:

"Wasn't that. Oil I can manage. 'N I've been buying greasy little Spik bastards since before you was born. 'Course them A–rabs done set 'em a mighty bad example; but I kin still manage. 'N even if I couldn't, how much difference d'you think it would make to me now?"

"Not much, I suppose," Jim said.

"Son, I'm sixty-three years old. I was to give away a million bucks a year, I'd still have to live another hundred years or so to die broke. Nope—more'n that. The interest on my money automatically doubles my capital every ten years. But you're dead, damned right. I did get you that ambassadorship. Only oil didn't have a clinking dingdanged thing to do with it—"

"Then what did?" Jim said.

"Jenny. She's down there, Son. Joe Harper—brother of th' fella I sent to meet you at the airport—got her outa th' country for me. She's livin' in a nice house on a quiet street in Villalonga City—with a young army o' bodyguards to keep her safe. Only she wants to come back home— wants to stand trial. Swears she didn't have nothing to do with butchering them poor little orphan girls—"

"I believe her," Jim said.

"Me, too. 'N she says she didn't kill th' nigger, neither. 'N that's just *why* I can't let her come back . . ."

"I don't follow you," Jim said.

"Hell, Boy, you'n me both know that Jenny is too tenderhearted to blast even a pore badhurt hounddawg, not to mention a critter as nigh onto human as a Spade. But it's the *way* she's aiming to clear herself that I purely can't stand . . ." He stopped, peered at Jim speculatively, let out a gusty sigh, went on: "Hell, you always was one of them pointy-headed Liberals yourself, so I can say it straight out 'n ugly with th' hair 'n hide left on. She was *livin'* with that burrheaded black bastid 'n she can line up dozens o' smelly freaks to prove that she 'n th' Spook was happy as all getout together. Never a fuss nor a fight. She swears some white fella she didn't even know come along 'n seen her 'n the Dinge necking in the car. 'N couldn't take it; so he yanks out his hawgleg 'n blasts th' nig—"

"I also believe that," Jim said.

"Me, too. Would of done the same thing myself if I come up on a white gal playin' around with a Dinge. But, Jesus, Jim! I don't want every scandal sheet in th' country printing *that* story. You can understand me there, can't you?"

"Yes," Jim said, "on a gut level, I do understand it. Doesn't make me especially proud of myself, but there it is . . ."

"Okay, Son; since we're together on *that,* here's what I want you to do: Marry my filly, will you, Boy? You always was rightly fond of her, 'n Grace tells me that th' poor little critter was plumb, downright in love with you."

Jim heard his own voice, coming from somewhere else, somewhere very far away, speaking flatly, cooly, clearly, with what was, under the circumstances, astonishing calm, say quietly:

"I don't believe that."

"Grace swears to it, Son; and what Grace swears to, you'd better believe!"

"I'll concede that *she* honestly believes it, which only means she's honestly mistaken. Brilliant people get their beliefs confused with facts almost as often as we plain morons do, Ed. But hasn't it occurred to you even yet, that you, yourself, fouled that particular deal up nicely—for everybody?"

"Yep. Went off half-cocked that time. Should of known the kid she was carryin' wasn't yourn, 'n that her being in your bedroom had another slant to it than plain ordinary screwin'. You'd of been layin' my girl, you'd of done it someplace *else*—"

"Thanks," Jim said. He stood there, studying his ex-employer. That, and something else. Only the something else was—strange. Because he wasn't really thinking. Nor planning. And certainly not calculating the really immense material profit he could have extracted from the highly unusual situation of being offered the daughter of the fourth or fifth richest man in the whole damned world, and by that man, himself. He was aware that most men would have considered the opportunity priceless. He was realist enough to wonder how he would have responded to that offer if it had come before his father's death had relieved him of most of the burdensome aspects of having to earn a living. But now one of the things his realism told him was that once you'd got past a certain fairly high level of comfort, being filthy rich wasn't very likely to add to the sum total of human happiness; that, in sober fact, it was more likely to detract from said total, especially when the wealth in question came accompanied by the kind of package deal that this one did.

But he really wasn't thinking, because thinking involves making decisions, and, about this, he didn't even have to decide. For one thing, if he were to remarry, the income—after taxes—from the trusts was enough to keep him, his wife, and any hypothetical—and, by now, highly improbable!—children on a fairly decent plane of living, whether he went back to work or not. So it followed that the only reason for his risking matrimony a second time would be a chance, or planned, encounter with a woman capable of gracing his declining years with serenity, with peace, if not with the dubious joys of passionate love. He didn't dare hope or believe that such an encounter had already—perhaps!—taken place that very day; but the idea hovered about the outer edges of his consciousness, warming him, and arming the ramparts of his will against his own weakness, pity, pain—the only considerations that conceivably might bind him, against his better judgment, to the kind of walking wounded, the all but living dead, that alcohol, drugs, and marathon promiscuity had reduced poor Jenny—his Jenny with the light brown hair!—to now.

He said: "Ed, tell me a couple of things, starting with why, in the name of everything unholy, you think my marrying Jenny—even granting that she'd marry me, which I doubt—would change or help the godawful mess she's in *this* time?"

"Would though. You could keep outa th' country. Being with you, 'n happy, she'd be willin' to stay away. You finish your stint down there, 'n I get you another appointment—to any damn country you name, long as it's a helluva ways from *here*!"

"Ed," Jim said, slowly, thoughtfully, quietly, "aren't you forgetting something? I have to travel, you know. I'm even called back to Washington for consultations fairly frequently. And Jenny, as your daughter, is certainly one of the world's most photographed young women. Someone would recognize her, even in the unlikely event that my marrying her could be kept secret, which is another thing I doubt."

"Jim, you plain just don't know how to pull a fast one, do you?" Ed cackled. "You won't be marrying Jen. You'll be marrying Isabel Rodriguez, daughter of my general manager down there in Costa Verde. Fact, Boy. Legal. Adoption papers 'n change o' name, recorded in the Costa Verdian Supreme Court. Cost me a cool half million, that did—"

"Ed—" Jim said.

"I know, I know. Jenny don't look like no Spik broad. But that can be fixed, too, you up to sweet-talkin' her into it . . ."

"Talking her into *what?*" Jim said.

"Nose job. Plastic surgery. Dave Goldstein will fly down there to do it in Doctor Vicente Gomez' flossy hospital, 'n keep his mouth shut afterwards, in return for enough folding money. Swears he's tempted to do the job for nothing since it'll be the first time since he got outa Med School that he'll be building a hook into a babe's sniffer instead o' taking one out. You won't mind your Missus lookin' a little like a Hebe, will you, Son?"

Jim stared at Ed Crowley in pure, aching wonder. He said, dryly:

"I've always *liked* Jewish girls. The only trouble is that they don't reciprocate."

"Good. That's settled then. Here's how we'll work it . . ."

"Wait a minute! Jenny, even with a hooked nose, isn't going to look like—"

"A Hot Tamale? Dye her hair black, stock up on the kind o' dark makeup all th' big stores is carrying for the cullud trade nowadays 'n she will. Long as you don't pull her drawers down in public, you'll be perfectly safe. Now shut up 'n listen, will you, Son? We's got a mighty heap o' planning to do—"

"Ed—you're the one who'd better listen. Do you realize the kind of proposition you're asking me to let myself in for?"

"Yep. The kind any *smart* fella would grab with both hands 'n both feet. I'm asking you to marry my daughter. 'N that includes cutting yoreself in for enough o' th' long green so's you won't hafta hit a lick at a snake while I'm still around, 'n after they haul my pore mangy carcass out onto th' lone prairie 'n put it to bed with a shovel, you—"

Jim sat there. What rode over him wasn't rage. Instead it was sadness. He was seeing, as though for the first time, how limited any man's options were. Ed Crowley's. His own. Any man's at all. He thought with something closely akin to sorrow: 'You think you can buy me, too. As you've bought everything and everyone you've ever needed, or thought you needed, or merely even wanted. That you can reduce me to goods for sale. And it's never so much as occurred to you that the kind of people who can be bought aren't even worth having in the first place, because they're whores, if women, and, if men, an even more pitiful obscenity still: slaves . . .'

He went on, thinking: 'Am I *that*? Is that what's wrong with me? The visible chancre—or the noticeable smell—of littleness, meanness, cowardice, that makes women instinctively despise me? I am—or *was*—fond of Jenny. But what would this way out do to both of us? In God's name, what?'

He said:

"No, thanks, Ed. I'm nothing much; but I can do better than your daughter. At least better than what poor Jenny is now. So again you've run up against another case where money just doesn't count. Hard to believe, isn't it? A little like dethroning God. The only God *you* believe in, anyhow. You haven't got enough money to buy me. There isn't that much money in the whole world . . .

Ed stared at him. When the old man spoke, a little quaver had got into his voice.

"Ain't tryin' to buy you, Son. Just tryin' to persuade you—to help me save my daughter. Oh I know she's a helluva handful. Worse disposition than a catamount's 'n a she-bobcat's combined. But since she fairly dotes on you 'n is the richest lil' ol' piece o' fluff who—"

"Ever had her heels designed in a ballbearing factory," Jim said dryly. "Tell me something, Ed: Would you marry a girl who's lost count of the number of men she's been to bed with? Would you be interested in Grace Nivens if she had a face like the one the papers print as Jenny's now? I don't even recognize it. It's ugly. Mindless. Eyes like two pieces of glass. Emptied of everything I thought Jenny had in her: all that gaiety, spirit, intelligence, will . . . A drug addict's stupid drooling smirk on her lips. Reduced to untidy, slovenly—hell!—plain stinking human garbage. That is, if she's even human anymore. A thousand men's leavings—the estimate's conservative!—and at least one of those men—a *Black* man, Ed—"

"Jesus!" the word was an actual scream, so shrill it made the windows vibrate.

"So count me out," Jim went on, whispering the words, talking more to himself than to Wildcat Ed Crowley; "as I said before, I'm not for sale. I don't especially need money, anyhow. And all the many things I haven't got, I've learned to do without. There's a line I could give you that you probably wouldn't understand. But take it from me, anyhow, as a gift. Maybe the most important gift anyone ever offered you: 'True wealth consists not in the magnitude of a man's possessions; but in the paucity of his desires.' By that measure, I'm richer than you are, Ed; because I don't want anything. Especially not your daughter—"

He stopped short. Stared at Ed Crowley with real concern. For a long moment he was afraid the old man was going to have a stroke. For Worldwide Petroleum's owner and president had bowed his head. He peered owlishly at the toes of the high heeled cowboy boots he wore even in New York for what was, to Jim, a lung cracking age. Looked up again. Astonishingly, Jim saw his watery old blue eyes were filled with tears.

"You was my last hope, Son," he croaked. "Now I don't what what I can do. I purely just don't know . . ."

Jim sat there, pity in him like a blade. 'Another Baudelairean metamorphosis,' he thought. 'The last Tycoon, the second or third richest man on the face of Creation transmogrified into this weary, defeated, broken old wreck, whom you—with your small-minded, smirking, your so-called moral superiority!—have been sitting here and condemning for trying—by the only methods that he knows!—to save his daughter . . .'

"You win, Ed," he said softly. "You just paid my price. Pity. The only coin I can be bought for. Part of the way, anyhow. Wait! I'm not saying I'll marry Jenny. God knows I don't want her now. All I'm saying is that I'll do my damnedest to help her, get her out of the murderous mess she's in—"

"S'pose th' only way you *can* do that is to marry her, Jim?" Ed husked.

"Then, all else failing, I'll at least consider it. Maybe I'll even go through with it—who knows? And if I ever do, if I'm ever that big a jackass, I promise you one thing, Old Party: I'll honestly try to make a go of it. Try to make up to her for the really raw deal the Fates—or the Furies!—dished out to her: having you for a father, Ed. Even try to change or cure all the unlovely things your combination of polecat's and turkey buzzard's blood makes her do—"

"Son, you won't regret it! I'll—"

"You won't do a goddamned thing, Ed. You see, I agree with Grace. I don't want your money, either. In fact, the only thing you've got— that is *if* you've got her—that I really want is Grace, herself."

"Jesus!" Ed said, again. "You play *rough,* don't you, boy?"

"No. What I play is fair. Which I've just proved by telling you that. Don't worry, I'm not asking you to give me Grace in return for whatever I can do for Jen. You can't do that. If you don't know by now she's her own woman, you don't know anything. And if you *could,* I wouldn't want her. All right. You'll leave this business of Jenny in my hands? Let me do it *my* way? In any form, shape, or fashion I see fit?"

"Well now, I don't know—" Ed began; then, "Oh, hell! What choice have I got? You'll keep in touch, won't you, Son? At least let me know what's goin' on?"

"No. Not a damned word. When I spring this on the world I want you as surprised as everyone else. Really surprised, or else it won't work—"

"Son, I—"

"Good-bye, Ed," Jim said, and put out his hand to the old man; "I really must be going now."

"Hell, Boy, I give orders for my folks to put you up in the guest suite and—"

"I know. I countermanded those orders. I'm going home. To take a bath. Get some sleep. You see, I have a date tonight."

"With Grace?" Crowley said.

"With Grace. Be seeing you, Ed."

The old man stood there. Then he grinned. It was a grin of almost infinite evil.

"Son, you shore Lawd ain't no poker player, are you?" he cackled.

"No. I don't suppose I am. Why?"

" 'Cause, you was, you'd of learnt to hold yore cards closer to yore chest by now," Wildcat Ed Crowley said. "Telegraphing yore moves afore you makes 'em can git to be expensive, Boy."

Jim looked at him and said, very quietly:

"That's so. But maybe you'd better take another look at what kind of hand you're holding, Ed, before you call me."

Ed Crowley rubbed a bony hand over his chin. Although he was freshly shaven, the motion made a rasping sound.

"Don't aim to call yore hand, Son," he said mildly. "What good would that do? Way I figger it, more'n likely you're gonna be family soon. But I just might hafta head you off, side-track you a little. For yore own good. 'N for my baby's. 'N to say it straight out 'n honest, in self-defense. You're a powerful sight younger'n than I be, 'n even a mite better lookin'. 'N you likely makes enough money to satisfy a gal what don't want much—"

"Grace, again?" Jim said. Then he smiled; and put out his hand to the oilman. "Don't worry about it, Ed. I'm no threat. To her I'm only a different kind of a bug squirming under a microscope. Or the materials for another case history for her files . . ."

"Who *ain't?*" Ed said morosely, and shook hands. "But you will give th' matter o' Jenny some thought, won't you, Boy?"

"Yes, Ed; I'll give it thought," he said.

CHAPTER

6

*H*e lay there in the huge Castilian bed that his father had brought back from Spain, and stared at the ceiling. The bed had the date 1586 carved into its ornate and decorative headboard. Jim didn't doubt that the date was authentic, because trying to sleep in that bed had been a form of masochism until Jim Rush, Senior had had a cabinet maker adapt it to modern innerspring mattresses.

But then, considering what Inez Montero (the twenty-eight-year-old stepmother Jim Rush, Senior, had inflicted upon his outraged son upon retiring from a really brilliant diplomatic career at seventy years of age) looked like, it was more than probable that sleeping wasn't exactly what the old man had had in mind.

"*¡El viejo verde!*" Jim chuckled, fondly. The words meant "The Green Old Man," and were a fine example of how much more compassionately the warm—and realistic—Mediterranean temperament looked upon enduring human folly than the Anglo Saxon mentality did. The English-speaking peoples with their ingrained and bitter puritanism reduced that to "Dirty Old Man," which only proved what was wrong with Anglo Saxons, not with men like Jim Rush, Senior, who retained green and flowering youth, and wine and joy and laughter in their veins until they died.

'Of gallant uxoriousness! Jim thought. 'Lord, how poor Inez cried

over him! Only thirty-two years old at the time, and so damned beautiful she could stop any man's breath, and yet I actually thought she was
going to die of pure grief when the old man went. Thank God she got
over it finally; and even more that she's happy now. I should call her.
Take a day off and go visit her and Manny and the kids. But New
Hampshire's too damned far and—'

And no woman, he remembered suddenly, bleakly, had ever cried
over him like that. Not even once. The only tears he'd ever seen on
Virginia's face had been of pure exasperation or of rage. Or, worse still,
shed for someone else. And now he was about to commit the unequaled
folly of dating a really splendid woman like Grace Nivens! He who had
absolutely nothing to offer any woman, born as he was of his mother's
bleak, resentful loathing for life, love, sex; being, as he was, blood of
her icy blood, bone of her bitter bone!

Panic fluttering his gut, he stretched out his hand to pick up the telephone. He'd invent some excuse, plead illness, say—

But, before he could touch it, the phone buzzed cheerfully. He picked
it up, said:

"Yes?"

"Is this Mr. Rush's residence?" Meg's clear soprano came over. "Ambassador James Rush, please?"

"Speaking," Jim said. "How are you, my dear?"

"Oh, thank heavens!" Meg said, her voice breathless with pure relief.
"This *is* your home address, isn't it? Two-sixty-eight East Seventy-
second Street?"

"Yes. Why yes, of course, Meg. Why?"

"No reason. That's all I need to know. 'Bye now, Sir!"

"Oh no; you don't!" Jim said. "You're going to explain this, young
lady!"

"Must I?" Meg teased. "Couldn't I just keep it a secret? A deep,
dark, *romantic* secret, Mr. Ambassador?"

"Girl-child, at my age secrets are bad for the digestion. And the
blood pressure. Especially romantic secrets. You wouldn't want to bring
on an infarction, would you?"

"Heaven forbid! Grace would never forgive me! Really, Mr. Ambassador, it's very simple, oh, quite! We let you get away without asking
your address. So how then was Grace to call for you?"

"Call for *me*?" he said; "but I was going to—"

"Drop by her place? Tell me, Sir, d'*you* know *her* address?"

Jim hung there, helplessly. He didn't. And that really monumental
catch hadn't so much as occurred to him.

"Good Lord!" he said. "As a matter of fact, I don't!"

"You see!" Meg laughed. "And yet we allow you men to believe you run things. But what would the world do without us women to tidy up the messes you generally make of things? Ever thought of that, Mr. Ambassador?"

"I *have* thought of it," Jim said solemnly; "in fact, I know."

"What would it, Sir?" Meg said.

"Collapse into ruin and utter desolation," he said. Then he added, to see if she would recognize the quotation, "and not with a bang, but with a whimper . . ."

She didn't. But neither did she now seem in any especial hurry to end the conversation. She said, the tone of her voice changing, becoming a trifle higher, edged with—nervousness, he guessed—

"Mr. Rush, may I ask you something? Something that's definitely none of my business, so you don't have to answer it if you don't want to. But I do wish you would. It would make me feel better about—about a thing that's troubling me. Or rather, let's say I hope it would. Because it could make me feel worse, come to think of it! It all depends, doesn't it?" Her voice trailed off uncertainly.

He lay there, thinking. So long that she burst out:

"Oh, I say! I *am* sorry! I—"

He said, quietly: "Suppose you ask me, my dear."

"Oh! Quite. Very well. Mr. Rush—Grace. What, actually, d'you think of her?"

The silence lasted even longer this time. And was so deep that he wondered suddenly, oddly, if she were holding her breath.

"What do you want me to say, Meg?" he said.

"Anything you like, Mr. Rush," she murmured. "As long as it's—the truth—"

"Then," he said slowly, sadly; "I'm afraid I've fallen in love with her. A thing I'd sworn I'd *never* allow to happen to me again as long as I lived. My past experiences haven't inclined me towards the view that felicity automatically results from letting one's heart get ahead of one's head, Meg. Quite the contrary, in fact—"

"Oh!" she said. "That makes two of you, then. Who have more or less the same attitude—the same *negative* attitude—towards life—and love, I mean. A pity. But, Mr. Rush—"

"Yes, my dear?"

"You will be—careful with her, won't you, Sir? She's had rather a bit of a bad time of it, before, I gather. I shouldn't like to see her—hurt—again."

He said: "Of course. That goes without saying, Meg. But what on earth makes you imagine that I *could* hurt Grace? That is, setting aside as irrelevant the obvious fact that no conceivable set of circumstances could make me want to?"

She said, tartly: "I don't *imagine*, Mr. Rush; I *know*. Good Lord! Why are you men so dense?"

He hung there, until her voice came over the wire again, saying, sadly:

"I guess I'd better ring off. This conversation has got a trifle out of hand, hasn't it? And I'm sorry. I didn't mean it to . . ."

"No," he said; "please don't. Not yet. Not until you explain that last remark, anyhow. I make no claim to extreme lucidity, of course; but just what am I being dense about, now?"

The silence hurt his eardrum. He pulled the receiver a little away from his ear. Then he heard her soft voice purring and put it back, jamming it into his flesh, hard.

"Mr. Rush—Mis–ter Rush—didn't you *see* the way she reacted to you? Or rather—responded. A better word, what? Warmer, some-how . . ."

He said, slowly: "Yes. And rejected the—impression—as illusion. As one of those tricks that hope—fond and foolish hope!—plays on the senses. Unlike most men, I tend to be realistic about myself. I've had that realism ground into my face by more than one dainty pair of spike-heeled shoes, shall we say? I have, unfortunately, to look into my mirror every morning, in order to shave. I've had it pointed out to me consis-tently and continuously over a goodly number of years that the kind of temperament I'm cursed with would drive the average woman straight up the nearest wall—"

"Which only means you should stay away from the *average* woman, Mr. Rush. Tell me, does Grace seem average to you?"

"No," he said fervently; "God, no!"

"That's wizard, as Mum used to say when she was trying to make the whole Royal Air Force happy! That line came across beautifully. Clear and ringing. Audible even in the half-shilling tiers." Then she added, her young voice suddenly—and oddly—serious; "I really must ring off shortly. Mr. Crowley's in conference now, but I really shouldn't like for him to come out unexpectedly and catch me gabbing over the phone. But before I do, may I build your morale up a bit? My contribution—to—tonight. Because I want it to go—well. I truly do."

He said: "Why?"

"Because I'm most awf'ly fond of Grace. And I—like you. All right?"

"I thank you," he said solemnly.

"Let me see. How shall I go about it? Mr. Rush—you're not very tall. And you're not very handsome. Right?"

"The understatements of the year," he said. "Or of any year. Go on, Child."

"And you're quite charmingly timid—a fact that you try valiantly to hide."

"Go to the head of the class, my dear!"

"And those facts aren't likely to change, are they?"

"I'm afraid not," he said, sadly.

"But, Mr. Rush—*women* are changing. In fact, a good many of us have changed."

"Meaning?"

"That the type of man you probably envy—the tall, oh so good-looking chaps who're terribly sure of themselves, who fancy themselves as God's gift to women—rub today's women the wrong way, most of the time. Nearly always, actually. We prefer—simple kindness. Comradeship. We'd much rather that when our lovers gaze into our eyes they didn't use them to reflect their own images in—"

"That's a good line," Jim said soberly.

"It's Grace's. I'm not that smart."

"Thank you," he said; "You're saying—I have a chance?"

"I'm saying I've never known Grace to react as favorably to any man as she did to you today in the whole time I've known her. She'd be furious with me if she knew I'd told you that. So you mustn't give me away. Promise?"

"I promise."

"Good. Mr. Rush—Mr. Ambassador Rush—may I say something absolutely outrageous?"

"Please do!"

"If things—don't work out—between you and Grace—may *I* be next in line?"

"Good Lord!" he said; then: "I'm sure you don't mean that, Child . . ."

"I'm *not* a child, and I jolly well *do* mean it. Which brings this conversation to a screeching halt, doesn't it, Mr. Ambassador? 'Bye, now!"

"Please! Answer me one last question, Meg—"

She said softly, slowly, sweetly:

"Only if that one last question is *not* about Grace. Or about *me,* Mr. Ambassador!"

"Oh, damn!" Jim said; then: "All right. You win. But this, then: How'd it ever occur to you to call this number? There are a good many Rushes in the phone book. Don't tell me you called them all?"

"No, Sir. It came to me that Mike Harper might know where you lived, since he'd spent the better part of half an hour complaining to me about what a chore it had been to convince you to come here to the Towers at all. Said you'd insisted upon his taking you home. So I asked him; but all he remembered was somewhere in the East Seventies. Even so that narrowed things down greatly. Got it right on only the third try. Grace is in conference with Mr. Crowley, which is why she couldn't ring you up, herself. But she'll pick you up about eight—at your place, now that we know the number. All right, Mr. Ambassador?"

"All right. Better than all right. That's marvelous. I'll dance at your wedding, my sweet!"

"And I at *yours.* 'Bye, now!" There was a click. The line went dead. Then, again, the dial tone. Jim lay there staring into the mouthpiece of the telephone. Then he lay it back on its cradle as though it were made of wine goblet crystal, blown ruby stemware, infinitely fragile, delicate, precious . . .

After that, sleep was out of the question, so he set himself to transcribing into writing the notes he had taken from the Reynolds' and the O'Rourkes' briefings on his tiny pocket tape recorder. He was concerned at the moment with getting down the names of the chief terrorist organizations in Costa Verde which were DRAP, EMMA, and ERL on the Left side of the political spectrum, and the JOCR on the far Right. The initials in every case stood for words. Supplying the missing prepositions which Spanish-speaking peoples generally leave out of these sorts of abbreviations, he jotted down the full titles after the initials. DRAP was *Defensores Revolucionarios Armados (del) Pueblo,* or "Armed Revolutionary Defenders (of the) People." EMMA was not a woman's name but the letters for *Ejercito Maoista (de) Militantes Armados,* "The Maoist Army (of) Armed Militants." And ERL was *Ejercito Rojo (de la) Liberación,* "The Red Army (of the) Liberation." This last, of course, was Japanese trained; just as EMMA had Chinese experts instructing them in strategy and tactics. DRAP's technical advisers were less distinguishable; but Peter swore they were much too good at their jobs to be Costa Verdians. Which meant they had to be Cubans—the number one satraps of the Russians, these days.

Not so strangely, granted the greater cohesiveness of the far Right, its anti-intellectualism, its paucity of ideas, as contrasted with the far Left's perhaps fatal tendency towards too rarified a theoretical philosophy, its almost suicidical fragmentation, there was only one far Right organization, the JOCR, which had quickly and easily absorbed the two imitations of Spanish Fascism, the *Falanje Costa Verdense* and *Los Hijos de Cristo Rey,* the "Costa Verdian Phalange" and "The Sons of Christ the King," into one well-armed, well-financed—by the CIA it was openly rumored—band known as the *Juntas Ofensivas Contrarevolucionarias,* or "The Union for the Counter-Revolutionary Offensive."

But every damned one of them spelled trouble. Bad trouble. Since the year had begun, there had been close to one thousand political assassinations in Costa Verde. And three hundred fifty public executions—by garroting or the firing squad. "And that," he could hear Tim O'Rourke's voice, rough with pity, saying, "doesn't count the poor devils who couldn't even make it to *la Plaza de la Liberación* to give the crowds a good show. The ones Butcher Boy García's interrogators were a mite too rough with in those soundproof cells down under *la Jefetura de la Seguridad Nacional* where you can scream your bloody guts up and nobody will ever hear you, except the Neanderthal-type throwbacks who're playin' around wity you in the first place. Having a red hot wire run up your dong and your balls squeezed flat with wooden nutcrackers ain't likely to leave you feeling like the power 'n the glory, Chub, me boy. 'Tis a wonder anybody survives to be sweetly shot in th' back of the neck for the edification of the loyal people of Costa Verde—"

"No, it isn't, Tim," Marisol O'Rourke had said then; "there are other, more effective ways of breaking a man—or a woman. Indirect ways that leave one's body unmarked. As they—broke me—the night I received Roberto's finger—packed in cotton—in a little box—with the ring from our double-ring wedding ceremony still on it. That night I easily and quickly consented to play the whore—to lend my body—to Peter here, in order to influence him—in order to—save what was left, or what I had been deceived into believing was left of poor Roberto, then . . ."

"Only you never got around to it," Peter said quickly.

"No. But only because Alicia intervened."

"Selfishly. To protect my own interests," Alicia said.

"No matter. But the use of physical force, of the cruder forms of torture, is not always necessary. For, if a man has three daughters, say, he is unlikely to permit that more than one of them—usually the youngest one, twelve, thirteen years old—be violated before his eyes by seven or eight burly policemen before giving in, before confessing to any crime they want him to. Or if he has only a wife or a sister—witnessing what those two-legged animals do to a woman with the—electrodes—with the vibrators, with—"

"Mari, please!" Tim had said.

Jim put down those notes. For a long moment he lay there, trying to decide whether or not to ring for Rad—Radcliffe Harkness, which was the stately, aristocratic name that the equally stately, and inky black, manservant whom he had also inherited from his father—to bring him a stiff Scotch on the rocks to calm his nerves. But he decided against it. Rad was in a sad state of mind these days, as was Bessie, his wife. The couple, who ran the townhouse for Jim, as they had for his father before him, in impeccable style, had invested nearly all of their considerable savings in a hotel on one of the Bimini Islands in the Bahama archipelago, a logical enough choice, since both Rad and Bessie were from the Bahamas in the first place. The hotel was currently being run by their only son, and was designed to be their sustenance when they retired, and their legacy to their son and grandson after their deaths.

But again that dreary old saw about the best laid plans of mice and men applied. Now that the south Atlantic and Caribbean islands were free of England and under black rule, the tourist business had gone straight to hell. For not only were the younger Blacks, seething with vengeful racial hatred after centuries of White oppression, contemptuously abusive—"Sheer insolence!" the Whites called it—to anything in a white skin, but they were continuously rioting against the Hindu business colony who, they claimed, sucked their life's blood. Occasionally they kidnapped, whipped, and—infrequently!—murdered some bumptious White who hadn't learned his lowly place in the new scheme of things. They called themselves "The Black Panthers" after that North American Black revolutionary organization. And, as a result of their activities, poor Rad was losing the shirt off his back, with the additional insult of knowing that his grandson, to whom the hotel was ultimately supposed to go, was not only a member of "The Panthers," but openly referred to both his father and his grandfather as "Handkerchief-Head niggers" and "Toms."

So Jim didn't call Rad. His own mood was too troubled to endure the sight of that mournful black face. But, almost exactly in the same fashion that the telephone had rung just as he had been reaching for it in a fit of panic to call off his date with Grace Nivens, at that very instant he heard the dry, raspy brushing of Rad's knuckles on the bedroom door. 'This place is psychic,' he thought. 'Or I'm psychotic. One of the two. Or both, maybe . . .'

"Come in, Rad," he called.

Rad came in. Jim was relieved to see that he wasn't, this time anyhow, close to tears.

"Gentleman to see you, Sah," he said. "Young gentleman. Not anybody we know. Show 'im up to your study, Sah?"

Jim started to say, "Get rid of him, Rad, whoever the hell he is!" But a certain sixth sense that had served him well and even, at times, had keep him alive throughout his career, warned him not to.

"All right, Rad. Show him into my study. Offer him a drink if he'll take it. I'll be with him in a minute. But first, bring me my bathrobe, will you?"

The young gentleman, Jim saw, when he came into his study, really wasn't anyone they—they being, of course, Rad, Bessie, and himself—knew. Nor was he quite a gentleman. His clothes were—well—a shade *too* smart. A Cardin suit. Tie a shade too wide. His long hair showed only the bottoms of his ears, and had obviously been sprayed with a fixative to hold every strand of its rounded, exquisitely razor cut coiffure in place. Impeccable white silk shirt. Hand-stitched box calf shoes. Manicured nails gleaming faintly rose . . . The most expensive attaché case made.

'Looks,' Jim thought, 'like a Hollywood actor got up to play the role of a modish young business executive . . .'

"Yes?" he said. "What can I do for you, Sir?"

The young man jumped up. Smiled. He had a good smile in a strong, handsome young face. There was no softness there, no effeminacy. A little—a very little—of that special paranoiac look Jim had come to know so well. But much less than usual. So little in fact that Jim was not too sure it was there.

"Mr. Ambassador," the young man said; "my name's Bill Carter. And I'm from the Federal Narcotics Bureau . . ."

"Good Lord!" Jim said.

"That's confidential, of course, Sir. I only told you that so quickly to keep you from thinking I was FBI or CIA."

"Exactly what I was thinking," Jim said. "But sit down, Mr. Carter. And tell me what I can do for you."

"A lot—if you're willing to. But Mr. Townley warned me that you weren't too inclined to be cooperative with other Government agencies when the policies of those agencies don't meet with your approval. And what's more, he feels—and my own investigation sustains him—that you're practically immune to any pressure that the State Department, our agency, or either of the cloak and dagger outfits could bring to bear . . ."

Jim stared at him. Said, very quietly:

"Care to explain that one, Mr. Carter?"

"Gladly. Your record's as clean as a hound's tooth. You've never ducked a striptease dancer in the Washington Monument Pool as far as we've been able to ascertain—"

"Nor anywhere else, more's the pity," Jim said dryly.

Carter laughed at that.

"You're unmarried. Or rather you've been married, divorced, and widowed, in that order. So whatever pressure we might have been able to exert through your natural—and entirely praiseworthy—inclination to cover up your late wife's unfortunate tendency to indulge in fun and

72

games during your absences no longer exists. In fact, if we tried such a tactic now, it would backfire and put us in a bad light."

Jim kept an iron grip on the anger rising in him.

"I'm glad you realize that," he said.

"We do. And that effectively eliminates any pressure that we, or either of the Intelligence agencies might have once considered using to—well—persuade you to help us out . . ."

Jim waited. After twenty-odd years in the State Department, waiting was a thing he did superbly.

"On the other hand, Assistant Secretary Townley is unwilling to intervene. Says you're operating with a bit too powerful backing from a source outside the Department, a source anyone in the Government who thinks realistically would have to reckon with these days . . ."

"He's wrong," Jim said flatly. "Not in his statement of the case, but in the implication he's putting on it. Ed Crowley of Worldwide Petroleum lobbied openly to get me appointed Ambassador to Costa Verde. He wanted—and wants—me to do him a favor in that general geographic area. And, to be entirely frank, I've already consented to do him the favor in question, if it can be done at all. But, Mr. Carter, it's a personal favor, not an economic or political one. Or else I shouldn't have agreed to do it. An Ambassador's duties don't include lobbying for a multinational concern. Or for any kind of a concern for that matter, even a national one . . ."

Carter smiled.

"I quite agree, Mr. Rush! But you'd be surprised at the number of Ambassadors who bend that particular rule a little, shall we say?"

"I shouldn't be surprised. Not at all. I've been in the State Department a long time," Jim said.

"Only *you* have never done it," Carter said.

"One of the better reasons why neither you, nor anyone else, has a stick to beat my head in with," Jim said.

"True. And last of all—a man who has an income of between seventy-five and a hundred thousand dollars a year, *after* taxes, enjoys the blessed and enviable liberty of being able to quietly and cheerfully resign if his departmental heads try to order him to do something he really doesn't want to . . ."

"A masterly exposition of the facts in the case," Jim said; "so?"

"So I can only appeal to your—patriotism and to your better nature. Mr. Rush, have you ever known—known well—a drug addict?"

"Yes," Jim Rush said.

"Mind telling me who this person was?"

"Yes, I do mind. It's none of your goddamned business."

"Sorry! Didn't mean to offend you. And you're entirely within your rights. I apologize, Mr. Ambassador."

" 'S all right. Forget it," Jim Rush said.

"You do agree, however, that the drug traffic into the States has to be stopped, don't you?"

"Yes. But I might not agree with you over the method of doing so."

Bill Carter stared at him.

"How do you think it ought be done, Mr. Rush?"

"By changing the social and moral climate of our times. By educating our youth to the fact that there are no inalienable rights in life, only inalienable obligations. And that among these are the basic ones of conducting one's life with order, dignity, and decency, even though these qualities are seldom, if ever, adequately rewarded. Hell! They're never rewarded at all. Which doesn't matter. What I mean is, I'd try drying up the market first, before tackling the source—"

"Would that *work?*" Carter said.

"I don't know. How could I? It's never been tried. Do you think that what your Bureau does, works?"

"Frankly, no. Or, at least, only in part. But it's less of a tall order than what you're proposing, Sir!"

I know. Jesus, Moses, Isaiah, Buddha, Mohammad and quite a few others have failed at what I'm proposing. Which is no reason to stop trying. Life is inevitable failure, inescapable defeat. We never get out of it alive, do we? My slant is that noble failures are worth a damned sight more than cheapjohn quickie successes—and only apparent successes at that! Sorry. End of sermon. What is it that you want of me, Mr. Carter?"

"That you cooperate with our man in Costa Verde. General García's police are pretty sophisticated types. They should be: They were trained in Spain by the late General Franco's *Segunda Bis,* a sort of technical lend lease between extreme Rightists. So our man hasn't been able to get anything out to us in months. Now, if you could save us a little space in your diplomatic pouch—"

Jim stared at Carter. His gaze was ice cold. And unbelieving.

"Good Lord, Sir! Do you realize to what extent we're being flooded with heroin?" Carter burst out. "Hasn't it ever occurred to you that it could be a conspiracy?"

"No," Jim said; "it hasn't."

"Look at the facts, Mr. Rush. All of a sudden, *somebody* flies a whole laboratory into the southern part of Costa Verde on Tupolev An 16s, six-engined Russian propjets. A laboratory, hell! More nearly a factory, as far as its productive capacity is concerned. From Cuba, surely, after its component elements have been brought into Cuba from somewhere else . . ."

"So?" Jim said.

"So those big buzzards come in above fifty thousand feet with their turbines cut and their props feathered. At night. Parachute their cargos down—on *black* parachutes, the ultimate touch of sophistication—into the jungle. Into the triangle between Xilchimocha, Chizenaya, and Tarascanolla."

"The concentration camps. Correction: The Extermination Camps. García's murder factories. Improvements on Dachau, Auschwitz, and Treblinka."

Carter looked at him. Said:

"How'd you know about that, Mr. Ambassador?"

Jim shrugged. "Say—I have my sources. Private sources. *Not* the Department's," he said.

"Then they're damned good ones," Carter said.

Jim didn't answer that. He said, quietly:

"Get on with it, Carter!"

"All right. At first it looked as though Fidel and Company were out to ruin García's Armed Forces for him, that was all. Because, four years ago, the babes at the Blue Moon started pushing shit—Oh, I mean—"

"I know the meaning of the word 'shit' in that connection, Mr. Carter. Harlem pushers' terminology, meaning heroin."

"Right. Anyhow, the whores were not only shooting it up themselves, but passing the purest stuff you ever saw—even better than the stuff from Viet Nam's Golden Triangle—out to García's officers, free of charge. Getting them hooked fast . . ."

"So?" Jim said.

"So García cracked down. Male pushers, when caught, were shot. Drumhead trials. One hundred percent guilty verdicts. Then off to *la Plaza de la Liberación,* and Bang!"

"I don't believe in capital punishment," Jim said dryly; "but in this case, I can support the idea . . ."

"It is—effective," Carter said. "Female pushers were whipped. Hung by their wrists from a scaffold, with their feet dangling forty centimeters off the ground. Stark mother naked, of course. The crowds loved that detail. Fifty lashes for a first offense. Thirty percent of the girls died of less than fifty lashes. The whips were leaded—and the executioners, graduate sadists. One hundred lashes for a second offense. Only two culprits ever tried it twice. Both died. One took sixty-one lashes. The other, sixty-eight. Tough girls. Their *bones* were showing, Mr. Ambassador."

"Sad," Jim said; "I'm crying."

"All right. So Villalonga City became drug free. Only nobody put that laboratory out of business. The best equipped, most modern opium to heroin conversion lab on earth. It would make those Marseilles attic, basement, and garage outfits look like kids' chemistry sets. We think someone got to Garcia. Paid him one of the biggest bribes in history. Because he hasn't stopped the raw stuff from coming over the Sierras from Colombia—which would be difficult, I admit, especially the way they bring it in now. But more to the point, he's left that lab untouched and he must know where it is!"

"I follow your narrative well enough; but I simply don't see your, my, or even our country's connection with the whole filthy mess," Jim said.

"What cheaper or better way to win the Ideological War, Sir? They'd reduce the last great capitalistic country, *ours,* to a crawling mass of witless addicts. Without the desire, the will, or the capacity to fight. End human liberty forever; terminate the last great hope of man—"

Jim stared at him, his brows rising in what Carter didn't know was a characteristic expression of pure amazement at the depths of human stupidity.

"Mister Carter—Mister Carter," he said gently, "you disappoint me You have obviously investigated me, but not in depth, have you? Or else you'd know I'm allergic to cant. From the Know-Nothings to the Ku Klux Klan, the U.S. has never been a bastion of human liberty. Talked about it, yes; practiced it, no. Eleven years after the Pilgrim Fathers got here, seeking freedom to worship God as they saw fit, they hanged their first Quaker for trying to worship presumably the same God, as *he* saw fit. Apart from the hypocrisy of mouthing ringing phrases about 'Liberty or Death' while gaining their bread from the sweat of other men's faces—living as both Washington and Jefferson did upon the fruits of that monstrous obscenity, human slavery—there was something sadly comical, if not farcical about contrabandists and smugglers defending their rights to break the laws by talking about 'Taxation Without Representation' and other such pure undiluted fecal matter. So don't try to appeal to my patriotism. I have very little. I am, by accident, a citizen of the country that has talked liberty while practicing lynching, race riots, and genocide. Take that appeal to the Apaches, the Sioux, the Navajos, the Blacks. Say it above the graves of the millions of European Jews who were flatly denied entry into this country by our State Department although we knew the Nazis were killing them. Or else—"

"Or else?" Bill Carter echoed.

"Chant the names of Nagasaki, Hiroshima, Song My, My Lai, every time you're tempted to give off with a phrase like the last great hope of man, Mr. Carter. Patriotism has been called the last refuge of fools and scoundrels. I like to think I'm neither . . ."

"But, Sir," Bill Carter said, a little stiffly now, "you're saying our country is not *worth* saving?"

Jim smiled.

"No," he said; "because it is. But no more than any other country, composed of human beings, is. I'm saying that I doubt the danger. I don't believe it's possible to turn even a sizable minority of any nation into addicts. Physical craving can be induced, of course; but normal people break the addiction quite easily even when it's been deliberately or accidentally caused. You ought to know that. You ought to know also that addiction is practically unknown in Turkey, one of the world's great opium producers. And that China, which had the world's greatest number of addicts—thanks to our British cousins who fought a war to insure their right to dump Indian opium into that then defenseless country—is now totally free of addiction, as is Japan. My questions are these: Can any product be sold in an area where people don't want it? And whose fault is it that our country produces neurotic, whining, spineless idiots—I won't say scum, though the word is fitting!—who think society has to support their nonproductive, parasitic lives, allowing them to live without work, basking in a mainliner's witless dreams—produces them in wholesale lots? Because you must know that the *sine qua non* of addiction is the psychotic personality. What right, in the final analysis, Mr. Carter, has a morally inferior society that turns out morally inferior people to survive?"

"You're turning the thing around," Carter said angrily; "you're blaming us, instead of the people who deliberately dump on us—"

"A lethal product that all too many of our citizens—especially the young!—pay hundreds of millions of dollars—stolen or conned from other people—to get their hands on. Dumped? Of course. But not because of anything so complicated as a conspiracy. Very simply because it's profitable. So don't try to sell me the Demonic Theory of History. I've lived too long and in too many countries not to have learned that any conspiracy involving more than three people always breaks down from the sheer weight of human stupidity. Look, Mr. Carter, you waste my time and your own with this approach. I'm against drug smuggling, drug addiction, because they're evils, *per se,* anywhere and everywhere. Don't try to hard-sell me. When you do, you reenforce my belief that people who let too damned many things happen to them, maybe have it coming. All over the world—a point you made quite neatly earlier—a cuckold is a joke. And rightly so. But then so is any nation, any group, ethnic, religious, social, or what have you, that lends itself too easily to victimization. A sad joke. Even, at times, a tragic one. Or a big, fat, fatuous one—like this country. So, since I'm partially on your side, anyhow, let's get to the point, if you have one."

Bill Carter studied him, sighed.

"I was told you'd be a hard nut to crack. All right. Let me put it on a more pragmatic basis. All we can do now, Sir, is to stop the leaks. We've stopped Turkey. Lebanon has taken care of itself by political suicide. The French connection is well under control. We work with the police of Marseilles and Corsica in perfect harmony. Viet Nam is no longer a threat because, since our pullout, the logistics of getting their narcotics to the States is just too difficult. Which leaves the South American connection as our number one problem. And the worst plague spot of all is Costa Verde. That laboratory, Sir: What it means is that it's no longer opium or cocaine they're flying in to us, but heroin, itself—"

"Flying in?" Jim said.

"Yes, Sir. Light planes. Single-engined or at best twin-engined Pipers, Cessnas, Beechcraft. They come in at night *under* our radar. Wave top high. Too low for our beams to pick them up—"

"From *Costa Verde?*" Jim said.

"No. No, of course not! Light planes haven't the range to fly that far. The stuff goes by fishing boat to any of two hundred islands, ninety, a hundred, two hundred miles off Florida. A rusty old shallow-draft landing craft butts up to an island's beach and puts down a bulldozer. In two days they've scraped out a flight strip. In the unlikely event that the Coast Guard locates it—and most, Mr. Rush, stay operative from six months to a year before they're found—they simply abandon it, and scrape out another on another island. With those kinds of profits they could afford that, even if the Coast Guard put the strip out of action after a single day's operation. Or they use float planes. Which is where that laboratory comes in. Look at the arithmetic of it, Sir: Opium's bulky, and still has to be processed after you get it into your potential market. But heroin! Hell, Sir, a Piper Cub can bring in ten kilos of heroin from a hundred miles away; and ten kilos after it's been cut, and recut, and recut again, works out to ten million dollars."

"Whew!" Jim whistled. "Then your idea for operating inside of Costa Verde is?"

"To nail the Big Fish, first. After that, infiltrate one of those alphabet soup terrorist organizations—Left or Right, depending upon which can be more easily influenced at the moment—and talk them into a search and destroy action against that laboratory . . . But first the Big Fish. One of the Big Fishes, anyhow. He, we've reason to believe, is an American. And his cover is—perfect . . ."

Carter stopped. Stared at Jim. Shrugged.

"Hell, I've gone this far, so I have no other recourse than to level with you, Mr. Ambassador. He's down there doing a job, a perfectly legitimate job, for a friend of yours, the—ah—gentleman who was so interested in your becoming Ambassador to Costa Verde."

"Good God!" Jim whispered.

"One moment, Mr. Ambassador! We're not interested in the—young person—he is living with, and supposedly guarding. I use the term 'living with' advisedly, for your information. I don't think it should surprise you."

"It doesn't," Jim said.

"Good. Her case is a matter for the FBI—through Interpol. You have the personal assurance of the Chief of our Bureau that your helping us out will not prejudice, or endanger her, even slightly. General García, for reasons of his own, has up until now flatly refused to permit extradition. And your department heads feel that reviving that peculiarly unsavory mess at this juncture wouldn't help our country's international standing, might cause our enemies to believe we'd become excessively decadent, and hence something of a paper tiger, shall we say? In other words, State feels we'd be better off if Jenny Crowley *stayed* lost. So your heads aren't leaning on General García too hard. And His Nibs apparently wants to keep a check rein on Ed Crowley, or—"

"Is screwing little Jenny himself," Jim said bitterly.

"I don't think so. It's possible, of course; but we've had no report to that effect. Well, Sir?"

"Let me think. In principle, I'm on your side. You're the one agency I know that's generally on the side of the angels, but—"

"But look at this, Sir."

He handed Jim a photograph. Jim studied it quietly. He didn't shake. Or throw up. But he wanted to. Both.

"Explanation?" he said.

"The Costa Verdian frontier patrol stopped this rattletrap truck converted into a school bus as it came down a mountain trail from Colombia. It was filled with kids. Two adults, a man and a woman—not counting the driver, of course—with them. They had papers that seemed to show that the Colombian kids, Chibchas, *Mestizas,* Blacks, had been invited to Ciudad Villalonga by Padre Pío, the Archbishop, for some kind of a youth festival. Not unusual, Padre Pío's always doing things like that for poor kids . . ."

"And?" Jim said.

"One of the kids got sick. Only he spoke only Chibcha, a form of Inca, really, not Spanish. So the *Aduaneros* took him to their first aid station over the loud protests of the three types on the school bus. Just after they got there, the kid threw up. A sealed tube, filled with grey-brown powder . . ."

"Opium?" Jim said.

"No . . . morphine. The first stage in the refining process. Opium would weigh too much. So the customs men dashed back to look for that bus—"

"Now wait a minute! If García's getting his cut from the narcotic trade wouldn't he order his customs men to let it through?"

"Not being a fool, no. He knows that enough raw opium or low-grade morphine will always get through to keep that lab working over-time, no matter how much stuff his underpaid and understaffed border men capture. So he has it both ways—gets rich off bribes from the lab operators and the types who're smuggling heroin out of Costa Verde and into the States, and preserves his image as a Public Benefactor and Enlightened Statesman by making loud and showy war on the drug traf-fic. Hell, his methods have been repeatedly cited by *our* conservatives as the way to end the drug menace. You know: 'Cold Turkey' for addicts, and death to pushers—"

"I more than half agree; but I suppose it's much too simplistic, isn't it?"

"Yes; it is. So García *rewards* his frontier men who catch opium smugglers. Pins medals on them, personally. Raises their pay. Every-thing except quadrupling their numbers, and giving them decent equip-ment to work with, which might—mind you, I said *might*—end the traffic . . ."

"All right. Back to that school bus. Did they catch it?"

"Didn't have to. It hadn't gone more than five kilometers further into Costa Verde. They found it parked under a tree with the kids lying on the ground beside it. Sixteen of the poor little bastards dog sick, but alive. The types were gone, of course. And three kids were dead. Like this one in the picture. Apparently they couldn't bring the test tubes up . . ."

"So they—eviscerated them," Jim whispered. "Ripped them open like goats—or pigs—"

"Yes," Carter said. "Three hundred thousand dollars' worth of base morphine or three nigger, *Mestiza,* Indian kids' lives. I'm not God, but—how would you equate it, Mr. Ambassador?"

Jim looked at him. A long time. A very long time. Said:

"You're a dirty fighter, Carter. But you win. I'll cooperate with your man. Through a go-between—so I can honestly say I've never seen his face, or heard his name. Fair enough?"

"Fair enough!" Carter said, and put out his hand. Jim took it. And it was then, at that moment, that Rad opened the door without even knocking, and pushed his grizzled head through the doorway. He was grinning from ear to ear, his white teeth dazzling in his inky face.

"Lady to see you, Sah!" he cackled. "And my, my, *what* a lady, Sah! Just what this old place needs! Sure hope you won't let this one git away!"

"Don't mean to," Jim said soberly. "Mr. Carter, if there's nothing more—"

"Nothing at all. Except the Bureau's thanks, and my own. Oh, one thing—could your man show me out some other way? I'd much rather that—your lady—didn't see me. You understand, don't you?"

"Of course. And that's another point on which we're in perfect agreement, Mr. Carter. I'd prefer she didn't see you, either. Rad, show Mr. Carter out through the basement entrance, will you?"

"Yes, Sah, Mister Jim! That I will!" Radcliffe Harkness said.

CHAPTER

7

*H*e decided at once that he was neither going to send Rad downstairs with a verbal message for Grace, explaining that he had been unexpectedly detained, nor—most certainly not!—simply let her wait without any explanation until he could get dressed and join her, a tactic that many another man would have considered but one more happy stratagem in the war between the sexes. Instead, he simply gave way to a normal—if somewhat irrational!—impulse, born, as it was, of his overwhelming desire to see the object of his newly conceived idolatry as soon as humanly possible, and came racing downstairs just as he was, in his pyjamas and dressing gown.

"Grace, I'm sorry!" he began breathlessly; but, by then, he was close enough for her to reach up and finger the lapel of his dressing gown. It and the pyjamas were of the purest mainland Chinese silk, smuggled out through one of those attacks of benevolent blindness on the part of the Red customs authorities that earns the Peoples' Republic so much hard Western currency in the markets of Hong Kong, and both of the same tawny shade of beige, so deep and rich that it looked, in some lights, like old gold.

One of Grace's heavy brows crawled upward. Her wide, humorous mouth spread into a mocking grin.

"Hmmmmmmmnnnn—sexy!" she breathed. "Now what? Am I supposed to chase you round and round this gorgeous sunken living room, Jim Rush? Hurl myself upon you with a fiendish howl? Or—"

Then she saw his face. At once her hand dropped away from his lapel and caught his forearm in a grip powerful enough to make him wince.

"Jim," she breathed, "I'm sorry! Forgive me, will you?"

"For what?" he said dully. "You didn't—"

"Oh, yes; I did!" she laughed. "I actually thought you put on these sexy pyjamas with unconfessable intentions in mind, as my mother used to say. Oh, no! Not my mother. My mother was a belle of the early thirties. And probably not my grandmother, although she lived in the days of hip flasks and rumble seats . . . Anyhow, I should have known better. I suppose you sleep in these all the time . . ."

"Or in others just like them," he said; "different colors, but the same material. I like the way they feel. A harmless enough pleasure for a man who has so few . . ."

His voice, saying that, was so sad that, moved by genuine compassion, she tugged at his arm.

"Come, sit beside me a moment, Jim—and talk to me," she said. "There's no hurry—now. We'll have to find some all-night place anyhow, because by the time you get dressed, it will be too late for the place I was going to take you to—"

"Grace, I'm sorry," he said; "it's just that a chap from one of the other Government agencies flew up unexpectedly from Washington to see me. His errand was at least important enough for me to listen to. So—I didn't get the *siesta* I was planning, as well as not having had time to dress. One of the reasons I'm jumpy, I suppose . . ."

She smiled at him almost tenderly; said:

"Jim, we don't have to go out, if you're tired. Let's stay here, and raid your frig. Or send your man out to the corner delicatessen . . . Then I'll go home early and let you get your beauty sleep."

He looked at her, and his eyes were naked.

"I wish you'd *never* go home," he said.

He saw her face tighten; said: "What's wrong?"

"That," she said evenly. "What you just said. Under your present circumstances, one could take it—as an insult, Jim Rush. But—let it pass, let it go! We've time for explanations, if you care to give them, later. Time for all sorts of chitchat: even a discussion of the price of—orchids. The value of *objets d'art*—"

He stared at her. Whispered: "Grace—" making of her name a mourning sound.

She patted his arm, laughed, said:

"I'm hungry! And when I'm hungry I become *mean*. Bitchy—mean. So you'd better get dressed, so we can go out, or at least feed the famished she-beast—"

He reached up and pulled the bell cord. Rad appeared as if by magic, so quickly that Jim knew he had been eavesdropping just outside the door.

"Rad," Jim said, "Go tell Bess that Mrs. Nivens is staying to dinner. I don't know what we have on hand, but if the way you fix it is not absolutely perfect, I'm personally going to repeal the Emancipation Proclamation and sell both of you down the River. To the Governor of Mississippi, at that!"

Rad laughed, happily.

"Don't think me 'n Bess got to worry too hard about that, Sah! But anyhow we do our level best . . ."

"See that you do. By the way, have we any champagne in the refrigerator downstairs?"

"Yes, Sah. We've got some Piper Heidseck, forty-seven. Some Veuve Cliquot, that's for sure. And maybe even some Mum Brut, too; but I'm not too sure about that—"

"Lord!" Grace said. "This *is* a den of iniquity, isn't it?"

"A damned unsuccessful one," Jim said, "what with Bess watching Rad like a hawk, and my lacking the knack—totally. All right, Rad; get a move on, will you? I'm counting on you and Bess tonight to help me persuade Mrs. Nivens—Miss Grace—to become the co-titular head of this household. To stay here with us—forever."

"We're on your side far as that's concerned, Sah!" Rad beamed. "Be mighty glad to have her here for keeps. Just what this old place needs— a Mistress. And a pretty one like Miss Grace—Lord, Lord! Yes Sah, mighty glad! 'Scuse me now, Sah, Ma'am—I better go get busy with that dinner. Sure hopes it'll be an engagement feast!"

Grace stared at Jim. At first her gaze was appalled. Then angry. Then it stopped being either one, became merely puzzled.

"Jim—" she said; "you—" Then: "No. It doesn't add up. You simply aren't that—crass."

"What doesn't add up?" Jim said. "What aren't I crass enough to do?"

"Later," Grace said quietly. "If explanations get to be in order, even then. I confess I'd like some, from you. But only—voluntarily, Jim. I won't ask them. I can't."

"Why not?" he said.

"Because for a woman, even for a modern woman—some things are just too demeaning, Jim."

"Such as?"

"Such as *asking* certain explanations of a man."

He stared at her.

"Then I must guess what the explanations you want are?" he said.

"Something like that. Though if you really are as perceptive as your Jenny said you were, you'll know . . ."

He heard that "your." Caught the slight, almost understated emphasis she'd placed upon it. Saw for a flickering instant how her voice had italicized it upon the naked air. *"Your* Jenny." What did she mean? But he didn't ask her. Every nerve in his body, every overbred instinct was hissing at him like a nest of snakes: 'Not yet, you fool! Not now!'

He said:

"Would you like a drink before dinner? I can ring for Rad to bring you one while I run upstairs and get dressed."

"You," Grace said solemnly, "don't have to get dressed, Jim. I promise you I won't chase you round and round the living room. Word of honor!"

He smiled, said dryly:

"More's the pity!" Then: "Unfortunately, I *do* have to get dressed. I don't know whether you're good at accents; but Rad and Bess are West Indian Blacks, not ours. Conventional as all get out; even a bit straight-laced. Wouldn't do to shock them. And—for your own good comfort— as a consequence of the way our British cousins brought them up, it goes without saying that *here* you'll be most strictly chaperoned!"

"More's the pity!" Grace said in a perfect imitation of his own dry tone. "Very well, since my sacred honor's per–fect–ly safe, I'll venture one small sherry. Very dry."

Jim rang for Rad; noted with satisfaction that the interval it took him to get there meant he'd actually been out of earshot—this time.

"Rad, bring the *Tío Pepe,*" he said. "And just one glass—for Miss Grace . . ."

"One moment, Rad!" Grace said. She turned to her host. "Jim—" she began; paused a long, long moment then added, with wicked deliberation, "Darling, d'you mind if Rad shows me around your house while you're getting dressed? What I've seen of it seems lovely. I'd like to see the rest. Especially—your bedroom. That is, if you haven't some charming little visitor up there tonight. But you can't now, any more, can you? Your fate's already decided, isn't it?"

He had that feeling again, but now he was sure. She was baiting him. And under her warm alto voice ran an undercurrent of anger. Real anger, not unmixed with sadness. Which was why, perhaps, she didn't get the note of light, playfully feline mockery quite right. Most women could manage that tone beautifully, he knew. Especially women like— Virginia. But Grace couldn't.

He thought: 'She's basically honest, so this just isn't her style . . .'
He said:

"Is any man's fate ever decided before *rigor mortis* sets in, my dear? Of course you may see the house. Rad will show you around. All over. So that you may convince yourself that there's no visitor. Not tonight. That is, unless *you* care to stay . . ."

Then he turned on his heel and marched out of there.

When Jim came back downstairs he was dressed in fawn-colored slacks and a burgundy silk lounging jacket with velvet shawl collar and cuffs of a slightly deeper shade of the same color. A white, ruffled shirt, open at the neck. No tie. Soft grey glove-leather slippers. He looked rather like an Edwardian dandy, except that most Edwardian dandies had been large, corpulent men. A pint-sized Edwardian dandy, then—

Or, the mischievous and mocking thought stole through Grace's mind, 'Little Lord Fauntleroy!'

She took his hand, laughed gaily, said:

"Jim, you're positively beautiful!"

And bending swiftly forward—and slightly downward!—kissed him on his forehead as a mother would a handsome child.

He stared at her, and his eyes were very bleak.

"Please, Grace," he said; "don't make fun of me."

The hurt in his voice got through to her. She looked into his young-old face, physically so much younger than his actual age until you saw his eyes. Then it became older. Older than time itself, than anything at all, except the loss of hope, the immutability of pain.

"Sorry!" she said. "Look, Jim, I—"

Then Rad came parading into the living room bearing the silver ice bucket, already well frosted over, and a magnum of champagne protruding from it, its neck covered with a snowy napkin.

"Open it, Rad!" Grace said. "Lord, how I need a drink!"

Jim's brows winged upward. But he didn't say anything. He waited until Rad had shot the cork thunderously ceilingward, then took, in his turn, the champagne glass—it, too, properly frosted, since it had been resting like its fellows in a special dry ice chest, designed to chill champagne, white wine, and *vin rosé* glasses. The red wine goblets, of course, stood apart, on their own heavy silver tray. The brandy snifters reposed on their cradles of solid, massive silver, with the ornate sterling alcohol burners beneath them, ready to heat them to the proper temperature that the one-hundred-and-twenty-five-year-old silver ribbon cognac beside them called for.

Grace took those details in with one swift and knowing look.

"Jim, you're a true sybarite, aren't you?" she said.

"No," he said quietly, "for a sybarite's chief pleasure always manages to escape me. Say a sybarite *manqué,* Grace . . ."

"Hmmmnnn!" she said. "We'll have to do something about *that,* later on!"

He stared at her. He had the sudden, startled feeling that she wasn't really joking. But his sense of timing told him it wasn't the moment to push that one any further either. He had to play this evening by ear. There wasn't any score to go by.

After a longish interval spent in carefully meaningless small talk, punctuated by even more careful silences, Rad came in to announce that dinner was served. They went into the dining room. Jim held Grace's chair for her to sit down, instead of waiting for Rad to do it. She glanced up at him with a tiny frown; but then she realized it was the sort of thing that he would do naturally, that it would never occur to him not to. Watching, as Rad in his turn pulled back the chair for Jim with grave ceremony, she thought: 'He's a holdover from another century—another world. I'd never get used to him, never!'

She gazed around her—again—at the furniture, drapes, tapestries, pictures, that Jim Rush, Senior, had accumulated in a lifetime of sure and disciplined catering to his nearly flawless taste, and the next thing she thought was contradictory to what she had thought before, or almost: 'But, I *could* get used to this house. In fact, I already have. It—suits me, even though I simply don't know enough to have planned it—'

"How—beautiful!" she breathed. "Oh, Jim; I just *love* your house!

He said, quietly:

"Allow me to make you a present of it, then."

She had an excellent ear. She heard what vibrated just below his voice. She said, evenly, flatly, coolly:

"There's a catch to that, isn't there?"

"Yes. That you have to take *me* along with the house—"

She laughed. But her laughter had lost its usual music. There was an edge to it.

"That, Jim Rush, is just about the neatest proposition I've had so far this year!" she said.

Again the expression on his face stopped her.

"Jim," she said; "I don't understand you—truly I don't!"

"I know," he said; "you've just proved that. For your information, my dear, that was a proposal, not a proposition. *Gauche* of me, what? Hardly the time, or the place—forgive me, won't you?"

Then, before her astonishment had ebbed enough to loose her halted breath into speech to say—what? What could she, should she, say to *that?*—or memory had supplied her with the renewed defense of anger, he'd touched the electric bell set into the floor beneath the table with the toe of his slipper. Rad appeared like an inky Djinn conjured up from some magic lamp.

"You may serve dinner now, Rad," Jim said.

The dinner was a marvel. A *bouillabaisse* served with a Domaine d'Ot white, almost golden, really, and chilled to a breath-smoking degree that contrasted wonderfully with the *bouillabaisse's* spicy fire. Then, *pompano en papillotes,* filets of white fish, sautéed in butter with green onions, mushrooms, truffles, and white wine, then baked—with all these ingredients, plus two more, crabmeat and egg yolks, added at this point—inside a brown paper bag, then served with the bag unbroken to preserve all its matchless flavor, and accompanied by a Chablis *Premier Cru* that was almost silver, and even colder than the Domaine d'Ot had been. After that, leaving France—and Louisiana!—far behind, as the main course, roast suckling pig, West Indian style, with candied yams, and all sorts of herbs and spices Grace had never tasted before, and which caused Jim to glare at Rad, because he strongly suspected that those two Machiavellian matchmakers in his kitchen had added at least some of them for their aphrodisiacal effect. The pig was served with a Burgundy red that had weight and body, and a rich, dry, smoky flavor.

Sometime later, or about three-quarters through the main course, Grace noticed three things: that another mouthful was going to cause her to burst, that her eyes weren't focusing properly, and that Jim Rush was scarcely tasting all that marvelous food, and had taken only a sip or two of each of those miraculous wines.

'The classic tactic!' she raged inside her mind. 'Candy is dandy; but liquor's quicker! Get the stupid bitch stuffed *and* drunk, then—'

"Jim—" she said accusingly, anger shaking her voice, "you're not eating at all! Nor drinking! Mind telling me why?"

"Another of my complexes, Doctor!" he said soberly. "An overreaction, triggered by my painful memories of my former obesity. I guess I've become conditioned against food. Turns me off. And, frankly, my dear, *your* presence doesn't help my appetite—"

"Now *that's* a left-handed compliment if I ever heard one!" she said.

"It *is* a compliment. I find myself—uninterested in anything else. Unable to concentrate upon such mundane matters as food and drink. The problem at hand is too grave: how to prevent the one person who could—sustain my existence—give it meaning, from slipping away from me. I've very little to offer, I know, still—"

And, at that moment, as if on cue, Bessie appeared, beaming, and bearing a *soufflé* lighter than an angel's breath, on a platter held high in her black hands.

Jim didn't even pretend to taste it. But at the risk of really bursting, Grace ate a huge mound of it. Then she saw Rad was lighting the minature burners under the brandy snifters.

Jim saw her look.

"Can you?" he said. "It's a great old cognac, but I'd rather you stayed conscious, my dear—and sufficiently awake to *hear* what I'd like to say—"

She said, defiantly:

"Yes, Rad—I *will* have a brandy!"

"You, Sah?" Rad said.

"Well—all right; but a very small one, Rad. And serve us in the living room, not here. Miss Grace and I have some serious talking to do. Oh, by the way—bring us some coffee too, will you? For me *espresso*— black, and as strong as you can make it . . ." He put out his hand to Grace; said: "Come along now, my dear—please?"

Grace got up, a little unsteadily, took his arm.

"No coffee!" she said; "I wouldn't sleep in a week!"

She was, Jim saw, disposed to be contrary.

"My dear," he said "it would be wiser to have some coffee before that cognac. Or else a rather quick paralysis will set in. And I do want to talk to you—"

She dropped his arm, strode ahead of him. Sat down on the sofa. Kicked off her shoes.

"You mean," she said venomously, "that you want to propose to me again? Or is it proposition, this time? Of the two, I'd much prefer a proposition. That comes under the heading of mere extracurricular activities, doesn't it? While a proposal's serious. So serious that you no longer have the right to make one, Jim Rush! Not *another* one, anyhow. Speaking of which, let me be the first to congratulate you! I hope you and dear little Jenny will be very, very happy!"

She was aware suddenly that she could no longer see him. She almost never drank, and now, to her bitter shame, she realized that all that wine had been too much. She wasn't really intoxicated, but she had reached that curious plateau of pre-intoxication where alcohol numbs the critical faculty, that autodidactic center that lends one prudence, tells one what *not* to say. The cruel part about it was that she was acutely aware that she was being a fool, letting her feelings—especially the way she had come, completely against her will, to feel towards this absurd, quaint, almost comical, but for all that, distinctly charming little man—flood through to the detriment of all sense.

"Oh, damn!" she wailed; but then he was kneeling beside her, touching gently, tenderly, his handkerchief to her flooded eyes.

"Lie down," he said firmly; "and give me that damned cognac, will you? Rad will be here with the coffee in a minute. And you, my dear, are going to drink a whole pot of it. Because I refuse to let *anyone* spoil tonight. Not even you."

The coffee made her sick. Jim rang for Bessie, who escorted her to the nearest bathroom. She brought up all of the coffee and most of the food and the wine. After that, she felt better. In one way. In another, she felt worse.

"Jim," she said, when she came back into the living room, "will you call me a taxi, please?"

"No," he said; "I'll take you home in my car. But not now. Later. When you're feeling better."

"Jim—" she whispered; "I'm sorry! For if there is anything on earth more disgusting than a drunken female, I'm sure I don't know what it is—"

He smiled at her, said:

"You're forgiven. In fact, I can't imagine anything I couldn't forgive you for. But, then, you see, I love you."

She said:

"Jim, please!"

"Sit down. Here beside me. Put your head on my shoulder. Please Grace . . ."

"I'd have to be a contortionist to manage that," she said bitterly; "as tall as I am—"

"And as short as I am," he said quietly.

"Yes, that, too," she said. "You'd might as well face the fact that you and I would make the most mismatched couple in history. Physically, anyhow. That's why you and —Jenny—"

"Don't start that again!" he said sharply, his voice firm, commanding. "Sit down, will you?"

She did so; but not beside him. With that astonishing physical grace that made every motion of hers slow ballet, mobile sculpture, she sank to the floor at his feet, rested her head on his knees, staring away from him. She hoped he wouldn't see she was crying again, very quietly.

"Grace!" he said.

She turned to face him, angrily. She was still crying.

He bent and kissed her.

She did none of the things he more than half expected her to. She neither jerked away, nor slapped his face, nor threw furious denunciations at his head. She simply kissed him back, slowly, softly, sweetly—and, at the last, for the briefest of moments, hungrily. Then she drew back, and said:

"Jim—"

"Yes, Grace?"

"Don't do that, again. Please?"

He said, dully:

"All right. As you wish, my dear."

She said:

"*Not* as I wish. I liked it. That's *why* you mustn't do it again."

"Meaning?"

"I'm old fashioned. I believe a man's pledged word should mean something. So even if you were inclined to break yours, I shouldn't let you. Besides—Jenny *needs* you . . ."

"And I need *you*," he said quietly. "Or do you hold that what I need or merely even want is without importance in this world? Does Jenny Crowley's hypothetical needs take precedence over yours, or mine? Grace, let's have this out. The pledge you're accusing me of breaking doesn't exist, because it was never given. Do you mean to tell me you've worked for Ed Crowley all this time without finding out he's the biggest liar on two left feet?"

She sat there, considering that. Said, finally:

"All right. He does misuse the truth with distressing frequency. I know that. So, now, you—you're implying that—"

"Implying, hell! I'm flatly stating that I am not engaged to Jenny Crowley. That I refused to be bought. I did promise Ed I'd do what I could to help Jen out of the mess she's in. But that help doesn't include marrying her. I'm fond of her, of course; but, item one, I don't love her. I love *you*. Item two, I suppose, is that being an orderly, rational man, I could never stomach the idea of having a drug addict as a wife. And I was married to one promiscuous woman. One, I assure, was quite enough. So now, tell me, are you entirely sober? Sober enough to hear and understand what I have to say?"

"Yes," she whispered; "only I don't want you to say it!"

The silence stretched out between them, nerve tightening until it twanged. He broke it.

"Why not, Grace?" he said.

And she, slowly:

"Not—what you're thinking. Not because of Jenny. Though I do think that if your marrying her would save her, you should. I still believe you'd make her happy and—vice versa—"

He said:

"You don't need that way out, Grace. All you've got to do is to say, meaning it, 'No, Jim . . .' "

She turned, faced him.

"Then I *do* say it. No, Jim. And please don't tell me I've broken your heart. It doesn't break very easily. It only—feels like it does."

He sighed then, deeply; said, with infinite weariness, but with no bitterness at all, his tone free of both irony and anger, yet flattened and slowed by a resignation much more painful to her than those more normal reactions would have been:

"How would *you* know that, Grace?"

She didn't hide her face. She let her clear eyes flood, brim, spill.

"Because that's how *mine* feels now," she said.

"Grace!"

"When Ed Crowley told me that, I literally couldn't breathe. Part of it was, of course, shock at—at the intensity of my own reaction to a piece of news that, up until two days ago, *I* was actively promoting as an ideal solution to at least the emotional side of Jenny's problems. But then, two days ago, I hadn't yet met *you*, had I?"

"No," he said; "you hadn't . . ."

"Oh, I brought it off well enough! Told him how happy I was—for Jenny, and for you. Said I was sure it would work out, that the two of you were so right for each other, *et cetera, et cetera, et cetera,* and so forth, and so on—"

"And?" Jim said.

"I got away as soon as I could. Went back to my office. Sat there all afternoon long, staring off into space. I didn't work, because I couldn't. All I did was to sit there and chant to myself: 'You fool you fool you fool!' "

"Grace, listen! We—"

"No, Jim. There's no 'we.' Nor 'us.' There can't be. Just you and I, separate and apart. Parallel lines that must never meet, nor touch. Let me finish this, will you, Jim? I've got to. You—you've been hurt—badly hurt, by that horrible bitch you married. Jenny told me all about her—"

"Jenny didn't *know* all about her," Jim said.

"She knew enough. More than you think. I know you didn't talk about it. But the little you did say aroused her interest, her curiosity. And the very rich, Jim Rush, can find out practically anything about us ordinary mortals they want to. All it takes is enough money to pay a sufficient number of first class investigators—private eyes, Jenny called them . . ."

"My God!" Jim said.

"It's not important, now. What is important is that your past has set up a self-perpetuating pattern of defeat in you, as far as your emotional life is concerned."

"Doctor, I thank you," Jim said.

"In other words, you feel rejected. And I—damnit all to deep blue hell and back again!—come along at a time, and under such circumstances, that I'm literally forced to reenforce that rejection psychosis, the last thing on earth I want to do!"

"Grace, I won't accept—pity," he said.

"Nor do I offer it. Because—oh hell! how can I explain it?—it's not *you* I'm rejecting. Rather I reject *me* for you. As—as not good enough!"

"Grace—" he began.

"Listen! I went back to my office and sat there trying to analyze, sort out, clarify the way I felt—feel—about you. To decide what, if anything, to do about it. Took me less than an hour to reach the conclusion that the only sensible, sane, humane, *safe* thing to do—was nothing. It was at that point that Meg came into my office and saw my face. She said: 'Cry, Grace. It helps. Believe me it does. Truly.' So I cried. In poor little Meg's arms, with her trying to comfort me. Can you picture that scene, Jim? A big, overgrown horse like me, blubbering like an idiot-child, bathed down in tears over something I knew from the outset was impossible! Can you imagine anything more utterly ridiculous? Comic, isn't it? Farcical!"

He put out his hand and let his fingers stray along her cheek.

"Wrong word," he murmured; "try—'glorious' on for size, Grace . . ."

She reached up and snatched his hand from her cheek. Her fingers bit into his wrist. She saw the involuntary grimace of pain he made and dropped his hand. "Sorry!" she said. "I always have to remind myself to be gentle with normal people. All the way through college, I used to refuse to shake hands for fear of leaving people maimed! My ex-husband said I belonged in the circus. Or in a carnival sideshow. Y'know, the Strong Woman. Breaking chains across her chest. Or the Lady Wrestler. Or something else—equally—physical—"

"Then what would you have done with that mind of yours?" he said. "That brilliant, wholly admirable mind?"

"Don't know," she said morosely. "Doesn't it frighten you? It does most men."

"But I am not most men. And it delights me. Which is why I want to add it to my *objets d'art*. Along with the rest of you, of course."

"Oh, damn!" she said feelingly. "Jim—you—you *really* believe that you're in love with me?"

"I don't believe. I *know*."

"While I—I don't know whether I love you or not. I—probably do. Or why else did I react the way I did to Ed's telling me that?"

"Grace—" he breathed.

"Wait! I—I've always been terribly fond of Jenny. Pitied her, of course; but loved her, too. Jenny's lovable, Jim."

"Agreed. I also love her. As a daughter. A pitiful, emotionally retarded child. Who needs all the protection, help, counsel, defense, guidance, she can get. All of which I'll gladly give her. But not my body. Nor—my life . . ."

She peered at him through her glasses; whispered:

"That's well put. What I started to say is that I've always loved Jenny. But, all of a sudden, listening to Ed announce *your* coming wedding to her, I was seized with a feeling of black, abysmal hatred for her, found myself possessed by a pure, bitchy, feline, female desire to wring her little neck!"

"Grace—" he said; "kiss me?"

"No," she said. Like that. Flatly.

"Why not, Grace?"

"Because I don't propose to start something that is sure to end badly, Jim. It's quite possible that I love you. Or that I could—hungrily and desperately like the great starved bitch I am!—if I'd let myself. But I don't intend to permit myself that luxury. Or that folly. It's one I can't afford. And that I *refuse* to inflict upon you. You deserve better. Much better . . ."

"Like—Jenny?" he said bitterly.

"No. Jenny has nothing to do with it. I don't suppose she ever did, really. She was just an excuse my defense mechanisms seized upon. Believe me, Jim, you and I could *never* work . . ."

He said:

"Same question: Why *not,* Grace?"

She got to her feet, swayed there, all long, lanky grace; put out her hand to him. He got up, stood there, facing her. She caught him by the shoulders, whirled him effortlessly around until they were both facing the mirror. Even in her stocking feet, she was close to a head taller than he was.

"Look," she said. "I'm five feet eleven and one half inches tall. No; that's not true. I'm an even six feet. When I wear high heels, I'm well over six feet two. And you're—"

"Five feet six," he said bleakly, "barefooted, anyhow. Lord God, Grace! That's not important! Why—"

"Oh, yes; it is!" she said, crying now, the slow tears pencilling her cheeks; "Because it has always spoiled my life! It's likely to go on spoiling it. Why d'you think I became a psychiatrist in the first place, Jim? Because I had the idiotic idea that understanding my complexes would eradicate them. Only it doesn't. It can't."

"So," he said, "because I'm a miserable little runt, you can't—"

"Love you? Of course I can! I probably already do! I told you *that,* Jim. What's size got to do with love?"

He stared at her, whispered.

"Aren't you contradicting yourself now, Grace?"

"No. Not really. Because, you see, you're *not* a miserable little runt. You're a living *doll*. A sweet little fellow. Good-looking—to me, anyhow. Gentle. Even—kind of cute. I want to take you in my arms—and sort of *cuddle* you!"

"Oh, Jesus!" Jim said.

"You see?" she said with wicked, tender, female malice, blinking back the hot tears in her eyes. "The whole thing's all wrong, Jim. The *way* I love you is more than half maternal! Sleeping with you would probably feel like incest—"

"The hell it would!"

"To me, it would. But let's say that mental block could be overcome—as it probably could. One fine busy night would probably fix *that* quite nicely, thank you! I could love you. Granted. But what I can't do—is to inflict an outsized Junoesque female with a lifetime's accumulation of even more outsized complexes upon you as a *wife*. I—I *couldn't* marry you, Jim. I'm just not brave enough."

"Grace—" he began.

"Sit down!" she said sharply. "Listen to me! In high school, I *never* had a date because I was a clothier's yard taller than any damned boy in the school. Just once, a very nice boy, Dave Tyler, got up the nerve to ask me to the Junior Prom. When we tried to dance, he came up to *here*. And, after that, they called him "The Breast Fed Baby" until he broke down and actually left school . . ."

"So?" he whispered.

"So I became an overachiever, which endeared me to *nobody*. Dean's List. Highest grades in the history of the school. Went out for track; broke even some of the men's records for that age group. Tennis champion of the whole miserable state. There wasn't a boy who could stay on the same court with me, and you can imagine how that helped my popularity with the male sex! Led the girl's basketball team to the regional, state, and finally national championships. I understand my scoring record's *never* been broken, not even yet. Lord, Jim, I could go up on tiptoe, give a little hop, and stick my big red paw, and the rest of my skinny arm up to the elbow, through the damned basket before even turning the ball loose, so how could I miss?"

"And in college?" he said.

"Same story. Except in college, there *were* boys who were tall enough for me. A very few, but some. Only even they preferred little, cuddlesome girls. As a result, my—well, call it my 'love life,' was an unmitigated disaster. I willingly—even eagerly—surrendered my frozen, rigid, sickened, and revolted body to a huge, muscle-bound oaf of a football hero on the back seat of his car. Frightened him completely out of what little wits he had. I hemorrhaged like hell, and he'd never imagined that a big strapping horse of a girl like me could possibly still be—at twenty years of age—a virgin. Nor did he realize that a woman's internal structure doesn't necessarily match—as far as size is concerned!—her outer contours. Result, he dropped me like a hot brick."

"He was a bastard," Jim said grimly.

"No. Just a fool. Bastardy calls for a certain degree of talent. I've often admired bastards. Fools, never!"

"Go on," Jim whispered.

"After that I found myself blessed or cursed with a certain highly suspicious popularity. A quick check instantly revealed that they were *all* friends of his. The oaf had passed the word around. Grace Foster is 'putting out.' Brother, Grace Foster can be *had*!"

"And?" Jim said.

She laughed.

"You've already noticed how strong I am? After I'd crippled the first two or three of them, the rest gave it up. Which ended my 'love life.' I kept to myself. Or went around with the type of girls that your BMOCs—"

"Your what's?"

"BMOCs—Big Men on Campus—describe as 'real *dogs*.' Which, of course, promptly got me tagged as a Lesbian . . ."

"And were you?" he said gently.

"No! Of course not! I like women, but I'm definitely not attracted to them sexually. Then—my career. One long, ice cold Eskimo's Hell of wearying my poor sex-starved body into sleep. Piling sublimation upon sublimation. Jim, does my frankness distress you? I *am* a psychiatrist, remember, and it's quite normal for me to call things, states of mind, emotions, by their right names . . ."

"Not at all. It's refreshing," he said.

"Good. Say that out of my frustrations, complexes, repressed desires, I built a career. My lovely, lonely, brilliant career! Until I met Jon. Jon Nivens. Physicist—one of the world's outstanding authorities on subatomic particles. Six feet seven and one half inches tall. As—beautiful— as a Norse god . . ."

"All right," he said sadly, "I get the picture . . ."

"No, you don't. Or at least not entirely. The connection between male beauty and female response is not nearly as direct as you men think. That is, when it exists at all. A lot of the time it doesn't. I've known a good many absolutely stunningly handsome men whom I've loathed on first sight. And so has any other woman who is a woman, Jim. Which was one of the things I'd meant to explain to you if I'd had the time—that whole very nearly uncharted area of female response; I mean how our hearts and minds respond to the men we love, not merely how our genitalia do, a thing those obscenely voyeuristic machines of Masters and Johnson *couldn't* measure—because it has all the bearing in the world on the problem that you mentioned. Voluntarily, which was quite the finest compliment I've had from *any* man in my whole life . . ."

"Finer than my wanting to marry you?"

"Yes. Why yes, of course! Because it meant you trusted me. The majority of men marry women they don't trust, don't even *like,* but merely, on one—appallingly primitive!—level anyhow, *love.* We human beings can fall in love with the goddamnedest people, Jim! If you don't know *that,* you don't know anything. As I fell in love with Jon."

"Because he was as beautiful as a Norse god?"

"In part. But now I think it was more likely because I had *good* sex with him. Before we were married. As his mistress. Made me decide to marry him, I suspect . . ."

"In short, besides being beautiful, he was also an A-One Stud?"

"Don't be—bitter, Jim. Not about that. That problem's curable, nearly all the time. As a matter of fact, he *wasn't.* As far as I can judge from my own distinctly limited experience, he was just—average, or maybe even not quite average. And that's the main thing you men don't understand about us women. How subjective we are. With us, it's the 'Who' that counts, not the 'What' or the 'How.' All you have to do is learn the basic minimum of relaxation, self-control—and *we'll* do the rest. Or our imaginations will. Forget technique. It turns a sensitive woman off. Just—*like* us, please? Really like us, as *people.* Be glad to be around us, even when we've not only got all our clothes on, but have no immediate intention of taking them off! Be amusing, gay—in the old fashioned sense of the word, not the modern usage!—tender, loving. Love *us.* Our minds, our personalities, even our quirks, follies . . . We're more, much more than *this,* and *these,* y'know." She swept, as she spoke, her hand wryly, disdainfully, across her pelvis and her breasts.

"Grace," he said, "you've just said for me—beautifully—what I've been trying to say all night!"

"I know. I understand that. But what you won't see is that I must not, cannot, inflict outsized *and* damaged goods on you! Jim, my marriage to Jon Nivens lasted all of eighteen months. Until I came home from a National Convention of Freudian Psychiatrists and found one Dolly Mirkus in *my* house, in *my* bed, with *my* dearly beloved husband. They were rutting like pigs—and in the same general position. Ugh! I've never understood voyeurs. As a spectacle, it's most unpleasant, Jim. Since then—nothing. An affair or two, entered into coolly with no idea or desire to let them get out of hand. I am after all, a normal mammalian female, with a normal female's purely physical needs, though, thank God, I manage to suppress them most of the time. Besides—" she added wickedly, throwing a sidelong glance his way, her wide mouth curling into a sad, mocking, self-depreciative smile, "the electric vibrator is a most useful safety valve against being pressured by sheer biology into the grosser forms of folly!"

He ignored that; said:

"Grace, *we* could be happy. I'd never look at another woman. I'd never even be tempted to—"

"I know. Only—could you stand the stares, the grins, the chuckles, the winks, as we walked down a street together? I *love* dancing, possibly because it, too, is a useful sublimation! D'you realize how you'd look with *me* on a dance floor, Jim? Another 'Breast Fed Baby!' And—I'd want children. I'm just too female, and too primitive, to forego that privilege. I'm not yet too old. Almost, but not quite. Imagine us—you, me, and a gaggle of kids like an inverted staircase straggling along through a supermarket, and—"

He bowed his head. Stared at the toes of his grey slippers.

She said, her voice rough, grating, harsh:

"*Will* you take me home now, Jim Rush?"

"Of course," he said quietly, He got up, rang for Rad, said when his manservant appeared:

"Bring the car around, Rad. Wait in front of the house. Double-park if you have to. We'll be down in five minutes . . ."

He turned to Grace then, added:

"Excuse me a moment, Grace? I must slip on a jacket, a tie, a pair of shoes—"

She smiled at him, murmured:

"May I come up with you? I still haven't seen your bedroom . . ."

He searched her eyes, in an effort to discern her intent. She looked back at him, serenely. He sighed.

"All right," he said; then: "I was thinking how easy it would be to redecorate it to—suit you . . ."

"Jim, please!" she said.

"Sorry!"

But when they came into his bedroom she went immediately to the big Castilian bed, and lay down upon it, her hands behind her head, staring at the ceiling.

"Go on," she said mockingly; "say it!"

"Say what?" he said.

"That all women are the same height lying down."

"Never thought about it," he said dryly. "Besides, I'm not concerned about all women. And since the one I was prepared to give my undivided attention for the rest of my life wants no part of me—"

She raised up, on one elbow, said:

"I didn't say *that*, Jim. I only said I wouldn't marry you. And that's wrong, too. I would marry you, if I could. Only—I *can't*."

He finished knotting his tie. Sighed. Said:

"So be it, then. Come."

The car was a Rolls—an old but perfectly kept Silver Phantom inherited from his father. Rad, splendid in a chauffeur's uniform, drove.

She lived on Central Park West, in a fancy modern condominium. Jim got out of the car and walked with her to the doorway. An imposing doorman saluted her with grave respect, opened the door for them. Jim hesitated, then walked with her to the lifts.

She said:

"When do you leave for Costa Verde, Jim?"

"Day after tomorrow," he whispered.

She smiled at him. Her smile was dazzling. And heartbreaking. The saddest smile he had ever seen upon a human face.

She said, her voice—gentle? Sad? That surely; but something else, something more. It had another quality to it now, the quality of—of longing. But not, he was quite sure, in any sensual sense. As though she simply wanted him there. With her. Where she was. Close to her. Not necessarily touching. Though she would permit him that, if she thought he wanted it. That and anything to keep him there just a little longer—an hour, a day, a week—

"Come up with me. No, wait. Go send Rad and the car home, first. Then come up with me. To stay—'til day after tomorrow. Until plane time. Rad can bring your bags over when he picks you up."

He passed a sand dry tongue over bone dry lips. Said:

"No, Grace."

She looked at him and the pain in her eyes matched that in his own. She tried a smile. It didn't work.

"I had that coming," she said; "but—mind telling me—why?"

"Various reasons. On various levels. The honest ones first?"

"Please!"

"My nerves are shot. I probably couldn't. I should hate disappointing you. And loathe myself for—failing."

"You wouldn't fail. *I* shouldn't allow you to!"

"I'd fail. Because the other reasons—less simple, but just as honest really—would get in the way."

"And those are?"

"Hard to say. The words—have been tarnished. Lost their luster. And I can't think of any new ones . . . ."

"Try! Or say the old ones. They may be new—to me."

"All right. To love—to honor—and to cherish. Until death do us part. *Not* a one night stand. Not with *you,* Grace. Never with you. With you—it's forever. Or no time. You chose—no time. And I'm sorry . . ."

He half turned, but she caught his shoulder in her strong, athletic clasp, whispered:

"At least—kiss me—good-bye, Jim?"

But he shook his head. Put up his hand and broke her grip; said:

"No. Even that—would hurt too much—remembering . . ."

And turning, he walked away, his small, slight figure a shadow without substance.

CHAPTER

8

*L*ooking downward and backward out of the window
beside his seat in the first class cabin, Jim Rush could
see the sharp, compression-retarding sweep of the DC 10's wing, with
the gaping maw and the streamlined housing of one of the plane's fanjet
engines beneath it. Just below the engine—or so it seemed to him, his
vision flattened by the lack of any intervening object to give the sweep
of that sky and sea perspective—a swarm of sea-going tugs crawled,
their snowy tracks distinctly visible even from the height at which inter-
continental jets usually fly, as they towed an ungainly structure behind
them through the metallic sun glare, mist-blue, and pale, milky green
of the Caribbean waters.

He knew what that meant: that his flight was nearing Costa Verde
now. For that structure, ugly, ungainly, awkward, and completely unnatural—for anything seaborne, anyhow—was an offshore drilling rig.
And those tugs had towed it all the way across the ocean from Norway,
where the world's best and finest deep-sea platform rigs are built, on
Worldwide Petroleum's direct order. He knew that, because Ed Crowley
had told him so. And he believed him, because Ed was too canny an old
pro to settle for anything less than the very best.

"Cost you too damn much down time, they ain't jes' right, Boy," he
had said yesterday when unexpectedly, and astonishingly, he had per-

sonally dropped by Jim's townhouse to say good-bye, a thing no one who knew him well had *ever* heard of his doing before. "Them shitty lil' rigs they build over here can't take a real blow. 'N when I starts bringing in that there oil under them shoal waters off Costa Verde, I don't mean to stop even if I sees an angel's pearly-white underdrawers blowin' pass my head . . ."

Jim smiled grimly, remembering that visit. He hadn't been bored. He had spent the first half hour of it trying to figure out the *real* reason Ed had come to see him. To calculate some new way that he, Jim, might still be roped and hogtied into marrying poor Jenny and thus insuring her—and his!—permanent exile from the States? Of course. But that wasn't all. There was something else, something more. As usual, Ed Crowley was out to exterminate the entire avian species with but a single stone. 'Stone, hell!' Jim had thought; 'a pebble.' He had studied his ex-employer. There was a lack of ease in the oilman's voice; a disquietude in his gaze that had made Jim decide that he was mounting a defensive rather than an offensive action—in itself, unusual. Jim had thought: 'I wonder what's eating the old buzzard, now?'

Then, with elaborate casualness, Ed had drawled:

"Mighty fine place you got here, Son. Yessirreebobtail, mighty fine! Don't reckon you'd think o' selling it, would you? I mean, seeing as how you hardly lives in it at all . . . I could use a place like this. Homey—not like that damn too flossy suite I got in th' Towers. Say, Son, show me th' rest of it, will yuh? Or have yore cullud boy do it—"

And the answer to the whole puzzle of Ed Crowley's uncharacteristically civil behavior had hit Jim right between the eyes.

He had grinned at his ex-employer; said:

"What's the matter, Ed? Grace didn't come to work today?"

"Now, Son, don't you go ajumpin' to conclusions! I really want to see this here place o' yourn, and—"

"And I'll show it to you. All of it. But with two points made very clear, Ed: It's not for sale. Not to you, not to anyone. And—Grace is *not* here. That's the main reason I'm going to show it to you, so you can convince yourself of that simple fact. Last night, I fed her a meal a little too rich for her digestive system. And, incidentally, spoiled my own evening, because it made her so sick I had to take her home. I suspect she's still got an upset stomach, so—"

"So you outsmarted yoreself, Son!" Ed had cackled, "You'd of asked me, I coulda told you that! All Spanish fly *ever* does is to throw a filly off her feed. Any fella what tells you he ever got hisself a piece o' tail usin' that stuff is a barefaced liar! 'N me thinkin' you really wuz *smart*! Meg told me this mornin' Grace wuz laid up, but I didn't believe that frizzly-headed lil' Limey. She always sticks up for Grace. Besides, when I asked her, I'd already done called Grace's flat, 'n nobody'd answered the phone . . ."

"She probably didn't feel up to talking," Jim had said.

But now, as he turned away from the plane's window, he was suddenly appalled. Needless to say *he* hadn't put cantharides, Spanish fly, that obscene concoction made of dried and powdered *Lytta vescatoria,* the blister beetle, and used since ancient times as an aphrodisiac, in Grace's food. Not only was the idea foreign to his very nature, but he was well aware that, one: *never* in the long history of human venery has anyone ever come up with an aphrodisiac that actually works; and two: cantharides is close to a poison, anyhow. He hadn't; but what about those two Obeah-Witch Doctors in his kitchen? 'Lord God!' he thought miserably, 'I should have called her! I—'

Then he remembered with relief that nothing Grace had eaten or drunk had stayed down, and that she had been perfectly all right—at least physically—when he had left her before the elevators in that coldly modern condominium in which she lived.

'Even so, I should have called her,' he thought. 'Not to offer her my regrets for having suffered a mild attack of nausea brought on by mingling too many varieties of wine. But to say—' Then he stopped. 'To say what? What was there really to be said?'

He gazed diagonally forward out the window. But since it was the very first window after the bulkheads that separated the pilot's cabin from the rest of the aircraft, he really couldn't see very much. He had the regretful feeling that it was going to be impossible for him to get an early view of Ciudad Villalonga from the air; because, by now, the pilot should have already made the usual weaving identification turns for the benefit of the Control Tower's radar. But, judging from the announced arrival time, it was apparent that he was going to bring the big plane in straight ahead without making them at all. 'Probably unnecessary, considering how light air traffic must be down here,' Jim thought; then he added, 'I wonder if *Bahía Linda Aeropuerto* even *has* radar?' But a moment's additional reflection made him decide that it did, that it had to, or none of the three major airlines—TWA, Pan Am, and Air France— that still flew into Costa Verde would consent to land jet aircraft costing from thirty to fifty million dollars each there.

The airlines, he knew, had troubles enough, even so. They had to fly into Costa Verde a certain number of times a month in order to keep their franchises for some future day when, order and stability conceivably having descended upon Costa Verde, said franchises might become valuable. But, at the moment, directly as a result of this rule, imposed by the Costa Verdian Government itself—which, in practice, meant that said rule had been imposed by General Manuel García Herredia who *was* the Costa Verdian Government!—the airlines were losing money hand over fist for the very simple reason that nobody in his right mind wanted to go to Costa Verde anyhow.

In fact, the only times that even a majority of the seats on the planes were filled were on the return trip flights to the States or to Europe when the General sporadically exiled another several hundred of his less dangerous enemies—the dangerous ones being, of course, shot, or disposed of in more artistic and leisurely fashions, the processes involved being deliberately leaked to the general public in order to impress upon any would-be rebel among them the extreme inadvisability of saying anything about General García that wasn't couched in terms of total adoration, even in one's sleep—or, again, when His Excellency was in a sufficiently complaisant mood to accept the ruinous bribes from those few Costa Verdians who could scrape up the huge *mordiscos*—literally, "bites"—that were the price of an exit visa out of the country.

The *bromistas,* wags, held that General García was forced to keep the bribes so high because, if he didn't, he would soon be presiding over a country whose citizenry consisted solely of monkeys, since any creature having a degree of intelligence even approaching that attributed to humanity, would immediately flee the country if given the remotest opportunity of doing so.

To which the good citizen of all those countries having frontiers with Costa Verde replied that he probably already was, because who the hell could tell a Costa Verdian from a monkey, anyhow?

Jim smiled wryly, remembering that one. 'They're somewhat less than just,' he thought; 'at least as far as the women are concerned. For God knows, there's nothing simian about Alicia. Or about Marisol . . .'

Then he stiffened, because, for the first time since he had met Grace Nivens, he recalled the Polaroid photo that Tim O'Rourke had made of him standing between Alicia and Marisol; recalled it, and what he'd more than half intended to do with it. But now, revulsion was in him to the bitter bone. 'No!' he thought. 'God, no! I've had it. I won't be a fool again. Not *ever.*'

He bent swiftly forward, picked up his attaché case. Opened it. Took out that photo. Then, without even looking at it, slowly and carefully he tore it into tiny pieces.

Immediately, he was confronted with the problem of what to do with those pieces. He felt a certain repugnance against taking them into the lavatory and flushing them down the toilet. And, beyond that mere repugnance, he had to consider the fact that since aircraft toilets have very little flushing power, depending largely upon the chemical septic tank beneath them to maintain a reasonable degree of sanitation and freedom from offensive odors, a material as heavy and as indissoluble as the cardboard backing of that photo might well stop the whole works up. Then it came to him what to do. He took an envelope out of the attaché case, put the pieces in the evelope, sealed it up, and stuck it in his inside breast pocket, behind the felt-tipped and the conventional fountain pens he carried there. As soon as he deplaned, he would drop the envelope in the first wastepaper basket he passed, and that would be that.

He was conscious of a feeling of relief at having torn up that photo. Now, no matter how cruelly he might be tormented by loneliness in the near future, he *couldn't* show that picture to Tomás, say:

"Look, Tomás, could you find me a girl, who—"

But upon that word "girl," there was a sudden, jarring dislocation of his thought processes' normal continuity; his senses did a cinematographic lap dissolve: the visual image "girl," wearing the maddeningly exotic and erotic tribal mask that was Alicia Villalonga de Reynolds' face melted abruptly into a perceived presence that was no longer visual but olfactory, assaulting his nostrils with a cloud of perfume noticeably mixed with a strongly acrid—and damned unpleasant!—smell of sweat. He whirled and stared into the face of one of the airline stewardesses. She had bent over him close enough to kiss him, if she'd wanted to. But, he saw at once, romantic intimacies were the last thing she had in mind.

She was trembling. Her lips were white. And the reason she smelled of sweat wasn't anything so unlikely in a trained airline stewardess as a lack of personal fastidiousness; she, Jim realized, would never have got through the airline's training school if she had been guilty of that. Rather, it was the elemental fact that terror visibly gripped her, made her sweat so heavily that neither her preflight bath, her colognes, nor her deodorants were doing her a damned bit of good. Her uniform showed great dark splotches at the armpits. Beads of perspiration were dripping off the tip of her adorable little nose.

"Gentle down, baby," he said in an easy, conversational tone of voice; "tell old Uncle Jim what's wrong."

"Can't!" she whispered sharply. "Not here! You *are* Mr. Rush, aren't you? Ambassador James Rush?"

"Yes," Jim sighed, realizing that the New York Consular Service that had procured him his ticket and seat reservation had again sent a VIP notice to the airline, a practice that he, personally, would have liked to have seen abolished. "What can I do for you, Miss?"

"Captain Wilkinson asks that you come forward into the 'office,' Mr. Ambassador. He'd come back here to talk to you, but it would attract too much attention—and some of the other passengers might try to listen in on your conversation. Can't risk—a panic, you know. So Captain Wilkinson asked me to present his apologies and request that you—"

Jim stared at her, and an ice cold blade of fear whistled in, stabbing deep between his breathing and his life. Then he stopped that. Whatever she was afraid of didn't and couldn't involve a technical failure of the aircraft, because there was no conceivable reason for the pilot to consult him about that. While the other grim possibility, a skyjacker, would have had to pass through the first class cabin to get to the "office," as pilots called the control nacelle. And none had. Jim was sure of that.

"Very well," he said, and stood up. "Let's go, then."

She led him forward. Jim had never been in the pilot's cabin of a multiengined passenger jet before. His first thought was the same thought that absolutely every layman who enters one for the first time has: that it was a physical impossibility for any two men to read the illuminated dial faces of even one-tenth of the literally hundreds of instruments with which every available millimeter of the walls and ceiling of that cabin was covered, and at the same time handle what seemed to him a perfectly endless series of push buttons, levers, throw switches, pedals, and wheel-yoke controls.

But he didn't say that. He said:

"Well, Captain?"

The Captain gazed at him with blank, uncomprehending grey eyes. Even from where he stood, Jim could hear the staccato squawk of mixed Spanish and English pouring through the earphones the Captain wore. Whoever was radioing from that Control Tower—most likely the one at Bahia Linda Airport, the only international-size airport in Costa Verde—sounded wildly excited.

"Roger!" the Captain said into the throat microphone he wore. Then, very slowly, he took off both earphones and microphone, which were a unit really, connected through the same headband, unfastened his seat belt, stood up. The copilot stared straight ahead, intent upon managing the big bird.

"Mr. Ambassador," the pilot said in a marked Southern accent, Alabamian or Georgian, Jim guessed; "I'm mighty sorry to have to bother you, but this is an emergency. And since, in a way, *you're* the main cause of all the trouble, I thought I'd better consult with you before makin' what could be th' wrong move . . ."

Jim stared at him; said:

"I'm listening, Captain."

The Captain turned, pointed forward, and to the left through the vast panoramic windshield of the plane.

"You see that, Sir?" he said grimly.

Jim leaned forward. He saw the blue-green-violet shoal waters of

Bahia Linda—"Pretty Bay"—first; the golden sands of the beach; the dark green of the jungle; then, abruptly a sprawl of white buildings, brilliant in the sun, and above them the pale blue, dazzling white, grey smoke-plumed cone of the—maybe!—extinct volcano, Zopocomapetl. It was all, from the air, anyhow, almost unbelievably beautiful.

"Not there. Further to yore left," the Captain said.

Then he saw it: A tower of inky smoke boiling up ferociously through the limpid air, higher than they were already and mounting furiously higher every second, dirtying blue heaven.

He dragged his gaze down that midnight column to where it started, saw the red-orange-yellow leap and whip and burst incredibly bright at the base of it and the little red bugs of the fire trucks surrounding it, pouring their ineffectual, useless, and worse than useless streams into that inferno, only to have them explode instantly into grey-white clouds of steam.

And there, scattered, some meters to the right and to the left, completely off the runway, a pair of silver wings, broken, crumpled, smoking. Beyond them, the empennage: the stablizer, elevator, vertical fin with the aft jet turbine still intact in it, showing that the wrecked plane had been a trimotor jet rather like the one he was on now, only it looked different somehow, smaller . . .

"A 737," the Captain said. "Pan Am's—"

"Why?" Jim got out. "The visibility's perfect. Even if a motor failed, they ought to have been able to—"

"Those motors don't fail, Mr. Rush. Not with the kind of upkeep Pan Am gives 'em. That there airplane didn't crash. It was—shot down," Captain Wilkinson said. Then he added, softly, slowly: "You see, Mr. Ambassador—they thought *you* were on it . . ."

It took Jim Rush a full thirty seconds to get that all but soundless, breathgone "Dear God!" out. Then he tried the next question; but, by then, the Captain had to read his lips.

"Who? Some crazy Red terrorist outfit, likely. Costa Verde's full of 'em. Probably had a man planted among the Cuban refugee colony in Miami. Bet I know what happened: He went out to the Miami Airport 'n checked. You deplaned there while we were refueling, didn't you?"

"Yes," Jim whispered.

" 'N we 'n Pan Am were parked side by side. Scheduled to take off almost at the same time. So two lines o' passengers start out for two planes, 'n the bastard got mixed up. Or maybe he didn't even know the difference between a Boeing 737 and a DC 10. They're both trijets, but beyond that they aren't anything alike. Don't even have the motors in the same places. 'Course both of 'em got the center turbine in the tail, but that's the only way they're even a little alike. The Ten's fanjets are underneath the wings, while the 737's got 'em aft, grouped under the stabilizer and—

"For God's sake, Captain, spare me the technicalities! You think he—"

"Radioed ahead? Don't think. I know. 'Cause they captured the kid that did *that* alive. Skinny little fella with a Chinese-made rocket launcher—shoulderfired, like our old bazookas. Damned good one. Missile's a copy of our Sidewinder. Heat-seeking gizmo in the nose. They *never* miss. You got your engines on, you've had it. Hell, even if one of yore stewardesses is a hot little number those damn things will home in on you . . ."

Jim didn't appreciate the joke. He hung there, feeling the sidewise tug of gravity as the copilot banked the big plane, circling the airport, not losing any altitude, keeping her high.

"We're stacking up for the moment," the Captain said; "but we got to make up our minds about what to do real fast. The way these big bastards of fanjets eat fuel we—"

Jim found his voice.

"But—the people on that plane, Captain? The crew? The—"

"I'm sorry, Sir," the Captain said.

Jim couldn't see. There was an abrupt shifting of the converging point of focus. His eyes couldn't fix it in space. It kept moving away. He couldn't breathe, either. The constriction of his nostrils, throat, bronchial tubes, lungs, was total.

"Git yoreself together, Sir!" the Captain said gruffly. "Ain't a damn bit of it yore fault. Nary a—"

"How many?" Jim screamed at him. "Goddamnit, man; how many?"

"Forty-three," the Captain whispered. "Pilot was—a good friend o' mine. Some of the passengers was—kids. Hell—babies."

Jim stood there. That was all he did. He stood there.

The stewardess' face came clear. She was sobbing aloud.

"Friend of hers on it, too," the Captain said. "Stewardess . . ."

Jim straightened up.

"What do you want of me, Captain?" he said.

"Tell us what to do. Fact is, Mr. Ambassador, the *only* runway at this here airport long enough to put a DC 10 down on is *that* one. The one with a wrecked aircraft right slapdab in the middle of it. Now, we've got enough fuel to get back to Miami—with luck. Havana, sure. But we land in Cuba, you know what kind o' trouble we're gonna have. Hell, the Company'll practically have to buy back this airplane . . ."

"Go on," Jim said quietly.

"But I been flying thirty-five years now, and I say we *can* put this airplane down in that airport. Other runways are all mighty short; but if we sort of drag in on full flaps a couple o' knots above stalling speed, touch down in the first ten feet o' that damn East-West runway, and reverse thrust the second th' gear scrapes cement, we can make it. Be a sight rough, of course. Shake up the passengers a little. Maybe even blow out a tire o' two; but it can be done . . ."

"Good God, Man; why are you telling *me* this?"

"Because it could be the best thing to do. The crazy kid with th' bazooka has bought his share o' th' farm: six feet with unslaked lime in it . . ."

"But you told me they took him alive!"

"They did—some time back. Kid took th' easy way out. Bit down on a cyanide capsule he had in his mouth—after bragging about *why* he did it. That was what the Tower was telling me when Josie brought you in here—and how come we knew he was after *you*. Reckon he had a mighty fine idea of what they were going to do to him once they got him downtown—"

"God!" Jim whispered.

"So, it's safe enough. Army's all over the place. The point is, Mr. Ambassador, them folks down there don't *know* you ain't in that smokin' heap o' junk that was a mighty nice airplane half an hour ago. They don't because I haven't told 'em, and don't mean to tell 'em 'til I deliver you safe 'n sound to yore own Marine guards. But it sure as hell would calm things down a mighty heap if you was to show up safe 'n alive without a scratch on you, Sir . . ."

Jim thought about that. A long time. Maybe too long.

"If you want, we can raise Miami from this altitude, and they can phone-patch into Washington. You can get instructions from yore Department and—"

"No," Jim said finally; "I make my own decisions, Captain. Take this aircraft in. Land it."

He smiled suddenly. It was a hell of a smile, but he managed it. He put out his hand to the Captain.

"Just in case there's another crazy kid down there with another Chinese-made bazooka, I'd like to say it was nice knowing you, Captain—even for a little while," he said.

"Likewise," the Captain said; "but we ain't a going to have no more trouble, Mr. Ambassador. You can bet on that . . ."

No more trouble. Except one more half hour that redefined all those words in the English language that need substitutes coined to replace them, or the force they have lost through centuries of careless use restored to them. In that half hour, Jim Rush neither died nor went mad. He wasn't that lucky. He simply sat in an airplane's seat and thought about how it was going to be to live the rest of his life knowing that forty-three men, women, and children had burned into unrecognizable, vaguely human shapes of charcoal, because all over the world vast numbers of people have learned to hate the United States of America so damned bad that if to kill one of its representatives—namely, in this case, one Jim Rush—they had to murder forty-three other people, then murder them they would, because that concrete demonstration of the degree and intensity of their hatred seemed to them well worth the price.

He sat there and contemplated that and the miserable fact that he was scared absolutely shitless, so that a small amount of urine escaped his urethral sphincter and stained his shorts, plus the even more unpardonable fact that, as a result of his sick need to demonstrate a courage he damned well didn't have, on his direct order several tons of aluminum and steel with over one hundred other people in its fragile guts was whining and groaning and shuddering about three meters above the wave tops just off Ciudad Villalonga, with the smoking cone of the semiextinct volcano Zopocomapetl towering several thousand feet higher than the aircraft off to their left, and the trees of the jungle which could hide a thousand crazy kids with a thousand damned fine Chinese rocket launchers to their right, across the limpid, multicolored waters of Bahia Linda.

And, last of all—hearing the rumble as the gear trains dropped out of their niches and locked into place, and the whining of the fanjets grow shriller as the pilot poured it on to compensate for the loss of speed caused by the drag of the now exposed landing gear, calculating to the millimeter the amount of throttle necessary, because if he didn't give those big turbines enough fuel, the plane, clawing in with full flaps down, was going to stall and crash into Bahia Linda, "Pretty Bay," transforming it into a pretty place to drown in, and if he gave those jets a hair too much, the plane was going to touch down too fast, scream down that murderously short runway that was all they had left now, burning all the rubber off the fat balloon tires, and slamming head on into the tool sheds and hangars that some idiot had built at the end of it, converting them and itself into a hundred-odd-man hecatomb, an enormous funeral pyre—he, Jim Rush, had to live one dead-stopped aeon and three gut-crippling eternities with the thought that if the pilots failed at this one last, almost superhuman test of skill, the deaths of more than one hundred other people were going to be on his head too, to be added to the forty-three he already had on his conscience, the only comfort being that he wasn't going to be around to think about it.

About that—or about anything.

He heard the tires screech. Felt the plane lurch. Behind him heard a muted shriek or two, vibrant with terror. The bellow of the engines, as the copilot threw them into reverse thrust, drowned out the screams. The big plane slowed, slowed—stopped. The passengers ripped out a ringing cheer. They had made it. They were safe.

Somebody found the young Embassy Under Secretary, and the Vice Consul, who had come out to the airport to meet the new Ambassador. They were in the airport bar trying to get as drunk as possible as fast as possible in order to calm what the sight of those—*things*—the firemen were bringing out of the wrecked aircraft now, without having on hand even a sheet or a blanket to cover them with, had done to their nerves. It took the *Azafata de Tierra*—Ground Stewardess will do for that— several long minutes to convince them that the Honorable Mr. James R. Rush, Ambassador of the United States of America to *la Republica de Costa Verde* was unhurt, alive, and breathing air.

Then they came rushing out to where the big DC 10 had stopped, far from the main terminal, on a distant runway generally used by bimotored propeller and jet aircraft no bigger than a French Caravel, say, or a Boeing 727, or a DC 9, since nobody had believed it possible to get giant craft like the 727 Jumbos or the DC10s onto it.

Behind them ran a short, dark, uniformed, bemedalled, and beribboned Costa Verdian army officer who had been drinking with them, Colonel Elias Garay Bustamontes, General García's Chief of Protocol. Seeing him on the run, soldiers converged on the plane from every direction, their fingers on the triggers of their 9 mm Schmeisser submachine guns, the safeties already off. Though he didn't know it, when he appeared in the doorway of the plane, flanked by the two wanly smiling first class cabin stewardesses, Jim Rush's life was in far greater danger than it had been at any time prior to that moment. Because those soldiers didn't know why Colonel Garay was running towards that plane, and their response to practically anything that could have happened at that moment, as, say, one of their own number's stumbling, falling, and firing his weapon accidentally, would have been to riddle the giant craft and every one aboard it.

But since the Old Gods, who the Tluscolans swear live inside Zopocomapetl's fiery cone, are occasionally kind, no one stumbled, no shot was fired, and Colonel Garay was able to take control of the situation, forming the men into ranks, and having them present arms at the foot of the landing ramp. As was to be expected under the circumstances, the welcoming ceremony left a great deal to be desired. Only about a third of the military band could be found, the others having wisely decided that an airport where people shot down aircraft with rocket launchers was no place for men armed only with musical instruments. And that remaining third made a picturesque atonal tropical stew of both "The Star Spangled Banner" and *"El Lider Glorioso"* the Costa Verdian national hymn.

Colonel Garay and Ambassador Rush reviewed the troops. Colonel Garay welcomed Ambassador Rush on behalf of the Head of the State and the People of the Republic of Costa Verde. Ambassador Rush expressed his satisfaction at being in Costa Verde and his confidence in a tightening of the already close bonds of friendship uniting the peoples of the two republics, in a voice that even the microphones six inches from his lips had trouble picking up.

Then the little group started towards the terminal. By then, a swarm of reporters, both national and foreign, was out in force. Ambassador Rush graciously consented to hold a brief press conference in the waiting room reserved for visiting dignitaries.

On the way there, he put his hand in his inside breast pocket to see if he had his felt-tipped pen with him. Experience had taught him the wisdom of jotting down the questions that reporters asked him so that afterwards they couldn't claim they'd asked him something else. The pen was there all right, but his fingers also touched the envelope with the torn pieces of the photo of Alicia, Marisol, and himself in it. He looked swiftly around, located a waste disposal basket ahead of him and to his left, slanted his steps casually towards it, and once he was close enough, quickly and furtively dropped the envelope in. He did this very smoothly and well, but Colonel Garay who, naturally enough, was a member of the Costa Verdian Secret Service, had the eyes of an Andean condor. He saw instantly what Jim Rush had done. Just as smoothly, he raised his own eyes and glanced around until he saw a certain face. Absently, indifferently, slightly, he nodded in the general direction of that trash basket.

One minute and thirty-seven seconds later, that wastepaper basket was on a light truck on its way to the National Security Headquarters of the Republic of Costa Verde.

Three hours after that, every single piece of that photograph had been fitted back together again upon a glue-coated cardboard backing by a Tluscolan female Secret Service agent whose fingers, the Director General of National Security swore, were a miracle of God.

Twenty minutes more, and General Manuel García Herredia, Chief of State, was himself studying that picture.

Very, very carefully.

CHAPTER

9

Jim Rush sat in the big, wonderfully soft and comfortable armchair in the bedroom of the Ambassador's residence—which was not the American Embassy, but rather a lovely villa several kilometers out from Ciudad Villalonga, and, better still, fifteen hundred meters higher in the foothills of the Sierras, so that the air was relatively cool and practically free of insects. He was, at the moment, watching Tomás—Tomás Martinez Galán, the Embassy's majordomo, or butler—unpack his clothes and hang them in the closets. From the way Tomás did this, Jim could see that as a butler-valet, he was very expert indeed.

"And—your Lady?" Tomás said smoothly in his nearly perfect English; "I mean—" he stopped; but apparently an English term polite enough failed to occur to him. "*¿Su Señora la Embajadora?* She will come along later, doubtless, Sir?"

Jim thought about that. Not, of course, about the wife he didn't have, but rather about the question itself. It was a perfectly normal question, and in any other country in Latin America he would have answered it at once, without even thinking about *why* it had been asked. But he wasn't in another country; he was in Costa Verde. And given the highly peculiar history of that highly peculiar country, he *did* have to think about why it had been asked, because not only could the correct and true answer to it cause him more trouble than he was emotionally prepared to handle, but that Tomás had asked it at all meant that from now on he had to consider his own relations with the majordomo very, very carefully.

He thought about both considerations so long that Tomás burst out:

"I'm sorry, Sir? It was not my intention to pry! I only asked that because—"

"Lord, Tomás, I was thinking about something else!" Jim said. "*¡Se me fue el Santo al Cielo!* What was it that you asked me?"

Tomás looked at him with an expression of surprise, and Jim knew he'd given himself away, blown at least a part of his cover. He had allowed Tomás to assume that he spoke only the slow and halting elementary Spanish that most North American diplomats assigned to Latin America pick up over the years. But a man who said, "The Saint went from me to heaven!" to express what English-speaking people mean when they say, "My mind was a thousand miles away!" spoke the kind of Spanish that people who imbibe the language with their mother's milk do, and had, therefore, to be considered in an entirely different light.

"You speak Spanish, do you not, Sir?" Tomás said in that language; "that is to say, you speak it truly, as *we* do."

Jim sighed. Then he said, making no further efforts to hide the double-distilled perfection—upper-class Latin American, plus the formation that Castilian *Academia de la Lengua* linguists from Spain itself had imposed on top of that—of what was, after all, his first language, the one he had been practically born speaking:

"Yes, Tomás. I was born in Bogotá, Columbia. I first began to learn the language of my fathers, that is, English, when I was ten years old. There are those who swear I have not mastered it, even yet. Or at least not very well."

"Your Spanish *is* the better of the two, Sir, if you will permit me the observation," Tomás said. "I felicitate you upon it, Mr. Ambassador! But, just the same"—he switched abruptly back into English—"*here* it would be better if we spoke only English. Rapidly. Using as many idiomatic expressions and as much slang as possible."

Jim stared at him. But he knew instantly that that last observation—spoken very fast through almost motionless lips, aimed straight at him as though he were a ventriloquist's dummy, and so flat-toned, uninflected, quiet that the most sensitive microphone made would have difficulty picking it up—was not to be answered. So he said, calmly, casually:

"Tell me, Tomás: What was that question you asked me just now, that I really didn't hear?"

Tomás smiled, relief in his eyes.

"You Lady, The Ambassadress? Your wife, Sir? She will doubtless join you shortly?"

Again Jim considered both horns of that dangerous question. Horn one: Was Tomás, in spite of Peter Reynolds' faith in him, a spy, after all? That the majordomo had just warned him that the house was bugged meant little. A trained Secret Service man might well employ such a revelation as a giveaway move, a ploy designed to disarm suspicion, until his real objectives could be carried out. Horn two: What use did García and Company intend to make of the answer? For Jim already knew that any American diplomat, single, or—what in his case amounted to the same thing—widowed, free, and unattached, was fair game in a goodly number of countries where his sexual proclivities—hetero or homo!—might lend themselves to a little useful blackmail.

And in no other country whatsoever was that latter aspect of the question more true than it was in Costa Verde. He knew that very well because both Peter Reynolds and Tim O'Rourke had briefed him very thoroughly in the ways that the Costa Verdian Intelligence Service made use of women to pry information out of any foreigner sufficiently unattached to make the tactic feasible, or even disaffected enough with his own wife or mistress to make it possible. Often the task of these female agents extended even to the first stages of brainwashing.

"And what makes 'em so damned dangerous, Chub," Tim had said, "is that they not only look, act, talk, and think like small brown flakes on th' Upper Crust, they *are. Damas de alta cuna, y alta sociedad.* Blood so blue it's practically purple. Soft, sweet, appealing. So damn' beautiful that you don't believe 'em even *after* you've seen 'em . . ."

"But why should girls like that consent to—" he had begun.

"For the same reason *I* consented to it," Marisol had whispered, then. "To—save the lives—of the men they love. To save them from nothing so gentle as a firing squad, Señor Rush! But from—unspeakable tortures that reduce a man out of manhood. That go on—for weeks. Until—he dies, finally. Or, if he survives—he has become a—a *thing*. Less than human. A zombie, one might say. One of the living dead. A— a *nothing*—whose touch—incites nausea. Or freezes the blood—"

But Peter had said Tomás could be trusted. Could he? Could any man?

"No tengo esposa," Jim said slowly, carefully, clearly, thinking, 'I'll make it easy for you, you bastards. Now you won't even have to trust your interpreter.' *"Soy—viudo. Desde hace cinco años."*

"I am sorry to learn that, Sir!" Tomás said with a slight smile. "But surely five years of being a widower is enough, do you not agree, Your Excellency?"

A shudder of pure revulsion shook Jim's slight frame. He was remembering the young Under Secretary's words: "*It* had on shoes. High-heeled white shoes. Smart as all get out. That's how you could tell it had been a woman, Sir. Neither the shoes, nor the feet had burned. Don't know why. Some of the others who'd been sitting back near the tail of the aircraft they had to—sort out. The pieces, I mean. Whose arms and legs belonged to whom. You see, that rocket went right up the afterburner of the starboard engine and blew it to bits. Took the stabilizer and the rudder with it. *And* those poor devils in the aft tourist section. So they piled in from a little under a thousand feet and—"

'I,' he thought, 'will *never* be able to touch a woman again. Not after having caused the deaths of so many . . . But let's have fun, Tomás! Let's play the game!' He said, with a convincingly rueful little laugh:

"*I* agree. In fact, I agreed after the first two years of having been forced—by my poor dear wife's untimely passing—" At that, he stopped; thought: 'Pour it on, you goddamned liar! Shovel it all over him!' Then he went on, smoothly, "—to live alone. Unfortunately, however, the ladies seem not to be of the same opinion . . ."

"Then, Sir, you have come to the right place!" Tomás laughed. "Here in Costa Verde, for various historical and sociological reasons, we have an enormous surplus of women, many of them young, and exceedingly beautiful—"

"And many of them *widows* for the same historical and sociological reasons you mentioned. Right, Tomás?"

Tomás stared at him. Shook his head. Said very softly:

"Right, Sir; I see that you've been well informed."

Jim looked at the majordomo. When he spoke, he realized to his own surprise that he was telling the truth—as of yesterday, anyhow. And that what he was saying could, under reasonably favorable circumstances, get to be the truth again. When the horror in him, the revulsion, turned him loose. When the shocked guilt feelings ebbed enough for him to admit emotionally what he already knew rationally: that though he was sorry to the depths of whatever the hell it was he meant when he said his soul that those people had died, though he would remain so until the hour that he, too, drew his final breath, the fact remained that *he* hadn't killed them, or planned, sought, caused, or wished their deaths, and, more importantly, that if the American Ambassador to Costa Verde at that fatal juncture had been any other American diplomat whosoever, those murderous maniacs would have downed that plane just the same.

So he said, slowly, bitterly, clearly, backing off a bit from the tactic of crowding poor Tomás into an irrevocable error, conceding that Peter's faith in the man had not yet been proven unjustified:

"I hope you're right, Tomás. I admit I'm tired of being lonely. But I should much prefer a woman of a certain age. Preferably a widow. After all, she would be accepting a small, not excessively good-looking—to put it mildly!—middle-aged gentleman who is not always in there cooking on all four burners. You get what I mean, Tomás? Hardly a 'blue-flame' boy on any level. Inclined to be, frankly, dull. Therefore, a woman who has lived enough, friend Tomás, to have learned resignation, accept disappointment. One who would not find the man I have described impossible to put up with. Do I make myself entirely clear?"

"You do, indeed, Sir!" Tomás said, and his voice to Jim sounded convincingly sincere. "But you mustn't play yourself down, Sir—nor hold what you have to offer, cheap. Here, we do not have prejudices against a certain disparity in the ages of a married couple, Mr. Ambassador. You will surely find any number of gloriously beautiful young women, in their early twenties even, *never* married before, who would be honored, even delighted, to become the Lady of the Most Illustrious Ambassador of the Richest and Most Powerful Nation on the face of the Earth!"

"I know that," Jim said sadly; "I've run up against it before in Latin America. Unfortunately, I ask too much. I insist that my wife be—fond of me. Even—if possible—love me a little . . ."

"That is not to ask too much. Nor is it even difficult to accomplish. Many of the girls you will meet will be—well—unaccustomed to gentility, kindness, on the part of men. Oh no, don't mistake me, not because of our political formation, but rather, a cultural deformity—an extreme kind of—of *machismo*. I know not the word for that in English."

"We use the same one. We borrowed it from you *Latinos.*"

"I knew a girl once, who killed herself when her more than middle-aged foreign husband—English, or North American, or perhaps even Canadian, I don't know which—died. Because he had been unfailingly kind to her, unfailingly gentle. She knew she could never find *that* again. Not here; not among us. And because of that quality, that to her very rare quality, she had learned to love him with all her heart. A man considerably older than you are, Sir; considerably less handsome . . ."

Jim grinned at the majordomo. Said:

"You're quite a salesman, Tomás! But—two things: I am no longer sure I wish to remarry. And, in any case, it seems to me wiser to avoid any woman so young and so beautiful that she might be employed in 'The Treatment,' as I believe it's called down here . . ."

Tomás stopped hanging up the clothes. Stood there. He was, Jim saw, not even breathing. Then he let his breath out again, very slowly. Measured it out upon the afternoon air. Carefully. So it wouldn't make a whistling sound.

"Look, Sir!" he said brightly. "Now that I have finished arranging your clothing—" He hadn't, of course; but Jim knew that this was another misstatement damned well not to be commented upon. "—let me show you the garden! The *fountain* is especially beautiful, and—"

'And makes enough goddamned noise so that close to it the bugs these swine have planted all over can't pick up what we say,' Jim thought. He said:

"Of course, Tomás. In fact, I need a breath of air. I've been cooped up all day, first in the airplane, then in the waiting room of the terminal, fielding some rather impertinent questions, from even more impertinent reporters . . ."

"Not *ours*, I hope, Sir!" Tomás said piously.

"No; yours were most polite. Journalists from my country. And certain European ones—"

"Out to make trouble, as usual. Coming, Sir?"

The garden was crawling with soldiers, without counting the U.S. Marine guards stationed before the front and back doors. General García, Jim saw, was taking every precaution to see that he lived long enough to at least present his credentials—in a ceremony to be held day after tomorrow, Friday, in the early afternoon. Tomorrow, Thursday, was the mass funeral for the victims of the Pan Am crash—or more truly for the victims of that mass assassination. Jim knew why the funeral had been put off twenty-four hours, although the charred bodies couldn't be embalmed, and had had to be put in plastic bags to make their stench remotely bearable: Both U.S. major television networks were flying camera crews down to Costa Verde to film it, live. Which meant he had to be present. He had intended to go to that funeral anyhow, but now he had to. There was no getting around it. His absence, considering the brutal fact that all those people had died in his stead, would be from any standpoint, including the diplomatic one, unpardonable.

He walked up to the fountain with Tomás, seeing as he did so that the soldiers were going to let them strictly alone, as they'd been ordered to, probably.

"Sir, I ask you—I beg you not to make statements like that in the house!" Tomás whispered. "Nor in the Embassy! You know, you must know, they're both—"

"Bugged. All right. Tell me, how many of the domestic staff are on *his* payroll?"

Tomás considered that. Then he said, very quietly:

"*All* of them, Sir." He paused; then added flatly, "Including *me*, Sir."

Jim studied him.

"In which regard, Sir," Tomás said, "I'd suggest that you give me occasional bits of information—true information, of little importance, which I can feed to them. I will, of course, build it up, exaggerate its importance." He stopped; then went on quietly. "Your predecessor always did me that favor. That enormous favor. Which is why I am alive."

Jim went on studying him.

"What do I get in return, Tomás?" he said.

"Real information. That you can check and prove. Help. Protection from your—from our mutual—enemies, by my friends. Protection which may save *your* life, Sir!"

Jim's still gaze didn't move. Or waver. He said:

"Why, Tomás? You're from *here*. This is *your* country. I'm a representative of a foreign power. One that many of you have no cause to love . . ."

Tomás sighed.

"I know," he said. "But this is *not* my country. It was. But now it's *his*. And I'd like it back, Señor Rush. With the help of—the *decent* people in your country. The people who ousted Nixon, pulled you out of Viet Nam. I am sufficiently sophisticated not to believe all North Americans are swine. I am more than sure that Peter Reynolds' best friend could never be a traitor—or an oppressor of the people. Which is why I've placed my life in your hands, Señor Rush. What do you intend to do with it?"

"Use it well," Jim said; and put out his hand to Tomás.

Stonily Tomás ignored that outstretched hand.

"Another error, Sir!" he hissed. "Ambassadors don't shake hands with butlers in Costa Verde! But thank you. And, Sir—since I see you're still wondering at least a little about me, I shall tell you this: My sister Josefina—my only sister—was in the Women's Detention Camp at Chizenaya when Peter Reynolds' little band took it in 1963. They got there in time, in the sense that she was still alive. In fact, she still is. What she isn't any longer, my friend, is quite—human. My wife and I go to visit her at the State Insane Asylum from time to time. The next time we go, you are invited to accompany us, Mr. Ambassador! The sight is—instructive. Helps one's formation—politically, and as a human being, Sir. And now—"

"And now, one thing: Can you drive?"

"Yes, Sir. Why yes, of course. But, there is, after all, the Embassy Chauffeur, and—"

"Don't want the Embassy chauffeur. Not tonight. I want *you* to drive me. In a small, cheap, dark-colored, rented car. One that has not been implanted with miniature VHF transmitters which enable a Security Technician to sit comfortably in the radio room of the National Security Headquarters and follow its progress across the entire city with ease. In short, I want to be driven to a couple of places I'd rather His Nibs and Playmates heard about later. Much later."

Tomás smiled. "Very well, Sir!" he said.

"Good. First, do you know—do your friends have an electronics technician among them? One who knows how to debug houses and offices?"

"Of course. Trained in Prague—and in Moscow. Only he does not love *norteamericanos.* Especially not *official* North Americans . . ."

"Lead me to him. I'll convince him."

Tomás hesitated. Then he said:

"All right. But you'll have your work cut out for you there, Sir!"

"I'll risk it. Next: Do you know where Jenny Crowley lives? The American oil heiress who—"

"Is wanted for murder—but only *slightly* wanted, since the victim was a Black—by your FBI. Who is now living with the chief of her body guards, though it is said that when he tires of her, he lends her out to all his subordinates, who amuse themselves vastly with her, since when she is under the influence of the various drugs she is addicted to she is capable of the most interesting vilenesses and multiple perversions with various partners simultaneously without ever becoming fatigued. One story which I, quite frankly, do not believe, is that they once tried a live snake with her—as a sort of substitute for the role usually performed by her, well, call them human, anyhow, male partners. The snake, say the local *bromistas,* died of exhaustion . . ."

Jim looked at him; said, his voice flat, calm, unperturbed:

"The same. She's a friend of mine. I'd like to see her."

Tomás stared at him. A long time. Shrugged.

"When?" he said.

"Also tonight. When we come back from visiting your debugging expert."

"It—may be dangerous, Sir. They—those of the airplane—will not give up easily, you know . . ."

"I know," Jim said; "but I still say tonight, Tomás. I want this place and the Embassy clean before I even present my credentials. And I've got to do something about Jenny. In part she's what and where she is because *I* failed her before. *Moral* obligation. Can you do it?"

"I think so, yes. At least we can try, Sir," Tomás said.

When they came back into the villa, the phone was ringing. Shrilly, insistently, in a very special way. Tomás picked it up, said:

"*¿Diga?*" Then, in English: "What's that? The residence of the American Ambassador to Costa Verde? Of Mr. Rush? Yes, this is his residence. Who's calling, please? Mrs. Nivens. Mrs. Grace Nivens. *¡Bien!* Good! And you are calling from—New York? Very well. One moment, please. I will see if I can locate him. What's that? Of course he is not dead, Señora! I mean Madame! I have just talked with him a little while ago. Yes, yes. Amen to that! I, too, say Thank God, Señora—but, but—it is not for crying! Please! Wait, I will try to—"

"Give me that phone, Tomás!" Jim Rush said.

She said: "Jim." Then she said it again. Three times. Just his name. He could hear her voice strangling over more than four thousand miles of wire; hear it—drown.

He said, quietly:

"Grace, I'm all right. They blew it. Got the wrong airplane."

She tried to talk. She couldn't.

He said:

"Go lie down. Take something. A tranquilizer. I'll call you back later. When you've had time to calm down. Say—about midnight. All right?"

She said, fiercely:

"No you won't, Jim Rush! Because by midnight I'm going to be on a plane!"

He thought about that; said:

"Grace—no. Please?"

He heard her voice, whispering:

"Why not, Jim? I'm coming down there—on *your* terms. Forever. That *was* what you said, wasn't it? You can even keep that 'and obey' in the ceremony, if you want to. Or you can skip—all ceremony. But I will not, I repeat, *will* not, suffer the way I have today again!"

He said:

"Grace, listen to me. One, you can't because there's not another flight down here for at least two weeks. Two, I don't want you to—not under the pressure of—the wrong kind of emotion."

"Jim," she said quietly, and he was sure that this was a satellite connection because the line was so unbelievably, astonishingly clear, "you haven't the right to decide that. I mean, what kind of emotions are right for me and what are wrong. And, anyhow, you're too late. I have decided. No. That's not true. I had it decided for me. Do you know —how?"

"I can guess," he sighed. "It was on the radio, wasn't it? That I'd got mine?"

"Yes. And on TV. Meg came into my office. Without knocking. With the tears pouring down her face. Walked over to my TV set without a word, and switched it on. The announcer was saying: "The Costa Verdian authorities claim to have hard evidence that the aircraft was shot down *because* Ambassador James Rush was on it. So far Mr. Rush's—body—has not been—conclusively—identified. The aircraft was—completely—destroyed—by—by fire—after crashing, making identification—mmmmaking identific—"

"Grace!" he said.

"You see? You see, Jim? I—I *still* can't bear it!"

"Grace," he said desperately; "I'm—touched. And—honored. *Too* honored. But—but *please* don't come down here. I—I don't want you to!"

She said: "Oh!"

He said: "Grace—" And he stopped, not knowing how to go on, what to say.

"Jim," she said slowly, quietly, "you've had—second thoughts, haven't you?"

"Yes," he said, "and first thoughts, and third thoughts. I say, is the connection on your end as good as mine? I can hear you perfectly."

"Yes, Jim," she said; "Ed—I mean Worldwide—paid Intersat half the cost of putting a geostatic satellite in orbit over the Caribbean to cover that area. Business as usual! So—perfect connections. For which I thank him. So now you can—without difficulty—give me your first, second, and third thoughts. But not in that order. The *second* thoughts first. Those are—the ones that interest me."

He said:

"No. First thoughts first. Because they're the important ones. Grace, I don't want *you* in Costa Verde. People who have the determination and the know-how to shoot down airplanes with Chinese-made rocket launchers aren't very likely to give up because they failed *once*. Which makes this place—rather a bit on the dangerous side, shall we say?"

He heard the sharp intake of her breath; then:

"Oh. Oh, my God. Jim—resign. Come home. Come home—to me. Now. I—I'm not brave, darling. I told you that. Don't—do *this* to me, Jim. Please."

"Grace, listen. I'm very well guarded. There're soldiers all over the place. But the main point is—I simply can't let a band of crazy terrorists run me out. I'd despise myself. And you'd despise me, when you'd have had time to think about it. A rain check, then, my dear? Until Christmas, say? I'll have vacation time accumulated by then. And between now and Christmas, I'll have time to—to get a grip on things. And you'll have time to think—long, and carefully, the way you ought to—about us. About whether there even ought to be an 'us' now . . . Then I'll fly up there and—"

She was silent. Intensely silent. His eardrums ached. Then she said:

"Which brings us to those second thoughts, Jim. *Your* second thoughts. Because I haven't any. And I never will again. So tell me—why are you going to—to leave me. Or—for whom?"

"Grace," he sighed, "I'm a kind of a complicated little guy. So don't try to oversimplify me, please? Say—at the moment, anyhow—my mood's all wrong. Between the airport and here, I was treated to a—detailed description of how forty-three charred lumps—of meat—looked when they dragged them out of a mass of still smoking, twisted junk that had been an airplane—through my fault, through my fault, through my most grievous fault, my dear! Does it surprise you that right now—under *those* circumstances—love and happiness don't seem states I'm exactly—entitled to? That they strike me—at present, today, now—as a trifle—blasphemous, shall we say?"

She considered that.

"No," she said gently, "it *doesn't* surprise me. I already know you that well, Jim. One of the reasons I love you, I suppose. Oh, but this is wrong! So wrong, darling. To force a decent man to—burden himself with extraneous guilt! Jim, *you* had nothing to do with it! It is *not* your fault! You mustn't blame yourself for this, too! You simply mustn't! Jim—I *won't* promise to wait 'til Christmas! You—you *need* me too damned bad . . ."

"I know," he said; "I do. But you must, Grace. Let me work this out. My way. Cure myself. Even—redeem myself. Or else—I shall never be—whole again . . ."

She said, her breath shredding his name, her tears drowning it:
"Jim, please!"

"Turn on the tele tomorrow. At four thirty P.M. The time's the same, isn't it? Doesn't change North to South, only East to West, I believe . . ."

"Yes—it's the same. Why, Jim?"

"I'll be on it. At the funeral—of all those people. And you can look into my eyes. By remote control. I can't look back, except in imagination. But knowing that you're watching—will help me bear it. Please, Grace?"

"Yes. Oh, yes. Jim—write me? Call me? Any time. Any time at all! And I—"

"I love you, Grace," he said, feeling it, meaning it. 'For all the good it's ever going to do me now,' he thought.

And hung up the phone.

CHAPTER

10

*I*t was Tomás who suggested the operative procedure, because, although Jim Rush had been posted to more than one dictatorship during the more than twenty years he had served in Latin America, never before had he lived and worked in one as paranoiacally oppressive as Costa Verde was.

"Sir," Tomás wrote on a notepad, and passed it over to him, since they were inside the house now and the voice-masking effects of the fountain were unavailable, "you must call the Embassy and ask them to send you a car. The car will, naturally, be driven by your chauffeur, one Roberto Henriques, who is, actually, a Lieutenant Colonel in the Secret Service, and a very clever and dangerous man. You will ask to be driven to the Embassy, itself, which is in *la Plaza de la Liberación,* a great convenience, because it means that from the Embassy's balcony you will have a most excellent view of the frequent public executions carried out in that most historic square. Your failure to assist at such gloriously patriotic occasions would, of course, be deemed a grave discourtesy . . ."

'Fornicate the discourtesy!' Jim thought, 'And, also, a little lighter hand with the irony, will you, Tomás, please?'

"You will tell Henriques that it is your intention to work until very late, past midnight, probably in order to aquaint yourself with the problems pending in the Embassy files. This he will accept as normal and not be troubled about, since he has personally photographed every single paper in those files and forwarded his photos to Headquarters for detailed study . . ."

Jim glanced up at Tomás, who nodded his head emphatically towards the closely written legal-sized yellow pages. Jim went on reading:

"You will tell him that he may go home, and take the car with him, stating that you will phone him to come back for you when you have finished. But sure to ask him for his phone number. For you to know it already would perhaps alert him."

Jim again looked up, grinned approvingly at Tomás, continued:

"If he offers to procure you a secretary, refuse with the believable excuse that you are only going to read the files, not give dictation, and that whatever notes you need, you can easily jot down yourself. You might remark that it seems to you excessive to trouble a poor working girl at that hour of the night . . .

"After he has gone, you will leave the office, *without turning off the lights.* Also *you will leave the air-conditioner running.* You see, it is old and noisy, and the sounds it makes will prevent them being able to distinguish between your presence and your absence, as said sounds are sufficient to hide the small noises that a man alone, not talking to anyone, would normally make. This, of course, only after having opened and closed the drawers of the files several times *with considerable force,* during the first half hour that you remain in the office . . ."

'Jesus!' Jim thought. 'You *are* expert, aren't you, Tomás? Well, I've got to trust you—and all the way. There's no other way out, now . . .'

"You will descend by the back stairs to the servants' entrance. Open the door very quietly. Stand still until your eyes have accustomed themselves to the darkness. Make sure that you neither see nor hear anyone. Walk very quickly to the back gate of the wrought iron fence, making as little noise as possible. That gate, though normally locked, will be open tonight, since *I,* as majordomo, have a key to it. Walk down the alley until it comes out on the street of *Los Mártires Concepcionistas.* Enter the back seat of the small car that will be parked there—a Volkswagen, because that type of automobile is fabricated under license here in Costa Verde, and hence is the most common of all the less expensive cars. I will be driving it. That is all. Now please burn this note!"

Jim looked around the bedroom until he saw a massive silver cigarette lighter on an end table. Picked it up. Walked to the fireplace. Burned the papers to thick grey ash. Seeing how that ash clung together, he scattered it with the poker.

Tomás nodded with pleasure at that detail, then put out his hand towards the notepad. Jim gave it to him. He wrote on it again, his ballpoint flying. Jim frowned. To use a ballpoint was a mistake. It was strange that an agent—or counteragent—as well trained as Tomás appeared to be, didn't know the fatal defect that type of pen had as far as secrecy was concerned.

He took the note from Tomás, read:

"It is possible that when I leave here, they will pick me up for questioning. It would help if you could give me something to tell them; something harmless, or better still, confusing, but which they can verify."

Jim tore off that sheet. Burned it. Smeared the page beneath it with ink from his felt-tipped pen, stroking lightly. Instantly the letters Tomás had written on the previous page reappeared as light yellow against black, because Tomás' ballpoint, which, like all ballpoint pens, required a considerable degree of pressure to make it write, had indented them not only into that sheet, but probably into the two or three following ones. Beneath that clear, reversed-toned copy, Jim wrote:

"*Never* use ballpoints, Tomás!"

Tomás stared at that sheet, his eyes appalled. Took it to the grate. Burned it. Twisted his heavy silver—and very handsome—ballpoint between powerful fingers until it broke. Started to throw it into the fire. But then, realizing that it would neither burn nor melt, and that its remains would excite curiosity, put it back into his pocket.

Jim wrote:

"I will procure you a felt-tip like this one. Can refills be obtained here?"

Tomás nodded, reading that. Jim took the pad, wrote:

"Give them this: Edward Crowley, President of Worldwide Petroleum, used all his considerable influence to get me appointed Ambassador to Costa Verde. This is a fact that their people in Washington can verify in an hour. Or less. That is, if they haven't passed the word along already. He did so because he wants me to get *Jenny* out of here to some other country. I shall allow them to believe that he did this to get me to lobby for still greater concessions from your Government to Worldwide. You needn't state an opinion. Allow them to draw their own conclusions. That way, you're clear."

Tomás read that. Clasped his two hands together above his head and gave them a vigorous shake like a victorious boxer, to express his thanks. Then, after having burned that page, too, he said, speaking slowly and clearly for the obvious benefit of those hidden microphones:

"Sir, if you have no further need of me for a while, I should like to go home. Laura—my wife, Sir—will be worried, what with all the excitement of today . . ."

Jim said:

"Of course you may go home, Tomás. In fact, I shan't need you until about noon tomorrow—to lay out the proper clothing for the funeral of all those people who died in *my* place. I shall never reconcile myself to that. Oh, damn all *Reds* anyhow! No other political philosophy is so murderously cruel!"

Tomás smiled; said:

"Oh, I quite agree, Sir! 'Til tomorrow, then?"

"Until tomorrow, Tomás," Jim Rush said.

Riding in the almost soporific luxury of the Embassy's air-conditioned black Cadillac, Jim had to admit to himself that despite all the horror stories people told about it, Ciudad Villalonga was actually a beautiful city. Then he realized that you could say the same thing about every major city in Latin America if your driver chose his route carefully enough. 'And,' he added wryly, 'about most major North American cities except that you'd have to reduce beautiful down to handsome. But ghettos, favellas, bidonvilles—stink, filth, eyesores, rampant crime, and at least near hunger—are constants of modern urban civilization. You find them everywhere: New York's Harlem; Chicago's South State Street; those bidonvilles full of Portuguese refugees outside of Paris on the route in from Orly; London's Nottinghill Gate; Rio's favellas—'

Then, abruptly, he stopped thinking about such things; leaned forward, said:

"Good Lord, Roberto! What's *that?*"

That was a free-form modern building that looked, if anything, as though it had been copied from the TWA terminal at Kennedy International Airport in New York. It was, of course, much smaller, and its lines were considerably more graceful. More—feminine, somehow, Jim decided. You could see all the way through it, because, except for the soaring, semicircular. and oval projections of its roof, it was all glass. Late as it was—after nine o'clock at night, he saw from his electronic watch's illuminated L.E.D. digital numbers which glowed bright red when he touched a button—all its lights were on, and a considerable number of well dressed women were inside it, apparently looking at other even better dressed women who strolled about with a curiously pantherish, stalking stride.

"Oh, that, Sir!" Roberto—*Teniente Colonel* Roberto Henriques *de la Seguridad Nacional,* and official chauffeur for the American Embassy— laughed. "That is the Seven M, our most fashionable boutique. It is run by a fellow countryman of yours—though country*man,* is not quite the word to use, one could say . . ."

"You mean that's Geri Pyle's shop?" Jim said. "Stop the car, Roberto! I must say hello to him. He's an old, old friend of mine—from the days when I was stationed in Chile. Park where you can. I'll only be a moment."

He saw, with grim satisfaction, the way Roberto was looking at him now. 'Trying to decide whether *mariquita, marica,* or *maricon* applies!' he thought. 'Good! The more I confuse you Neanderthals, the better!'

He got out of the car, throwing a sidelong glance at Roberto's carefully impassive face as the "chauffeur" held the door open for him. He could almost read Henriques' thoughts:

'This presents a problem. Women are a centavo the dozen, but—a pretty boy for this middle-aged pederast? That is going to be difficult. By now we've killed off nearly all the known homosexuals. And the unknown ones have gone underground. Where on earth will we find—on such short notice—a pliant Catamite who—'

He walked into the Seven M. As he did so, the reason for the name struck him: Seven M, for *"Siete Machos"*—the not so subtle gibe that *Latinos* had long ago applied to Geri for the very simple reason that he wasn't even *one* male, not to mention seven.

There wasn't another man in the place. And when—attracted by the fact that all his *distinguidísimas e illustrisímas clientas* had turned as one woman to stare at this small, dapper apparition suddenly there among them—Geri came rushing towards him, there still wasn't. Geri wore mauve slacks that fitted him like a second skin. Jim noted that he was quite respectably well developed as far as his genitalia were concerned, a fact that those slacks had obviously been designed to advertise. He wore a loose silk blouse-shirt, opened to his clearly visible navel. An enormous chain of heavy gold circled his neck, and dangled down his lean belly to end in a massive gold bas-relief of one of the more hideous of the old Tluscolan gods. And his blond, naturally curly hair had been puffed out and teased into an Afro. The effect of that huge ball of blond hair above Geri's White, Anglo Saxon, Protestant, and rather aristocratically good-looking features was either comical—or sad. At the moment, Jim couldn't decide which. Geri wore, Jim could see, marvelously discreet makeup. His lipstick was transparent, faintly rose, with just a hint of silver in it.

As he came towards Jim, he was frowning, until he was close enough for his mildly myopic vision to make out who his visitor was. Then he let out a delighted squeal that caused, as Spanish-speaking people would have put it, a grave peril to the physical integrity of all that window glass.

"Why Jim—meee!" he shrieked. "Don't tell me it's reealee *you*! What a joy!" Then, bounding forward, he clasped Jim in a fond embrace.

"I'm glad to see you, too, Geri," Jim laughed; "but come off it, will you? You're ruining my chances with all these gorgeous dames you've got in here!"

"Hmmmn!" Geri sniffed. "Fish!"

That, Jim had long since learned, was the ultimate insult that male homosexuals hurl at womankind. Fish, pronounced "Feee-ish!" was what they claimed women, or at least the female sexual apparatus, smelled like.

"I'm a fish-lover, Geri-Boy," he said solemnly; 'I thrive on marine life. That aroma ought to be bottled. Distilled. Put in spray cans. So I could perfume the whole damned Embassy with it."

Geri clapped both hands to his well tanned cheeks.

"Why!" he gasped. "But of course! You're the new Ambassador! The one they tried to—"

"Kill," Jim said grimly. "Look, Geri, I—"

But Geri Pyle had whirled like a ballet dancer. It was one of the most graceful pirouettes Jim had ever seen, so perfectly executed that it looked like a bullfighter's *media veronica*.

"Ladies!" Geri cried, his voice descending two full octaves into a pleasant baritone that was, or would have been, if he'd have let it be, natural to him. "We are singularly honored tonight! May I present to you His Excellency, the Most Illustrious *Don* James Rush, the new Ambassador from *my* country to yours!"

He said all that in Spanish, of course. And his Spanish, Jim was not surprised to note, was very good indeed. There was a soft, rising murmur from the Most Distinguished and Most Illustrious Dames of Costa Verdian High Society—and, Jim saw, from Geri's models, as well.

Then one or two of the bolder or more self-confident ladies came forward to greet Jim—or rather His Excellency, the Ambassador!—personally, and the others immediately joined them, forming an impromptu reception line. They ranged in ages, Jim saw, from the middle twenties to the late sixties; but one thing was very sure: Joke as their neighbors might about Costa Verdians being indistinguishable from monkeys, at least here, in Geri's boutique, at least now, tonight, there wasn't even a plain woman present, not to mention an ugly one, and most of them were glorious.

The first of them to reach him murmured something like:

"I am veree sorree that I your language cannot well speak, but—"

To which Jim replied smoothly, easily:

"Eso carece de importancia, Señora; creo que puedo defenderme—por lo menos, un poquitin—en lo suyo . . ." A politely modest phrase that meant, more or less: "That doesn't matter, Madam, I believe I can defend myself—at least a little—in yours . . ." And all the murmurs rose into a purr of really appreciative approval; a curiously feline sound, rather like that which high bred cats, Persians, Siamese, Angoras, make when they've

been fed and petted to their lordly, spoiled, and selfish hearts' content.

But it was only the fourth of them in line, a really imposing *Gran Dama* of sixty-five or so, who had both the nerve—and the years!—Jim realized wryly, to put the fatal question, the one the answer to which they were all literally burning to know:

"And—your Lady, the Ambassadress? We are to have the privilege, and the pleasure, of meeting her soon, Your Excellency?"

"Unfortunately, no, my Lady," Jim said quietly; "for that would necessitate your making a voyage—to heaven, I like to believe—since my beloved, and eternally wept-for wife—died—these five years ago . . ."

The phrasing of that reply was classical, even literary Spanish. Deliberately so. He hoped that they, at least some of them, would take that *"mi querida y eternamente llorada esposa"* as evidence of a romantically permanent and not to be consoled grief. But in Costa Verde he had all of recent history working against him. Hearing that answer, even the models were looking at him with—'damned hungry eyes!' he thought bitterly.

As all those women, well dressed, groomed, coiffed, perfumed, with a standard of physical beauty that any major capital in Europe or the Americas would have been hard put to match, descended upon him with soft, dovelike coos, saying the classical expressions, "I join you in your grief," "Permit me to offer you my most sincere regrets," and so forth, he knew what he was in for. Every older woman in the place was running down the list of daughters, nieces, even, in some cases, granddaughters she had on hand; the younger married women considered unmarried sisters and friends; and the few single girls among them, as well as the astonishingly high proportion of them—high, that is to say, for almost any other country on the face of earth, except Costa Verde!—who were widows, took sudden stock of their own makeup, dress, and general appearance at that crucial moment.

At which same crucial moment, Jim Rush could have cheerfully strangled Geri Pyle with his bare hands. But another instant's reflection made him realize he was being unjust. After all, the fact that he was a widower could not possibly be concealed. Nor was Geri responsible for the conditions that made *any* male foreigner with a valid passport enabling him to leave Costa Verde and take, as Costa Verde's own legal code permitted, his wife with him, a prize, a catch, or as the women of Costa Verde themselves would have put it—*un partido*—beyond all price.

Which was why, confronted with a situation that would have made many another man, less thoughtful and less sensitive than he was, chant hosannas to the Most High for granting him such luck, Jim Rush felt cold and more than a little sick. He realized at that moment with brutal clarity just why it was that modern women hate being considered mere "sexual objects" with such intensity. Except, he recognized sadly, to add the adjective "sexual" would actually have been an improvement in this, his present, case. Because he was absolutely sure that asked, an hour later, not one of those sleek, dark, exquisite Costa Verdian women would have been able to describe *anything* about him, neither his face, his build, his way of carrying himself, his voice. They'd all say, of course: "He speaks Spanish beautifully!" That in a *Gringo,* even a *Gringo* Ambassador, was sufficiently unusual to make the detail cling in their minds.

But beyond that, *nothing.* An object. An economic object to provide the lucky winner the ease and luxury most of them were born to. A socio-political object to provide her with physical safety. A foreign object to take her away from the enormous green concentration camp into which her country had been transformed. Waft her away to—somewhere else. Anywhere else. Where she could live, breathe air, instead of existing—regardless of the social class to which she belonged!—always on the ragged edges of pure terror, forever just out of earshot of tortured screams . . .

And, thinking all that, while arming his mind and heart against them—more than a little unjustly, because, considered coolly, a loveless marriage into which a woman enters with every intention of complying fully with all her obligations as a wife is very far from being a dishonorable estate!—he found a means to beat a graceful enough retreat. Turning to Geri, he said:

"Geri, will you send me a list of the names and addresses of all the ladies present tonight? To my office at the Embassy? I'd like to invite them, and their husbands or—well—escorts to a *soirée* very soon—"

"Of course, Jimie! Ooops! I mean Mr. Ambassador!" Geri gurgled. "Anything I can do to help out, you may count on . . ."

Jim noted suddenly the expression of disappointment on several faces, and, abruptly, it came to him why. In Costa Verde, not a few women like these, women who, in any other country would have been under perpetual siege by a host of eager males, hadn't any escorts at all. Because, between them, the extreme Right, under García, and the extreme Left, under a scattering of minor *Caudillos,* Leaders, Chiefs, were committing what sooner or later would develop into actual genocide. If not in this generation, Jim realized with aching pity, then in the next. 'With perpetual, ferocious civil war—for it is that, for all its being conducted as guerrilla action—killing off the majority of the young men, far too few are left to father the babies that most of these glorious creatures should be having now . . . Too few? Hell, there're practically none!'

He grinned with wry self-mockery; thought:

' "Once more into the breech, Dear Friends! Once more!" *What* dear friends? Who's around to take—or rather undertake—remedial action? Not old *Siete Machos,* that's for sure! Which leaves—me. Girls, your Secure Servant is perfectly willing to give the matter his undivided attention; but he warns you from the outset that as a lover, he is three zeros to the left of the decimal point—an infinitude of nothing. And disappointing sweet young things in a horizontal position is not only shameful, it's a crime!'

He turned to Geri, said quietly, in English:

"Geri, after I've gone, tell 'em they don't *have* to be escorted. I know Costa Verde. A lot of their boy friends are in jail, or dead, or I miss my guess . . ."

"Or in the Sierras, Jimmy," Geri said.

"Yes. I'd gathered that even a segment of the upper class has gone Left, these days . . . Look, Geri, I have to run. But one more thing: When can you stage a *desfile,* a private showing for *me*? Of all your models in bathing suits?"

Geri cocked a mocking eyebrow at him.

"For whom, may I ask, are you buying bathing suits, Dear Boy?" he said.

"I'm not. I merely want to see as much of your models' cute little figures as possible. I have to buy four of your specials—the Andean line, I believe you call 'em—for a friend of mine. And she's—well—very small. Quite thin, too. So I have to see which of your models is really close enough to her in build so that we can try my selections on her . . ."

"Tomorrow morning. Elevenish, say? And, if you like, I'll parade 'em in bare-assed, Lover-Boy! They'd *adore* that, the little bitches! They're all whores, anyhow. Make more money going back on their dainty backs for García's officers than they do working for me."

"Then why do they?" Jim said. "Work for you, I mean?"

"Gives them a facade of respectability. Of course, I can't *prove* they're hustling. They all swear by their favorite statues of the Virgin that they're not; but if you want to see 'em, warts, moles, birthmarks, *jusqu'au poil,* bouncing their tits and tails about to turn *you* on, Dear Boy, I'll—"

"No, thank you! Bikinis will do. That way I can judge well enough. 'Til tomorrow morning then, Ger—"

"Wait, Jimmy! This special friend you're buying my Andean dresses for: Are you going to take her on—permanently?"

"Can't. She's my best friend's wife."

"Why, Jim—meee! You naughty, naughty boy!" Geri cooed.

"Oh, come off it, Geri! Ladies, your Secure Servant!" Jim said, and got out of there.

Tomás' operative procedure for leaving the Embassy unobserved, for eliminating the very real danger of the Secret Service's hanging a tail on Jim Rush, worked, but with one minor hitch. The trouble was that when you were dealing with Costa Verde's *Seguridad Nacional,* one minor hitch could add up to a major catastrophe. In fact, it almost did.

Jim did everything by the book and to the letter. He left the lights on and the air-conditioner running. Came down the back stairs. Opened the door to the servants' entrance. Stepped out into the dark garden. Stood there, not even breathing. Held his eyes shut for a count of ten. Then twenty. Then fifty. By then, he could see a little.

He stole to the back gate. Pushed on it. It swung open with a rusty, creaking groan approximately as quiet in that stillness as a twenty-one gun salvo of artillery. Jim hung there. He was sure the noise his heart made could be heard beyond the Street of the Conceptionist Martyrs, beyond the Plaza of the Liberation, beyond the city, the volcano, the mountains.

He wondered whether to leave that damned gate open, or to close it. Why in the name of everything unholy hadn't Tomás thought to oil those infernal hinges? He'd have to close it. For, if a policeman passed and found it standing open, he'd—

Jim closed that gate. It groaned louder than hell's own hinges. Clanged shut with a sound that echoed out to the sea, across the bay, into the jungle. Then he started away from there.

And saw, as he half turned, the firefly dancing of the two flashlights coming up the alley behind him, sweeping each doorway, garage entrance, service gate, with slow deliberation as they passed.

He froze. Then he saw the row of the Embassy's garbage cans. They were three-quarters as tall as he was anyhow. And there were three or four of them. He dived behind them. Crouched there unbreathing. The worst of it was knowing that if the men with the flashlights were policemen—as they probably were—he was in no danger at all, physically. And yet his effectiveness as an Ambassador would be over. Terminated. Finished. Because he'd have done the one thing no man in an official position can get away with in Latin America, which was to make himself ridiculous. The story that His Excellency, the Illustrious Ambassador from the Most Powerful Nation on Earth, had been found crouching behind the Embassy's garbage pails would be far too rich to expect any minor official—even one as disciplined as a policeman ordinarily is—to be able to resist the sheer pleasure of telling all over town. And the story would grow and grow until whether the State Department believed that his companion in sin was a pretty boy, or the fat, inky-black wife of the Ambassador from Uganda, or that he was innocent of any wrongdoing whatsoever, would become irrelevant. In defense of his country's dignity, he'd have to be recalled out of pure necessity and in deepest disgrace.

The flashlights came closer. Policemen, all right. Two of them. One of Ciudad Villalonga's justly celebrated *"parejas,"* "pairs." Making, doubtless, a routine check. No—not so routine. Henriques had probably called Headquarters and suggested that they double the guard, send twice the usual number of patrols, because the new Ambassador was working in his office late tonight.

Of course. Surely. And they'd go on circling the Embassy all night long until those damned lights in his office windows went out. They passed him, directing those powerful beams on everything. Even on the garbage cans. Went on by, treading heavily, firmly, in their leather boots. He let his breath out. They hadn't seen him! So now the thing to do was—

To time them. Let them get out of the service alley. Make a rush to the end of it while they were doubling back through *la Plaza de la Liberación* in front of the Embassy. Get in the car and—

He waited very quietly until they reached the end of the alley, turned the corner, were out of sight. Then in one long, smooth rush he came flying down the alley to the place where it came out on *la Calle de los Mártires Concepcionistas.*

Only there wasn't any Volkswagen there. In fact there wasn't any kind of automobile at all.

He hung there, cursing in Spanish, the world's best language for cursing. He examined the sexual morals of all Tomás' female ancestors and found them gravely wanting, the virility of the males encountering them, nonexistent. He was just pausing for breath when the Volkswagen rolled silently up beside him, coming from the wrong direction, the one opposite the way it should have. He tore open the door, leaped into the back seat. Tomás gunned the flat four-cylinder air-cooled rear engine until it sounded like a sewing maching gone berserk.

"That pair," he said to Jim with evident satisfaction as they tore through the empty streets, "got the matricula. I saw them write the numbers down just as I was moving off. Didn't dare wait for you that time around, Sir . . ."

"You sound happy over it," Jim said. "What's so great about their writing down the license plate numbers of this heap, Tomás?"

"It's stolen," Tomás grinned. "Belongs to the mistress of the Minister of Justice. And it's going to be back in her garage before she even wakes up tomorrow morning and misses it. She's going to have some explaining to do, the little bitch!"

"Poor thing," Jim said. "Tomás—about your electronics expert—"

"That's going to be tough, Sir," Tomás said; "I suggest we sort of play it by ear. Go slowly. Maybe we'll hit upon some approach that will give us a reasonably convincing argument."

But here, again, Tomás was wrong. Not entirely; but still somewhat off the mark. For, surprisingly enough, engaging the services of the PCCV's—*el Partido Comunista Costa Verdense's*—electronics expert didn't prove nearly so difficult as either of them had anticipated. In fact, Comrade Carlos Suarez Calvo seemed definitely inclined towards sweet reason. Tomás got the message at once, from the very fact that Suarez received them in his isolated little white stucco villa with something approaching politeness.

He was a small man, as quick and as graceful as a cat; but with a face so typical of any Costa Verdian of mixed Spanish and Tluscolan ancestry that identifying him in a police lineup would have been difficult indeed, a protective coloration that, Tomás knew, had enabled him to do many astonishingly dangerous things in the past and bring them all off.

He said, calmly:

"I am a Communist, Mr. Ambassador. Why should I do anything to aid the representative of a decadent bourgeois so-called democracy which is the worst enemy of everything I stand for?"

And Jim shot back at him:

"I am a Capitalist, Mr. Suarez. Why should I seek the aid of an agent of a hyprocritical, oppressive, tyrannical regime that suppresses the last vestiges of human liberty in any country in which it comes to power?"

Carlos Suarez laughed.

"A worthy opponent!" he said. "I'll bite, Mr. Ambassador; why should you?"

"For the same reason you should be willing to collaborate with me: to help destroy a mutual enemy who, at the moment, is far more dangerous to both of us, than either of us is to each other. We can resume cutting each other's throats later, after we've got rid of García."

"But," Suarez said, "does not your government *love* General García, as it generally loves all the oppressors of the people?"

"A naïve question, Comrade Suarez! You've been to my country dozens of times. You buy a good bit of your electronic counterespionage equipment from Carl Lintz' Electronic Hobby Shop on Fourteenth Street near Eighth Avenue—"

Tomás and Suarez stared at him. At each other. Among the things they both knew was that Tomás Martinez simply hadn't known that fact. Not before that very instant anyhow. And both of them revised their opinions of Jim Rush upwards. Gave him, as a beginner in the very peculiar business they were both engaged in, better than passing marks.

"Continue, please, Mr. Ambassador," Carlos Suarez said.

Jim noted that the technician made no attempt to dispute what he knew perfectly well was accurate information. Being a professional, he neither admitted nor denied it. He simply let it pass, which, in itself, was a concession of sorts.

"Therefore," Jim went on, "you must know that we're not a monolith, politically. We're a democracy. A real—if somewhat imperfect one. We have no—effective, anyhow—Gulags for political dissenters. Nor psychiatric hospitals for those mad enough to disagree. We have a press existing in a state so closely approaching freedom that it's capable of— stopping a war, wrecking a Presidency, forcing *our* trained paranoiacs to operate with a commendable degree of caution, even exposing corruption in high places."

"You mean wasting the public's time and their own writing stories about events of such world-shaking importance as the excessive fondness your Congressmen seem to have for their secretaries?" Suarez said.

"Even to so small a matter as that," Jim said. "Therefore, it should be conceivable even to you that a man could reach Ambassador's rank in spite of holding a few relatively unpopular views, such as a belief in the desirability of a policy of intelligent flexibility towards the Left. I don't believe, Comrade Suarez, that all Marxists sport horns, hooves, bat wings, a pitchfork, and a tail . . ."

"Horns, I'll grant you!" Suarez quipped. "Having as we do to work nights so often to keep you Capitalist Devils in line! But what you say interests me, Mr. Ambassador. Is this viewpoint of yours the reason it has taken you so long to reach Ambassador's rank?"

Jim thought about that.

"I don't know," he said; "but it could well be."

"Good! I'd heard as much. All right. My fee is five thousand dollars, your currency, for both places. In advance."

"You'll take my personal check?" Jim said.

"Gladly. I'll cash it, and spend it, in New York, the next time I go there," Suarez said. "When do you want the jobs done?"

"Tonight," Jim said.

Suarez didn't blink an eye.

"You can provide me with keys?" he said.

Jim hesitated; then said: "Of course." He took out his leather key-holder and unhooked the two keys. It was then that he saw the problem involved.

"Tomás," he said, "do you have yours? Or else I won't be able to get back in . . ."

"Don't worry about that, Sir," Suarez said; "I will make duplicates and give you these back. Now. Within five minutes."

He saw Jim's look. Added, dryly:

"You can always change the locks afterwards, you know."

"I don't think that will be necessary," Jim said. "You don't impress me as being a stupid man. But one thing, Comrade, since the excellent marksmanship of one of your friends out at Bahia Linda Airport early this morning, my residence and the Embassy grounds are crawling with policemen. I had great difficulty even leaving the Embassy without being seen . . ."

Suarez smiled.

"The lights at both places will fail. After examining the fuses and finding them all intact, someone will call the power company. A truck bearing a repair crew will arrive. *I* will be among the repairmen. The rest will be friends of mine. All our documents will be authentic. I actually work for the electric power company, you know. And *everyone* on the night shift is a friend of mine. Now, if you'll write me that check, I'll be on my way. These matters require a certain amount of time . . ."

Tomás drew the Volkswagen up before a villa in the *Puerta de Oro* district of Ciudad Villalonga. It was the kind of a villa you'd expect to find in a residential section known as "Golden Door." Luxurious. Quietly luxurious. The kind of a house that only *old* money could build, since the wherewithal had obviously been accompanied by exquisite taste.

"This," Tomás informed Jim, "used to be the home of los Miraflores. They were at that time the richest family in Costa Verde. And they remained so until Moscow sent in Ernesto 'Rubles' Ramirez from Cuba to advise the Reds who had come to power. Then they were all shot. Including—"

"Carmencita Miraflores, who was a friend of Alicia Villalonga de Reynolds, the wife of our mutual friend Peter," Jim said dryly. "I know the history of the revolt of 1963, Friend Tomás, including *your* part in it. Wait for me, down the street. There, in the shadow of those trees, where the street lights won't reflect on this car . . ."

Tomás stared at him. Said:

"Don't you think it would be wiser if I accompanied you, Sir? Those animals in there aren't to be trusted."

"No. I can manage. I don't think they'd dare do me—or rather the American Ambassador—any harm."

There were a series of factual errors, or at least misapprehensions, involved in that statement that neither Jim nor Tomás realized at the time: No one in that house knew who *any* Ambassador to Costa Verde from any country whatsoever was; and given the marginal, if not obliquely tangential, relation that the present occupants bore to existing society, to ask them to even consider any attribute of a visitor beyond his brute physical force or the caliber of his armament was to make completely unrealistic demands upon their alleged intelligence; and, finally, among those present, only Jenny Crowley had ever seen Jim Rush before. To top all that off, even she didn't know he had been appointed Ambassador to Costa Verde. In fact, at that stage of her existence, she didn't know much of anything. If the entire world outside the Villa Miraflores' walls had that day been suddenly destroyed, Jenny would have discovered the catastrophe only after the onslaught of withdrawal symptoms, induced by the disappearance of all sources of the heroin that kept her in a state of apathy, had driven her—in sweating, shaking, frantic desperation, a prey to nausea, diarrhea, copious menstrual bleeding from a period brought on out of season, and a dozen more equally unpleasant manifestations of the state addicts call "cold turkey"—to look beyond those walls.

To look beyond them not, of course, to see what had happened to the world, but only in mindless, hopeless, helpless search of the poison that was killing her by inches for another "fix." For enough powdered joy to shoot into her hideously scarred, badly collapsed veins, achieving thus an instant solution to all the problems flesh is heir to, a total substitute for the one thing that, for so much as a single wholly conscious instant, she dared not face, nor for an even brief fractioning of time could bear—

Which was her life. Her life.

Jim came up to the door. Rang the bell. A maidservant answered it. The army of bodyguards Ed Crowley was paying to guard his darling daughter weren't—fortunately for Jim Rush, or unfortunately for Jim Rush; who in this world of total insanity would dare decide which term applied?—even there. They weren't because Joe Harper—or *Don* José as that band of illiterate, drunken, louse-infested scum he'd personally hired called him—had sent them away. He did that quite frequently now. When he'd got sick of the sight of them. Or when he wanted enough privacy to try some extra fancy variation on the basic theme— become as deadly a bore as it always does when it involves no more than the distinctly limited uses to which the complementary apparatuses of male and female flesh can be put—of sex with poor Jenny. He had con-

138

vinced himself that there was absolutely no danger of the Reds' or of any other groups' abducting her. In the first place, her very presence in Costa Verde had—with and through the devoted cooperation of the Secret Police—been kept a secret from the general populace. In the second, Joe held the abysmally contemptuous conviction that if anyone ever found it out, and made off with "that stupid cunt," which was the tenderest phrase of endearment he ever called her, they'd bring Jenny back voluntarily after having been forced to put up with her for as long as two hours.

All of which, of course, Jim Rush didn't know as he stood there facing the maidservant.

"¿Señor?" the maidservant said.

"Miss Crowley. Miss Jenny Crowley," Jim said in Spanish. "She is at home, no?"

"Well, Sir—" the maid hesitated.

But Jim had lived and worked in Latin America too long not to know how to deal with maidservants.

"Let me in!" he snapped. "Go tell your mistress that Mr. James Rush is here. And at once, woman! You have understood that which I have said?"

"Yes, Sir!" the maid wailed and fled.

Jim walked through the door the maid had left open. Into that magnificent foyer. Into the grand salon. Both gave every indication of having been occupied by a herd of pigs. Dust and dirt were all over everything. The cushions of the expensive, antique sofas and armchairs were knife slashed. Stained with wine, shoe polish, mud. With what looked like dried blood in some cases. Like feces in others. Someone, quite recently from the smell, had urinated on that priceless Persian rug.

Then Jenny came flying through one of the archways. She did have on, Jim was relieved to observe, a pair of panties. Said panties, he was somewhat less pleased to note, hadn't been washed in a considerable length of time. Nor, his nose told him, had dear Jenny. But by then she had hurled herself upon him like a wild thing, was crying like a whipped child, and kissing him every place she could reach.

"Oh, Uncle Chub!" she wept. "Oh, you sweet Old Thing, you! Oh, I'm so glad! So glad!"

"This isn't the way to act like it, Jenny," he said sorrowfully.

"I know!" she sobbed; "I'm outta control, Uncle Chub! I—I need a fix! And that bastard Joe won't give me any shit until I—"

"Jenny!" he said sternly.

She shoved him away from her, holding him at arm's length.

"Lemme look at you, Uncle Chub!" she breathed. "Ohhh Lord, but you're beautiful! You've got thin—and young—and—and sexy! Oh, but Grace was right! I *do* love you. *That* way, too—only—"

He looked at her with aching sorrow. She wasn't merely thin, she was emaciated. Her breasts were the size of oranges. Small oranges. One of them was blue, bruised around the nipple. 'Where some bastard bit her, sure as hell,' he thought. He looked at her left arm. The inside crook of her elbow was tattooed with needle marks. So many of them he couldn't count them. A collapsed and clotted vein showed black-blue through the dirty white of her skin.

He said:

"Go put some clothes on, Jen. I'm taking you away from here. To a hospital. Where you can kick the habit. Where—"

She wrapped her bony arms about his neck. Ground her skeletal, all but naked body into his fully clothed one. Writhed against him, moaning in a hideously obscene counterfeit of passion, designed, he was sadly sure, to take his mind off hospitals, cures, or anything else that might throw a check rein on the white-winged dream horse she was riding.

"Love me, Uncle Chub? Right *now*! Huh, please? I want you to do it to me. Always *have*, y'know. Grace says—"

Then she raised her eyes to his face. Turned. Followed his gaze to the exact point in space on which his eyes were fixed. To that ugly 9mm Beretta automatic dangling carelessly floorward in Joe Harper's hand.

"Who's th' Creep?" Harper said. "Lord, Baby, you sure can pick 'em! But what's a guy to expect from a dumb cunt like you? Look, Buddy, turn my Old Lady loose, will yuh? Whatcha lookin' so worried about? This? Hell, Mac, I wouldn't blast anybody over this cunt . . ." He stuck the Beretta into the waistband of the blue jeans that was the only garment that he wore. "She plain ain't worth killing nobody over, 'specially not a poor, tired, little old Creep like you. Say—what's your name, anyhow?"

"That," Jim whispered, "doesn't matter. You're Harper, aren't you? Joe Harper. Michael's brother . . ."

"So you know Mike? Lord, what a square! Still up there lickin' Crowley's ass and lovin' it! Never could teach him anything, even though he's my brother. Okay, Creep—no names, if you don't want to level with me. But, tell me, whatcha doing down here?"

"I'm a friend of Mr. Crowley's," Jim said quietly. "He asked me to check. Look, Harper, this girl needs treatment! There's a first class hospital right here in Villalonga City and—"

"I know. Vince Gomez'. Only Jenny ain't going there. You read me, Creep? D'you get th' message loud 'n clear?"

"Jenny," Jim said, "is considerably older than twenty-one, Harper. In fact, she's twenty-seven, if I remember right. So you can't stop her if she—"

"Can't I, Creepie-Poo?" Joe laughed. "You know Costa Verdian law? Down here a Babe can't go to the john to take a leak she doesn't ask her Old Man's permission first. Ain't that right, Baby?"

"Tha's right, Joe-Honey," Jenny said.

"Her Old Man?" Jim said; "you mean that you and she—"

"Are married? Yep, Creep; you got th' idea. Legal. All the ribbons and the papers. In the church, yet! Don't that just grab you by your balls, Creep? That is, you got any—which I doubt . . ."

"Harper, for God's sake. Jenny's *sick.* Since you've married her, you ought to care if she—"

"Well, I don't. She's already made her will in my favor. And right now, I don't even know if I've got patience enough to wait 'til that oil-swillin' old fart up there gets his. Putting up with this crazy cunt maybe ain't even worth that much bread. Besides, I'm making my own pile down here. Nice country, Costa Verde, you plugged into the right connections . . ."

"Jenny!" Jim said. "You can't! You mustn't let this madman keep you from—"

"I'm not keeping her from anything, Creep, Old Chum! She's stayin' away on her own. 'Cause she loves shootin' shit into these cute little veins of hers. Loves stayin' stoned out of her ever-lovin' skull. But most of all she loves *me.* Loves what I do to her. Loves how I do it. She's my slave. More slave than any Spade chick *ever* was. Ain't you, Babe? Won't you do *anything* I tell you to?"

"Yes, Joe-Honey," Jenny said.

"Come here, Bitch. Let's give old Uncle Creep a demonstration. Show the dried up li'l old bastard a trick or two. Like I say—a li'l *expert* knob polishing. You're good at *that,* I have to admit. C'mon, I kinda feel in th' mood . . ."

Jim stood there. He could feel the shaking, starting somewhere below his knees, climb up his thin body in obscene waves. He couldn't move. He saw that—zombie, that mindless apparatus of vaguely female, somewhat human flesh, stumble forward to where Joe stood, wide-legged, waiting; drop to her?—its?—knees before him; put up a hand, red, scaly, scabby, the nails chewed off below the quicks; and fumble at the buttons of his fly.

'I am a coward,' Jim told himself soberly; 'but what am I afraid of now? Dying with a bullet in my guts from this degenerate swine's gun? Or—living—and remembering I stood still—watched—witnessed— *this?* To save—my life. A life that's been paid for forty-three times over now . . .'

He heard the choking, mewing sounds she made. Saw her long hair—
Jenny's light brown hair he'd dreamed of!—jerk and sway. And was released. Strode forward, caught her by that still lovely mane of hers—the
only thing left of her that was—and jerked her up and away. She stared
at him wide-eyed, her irises so much blue glass with nothing behind
them remotely resembling a mind, her mouth slack-lipped, open, wet,
moaning:

"Whatcha wanna go 'n do that for, Uncle Chub? I—"

And something iron-hard crashed into his face. And something else
exploded inside his mind. A weight of darkness. Utter night. A leitmotif for a fugue called death. Or a prelude, anyhow.

When he came back, he found that he was lying on the floor near the
doorway. They, his clearing eyes saw, were on the sofa. Or at least Joe
was. Jenny was on her knees, on the floor, the upper half of her pitifully
emaciated body draped over Joe. She was making those sounds again.
Soup sounds, yolk-thick moanings.

Jim tried to stand up. He couldn't. He crawled to the doorway,
clawed himself up by his fingertips, digging into the flutings of a column. Reeled out the door. Onto the veranda. Hung there.

Tomás got there in time to catch him as he fell. To ease him down
into the second movement of that fugue. Well beyond the prelude now.
Into the contrapuntal treatment of that leitmotif, maybe.

Become *his* leitmotif now. His fugue. A marvelously complex form
for dark voices crying. His, forever. Until one last cymbal clash should
end it.

'Soon, God; soon!' he prayed.

CHAPTER

11

Are you all right, now, Sir?" Tomás said.

'Am I?' Jim thought. 'Will I ever be all right again?'

He said: "Yes, Tomás."

"Your face is badly bruised," Tomás said. "Colonel Henriques will notice it."

"So?" Jim said.

"We had better think up a story to tell him. One that he will believe."

"*You* think up one," Jim said; "my head aches."

Tomás frowned. Sat there very still behind the wheel of the car. Then, very slowly, he smiled.

"Let us engage in psychological warfare," he said. "I will accompany you to your office. We will remove from your files all the dossiers on their most active spies, the people they have planted in the Embassy as domestic help. Including Henriques. Including *me*. You will tell Colonel Henriques that you descended to the garden for a breath of air. Upon your return to your office you surprised two masked men rifling your files. One of them hit you with the flat of his pistol—"

"Jesus!" Jim said; "that's just what the bastard did hit me with, come to think of it!"

"It is obvious. I have seen this type of bruise before—many times. All right. When you regained consciousness, they were gone. Can you remember all this, Sir?"

"Of course. The concussion, if any, seems to have passed. At least I'm not dizzy any more," Jim said. "So, come on. Let us set up our little comedy. I only hope it works . . ."

"So do I," Tomás said.

He gave Tomás a good half hour's start before phoning Henriques. When he heard the "chauffeur's" voice on the telephone, he said, faintly: "Roberto—Roberto—"

"Yes, Sir?" Henriques said.

"Come—over here," he whispered; "bring—a policeman—and a doctor—I—I'm hurt . . ."

Then, without hanging it up, he let the telephone fall so that it dangled from the end of its cord, and sprawled across his desk before the opened, obviously ransacked files. That the scene he was staging for Lieutenant Colonel Henriques' special benefit was pure Hollywood, a Class B thriller, he realized, and, to make things even worse, that dying gladiator pose he had assumed was damned uncomfortable. He hoped Henriques wouldn't be too long in getting there. From the dangling telephone, he could hear his "chauffeur's" voice squawking:

"Sir! Sir! Mr. Ambassador! Now what the devil's gone wrong?"

He thought: 'Why is it that life in our times always seems to reduce a man's options—and his acts!—to the level of children's games?' And, after that, within minutes, he heard the sirens screaming in, from every point of the compass.

The doctor whom Henriques brought was none other than Vicente Gomez Almagro, himself, the head of the one institution in Costa Verde that was spoken of with awed respect throughout all Latin America: the famous—and deservedly so—Hospital *Miguel Villalonga*. Presidents of other countries, millionaire industrialists, businessmen, cinema and stage stars, the celebrities and elite of nearly every country in the Western Hemisphere where Spanish or Portuguese is spoken, had themselves, their wives, children, loved ones, flown into Ciudad Villalonga to that particular hospital from thousands of kilometers away when faced with any serious medical emergency, especially one that involved surgery. Nor was Vince—as his friends called him—Gomez' fame confined to the southern half of the hemisphere. He lectured, taught brief seminars, and demonstrated his brilliantly original surgical innovations at Harvard Medical School—incidentally, his own alma mater—as well as at the Mayo Clinic, Tufts, and at Dr. Cooley's world famous establishment at Houston, Texas.

And yet, Roberto Henriques had dragged this great surgeon, this *Eminencia,* as the Spanish-speaking medical profession justly considered him, out of his bed in the middle of the night to attend a bruised face that any first-year medical student could have treated with ease.

"Doctor, I apologize!" Jim said. "I had no idea that Roberto was going to call *you*! Why—"

"He did well, Mr. Ambassador," Doctor Gomez said, "at the time. He knew only that you'd been hurt, not the nature of the wound. Even so, if you don't mind, I'd like you brought into the hospital. I should like that side of your face X-rayed. Nasty blow you've got there. There could be at least a hairline fracture beneath that bruise . . ."

"All right," Jim said; "as long as you'll promise to let me out before tomorrow afternoon. I simply must attend the funeral of those people who—"

Vicente Gomez stared at him; said quietly:

"Don't tell me you're blaming yourself for *that*, Mr. Ambassador?"

"In a way, yes; I suppose I am," Jim said. "It's not—pleasant to have forty-three deaths on one's conscience, Doctor."

"Don't see why they are, or even should be; but we can argue that later," Dr. Gomez said. "Now I'd better phone for an ambulance . . ."

"Good Lord, Doctor!" Jim said. "Say I *do* have a fractured cheekbone; that doesn't seem to me sufficient reason to call an ambulance! Roberto can drive me to the hospital in the Embassy car. I'd like this—incident—played down, if it's at all possible. No need to give unnecessary aid and comfort to the types who did it, you know."

Dr. Gomez considered that.

"All right," he said; then turning towards Henriques added: "But drive slowly, Roberto. No violent starts and abrupt braking. This doesn't look dangerous, and it doesn't require haste. But a rough ride could play havoc with internal injuries, if any—"

"Yes, Sir, Doctor!" Henriques said; quite the humble, efficient chauffeur once again.

But *Capitan* Carasco of the police said, sharply:

"One moment, please! Mr. Ambassador, have you any idea of what's missing from those files?"

"No idea at all," Jim mumbled. "Quite a lot seems to be, though . . ."

"Your Excellency," Captain Carasco said, "would you object to our taking the files down to Headquarters temporarily? Our clerks could make a list of what's there, and from that, you—"

"Not at all," Jim said. "There's nothing secret about these particular files. Seem to be mostly personnel. Names, addresses, vital statistics. Citizens of your country who work for the Embassy . . ."

Carasco and Henriques exchanged looks.

"That could be important," Captain Carasco said. "You'll have the files back first thing tomorrow morning. And our list. We're going to have to work on this all night, I'm afraid . . ."

"All right. Send the list to my residence, not here. I'll phone you if it gives me any lead . . ." Jim said.

So it wasn't until two o'clock in the morning that he got to bed, finally. His cheekbone, the X rays showed, was not fractured; but from the way he felt by then it was the only bone in his body that wasn't. Yet the very degree and intensity of his fatigue helped. He slept without moving until nine thirty that next morning. Woke up clear of head, and eye, feeling that he could at least function on a level somewhat above the amoebic, even pass muster—if the inspection were not too thorough!— as a reasonable replica of a human being.

Tomás, himself, brought him breakfast. Jim glared at him, said:

"This wasn't necessary, Tomás! I told you that I wouldn't need you before noon . . ."

"I know that, Sir," Tomás said; "but on the radio this morning, I heard the report of this new attempt upon your life, so I called Roberto. He picked me up, brought me here . . ."

Tomás opened the short, folding legs beneath the tray, placed it across Jim's legs. Then he turned, and switched on the radio on the night table beside the bed. Jim stared at him, then at the radio. He realized at once that the gesture hadn't been idle. 'Some special item in the morning newscast,' he thought. But no sound came from the radio at all.

"It's a transmitter," Tomás said in a calm tone of voice; "tuned to exactly twenty-seven thousand, eight hundred kilohertz, which is the frequency all the hidden microphones and their VHF band radios are tuned to, Carlos says. It sends out an ultrasonic signal at that frequency which produces a kind of Lawson Effect in those microphones. In other words, anyone listening at this moment will hear only a squeal of such intensity that listening to it for as long as thirty consecutive seconds could permanently damage his hearing . . ."

"Good Lord!" Jim said.

"A much better idea than removing the bugs, Sir. When there is something you *want* them to hear, you cut off the transmitter. In fact, you should leave it off except such times that you wish to tell me something secret. This procedure will convince them that their surveillance system works, but that some accidental interference occasionally affects it. With thoughtful planning, it should take them months to realize that nothing they hear is of any importance . . ."

"Especially since we're going to let them hear some *very* important things, at least from time to time," Jim said.

"Such as?" Tomás said.

"Such as that we believe Joseph Harper is the head of Costa Verde's drug traffic. That he hasn't been arrested because he and General García have a profit-sharing deal worked out between them. We're going to wonder out loud why nobody can find what I've been told is the world's biggest and finest heroin-processing laboratory, even though it must be within ten kilometers of one of the three major detention camps. I don't exactly believe His Nibs can afford letting even his most loyal lackeys, the boys who monitor his surveillance set up, chew on that information for very long—"

Tomás stood there. A slow grin spread across his face.

"*When,* Sir?" he said.

"Within the next two weeks. After I've presented my credentials. After things have calmed down a bit. After we have more definite information, or even proof. Can Carlos and Company hang a round-the-clock tail on Harper? Bug his phone, his house, his car?"

"Easily. But, Sir—his house? Well, *that,* Sir—"

"Some of the things they might pick up there could make me unhappy? Yes. But you needn't bring those particular items to me. I'm not interested in the gentleman's sex life, Tomás. I'm interested in doing what I can to stop the drug traffic from here into my country. Even though that lies well outside my ambassadorial duties. For—personal reasons, say. And, being human, in instructing Mr. Harper that hitting at least certain people in their faces with the flat side of a gun can get to be an expensive pastime. As well as convincing him that keeping a young woman in a state of witless addiction for—his own purposes, call it—can become a trifle more costly than that. Now please go draw my bath, and lay me out some clothes. I've one small errand to run this morning—"

"An errand, Sir?" Tomás said.

Jim pointed at the transmitter. Made the gesture of shutting it off.

Tomás did so; said again, loudly:

"Just what is it you have to do this morning, Sir?"

"Go take a good look at five or six of the finest young female anatomies in Costa Verde," Jim said solemnly. "Speaking of which, you'd better tell Roberto I'll be needing the car within three-quarters of an hour . . ."

He saw with real pleasure that Henriques was going to be able to park the Cadillac close enough to the Seven M to get a perfect view of the proceedings inside the boutique. 'Now to see if I can't get you to remove my name from your list of the Members of the Ancient and Honorable Sisterhood of Closet Queens,' he thought. He said:

"Wait here, Roberto; I shan't be long . . ."

The occasion was a huge success. Of course, true to his nature, Geri had to complain:

"Now look, Dearies, can't any of you move with a little more grace than a *cow?*" he said airily. "Oh, *María Santísima,* what wouldn't I give for a model who didn't clump along like a pregnant elephant!"

But Jim paid no attention to his grumping. The truth of the matter was that Geri's models were all really striking girls with what would have been lovely bodies except for the fact that he, like all high-fashion designers, tyrannically insisted upon their keeping themselves much too thin.

They paraded Geri's current line of bathing suits before His Excellency, the Ambassador, with such verve that Jim saw, with wry amusement, that they were actually competing with one another to gain his attention. After all, *Gringos* were completely insane, anyhow. It remained well within the realm of possibility that this strange little Ambassador—not really half bad, all things considered!—might be sufficiently smitten by their charms to forget social and class distinctions—never very strong in his country from all they had heard!—and falling madly in love with one of them, take her as his wife. And for a girl of the social stratum to which they belonged, to snatch him away from under the aristocratic noses of the clients of the Seven M would be a coup never to be forgotten in Costa Verde; a blow of pure theater to be all the more savored, given the fact that they, *las maniquies,* the models, came, without exception, from the lower fringes of the middle class, and therefore, naturally enough, hated the distinguished Dames of High Society with all their envious and malicious little lower-middle-class hearts.

So it was no accident that each series of bathing attire they paraded became a little more daring than the one preceding it. By common if unspoken agreement, they had arranged the bathing suits in piles by order of weight—a simple matter for professional models to do merely by hefting them in decidedly experienced hands. Which meant each series of suits had less material, less cloth, and thereby exposed greater areas of lissome flesh to sunlight and air—and Jim Rush's bemused gaze!—than the one before. At the very last, one of them appeared in a *Tanga* that she, herself, had sneaked out of the boutique last night upon being told by Geri of the proposed *desfile,* and modified for maximum effect. Now a *Tanga* is the type of bathing suit that *Gringos* call the "String"—a garment so near to actual nonexistence that modifying it in the direction of greater nudity should have been an impossibility, but she had managed it. This one consisted of a black, elastic *cache sexe,* a sort of triangular G-string which concealed—somewhat—that part of her which even in today's permissive society generally *is* concealed in public, said triangle being held up by a pair of halter straps that widened and formed a pair of miniature cups in order to substitute—inadequately—for the, esthetically, anyhow, essential item of feminine attire, that Americans who think they know French call a *brassière* and the French, conceding them a slightly superior knowledge of their own language, a *soutien gorge.*

Now to the bottom of said *Tanga* or "String." From dead astern—the position from which all males drawn to view a *Tanga* by sheer instinct—it disappeared completely between her delightfully callipygian callipygiousnesses—or is it callipygialities?—And absolutely nothing could be done to make further reduction possible, so she'd gone to work on those straps. Which, as a result of her artistry, and by the time Jim was awarded the distinct privilege and even greater pleasure of viewing that particular *Tanga,* had been, from the place where they started, at the top of that microscopic black triangular front piece to where they looped and tied in a bow around the back of her neck, diminished to a uniform two and five-tenths centimeters—almost exactly one inch wide. To keep them in place where they climbed, crossed, and caressed the gentle globular swellings of two more of her strategic and/or erogenous zones, she had stitched a slightly narrower strip of adhesive surgical tape beneath each of them, forgetting—poor dear!—that adhesive tape is one of the most maddeningly irritating, not to mention itchy, substances known to medical science, and that the zones to which she'd forced them to adhere are, after all, in the human female, anyhow, distinctly erectile tissue. The results, to say the least, were a trifle startling.

Jim threw back his head and laughed aloud.

"Bravo!" he said, and putting out his hand, gave an affectionate squeeze to that part of her that placing on public display is a *Tanga's* only *raison d'être,* thus proving to his own satisfaction that under the stimulae of the conditions extant in Costa Verde his painful timidity was rapidly disappearing. "This one will do, Ger! Now bring out your Andean line in her size and drape 'em over her . . ."

When he came out, he had bought four rarely lovely dresses for Alicia. He had also been forced by her obvious disappointment to explain to the model that he'd bought them for a niece just her size. The lie was ill chosen, for it demonstrated—again—the futility of any man's trying to have the last word in even a concealed dispute with a woman. For she made an impish face and said:

"But, Mr. Ambassador, I didn't know you were a priest!"

And he had to admit defeat. All over Latin America—in fact, wherever Spanish is spoken—*sobrina,* "niece," is a code word, as far as any sworn to celibacy Catholic priest is concerned, for *querida,* "mistress." And *every* priest, from the Archbishop on down, is conceded by kindly and understanding common consent the privilege of possessing at least one. It was useless to argue that he had no mistress, and worse than that to state he was buying the dresses for his best friend's wife—with said friend's full knowledge and consent. That no woman of Latin blood, or no man, for that matter, was even going to listen to, not to mention believe.

But when he got back to the car, he saw he'd won that round of his psychological war with García and Company hands down. Roberto Henriques was grinning all over his square-jawed, classically policeman's face.

"I say, Sir!" he blurted out. "You've certainly relieved my mind!"

"How so, Roberto?" Jim said.

"Well, Sir, down here, to be—well—friendly—with a known homosexual—is often misunderstood and—"

"Oh, that!" Jim said. "Look, Roberto, hasn't it ever occurred to you that a man who had anything to worry about as far as his own tendencies were concerned would be precisely the one who'd stay as far away from those poor devils as possible? Or that people always try to boast of and exhibit the qualities they fear in their heart of hearts they lack? I like Geri. He's a brilliant man. Amusing. His—sexual proclivities I consider unfortunate. But they are his worry, not mine. I have other and more serious things to worry about—"

"More serious, Sir?" Roberto said.

"Yes. Such as why someone stole *your* dossier from my files last night, Roberto. And Tomás'. And the maid's—what's her name? Oh, yes; Maripaz'. And two or three others' on my household staff. I think maybe I'd better consult with the Director General of Security. I shouldn't like any of you—hurt—or killed, you know."

"Oh, I don't believe any of us is of sufficient importance for the Reds to—"

"Were the people in that airplane of sufficient importance, Roberto? Hell, man, they didn't even know their names!"

"That's true, Sir," Roberto said uneasily. "Shall I drive you down to Headquarters?"

"No! Of course not! Look, Roberto, since it's well after midday now, suppose you leave me at *Les Ambassadeurs*. Then go get the Director General. Ask him to drop into that restaurant casually. As though it were by accident. He can come in alone, or with some of his officers. Then, after seeing me at my table, he can send the *maître d'* over to invite me to join him. Better like that, don't you think?"

Roberto was staring at him. This time he actually said what he thought:

"You—know how to operate, don't you, Sir?"

"Roberto, I've been stationed in eight Latin American countries before now. What's more, I was *born* in one, where my father was stationed as Ambassador. So I tend to think as you do . . ."

"You surely do!" Roberto said. "But, Sir; I suppose you know—that I'm armed. That one of my duties is to guard you . . ."

"Yes, I did know that," Jim said. "So?"

"So I cannot leave you to get the Director General. Couldn't you phone him from the restaurant?"

"No. You know better than that, Roberto. Every line in this town's bugged. Look—cruise around a bit. Pick up a motorcycle policeman. One you know. Send him to the Director General with a written note. All right?"

"All right, Sir—as long as *you* write the note!" Roberto Henriques said.

The lunch with the Director General of Security was also successful. Jim planted a couple of extremely worrisome questions in the right spots as neatly as a *banderillero* places his gaily festooned little harpoons in the great hump just behind the neck of the bull. His government was exceedingly troubled by the tremendous increase of narcotics coming into the States from a source that Bureau experts had pinpointed as being inside Costa Verde. He could not, nor would not, interfere with the internal affairs of a friendly sister republic, but his Government would appreciate a crackdown on the part of Costa Verde's own law enforcement bodies, especially the expulsion or arrest of certain *foreigners* believed to control the traffic. General García's praiseworthy attitude towards drug smuggling was well known, but of late Washington felt that the facts were possibly being concealed from His Excellency because certainly the increase was noteworthy . . .

The recent attempts on his own life, together with the tragic deaths of so many innocent people that had resulted from them, could, in his opinion, only increase the inclination of certain acquaintances of his in Congress, men who had a say in all military appropriations, to believe that the degree of desperation shown by the Reds was perhaps at least somewhat engendered by the rumored disregard for individual civil rights widely held to be part of *Seguridad*'s own police procedure—

'You spell it torture, *Amigo*!' he thought grimly.

If the Director General could provide him with a confidential assurance, together with—ah—certain corroborating evidence that such was *not* the case, perhaps Congress' foot dragging over the release of more sophisticated armament to Costa Verde, especially the type of special antiguerrilla weapons that the Costa Verdian Armed Forces were requesting, might well convert itself into a speedy and wholehearted expedition of the materiel in question . . .

The Director General listened gravely, nodded frequently, and promised that he would personally take Ambassador Rush's suggestions up with the Head of the State. And Jim Rush left *Les Ambassadeurs,* surely one of the world's finest French restaurants outside of France itself, with the heady feeling that he had been damned effective, had handled himself very well indeed. As, in sober fact, he had. But his self-satisfaction would have been sharply lessened had he been able to hear what Don Raoul Pérez de la Valle, *Director General de la Seguridad Nacional,* remarked to his Chief Aide:

"That little man—is dangerous. This is the first time to my knowledge that Washington has sent us one such as this. One who—"

"*Speaks* Spanish," the Aide supplied; "truly speaks it. Even to *modismos,* idiomatic expressions, turns of phrase, plays upon words—"

"And who, additionally, has a mind. A mind which functions. So now, as of this morning, SN-2 informs me, the surveillance microphones in his residence and the Embassy squeal unbearably—"

"Not all the time," the Aide said.

"True. But when they do not, the conversation is of an insupportable banality. And, additionally, he asks questions whose answers *I* do not know, and which could be—perilous. This big blond swine of a North American—Harper. He runs down to the docks in a car which is *never* stopped—or checked. Because even *I* have been requested to leave it alone—"

Pablo Fuentes Toralba, Chief Aide to the Director General, his confidant, closest friend, and the one man in Costa Verde privy to, and already an active supporter of, his ambition to become Chief of State in his turn, by the only methods that feat could be accomplished in Costa Verde, which was to say by overthrowing and subsequently murdering the present Chief, smiled.

"Requested by *whom,* Sir?" he said.

"Ah! *That* is an interesting question, is it not, Friend Pablo? But I did not ask it. A certain instinct instructed me not to. A strong desire to die in bed of the normal weaknesses of old age, surrounded by my weeping children and grandchildren. Say—it came through channels. One of those requests whose original source one is given to understand with a degree of ambiguity—with an unclarity sufficient to protect its immediate bearer, who can always say: 'You misunderstood me, *mi General*! That is not what I meant—nor *whom*!' "

"I see. But still, considering Our Glorious Leader's well-known hatred for the drug traffic—the Draconian methods he has employed to curtail it—to me it seems strange—"

"That this arrogant pig of a *Gringo* operates with such total impunity? And to me, Pablo; and to *me*! He flies *inland* in one of the helicopters of Worldwide Petroleum, helicopters whose normal use is to transport men and materials out to the offshore drilling platforms, for which, and *only* for which, they have permits. He does *not* file a flight plan with the civil or the military aviation authorities. Once he is across the Sierras, the Tower radar, of course, loses his image. But helicopters are slow. Long before he gets that far our fighter planes have time to spare to take off, intercept him, challenge him by radio, shoot him down—"

"Yet they don't, do they, Raoul? Hmmmnn—strange. And now, His Excellency, the American Ambassador, concerns himself with the narcotics traffic, and specifically requests the expulsion—or arrest—of certain *foreigners* who—"

"Exactly," the Director General said. "Look, Pablo, may I have the benefit of your rarely corrupt and Machiavellian mind in this matter?"

"Raoul—" Pablo said; "hadn't we better *cooperate* with the American Ambassador?"

"Pablo—" the Director General said; "you disappoint me. Hadn't we better *make use of* the American Ambassador?"

"Which was what I meant in the first place, *mi General!*"

"Then you should have said so. We cultivate this strange little Anglo Saxon gentleman. We find out what he knows. If what he knows leads where and to whom I think it does, we encourage him—verbally—"

"In some place free of electronic surveillance—"

"That goes without saying, Pablo! We encourage him to make use of it, while keeping *our* hands scrupulously clean."

"As clean as Pilate's after he had washed them before the Crucifixion," Pablo said.

"That's an unfortunate simile, Pablo!"

"I withdraw it, *mi General.* Sorry."

"All right. In the resulting explosion, we proceed as already planned, greatly aided by public and official revulsion caused by His Excellency's, the United States of North America's Ambassador's relevations. Thereafter, we get rid of *Su Excelencia el Embajador Estadounidense,* as well . . . ."

"How, Sir? By becoming a trifle lax at frustrating the Reds' sterling assassination attempts, say?"

"No! God, no, Pablo! We don't want to get the *Gringos'* backs up. We, too, will need that sophisticated stuff to eliminate those Red swine after we come to power. Neater to—induce his own Government to recall him. Some—juicy scandal say—"

"But Henriques says he doesn't seem to like women very much. And beyond his friendship with that *Invertido Gringo* dressmaker, there's no proof that he—"

"Henriques is a fool! I monitored that call our diminutive Ambassador got from New York. A man who can cause a woman—especially a frozen-tailed *Gringa*!—to cry like that, not only likes women, but knows how to handle them. Tell me, have you been able to discover who the two women in that photo he tore up are?"

"Not yet. But our people in the States are working on it," Pablo Fuentes said.

"*La Morena*—the dark one, her face haunts me. I'd swear I'd seen her—and in the *flesh*—somewhere, before . . ."

"So would I," Fuentes said; "still—"

"Still, come on. We've got to attend that bloody funeral, y'know. For, my dear Pablo, it *will* occur to Our Glorious Leader to request a videotape from the television people so that he may check who among us were present, as well as who *weren't,* holding the latter guilty *a priori* of insufficient sensibilities, patriotism, and loyalty to his Most Illustrious Person. So, in the shrewd assumption that you have as little nostalgia for our Heavenly Home as I do, let us be on our way, my friend!"

And now, standing there sweating in his dark cutaway frock coat and hickory-striped trousers, with his black homburg posed reverently over his heart, listening to the tired, rasping voice of His Grace, the Archbishop, Father José María Zaratieguí Istúriz, better known as Padre Pío, Father Pious, the beloved little Father of all Costa Verde's poor, as he intoned the prayers for the dead, under the obscenely watchful eyes of the television cameras, Jim Rush knew that the feeling of near happiness, of assurance, belief in himself, that had gripped him all morning had been an illusion.

The reality was another thing. The reality was forty-three dark, oblong wooden boxes laid out in neat rows before forty-three gaping holes in the ground. Forty-three lumps of charred meat, clinging in tarred viscosity to some exponential number of blackened, splintered bones. Forty-three unidentified and unidentifiable, not even recognizably human corpses that constituted an insoluble mathematical problem, because you couldn't add them up, or subtract them down to one living man named James Randolph Rush, or divide the breath, life, spirit, thought, hope, dreams, that they'd been possessed of into one forty-third part of these qualities and award them to him; nor multiply their love, lust, longing, by an infinitude of zeros to fill a universe with nothing, and cram that aching vacancy into the one small desolation he called his heart.

'I'm living on borrowed time,' he thought, 'the time you lent me, friends . . .'

He felt the tears sting his eyes. Shook his head to clear them, turned his face away from the raised platform about twenty yards to his left on which General García, Head of State, and a group of high ranking officers stood, with their wives behind them in a compact group of sober, dark-colored, silk-clad figures, raised his eyes to a clump of trees, part of that tropical rain forest, that jungle that had to be hacked back almost daily to keep it from actually invading Ciudad Villalonga on this, the landward side, and saw very clearly the tiny figure in jungle camouflage fatigues who was sighting through the telescopic sight of that Czech-made, twenty-five-calibre Olympic target rifle, a clumsy-looking, single-shot, long-barreled gun that was a problem to reload, but that if you were any kind of a marksman at all you didn't need to reload because from that distance—two hundred meters more or less—it could put that one shot dead center through a fifteen-millimeter-diameter bull's-eye.

He saw that the rifleman was doing it right: lying on his belly with the barrel of the rifle resting on a soft sandbag to absorb whatever little recoil it might have. And he didn't even need to judge the angle to know whom the trained assassin was aiming at. Him. Jim Rush. The elevation was far too low for García or the Archbishop, or anyone else to be the target.

And, seeing that, he couldn't move. Somehow, deep inside himself, not inside his mind, but within himself, he didn't even want to. All the years of disillusion, sorrow, loss—the failure of hope, his ingrained self-loathing—held him there. Forty-three nameplateless coffins anchored his will. The suicide note Virginia had left him. Jenny's light brown hair jerking and swaying as she—

He saw the flash, the sudden stabbing tongue of flame; felt a razor slash across his forehead above his left eyebrow, just below his hair, heard *after* that, noticeably after, the sodden long-drawn-out craaaaack! of the shot; and all the world disappeared in blinding pain, in a hot, wet slithering curtain of red.

He did not fall. He dropped his homburg, fumbled for his handkerchief, wiped the flooding, solid sheet of blood from his face. Heard the screams, saw the dark, blurred figures dashing towards him, and another kind of pain stabbed into his gut as he saw those trained professionals on the TV camera dollies twirling their long focus lenses in for a close-up of his bloody face.

"Grace!" he whispered; "I told her to—"

He found his voice; said clearly, calmly, not shouting, but cutting through the rising babble with sudden authority:

"I'm all right. Gentlemen, I beg you to respect these dead!"

Behind him, up that wooded hill, he heard the stutter of submachine guns: Schmeissers from the ripping sound they made, which meant that the soldiers General García had stationed all around the cemetery had already gone into action; and the slower, heavier, jerking tattoo of the guerrillas' Ak-47s answering them. It lasted not even a minute. Then the silence roared in upon him. Echoed.

Hands reached out to take him, support him, bear him away. But his flat, terribly calm voice stopped them.

"It's—a scratch. No more. Let—the funeral continue. I won't leave. I cannot. Not until all these who died—for me—in my place—are laid—to rest . . ."

They fell back. Three of the five TV cameras never left his face. He stood there, pressing his absolutely soaked handkerchief to his forehead in a way that served only to detour that red flood around his eyes as Padre Pío said:

"Father, receive these, thy innocent children, so cruelly slain!"

And those forty-three coffins were almost hurled into those yawning graves with absolutely indecent haste. And Vicente Gomez was upon him, ripping off his own frock coat, hurling it to the ground, saying:

"Lie down, Jim. On my coat. I'll send someone for—"

And he: "No, Vince. Not yet. Tell the *sepulceros* to cover them. This is not right. I—took their lives. By merely—existing, I took them. Can't—can't spoil their funerals—on top of that. 'S wrong, Vince. Can't—"

"Jim," Vicente Gomez said quietly, "there are times when it is not useful to be brave. And this is one of them. You are hemorrhaging—badly. So do me, and yourself, the favor of lying down, will you?"

"Vince," Jim said, "you're wrong, you know. I'm scared shitless. It just hasn't caught up with me, yet . . ."

"Somebody get me my bag!" Vince said. "You, soldier! Take these keys! Bring me my bag out of the trunk of my car. You know it, don't you? Good! Run, man! I've got to stop this bleeding!"

"Doctor—" the Director General of Security said; "his wound—is it—"

"Don't know," Vicente Gomez said. "Look, *mi General,* you have a patrol car outside the cemetery gates, haven't you?"

"Yes, Doctor; why?"

"Have them radio for an ambulance. He's losing too much blood. *Amigo,* Jim, do you know your blood type?"

"Yes," Jim said, "it's A positive."

"Good. That's easy enough. Here comes that military snail with my bag at last. Jim—Mr. Ambassador—"

"Jim—please," Jim whispered; "they just—shot—Mr. Ambassador, Vince. And—and—now I *will* sit down—or lie down—if you don't mind. I—I'm afraid I'm going to faint . . ."

The rest of it was confusion, a blur of impressions in which time and space telescoped, collapsed in upon themselves. When he came back, he was in a white room, in a bed with a plasma bottle on its stand beside and above it. From the bottle a clear rubber tube descended. On the end of the tube was a needle surely designed for the easy and rapid disembowelment of elephants; but at the moment, they had stuck it into a vein in his left arm.

A pair of young nurses, or more likely nursing students, he judged from their extreme youth and noticeable nervousness, hovered solicitously about him. A nun—a nursing sister—sat tensely watching him from a chair by his bed. Through the opened doorway he could see the two uniformed gorillas who justified every bad joke their neighbors told about Costa Verdians, fingering the triggers of their submachine guns as though having to refrain from shooting somebody, anybody, was causing them intolerable pain.

The moment she saw his opened eyes, the nursing sister raised her great, stiffly starched headdress, which looked rather like a racing sloop's balloon spinnaker placed in a horizontal position and quick frozen, Jim thought, and stared at him. Then with a soft *"!Jesus y María!"* she flew out of there in a great flapping of her pious robes. Within seconds she was back with Doctor Gomez.

"So you've decided to postpone your departure for a better world, eh, Jim?" Vince said in his accentless American English. "Good. Only now we've got to give you a couple of transfusions. Wound's not bad, but you've lost too much blood. Incidentally it's *not* a bullet wound. A chip of granite off a sculptured angel's wing did that, when it was clipped off by the bullet. I suppose the heat waves rising from the cemetery must have confused that sharpshooter's aim . . ."

"Vince," Jim whispered, "may I have—a telephone? I need to call— someone—in New York . . ."

"Hell, no. Not 'til tomorrow, Jim. If then. Maybe not 'til day after . . ."

"Oh, Christ!" Jim got out.

"Give me the number," Vince said; "I'll call her. Tell her you're all right. I've already talked to Peter Reynolds. Had a long distance call from him an hour ago, asking how you were. Said you're his very best friend . . ."

"Thanks—Vince," Jim said.

"Alicia—his wife—was quite dreadfully upset. They had the TV on and—"

"Oh Christ!" Jim said again, even more faintly. "Vince—call 212-586-5959. Ask for Mrs. Nivens—Grace. Tell her—I'm—all right—I— told her to—watch."

"Done. Now shut up, will you? Dr. Guttierez, my assistant, will perform the transfusions in about twenty minutes from now. By tomorrow, you'll be feeling great."

He was back after the first transfusion. Stood there, looking at Jim. He said:

"Jim, goddamnit, you marry that girl!"

Jim smiled.

"That's—unscientific advice, Doctor," he said. "You don't know her—have never seen—"

"Don't need to. I prescribed for her over the telephone. She was in—deep shock, Jim. Her friend—English girl from her voice—came on and promised to buy the stuff. Only *she* was crying so hard I'm not sure she'll get it right. Lord God, Jim—how d'you do it?"

"I don't," Jim said sadly. "With women, my score's zero minus, Vince."

"*¡Mierda!*" Vince said. "Call her tomorrow, Jim. About noon. Her flat. I was damned high-handed with her. *Ordered* her not to go work until the middle of next week—"

"Thanks, Vince," Jim said.

"Jim," Grace said. She wasn't crying. It would have been better if she had been. This was worse. Far worse.

He dragged breath back into his lungs; said, his voice all gone, dead stopped by just the way hers had sounded, saying his name:

"Grace—I'm sorry I told you to watch that. But after all—"

"You didn't know," she said; then: "How are you, Jim?"

"All right. I've a headache, of course; but you can't crack a Rush's skull with only a chip off an angel's wing . . ."

She said, dully:

"A—chip—off an angel's wing?"

He explained. Her only response was: "Oh!"

The silence hummed. Stretched out between them.

He said, almost crying:

"Grace—please!"

"Jim," she said softly, clearly, slowly: "This—is—an ultimatum. I'm sorry, but that's the way it has to be. Either you resign, *now;* catch the next plane; come home—to *me*—or—it's good-bye. Good-bye, forever, Jim . . ."

"Grace!" he said.

"I can't stand this. You have—no right to—to torture me to death, this way. To make me lose—what's left of my mind. I had to—to sit there and watch you—standing like a rock with the blood pouring down your face—and being—that brave. That criminally, idiotically brave.

I've no use for—heroes, Jim. I want—a man. A simple man. Good. Gentle. Who—won't kill me like this—"

"Grace," he said; "I *can't* come back now. Grace—listen! I simply can't—"

"Then—it's good-bye, Jim. I'm not going to watch TV any more. Nor read the papers. So—when—somebody tells me—maybe it—will be a long time—afterwards, and I can say—can say—"

"What, Grace?"

"That—you—were—just—someone—I *used*—to know."

"Grace!" he moaned.

She said, whispering the words:

"Good-bye, Jim . . ."

There was a click.

Then—silence.

'Which is the way the world really ends, doesn't it?' he thought.

CHAPTER

12

*H*e remembered that Peter Reynolds had said that General García kept Padre Pío shut up in the Ecclesiastical Palace and wouldn't let him out. But relations between Church and State in Costa Verde must have improved since then, or anyhow changed, for here the Archbishop was, dressed in an old, rusty black soutane with a badly frayed hem like any village priest, and sitting by his bed.

"How are you, Son Jim?" the Archbishop said.

Jim smiled to himself. Not, "Mr. Ambassador"; but *"Hijo Jaime"*, "Son Jim." It was a measure of the quality of the old priest. Padre Pío had got the name from Vince Gomez, surely. And used it, because at the level of saintly simplicity on which he lived, rank and titles meant very little. As little, maybe, as they meant to God.

"Very well, Father," Jim said. "I thank you for coming. Your visit honors me."

"Nonsense!" Padre Pío laughed. His laughter was full and strong. If you'd heard it from another room, you'd think it came from a much younger man. He peered at Jim out of eyes that were small and black and merry and shrewd and compassionate and filled with—love. The kind of love that passes understanding because it continued, went on, existed unshaken, in spite of knowing *exactly* how and what people are. Those eyes peered out of a face that had been gouged out of brown granite by the sand-laden scourings of a desert wind; and blasted out of the bole of a tamarind tree by lightning.

"You do not *look* very well, Son Jim," the old priest said. "In fact, you look like the bad death!"

"Of a verity I am all right, Father," Jim said. "Doctor Gomez is letting me go home tomorrow."

"Ah, so? But that, my son, only means that your *body* is all right—or nearly so. And why not? You are young and strong. But it does not please me, this look in your eyes. It means that I must hasten. And at my age, Son Jim, haste is not recommendable. My old bones creak, you know. Like the wooden axles of a Tluscolan oxcart. And my breath is short . . ."

Jim stared at Padre Pío. Said:

"Just what is it, Father, that you see in my eyes that causes you to believe you must make haste?"

Padre Pío peered back at Jim, gravely. His raspy, breath-gone, old man's voice steadied. Became full and deep and musical. Warm, somehow. Comforting.

"The bad sadness, Son Jim. The loss of hope. Which is—to insult God."

Jim lay there.

"I—am not a believer, Father," he said.

"Ah, so? Hmmmnnnn—well, in a way, that could be better. Come to think of it, it *is* better. At this very rare moment. And for you."

Jim studied the old priest. He saw what Alicia had meant now. Even understood it vaguely. This old man *was* magnificent. If believing nonsense built a personality like this, created such character, then nonsense had much to recommend it. He said:

"Father, you astonish me. You hold it is better *not* to believe?"

"No. I do not hold it better. I merely say that in your case, now, under your circumstances, it is the lesser of two evils—at least if you do not persist in it too long. For surrendering to the idea that life is meaningless, that living has lost all savor, is in you, as an unbeliever, less than a blasphemy, perhaps not even quite a sin. But, for a believer to do so would be to reject God's mercy, His forgiveness, His understanding, His endless power to set things right again. And that, *Hijo Jaime,* would be a sin—such a sin as would cost me much struggle—and even God a little to forgive it!"

"Father—these ideas are beyond me. My head has been cracked, and functions badly. Which is no excuse. About the concepts of religion—and of God, it functions badly even when it is well. I simply do not understand them—or you, Father . . ."

"Don't try to, Son Jim," the old man laughed; "because when I talk like that, God speaks through me. And we aren't even supposed to understand Him. No, no! I'm not going to preach you a sermon. It has been my experience that sermons do no good at all. In fact, they get people's backs up, and drive them into greater mischief. Son Jim, I was very close to you in the cemetery, probably because you had left the platform of the dignitaries and come down to the opened graves to be nearer to those who'd died *for you* and *in your place*. Am I right?"

Jim looked at that ugly old gargoyle's face. That marvelously ugly old face.

"Yes, Father," he said.

"So I know you had time to spare—to hide behind a tombstone, throw yourself down, run, at least try to escape. And you did not. I ask you only this: Was that a—decision? I mean, was your failure to take evasive action conscious, reasoned?"

Jim lay there.

"And if it were, Father?" he said.

"It would make my task much harder. But I should *not* give up, Son Jim! God does not offer me material such as *you* every day."

"God must be—hard up. Suffering from penury, then," Jim said.

"Or, perhaps, in His infinite wisdom, He knows far better than we do which material is good, and which bad. Even which is—excellent. Now stop begging the question, my Son! Did you, or did you not—decide to accept your own assassination, thus converting it—into suicide? Or at least into attempted suicide in this case?"

Jim thought about that. Said, slowly:

"No, Father. Not—consciously. Or not entirely. The question's—hard. I was terrified. Shocked. I *couldn't* move, Father. But—yes. There *was*—an instant, a flash, half a heartbeat, when I didn't want to. When to die—seemed so—so simple. And such—a relief . . ."

Padre Pío leaned close, looked into Jim's eyes.

"And now," he said sadly, "it seems—even more simple. Even more of a relief. And—consciously. Am I right, my Son?"

"Yes, Father," Jim said.

"Why?"

"Does it matter?" Jim said tiredly.

Padre Pío thought about that.

"No," he said; "it doesn't. The reasons for being wrong seldom do. Son Jim, do you believe in *me*? Not as a Servant of God, but as a man? As one who is unlikely to deceive you, or to lie to you? Even as an old, old Party who knows a thing or two? You know the saying: 'The Devil knows more from being *old,* than he knows from being the Devil.' ?"

" 'El diablo sabe más por viejo que por diablo . . .' ? Yes, Father—to both questions: I know the saying; and I do believe in you."

"Good! I'm going to make you a sporting proposition, then, Son Jim. It's very simple, *Hijo*: that *you* play fair. That you give God a chance. For, if you remove yourself from this world—or allow our mutual enemies to remove you—*nothing* can be changed, resolved, or proved. For I will wager you anything you will, at any odds you wish, that within the next two weeks, things will have changed for you. Changed so greatly that you will begin to see life for what it is—a privilege. An opportunity—for service. For doing good. For forgetting your small hurts before the enormous sufferings of humanity . . ."

Jim lay there. Said, whispering the words:

"Will—that change—lift forty-three deaths—from off my heart, Father?"

"No. And it shouldn't. Nothing should do that, Son Jim. That memory is yours to keep. To suffer. To be burdened with, forever. To cherish, even—as the blessed Saints cherish their *Stigmata,* even though they burn and bleed. God—has given you that, to remind you how greatly you are *His.* And that you must be—worthy of those deaths, my Son. And now, I go!"

Lying there on his narrow bed in the hospital room after Padre Pío had gone, Jim realized that he felt better. He didn't know why. There was no reason for it except the sheer impact of Padre Pío's personality, maybe. He was lying there, thinking about that, trying to analyze why it was so, when Tomás came through the door with a plump and pretty brunette in her early forties beside him.

"*Laura, mi esposa,*" he said.

"I'm honored," Jim said.

"*¡Encantada, Señor Embajador!*" Laura said.

"Now sit down and shut up," Tomás said to his wife, in English.

Then he took a small black transistor radio out of his pocket and showed it to Jim. Turned it on. It made no more sound than the ones in the Embassy and the Ambassador's residence did. Tomás put it back in his pocket without turning it off.

"Just in case," he said to Jim.

"The guards?" Jim whispered, nodding his head towards the door.

"Speak no English," Tomás said.

"You're sure?" Jim said.

"I'm sure," Tomás said.

"All right. What is it this time?"

"That's just the trouble, Sir; I don't *know.* They're planning something—but since their investigations center around a person who doesn't even live in Costa Verde, I don't see . . ."

"And that person is?"

"*Doña* Alicia Villalonga, wife of our mutual friend Peter Reynolds."

"Good Lord!"

"Sir—they know about those four dresses you bought for her."

"How the devil could they know that, Tomás?"

"Because *I* told them, Sir . . . Remember, last week, in fact the very morning of the day you got shot, you instructed me to pack them and send them off to her through your diplomatic pouch. I had to tell them that, Sir. One of the *maniquies* had talked, Sir. The little one with the gorgeous behind, Sir!"

"Tomás," Jim said, "that model didn't *know* to whom I was going to send those dresses. She only knew that I'd bought them."

"I know that, Mr. Ambassador. But the purchase itself was enough to arouse their curiosity. An Ambassador buys four women's dresses. Expensive. Quite—sexy. An Ambassador who hasn't a wife. Nor a sister. Nor a daughter. Nor any female relative of any variety. What supposition is left to them, Sir?"

"*Una Querida.* A Mistress."

"Right, Sir. Logically, the next step would have been for them to investigate *La Señora de* Nivens, wouldn't you think? There is no doubt that they know about—your relations with her. To monitor incoming long distance telephone calls is an automatic reflex for Security . . ."

"Yet, they—didn't?"

"I don't know. Maybe they did. I only know they didn't ask *me* about her. Not one word. Can you think of any reason for them to—discard her as the possibility, Sir?"

"Yes. Two. She and I have broken off relations."

"I'm sorry to hear that, Sir!"

"And I'm sorrier. But an even better reason is, if their people in the States have—seen Grace, they'd know instantly those dresses weren't for her."

"Why would they know that, Mr. Ambassador?"

"Size. Mrs. Nivens is one meter eighty."

"Lord, Sir!" Tomás laughed. "That must make kissing her a bit awkward for you, doesn't it?"

"When she feels inclined to cooperate, no. But get back to the point, Tomás. Why did you think you had to tell them I bought those dresses for Alicia?"

"Didn't *think,* Mr. Ambassador! I *had* to. Or blow my cover. Not to mention putting my neck in *el Garrote Vil.* You see, they asked me if the dresses weren't for her. For *Doña* Alicia Villalonga, widow of *Don* Emilio Duarte y Marin, now wedded in second nuptials to *Don* Peter Reynolds, the celebrated North American journalist. All that, Sir. Textually."

"So you said, 'Yes.' Hmmmnnn, you're right. You had to. But how the devil did they—"

"Get her name? I'm sure I don't know, Sir, any more than I know why they had eliminated Mrs. Nivens before they called me in for questioning. Did you ever telephone *Doña* Alicia? Or did she—"

"Ever phone me? No; to both questions, Tomás. I can't think of any way they—oh, Christ!"

"Why, 'Oh, Christ!' Sir?"

"Because I just realized how they got Alicia's name. Peter called Vince Gomez, to ask how I was. You see, he and Alicia were watching TV while I was playing 'Death in the Afternoon' or 'The Man on the Spot' for the benefit of the *telespectatores*. And he mentioned to Vince that seeing me get shot had upset Alicia terribly—"

"So now they probably think that *she's* the lady in your life, Sir," Tomás said. "And the question becomes: What do they plan to do about it? She's *there;* you're *here*. Unless they plan to remedy that very aspect— I mean the obstacle of distance—"

"You think they'd actually dare *kidnap* Alicia?" Jim said.

"Don't know. They'd dare do absolutely anything, Sir. What I can't quite see is how they could use such a tactic profitably. Threaten to kill her if you didn't do what they want you to? To do that, they'd have to reveal it was *they* who'd abducted her, thus bringing the wrath of your Government down upon their heads. Lock her in your bedroom after having removed all her clothes and say: 'Here, *Señor Embajador*—a present for you! Enjoy her thoroughly! But thereafter express your gratitude by persuading your Congressmen to provide us with the superscientific arms we need!'?"

"Makes no sense. It would backfire. How could I do them any good if my Department recalled me for getting mixed up in a scandal that juicy? One that involved kidnapping a married woman away from her husband and three children in order to indulge in a little plain and fancy screwing? Because my Department sure as hell would recall me for something that outrageous. García and Company have never impressed me as being stupid, Tomás. They'd know a caper like that one couldn't work. But in any case, maybe I'd better warn her, warn Peter—"

Tomás looked at him. Said:

"How?"

"Good Lord, Tomás! I never thought of that!"

"A letter would be opened. A cable copied by the operator. Telephone calls and radio messages monitored. The diplomatic pouch? Too slow. And who knows whether they *really* respect it?"

"Then?" Jim said.

"I vote we—do nothing, Sir. For the moment, anyhow. Until we have hard evidence they're planning some action against *Doña* Alicia. Somehow I don't think they are. Nor—against Mrs. Nivens. If you had someone—dear to you—in this country—especially a *native* of it, who'd have absolutely no defenses, that would fit in perfectly with their usual style of operating. I say, Sir—you haven't got seriously involved with that little model, have you? Roberto says you were fondling her cute little—"

"Tomás, please!" Jim said, glancing sidewise at Laura.

"Oh, she doesn't understand *that* much English, Sir! Well, Sir, about that little *maniqui,* you—"

"No, Tomás."

"That's a relief. Well, Sir—I guess that's all, unless there's something else you want me to—"

"No, Tomás. Just have everything ready for me at the residence, to-morrow," Jim said.

After Tomás and his wife had gone, Jim lay there thinking:

'*¡La Republica de Paranoica!* Damned if this place doesn't get anybody wild. Maybe Grace is right. Maybe I should get out of this madhouse. Resign. Go home—

'And leave poor Jenny in the hands of that bastard. Leave Harper and friends to flood the East Coast with heroin. Leave in power a Government to whom torture is a way of life. Or see decent people—like Vince, like Padre Pío, like Tomás—fall into the hands of murderers when the *next* revolution comes . . .

'Ha! Speaking of delusions of grandeur! A forty-six-year-old miserable little runt named Jim Rush is going to right wrongs, rescue damsels in distress, slay dragons, tilt against windmills!

'No. A forty-six-year-old runt *and* coward is going to—try. To at least not knuckle under to—evil, even when it rides out in overwhelming force. And—fail, surely. But at least making of his failure—how was it that Padre Pío put it? Oh, yes: making of his failure something—worthy of—his forty-three dead. That they cease to haunt him finally. That they lie very quietly there upon his heart. And allow themselves—and him!—a little rest . . .

Upon his return to the Ambassador's residence in the foothills of the Sierras that next day, he followed Doctor Gomez' advice and went back to bed, although he felt very well except for a dull, never-ending headache that resulted from the hairline fracture that granite chip had left in his skull.

Tomás brought him a light lunch on a tray, but before he could eat it, they heard shots. Up the hill behind the residence. Not too far away. Close enough for them to distinguish between the ripping snarl of the

Schmeissers, those World War II surplus Nazi "burp guns" with which the Costa Verdian police were equipped, and the much slower, heavier, staccato kettledrum beat of the modern Ak-47s the guerrillas used. The Ak-47s could be fired as a rifle, shot by shot, thus conserving ammunition, or as a submachine gun, in bursts. They were much more accurate than the Schmeissers, which meant police casualties were becoming heavier every day. But, so far, the guerrillas didn't try to win pitched battles. They hit and ran, leaving death and destruction behind them.

"Again?" Jim said.

"Yes." Tomás said. 'I think it's the same band as of the cemetery, Sir. They never caught up with them, you know. Listen! Quite a fire fight, isn't it? I've never known guerrillas to keep it up this long before . . ."

The gun battle up that hill went on for five full minutes. Jim sat there, sweating, and trying not to shake too visibly, until it died down. Until the silence rode in upon him.

"Tomás—" he began; but the phone rang shrilly. He picked it up, recognizing immediately the sound of an international call.

"Mister Rush?" Grace's voice said.

"Grace!" he said, joy almost strangling him.

"So it's you?" she said. "All right. I swore I'd never call you again. And I won't, after this. Only—I didn't—still don't—believe you could be *this* big a bastard, Jim!"

"Lord!" he said.

"Anyhow, answer me one question: Did you, or did you not, buy four Geri Pyle dresses—for a—friend?"

He hung there. Then he said, sadly: "Yes, Grace."

"A *strange* couple came to my place, last night. Asked me if *I* had the dresses you'd sent. Said that there'd been a shipping mistake. That the wrong sizes, colors, had been sent. Different ones from those you'd ordered . . ."

He thought: 'The filthy swine!' He said: "Look, Grace—"

"*You* look, Jim! I told them that they were the ones who were mistaken. That you'd sent no dresses—at least not to *me*. They apologized profusely, in accented English. Then the woman said: '¡No puede ser ella! ¡Mirela, Juan; esa es demasiada grande!' "

"And you—understood that?"

"No. But I've an excellent ear. So I said it over to Ruth Pinilla in our office. She translated for me, very exactly: 'It can't be she! Look, John, this one's too big!' Therefore: my size again—"

"Grace, please!"

"It's not important, Jim. What is important is that *before,* there was already a girl. A cute, little, dark Latin girl, for who else could wear Geri Pyle's Andean dresses? Certainly not a big horse like me!"

"Grace, you're wrong! I bought those dresses for—the wife of a good friend of mine who—"

"Jim," she said tartly, "idle sex is not a pastime I'm inclined to be especially indulgent towards. You should know that from the sad story of my life. And—you *wanted* me to know, didn't you? To find out? So you could—get even with me—for that call the other day. For the things I said—while in a state of shock. All right, Jim; if it's any comfort to you, this *hurts.* You've cost me a few more—tears. But you won't again. I promise you that. Not *ever.*"

"Grace—" he began; but the crashing sound the phone made as she banged it down upon the cradle guillotined his voice. He said, softly: "Oh, goddamn!" knowing it was no use to call her.

The very next day, after having had the Embassy Secretary phone for an appointment, he presented his credentials to *Don* Manuel García Herredia, Chief of State of the Republic of Costa Verde, and Commander in Chief of its Armed Forces.

Like most career officers in Latin America—since military men of that rank always come from the economically favored segment of the population, and hence even from early childhood get rather too much to eat—the General dwarfed Jim in every dimension. Also, because he was a *Mestizo* of the same Tluscolan-Spanish mixture that Alicia Villalonga was, and hence an improvement over both the parent races, he added to Jim's ever-present inferiority feelings by being a remarkably handsome man as well.

Bending forward and slightly downward in the involuntary gesture that big people always employed towards Jim—and that, in consequence, always set his teeth on edge!—General García greeted the new Ambassador with grave courtesy. The General was accompanied by his Chief of Protocol, Colonel Elias Garay Bustamontes, the Director General of Security, *Don* Raoul Pérez de la Valle, and the Director General's Chief Aide, *Don* Pablo Fuentes Toralba.

"Mr. Ambassador," General García said, after they'd all been seated, "permit me to felicitate you upon your bearing and behavior at the funeral. I quite agree with the newspaper accounts. Show him the papers, Elias!"

Colonel Garay passed them over. *"Gesto Heroico del Embajador Estadounidense,"* one of the headlines read; *"Valiente Comportamiento del Embajador Norteamericano,"* said another; *"Valor y Dignidad,"* the third had placed above a huge photo of his remarkably bloody face.

"I thank you, Your Excellency," Jim said.

"Therefore," General García continued, "I am taking the opportunity to award you *La Orden del Merito Caballeresco,* the highest *condecoración* we are allowed to offer foreigners. Elias, summon the photographers, please!"

"But, Your Excellency!" Jim protested. "Such an honor seems to me entirely undeserved! It hardly seems fitting to receive a medal for merely serving as the bull's-eye for an assassin's bullet!"

"Let us be the judge of that!" General García said. "Your refusals to leave the cemetery and to permit the funerals to be halted even though you were badly wounded have won you the respect of all Costa Verdians and their admiration as well. Have the goodness to stand, Mr. Ambassador . . ."

Jim stood up. General García draped the broad purple ribbon with the huge enamelled gold cross around his neck, embraced him in a rib-crushing *abrazo* while the flashguns of the press photographers made sudden lightnings.

That picture would appear in all the local newspapers, and in a good many foreign ones too, tomorrow, Jim realized. 'And I am sunk,' he thought bitterly; 'A Costa Verdian decoration will ruin a man in any halfway liberal country in the world. Now I need only collect one from Pinochet to finish me off . . .'

"I thank your Excellency, and the People of Costa Verde for this truly undeserved honor," he said.

"Sit and chat a while, Mr. Ambassador," General García said. "Perhaps, between us, we may come up with a solution to the deuced awkward social problem you present!"

"A problem? A *social* problem? I?" Jim said.

"Your lack of a wife, *Don* Jaime!" General García said with heavy joviality. "Quite a problem socially. Winter's coming on. We're below the equator, y'know, so our seasons are the reverse of yours. And winter, due to the fact that our climate becomes rather pleasant at that time of year, is our really festive season. Balls, theater, soirees, the opera, the ballet, horse races, the bull fights, what have you—"

"So I've heard," Jim said.

"But having an eligible bachelor as an Ambassador is, my dear *Don* Jaime, a hell of a note! You've already learned to your sorrow that we've a practically permanent Red insurrection on our hands. But having to handle a female Civil War on top of that is more than I'd bargained for! Raoul, what d'you suggest? That we lock all the unattached young women in the bullring one fine Sunday to engage in a no-holds-barred free for all and award *Don* Jaime here to the winner?"

"That would be hardly fair to *Don* Jaime, himself," the Director General of Security said; "I'd suggest that we stage a beauty contest with our gallant Ambassador as the sole judge. The winner would be awarded the

post of his official hostess for the Winter Season. What other—awards—
Don Jaime may care to confer upon her, or what other—ah—duties—he
may demand of her, would be, of course, up to him—"

"Gentlemen, you do me too much honor!" Jim said. "But may I state
that even your mode of jesting amazes me? I've been stationed in a good
many Latin American countries before now. In fact I was *born* in one,
and spoke your language before learning my own. So I know that the
house rule for operating anywhere Spanish or Portuguese is spoken is:
'Don't criticize the country, and leave the women the hell alone!' "

They laughed at that one, heartily.

"Ah, but we are different, *Señor Embajador!*" Pablo Fuentes said. "We
consider the type of jealousy displayed by our neighbors as primitive and
uncivilized. Not to mention its being *prima facie* evidence of personal in-
security and of an inferiority complex!"

"Jesting aside, *Don* Jaime," General García said then, his voice suddenly grave and fatherly, "I've been told that you lost your dear wife
more than five years ago. While respecting your grief, my friend, it
seems to me—rough old soldier that I am!—that enough of a thing is
enough. Don't you agree it's high time something were done about your
lamentable state of solitude?"

Jim stared at him, thinking: 'So now I'm to be set up for—"The
Treatment," eh, Gentlemen? Because this whole conversation, jokes and
all, is abnormal. It couldn't happen anywhere else in Central or South
America except *here*. No *Latino* I've ever known would invite a thrice
bedamned pig of a *Gringo* to make free with the women of his race! But
here it fits, doesn't it? For this, you investigate even a casual purchase for
a friend, send your spies to molest a woman—the woman I love!—four
thousand miles away in New York. So now, some home-grown Mata
Hari, surely. With, from what Tomás has told me, a striking physical
resemblence to Alicia, if you can find one, waiting in the wings for her
cue! The jest is rich, *Caballeros!* No, ripe's the better word! I'm to be
screwed both fore and aft by remote control, and, through me, my country!*¡De acuerdo!* I'll play along—at least far enough to see how you plan
to work it!'

He said:

"I came to that same conclusion at least two years ago, Your Excellency. But since marriage is a cooperative enterprise requiring a degree of consent from *both* partners, what I concluded is likely to remain
an exercise in futility in view of the unanimous opinion of the entire
female half of humanity—at least in so far as *I* have been able to ascertain!—that they wouldn't have me as a Christmas gift!"

"Nonsense!" General García laughed. "You underestimate yourself,

Amigo Rush! Now, tell me, which do you prefer: *¿rubias o morenas?* Of course, blondes would be more difficult, because we have so few; but even so, there are some . . ."

'That photograph!' Jim thought with sudden amazement. 'That Polaroid color shot Tim took! But I tore it up! So how—'

He said: "Why? Do you propose to find me a wife, *mi General?*

"Heaven forbid!" the General said. "Matrimony isn't a state I'd inflict upon any man! To tell the truth, *Don* Jaime, I am only relaying a question put to me by *my* wife. I run the country, but *mi* Luisa runs me. And your single blessedness has become *the* burning issue among the good wives of Ciudad Villalonga. They haven't had so excellent an opportunity to try their hands at matchmaking in years. I'll do what I can to protect you, of course; but what I—what any mere man—can do isn't much, *Don* Jaime! When the ladies—bless them!—scent the quarry running free in the sole blood sport they truly enjoy, only a miracle can prevent their dragging him to earth. So what shall I tell *mi adorable y adorada* Luisa, so that she may more accurately revise a list running to five folio pages now?"

"That—'In the dark, all cats are grey,' *mi General,*" Jim said solemnly.

"Ha! That's a good line! And it's true, isn't it? But enough of this subject—this tiresome subject of matrimony. I'd much rather help you find a gentle and submissive little mistress, though Luisa and her league of liberated women would probably drag us both before an all-female firing squad in *la Plaza de la Liberación* if I tried that! Anyhow, I have a present for you; one that I fervently hope you'll make use of in order to prevent any more—incidents like that of the cemetery . . ."

"A present, *mi General?*" Jim said.

"Yes," General García said, and rang for his manservant. "Bring me that box off the hall table, Matias," he said when the majordomo appeared.

The man was back within minutes with a large cardboard box. Coming up to Jim, he bowed and held it out.

Jim took the box, opened it. Inside was a sort of khaki bush jacket that looked thick and heavy enough to suffocate within minutes any man who tried to wear it in this climate.

"It's a bulletproof vest," the General said. "The very latest model. Pick it up, *Don* Jaime. See how light it is?"

It *was* surprisingly light. In fact it weighed less than a third of what he had expected it to from the way it looked.

"Lightest *Chaleco Antibala* made," the General said. "The sheet armor is very thin and flexible. Doesn't stop the bullets. All it does is give with them and slow them down so much that the fiber batting under the steel and plastic armor catches them. In fact the bullets actually spin themselves a cocoon in the fiber, thus stopping themselves dead in twenty of the one hundred millimeter thickness of batting available. Always works. We've tried .44 magnum, .357 magnum, and 9 mm full-jacket Parabellum ammunition against it, with a living man wearing it. He got a couple of bruises from the heavy stuff fired at point blank range, that was all. Want to try it?"

Jim stared at him.

"You mean you want me to put this thing on and let some one *shoot* at me?" he whispered.

"Not if you don't want to, *Don* Jaime," General García said. "Tell you what: We'll put it on the Director General here, and let you shoot at *him*."

Jim saw Raoul Pérez de la Valle's face turn grey.

'So—here we have the opposition!' he thought; 'Pérez de la Valle and Fuentes Toralba! And this wiley old bastard knows it. Neat trick to have the American Ambassador kill one of them . . .'

He said, ruefully:

"*Mi General,* you see before you the biggest coward in the Western Hemisphere. My hands would shake so that nobody in range would be safe. I'd probably shoot off my own big toe plus the Director General's nose and assassinate a passing nun. I thank you most sincerely for your gift, but I'll take your word for its virtues and leave it untried until the next time our Red friends take a potshot at me . . ."

Thereafter, as soon as he could gracefully do so, he pled fatigue and a lingering weakness from his wound and asked to be excused. Again General García embraced him as did the others. The Director General of Security with real gratitude, Jim thought.

Roberto brought the car around and they started back to the residence, no more than a pleasant hour's drive away. But, sitting there, engulfed hip deep in the almost sinful luxury of the limousine's back seat, and holding on his knees that cardboard box containing a perfect example of the kind of obscenely insane dead ends that the twentieth century of Western civilization seemed somehow to always come to, Jim Rush had the ice cold, unshakable premonition that they weren't going to get there at all, at least not alive, and the even bitterer conviction that whether they did or did not was a question of so little importance that it wasn't even worth thinking about. So he didn't think about it. He simply sat there and sweated like an overdriven horse, in spite of the tomblike chill the air-conditioner reduced the temperature inside the car to.

But his premonition turned out to be wrong. They got there on time and without anything's happening at all. Yet, looking back over the chain of events growing out of that night, Jim Rush wondered whether his own arrival at the residence alive and unhurt on that particular night was good luck or the very worst he'd ever had.

Thinking the whole thing over carefully, he finally came to the conclusion that it had been a little of each, injudiciously mixed.

The way a man's luck generally is in this world.

CHAPTER

13

*T*he first thing Jim saw when they came up to the gates of the residence was the little Volkswagen Golf parked just outside them. Now the Golf is the model of Volkswagen known in the States as the "Rabbit" and, he knew, was not yet manufactured in any of the Volkswagen plants outside of Germany, itself. Which meant this sporty little car had been imported, since only the ancient and much beloved "Beetle" was made in Costa Verde so far.

And that, in its turn, meant that the car belonged to a member of Costa Verde's idle rich, for the import duties on foreign cars—that is, cars not manufactured under license in the Republic—were absolutely outrageous. What's more, to judge from the paint job, lemon yellow with a vile green stripe nearly twenty centimeters wide sweeping from hood to trunk, from bonnet to boot, across the sides of it, this car belonged to some member of the younger generation.

"Now what the devil!" he said to Roberto.

Henriques let a slow and knowing grin steal across his face.

"Some youngster's car, Sir!" he said. "Out of gas, surely. Perhaps when your friend, *Señor* Crowley, starts piping the petroleum his prospectors have found offshore in to us, the kids will be able to wheedle enough *pesos* out of their fathers to buy sufficient gasoline to get back home . . ."

"But anyone who can afford an imported model like that one—"

"As a matter of fact, the owner of that Golf probably *can't* afford it, Sir," Henriques said. "Only his—or her—father can. And is using the dreadfully high cost of *gasolina* as a disciplinary measure, I'd say; rationing son or daughter so that he or she doesn't wander too far afield. Or— even as a punishment for some past escapade. The young, today, Sir, are difficult. I have teen-aged youngsters myself, and I know. Not even a peeled tamarind branch applied to their hides works any longer . . ."

"Roberto—" Jim said, "couldn't this be some trick of the Reds to—"

"Of course not, Sir! They'd never use such a flamboyant vehicle as this. A black Beetle, with altered license plates, parked around the corner would worry me; but this one doesn't. You can trust my judgment, Mr. Ambassador. I have had much experience in these matters . . ."

'I don't doubt that,' Jim thought; 'what I doubt is—'

But he didn't know exactly what it was he doubted. It was, somehow, a part of the premonition that had gripped him ever since they had left the Presidential Palace. It seemed to him that even Roberto's very complacency was suspect. He had never known his "chauffeur," bodyguard, security-spy, to be complacent about anything before. He would have sworn that Roberto left nothing to chance, that the big man wouldn't trust his own mother. And now here was *Teniente Colonel* Henriques of *La Seguridad Nacional,* accepting the presence of this little car parked before the very gates of the residence as though it meant nothing at all, or—

As though he had known it was going to be there.

The more Jim considered that thought, the more convincing it became. "The Treatment." Now. Tonight. Some daughter of a wealthy family who could afford an imported car, compelled to play the whore because García and Company had her father, brother, lover in their torture chambers and could—

The very idea made him sick. 'How little they know me!' he thought.

Roberto sounded the horn. The guards tumbled out of the sentry boxes, opened the gates for them. The big car swept majestically up the drive.

Roberto held the door open for Jim to get out.

"Sir," he said; "I don't suppose you'll be needing me or the car anymore *tonight,* will you?"

Had he really emphasized that word "tonight"? Jim couldn't be sure. 'Probably my goddamned nerves,' he thought.

"No, Roberto, all I need tonight is twelve solid hours of sleep," Jim said.

"Oh, I'm sure you'll get them!" Roberto said in a tone of voice that all but stated he was sure of the exact opposite. "A *very* good night to you, Sir!"

Jim went up the stairs. The two U.S. Marines he was permitted as guards, since the residence, as well as the Embassy, was included in the Extraterritorial Agreement between the two countries, grinned at him as they saluted. With—approval. With a damned sight *too* much approval, Jim decided.

But if there were any one thing that twenty-five years in the Diplomatic Corps taught a man, it was where to draw the line. However much he may have admired the clean-cut, sturdy young specimens of American manhood that most Marines were—and he *did* admire them— he knew only too well the dangers of fraternizing with them. Discipline—and dignity—could only be maintained by keeping one's distance.

He said: "Goodnight, boys."

And they: "Goodnight, Mr. Ambassador!"

Had he heard—or only imagined—a chuckle in their voices?

When he came into the hall, Tomás was there waiting for him.

"Sir!" the majordomo hissed. "Upstairs—in your bedroom! A—a young woman, Sir!"

He stared at Tomás. Said, reproachfully:

"And you didn't put her out?"

"Can't be done, Sir. Better to find out *who* sent her. And *why*. Besides—" Tomás stopped, grinned; "I thought I'd better let you have a look at her, Mr. Ambassador, before putting her out."

Jim stood there. Said:

"Good Lord, Tomás! Don't tell me it's that little model!"

"No, Sir," Tomás said. "But, rather a bit—better, for my money. No; a great deal better. If—our positions were reversed, Sir—and someone put an article of *that* degree of class out of my bedroom without letting me judge for myself the—well—advisability of such action, I should be annoyed, Sir—very!"

"Oh, don't be a fool, Tomás! It stands to reason they'd send a beauty. But you might have saved me the trouble of being ungentlemanly. Oh, I say! *Who* knows she's up there? Besides you, I mean?"

"The guards on the gates, Sir. The Marines."

"The *Marines*!"

"Yes, Sir. She let them search her handbag. Showed them her stocking tops. For—a concealed knife, y'know? They—enjoyed that. She finally let one of them—pass his hands—all over her—routine search. Only, from a couple of things she called him, I gather he got carried away . . ."

"But what did she *tell* them?"

"That she was—'Your Little Friend'—I think that was the way she put it, Sir . . ."

"Oh God!" Jim said.

"Sir," Tomás said, "don't be—hasty. I mean, don't be in too big a hurry to put her out . . ."

Jim stared at him. Said:

"Why not, Tomás?"

"Failure to accomplish her mission—could cost her a great deal, Sir. Her life, perhaps. The life of—someone dear to her . . ."

"Goddamnit, Tomás!"

"It's true, Sir. You *know* it is."

Jim thought about that. About the things Alicia Reynolds—but more especially Marisol O'Rourke—had told him. How Costa Verde's *Seguridad Nacional* recruited the last women on earth a man would suspect of ulterior motives to do its filthy work. Doubly filthy since the women so used were far more victims of the system's remorseless and implacable cruelty than were the foreign business executives, diplomats, military men, scientists, they were sent to corrupt, seduce, betray. And, in his own case, at least, a bitterly ironical core of futility lay at the heart of the whole operation, making the very idea of loosing one of their essentially pitiful little female spies upon him an error of appreciation of several orders of magnitude. That error lay in the fact—vastly compounded, of course, by their flat refusal to believe it even *after* it had been pointed out to them—that it was simply beyond his power to do *any* of the various things they meant to seduce or blackmail him into.

That he had friends of his own and of his father who sat in Congress and the Senate? True. That several of them, especially his father's friends, held positions of power and influence—were even, some few of them anyhow, chairmen of certain foreign aid and/or military appropriations committees? Likewise true.

But Catch Thirty-five—as he knew from sad experience!—grew out of the absolute impossibility of ever convincing people with authoritarian minds, dictatorial temperaments, and who, moreover, have spent much of their lives ruling countries like Costa Verde, how little that meant. It was inconceivable to General García that if he, Jim Rush, were to suggest to his best friend in Congress that military appropriations to Costa Verde ought to be increased, and that scientific antipersonnel and/or search and destroy weapons, specifically designed to combat guerrilla insurrectionists should be provided that country, his best friend would merely grin at him and say, "Jim-Boy, I wouldn't give those bastards the time of day!" and then invite him out for a friendly drink. What's more, he could *tell* the General that, textually, in so many words, and García wouldn't believe him. He'd simply assume that Jim was lying, for reasons of state, or of his own, as he, Manuel García, damned well would under like circumstances.

That said—or rather thought—the problem of what to do about the young woman upstairs became thorny. For many, if not most other men, the solution would have been simple: Drag the poor little bitch off to bed and make her no promises! But he wasn't most other men; he was himself. Never in his life had he been able to separate sex from love, a trick most men find as normal as breathing. 'In fact,' he thought now wryly, 'what they find difficult is combining them. While I—every damned time I've tried to make use of a whore—'

He'd failed. And he had tried. On several occasions, driven by abysmal loneliness, utter desperation. But he couldn't. He had never wanted merely a woman's body. He wanted the whole woman, both before, during, and after. He needed to talk with her, laugh with her, fight with her, cry with her, want her. Sitting beside him with her head resting against his shoulder, silently. Walking with him through a swirl of autumn leaves wind-driven down a country lane. Stopping in midsentence to smile at him suddenly, let a caressing hand stray across his face. Hold out to him the little, red, wrinkled, squalling bundle that was—his continuation in time, and hers—their joint immortality—the only kind there was, he suspected—certainly the only one that mattered.

What he might have had with Grace if only—

He sighed; said:

"Yes, I suppose it is true, isn't it? Don't worry, Tomás; I'll be very gentle with this young person . . ."

Then very slowly, he went up those stairs.

When he came into his bedroom she was lying sprawled out in his bed, smoking a cigarette. And her clothes were very carefully folded and draped over the back of a chair.

'The way,' he realized suddenly, bitterly, 'a real pro would do it. One who's got a dozen or so "tricks" scheduled for tonight. So that she can arrive at the flat of "John" Number Ten, not looking *much* more used than she had when she'd got to her first "John's" place.'

She wasn't under the covers. She lay on top of them, naked. And now he realized fully what the qualifying—and vulgar—adjectives "stark," "mother"—when placed before "naked"—meant.

As he crossed to the disguised jamming transmitter that Carlos Suarez had installed for him, to switch it on—he definitely wasn't going to have *this* conversation recorded for posterity!—he was thinking: 'Damned if she isn't the nakedest naked woman I've ever seen!'

He wondered why this was so. Part of it, he suspected, lay in her aspect of sheer animality. Most women, he knew, looked far more sen-

sual clothed than nude. And the more harmonious, slender, graceful
their bodies were, the more this was so. Unclothed they took on the
look of living sculpture, works of art, and, especially if they belonged to
the fairer, more Nordic segments of the Caucasian race, whatever little
sensuality, purely sexual attraction, they possessed, vanished completely.

He thought: 'I've known some beautiful blondes. But the 'Sexy
Blonde Bombshell' is a creation of Hollywood. In life she doesn't exist.
But this adobe-and-pitch fetish-doll, this image of unmitigated carnal-
ity—dear God!'

The girl there on his bed wasn't white. Start with that. She had some
white ancestry, of course. Spanish, surely. But at least two other strains
had gone into this creation, this masterpiece: Tluscolan and Black. Her
skin was tawny. Golden. She hadn't a surplus gram on her anywhere.
She was thin. Damned thin. The bones of her rib cage showed. And yet
her thinness wasn't unpleasant. Because she was also so—his mind
groped for the adjectives—lithe? Sculptured? No. Say trained down,
race horse fine.

And—animal. He kept coming back to that. Controlled, but, at bottom, a jungle she-thing. Feline. Watchful. But, when aroused, utterly
savage. Feral. Wild. The nakedest, bitchi-est, goddamnedest *female*
woman he'd seen in all his life. Lying there sprawled out, her skin glistening with a fine dew of sweat, peering at him above a pair of darkly
areoled, small and perfect breasts, out of slanted, almond-shaped Tluscolan eyes—and, now he saw it, saw like a fist-smash into his face the abysmal contempt of the gesture, twining one lock of the longest, blackest,
highest standing bush of pubic hair he'd ever encountered in any human
being (was she real? Or a Voodoo witch doll, devil made?) around one
slender finger, deliberately to catch his eye.

He tore his gaze away. Said:

"Get up. Get dressed. Get out."

She smiled; and his breath stopped. Because she *was* Alicia. Fifteen,
sixteen, seventeen years younger. And far more beautiful than Alicia had
ever been.

She said:

"I do not—do *this*—to divert myself, Mr. Ambassador. Nor do I find
Gringos attractive. Especially not short, dried up, ugly little *Gringos*. I
usually get paid, y'know. And you've made me waste my time."

He said, very quietly:

"How much?"

"A—hundred—dollars?" she said tentatively.

He knew she didn't get that much. Not in Costa Verde. Twenty-five
at the very best. An occasional fifty, maybe.

He took out his wallet. Counted out a hundred and fifty dollars. Said, evenly:

"The extra fifty's for your wasted time. Now I'll leave you to get dressed. But I want you out of here in ten minutes."

She took the money. Stuffed it into her handbag. Abruptly her expression changed. Her lovely, thick-lipped, sullen mouth tightened.

'With worry, surely,' he thought. 'Now she's remembering the consequences of—failure . . .'

"*Don* Jeemie—" she whispered, slumberously; "don't you like me? Am I not—pretty?"

"You're beautiful," he said honestly; "but no, I *don't* like you. I can buy—an animal. I prefer—a woman. The highest creation of God. Having one quality I find essential for communication."

"And this quality is, *Don* Jeemie?"

He looked at her. Said, very, very quietly:

"A soul."

Her eyes leaped and flared in the darkness of her face. Then they turned inward, lid hooded. But not before he had seen the pain in them. Bitter. And very deep.

"You are right," she said; "I am—a zombie. I have no soul. Men—starting with my father—killed it long ago."

He said:

"I'll leave you now. Get dressed. That's your car out front, isn't it? The little yellow Golf?"

"Yes. It was given to me by my Protector who was a Minister of the Government. Only the Reds ambushed his car on the road to Chizenaya last month. So now he is dead."

There wasn't the faintest hint of regret in her voice, saying that.

"Good," Jim said coldly; "then I don't have to call for a taxi to take you home." He started towards the door.

"*Don* Jeemie—wait! Don't go! Take back your money! I—I will love you—for nothing—"

He said, pointing at the transmitter.

"*They* cannot hear what we say. That radio prevents it. Drowns out our voices. So they do not know what you have said—or done. Nor, more to the point, what you have *not* done. And I have no intention of telling them. So be a good girl. Put your clothes on. Go."

"It—would be—better—if you made love—to me," she whispered; "or—at least—had sex—with me . . ." Then she added with aching bitterness, "Which is seldom the same thing—as making *love*, is it?"

"It would not be better. I do not want to," he said.

"I—I haven't a sickness," she said.

"I know that."

"Then—why not?"

He shrugged.

"Too hard to explain. And you're perfectly safe. I shall not tell them."

"Why not? Why won't you tell them?"

"Because I don't want you tortured. Or killed. Nor someone dear to you, either. I've enough on my conscience, now."

"Oh!" she said. "So you knew!"

"Yes," he said; "I knew. Come on now, get dressed."

"*Don* Jeemie—make love to me. I will give you great pleasure!"

"You will give me great nausea. Which is what fakery always does."

"*Don* Jeemie—at least—at least do not put me out. If I have to leave too soon, they—"

He studied her. Said, tiredly:

"You may stay the night. In another room. You may tell them I made love to you. I will not contradict what you must say . . ."

She stared at him, whispered:

"You are—very rare."

"I am very tired. Old. And I have forty-three burdens too many now, upon my heart."

"*Don* Jeemie," she said; "let me stay—in here. With you. I—I will not touch you. Or trouble you. Only—it is too sad, being alone . . ." She stopped, whispered: "*¡Dios mío!*"

He whirled at the sharp intake of her breath. Saw the boy standing in the doorway of his bathroom. Seventeen. Eighteen. No more. In jungle camouflage fatigues. Leaning against the frame of the door that had been closed up until that very moment, Jim was sure. The boy was trembling. Trying not to fall. Blood was still seeping out of him slowly. His uniform was plastered to his thin body with it. Some of it had dried. He stank. Of blood. Of sweat. Of urine. Of feces. Of the beginnings of gangrene, maybe. He had three days' growth of sparse boyish beard. His eyes were bloodshot. They seemed not to focus properly. He had an automatic pistol, a German Walther P-38, dangling from his hand.

"*¡Puta!*" he said. "Whore!"

She said, whispering the words:

"Who art thou?"

"Thy executioner," he croaked. "He who deals out justice upon such as thee. Upon—filth. Things of bad milk. Women of our race so wanting in honor that they couch themselves with *Gringos*!"

"No!" she said. "Oh, no! I—"

"What is thy name?" the boy said. "Who is it I am going to have the pleasure of killing? Go on, Thing Without Shame! Speak! Tell me: How art thou called?"

"Trini—" she breathed, her voice very nearly inaudible.

"All of it! All thy names, whore! That I may know if thou'rt she I sought. And didst thou know Ana Ferrero?"

"My names are María de la Sagrada Trinidad Alvarez Bermejo," she said then calmly, sadly, with perfect resignation; "and yes, I am whom you seek—the companion of—Anita."

"¡Sagrada! ¡Sagrada Puta! Sacred Whore! Wallowing with Gringo pigs! So say a prayer, little Trini! For I am going to—kill thee very slowly. Disembowel thee. Cut out with my knife—those parts of womanhood thou hast let a Gringo befoul. Pray—that God receive thee. As he—received the Magdalene. I—no longer believe in God—but pray, anyhow. Perhaps—"

"Look, Son—" Jim whispered.

"Thy mother, Gringo! Thou who hast befouled a woman of my people—thinkest thou I'll let thee live?"

"Let her go, Son," Jim got out. "It's not her fault. She was forced to—" His voice died.

"You're shaking," the wounded boy jeered. "You have no testicles, Gringo! You are afraid."

"Yes," Jim said slowly, sadly; "I am afraid. No man wants to die, Son. But I—I do not plead for me. Nor ask my life. Only hers. Trini's. Who had no choice. Who—"

"No choice? This companion of my sister's—at the Blue Moon? Who brought poor Anita—the drugs—that have enslaved her? This bitch? This born whore? ¿Esa sin vergüenza? ¿Esa impúdica, licenciosa, lasciva, deshonesta, deshonorada, vilemente vil cosa de toda mala leche?"

"¡Decarada!" he screamed, and whirling, slammed the gun across Trini's face, knocking her from the bed so that she lay collapsed and trembling on the floor. Stood there above her, aiming the Walther at the back of her close-cropped head.

And he, Jim, strangling on the vile green tide of nausea exploding upward in his throat, feeling the sudden scald of urine escaping his control and pouring obscenely down his legs, screaming to himself silently or maybe even aloud, he did not know which and it didn't matter a good goddamn:

'Move! Goddamn you, you miserable coward, move! Forty-three are damned well enough, so move, get going, go on, you ball-less wonder, move!'

And lurching forward through air gone viscous, clinging to his shoulder arms legs like slimy invisible tentacles, dragging against the strides he was not even sure he was making through that nightmare dreamscape prolonging itself endlessly along the dimensions of space of time, he nonetheless got there, by his own shame-filled self-loathing driven, well within that dead stopped interval with margin enough left over to—

Catch the boy as he loosened all over, slumped, gave out on his feet finally, falling.

Jim lay him down very gently on the floor beside Trinidad, took the pistol from his inert hand and dropped it into his own jacket pocket.

"Thou!" Trini whispered. "Thou hast killed him!"

"No," Jim said tiredly, "he lives."

"And now—thou wilt call the police. And they—dost thou know what they will do to him?"

"I know. Which is why I am *not* going to call them. Get some clothes on, Trini! You heard me, woman, move!"

She leaped to her feet. Whirled, snatching at her clothes.

'And I thought Grace was graceful!' he thought.

He picked up the phone, dialed Vicente Gomez' number. His house, not the hospital. When he had yelled and cursed his way through three servants, he heard Vince's voice finally saying with terrible weariness:

"*¡Diga! ¿Quien es?*"

"Vince. This is Jim. Jim Rush. Come over here. Now. Please."

"Jim! Good Lord! What's wrong? Are you dizzy? Seeing double? Can you focus your eyes? Does your head—"

"Vince—please. Now. The residence. Or it will be too late," Jim said.

"I've done all I can here," Vince said. "This fool kid should have been in the hospital since yesterday. He needs a transfusion desperately. Within the next two hours, or he won't make it, Jim. You could give him blood. His guerrilla dog tags list his type: A positive, the same as yours. Only I haven't the equipment here. So I'll have to call for an ambulance. And when the guards on the gates see that, they're going to alert Security so damned fast . . ."

Trini sat there, listening to all that flood of English, her eyes big with wonder.

"Tomás," Jim said in Spanish, "get these rags off him. Put my pyjamas on him. He's no bigger than I am. They'll fit . . ."

"But—" Vince began.

Jim grinned.

"I was—overambitious. Tried a few too many, and too vigorous, horizontal acrobatics with dear little Trini here, for a man of my age, who has an unhealed head wound on top of his—other disabilities. Such as being—short, dried up, and ugly—eh, Trini, dearest?"

"*Don* Jaime, please!" she said, and astonishingly, her eyes filled up with sudden tears.

"So—I relapsed. Passed out. The type on the stretcher is going to be *me* as far as both the Marines and the guards are concerned. Here, Tomás, put my watch on his wrist, and my ring on his finger. Let that hand hang out. But turn his head sideways and cover his face as much as you can. All right?"

"Good!" Vince said. "Whatever this poor, half starved little bastard may have done, it doesn't merit being tortured to death for. We're in perfect agreement on that point, my friend. And I can control my staff, most of whom have excellent reasons for not loving His Nibs and Chums excessively, anyhow. Besides, my people are personally loyal to me, every one of them. If this extravagantly ventilated little piece of Swiss cheese doesn't die on me on the operating table, we ought to get away with this caper handily enough . . ."

"Trini," Jim said; "you tell the guards you're going to the hospital to see after me. Act agitated, will you? Say a couple of times it was all your fault—"

"It *was*," she said morosely.

"Nonsense! Then drive that little yellow submarine of your all the way around to the back service entrance of this house. No guards there, are there, Tomás? Gates are locked, aren't they?"

"*Now*," Tomás said. "But they will be unlocked before you get downstairs, Sir!"

"Put some oil on the hinges, damnit!" Jim said. He turned back to the girl; said:

"Look, *Niña*, I'm going downstairs and out back *now*. Before the ambulance gets here and alerts the guards. You wait for it to arrive before picking me up. I'll lie down between the front and back seats of your car so I won't be seen. All right?"

"All right, *Don* Jaime," Trinidad said.

So it was done. And it worked, because like all really good plans its simplicity bordered upon elegance. An hour later, Jim lay on a hospital bed a little way from another in which they had put the unconscious boy, and watched the dark red tide of his own blood seep through the tubes and the flasks into the wounded guerrilla's arm. For the moment, he and the boy were alone in the room. Vince had gone to get more plasma. Out of consideration for his staff, he'd decided to involve as few as possible in the matter. Only those he couldn't do without, and them only much later, when he had to operate. Dr. Guttierez, his assistant, the anesthetist, and the head surgical nurse. That few he could both protect and control. So, therefore, Vince was procuring his own supplies instead of ringing for an orderly to bring them. What his people didn't know, couldn't hurt them. Or get them tortured, he thought.

Jim looked at the badly wounded boy. 'I am perhaps saving a life,' he thought. 'Better than taking one. A great deal better. One—for one, Padre Pío's God? But where will I find forty-two more to make up for the rest?'

He was thinking that when Trini came through the door and stood there staring at him. He thought: 'I don't like the name Trinidad, but what else can I call her? María? Hell, ninety-seven percent of all the women of the Spanish-speaking countries are named María, which is why, I suppose, we *never* call them that. No, it's always the "of the" part of their names that's used. Dolores instead of María de los Dolores. Mercedes for María de los Mercedes. De la Asunción. De la Anunciación. Del Carmen. Del Amparo. Del Buen Consuelo. De la Mar. Del Sol. Of every damned thing. Do I know even ten Spanish girls whose names *don't* start with María? Or even three? So, little Mary of the Sacred Trinity, we're stuck with Trini, now, henceforth, and forever more. And here we are, you and I. In the same room, but light years apart. And I'm sorry. I'm very sorry. We might have given each other something to remember, you and I . . .'

She came closer to his bed. He saw then, with a breath-stopping surge of pain, of pity, the tears that were literally flooding her dark face. Then, very slowly, with that absolutely incredible grace of motion that she had, that linked her in his mind with Grace Nivens, and contrasted at the same time the two of them because beyond that shared characteristic they were nothing alike, she drifted down, sighed down, a brown leaf blown, a wisp of storm cloud sinking, sinking, beside his bed, took his free hand and pressed the soft wet wine-scald of her mouth to his palm, let it cling and quiver there until the aching pity in him was a little death.

"Trini—no!" he said reproachfully.

"Thou hast much right, *Don* Jaime," she whispered, using the intimate *"Tú"* form of address to him, which she had no right to since he was neither kindred nor lover, though perhaps sufficiently a friend, forgetting that the differences between them, of rank, of station, of age, of respectability even, demanded that she say respectfully *"Usted,"* "You," instead of *"Tú,"* "Thou." "It is—a—a presumption of me to—kiss thy hand. To—dirty it—with the lips of—a whore . . ."

"Trini!" he said.

"But, allow me this—little—wilt thou not? Afterwards thou canst call for water and wash it. For I have *never* known another like thee— who liest there now, giving thy blood to save the life of one who would have slain thee . . ."

"He has suffered—much, the poor little fellow," Jim said.

"And thou—thou *art* much!" she stormed. "Thou whom I called little—and dried up—and ugly—"

"*¡Dios!*" Jim said. "And now I am no longer little and dried up and ugly?"

"No," she said solemnly. "Now thou'rt—beautiful, if a man can be called beautiful. For thy soul is. And all of thee hath become handsome in my eyes. For now, they see thee truly, as thou art. *Don* Jaime, may I say a thing?"

"Of course, Child," he said.

"It is—a grave thing, *Don* Jaime."

"Grave?" he said.

"*Gravísimo.* But may I say it, please? I—I *need* to say it. It—hurts within me, wanting to be said."

"Then say it, Child," he said.

"And thou—wilt not be offended? Insulted? Thou wilt not curse at me—or—or—strike me?"

"Good God!" he said. "Trini, I have never cursed or struck a woman in all my life! And I certainly don't propose to begin with you."

"No," she whispered; "Thou wouldst not. For thou art good—all the way through. Very well, I shall say it: *Don* Jaime, I—I love thee. I—am thine. I am thine, forever. For as long as I shall live."

He lay there staring at her wordlessly.

She kissed his hand again, murmuring into the palm of it.

"This distresses thee, I know. There is—no honor in the love—of a whore. But for me it is—grave. It—it changes everything. *Don* Jaime, dost thou know truth when it is said? Then hear this; I have *never* loved a man before. I did not believe I could. All I have known of men awoke in me only—disgust and hatred . . . ."

Hearing how she pronounced those two words, *"asco y odio,"* he didn't, couldn't doubt her. What he did doubt, could not accept was this sudden—fixation, this almost classically Freudian transference of the thwarted, all but crippled emotions of this lovely, forlorn child upon himself. It was wrong—all wrong. It spelt tragedy. 'Forty-six and what?' he thought. 'Eighteen, nineteen, no more. If that . . .'

But he didn't ask her her actual age. He didn't dare. In a tropical country like Costa Verde she could easily be fifteen and look the way she did. And that would have been too much. Insupportably too much. 'My little Electra,' he thought; 'and I the too beloved father figure, your substitute for dead Agamemnon? No, Child, it cannot be!'

"Trini—you mustn't," he said gently; "this is a madness. You do not know—"

"The man who *offered* his life for mine? The life of—an Ambassador—

a great man—for the life of a whore? Who said? 'I do not plead for me. Nor ask my life. Only hers, Trini's.' Thou didst not say that? I was mad, and my ears deceived me?"

"Well—look, Trini, there are things that—"

"And who was it who walked into the muzzle of a loaded gun? Took it from him at clothes-burning range? Two or three other people? The soldiers on the gates? Your filthy Marines who—pawed my breasts, and ran their hands all the way up between my thighs?"

"I did *not* walk into the muzzle of his pistol. He had fainted. I took it away from him afterwards. And you—whom equally he would have killed, begged me to save him from the police . . ."

"He is—of my race. My people. My kind. Poor like me. Helpless like me. And he—would have done well to have killed me. I should have thanked him for it."

"Now, Trini—"

"Thanked him!" she said, her voice a slow, deep shudder, the revulsion in it soul deep, maybe. "For that favor! What am I alive? A whore. Dirt. Offal. Two breasts to be slobbered over, bitten. Two legs with a hairy little slit between them for men—dirty, stinking, hateful men!—to pump their filth up into!"

He thought:

'What can I say to that? What, Padre Pío's God? Didn't *You* put ugliness into this world? Aren't *You* finally responsible—for evil?'

She looked at him, said, crying:

"Wilt take me as thy mistress, *Don* Jaime? For if thou dost not, I shall starve. No one would give me work. I am too well known. And this of—of selling myself to men is finished. I love thee, so I cannot shame thee, thus. Nor myself—for one who can feel what thou hast made me feel for thee, has—*must* have—a certain value!"

Vicente Gomez came back into the room.

"You get out of here, Trini!" he said.

"No," Jim said, "let her stay, Vince. I'm enjoying her company . . ."

"All right. But you will cease to yell, Trini. Or I shall call in the police and have you hauled downtown for soliciting on the premises!"

"Vince!" Jim said reproachfully.

"You have to handle these little tramps with a firm hand, Jim, my friend," Vince said, "or else they'll make bloody nuisances of themselves, and you'll have no peace . . ."

He bent down, examined the flow of the blood in the tubes.

" 'S all right. Another five minutes. I should keep a nurse in here, but for obvious reasons this transfusion must be neither recorded nor witnessed. I've the kid down as a hit and run accident victim. Found on the highway without identification. Trini will keep her mouth shut, I'm sure. By now she's learned how or she wouldn't have any teeth left. I'm going back to my office to head off the police should they come or phone. Trini, you be quiet, and leave *Don* Jaime in peace, damn you!"

After Vince had gone, Trini sat there by Jim's bed and cried. Silently, wordlessly, terribly, endlessly. It was not to be borne. At least Jim was not equipped to bear it.

"Trini—" he said.

"You see how I am treated?" she whispered. "Oh—if I were not— bad! If someone—anyone—God All-powerful Himself—could make me—decent—again.*¡Una chica honesta!* A—good—girl. A virgin. For thee—a virgin. So that I could give—*thee*—my virginity. And all my love—forever. And—and sons! Many sons!"

"Not to mention a daughter or two," he teased her solemnly.

"Yes! Yes! And daughters! Who would adore thee as daughters always adore their Papas. As I did mine, until—"

"Until what, Trini?"

"No! That is too shameful. It is not my wish to distress thee, *Don* Jaime . . ."

"Tell me!" he said, his voice commanding, stern.

"My father—" she whispered; "my father—" Then she sat there and shook. All over. It was very nearly the most horrifying sight he had ever seen.

"Tell me!"

"My father—violated me—when I—was—thirteen years old . . ."

"Dear God!" he said.

"There—was—a reason," she said softly, slowly. "When I was born—Miguel Villalonga was still Dictator . . . And he—and his half brother Luis Sinnombre—had the custom of driving through the streets—and simply bearing away—any *chica* who struck their fancy . . ."

"And?" Jim said.

"And—my mother—caught their eye. She was very beautiful, *Don* Jaime. So they took her to the remote villa they kept—for the purpose of amusing themselves . . . You understand that there was *nothing* my father could do to defend—or save—his wife, don't you? When they tired of her, they brought her back to him. Pregnant—with me. Gave him a high-sounding job with a huge salary . . ."

"And he *took* it?"

"He had to, *Don* Jaime. Or else—die. Very slowly, and very badly, you understand. So he took it, went on living with my mother, and watching me grow to look more like *them*, like *la muy zorra de mi tía* Alicia every day!"

"Now you're being unjust, Trini. I *know* your Aunt Alicia. She is anything but a bitch."

"She betrayed her own brother! Her country! Ran away with a pig of a *Gringo* and—"

"*I* am a pig of a *Gringo,* Trini," he said.

"No! No! Thou'rt my love, *Don* Jaime! From now on—my *only* love, for whom I'd die before I'd dishonor or betray! Ohhhh! If I only could get out of *la mala vida*! Live decently! So that one day—perhaps thou couldst—even—forgive my past—or forget it—for God knows I love thee so!"

"Trini," he said, knowing that this was a train of thought, a dream it was unwise to let her pursue. "You were telling me about your father—"

"Yes. He came home—drunk. He usually came home drunk. Whereupon I would hide, so that he would not curse and beat me. But that day we did not expect him to come home, so I was sleeping the *siesta*. I had on—only a white nightgown—very thin—and he saw—the—the shadow of the hair—y'know—down *there*—which told him I was—grown up—a woman. And that—inflamed him."

She bent her head, wept.

"It's all right, little Trini," Jim said.

"It is *not* all right!" she stormed. "It will never be all right again. For afterwards, when he had come to his senses—he—he killed himself. He put both barrels of his shotgun in his mouth. Pushed down on the triggers with his great toe and—"

"Dear God!" Jim said again.

"My mother hated me after that, *Don* Jaime. I—left home. Ran away. I had to. I could not—face her eyes. And I was not brave enough to—either—kill myself—or starve—so . . ."

Vince came into the room. Examined the plasma and the blood flasks, the tubes.

"That's it," he said, and shut the clamps. Slipped the needle out of Jim's arm.

"Now I'm going to put you in a private room until day after tomorrow. And send this little bitch home. What's she been doing, selling you a sob story?"

"The story of her life. Vince. Is it true that her own father—"

"Raped her? Yes. Incest isn't uncommon in Costa Verde, unfortunately, nor any other vice you can name, for that matter. But the truth of her story—and it is true *and* tragic, Jim—is no reason for you to get saddled with her. She's a dirty little bitch, my friend. I'm sure, though I can't prove it, that she's been a dope pusher. Hell, I could have proved it; but I didn't want to. She's too damned skinny to take fifty lashes and live . . ."

"Vince, may I have some writing materials? Paper, envelopes, and so forth?"

"Sure thing, Jim. But today you ought to rest. Write your letters tomorrow . . ."

"Not letters. A letter. Just one. A recommendation. For Trini. For a job I *know* she can do. So she can quit hustling. And pushing, if she does that. So it has to be today. She swears she wants to leave the bad life, Vince . . ."

"They *all* swear that. And they hold out at any occupation in which they have to maintain a vertical position for about a week. Two at most. Being a whore is the result of a certain kind of woman's natural inclinations, Jim, not of the immediate, accidental causes that pushed her into it. You can force *any* woman into whoring, my friend. But if she isn't a whore, a born whore, she'll die of sheer disgust, or by her own hand within six months. Or she'll go mad. Or she'll get out. If she stays, it's because she's found her natural occupation, that's all; the pain, filth, contempt that her basically masochistic personality craves . . ."

"You've a cruel streak, Vince," Jim said quietly.

"I've an accurate, scientific mind. Which is why I'm going to put the matter to the test. You'll have your paper and envelopes as soon as I've moved you into your private room. You want her to wait for her recommendation?"

"Of course. Vince—I *like* her! She—"

"Then screw her and get her out of your system. But not in *my* hospital, goddamnit!" Vicente Gomez said.

CHAPTER

14

*P*eter," Jim said into the telephone, "could you get me a complete rundown of Jenny Crowley's mad career out of your morgue, photocopy it, and send it to me?"

"Don't have it," Peter Reynolds said. "We don't run a scandal sheet, Chub. People like your dear little ex-girl friend are of no interest to us. By the way, Boy; how are you? They haven't blown the other side of your head off yet down there, have they?"

"No. And I'm all right. Oh, Jesus! I need that information on Jenny worse than all hell, Peter! Especially—her weddings. She's been married twice, hasn't she?"

"Yep. First time to some Italian kid. Old Wildcat had it annulled; she was about fifteen, then. The second time was a Big Howdy Do. To the FitzGibbons boy. You know, Jim, the shipping people. The only family in the world who've got boats and who aren't Greeks. The biggest Irish-American fortune. They give away in tips more money than the Kennedys have got . . ."

"Peter," Jim said, whispering the words, "the FitzGibbons—they—they're *Catholics,* aren't they?"

"You ever heard of a Son of the Auld Sod who wasn't? The wedding took place in St. Patrick's Cathedral, if I remember right. Only about a year later little Jen let Bob FitzGibbons catch her playing footsie with another guy. Footsie, hell. Handsy and titsy and tailsy and what have you. Bare-assed in the chaise longue by the swimming pool. So he divorced her."

"That's my Jen, all right!" Jim sighed. "Say, Peter; could you get me documentary evidence of all this?"

"I could; but damned if I see why you want it. Jesus, this call is costing you a fortune! Why don't you write me a nice long explanatory letter and—"

"Don't care about the cost. It's worth it. Look, Peter, she's *here.* Don't tell anybody that, not even—Alicia. Please?"

"Okay, Jim, I won't."

"And I've got to get her out. Promised the old man; catch? But she's married again. Down *here.* And you know the laws of *this* country . . ."

"Sure do, Chub—I mean Jim. She can't go to the ladies' room unless her hubby signs an affidavit of consent. And *he's* balking? Wants to keep his sticky fingers on all that long, folding green stuff, right?"

"Right. Only, Peter, what does Costa Verdian law say about—divorce?"

"Goddamn!" Peter said. "It says there *ain't* no such animal. So friend Hubby down *there* is merely 'Little Friend and Playmate,' and he can hang his affidavits up over the john to use for other purposes until such time as a young healthy fellow like Bob FitzGibbons, who's just thirty-two *now,* is gathered to his reward, thus giving said 'Little Friend and Playmate' down there a chance to jump over the broomstick with Jen all over again and make it legal even in Costa Verde. That's what you're getting at, aren't you?"

"Yes, Peter. But the fine points of the matter are that FitzGibbons is a Roman Catholic, and the wedding—that is, the wedding prior to this one—took place in the One True Church. Because if he'd been a Protestant or a Jew, and the rites solemnized by a man of the cloth of any such lesser breeds without the law, or in a civil ceremony, her present wedding *would* be valid under Costa Verde's legal code. I need to prove it isn't."

"You've done it. I'll put the stuff in the mail tomorrow. I'll get it out of *The Examiner*'s morgue. Professional courtesy. They'll let me photocopy it, considering all the years *I* was one of their galley slaves. Anything else?"

"No. Yes! Tell Alicia I'm—sorry about that Grand Guignol TV show I put on. I wouldn't have upset her for anything in the world . . ."

"But you sure *did,* Boy! Had to send for the local sawbones. Good thing you're down there, or I'd have to oil up my dueling pistols. Say— Jim! What's all this fuss about those dresses? A couple of oily types showed up at the O'Rourkes', asking funny questions. Marisol swears they were Costa Verdians, and—"

"She was right. SN-2, Peter."

"Jesus! How'd that get to be a matter of State?"

"Peter," Jim said flatly, "this line is tapped. Bugged. *Intervinido.* But I'll tell you, anyhow. I think they got their hands on that picture Tim took. The Polaroid of me standing there with a lecherous—and envious!—grin on my homely countenance, and squeezing two gorgeous dames as hard as I could get away with. And they wanted to find out who was who. Or more exactly, which of the two I was squeezing a little harder. To—well—duplicate her—for 'The Treatment.' "

"Well, I'll be goddamned!" Peter said feelingly. "Did they?"

"Yes, Peter. The duplication's perfect. *Pluscumperfecto.* Alicia, herself; but younger. Damned if I don't believe they cloned her! Only—they also sent the oily types to check out—there in New York—the girl I was planning to marry. So now, engagement's off. Busted. Grace got—the wrong idea. Found the possibility of a guy's buying dresses for the wife of a friend, with said friend's knowledge and consent, a little too odd-shaped and rough about the edges—to swallow . . ."

"Grace—who?" Peter said.

"Nivens. Works for Crowley. But leave it be, Peter. There's nothing you—or anybody—can do, now . . ."

"Me—nor anybody. Could be you're right, there. But me *and* Alicia, together, Jim? Dropping in on the lady? Inviting her out for a little chat at Enrico's Spaghetti Joint down in the Village over a bottle of Chianti Ruffino?"

Jim felt hope claw in, reaching for his life.

"If you do that, tell Alicia to *wear* one of the Andean dresses for the occasion, please!" he said.

When he hung up the phone, he was thinking: 'So now I've got what I wanted, and what the hell good is it going to do me?' What he had wanted was proof that under Costa Verde's laws, Joe Harper's marriage to Jenny Crowley wasn't legal. And he had that, all right, for in Costa Verde, in all matters pertaining to marriage and divorce, the strictest interpretation of Roman Catholic Canon Law prevailed. Remarriage could only follow annulment—granted only to the multimillionaires with the fortunes to spend and the long years of superhuman patience it took to push an annulment through the Ecclesiastical Courts, and then only for causes so esoteric that almost nobody had the sheer gall to allege them—or the death of one of the partners. So, as far as Costa Verde was concerned, Jenny Crowley was still married to Robert FitzGibbons; and, as a consequence, her paramour, one Joseph Harper, had no legal right whatsoever to forbid her to sign a paper committing herself to the hospital for the psychiatric and addiction rehabilitation treatments she so desperately needed.

'Which,' Jim thought sadly, 'matters not a good goddamn as long as the bastard's there to simply tell her not to sign it. Damned if I need any further demonstrations that she'll do *anything* he tells her to, no matter how perverted, nauseous, vile that anything is. And I can do without being converted into an unwilling voyeur anymore . . .

'So friend Harper has to go. Permanently, if possible; but anyhow for long enough for me to regain the moral ascendancy I once held over poor Jen. She wants to be browbeaten and cowed? Whipped into doing what she, herself, has not the will to do? She's got a masochistic streak in her a yard wide that craves rough handling, being dominated? Okay—glad to oblige. But for her own good—to get her out of the ranks of zombies, out of the walking wounded, to restore her to humanity again . . .

'All right, little friend! Let's cut out the dirt-cheap rhetoric and get down to cases: What all the previous diarrhea of the jawbone means is that Harper is *out*. If I weren't *me*, it would take half an hour. I'd simply contact, through Tomás, Suarez, and other Pinkish Pals, a cut-rate "hit" man and pay him fifty crisp, green American dollars, which is all a man's life costs down here. But, being me, I can't. Damned if I wouldn't like to *stop* being me in this case! But I can't. So—railroad the bastard, with his *own* devoted assistance. Because, according to Suarez and his Prague cum Moscow-trained electronic Wizards of Oz, Joe delivers the stuff—several kilos of the purest heroin anybody ever saw—down to the docks himself, in his own car.

'Stupid? Or—smart? Having an iron-clad guarantee from *El Lider Glorioso* himself that nobody's going to touch that black Buick—ever? Or simply that contemptuous of these "damned little monkey-chasers" as he calls all Costa Verdians?

'But therein lies my opportunity. Because with the help of my Red Brain Trust, Tomás, Suarez, *et al.*, I can set it up so that the police have to arrest Harper, so that they can't possibly avoid doing so. And once arrested, nobody, not even García will dare come to his aid, because to do that would be to publicly proclaim they are involved in the traffic themselves. And with Joe safely tucked away, I—'

He stopped still. Thought about that. Whispered:

"Oh, Jesus!"

For getting rid of Harper involved Catch Thirty-*six*. Costa Verde's law didn't condemn a man to a few years in prison for pushing narcotics; it stood him up against a stone wall about three meters away from twelve competent marksmen with twelve loaded rifles in their hands. And as much as he, Jim Rush, disliked Joe Harper, as many A-One, First Class, Good, Fine, Excellent reasons he had to hate that unmitigated bastard's wormy tripes, he simply was beyond the place, and the stage, where he could accept the moral responsibility for one more death.

He thought, slowly:

'So? So a little plea bargaining *before* the fact, Attorney Rush! I deliver Harper to Pérez de la Valle and his pal, Fuentes Toralba, give them the priceless opportunity they're surely looking for to put García's male attributes in one of those big, wooden nutcrackers I'm told they use, and convert his voice—permanently—to a lyric soprano, in return for their promise to reduce the penalty to three years in the hoosegow plus deportation like it is everywhere else . . .'

He put up his hand, pulled the bellcord. Tomás appeared almost instantly.

"Tell Roberto to bring the car around, Tomás," Jim said. "I'm going to pay a call on the Director General of Security—in his office."

"Yes, Sir," Tomás said; then reaching across Jim's desk, he switched on the jamming transmitter.

"Sir," he said, "what are you going to *do* about little Trini?"

"Jesus!" Jim said with real exasperation. "Haven't I done *enough?*"

"No, Sir; you haven't. Because nothing you've done really solves the problem. You got her that job as a model with Geri Pyle; that's true enough. Incidentally, he's delighted with her. Swears she's the very best model he's ever had. Besides which, the publicity is worth a fortune to him. Every Great Lady in town has been in within the last two weeks to see *la Protegida del Embajador Estadounidense . . .*"

"Good God!" Jim said.

"Natural enough, Sir. *Your* mistress would naturally invite both curiosity—and envy, Sir."

"Goddamnit, Tomás; she's *not* my mistress!"

"I know she's not, Sir. Which makes me one of the two people in all Ciudad Villalonga who do know that. Or who're willing to believe it. The other being *you,* Sir. Which makes the fact that she's not rather useless, doesn't it? Not to mention, from my point of view, Sir, *most* unfortunate!"

"Tomás, she's a child!"

"A beautiful child, Sir—who loves you, rather desperately, Sir."

"Tomás—she's sold herself a bill of goods. Pure autosuggestion, reenforced by the dramatic circumstances under which we met—"

"Plus the truly admirable manner in which you behaved upon that occasion, Sir!"

"Hell! Whatever the reasons, she—"

"Loves you. Really loves you. I've tested her feelings every way I know how to, Sir, and they ring absolutely true. Which means you're breaking her heart. Look, Sir; she drew all of her money out of the bank and made a down payment on a little studio apartment: One room, kitchenette, bath. But *she* didn't make the payment. She gave the money to *me* and asked *me* to make it. Can you guess *why?*"

"Yes, goddamnit!" Jim howled. "Every blessed son of his mother in this town knows you're my majordomo. So now it's all over town that I'm keeping her, which is exactly what she *wants* people to believe, right?"

"Right. She had to save face, Sir! And, Sir—*nobody* visits her at that apartment. She sits there night after night—waiting for *you* to show up—and crying because you don't."

"Oh, Jesus, Tomás!"

"Sir—you're being unkind. You *really* are. You see this key? It's yours. She sent it to you. She has the only other one. And this telephone number. An unlisted number. Not in the telephone book. For you, Sir. And Sir—if you'll permit me—the—well—unfortunate way she was forced to make a living—has ceased, Sir. Terminated. She—doesn't, any more. She really doesn't—"

"Well, I'm glad of *that!*"

"So far, she's not being—molested, Sir. Which is at least one of the reasons you *ought* to be seen with her occasionally, take her out. If our sporting gentlemen believe she's your mistress, they'll leave her in peace. And, besides, Sir, you're forgetting the principal thing: If *Seguridad Nacional, Sección Dos, Actividades Políticas,* get the idea that she is not complying with her original mission, it could go very hard with her, Sir . . .''

Jim stood there. Then he sighed.

"You win, Tomás. *That* argument is convincing. Get me the boutique on the telephone. I'll speak to Geri, first. Then to her. And after *that,* go tell Roberto to bring the car around, that is, if you *really* don't mind, Tomás!"

Tomás grinned at him shamelessly.

"Sir, I *have* to run your life for you a little," he said. "Can't let you make *too* big a mess of things, y'know!"

"Oh—get me that number, Tomás!" Jim said.

"Why—Jimmee!" Geri squealed. "What a joy! I've been meaning to call you, but I didn't dare. An Ambassador's so-ohhh imposing, y'know!"

"Oh, come off of it, Geri," Jim said; "I only called to ask you about little Trini. How's she doing, Boy?"

"A Love!" Geri gurgled. "An absolute Love, Jimmee! *The* most marvelous walk! Just perfect. Such grace! Best model I've *ever* had in my whole career. So thank you, Dear Boy, thank you! Where'd you *ever* find her? No! Don't tell me! I don't want to know! I've grown soohhh fond of her, that it would distress me no end to learn you found her in some cathouse!"

"As a matter of fact, I didn't," Jim said solemnly. "She paid me a visit one afternoon—to ask a favor. You know, Ger; happens all the time. And I saw the possibilities—"

"I can just bet you *did,* you naughty Boy! I had to protect her from the other girls at first—especially from little Petra, who fancied you were smitten of her . . ."

"I *was,*" Jim said; "of part of her, anyhow. Only I forgot to check her face out. What it looked like, I mean—"

"Jimmee, you are a card! But now they've accepted Trini; she *is* sweet, y'know. And the clients! Dear Boy, d'you know what they ask me?"

"No; what?"

" 'I say, *Señor* Pyle, will you let the Ambassador's little mistress show us this line?' "

"Oh, Jesus!" Jim said.

"Now, Jimmee! Hardly a secret, y'know. *La Querida del Embajador,* or *La Protegida de Su Excelencia Don* Jaime Rush. I'm delighted. Gives the boutique a little of that old *je ne sais quoi,* y'know. Chic, say; tone . . ."

"All right. Ger, can you do me a favor?"

"Of course, Lover! You need only to ask!"

"Lend her a dress. For tonight. Or better still, sell it to me, for her. I'm taking her out—to *Les Ambassadeurs,* first. Afterwards, to the Verdian Hilton—the Obsidian Room. And her clothes are awful. Can you do that?"

"Jimmee, Love, I should *pay* you! You give me and my rags the very best publicity I've ever had, and put it as if I were doing you a favor! Of course, Dear Boy! You can have the dress I've in mind at cost. And what's more, I'll personally make her face up for the occasion. She tends to be a little crude about those details, so far; but then, she's such a child, y'know . . ."

"Thank you, Ger. Now, may I speak to her?"

"But, of course, Dear Boy! One moment!"

He could hear before she got there, the clatter of her heels, literally flying towards the phone.

"Trini—" he said.

"Don Jaime—" she whispered; "oh, *Don* Jaime!"

He heard her voice choke on his name, strangle, drown.

"Now, Trini—" he said reproachfully.

"Yes! Yes!" she stormed. *"¡Estoy llorando!* And—my makeup will be spoiled—and *Señor* Pyle, *Don* Geraldo—will scold me! But *you* called me! Finally you called me! Oh, *Don* Jaime, I am so very happy!"

"And for this you *cry,* little Trini?"

"*¡Sí! ¡Sí!* I cry for this! Too much happiness also—hurts, *Don* Jaime! Though not as much—as loneliness does! *Don* Jaime—I—I love thee! Oh, how I love thee! Forgive me—for saying it again. But I have to. I must. It—*feels* so good to say it, *Don* Jaime! Besides, if I try to keep it in, it will burst my heart, and I shall die!"

"Lord!" he laughed, to hide how deeply her vehemence had moved him. "Trini, I shall call for you tonight. After work, and—"

"Ohhhhhhhhh!" she wailed.

"Now what the devil passes with thee?" he said.

"I—I—must sit down. I think I am going to—to faint . . ."

"Trini, don't you dare!"

"Yes, *Don* Jaime. I will not, *Don* Jaime. As thou wilt, *Don* Jaime . . ."

"Oh Jesus!" Jim said.

"Forgive me, *Don* Jaime," she whispered.

"All right. I shall call for you at ten, at the boutique, since that place stays open half the night. Mr. Pyle will give you a dress, because we're going out to dinner and to dance—"

"Where?" she said sharply.

"*Les Ambassadeurs.* Afterwards, the Obsidian Room. You know: at the Hilton."

"Ohhhh!" she gasped. "Now thou hast made me cry again! Dost—love me— a little, *Don* Jaime? Art thou—beginning to? A little bit? *¿Un poquitín?*

"Yes," he said sadly; "and more than a little, I'm afraid. Good-bye, Trini. Until tonight, my dear . . ."

"*¡Hasta esa noche!*" she whispered; then: "God grant it *never* ends!"

"Hmmmn—" the Director General of Security said; "you will deliver your fellow countryman Harper to us under such circumstances that a conviction will be guaranteed, so long as we promise not to shoot the filthy swine. And why not, *Don* Jaime? I mean, why should we promise you that?"

"Because," Jim said slowly, "it could—conceivably—make for difficulties between your country and mine. I'd like to avoid that. I presume you would, too, *Don* Raoul. All I'm interested in is stopping the drug traffic—"

"And *not* in getting your well manicured hands upon the young person Harper is living with, and is somewhat married to? You amaze me,

Don Jaime! I should have thought that dear little Trini would have been more than enough for you! Tell me, isn't she—satisfactory?"

"Trini is a—delight," Jim said carefully; "and—a joy. But yes, I *am* interested in getting my hands on Jenny Crowley, though only because I promised her father I would. To commit her to medical care, *here* in Ciudad Villalonga. Doctor Claudio Lopez Basquez is a first class psychiatrist, and especially expert in these matters. Doctor Gomez recommends him very highly. And Harper is deliberately keeping Miss Crowley enslaved to the drug—"

"But, as her husband, unfortunately, he has every right—"

"He, under *your* laws, is *not* her husband, and has *no* rights. I shall submit you within days proof of a previous *Catholic* marriage on the young woman's part. Dissolved by divorce. Which means *nothing* to the Church, or in Costa Verde . . ."

"Ah! There you have much right, *Don* Jaime! Let me see, let me see . . . *Don* Jaime, could your friends or agents arrange matters so it would be *marijuana* found on Harper instead of heroin?"

"Good God, man! I'm not going to frame the bastard! He really *is* running the stuff, you know!"

"I know he is. What I'm suggesting is only that you save his miserable life, *Don* Jaime. The death penalty only applies to heroin, morphine, and cocaine. Lesser drugs—lighter sentences. If, at the moment of his arrest—a substitution could be made—we'd be spared the unfortunate and politically embarrassing necessity of—shooting Harper. You see that, don't you?"

Jim sat there. 'Have I become a man of action, or haven't I?' he thought.

"Yes. And I'll see what can be done about it," he said.

CHAPTER

15

*A*s Jim Rush came out of the Director General's office, he realized suddenly that he hadn't the slightest desire to go back to the Embassy. 'I,' he thought with wry amusement, 'have developed a taste for excitement in what is still—in spite of all the really first class attempts the types down here have made to liven it up for me—the world's dullest job . . .'

Nor did he have to. There was absolutely nothing pending that even the Vice Consul's—certifiably moronic!—secretary couldn't handle through a couple of phone calls, or, for that matter, really required handling at all. He stood there thinking a long moment before it occurred to him what he wanted, and probably even needed, to do. Then he walked over to where Roberto stood holding open the door of the Cadillac.

"Take me to the hospital, Roberto. I have to consult Dr. Gomez," he said.

"Of course you may see the kid, Jim," Vince Gomez said. "He's doing great. So great, in fact, that pretty soon I've got to figure out how, where, and to whom to deliver him . . ."

"Does he still entertain ambitions of perforating me? Or poor little Trini?" Jim said.

"You, no. Definitely not. Trini, I'm not too sure. He has excellent reasons for disliking that little piece of commercial goods," Vince said. "Speaking of which, I'd advise you to listen to those reasons—from *him,* my friend. I'd rather not relay them, second hand, except to say that what you're doing just isn't *smart.*"

"And what, exactly, is it that I'm doing, Vince?" Jim said quietly.

Vince stared at him. Said slowly, thoughtfully.

"As a scientist, I have to admit that I don't know. Is it always true that, as *we* say, 'When the river sounds, it's carrying water.' Or as you Anglo Saxons say, 'Where there's smoke, there's fire'? Rumors, Jim. Women's talk, which, unfortunately, has reached even my Paloma's ears. I say 'unfortunately' because it increases my problems: Paloma's up to her ears in our local Women's Lib movement, which isn't exactly distinguished for either its sweet reasonableness or its moderation, Jim!"

"I'm sorry," Jim said.

"Don't be. Anyhow it's I who must apologize. Whether said rumors are true or false, they really aren't any of my goddamned business. Forgive me for sticking my nose in. Funny—I seem to have transferred my friendship for Peter Reynolds—my actual fondness for him—onto you. Or extended it to include you, Jim. In spite of your differences, you're strangely alike. You've both managed to tie my guts in knots by being too bloody brave at the wrong fornicating times. It's a trait I simultaneously dislike—because of its uselessness—and admire—because of a strong atavistic streak in my own makeup, I suppose—"

"Vince, thank you. I'm honored. And touched. And the friendship, even the fondness, is fully reciprocated, I assure you. But you actually know very little about me. I'd have to bore you with the excruciatingly dull story of my life to explain my present conviction: that I have a perfect right to be as absolute a jackass as I want to. All my life I've been the perfect picture of sobriety, of caution, correction, courtesy, the boy who's *never* out of line. And what has my angelic—read cowardly!—behavior ever got me? A bruised and bleeding ass, and a monumental collection of horns! So, it is not smart to get involved with Trini Alvarez? I agree. I agree two hundred percent. And if you can show me what good being smart has ever done me, I'll raise the ante and agree three hundred percent.

"Incidentally, if it'll relieve your mind, I'm not *that* involved with her. You've heard I got her that job at Geri Pyle's. That's true. The rest—isn't. And, as of now, my intentions are *not* to get too deeply involved with her. Though, frankly, whether my will power is on a level with my intentions is a thing I shouldn't like to bet on. She's a living doll, you know . . ."

"She is—almost extravagantly beautiful, physically," Vince said slowly; "exotic as all get out. And—there have been members of the

World's Oldest Profession who've reformed, I suppose. I've never actually met one who didn't fall back into that life sooner or later; but let's admit at least a statistical possibility. So, ordinarily, I'd even *advise* you to have a quiet little affair with Trini—if I could be sure you wouldn't fall in love with her . . . ."

"And what," Jim said quietly, "would be wrong with my falling in love with her? That I couldn't marry her because she's been a whore?"

"No. Because you damned well could if you wanted to. Many's the man who's done it before you, Jim. And under *your* circumstances—the fact that you can quite easily take her away from the geographical area where her past is known to a totally new environment where it isn't, and where there'd be almost nothing to yank her back into it—I'd give such a marriage a better than even chance of working out. What bothers me in this case is that you—a decent man by every test I can apply—might get saddled with a girl—so—to put it charitably—damaged—that inevitably your life would become a hell. I can and do forgive little Trini the whoring that she damned well *was* forced into, Jim; but this business of procuring heroin for a kid who had almost kicked the habit, I, personally, find unpardonable . . . ."

"So do I—if true," Jim said. "Are you sure, Vince?"

"Go talk to Alvaro. That's the wounded boy's name. Alvaro Ferrero Muñoz. Form your own opinion," Vicente Gomez said.

"How are you feeling, Son?" Jim said and put out his hand to the boy.

Alvaro took it. Said:

"Like dirt. Now, at this moment, before you, *Don* Jaime—like dirt. I would have killed you. I meant to kill you. Seriously."

"I know. But you only meant to kill the North American Ambassador—which is occasionally even a pardonable idea. If I believed in killing anyone, which I *don't,* I could think up quite a list of Ambassadors I've known whom it seemed to me killing was too good for. However, I don't believe you meant to kill *me.* You didn't even know me, so how could you desire my death?"

"Say rather the death—of a man I found with a woman of my people. Is *that* more convincing, *Don* Jaime?"

"Not *your* woman. And the man, incidentally, not yet guilty of her. You got there too fast, Son!"

"You have an Anglo Saxon sense of humor, *Don* Jaime. It is, I'll admit, charming. And I no longer wish to kill you. You got me past the guards—in your pyjamas. Put your watch and ring on me to fool them. Gave me your blood. Saved my life after I'd threatened yours. I find all this—rare . . . ."

"I was brought up—as a Christian, Son," Jim said quietly. "That much, at least, stuck. All right—we've signed a truce, you and I. We grant each other the right to differ politically and stay alive. Within the difference of our concepts, we can even be friends. At least I hope so. I admire courage. And you were very brave, Alvaro. It is one of the things I envy you."

"I thank you for that, *Don* Jaime," Alvaro said.

"Does our truce extend to—Trini?" Jim said. "Are you also—willing—to spare her life?"

"No. Never. The next time I see that little bitch, she dies!"

"Why, Son?"

"Because of this—of my sister, Anita. When my father was shot by *el Carnecero*'s soldiers, my older brother and I took to the jungle. So García's men arrested Anita. Do you know what they do to the women of guerrillas?"

"Yes," Jim said; "I know."

"You lie!" the boy burst out. "You cannot! No foreigner could know—"

"To mention but one item in a rather extensive *repetorio:* They 'beerbottle' them. Right?"

"So—you—you *do* know!" Alvaro whispered. "How is it then that—your Government—that *you* support—a beast like García?"

"My Government does not know the facts. Proof is difficult to obtain. And I, personally, *don't* support General García. I am trying to obtain that proof. When I have it, I shall submit it to my Government with the strongest suggestion that diplomatic relations be broken, and all aid—especially military—be withdrawn. Which is—too nebulous, I'll admit. But tell me, Son: Would you be alive now, and relatively safe, if *I* were a friend of García's?"

"There you have much right, *Don* Jaime," Alvaro whispered.

"Continue the story of your sister," Jim said.

"When—they had done with her—after the months when our leaders kept my brother—who is dead now, *Don* Jaime!—and me under guard so that we could not give way to our natural sentiments and surrender—they transferred her to a hospital. In that hospital they converted her into a heroin addict while patching her body up enough to be—useful—again. Then they—installed her in *La Luna Azul.* The Blue Moon. The worst whorehouse in all the Americas—or the best. Depends upon your point of view. Trini was there. She had not yet risen to being a motorized call girl, attending her clients at their flats. Nor the mistress of a Minister of the Government. Nor yet—*yours, Don* Jaime!"

"That's my business, Son," Jim said mildly, "and my worry, don't you think? Go on, please."

"Anita—fought against the habit. Desperately. She had won, almost. Got to the place where she could do without the drug. Did not *seek* it, you understand. Only—dear little Trini—at the instigation of one of her official lovers—brought it to my poor sister. Free. In great quantities. Of the purest quality. Finished Anita—terminated every hope she might have have had. Do you wonder, *Don* Jaime, that *esa maldita zorra* of a Trini must die!"

"No," Jim said sadly, "I don't wonder. I even grant you your reasons. But I don't believe that killing people solves anything. Alvaro, grant me a normal man's weaknesses, will you? Son, I just don't want Trini dead. Whatever she's done. So—a bargain? You—forget your vengeance. I'll not even add that revenging himself against a woman is demeaning to a man. A lessening of his manhood, it seems to me. You—refrain from butchering poor little Trini, and I will guarantee the removal of your sister from *La Luna Azul,* plus her acceptance by Doctor Claudio Lopez Basquez in his Psychiatric Clinic for a drug addiction cure. I'll undertake the negotiations—and the expenses. But you must agree to leave Trini—in peace . . ."

"You—you *love* that little bitch that much, *Don* Jaime?"

"I don't know. Yes. I suppose I do. At least I cannot bear the thought of her—being killed. Don't you—love your sister sufficiently to try to save her, Alvaro? Is not the bargain—fair?"

Alvaro lay there, staring at him.

"It would be, *Don* Jaime," he said quietly; "but for one thing: My sister died—of an overdose of heroin, the morning before that same night I persuaded my friends to put me over the back wall of your residence. On the score that I was too gravely wounded to survive in the jungle—and that my death would be useful if I took you, and Trini, with me. So, therefore, *Don* Jaime, I have nothing to bargain for. You, it seems, love the murderess who almost directly killed my sister. So now, do you know what you have to do—to save her?"

"No," Jim whispered, "what must I do, Alvaro?"

"Go to the nearest telephone. Call the police. Tell them I am here. By tomorrow morning, or even before, I shall then be dead. I shall die very well, *Don* Jaime. With as much dignity as their tortures will permit me. And you will have *that* to remember. And Trini to thank you. What are you waiting for? Go on! Call them!"

Wearily Jim shook his head. Said:

"No, Son. There are a few things that are beyond me. And that one heads the list. I—I have never had a son, and I admire thee. It saddens me to think that now, between us—there must be—war . . ."

Alvaro lay there.

"A war—that thou hast already won, *Don* Jaime!" he said slowly, softly, bitterly; then, his voice rising, grating, going metallic, harsh: "Keep thy filthy *zorra*! And may all thy daughters be—her image!"

Then he turned his face to the wall.

Jim stood there looking at that small, too rigid figure. A long time. A very long time. Then he whispered, feeling it, meaning it:

"Son—I thank thee," and got out of there.

CHAPTER

16

On the way back to the residence, Jim had Roberto stop the car before a florist. He went in and bought a bouquet of brown, speckled orchids for Trini. He didn't know why he chose that particular flower, except that it seemed to suit her, to reflect her own rich, dark coloring, to be as jungle born as she was, as exotic, tropical, rare . . .

As he took the bouquet from the florist, he thought suddenly of what Alvaro had told him. Was it—true? Yes. Very likely. Next question: Did it—matter?

'Yes,' he thought sadly; 'it does. But maybe not enough. Certainly its—impact—is insufficient to halt—my autumnal madness. To smother the dead-leaf fires blue-smoking all my lanes . . .' He walked back to the car with the bouquet in his arms, thinking:

'Trini—I forgive you. Whatever the hell you've done. Why ever the hell you did it. I have no right whatsoever to—play God. Hand out pardons. Still—I do. To—thee. For the crime of being born. The sin—of living. The insanity of even dreaming you could love me. Which is—a very great folly. But I thank thee for it. Tonight, I thank thee for it with all my heart . . .'

When Roberto drew the big car up before the boutique, she came out at once to meet him, not running this time, but walking slowly, step by

206

step, somnambulant, dream-wrapped, her eyes enormous in her small, thin, exquisitely sculptured face, her great flesh wound of a mouth a little parted, showing a pearly sheen of perfect teeth between those too thick, almost Negroid lips of hers, visibly atremble.

The dress—a formal ballroom model of Geri's famous Andean line— how could a man who professed nothing but contempt for women flatter them to this degree?—was a miracle. It was the color of cream and of silver, the old off-white of cherished memories. Her makeup was perfect. Everything she wore—the accessories he had forgot to ask Geri for!—was perfect: shoes, handbag, gloves, a tiny, jaunty, pill-box shaped, cute, funny joke of a hat; and *she* was perfection's very self. So much so that the whole time she employed to reach the car, Jim Rush forgot to breathe.

When she was close enough, he held out the orchids to her, jerkily, awkwardly, like a schoolboy on his first date.

"For—me?" she breathed, and took them. "Oh, *Don* Jaime!" Then, leaning swiftly close, hissed at him, fiercely: "Kiss me! Oh, please *Don* Jaime, kiss me! That the girls may see! That tomorrow they cannot mock me! For me, this once, please, please, please!"

He kissed her. Very gently. With aching tenderness.

And the great tears, bursting, exploding from her eyes, streaked her makeup all to hell.

"*¡Viva!*" the other models cried. "*¡Bravo! ¡Viva la Trini! ¡Viva el Señor Embajador!*

He almost pushed her into the car. Got in beside her. Said:

"To *Les Ambassadeurs,* Roberto!" Then he took out his handkerchief, and tried to dry her flooded eyes.

"*¡Mi pequeña regadera!*" he said fondly. "My little watering pot!"

"*¡Ay, sí!*" she sobbed. "It is so, no; *Don* Jaime? Since I have known thee, I have done nothing but cry! From—too much sadness, at first— and now, from too much joy!"

"Stop crying," he told her with mock sternness. "You will spoil your face. How then can you make all the Great Ladies swoon with envy at your beauty if you arrive with your eyes swollen and red, and your makeup a mess? Tell me that, *Muñeca mía?*"

She squeezed his arm, smiled at him through slowing tears.

"Do not call me thy doll!" she said. "I should rather be thy watering pot. For there is a thing we say: 'She is as crazy as a watering pot!' And I *am*—for thee, *Don* Jaime!"

She looked at Roberto's broad back, through the thick, probably even bulletproof glass partition separating the driver's compartment from the back seat.

"Can—he hear us?" she whispered.

"No," Jim said. He really didn't know whether Roberto could or not. Given the official tendency in Costa Verde to bug everything, he suspected that his so-called chauffeur probably could. But he didn't give a tinker's damn what Henriques heard, and he wasn't going to spoil things for Trini by telling her what he thought.

"Good!" she said mischievously; "*Don* Jaime, to thee I give thanks. For thou hast kissed me very nicely and sweetly and tenderly and all the girls saw it. Didst—like it? Was it—nice, kissing me?"

"Very," he said solemnly.

"Then it—would not be—burdensome for thee—to do it again? Now? But—for *me,* this time? I want thee to. Oh, so very much!"

"Now look, Trini—"

"Please? *¿Por favor?*"

"Let us wait a while. For when there are not—chauffeurs with rear-view mirrors in which to observe things that are not their business, eh, *Niña?*"

"No!" she said; "I do not care. Just one? A little one, *Don* Jaime?"

He kissed her.

She drew back finally. Stared up at him. Whispered:

"Enough! That—made me feel—wicked. And with thee, I do not want to feel wicked. With thee I wish—to imagine—to pretend that I—that I am thy *Novia.* Thy—promised one. A good girl. *Una chica honesta* of whom thou art *not* ashamed!"

"I am not ashamed of thee," he said slowly. "Truly, Trini. Believe me, I'm not."

"Thou'rt—kind," she murmured. "But that is too difficult to believe . . ."

"Then don't," he said; "I care not. As long as *I* believe it, which is what counts . . ."

"Dost thou believe it?" she said morosely. "How canst thou? I—am a creature of—of great wickedness, much ill fame, no reputation at all, who—"

"Has never been inside *Les Ambassadeurs* before. Nor, the Obsidian Room. Mind telling me—why?"

"Because men—my lovers—were ashamed to be seen with me. Whilst thou—"

"While I—what?"

"Art taking me to—to places—where all the best people go. Where thy friends and their *wives* and all the great ladies are *sure* to see us together and—Ohhhhh! *Don* Jaime, tell him to turn the car around! Thou canst not do this! I will *not* ruin thy life! Nor disgrace thee forever! Nor—"

"Love me?" he said quietly.

208

"That—yes. Because I do. Oh, I do! But—apart. In—secret. Where I cannot harm thee. *Don* Jaime, tell me—a—a thing?"

"What thing, child?"

"A grave thing, *Don* Jaime. *Gravísimo.* But I—I need to know it, *mi Amor—¡No! ¡Mi Dueño y Señor!*"

"Thy love," he corrected her sadly, *"not* thy Lord and Master. Not ever, those things, Trini."

"Yes, yes! Both! For thou'rt both and I want thee to be! But wilt say it, *Don* Jaime? Wilt answer me? Because it is a thing I *want* so much! A thing I have *never* wanted before. That I was sick from fear each time I—I thought it had happened!"

"Wrongly?"

"Wrongly—to God the thanks! But now I want it. From thee—and for thee. If—it would not—anger thee—or disgust thee—or make thee ashamed . . .

"Lord!" he said. "What thing is this, little Trini? Go on, say it!"

She wrapped both her arms about one of his, clung to it, peering upward into his eyes, her own filled with doubt, fear, hope—he did not know; whispered, her voice a rustle of velvet, a ripple on the surface of dead still waters:

"Don Jaime—if—if *we* should—make a child, can I—*have* it? Keep it? And—and wouldst thou—acknowledge it? Give it—thy name?"

"And dance through the streets from sheer joy, with it in my arms, showing it to all the world!" he said.

"Ohhhhh!" she wailed; then: *"¡Dios mío!* Why does being happy *hurt* so much? Thou—thou hast wished for a son, hast thou not, *Don* Jaime? A—long time, perhaps?"

"Yes. All my life. But now I wish for a daughter—who will look exactly like *thee.*"

She squeezed his arm, whispered:

"Then—*tonight* we will make one! Or at least try to—"

"Tonight we will do nothing of the kind," he said firmly.

"Why not, *Don* Jaime?"

"Because I do not wish to spoil tonight. I don't want it—confused—with other nights in your mind. I want you to remember it as—different. To say: 'There was a man once—a little, old, dried up, ugly man!—who believed I was a lady. A very great lady. And treated me as such . . .' "

She crushed her face against his Adam's apple, wound both arms around his neck, all but strangling him, cried, sobbing aloud, wildly, like a child.

"You stop that, Trini!" he said.

She turned him loose. Sat up. Peered at him out of eyes become so enormous in her small face that they made her seem a creature from another world, especially when the way they slanted was added to their dilation.

'Paint her green and she'd make a perfect Martian,' he thought. 'That is, if Martians *are* green. And—tiny—and defenseless—and doelike—and beautiful—' he added in his mind.

"It is—stopped, *Don* Jaime," she whispered. "Art—angry with me? *Por favor, Don* Jaime! Don't be! I could not bear it if thou wert!"

"I'm not. I find it difficult to become angry at you, Trini—and impossible to remain so. But I do wish you'd behave differently."

"Differently, how? Tell me and I will do it! I am—thy slave, *Don* Jaime. Thine—to command. The day that thou commandest me to cut my throat, my life will be over. For I will do it, *Don* Jaime! With a razor—zzzzhaaash—so! And bleed and bleed and bleed until I died. Tell me, wouldst thou—cry?"

"Trini, you are mad!" he said.

"Yes. As a watering pot. And for thee!"

"Well, I won't order you to cut your throat," he said solemnly. "You're too skinny to make good steaks out of. Let me see. What shall I order you to do? Something terrible—to punish you for your bad behavior. There, I've got it!"

"What is it—that you wish of me, *Don* Jaime?" she said, her voice humid with choked-back tears.

"I order thee—to smile. To laugh. To be gay. To have a perfectly wonderful time, so that I may enjoy watching thee have it."

She gazed at him, her eyes bigger than ever. Filled with—wonder. With—he was absolutely sure, now—real tenderness.

"I—will—try, *Don* Jaime," she said.

From across the table at *Les Ambassadeurs* he could see her trembling. She was ill from nervousness and it showed.

"Now, Trini—" he said.

"So many knives and forks and spoons!" she almost wept. "I know not which to use—nor in what order! I will disgrace thee, *Don* Jaime!"

"You will very simply and quietly observe which one *I* use, and employ the same one at the same time. Simple, no? And you will drink your champagne now, at once, but not too fast, nor too much, only enough to make you gay. And you will smile at me so that everyone in this room will cease to believe that it is my custom to beat you bloody three times a day, which is the one thing the expression on your lovely little face has them totally convinced of now!"

"But you don't, do you, *Don* Jaime?" a woman's voice said in very nearly accentless English, from just behind his chair.

Jim turned, stared up at her. Got to his feet, said:

"I'm sorry, but I don't seem to recall—"

"Having met me?" the woman said. She was, Jim saw, the type that Anglo Saxons mean when they say a person is typically Spanish. That is, she had straight black hair, dark eyes, and olive skin. Which meant that she was typically Andalusian, or typically Gypsy, but not typically Spanish because there isn't any such thing, for the Spanish, aside from being brunettes more often than they are blondes, vary as widely from individual to individual as most European peoples do. She was also quite tall, and in her early forties.

None of which was especially unusual. More than unusual, however, actually astonishing in any Latin American country, was for a woman obviously a member of Costa Verde's very highest social class to come alone and uninvited to a man's table in a public restaurant, and strike up a conversation with said man, even if they *had* been previously and formally introduced, and especially so when the man in question was accompanied by another woman. And, in this case, Jim was grimly aware, the whole onslaught was raised past mere unconventionality to sheer impossibility by the fact that his company was—what poor Trini was or at least—he hoped fervently that the past definite actually applied!—had been.

"Exactly," Jim said crisply. "Of course, I cannot boast of a flawless memory, but—"

"Your memory is not at fault, *Don* Jaime," she laughed. "We haven't met. But I'm not to be blamed for that, either. If you'd have taken a vacation from serving as the Reds' favorite target long enough for Vince to bring you home to dinner instead of having to forever patch you up, we should have met long ago . . ."

"Good Lord!" Jim said. "Then you're—"

"Paloma Gomez. Vince's better half. No, better three-quarters, as I frequently remind him! Mind if I sit down? Don't worry! I'll only stay a minute! I don't mean to spoil your—fun, *Don* Jaime. Even my position as Second in Command—Vice President, actually—of Costa Verde's League for the Liberation of Women, doesn't entitle me to be *that* unkind! Besides, if I stay longer, Vince might give way to his naturally atavistic impulses—not to mention his dislike for my political and social inclinations!—and beat *me* bloody as you were threatening to do to this poor baby . . ."

"Please do join us, then!" Jim said; and signaled for the waiter to bring another chair. As he did so, he looked around the room for Vince, but he didn't see him.

Paloma saw the look.

"Oh," she laughed, as she sank into the chair the waiter held for her, "my Lord and Master's probably hiding downstairs in the men's room and foaming at the mouth with *rage* at me! He really *hates* the things I do, Old Reactionary Male Chauvinist Pig that he is! Incidently, *Don* Jaime," she added with absolutely venomous sweetness, "*one* of those things is heading—officially—Luisa García's Organization for the Defense, Help, and Rehabilitation of poor girl children like this one—who've been pushed, beaten, starved, and otherwise forced into this filthy business!" Then she leaned forward and peered into Trini's face with an expression of real kindness.

Not only was Trini trembling, Jim saw now; but, quite visibly, beyond her lipstick, the edges and the inside corners of her lips were snowy. 'My God! She's going to faint!' he thought.

"You are Trini, aren't you?" Paloma said gently, but in Spanish, now. "How are you, my dear?"

"Very well, thank you, my Lady," Trini said, or whispered, or perhaps only breathed, because her lips formed the shape of the words without the sound.

"Don't be afraid of me, Child," Paloma said. "*I* would never harm you . . ."

Trini bowed her head. When she looked up again the tears were already on her cheeks, star tracks in the candlelight.

"I—know that, *mi Señora*," she said slowly. "In a way—you cannot. For what harm is there in life—what bad thing—that has not already happened to me—long ago—and many times?"

"But since I have investigated your case and know that nothing—absolutely nothing!—that has happened to you was your own fault, there is no need for crying, Child . . ."

"Ah, but there is, *me Señora*! *Now,* there is! For you have made me realize—again!—the great harm I have done *Don* Jaime. Now. Tonight. By merely being here with him. At his side. I thought that—that I love him—truly love him, *mi Señora;* you *must* believe that! *¡Por favor!* Tell me you believe me! Oh please, my Lady, please!"

Paloma stared at her. Said, slowly, her voice passing through doubt, hesitation, growing astonishment towards—conviction, reluctant at first, unwilling, fought against, but surrendered to, finally, accepted; then—almost joyously!—embraced:

"I *do* Child. Truly."

"God bless you, my Lady! I thought that—my loving him—truly—and with all my heart—would be enough. I was glad that he—is not ashamed of me, does not wish to hide me. But now I see I was wrong. I should have stayed in my little flat—on a quiet street and been content—with—some secret hours—stolen from his life. Because all I have done now is to ruin him!"

"Not in my eyes, Child!" Paloma said. "Besides, it's *you* I came to defend, not him, nor any *maldito* man!"

"Paloma, Mrs. Gomez—" Jim began.

"Don't interrupt, Jim!" Paloma snapped. "This is important!"

"No—perhaps not to you," Trini whispered; "but look around you, *mi Señora!* At the others! See their faces!"

Involuntarily, Jim looked round the room. Half a glance was enough to catalogue the expressions of pure outrage on the faces of the women present, the look of ill-concealed envy on the men's.

"I don't think that their reactions matter as much as you think, Trini," Paloma said gravely. "Now, if you'll forgive me, I am going to speak to *Don* Jaime in his own language. There is a thing I want to ask him that—"

"No," Jim said quietly. "You will ask it in Spanish so that Trini may understand every word, or I will not answer it, Paloma!"

Paloma stared at him.

"You're a brave man, Jim. Or a fool. Usually synonyms, aren't they? Very well. In Spanish, then: What are you going to *do* with this poor baby?"

Jim studied Paloma's face, her eyes.

"I'm not sure I understand your question," he said slowly. "Would you care to rephrase it?"

"I mean do you intend to—marry her?" Paloma said, her voice a whipcrack. "Father her children?"

Jim hung there, thinking: 'Do I have *that* much in me? That much—charity? Forgiveness? Pity? Pain? That much—love? Grace is—gone. Surely gone. And this child—this forlorn, tormented, badly damaged child!—thinks, believes she loves me. Confuses gratitude—for what ought to be a commonplace, but isn't, come to think of it, not anywhere: some human warmth, a little kindly treatment—with whatever the hell love is. While I—'

He literally *felt* then, Trini's gaze upon his face. Her eyes (eyes of a little green female Martian, doe-thing's eyes, big with desperate hope, blacker than ten thousand nights of utter pain, slanting Tluscolan eyes, dying wide open of all the awful ways there are to die) locked into his, holding them, searching his face, searching his mind, his heart . . .

He put his hand across the table and took hers.

"Trini," he said, "I am going to try to tell the truth. And that's very hard. So I say it to you. Directly. I don't *know* the answers to *Doña* Paloma's questions. I don't know whether I have that much love left in me. To offer you—or any woman. It's been bled out of me—through too many wounds. Starved out of me. Tortured out—even to the death, perhaps. But—maybe—yes. To both questions. If that's what you want of me. If that's what you need . . ."

"The—the children, yes! *Thy* children, *Don* Jaime! That they be— little like thee, and blond like thee, and as ugly as thou art, and as beautiful! Inside, as beautiful!" Trini whispered. "With *thy* soul which is enormous, and thy kindness, thy goodness, thy love! That they be *all* thee, and none of me—"

"Then I wouldn't want them," he said.

"That they be—as little of me, then, as is possible," she sobbed, "so that they may be *honorados y honestas y decentes y*—"

"Trini, you stop it!" he said.

"It is—stopped, *Don* Jaime," she whispered, and bent and kissed his hand.

"And *that*," he said.

"Equally. Likewise. The—children. *Thy* children, yes, *Don* Jaime! That they be many! Ten at the least! Twelve! Twenty!"

"Lord!" he said. "You'd have to put a couple of other workers on the job then, *Niña*!

"No and no and no! Thou! Only thou forever! If any man attempts to touch me who am thine, I will kill him, *Don* Jaime! But this—of marriage—is not necessary, *mi Amor*. I will not ruin thee—spoil thy life—as such a misalliance would surely do! That thou wilt acknowledge them is enough! That—"

"That you shut up, baby!" Paloma said her voice rough, breath torn, ragged. "Jim—I salute thee. Verily thou art—rare. Mad, of course; but I like such madness. It is a thing that Vince and I have fought over for years: his acceptance of, his complacence at, the way women are *used* down here . . ."

"I thank you, Paloma," he said.

"But—one thing—if it comes to a child, to children, you won't accept this arrangement that she offers, will you? Take her away, Jim. To your country. Where no one knows her. Instruct her. Teach her. Can't you *see* how bright she is? She can learn. Do that—and you'll have a wife, my friend. A real one. Forever. And *I* and every woman who *is* a woman, will bless your name."

"Like these present tonight?" he said.

"They *aren't,* and therefore they don't matter, Jim. They don't matter at all."

Then abruptly she leaned over and kissed Trini's cheek.

"I shall stand as Godmother to your firstborn," she said.

She got up. Stood there smiling at both of them. Whispered:

"God bless you both!"

And left them there.

CHAPTER

17

At the Obsidian Room, they danced.

'You could put it that way,' Jim thought. 'But in the interests of accuracy, respect for absolute truth, how can I put it? That she—Trini—works Black Magic. Turns on her Voodoo witchcraft, so that even *I,* who have never danced before, am dancing! Good Lord! She—'

Melted into the music. Flowed into all his hollows. Fitted into contours he hadn't even known he had. Eyes closed, remote and dreaming. Mouth a little opened, adhesively soft and scalding, clinging to the flesh of his throat, quivering there lost—helpless, hopeless, yearning—branding him forever, while all the rest of her made devil-doll's mockery of their clothing, fusing their separate lonelinesses, so that the beat of the music, its subtle tropical rhythms, became tactile and flowed along conjoined flesh, converted nerves—become linked and mutual!—into the whiplashes of the Penitentes, rolled in staccato drumbursts through all their veins.

In one sense, it wasn't true that he had never danced before—or at least not entirely. He had had dancing lessons, as most diplomats' sons do, as a matter of course. He had learned everything that such lessons teach: which is to convincingly fake doing a thing that, if you aren't *born* with its essentials in you, if rhythm, passion, fire, swooning tenderness, night, damnation, death, and pain, didn't go into your making at conception's blinding instant, no being whose membership in the human race is not subject to grave doubt could even begin to teach you to do it well, for without these gifts from God, from the Devil, a pair of blessedly lusty parents, there is not the faintest hope you'll ever learn.

'And if you *are* born with Flamenco guitars strumming in you, African Voodoo Tom-Toms in your blood, Tluscolan seed-gourds swishing magic along every wire-taut and twanging nerve you own, like this little miracle in my arms—Jesus! I'd swear she's floating two full centimeters *above* the damned floor!—it's a mortal sin for anyone to try to teach you, to interfere with what you've got, for all they'll ever do is spoil it. But I'll be blessed if she hasn't got *me* doing it! By osmosis, maybe . . .'

The music stopped. She hung there, glued to him from throat to knee, warmsoft, quivering.

"Trini—" he said.

She opened her eyes. They glowed in the dark. Black pearls. Jet.

"I love thee, *Don* Jaime," she said.

"And I, thee," he said honestly. He did now. He couldn't help it. What had caution, common sense, the sure ruin of what was left of his career to do with this? Nothing. Absolutely nothing at all.

He touched her arm to lead her back to their table.

"Oh, no, *Don* Jaime!" she wailed. "Let's go on dancing! Let's never stop! Never, never, never!"

"*Niña,*" he said; "I'm an old, old man. Dancing—with thee—is maybe too much for me. One more like that last one and I'll have a heart attack. And you can cry over me in the cemetery tomorrow as they lower me into the grave."

"But I should *not* cry over thee in such a case, *mi Amor,*" she said solemnly. "Not at all. Dost know why?"

"No. Why not, Trini? Aside from the probable fact that you've already ceased to love me. That is, if you ever really did."

In answer to that, there on that nightclub dance floor, in full sight of the few other dancers, and the many, many other people sitting around it, she went up on tiptoe and kissed his mouth. A long time. Mischievously and expertly and with real relish, enjoying herself, truly enjoying herself, having female, sensual, very nearly sexual fun; then, abruptly, stopping *that,* letting a wave of pure, sweet, childish, almost crippling tenderness steal through . . . As she drew her mouth away, stared up at him, he could hear the titters of delighted—and malicious!—laughter run from table to table all around the dance floor.

"Trini!" he said.

"That was—a very small sample of how much I love thee," she said. "And the reason that I would not cry for thee if thou shouldst die is that I would be lying beside thee in another coffin. Or in the *same* one if that is permitted. So thou must be very careful *not* to die, *Don* Jaime, for that would be to cheat me. Thou owest me *ten* babies, remember?"

"Good Lord!" he laughed. "Then, Trini *mía,* we'd better sit the next few out in order to restore my strength. Besides, I'm parched. Let's have some more champagne . . ."

"*¡De acuerdo!*" she said. "But *thou* must drink most of it, and become a little drunken, thus making it easier for me to seduce thee. For tonight I am going to seduce thee, which is necessary for the making of babies, *no es así, mi Amor*? And is even better than merely feeling as though one were making them—and by the hundreds!—which is what dancing with thee does inside me!"

"Lord!" he said again. "Trini, you're impossible!"

"No. Thou hast it wrong, *Don* Jaime, the Great *Don* Jaime, *Embajador Extraordinario de los Estados Unidos de Norteamerica*! Tonight, for thee, I am possible. No. That is wrong, too. Tonight, for thee, I am certain. Art thou certain—or even—possible—for me?"

"I don't know, Trini—" he said sadly, a blade of sudden, inexplicable near terror driving deep between his breathing and his life. "Thou'rt so—young. And so very lovely that—"

"That what, *Don* Jaime?"

"There comes upon me—a—a fear. Of harming thee. Of spoiling— all the rest of thy life . . ."

"Yes," she said gravely; "thou *couldst* harm me. That's true. The danger exists. But the harm would be—total. And the only way thou couldst spoil my life *now* would be to—end it. Thou canst accomplish both things very easily. By—leaving me. I would not support *that*—nor survive it, one full hour."

"Trini!" he said.

Again he saw those matchless eyes fill up, brim, spill. And as always, the sight was intensely moving.

"*Don* Jaime," she whispered. "*Mi querido, amado, y adorado Don* Jaime, dost not know even *yet* that without thee I would die?"

"Don't say that!" he said sharply, the fear in him deeper still. "To speak—a horror is to invite it. Come, let's rest a bit. Have more champagne . . ."

And it was then, at that precise moment, that their evening started to go wrong; for, when they got back to their table, Jenny Crowley was sitting there at it, waiting for them.

She was neither drunk, nor—to use the drug culture's favorite phrase—stoned out of her skull. She was completely sober, neatly, even attractively dressed, bathed, perfumed, made up, brushed, and combed. In fact, aside from her terrible emaciation, the result of the heroin addict's total loss of appetite, she looked almost human. Her eyes were not two mindless bits of blue glass, but clear, alert, alive, except that the sadness in them was very nearly unbearable.

" 'Lo, Uncle Chub," she said. "Oh, Lord! I *must* stop calling you that! You're so nice and thin, now—and so good-looking! Sexy-looking. So— Uncle Jim. All right?"

"All right. Jenny, this is—"

"Trini. The people at the table next to mine—ours; Joe *was* with me, but he got one of those spooky telephone calls he's always getting and had to leave for a while; reckon he'll be back soon though— Where was I? Oh yes. About your date. The people at the table next to ours were telling me about her—after she'd got through swabbing your tonsils for you on the dance floor. They could see how shocked I was, and they spoke English so—"

'You're shocked because Trini kissed me,' he thought grimly, 'but that little exhibition you put on for my special benefit with Joe was not shocking? No—I don't suppose it was. Shocking things have to be conscious, don't they? And you probably don't even remember *that* . . .' He said, quietly:

"Go on, Jen."

"I'll bet you don't know much about her, d'you, Uncle—Jim? They said she's the American Ambassador's *mistress.* And just in case you don't know—but you *couldn't* know, could you? Or else you wouldn't *dare* bring her to a place like this! She's your friendly neighborhood *hooker*! Now really, Uncle Ch—Jim, you—"

He thanked high heaven that Trini knew not one word of English. But then he saw she didn't need to; that Jenny's mere presence alone at their table was enough. She turned to him and her eyes went absolutely sick with sudden hurt.

"Who is this woman?" she breathed—and all that breath ashudder! "Who is this *Gringa, Don* Jaime? *Thy* woman? But no; she cannot be! Thou'rt a—widower—or so thou hast let the world believe. But if thou hast lied, I shall make thy lies the truth! For if she does not leave here *now,* this instant, she dies!"

"What's she saying, Uncle Ch–Jim?" Jenny said. "I know some Spanish, but she talks faster than a machine gun!"

"Later, Jen," Jim said flatly. "Trini, do me the favor of shutting up, and otherwise behaving thyself, or I shall beat thee. Which would be to spoil all we've had together, so I'd rather not be forced to. But hear this, little Pepperpot: Thou wilt kill no one, and especially not this poor, sick girl . . ."

"Ohhhh, *Don* Jaime!" Trini moaned. "She—she *is* thine! This skeleton dancing around inside that cat-vomit-colored skin! This quarter kilo of bones! This ugly, disgusting—"

"Wrong words, Trini. Have you no charity? Say thin, sick, pitiful—daughter of one of my oldest friends. Whom one of my first missions to this country was to try to save. But not—my woman, wife, or lover. Nor has she ever been. My pupil, yes; but nothing more. Now, sit down, will you?"

Trini sank into a chair. She was staring at Jenny with horrified eyes. Immense tears were stealing slowly down her cheeks—one by one by one. In the candlelight they made blood rubies, orange and silver fire.

"She *is!*" she wept. "*Thine!* Oh, *Don* Jaime! I never thought *thou* wouldst lie to me, deceive me!"

"Trini," Jim said, "this is getting tiresome. The comedy is not amusing. And I lost my taste for melodrama years ago. So, stop it, will you?"

Trini turned, stared at him, searching his face, his eyes. Whispered:

"It—is—stopped, *Don* Jaime, *mi Señor*! But along with it—my heart. And—my life!"

"What's she making it so *big* over, Uncle Jim?" Jenny said. "I don't hack *this* scene at all. Anyone would think she was shacked up with *you* instead of the American Ambassador."

"*I* am the American Ambassador, Jenny," Jim Rush said.

Jenny clapped both her hands at her thin cheeks.

"Oh, Lord!" she gasped. "I've *really* blown it, haven't I? When I saw you come in, there I was getting myself all set, trying to figure out the best way of turning you on, and— Ohhh, Uncle Jim—she—she's *so* damned beautiful!"

"Yes," Jim said quietly, "she *is,* isn't she? But that shouldn't trouble you, Jen. You are, I've been told, a married woman again. To—Joe Harper—"

"Only I—I *hate* him! He tricked me—forced me into—"

"Who th' ever lovin' hell," Joe's voice said wearily from above their heads, "ever had to force *you* into anything, you miserable cunt? Shit. You aren't even a good cocksucker any more. I'll *give* you to ol' Uncle Creepie-Poo, here, gratis. Hellll no! I'll swap you to him—for *this!*"

He leaned across the table, caught Trini's chin in his big, muscular hand. Turned her face this way and that, examining her as a buyer examines a horse.

"Take your hands off her, Joe," Jim said.

"Creep, Old Boy—*this* is too rich for your blood!" Joe laughed. "So I gotta suggestion: Why don't you quietly get lost like a nice *smart* little Old Party, huh? Take th' Cunt with you, I don't mind. But *this* is for *me!*"

Jim sat there. He was not, he realized with sudden wonder, afraid. Except for fearing the way he felt. He had never felt that way before. He had held himself incapable of such feelings. Believed they had been trained, educated, even bred out of men like him generations ago.

'I,' he thought, 'am going to kill this bastard. I don't know how or with what, but I'm going to kill him. I'm *that* atavistic. That primitive. And because—because *what?*' He couldn't think. There was no time. Action was indicated. Direct, effective action, now, at once, in this world of obscene violence where the Hamlets always lose.

"C'mon, Baby, let's you 'n me split this scene!" Joe was saying to Trini.

"*¡No hablo Inglés! ¡No lo entiendo!*" Trini said.

"No sweat, Baby! *¡Ven conmigo, gatita mía! ¡Vamos, zorrita linda, ven acá!*" Joe said.

"I," Trini said quietly, "am neither thy pussy cat, nor thy pretty bitch, nor anything of thine. I am— *his. Don* Jaime's. *All* his. In *all* ways. Hast comprehended, *Gringo* pig? Hast thou well understood this which I have said?" She was *"tuteándole,"* using the intimate form of address not because she liked him but the reverse. You also said "Tú"—but in a vastly different tone of voice!—to people you didn't have to be polite to, inferiors, lackeys—scum. Like Joe Harper, for instance.

"Baby, I dig!" Joe laughed. "But you know how long it's going to take me to change all that, *Putita mía?* Five minutes. No—three!"

And *because* the situation was impossible, utterly impossible, he, Jim Rush, had no lesser out. If he tried to defend Trini, defend whatever hold he had on her by engaging in an ordinary—and abysmally stupid!—fist fight, this big bastard, trained as a professional bodyguard in all the martial arts, would knock him unconscious with the first blow and bear Trini away by main force. And because of his position as American Ambassador, the subsequent chain of events would be just as inevitable: He'd be recalled inside of three weeks for—try as he would he could think of no more gentle or less merciless way of putting it— engaging in a vulgar public brawl in a night club over the favors of—a whore.

Of course, he admitted to himself—Was it then, at that exact instant, that the range of his vision extended to those steak knives the diners at the next table, themselves still on the dance floor, their chairs unoccupied, had left beside their unfinished plates?—nothing would be changed by the appallingly primitive and irrational act of murder except—

Except that the vulgar brawl would be raised somehow into the dimensions, and the dignity, of—tragedy.

As it already was. Because what he had to defend was, at bottom, his self-respect. His integrity. His manhood. And—his pride. Ancient, atavistic, primitive words, with no meaning in a modern world. But he was going to defend them. Them—and his love. For this woman. For this little piece of damaged, shopworn goods. This—whore.

No! (His hand moved smoothly, slowly, carefully now, towards that table, trying not to attract Joe's attention, because his only chance against that Neanderthal lay in the element of unexpectedness, surprise, towards his deliverance from littleness, meanness, fear, even— dishonor—that big, fat, solemn, hopelessly archaic word!) For this lovely, forlorn, pitiful child. Angelic face of a Martian female, night-black slanting Tluscolan eyes, mouth—

Halfway to her feet, drawn upward by Joe's immense—and immensely brutal—strength, perhaps because she was looking at Jim out of love, loss, longing, pure despair, Trini saw what he meant to do. And wrenching herself—all whipcord, vibrant sinew, midnight, abobe, snow and fire—free of Joe Harper's grasp, she threw herself sidewise between Jim and those knives, crashing into that table, almost knocking it over, bending across it, her back to them. By the time Joe recovered from his surprise, reached out, caught her by the shoulder, whirled her effortlessly around to face him, she had one of those knives in her hand.

"Ha!" Joe chuckled. "Put down th' hardware, Baby. Be a pity to have to break your pretty little arm!"

Her hand flashed blue lightning—but not at, nor even towards, Joe Harper. That knife sang upward, inward, buried its razor sharp point two centimeters or a little more deep in the soft, dark, lovely swelling of her left breast, while its serrated edge, following, before she could halt that thrust, slashed open, less profoundly, five full centimeters more.

"Trini!" Jim Rush screamed.

Her other hand came up, closed around the one already holding the handle of that knife.

"Try to take it away from me now, *Don Cerdo*!" she whispered. "Try, Mister Pig! Knowest thou what will happen, then?"

"Yep, Baby. *Sí, Chiquita.* I know. You'll—die. That is, if you don't already—of this. Okay. You win. *¡Tú ganas la partida!* But—explain me this—will you? *¿Quieres explicarmelo?*

"I—am *his*," Trini said. "*All* his—and I love him. And I am— Tluscola! At least—in part. We do not shame the men we love. We die first."

Jim was on his feet by then. He put his arms around her, hearing from afar off—thousands of kilometers away it seemed to him—the shrill screams of the women, the hoarse shouts of the men, and the pounding of feet rushing in towards them. He felt the whole room swirl dizzily about his head, his eyes go scalded, absolutely blind as if to shut out the sight of what was bubbling up, flooding up around the blade of that knife, streaking black red down that cream and silver, old off-white of cherished memories . . .

"I—I have spoiled my dress," she whispered, in an odd, grave little girl's tone of voice; then: "Oh, no; *Don* Jaime! Do not—cry! Men—do not cry! And especially not for—garbage. For—dirt-cheap goods—like me . . ."

Then, very quietly, she fainted.

He swept her up into his arms as though she were weightless—as she very nearly was—looked wildly around him for the nearest exit, and became aware that Joe Harper was struggling in the grip of four powerful men dressed as—waiters. Which they weren't. Very clearly, they weren't. Then a man wearing a chauffeur's uniform dashed in and smashed an absolutely expert and perfect karate chop to Joe Harper's neck. Joe went limp. And Jim saw, with no real astonishment, except to wonder when and how he'd come into the Obsidian Room, that the man who had put Joe out of the fight was his chauffeur Roberto. Correction! *Teniente Colonel* Roberto Henriques of National Security. And acting as such, now.

"Take that animal outside," he commanded; "and break all his bones!"

And it was then that Jim Rush had confirmed his own shrewd guess as to what the fatal flaw in the García-Harper axis for the control of the drug traffic would surely be: secrecy. Secrecy so tightly maintained that no one in any of the law enforcement bodies, not even in National Security, itself was aware of the connection. This was the flaw that made moving in on Joe Harper, and removing him from poor Jenny's path, child's play for anyone with the trained diplomat's skill that he, Jim Rush, had.

Not that he realized *then* that Roberto's unhesitatingly rough treatment of Harper had confirmed his supposition. That realization came to him days later when he had achieved the serenity to think about what had happened. Naturally *then,* at that awful moment, standing there holding Trini in his arms with her blood and perhaps her life— "Please no, Father Pío's God!"—pouring out of her, he thought about only those things he had to: preventing the situation from getting any further out of hand than it already was, and obtaining immediate medical help for Trini.

"No!" he said, "Please no, Roberto! For *her* sake, man—and mine! Creating a scandal won't help, you know. Don't arrest him. I won't press charges. Take him back to his table. This young lady," he nodded towards Jenny, "will show you which one. Leave him there. But first call the hospital—Dr. Gomez—an ambulance—"

"The car would be quicker, Sir!" Roberto said. "And I don't have to call Dr. Gomez. He's here with his wife, *Doña* Paloma. He's already gone for his bag. Meantime, better let *me* have a look at her. I have some experience of knife wounds . . ."

By then, hundreds of people, it seemed to him, were milling around, cutting off every breath of air. And every damned one of them, he was sure, saw and commented upon the fact that Trini's right hand was still clasped around the handle of that knife.

"*¡Se ha suicidado!*" they whispered. "*¿Pero—por que?*" "The big blond *Gringo,* of course! A former lover—surely. Showed up *inoportunamente,* to spoil the good thing she had going with *Su Excelencia el Embajador! Seguramente* that was why she stabbed herself! *¡Pobre zorrita!* She was far too pretty and too sweet—to die this way!"

"Stand back!" Roberto said authoritatively. "Give the little lady air!"

The waiters—the authentic waiters—not the ones who were hustling Joe Harper away, pushed three tables together, sweeping glasses, plates, napkins, cloths off them, swirling clean new tablecloths across. Jim lay Trini down on the three tables. Looked up and saw Vince Gomez pushing his way through the crowd with his satchel in his hands.

"Followed you here, you blithering jackass!" he snarled at Jim out of the side of his mouth. "Paloma, of course! Wanted to go on watching you having fun. Now get the hell out of my way, will you? Told you this little *zorra* would ruin you!"

Then he looked down at Trini. Looked back up at Jim. Said:

"My God!"

He opened his bag. Came out with a pair of surgical scissors. Cut down the front of that beautiful Geri Pyle creation to the waist as though it were so much floursacking, and the slip beneath it at the same time. Snipped through the front band of Trini's strapless bra, yanked it halfway around from beneath her, out, off, and away, threw it over his shoulder somewhere into the dark. Which left poor Trini naked to her panty tops before all those people, but the sight was hardly pleasing: with the amount of blood her breasts and belly were flooded with by then, she looked like a slaughtered she-goat.

"Bring more lights, damnit!" Vince roared.

Two waiters flanked him, holding high lamps from nearby tables. Vince unhooked her fingers from that knife. Drew it out. Dumped sulfa powder into the wound. The flooding flow of blood washed it away in seconds. He brought out hemostats and clamped the cut. Now you could see it was a long, clean, diagonally slanted gash, after he had mopped the remaining blood away. He fished into his bag for needle and catgut, turned and looked into Trini's dark, wide open eyes.

"Trini, *Niña,*" he said almost tenderly, "I'm going to have to sew you up. And it's going to hurt. I haven't any anesthesia to give you. Would you like—some brandy—or whiskey or—"

"No, thank you—Doctor," she whispered. "Do what you must. I am—mostly Tluscola. And *las Tluscolas* bear pain—very well . . ."

She did. Not very well. Magnificently. It was Jim who was shaking and shivering and on the verge of passing out before Vince got those seven stitches into that awful gash.

Paloma, almost angrily, it seemed to Jim, bundled Trini up in the remains of her bloody clothing, and two tablecloths. Vince said to Jim:

"Now I'll ring for an ambulance. You can ride along with her, if you like. I'm going to put *both* of you to bed—in different rooms, Jim Rush! Screwing is definitely not indicated for the next week or so, anyhow. I'll give you a shot that will knock you out at least until then. You're in a state of shock, my friend!"

"Couldn't I take her in, in the car?" Jim whispered.

"Of course! Be better if you did, considering where this damned hotel is anyhow: way the hell over on the far side of Bahía Linda, a good hour's ride from town. Cut the delay in half if we bring her in now instead of having to wait for an ambulance. She needs a transfusion, along with shots of vitamin K, for some odd reason—diet maybe, or the lack of it, considering how thin she is—her blood doesn't clot fast enough to do her any good. Jesus! Ever since I've met *you* I've done nothing but pump blood back into people. And this is, esthetically speaking, anyhow, the worst case of all from what Paloma calls my Male Chauvinist Pig's point of view. To ruin a gorgeous tit like this one! Why the hell did she do it, Boy? You were being mean to her, or what?"

"Explain it to you later, Vince. That is—if it can be explained. Some things can't, you know . . ."

"Jim," Paloma said, "may I ride in with you and her? I'm a trained nurse, y'know. Of course, I haven't practiced for years, but I know enough to help if she starts hemorrhaging en route. It's a long way. And she seems to be—a bleeder. And 'Gorgeous Tits' must be taken care of, mustn't they? In the interest of the next generation of Male Chauvinist Pigs— *and* their little sisters!"

"Paloma, for God's sake!" Vince said.

"I thank you, my dear. Please do," Jim whispered.

In the big car, Trini lay across the seat with her head in Jim's lap, and her legs across Paloma's knees. She was small enough to do that. Paloma had Vince's bag with her just in case. Vince had driven ahead to get everything ready. And, as instructed, Roberto drove very slowly and carefully.

"*Don* Jaime—art—angry with me?" Trini whispered.

"No—yes! It was a thing of men. You should have let me handle it!" he said.

"Of men? Perhaps. But more of *brutotes y bestias* like that one. But of—such as thou'rt, no; *Don* Jaime . . ."

"You mean," he said with aching bitterness, "it was not a thing for cowards."

"*¡Un corbade—Tú!*" she said with unfeigned astonishment. "Thou'rt the bravest man I've ever known, *Don* Jaime! And the best! But thou art—a gentleman. A great gentleman. *Un caballero. Un Hidalgo.* A *Grande,* surely, of thy country, because art thou not an Ambassador? I could not permit thee to intermix thyself in—" she stopped, and a little sob tore her throat, "in what the papers tomorrow are sure to call '*Una palea entre un chulo y una puta . . .*' "

"Trini!" he said, his voice anguished, for what she had said meant, "A brawl between a pimp and a whore."

"Trini," Paloma said crisply. "Do you still *do* that? Walk the streets? Solicit men? Go with them to houses of assignation? Inhabit The Blue Moon?"

"No, *Doña* Paloma," Trini whispered. "Since the very night I met *Don* Jaime, I have left the bad life. I work as a model at the boutique of *Don* Geraldo Pyle. I told *Don* Jaime—told this *gran caballero* whom I am presumptuous enough to love—"

"Stop it!" Paloma said sharply. "There is no presumption in the love of *any* woman for any man! We give our men great joy, and their continuation in our children. The boot's on the other foot, it seems to me! For what do they give *us* but misery and pain?"

Trini stared at her.

"I do not understand such things, *Doña* Paloma," she whispered. "But *Don* Jaime has given me—gives me—life. I'm alive all over, inside and out, so alive I tingle! I breathe, sing, skip, and dance instead of walk, for the first time since I was *born*—because—he's there. Simply because he's alive and in the same world with me! Is this strange—or rare?"

"No, Child; it's not. I felt that way myself when I was young. I still do—at times. God grant it stays with you! But what I was trying to point out to you is that you are no longer a prostitute. You *are* a decent girl, Trini. Vince—my husband, was talking with Doctor Basquez in the bar, and didn't see what happened. But *I* did. Thou, Child, hast washed away any lingering dishonor this night in thine own blood!"

"Amen to that!" Jim said.

"No—" Trini whispered, "this is not enough! I—I promised him, promised *Don* Jaime—that I would die, before I'd let another man touch me. And I will keep that promise, *Doña* Paloma. Still this is not enough. For what has it to do with the past? What thing is there—what act at all—that can scrape the layers—of—filth—from off my soul?"

"Trini, please!" Jim said.

"Listen! I wish I were *all* Tluscola instead of only part! For they have a way—"

"Thou'rt feverish," Paloma said. "What way is that, Child?"

"When a woman has been bad—*deshonesta, inmoral*—couching herself with men other than her *novio* or her husband, the Tluscola do a very cruel thing: They sit her on the stick. It is—thirty centimeters high, and of ironwood, and very sharp—"

"A form of—impalement," Jim shuddered. "Peter Reynolds wrote about it in his book on Costa Verde. But Trini, those women *always* die!"

"Not always, *mi Amor*. One in a thousand perhaps survives. And the Tluscola dress that one—in white. Declare her a virgin—again. Pure. Her husband then takes her back. Her *novio,* if she is not yet married, forgives her. And she is honored in the *Pueblo*. And she *never* sins again!"

"Here we are!" Roberto called back through the half-opened panel. He stopped the car. Came around, opened the door. Put out his massive arms to take Trini, and lay her down on the stretcher already waiting.

"No," she breathed. "Let *Don* Jaime take me. Oh! That is—if he—wants to . . ."

"I want to," Jim said and got out of the car. Lifted her up and out. Walked over to where the wheeled stretcher bed with the two orderlies waited. Stood there, holding her, as though he hated to put her down. He did. He wanted to hold her in his arms forever.

"I would—do *that* for thee, my love," she murmured; "accept the punishment of the Tluscola. Submit to it gladly. So as not to cheat thee. So that thou couldst have—*una chica casta, pura, decente, honesta, buena*—"

Which still less than the rest of it was to be borne. Swiftly he bent and flattened those hateful, hurtful words against her speaking mouth.

CHAPTER

18

"And the boy—Alvaro?" Jim said. "I'd like to say good-bye to him before I leave."

"Alvaro isn't here," Vicente Gomez said. "He's gone. He told me to tell you—good-bye—and thanks . . ."

"But, where? How? Vince, he was in no condition to—"

"You're right. But letting him go half healed was the lesser of several evils, Jim—or of several dangers. I got him a taxi, at his request. The taxi driver, whom I know personally—I've treated his whole enormous family at one time or another—later reported to me that he put the kid out, on a certain corner. Almost immediately, a truck picked him up. A truck from the Electric Light and Power Company. There were several men in it, dressed in blue coveralls. Strange, isn't it?"

"No," Jim said. "Not at all."

Vince looked at him; said:

"Then you know something that I don't."

"I know a good many things that you don't, Vince. Better like that. Safer. For you, anyhow. My slant is that Paloma's both too young and too good-looking to become a widow. Right?"

"I," Vince said gloomily, "sometimes think she'd be *the* Merriest Widow in Costa Verde. Ever since she started out to change my mental attitude, convert me into an advocate of equality between the sexes, our married life has gone straight to hell, Jim!"

"Then why not just let her do it? I'm on *her* side, Vince."

"You, Jim Rush, are a blithering jackass," Vince said. "And a romantic, which is maybe even worse. Number one: *Nature* is against it. The female of the human species, in case nobody ever told you, comes equipped with a womb—"

"And a delightful little snatch, not to mention a pair of gorgeous tits," Jim added solemnly. "And, oh, those lovely pear-shaped fundaments!"

"Oh, Christ!" Vince said. "Granted. But the *purpose* of all that equipment, Mr. Ambassador Rush, is to perpetuate the human race—for which it serves admirably. And that means that much of the time she's weighed down with two or three kilos of fetus, or a live brat, or both at the same time; and, as the result of the necessities of her organism, has a pelvic formation that makes her attempt at running laughable. Hence, she's easy pickings for any sabertoothed tiger—or his modern mutant named Joe Harper!—and needs and always will need defense by the stout club and/or stone ax wielding arm of her Lord and Master, and if she's smart, damned well ought *not* incapacitate him for said defense by de-balling him psychologically!"

"You know," Jim said, "you just might have a little something there, Doctor!"

"I know I have. Which brings us to the subject of dear little Trini. She's in love with you; right?"

"Vince—"

"I propose to be rough. I pay you the compliment of risking our friendship. I think you're worth it, Jim. I also think—hope—you're intelligent enough not to get *that* furious at me for trying to help you. In short, for attempting to open your love-besotted eyes!"

"Go ahead. Your approach—interests me. And the risk—to our friendship—is nonexistent. What is that you know about Trini that I don't?"

"Very little. Some questions of her health—her physical health—that since, fortunately, we've been forewarned about them, I should be able to control quite easily. They worry me, because left unattended, they could get to be dangerous. But they won't be left unattended. What *really* bugs me, Jim, my friend, is the psychological aspect of the whole question. Let's see: How would you rate this statement, true or false: '*Love* is the worst possible reason for getting married.' Come on, Jim! Answer me."

Jim thought about that. About—Virginia. About Grace. About—Trini. It was a complicated proposition because it involved—projection. And romantics are adverse to, if not constitutionally incapable of, projection. Trini—now. Glorious. But Trini—in ten years, after having struggled with the English language, trying to conceal the fact that she had barely a grade school education, was totally without any visages of culture, branded with the psychic scars of her past, oppressed with inferiority feelings, fears, bad memories—?

"I'd—say—true, Vince," he said.

"Good! The human race reproduced itself for thousands of years without that arrant nonsense. *I* shouldn't have married Paloma. *She* shouldn't have married me. I need a softer, more submissive woman. She needs a more liberal, more understanding man. But we loved—and, I believe—still love, each other. So what? Fine recipe for happiness! Statements Two and Three: Trini loves you. You love Trini. True or false?"

Jim sat there. Slowly he shook his head.

"Now you're oversimplifying, Vince," he said quietly. "Those aren't true or false statements."

"Then what *are* they?" Vince said.

"A witch's brew of infinite complications. Trini—loves, *really* loves, a—a Freudian father-image, she has created in her own mind. A surrogate for the father—correction!—for the man she then believed was, and had emotionally accepted as, her father, and who—destroyed her. D'you know that whenever she thinks about him, mentions him, she shakes? Physically. All over. It is the most horrifying thing to watch! He became for her the embodiment of evil—in its masculine form, anyhow. Her Aunt Alicia—Alicia Villalonga de Reynolds, Peter's wife—"

"I know her very well. She's one of Paloma's best friends. Great, great girl. Completely different from her late, totally unlamented bastard of a brother. But I didn't know she was supposed to be little Trini's *Aunt*. Jesus! You're right! She could be!"

"Have you ever known any two people who weren't actually identical twins who look more alike than Alicia and Trini do?"

"Goddamnit, no! I knew something was bugging me last week while the two of you were dancing—dancing, ha! staging a private porn movie on the Obsidian Room's dance floor. Hell, Jim, she'd moved in so close she was practically in back of you!"

"Yes," Jim said dryly. "A—lovely sensation, Doctor!"

"All right! All right! So—little Trini's the result of one of Miguel's and Luis' street raids, eh? Hmmmnn, accounts for a lot. That scandal—Teofilo Alvarez' suicide, and Margarita Balmes'—Trini's mother's—hysterical declarations of his motives for splattering his brains all over the ceiling—was major. Not the sort of thing that often happens in that kind of family . . ."

"You mean they were upper class?"

"Very nearly. Upper-upper-middle, anyhow. In fact, Trini is the *first* girl I've ever heard of from that particular stratum of society here in

Ciudad Villalonga to voluntarily become a prostitute. Of course, Miguel Villalonga forced a good many upper-class women into quasi-prostitution in order to revenge himself on *Alta Sociedad* because—"

"I know that story. All those stories. I've read Peter Reynolds' book on Costa Verde. But may I, Vince, object, mildly, to that 'voluntarily,' and then, if you please, go on with what I was trying to say?"

Vince studied him. Said:

"I withdraw that 'voluntarily,' Jim. And you've just made me understand something else: I've always been—well—unnecessarily rough on poor Trini. Because she—shocks me. It's too damned close to seeing one of my own daughters hustling. I suppose subconsciously I feel that *she* oughtn't to have. That a girl like that, one of our *own*, ought to have—"

"Starved, or committed suicide, after her mother kicked her out of the house?"

"Didn't know that last detail, but something like that, yes, Jim. I could live with the fact of one of my daughters taking her own life, better than I could with her doing—that."

"Don't say that, Vince!" Jim said sharply. "You've never been saddled with that kind of memory, so you damned well don't know what it's like."

"And you do?"

"And I do," Jim said quietly. "Which is why I can forgive Trini her decision to—survive."

"Sorry," Vince said. "I'm way out of line, aren't I? Go on. You were saying that Alicia Villalonga is Trini's aunt—"

"Yes—and no. I was saying that the fact that they look so much alike is another cause of Trini's deep-seated psychiatric—and I use the word advisedly; I *do* mean psychiatric, not psychological—problems. You see, to Trini, largely through her mother's carping, Alicia has become her father's counterpart. Evil—Female Gender. Capitalized. She *hates* the fact that she looks so much like Alicia."

"Hard to believe that any woman could hate looking like that! But I'll grant you the possibility; I've seen kids' minds warped often enough, God knows . . . What I don't see, though, is how her looking like Alicia affects *you*."

"It does, though. That resemblance has an almost crucial bearing on my own relations with Trini, a detail I'll get to, later on. Anyhow, *I* come along. The perfect Wish-Fullfillment Image to feed an Electra Complex. Old enough to be her father. Short, dried up, and ugly—I'm *quoting* her, Vince!—enough not to activate her built-in defense mechanisms against men in general. And we meet under dramatic—hell!—melodramatic circumstances: There stands Alvaro, bleeding like a stuck pig, and with a Walther P-38 in his hand! I was scared shitless, but apparently it didn't show. If she'd looked closely, she'd have seen I'd pissed my damned pants out of fear! But, being a sentimentalist, I couldn't turn that poor little bastard over to the police—"

"¡*Mierda!*" Vince said. "Being what you are, two hundred percent *decent,* you couldn't. So you saved his poor little skinny ass for him. Gave him your blood on top of that and thereby convinced that *pobre zorrita* you were a prince! Hell, you've convinced *me.* And Paloma. And convincing the two of *us* of the same thing takes some doing, Jim!"

"I thank you. All right. Does Trini love me? Some of my traits, tendencies, characteristics, yes. True. *Me:* who I am, living, breathing, suffering in this world? No. She doesn't even *know* me; so how the hell could she? Therefore, true *and* false, Vince, to the same statement."

"All right. I'll buy that one. Do *you* love *her?*"

"Yes. But again I have to qualify—nit pick—define. I love—youth. Beauty. Freshness. In spite of everything, Vince, she's still a breath of spring! I've *never* been able to make it with a whore. To me, they look used. I always imagine I can—smell—a thousand carnal sweats, the acrid odor of half-dried sperm, the billy goat stink of the poor, sick devils who have to buy that dirt-poor, pitiful counterfeit of love—on them. But Trini—"

"With her you can make it, so—"

"I don't know. You won't believe me, but I've never tried. I don't want to try. Dreams are such fragile things, my friend. You know that act most hookers put on? Wild excitement, badly faked? Professional skill—of motion, designed to get it over with, brother! Bring the poor, damned 'John' around in under two minutes flat so they can get dressed, rush out to find another 'trick'? That, would ruin—forever—what we have now. That is, if we have anything. Another aspect's—pity, Vince. I *hurt* with pity, my entrails bleed with pity for this poor, forlorn, abused, tormented, damaged child. Would I feel this way if she were— less lovely? I don't know. Quite frankly, I doubt it. So, again, I *love,* truly love—a dream image, at least in part of my own creation. She— that dream image—delights me. Everything about her does. But—is she real?"

"Okay. You're not deluded," Vicente Gomez said slowly; "at least not as deluded as I thought you were. But a couple of more rough questions, Jim: How'd you *meet* her? Was that meeting accidental, really? Or couldn't it have been a part of what's known locally as 'The Treatment'?"

"It was not accidental. It was 'The Treatment.' She confessed as much that same night. Though even her confession was superfluous. I knew, the minute I saw her, what was afoot."

"How?"

"That detail I mentioned: her resemblance to Alicia. You see, His Nibs and Playmates, through a series of fortuitous and completely casual happenings, got the idea that I was much smitten of Alicia—which is true; but, also, due to the really excessive weirdness of the official Costa Verdian mentality, they arrived at the conclusion, even the conviction, that she and I were conducting a discreetly adulterous affair. Which, I hope I don't even need to tell you, isn't."

"Ha! They don't know Peter, then! Unlike the Reds, he wouldn't miss!"

"They do know him. Peter Reynolds is a gentleman. A great and rather quixotic gentleman. I'm quite sure he'd hold to Kipling's advice:

> . . . Be loth
> To shoot when you catch 'em,
> For you'll swing by my troth!
> Make 'im take 'er and keep 'er
> And ye're quit of 'em both,
> Quit of the Curse of a Soldier
> Soldier of the Queen!' "

Vince grinned at him, said:

"Now you're making *me* wonder, Jim!"

"Whom they don't know is Alicia. Nor, I like to believe, me. For if I were the type who played around with his friends' wives, *Paloma* just might turn up missing one of these fine nights, Vince!"

"I'll tell her you said that," Vince said solemnly. "She'll be no end flattered, Jim. Go on. You're saying or implying that they selected little Trinidad on the basis of her resemblance to Alicia Villalonga?"

"I'm saying it. I *know* it's true."

"But now, 'The Treatment' has no bearing upon your affair? Now she's so overwhelmed with true and noble love for you, that—"

"I don't know, Vince. I very truly and humbly don't know. But— what did our latest episode from this Perils of Pauline cliffhanger we seem to be improvising straight out of the silent movie days!—look like to you? Wouldn't it have been both simpler, and less costly, for her to have held still, let me make my clumsy, nonathletic efforts to defend her, get knocked flat on my ass—with a broken jaw to boot, likely!— and then to have gone with Harper? What difference should getting raped, or even submitting quietly, have made to her? What *was* she defending? Her long lost virtue? Her nonexistent honor?"

"Not nonexistent, Jim. She was defending her—pledged word. To you. Or to the 'Father Image' you so scientifically described. And if that's not honor, then what the hell is? Only it was her *way* of doing it that troubles me, my friend. It never even occurred to her to simply

232

knife that big bastard and rid the world of so much vermin. No. She turned that blade—instinctively—on herself. Masochism, Jim. With psychotic overtones. Deep-seated loathing of self, induced, likely, by what she's had to do, to live. So, more questions! Could you save her, heal her, cure her, make her whole of heart again?"

"I don't know, Vince," Jim whispered.

"Who *does,* goddamnit! Another unanswerable question: Should you even try? Would you sink both of you, or save both of you, by trying? Aren't the risks too great?"

"Over to you. You answer that one, Vince."

"Can't. I'm not God. Nor even Padre Pío. Jim—she *sank* Ana Ferrero. Finished her. There's no doubt about that. None at all. She may have even set up Juan Comacho Zoraya, *Ministro de Hacienda,* the guy who gave her that little car, for the Reds. She was his mistress, just as she's—or will be—yours. And he left *from* the flat he was keeping her in to go to Chizenaya. The Reds were waiting for him at just the right spot. They *knew* he was going by road, instead of by plane, and what *time,* damnit!"

"I find—both statements—hard to believe," Jim said quietly. "But then, I'm prejudiced in her favor. Tell you what: Let's go ask her. Right now."

Vicente Gomez studied Jim. A long time, and very carefully. Said, finally:

"All right. But on your head be it, *Amigo!*"

When they came into her room, she was sitting on the edge of the bed, fully dressed. One of the other girls from the boutique—Petra *"Culo Lindo,"* Petra "Pretty Tail," as he always thought of her in his mind, surprisingly enough—was with her. From the plastic bags they were both folding, he gathered Petra had brought her the ordinary street clothes she was wearing. Shoes, stockings, underwear as well, he guessed, for at least two of the bags were full, probably with the soiled and still bloody clothing she had been wearing that night.

She jumped up and came to him, her eyes very wide and pleading. He knew she wanted him to kiss her—for Petra's benefit, a matter of saving face. So he kissed her. But not for Petra's benefit.

Petra—whose family names were Stevenson Verlayo, not as odd a combination as it sounded, because there is considerable intermarriage between Anglo Saxon businessmen and technicians stationed in Latin America and native women—stood up, and excused herself prettily.

"Wait for us in the downstairs salon, Petra," Jim told her. "We'll drop you off in the car . . ."

"Oh, thank you, *Señor Embajador!*" Petra said fervently. To be brought home—or to work—in the Embassy Cadillac, Jim realized with wry amusement, would truly make her day."

"Trini," Jim said soberly, after Petra had gone, taking both the full and the empty plastic bags with her, "Doctor Gomez wants to ask you a few questions."

"No, I don't!" Vince snapped. "I want *you* to ask them, Jim!"

"All right," Jim said. "Trini, what really happened between you and Alvaro's sister?"

She looked at him, and her lips went white. But she didn't cry. This time, for once, she didn't cry.

"I—killed her," she said slowly. "I—brought her—drugs—and she died of them. That's what you have been told, is it not, *Don* Jaime?" And she said "You" to him! *"Usted"* not *"Tú!" "¿A usted, se han informado así, no, Don* Jaime?"

"Yes," Jim whispered; "but is it—true?"

Her mouth went sullen. She looked mean, bitchy, almost—ugly.

"Yes. It is—true," she said, her voice flat, calm, resigned, "all of it."

"All right," Jim said. "And this of—*Señor*—"

"Comacho," Vince supplied; *"Don* Juan Comacho, Minister of Finance."

"Yes. And *Don* Juan Comacho?" Jim said.

"Likewise. I told—the Reds that he was going to Chizenya on that night. So they killed him. I was glad. I hated him."

"And I?" Jim said quietly. "Am I to be next?"

"Yes. No. I don't know. I haven't had my orders, yet."

But, by then, he knew her. He heard quite clearly what was beneath that flat, controlled, too calm voice. He bent forward, looking intently into her eyes. Saw what was in them. Perceived it. She was—dying. At that moment, quite literally dying. Of—torture. Suffering what was not merely unbelievable, but very nearly inconceivable pain.

He smiled at her. Said, very gently:

"Trini, I love thee. It matters not what thou hast done, or even what thou wilt do. With thee, from thee, everything is—sweet. Even—my death—if it comes at thy hands . . ."

She stood there. Started to shake. Horribly. Her eyes disappeared, walled out behind that sudden wild, white rush. Her mouth trembled like an idiot child's. She took one step towards him. Another.

He put out his arms to her.

Then she was in them and her own were strangling him. She was kissing his ears, the tip of his nose, his eyes, his throat, his mouth, every place she could reach, covering his face with great, hot, wet, salty kisses, sobbing aloud, moaning, babbling:

"I love thee! Oh how I love thee! I love thee venerate thee worship thee adore—"

"Trini—" he said reproachfully.

"I do. I am thy slave. And this life—my life—is thine to do what thou wilt with it! This poor, dirty life of this tattered rag doll of a girl belongs to thee, *Don* Jaime! For thou hast saved it again, since I should not have been alive one hour from now, if thou hadst not believed me!"

"Believed what, Trini?" Vince said sternly. "You gave no explications. Unless *Don* Jaime is to accept the awful things you said—these crimes—as truth."

She turned Jim loose. Faced Vicente Gomez.

"Me!" she stormed. "He had to believe *me*! Believe *in* me. For if he does not, what good are explications?" She stopped. Shivered like a wet dog. Cringed before Vince like a whipped one. It was totally unbearable.

"Why—do—you—*hate* me, *Señor Doctor*?" she whispered.

Vince sighed.

"I don't, Child," he said. "In fact, I rather like you. But *Don* Jaime is my friend. I don't want him hurt—or harmed. And you—could do both—"

She stared at Vicente Gomez. Whispered:

"Doctor, don't you *know*, can't you *see*, I'd die first?"

"Yes. But you still might do him harm unwittingly. Without meaning to. Trinidad, my dear, you are a sick girl. Not physically. No—not even that's true. You are also quite sick, physically, but I can control that, maybe even cure it. But mainly you are sick emotionally, perhaps even mentally . . ."

"Say—wounded," Jim said; "hurt, damaged . . ."

"All right. The terminology doesn't matter. The effect's still the same, and it's dangerous, Jim. Don't you see that she *won't* fight, *won't* defend herself, turns everything in upon herself?"

"You are saying that I am mad, Doctor?" Trini said. "I am. Mad. Insane. Crazy. Over—*Don* Jaime!"

"That's part of it, too," Vince said. "Suppose I decide now *not* to let *Don* Jaime take you home? Suppose I were to lock you up? What would you do?"

"Kill myself," she said unhesitatingly.

"Even—knowing it would grieve me?" Jim said. "Even—realizing that I could not possibly bear thy death?"

"Ohhhh!" she wailed, "*Don* Jaime, I—"

Trini, *maldita séa*! Listen to me," Vince said. "I want the exact truth out of you or I'll put you in a straightjacket! Why *did* you give Ana Ferrero that heroin?"

She stared at him.

"The *truth*, Trini!" he said.

"Please, Trini," Jim said gently. "Say it—for me."

"For thee, my life, itself, *Don* Jaime. All right. I will tell the truth. I swear it upon my love for thee, which is the most sacred oath I now can take. If I should lie, may I lose thy love, which is to say, May I go mad and die!" She turned once more to Doctor Gomez.

"You—you know what they—the police—the Political Action Squad—did to Ana, Doctor?" she whispered.

"Yes, Trini; I know," Vince said.

"Well, afterwards—for her cure—they put her in the hands of Dr. Karl Obermüller, Doctor."

"Oh, Jesus," Vince said. "That bastard. That swine. That First and Favorite Son of the Great Whore. That Nazi Unspeakable. That malformed abortion of a syphilitic mother. That—"

"Vince—" Jim said.

"He was at Ravensbrueck, Jim. He was in *charge* of some of the experiments they performed on women there. Jewish women. Polish women. Gypsies. Gas gangrene wounds. Bone grafts—without anesthesia, naturally. Freezing experiments. Flayings—alive—to get nice skins for lampshades. So, naturally, having escaped at the close of the war, he fled to Franco's Spain, where the worst Nazi scum were welcomed with open arms. But Doctor Obermüller was a little too much for even the *Falanje*—besides, there were Israeli execution squads on his trail. So he escaped again. And eventually, having proved more than even such homelands of casual, routine torture as Brazil and Chile were willing to stomach, ended up here—where his techniques—and his tendencies— his incurably sadistic tendencies—were, and are, highly appreciated. The one man on earth I've sworn on my mother's grave to shoot dead on sight the first time I run across him!"

He turned to Trini, said:

"Your friend Ana—*hurt* all the time, didn't she?"

"Yes, Doctor. Unbearably," Trini said.

"And you—brought her the drugs to ease her pain?"

"Yes, Doctor. And—and—also to—kill her. To allow her to—die. She had reached her limits. Passed them. I—I loved her. So I—gave her that. A good death, Doctor."

"Jesus!" Jim said, and put his arms around her.

"She—she asked me to, *Don* Jaime. I—I found out—how much it would take—to do that. From—a friend. No! I shall *not* lie! From a client. One of the men I used to go to bed with—for money. A—Doctor. A Green Old Man of a Doctor who was always drunk and smelt most disgustingly vile, since he never washed himself! And there was this—other swine—who *gave* me the drugs. Turn me loose now, *Don* Jaime, *por favor.* I cannot—say this with thou holding me. When I feel thy touch—I am—without strength. My—insides—faint. To say—so hard a thing—would be beyond—*mis fuerzas* . . ."

He turned her loose.

"He gave me the drugs, this unspeakably vile one, this Pig of all Pigs, to pass out, to distribute among the girls so that they could make addicts of the Army officers. He was a Red, so he thought—"

"We know what he thought," Vince said grimly. "And you did—*that?*"

She turned back to Jim. Went close to him. Looked into his eyes. Said:

"Yes. I did that. I—I hated them—those officers. They were such—brutes. And—so filthy. So vile. They demanded of us—all kinds of—perversions. I, *Don* Jaime—hear me, listen to me—then strike me down dead at thy feet, if that is thy will! I submitted—to—those perversions. To—stay alive. To preserve—this nothing that I am—that I was, until I met thee! I have done things so—disgusting, *tan nauseabundas, tan viles, tan—*"

"Do not speak of them," Jim said; "do not even remember them—for they are gone. Finished. Done with. Forever."

"Thou—canst—forgive—even *this?*" she whispered.

"There is nothing to forgive. Thou—art Trini. And I love thee."

Before he could even discern her intent, much less attempt to stop her, she had swooped to her knees before him, caught both his hands in hers, clawed them upward against her wildly trembling mouth, and was kissing them, kissing them, kissing them, branding and scalding them, backs and palms, endlessly. And pouring down a rain, a flood, an inundation from glazed and blinded eyes as if to heal even that. It was crippling, killing, beyond the endurance of a statue of stainless steel. He snatched away his hands from her grasp, dug his fingers into the flesh of her arms, yanked her none too gently to her feet, drew her to him, held her.

"Mi muñeca de trapo," he murmured; "my rag doll."

Vince Gomez said, harshly.

"Some of those girls—your companions—also became addicts, Trini!"

She brought both small fists up and ground them into her eyes, making them redder than they already were. Shook her head to clear away her tears. Mastered herself, finally. Said, slowly, softly:

"I know. That was why I refused to pass the drugs anymore, Doctor. He—that swine—gave me a terrible beating. Ask—your colleague—Dr. Luis Moreno, if this is not so. I was in Dr. Moreno's Clinic for more than a month. I had three fractured ribs—from the kicks of that animal, Doctor."

"Oh, goddamn!" Vince said. "Trini—another, the penultimate question: "After you came out of Dr. Moreno's Clinic, you *still* refused? You were brave enough?"

"I still refused. But I was not brave, Doctor. You see he—*el Cerdo este*—got into a gun fight with the police, and they killed him. Before I came out of the Clinic, Doctor. So I didn't have to be brave. I doubt I would have been brave enough to take another such beating. But since he was dead, I could refuse. And I did. By then, I had seen what drugs can do."

Jim looked at Vince. Said, his voice harsh, a little angry:

"Satisfied, Doctor? *Now* can I take her home?"

"Jim, I told you I proposed to play rough! And I think you're going to have to thank me for it. Because, right now, she's beginning to look pretty goddamned good, even to me. Let me finish will you? Let's clear everything up. There remains the case of Juan Comacho. Trini, you said you betrayed him. Did you?"

She bowed her head. Looked up again. Whispered:

"Yes, Doctor."

"Trini!" Jim said.

"I was—deceiving *Don* Juan—a little. *Don* Juan was—a very kind man, Doctor. I liked him. Only he was short and fat and not very attractive, so that his body—awoke a repugnance in me that I could not vanquish. I only became his mistress to escape from The Blue Moon. At the same time—I was seeing this boy. Forgive me, *Don* Jaime! But I told thee how and what I was! Dirt. Garbage. A liar. Deceitful. A whore. A real one."

"Trini, you stop it!" Jim said.

"It is—stopped, *Don* Jaime."

"Go on, Child," Vince said.

"I was seeing this boy. Felipe. A very nice boy. Handsome. And only twenty-two years old. I—I liked him very much. I thought—I could learn to—to love him—in spite of his being—an animal of a man. For you know, you must know, Doctor—out of your experience of treating us—as patients, that we of the bad life soon come to hate all men, which is why so many of us turn *Marimachos, Tortilleras, Lesbianas* . . ."

"Did you?" Jim said, teasing her.

"No. I am not—made that way, *Don* Jaime. Surely thou of all men should know that!"

"I was plaguing thee, Child," Jim said. "Please go on."

"I—liked Felipe. He was—always very gentle with me. And I did not realize, *zorra estupida* that I was—that I am!—that he—that he—"

"That he what?' Vicente Gomez said.

"Had been sent—to me. As I was sent to thee, *Don* Jaime!"

"Why?" Vince said. "Why were you sent to *Don* Jaime, Trini? And—by whom?"

"I don't know," she whispered; "neither why, nor by whom. The Political Activities Squad picked me up. Told me where to go—to thy residence, *Don* Jaime. And what to do. Which they—and even I!—believed was going to be very simple: to get thee to couch thyself with me. To enslave thee with my body. Only, since thou'rt a man of honor, a true gentleman, it proved—impossible, didn't it?"

"And Alvaro intervened," Jim said dryly. "Go on, Trini."

"But they must have told you something!" Vince said. "What, precisely, were your instructions?"

"That. What I have told you. To go to his residence. To—seduce him."

"Nothing more?"

"What would happen to me if I did not obey—or failed. I think they mean to give me further instructions later on. When they believe I—have progressed with *Don* Jaime sufficiently."

Vince looked at Jim.

"She's right," he said; "it figures."

"And when they do give thee thy instructions, *Muñeca?*" Jim said. "What then?"

"I shall tell thee what they are, word for word. Honestly. Then—I am very sorry, *Don* Jaime, for I know thou'rt beginning to feel a—a certain fondness for me—I shall kill myself. What else can I do? I am not—strong enough, nor brave enough, to bear—what those *bestias* of the Political Activities Squad do to women—for as long as even five minutes."

"Jesus!" Vince said.

"Thou wilt do nothing of the kind," Jim said. "For the very day that they give thee thy instructions, I shall install thee in the Embassy, itself, granting thee the right of political asylum, which under International Law, I can. Then, with the help of—friends—whose cleverness far exceeds theirs, I shall smuggle thee out of the country—to New York, where thou wilt wait for me until I can join thee. Is this clear?"

"*Clarísimo.* I thank thee, *Don* Jaime. Thou'rt very kind," she whispered.

"All right," Vince said, "that's settled. Let's now get back to *Don* Juan Comacho Zoraya, *Ministro de Hacienda,* and this boy you were adorning his forehead with. Giving him the horns of all known sizes, shapes, and convolutions, because poor *Don* Juan was short and fat and awoke a repugnance in you. Not to mention that like most fat men his performance of his manly duties left a great deal to be desired, eh, Trini?"

"Ohhhh!" she wailed. "To have to hear this! To be such a one as—people have the right to say such things to!"

"Vince, for Christ's sake!" Jim said.

"You're saying you didn't?" Vince said sternly.

"I did not. Never. I was—faithful to *Don* Juan the whole time I was with him. Only—" she turned to Jim, and her face was pitiful—"only I have now told the precise truth, which is also—a lie, *Don* Jaime. Because I was going to. I meant to. Betray *Don* Juan, I mean. Felipe—was very handsome—and even—creatures like me—feel the need for—for a little beauty in our lives. More than other women, perhaps; since we have to accept, submit to, such ugliness!"

"I find it perfectly understandable. And, additionally, it is of thy past which has nothing to do with thee and me. Not now," Jim said.

"*¡Eres un Angel! ¡Y un Santo!* It is for this, thy goodness, that I love thee," Trini said.

"*¡Eres un Idiota! ¡Y Un Bobo!*" Vince mocked. "Not to mention a jackass with long, hairy ears! But then, what man in love is not? Even I, I sadly fear! Get on with it, Trini!"

"He—Felipe—pretended he wanted to see me. To—to be with me. Yes—that too—to couch himself with me, *Don* Jaime!"

"That's natural enough, Child," Jim said. "You're—very beautiful."

"It was not natural, and I was a fool! For I did not realize then that 'The Treatment' could be reversed, that a man could be sent to—to seduce a woman, get her to—betray another who was—a kind protector, almost—if she would have let him be!—a friend . . ."

"Trini, *Niña,*" Jim said sadly, "there appears to be a certain—discrepancy in thy tale. Thou hast said that thou wert faithful to *Don* Juan. And now thou sayest that Felipe—seduced thee in order to induce thee to—"

"Go to the head of the class!" Vince said. "I hereby shorten your ears by two full centimeters!"

She bowed her head. Stared at the floor. Trembled. Wept. Straightened up. Faced him.

"This—is—so very hard, *Don* Jaime!" she whispered. "Yet—both things are true. I—betrayed *Don* Juan. Cost him—his life. But unwittingly, and accidentally, not knowing I was doing so. I did *not*, however, betray him with my body. That, too, was unwitting and accidental. That I did not, I mean. As I have said, I fully intended to. After so many old, ugly, smelly men, I thought it would be—pleasant—to couch myself with a boy as handsome, fine, and clean as Felipe was . . .''

"Yet you didn't," Vince said. "Why not, Trini?"

"Because when the occasion arose—" she stopped, and blushed, a warm red tide climbing up to the roots of her hair, "I was—with this *maldición* of women, Doctor. Especially a curse for me, because *every* month, I get so sick I almost die. I—I told you that, remember?"

"Yes, and we're going to do something about it," Vince said. "Continue, Trini."

"I—I'd promised to call Felipe and inform him when *Don* Juan was out of town. I decided to call him anyhow—even though—nothing would be possible between us. I didn't want him to get angry if he somehow learned that *Don* Juan had absented himself, and I hadn't called him. 'Better to tell him the truth,' I thought. So I called him—at the Power and Light Company, where he worked—"

"Ha!" Jim said.

"I get the picture," Vince said. "The Light Company is a Red cell, isn't it?"

"Yes," Jim said. "Go on, Trini."

"I called him, and explained to him very clearly why I could not be—his, for another five or six days. He said: 'Then why did you call me at all, Trini?' I said: 'Because we—could see each other. Have a drink— talk, anyhow. *Don* Juan is going out of town this weekend. He leaves— today.' "

"And?" Vince said.

"And Felipe said— *¡con gran interes!* so much interest that if I hadn't been—almost—in love with him, and hence, even more stupid than usual, I should have noticed it—'Where is he going, Trini?' And I: 'To Chizenaya.' And he: 'By road?' And I: 'Yes, Felipe.' And he: 'At what time does he leave, Trini?' And I—stupid fool that I was!—told him. 'At—midday, Felipe,' I said . . .''

"And that night, *Don* Juan Comacho Zoraya died, eh, Trini?" Vince said.

"Yes. When I—heard, I called Felipe again. Asked him if he—had done—this awful thing. He said: 'Yes, Trini—I passed the word along, to friends of mine. And you, Trini—have served the people of Costa Verde well. You are a heroine—a Jeanne d'Arc. Can you not catch us a few more such fat swine, my dear?' "

She looked Jim straight in the eyes. Said, slowly, carefully:

"I hung up the phone. I never saw him again. I have not so much as looked at another such as he. I went on with—my dirty life. Existing in disgust. Swimming in—vomit. Until thou camest, *Don* Jaime. And taught me that a man could be good, and gentle and kind and of an enormous nobility of soul, and—and beautiful! So beautiful inside that I see thee as such—with all *esa hermosura* shining out through the worn and tired *conturnos* of thy face. I love thee. And that love is—forever. Dost thou believe that? No! Dost thou believe me—and *in* me, Don Jaime?"

"I believe thee, Trini. And also I love thee," Jim said.

He turned to Vince:

"*Now* are you satisfied, Doctor?" he said.

"Yes," Vince said, "entirely." Then, seeing Jim take Trini's arm, he switched abruptly into English: "Jim, wait! You still can't go. There's still another problem, and now, of them all, contrary to what I thought, it looks like it's going to turn out to be the fat one! I'm talking about her—health, Jim."

"Her health?" Jim said.

"Yes. Her *physical* health, this time. If you're going to enter into any relationship with her, legal or not, that involves sex, it must be considered. I'll put the problem in a nutshell: Don't knock her up, Jim! I'm going to give her a year's supply of the Pill. You, my friend, had better make goddamned *sure* she takes them."

Jim stared at him. Said:

"Why, Vince?"

"Her blood doesn't clot. Or rather, it does clot, but much too slowly. I gather from what she's told me, she's been bleeding damned near to death every twenty-eight days since she was thirteen years old, and accepting that miserable state of affairs as perfectly normal. I found it out thanks to the fact that being as emotionally hashed up as she is, she stabbed herself in that damned nightclub instead of gutting Harper as she should have. She's terribly anemic and—"

"A hemophiliac?" Jim said.

"No. No, of course not! Women are *never* hemophiliacs, Jim. They only carry the defect and pass it along to their sons. But our Trini has— some hereditary, congenital defect, or has had some obscure virus infection, or any of two million other things medical science knows not one goddamned thing about, that has left her with *the* slowest coagulation time I've *ever* seen in an adult woman. Now, as she is today, she couldn't possibly survive giving birth to a child, Jim. I tell you this, because I've already learned from previous conversations with you, how much you want a son—"

"In this case—a daughter. Trini's image."

"How does *she* feel about it?" Vince said.

"Ask her. And—tell her the truth, Vince. Don't put that burden on me as well!"

"Trini," Vince said. "If—if things work out between you and *Don*

Jaime, if—marriage—becomes possible between you, do you want—a child?"

"A child? No, Doctor. *Ten* children. All—just like him. Good. Intelligent. Noble. Brave. With—enormous souls!"

"Trini—" Vince said sadly. "You—cannot. It is not possible."

She became a statue. Teak. Bronze. Ebony. As still as that. As—unbreathing.

"I—cannot—give *Don* Jaime—ten babies?" she whispered.

"You cannot give him even one, Trini. It would kill you. You would bleed to death, giving birth. Because of this defect of your blood."

She stood there. Breathed slowly, rhythmically. Said:

"Would—my baby—live, Doctor? Would it live, even so?"

"I don't know. I'm not God, Trini! Possibly. Even—probably. Your pelvic structure—is very fine. If it were not for this of your blood, its failure to coagulate properly, I'd say—"

But she had turned, was gone from them. To the headboard of the bed, above which, as in most Latin American hospitals, a crucifix hung. She took it down, kissed it, reverently, turned back to them. Back, specifically, to Vicente Gomez Almagro.

"Swear upon this," she said, her voice tight, high, almost strident, "that *you* will attend me, Doctor. And that you will save my baby. So that *Don* Jaime may have the son he has longed for. Swear also that you will give no thought to me, who, having done—this one truly fine thing in all my life—will no longer matter."

"Why, goddamn!" Vicente howled. "She's mad, Jim! You *see,* mad!"

"Swear it, Doctor!" Trini said.

"Swear to kill thee? To become an assassin? Go find thyself another executioner, thou stupid little fool! Besides, I am not a believer. So take this barbaric little image of irrationality—irrational cruelty at that—out from under my nose!"

"Ohhhhhh, Doctor!" Trini wailed.

"Look, Child," Vince said then, and Jim saw how suspiciously misty his eyes had become, "I'll tell you what: I'm going to put you on a treatment, which *you* must swear by this miserable little piece of whittled up firewood to follow. Massive doses daily of vitamin K for six months. Then, another blood test. If you've improved enough, I'll take you off the contraceptive pills. All right?"

"What would the risks be after such a treatment, Vince?" Jim said.

"Still too high for comfort. But I've another trick up my sleeve. The *first* time she skips a period, you bring her in and I'll give her a *total* transfusion. Replace all this goddamned miserable blood she's got. Rough and risky. But less, by several thousand percent, than trying to give birth to even so small a child as yours—and hers—would probably be."

Jim stood there, with one arm around Trini. Suddenly, almost happily, he grinned:

"Vince, you can bet on one of two absolutely certain propositions," he said.

"Which are?"

"That if Trini does get pregnant, she'll have cheated on me. Of if she *doesn't* hang a pair of magnificent antlers on my forehead—"

"I'm betting she won't, Jim. So make room in the ranks of sentimental jackasses, my friend! She's convinced me. *I* believe her."

"Thanks, Vince. You can't imagine just how much that means, coming from you—at least to me. And it will to her when I explain it to her. But let me finish. After the scare you've just thrown into me, if Trini doesn't put a couple of other guys on the job, and still comes up with an outsized belly some months from now, you, my friend, will have earned your niche in Medicine's Hall of Fame . . ."

"How?" Vince said.

Jim's grin widened.

"By delivering the first, certified, demonstrable product of parthenogenesis in the whole of human history!" he said.

CHAPTER

19

When Roberto stopped the big car in front of the economically modest—but clean, neat, and well kept, Jim noticed at once—condominium apartment house in which she lived, she leaned quickly close to his ear and whispered:

"Willst come up with me a while, *mi Amor?*"

Something in her tone came over to him, a note of hesitation, doubt, fear, he didn't know, so he looked at her to see if she meant it. Instantly and clearly, he saw that she didn't, that she was actually dreading that he might say "Yes."

"No, thank you, my dear," he said.

"Oh!" she breathed. "Why—not, *Don* Jaime?"

And now, just as clearly, he heard that her mood had changed. In half a heart beat, in the interval between the inhaling and the exhaling of a single breath, she had gone from fearing that he would come with her up into her little studio apartment to what was close to an actual terror that he wouldn't; perhaps not ever.

But he still had the feeling that she really didn't want him to; not at that particular moment, anyhow. It was only that she was willing to sacrifice her momentary reluctance—whatever its cause—to her greater fear of losing him.

He smiled, stroked her forearm, gave it a little squeeze.

"Two reasons, *Trinita mía,*" he said. "First, I have been away from my job for a whole week, too, so I'd better check up, and catch up, before my Government decides I'm spending too much time in hospitals, or in night clubs with pretty girls, and fires me."

"They won't do that," she said decisively; "they *know* they have the best Ambassador in all the world. But what is—thy second reason, *Don* Jaime?"

"That you don't really want me to," he said.

"Oh!" she said. "To thee, I am as transparent as a piece of glass, am I not, *Don* Jaime? Thou hast it right. I do not want thee to come up to *mi pisito* now. Dost know—why?"

He laughed.

"*Niña,* I sometimes have the unhappy feeling that I know women much too well. I wish I didn't. Too much knowledge subtracts from both their mystery and their charm. You have been away from your little flat a week. By now, there are perhaps two specks of dust on the commode, three on the dining room table, and the mirror could do with a bit of polishing. Additionally, since your absence was involuntary, or at least involuntarily prolonged, you have at least three pairs of panties, six of stockings, two bras, and a slip or two hanging in the bathroom. While in the kitchen—"

She surged against him, wrapped her thin arms around his neck, and kissed him.

"Thou *Brujo*!" she laughed. "Thou Sorcerer! In the kitchen there is a week's accumulation of dirty dishes! And the whole place is a mess! No; it is what the newspaper's call a disaster area! I shall ask *Doña* Paloma to ask *Doña* Luisa, la Señora del General García, to ask His Excellency the General to officially declare it one, and to proportion me disaster relief!"

She stopped laughing, abruptly.

"But—I will do better, *Don* Jaime," she said seriously. "From now on, I shall be very neat. For thee, I shall be the perfect housewife, so that thou shalt never have cause for complaint. I shall anticipate thy wishes, so that thou shalt always be content with me, and—"

"*Niña,*" he said fondly, "don't change. I love thee as thou art . . ."

"*Don* Jaime—" she whispered, "wilt thou—visit me—tonight?"

"Do you want me to, Trini?"

"Yes! Oh, yes! Please, *Don* Jaime!¡*Por favor!*"

"All right. What time?"

"Ten thirty. No, eleven!"

"Isn't that—rather late, Trini?"

"No. Of course not. In my house we have an electronic porter. You know how that works? There is by the front door a row of buttons. Each button is placed beside the name of the owner of one of the flats. Above all the buttons there is a little, decorative grill. Behind that grill there is a loudspeaker. You push the button beside my name, and then you will hear my voice coming through the *Alta Voz*. I'll say: '*¿Quien es? ¿Juan? ¿José? ¿Federico? ¿Paco? ¿Fernando?* Ohhhhhhhh! *Don* Jaime, forgive me! That was a *very* bad joke, wasn't it? *¡Oh, demonios!* What made me say *that?*"

"It doesn't matter, Trini," he said.

"It does matter!" she stormed. "No man has ever been in my little flat, *Don* Jaime! No man will ever enter it—except *thee*, my Love! I—I bought it for *that*. That it be—mine and thine—with no bad memories to haunt it. That—we—be happy there, Thou and I! But now I wonder if we *ever* can. Because wherever one goes, one takes oneself with one, does one not? And I take—*¡Trini, la Zorra! ¡Trini, la Ramera, la Fulana, la Qualquiera, la Puta!*"

He caught her by the shoulders, turned her again to face him, held her like that, looking into her eyes. He was thinking that of the four synonyms for the correct and formal Spanish word *Prostituta* she had used—out of the dozens, if not hundreds, available in the richest language of the Western world—that last, *"Puta,"* "whore," was the ugliest. Even the sound of it was. And the sadness—the bad sadness—was in him like a weight of darkness. Could a girl as—damaged—as this poor tormented child, ever really be healed, made whole of heart again? He doubted it. At that moment, he doubted it profoundly.

"Trini," he said quietly; "I love thee. And the thee I love is none of those things. She is—a rag doll, with the stuffing coming out of her in places. A *very* leaky watering pot. And a bird, a crazy little bird, no? But—a good girl. Truly a good girl, because she wants to be. I believe in her goodness, Trini. For a girl, who—" he pushed the V-neck of her dress open, touched the gauze and tape of the bandage with his fingertips—"did *this* has placed a very great value upon herself. Was *this* the act of—anybody's woman, cheap, commercial goods?"

"Ohhhh!" she wailed. "Now I am more ashamed than ever! *Don* Jaime—I love thee. That I am thine, that I would die for thee, thou knowest. But this is not enough! I must also—*live* for thee! Which means I must change—learn, grow. *Be* the woman thou shouldst have, such a one as thou canst love. No! More than love, for love is all heart and little head, and I would not entrap thee so! Such a one as thou canst—admire, respect, be—proud of! Thinkest thou I—can manage—all that?"

"You can try, Child," he said. "That's all anyone can expect of a mere human. Even God asks no more. Perfection's not attainable. Trying, meaning it, is enough. Even if you fail. You will, at times, you know. Everyone does. Now, come on; go straighten up that disaster area, will you? So that I can enter it tonight without falling over things. After that, lie down. Take a *siesta*. And your pills! The vitamins, anyhow . . ." He thought: 'The others, you won't be needing, little Trini. Not tonight. Not for a long time, if I can help it . . .'

"*Don* Jaime—" she breathed; "kiss me? Here, inside the car? I—I don't want my neighbors to see!"

He smiled, said:

"Why not, Trini?"

"They—believe—some rich man is—keeping me. I'd rather that they didn't know who thou art just yet. I don't want thy name in their filthy mouths! I—"

He kissed her. Murmured:

"Trini. My poor little Trini. *Mi muñeca de trapo* with the stuffing coming out . . ."

She half strangled him; whispered:

"Oh, how I love thee!" Scrambled out of the big car, fled into the house.

"To the residence, Roberto," Jim Rush said.

"There's a letter for you, Sir," Tomás said.

Jim looked at him. Said:

"*Here* at the residence, Tomás?"

"Yes, Sir. I thought that was odd, too; since all your mail comes to the Embassy. But it was addressed to you here. It's from our mutual friend, Peter Reynolds. I suppose he thought it would come to your attention more quickly, here . . ."

"He was right. Has it been opened?"

"Sir, have you ever known one of *your* letters not to be? It wasn't even well done, this time. I think they wanted you to know they'd seen the contents of that letter . . ."

He said: "Why, Tomás?"

"Don't know, Sir. That would depend upon what the letter says, wouldn't it? Sir: one other thing. I talked to Carlos. He has it all set up. A traffic accident, a collision between one of Power and Light Company's trucks and Harper's Buick. In the confusion—there will be much shouting and arguing and waving of arms and shaking of fists under noses, as is habitual in such cases—the substitution will be made."

"How?" Jim said.

"Carlos entered Harper's garage, while that gross animal and *la* Crowley were playing games with each other. Even filthier games than usual, I am told. Carlos' lookouts found the spectacle most diverting, and—"

"Get to the point, Tomás!" Jim said.

"The point is, Sir, that Carlos had plenty of time to remove the lock from one door, and the trunk—all he needed, Sir, since all the door locks and the ignition use the same key, only the trunk and the glove compartment having a different lock, so that only two keys are necessary for the whole car—tear them down, make wax impressions of their tumblers, reassemble them, refit them to the car, and get out of there. When the accident occurs, Carlos will be in possession of a perfect set of keys, thus greatly facilitating the speed with which the substitution can be carried out . . ."

"But, damn it all, Tomás! Since he was in the garage why didn't he just make the substitution then and there?"

Tomás smiled.

"Two reasons, Sir. Harper doesn't put the heroin into the car until just before delivery, and hence there was nothing for Carlos to substitute the marijuana *for*. And the second reason was—because of you, Sir."

"Because of *me*?"

"Yes, Sir. Several of the waiters in the Obsidian Room are friends of Carlos and—of mine, Sir. The Hotel's electrician, is, in technical matters, Carlos' Second in Command. And they all related to him, and to me, what happened the night you took dear little Trini there. So Carlos wishes to offer you the—pleasure of witnessing Harper's downfall, Sir. Which meant, that even if Harper had already placed the heroin in the car, the substitution would have been much too risky. Because of the time element, Sir. Before everything could be coordinated in such a case, that clever swine would have had too much of an opportunity to discover it. Now here's the setup, Sir: Harper always makes his deliveries to the docks on Tuesdays, and always at 4:30 P.M. sharp. Regular as clockwork. And since *today* is Tuesday, and moreover, since it's still only eleven o'clock in the morning, I need only make a telephone call and say, 'Uncle says he'd like to see that new film at the Bijou—' for things to happen. Right on schedule, Sir!"

Jim stood there. Said, finally:

"There won't be any slip-ups? I don't want Harper dead, Tomás. Behind bars for a good, long stretch, yes. But dead, no."

"No slip-ups, Sir! I guarantee it!"

But it, the whole thing, didn't *feel* right. There was somewhere, somehow, obscurely, something wrong. Afterwards it came to him it was the *hubris* in Tomás' guarantee that there wouldn't be any slip-ups. That the gods punish *hubris* implacably, any man with sense knows. But at the moment, he put that disquieting feeling down to nerves and dismissed it. He shook his head to clear it of all such arrant nonsense as premonitions.

"Yes, Tomás, make that call!" he said.

The letter from Peter Reynolds was a shock. He knew from the dull, leaden pain, sinking in slowly, crushing all the region around his heart, how much he had been hoping—despite everything, in spite of Trini (Or wasn't it maybe *because* of Trini? Hadn't he subconsciously hoped to be rescued, saved, from the consequences of what in his heart of hearts he *knew* was middle-aged folly?) that his once so promising relations with Grace Nivens could be renewed, could lead finally to a belated, autumnal marriage with a woman who was cultured, brilliant, strikingly good-looking, kind-hearted, good—and of his own *race*, people, kind!—perfectly equipped to bring serene fulfillment to his declining years.

But Peter's letter ended all that. Ended it forever. Its salient passages read:

"She brought along her new boy friend. Tall, good-looking type. Nice guy, Jim. Frankly, I liked him. Solid, honest, clean-cut. What most women would consider a damned good catch, I suppose. Engineer. Works for Wildcat, too. Another department, though.

"What was strange was that Alicia *didn't* like Wilkenson. That's his name, George Wilkenson. Swears that any woman who'd substitute him for you is an utter fool. Which brings me to the main reason our peacemaking session failed:

"Between Alicia and Grace it was *hate* at first sight! They spent the whole evening being sweetly, poisonously polite to each other, and eyeing one another out of the corner of their eyes. And d'you know why, my little *ex*-Chubby friend? *You,* damnit! That long, tall, gorgeous champagne bottle of a girl of yours is *still* in love with you. And so, subconsciously—I hope!—and in a left-handed sort of sublimated way—I hope twice!—is my ever faithful wife. When your Grace (Who is *really* something, boy; you should take a leave, come home, and fight off the opposition!) let fly with a really devious remark—I can't quote it; it was so goddamned feminine, female, feline, and downright complicated that its wording escapes me—to the effect that she'd always suspected there was a little Hot Tamale in your woodpile, my Alicia came back with one that if I didn't know positively you and she have never spent five minutes alone together, I, myself, would have taken as a damned near open confession that fun and games of a decidedly censurable nature—the kind that usually lead to messy divorces and/or even messier shooting scrapes!—had been indulged in all over the place, during my frequent trips away from home. She sat right there under my nose with her bare face hanging out and told Grace this although she knows damn well ever since we got spliced I've taken her with me even when she was big as a house with one of the kids, and the last couple of times with the whole, howling, car-sick tribe crawling all over me and driving me out of my mind!

"Jesus! Won't *Gringas* ever learn not to try to fight dirty against Latin broads? They're outclassed from the outset. Somebody should wise 'em up. Point out to them what racial stock both Machiavelli and the Borgias came from. And the Borgias were *Spanish* to start with. And so was Pontius Pilate, in case you didn't know. Hell, I'll bet one day they'll find out that Judas Iscariot was a Sephardi!

"No contest! My dearest, darling little *Witch*—after all, she *is* a Villalonga, come to think of it!—sent your gal home fighting back visible tears. And all the satisfaction I could get out of her when I got her back to that two-hundred-year-old termites' breakfast food type barn we live in and took her to task for bitching up the deal for you, was: 'That was what she *wanted* to believe, Peter! So why should I have disappointed her? Let her suffer a while. Maybe it will teach her something—such as which men are, and which men aren't, of value!'

"Sorry, Jim. We blew it for you. Blew it all to hell. I'm afraid your Grace will go for Wilkenson seriously, now. Sure you couldn't get an emergency leave?"

'No,' Jim thought sadly, 'I can't. And when I do get to New York, it will be far too late. So now—'

So now—his sadly lovely, hideously damaged—little piece of commercial goods. A blind alley affair that couldn't possibly work out. Half a generation of time between them, a cultural void stretching out to interstellar space. With whom, even good, honest lust wasn't really possible, unless he were prepared to risk her life. His broken rag doll with the stuffing spilling out . . .

From whom he felt a love that was three-quarters aching pity, a tenderness girt round about with pain. Whose *need* of him, of what she had mistakenly, blindly, falsely come to believe him to be, was actually terrifying; the responsibility involved in making her his mistress appalling.

He couldn't do it! He'd—

Leave this child, this glorious girl-child who'd pushed a knife halfway to her beating heart to keep other hands than his from her sweet flesh! Who loved him. Truly loved him. Or loved the man she thought he was, the man he'd never be. The man he'd been trying to be all his life.

'Hail, the conquering Hero comes!' he groaned, and started downstairs to go out to the waiting car.

But near the doorway, Tomás stopped him, again.

"Oh, Sir," he said. "There's one more item I forgot to tell you this morning: Your Secretary's just come back from her Stateside leave. A Mrs. Clyde, Sir. Mrs. Martha Clyde. A widow. Do you know her, Sir?"

"No. But you do, don't you? She's a holdover from my predecessor, isn't she? What's she like, Tomás?"

Tomás thought about that question. Said, judiciously:

"Well, Sir, during the Middle Ages, she'd have been burned at the stake. With—a great deal of justification, Sir!"

"Meaning she's a witch. I *always* seem to get them! Fifty-ish and *fat*, Tomás?"

"No, Sir. Late forties—*very* late, and slender. Not bad looking, really. Rather, it's a question of temperament. Determined to catch herself an Ambassador, Sir. And since all the recent incumbents have been married, Sir—rather a bit frustrated. A marked tendency towards sticking her nose into matters that don't quite concern her. It would be highly advisable that she never meets, or even hears about, little Trini, Sir."

"Oh, God!" Jim groaned. "I get the picture. And, thanks, Tomás. Believe me, I'll take care . . ."

From where the Cadillac was parked, near the intersection of the Avenida Juan Peron and the Calle General Pinochet, he could see the main approach to the docks, and also a group of dockworkers who were loading a small steamer about a half kilometer away. Much closer, not more than fifteen meters away, he estimated, he saw, and recognized, the big truck, sitting between two warehouses with its motor running. *"Union Electrica Costa Verdenese"* the sign on the side of it said.

Just in front of him, three workmen were busily tearing up the cobblestones. They were under the direction of a small, catlike man. Then the man turned, and Jim saw who he was: Carlos. Everything was under control. Carlos grinned at him, and swiftly turned away.

Jim touched the button on one side of his digital watch. The numerals flashed bright red: 4:29. As he released the button, he heard the sound of a heavy automobile coming on. A straight-through muffler! Sheer arrogance! Ordinarily a Buick wouldn't have made one-tenth that much noise. But was it arrogance? Hadn't Harper anticipated the necessity of having to run for it one fine day, and modified his car accordingly? A straight-through muffler cost considerably less loss of horsepower than did the baffles of an ordinary one. And from the sound of that motor, it had been hopped up: the heads shaved to increase the compression, another double carburetor added so that each bank of cylinders had a separate one, high-lift racing cams whining eerily—a real bomb.

It came on—black as a hearse, black as sin, as death, rumbling with power held in check.

Joe was driving it; his heavy, but, Jim admitted with honest envy, really handsome face, with the kind of granite-hard good looks that resulted from the genetic mutation caused by the possession of an extra y chromosome, whose effect was to exaggerate masculinity into pure bestiality, half hidden by aviation-type dark glasses. As usual, he was hatless, and his Viking-blond hair, cut fashionably long with heavy sideburns down almost to the point, or more exactly, the cleft, of his massive chin, shone like a beacon in the afternoon sun. He had a huge cigar stuck into the corner of his mouth, and, staring at it, Jim saw for the first time how thin his lips were. Hairline thin—the lips of a born sadist.

Jim tore his gaze away. Saw Carlos Suarez lift his hand, let it fall decisively. The truck's motor roared, thundered. It lurched forward, gathering speed.

The timing was perfect. It caught the Buick broadside, sent it over. The crash of that collision, the cacophony of mangled, crushed-in iron, the dry sleet splattering of broken glass, the secondary slamming of the far side of the Buick against the paving stone, the rumbling cough of the motor as it died, could be heard for hundreds of meters in every direction.

Jim saw Joe claw himself up through the opened window of the wrecked car. The dark glasses were smashed. Joe swept them off and away, and Jim saw he had blood on his face from a cut eyebrow. But with one huge wrench that burst the door completely off its hinges, he was out and free and racing for the truck. He tore the door open, reached up and yanked the driver out and down, slammed him up against the front wheel of the truck with a whistling left-hand smash, brought a knee up between his loosened legs that tore a scream, woman-shrill and terrible, from the truck driver's mouth; then Joe was all over him, smashing him backward against the truck, hooking his face right and left and right again with mulekick powerful punches, any one of which, Jim was sure, was enough to kill a man.

Which took him seconds only. But, even so, by then, Carlos and his crew, and the truck driver's helper were there. But, Jim saw with a stab of icy fear, they might as well have not existed. Costa Verdians of the working class are almost always small men, though strong and wiry. There were five of them all told: Carlos Suarez and his work crew of three men, and the truck driver's helper. But they were Liliputians trying to pull down Gulliver, ants attacking an elephant. But considered coldly, it wasn't Joe Harper's immense size and strength that made the decisive difference. Five determined men can always dominate one, no matter what his physical advantages over them as individuals may be. Rather, it was that Joe Harper's mastery of karate, jujitsu (as opposed to judo, which is merely a sport), Japanese and Graeco-Roman style wrestling, boxing, savate, commando hand-to-hand fighting, barroom brawling, rough and tumble street fighting, and every other known method for maiming, blinding, crippling, paralyzing, and killing people with one's bare hands, encircling arms, and leather-shod feet, not to mention the devastating use to which he could also put his elbows, his battering ram of a head, and his knees, was so far beyond the ordinary as to put him into a special class, not very far removed from that of a special cybernetic machine whose specific, designed-in purpose is murder. And when that was combined with the ice-cold killer instinct of the great beast his genetic oversupply of *y* chromosomes had transformed or mutated him into, no five unarmed men, who also lacked his precise and terrible training, nor any ten, stood the remotest chance against him.

Jim Rush found himself again, even under those appalling circumstances, gripped by his own nonathlete's envious admiration of perfect, even esthetically beautiful physical skill, for Joe Harper's movements as he struck down his foes had all the grace, precision, and effortless economy of a great *Premier Danseur* in some satanic ballet. In five seconds flat, with exactly five blows, whose expertness awoke in Jim a chilling sense of his own helplessness, a bitter renewal of the inferiority feelings he had all but overcome, Joe Harper put all five of his attackers down onto the cobblestones, and out of the fight for good.

Then he turned back to the truck driver, out on his feet, sobbing and coughing blood, hanging upright only by grasping the handle of the truck's door, and coldly and deliberately murdered him. Measuring the distance very exactly with his eye, Joe hit the absolutely helpless man twice, both karate chops, the first slanted in across the bridge of the truck driver's nose so that it crushed it in, just between his eyes. The result was an immediate hemorrhage, damaging fatally the brain's lower frontal lobes, so swift and heavy that not even Vince Gomez could have halted it even if he had been on the spot and standing by with his instruments ready and waiting. But, not satisfied with that, following the precepts of commando training which are based on overkill, or perhaps driven by his double *y* chromosomes, Joe chopped him again, but across the Adam's apple this time, the second chop smashing the larynx, causing irreversible strangulation.

Then leaving the dying man on the street beside the truck, Joe turned back towards his own wrecked car, his face calm, peaceful, even—and this was the most horrifying aspect of it all to Jim—happy. Clearly he meant to retrieve the hidden packages of heroin and then—

But before he got there, he saw the Cadillac. Saw, very clearly, Jim's face staring at him through the opened window of the back seat.

"Why!" he guffawed. "If it ain't little old Uncle Creepie-Poo!" He stopped, frowned, whispered: "Why, damn me for a nigger! *You* staged this! *You!* Uncle Creep! A caper like this one!" he grinned suddenly, happily. "Goddamn, Creepie-Poo, my hat's off to you! Cause I tried to relieve you of that fine little piece of shady snatch, eh? Great, Unc! I swear I didn't know you had it in you, and tha's a living fact!"

He started toward the Cadillac, still grinning broadly.

"All the same, guess I better teach you some manners, Creep, Old Chum, and a little sense. Ain't no little half-Indian, half-nigger broad worth tangling with Joe Harper over. Tell you what, you send her down to my pad special delivery tonight, and I'll let you off. So help me I will. Hell, I'll send th' Cunt over to your place to console you. Be just right for you. You don't even hafta be able to get it up. Th' cunt's tha greatest blowjob artist in th' business. Whatcha say to th' swap, Creepie-Poo?"

Roberto—*Teniente Colonel* Roberto Henriques of National Security— was out of the car by then. He had his flat, ugly German-made *Pistolle* M2 in his hand.

"You are under arrest, Harper!" he said in the English he wasn't supposed to either speak or understand.

"Why!" Harper laughed happily. "Th' Battling Chauffeur! It was you who hit me in that damn night club last week as I recall! Look, Fancy Dan, ain't nobody ever told you three-way crosses between Indians, niggers, and apes not to lay hands on a *white* man? Guess I better include you in the lesson, teach you to sing: 'My Momma is a She-Ape; I fucks her every night! From behind, Monkey-style, tha's how I do it right!' Ain't that th' truth, you dressed-up Chimp? Fine, big, black juicy tail your Momma's got!"

"He's mad!" Jim realized suddenly. "Stark raving mad!"

"Harper, stop! Stay where you are. Or I'll shoot!" Henriques said.

"Shoot away, Chimp. You monkeys couldn't hit th' left side of your Momma's big fat ass."

He took another step forward. Another, another.

That third step was too much. The *Pistolle* M2 bucked and barked in Henriques' hands.

And missed Joe completely. Then it hit Jim that Joe had been crazy like a fox. That he had been conducting not unskillful psychological warfare, that his careful and considered insults had been calculated to the word to send any Costa Verdian into an uncontrollable and therefore trembling rage. And now the proof of his tactics' effectiveness was in: Roberto Henriques, a trained Security Officer, and therefore, it went without saying, an expert pistol shot, had missed Joe Harper cleanly and completely from less than seven meters.

But Joe didn't miss. That squat, ugly Smith & Wesson .357 Magnum was out from under his coat and thundering before Jim even saw him draw it. A .357 Magnum slug will knock a man down if it hits him in his big toe, much less anywhere else. A gun like that isn't a mere revolver, it's hand-held artillery. The two shots Joe got off slammed Henriques back against the car door so hard his body dented it. They both tore fist-sized holes in his belly, came out his back, went through the outer panel of the door, and lodged in the padding inside.

But their impact, itself, or the realization that his death was upon him, made Henriques' finger tighten on the trigger of his own gun. The *Pistolle* M series is nobody's toy, either. This one was a special, made for the Waffen S.S. and the Gestapo. It was, therefore, chambered for 9 mm rimfire cartridges, instead of the more usual 7.9s. And a nine millimeter slug isn't *that* much smaller or lighter than a .357. The one shot Henriques got off before he died slammed into Joe's right shoulder, spinning him completely around. The big, short-barreled revolver slipped from fingers suddenly paralyzed, because Henriques' bullet had clipped or nicked the big nerve controlling the motions of that whole arm.

And Jim Rush, because he had to, because by then, out of sheer necessity, he was learning to act when action was necessary and indulge in sober thought and intimidating, cowardizing, fear-breeding speculation over the probable results of said action afterwards, came out of that car in a quite respectably smooth rush, bent and pried the automatic from Roberto's dead fingers, pointed it at Joe Harper, and whispered:

"Stay where you are, Joe. Don't move."

"Creep," Joe crooned, "you better shoot. Cause if you don't you're gonna curse your old, dried up, aristocratic whore of a Ma for ever letting Creep, Senior, or some of his gentle friends into her frilly lace pants. Curse her for ever birthing you, you miserable little turd! Because what I'm going to pin on you, you're *never* going to forget! You hear me, Creepie-Poo?"

Jim saw that even while he was saying all that, Joe's gaze was sweeping the cobblestones in search of the .357 Magnum. Then they both saw it, lying about three meters away from where Joe swayed. But, because Joe, actually, was in a state of shock—having a 9 mm full-jacketed slug plow into your shoulder and smash the ball and socket joint all to hell doesn't leave anyone, not even a man as strong as Joe Harper, feeling like the power and the glory—Jim Rush got there first. He kicked the big revolver into a far gutter. Said:

"Don't be a fool, Joe. Keep still."

But Joe Harper had whirled, was already running. Carlos Suarez and one of the others, back on their feet by then, but still dazed, made a futile grab for him. There was only one thing to do, but he, Jim Rush, couldn't do it. He hadn't got that far along, yet. Too many things *had* been bred out of him. Among them what it took to put a bullet—or the five of them remaining in the clip of that automatic—through the easy target Joe's broad back made. Essentially, he was a civilized man, and civilized men make heroes of an almost urinal poverty. He could have ended Joe's useless, parasitical, murderously criminal life easily enough. That is, he could have in the physical sense. He could shoot with sufficient accuracy for the task at hand. He had sat and shivered in duck blinds with his father, accompanied that august Victorian, even Edwardian, gentleman on grouse shoots in Scotland, deer stalking in Canada, boar hunts in the Schwartzwald—and hated every second of those essentially savage rites of passage into manhood so treasured by the upper class. But, in a real sense, being *who* he was, he could not. The thing was impossible. He lacked whatever it is a man needs to coolly and deliberately kill another human being.

So he let Joe Harper go. Saw the big man reach the end of the docks, and go off them in a dive that was almost as smooth and perfect as all Joe's physical acts were, in spite of the considerable handicap of an at least temporarily paralyzed right arm.

Even after that, he could have killed Harper. That bright blond head made a perfect target against the ink blue waters. But he stood there, his finger frozen on the trigger of the automatic, watching the worst enemy he'd had in all his life, or ever would have, treading water until that waiting speedboat slid out from under the docks and picked him up.

And still he, Jim Rush, stood there staring at that sleek, beautiful craft as it pounded off, its twin inboard-outboard motors bellowing, throwing up double rooster tails of milk white spray. Saw it grow ever smaller, disappear into the sea and sun mists, far out, going on. Only its dying wake was visible now.

'The worst enemy I ever had,' he thought. 'Except—myself. Myself.'

Then, slowly, sorrowfully, he turned, and went back to where the others were.

CHAPTER

20

*H*e didn't get back to the residence until well after nine o'clock that night. With him he brought the late Roberto Henriques' *Pistolle* M2, and Joe Harper's .357 Magnum. General García, himself, had presented the two guns to him, as souvenirs of his sterling heroism.

He called Tomás, gave him the two pistols, said:

"Take these two damned things out and throw them into the garbage pail. But break the firing pins, first. Plug the barrels. And the chambers."

"No, Sir," Tomás said. "I'll put them in the closet with your *Chaleco Antibalas.* Who knows? All three items may come in handy, some day. Especially the bulletproof vest."

"Jesus! I thought I told you to get rid of that obscene piece of idiocy as well, Tomás!"

"You did, Sir. But I disobeyed you. You are not living in the sanest country in the world, Sir. Obscene idiocies often prove most useful in *la Republica de Paranoia,* Sir!"

"You can say that again, Tomás!" Jim sighed.

"These pistols, Sir. I'd suggest we have them mounted. Display them prominently in your office in the Embassy. Excellent propaganda, Sir! It will remind people just whom they're dealing with . . ."

"Jesus H. Christ!" Jim Rush said.

"Sir, allow me to congratulate you. The story is all over town. The radio, y'know. The six o'clock newscast. Little Trini called. She was thrilled beyond words. And frightened past tears. Kept babbling, 'Tomás, watch him! Guard him! Don't let him do things like this again!' "

"*And* His Mother Mary!" Jim Rush said.

"And your secretary, Mrs. Clyde. She was all set to rush over here to congratulate you in person. I told her you were remaining in town overnight—with friends . . ."

"What did she say to that?" Jim said.

" 'Friends, Tomás. Or *a* friend? In—skirts?' "

"C'mon, Tomás; don't tell me you didn't have a comeback for *that* one. What did you tell her?"

"That I couldn't guarantee—the skirts, Sir. Or at least not their maintenance in their normal position. She shot back: 'You mean raised, Tomás? Or—removed?' I said, airily: 'Oh, I doubt they'll ever even be put on, Mrs. Clyde, since His Excellency's visit is—expected . . .' "

"Good!" Jim laughed. "Damned if that isn't the first and only cheerful note I've had all day!"

"But, Sir—after your feat of vanquishing Harper—"

"*¡Mierda!* Tomás, the whole thing got blown. Harper killed two men outright and knocked the others senseless. At the end of it, only I was in a position to stop him, to—kill him. And, by now, you know me. I couldn't. I simply couldn't. I let that bastard get away."

"Sir, eyewitnesses swear—"

"*What* eyewitnesses, Tomás? The dockworkers were half a kilometer from the action, and breaking every Olympic record on the books to put another kilometer or two between them and the fireworks when matters really got serious. Unless they have eyes in the seats of their pants, they didn't see a goddamned thing. Carlos and friends were decorating the cobblestones in various supine positions, out like lights. And the truck driver and poor Roberto were *dead.* Which leaves *one* eyewitness: *me.*"

"Sir, those dockworkers swear you took the gun from Henriques' hand—"

"True. At least they got *that* much right!"

"And shot Harper. Wounded him so that he dropped his gun—"

"False. I did no such thing. Henriques shot him before he died. All I did was to point poor Roberto's pistol—with a wildly shaking hand!—at Harper, who was both wounded and weaponless by then, and order him to keep still. Bur friend Harper has a very expert knowledge of my capabilities as a warrior. And a distressingly accurate estimate of my qualities as a man. He laughed at me. And walked—no, he did have the decency to pretend enough respect for me to at least trot!—away from the scene, knowing perfectly damned well that I didn't have the testicles to kill him . . ."

"Or were—too civilized to, Sir," Tomás said.

"All right. I thank you for putting it so kindly. Civilization is a good enough euphemism for cowardice, I suppose. But tell me this: What good does being civilized do in a savage world, Tomás?"

"Very little, I'm afraid, Sir," Tomás said. "But, Sir—I shouldn't contradict the story of—your splendid heroism too strongly, if I were you."

"And why *not?*"

"People *need* heroism, Sir. Just as they need religion."

"Which is why most of history is a pack of arrant lies, Tomás!"

"Truth is so—unkind, Sir. So—brutal. If you take away the myths men live by, Sir, what do you leave them?"

"Hmmmmmnnn—" Jim said. "Damned little. Probably nothing. That life is a not so prolonged exercise in futility, stupidity, and cowardice; and that we all end up as the *pièce de résistance* at that supper Hamlet accused Polonius of going to. You know: 'Not where he eats, but where he is eaten: a certain convocation of politic worms are e'en at him!' And so forth. And to spare them the pain of contemplating that, I'm supposed to pretend to be a hero?"

"Say you deny the whole thing with—an ironical twinkle in your eye. With charmingly becoming modesty. Sir, they aren't going to believe you if you deny it angrily. They need an authentic hero to compensate them for life's dullness. I'd say they won't believe your denials, whyever or however. So your position remains remarkably like that of the girl to whom the Male Chauvinist gave some very wise advice to. You see, Sir, she was in the throes of being raped. Forceably and vigorously violated, Sir. And this Male Chauvinist who happened upon the scene told her kindly: 'The only thing you can do *now* is to lie back and enjoy it, dear!' "

"Oh, damn you, Tomás!" Jim laughed. "You're really a treasure. Don't know what I'd do without you! By the way, can you stay a couple of hours overtime, tonight? I need you to drive the car. I must pay a short visit—to Trini. I promised her. Oh, hell, maybe I'd better just phone her and call the whole thing off. Take a rain check, anyhow . . ."

"Sir, don't. She's—too upset. The way she was sobbing over the phone was heartbreaking, Sir. Kinder to go and—*comfort* her, Sir . . ."

"Tomás, you will kindly remove all those implications you left dripping all over the word 'comfort'!"

"I rather think removing them—or removing other objects, such as certain rather delicate garments, say—is up to you, Sir! What time will you need the car, Sir?"

"Oh, hell; what's the use? An incurably filthy mind is an incurably filthy mind. At ten thirty, Tomás. And *yours,* not the Embassy's."

"Mine, Sir?"

"Yes. The Cadillac has at least two bullet holes in it, and nobody's got around to—washing poor Roberto's blood off the left front window, and the door. It's in working order, but it wouldn't help my mood, Tomás, nor my nerves. Tomorrow, you'll have to take it downtown to the Cadillac repair shop. Even so, I may get rid of it; buy another car. That one's going to give me the horrors for a good long time . . ."

"Very well, Sir. And, Sir, maybe you'd better take the smaller gun with you. Seems to use 9 mm ammunition, which is available locally. And with your great and good friend Harper still running around on the loose, who knows? Of course I have my own, a Spanish-made Astra-Star, 7.9 mm, long. But two guns would surely be better than just one, and—"

"Jesus! How'd I *ever* get tapped for a role in this Cops and Robbers Epic? I'll be damned if I will, Tomás! Haven't I already proved once today that, as a gunman, I make a first class Japanese Flower Arranger? Here, put these two greasy obscenities into the night table drawer until I decide what to do with them. Anyhow, get them the hell out of my sight! Even looking at them makes me nervous!"

When Tomás drew his little black Volkswagen Beetle up before the door of the apartment house where Trini lived, it was exactly ten thirty.

"I'll park there—on the top of that little rise, Sir," he said, "where I can watch both approaches. And, Sir—take your time! I'll be quite comfortable in the car . . ."

"Oh, come off of it, Tomás!" Jim Rush said.

He felt—drained. Utterly spent. He hadn't the slightest intention of making love—in the sense of having sexual intercourse—with Trini, even if *she* insisted upon it. As she might. For reasons having nothing to do with anything so simple and uncomplicated as mere physical desire. Reasons such as reenforcing her hold upon him, reducing the risk that he might leave her, which was what she seemed to chiefly fear . . .

He walked up to the door. As she had told him, entrance to the building was provided by means of what is known throughout the Spanish-speaking world as *El Portero Electronico,* for, what with the salaries real live human doormen demanded these days, only the very highest priced luxury apartment buildings could afford them.

Only, when he pushed her bell button, nothing happened. Looking through the glass of the door, he saw lights were on in the hall. He remembered that, as he'd come up to the house, most of the windows had shown the glow of lamps or the bluish flicker of television screens.

No power failure then. Moreover, from where he stood beside the door, he could see lights were on in all the buildings on the block. He pushed the bell, again. Held it in until his fingertip ached, was pounding. Released it. Tried it again. Twice. Five times. Ten. Twenty. He was beginning to sweat now.

He tried it one more time. No answer. He stepped to the edge of the sidewalk, waved towards the black Volkswagen.

Tomás was out of it at once and running towards him.

"Sir—what's wrong?" he said when he got there.

"Tomás—she doesn't answer her bell. And she *knew* I was coming here tonight. She was *expecting* me."

"I know. She said as much to me over the phone . . ."

"Tomás—she could be sick—or—or—"

"More likely her bell's out of order, Sir. They sometimes do fail you know."

"But what the devil does one do in such a case, Tomás? These economical apartment buildings have no porters, you know!"

"Ring her next door neighbor. Here, let me: 'Sr. Fernando Rojas Lupe, 7 B.' "

Tomás pushed the bell for 7 B. Almost at once a man's voice said: "*¿Quien es?*"

"Look, Sir; I'm the chauffeur from the American Embassy. I have a message for *la Señorita* Alvarez. And she doesn't answer her bell. I was assured she'd be in at this hour . . ."

"I know nothing about her! I don't want to get mixed up in it! Leave me alone! Good night!"

Jim Rush pushed the bell. Held it.

"*¡Maldita séa!*" the man's voice swore. "I told you—"

"Look, Sir!" Jim said sharply. "I *am* the Ambassador of the United States of North America! And I demand to talk to *Señorita* Alvarez! And if she's not there, to *you!*"

He could hear the man breathing. Then the voice whispered:

"Say something—in English. But first wait! I'll go get my son, who speaks it!"

They waited. Jim was shaking, now.

A boy's voice said:

"*¡Diga!*" Then, in English: "You will have the goodness to speak, Mr. Ambassador!"

"Look, Son," Jim said; "I'm James Rush, Ambassador of the United States to your country and—"

"You are—Trini's protector?" the boy said. "That is what we have been told—what all the world believes, *Señor* . . ."

Jim thought about that. Said, quietly, humbly:

"Yes, Son."

"Good. I will now open the door. Perhaps you will be in time—to save her . . ."

"Jesus!" Jim said.

The door buzzed. They pushed it open. Tomás had his hand on the butt of his gun, Jim saw.

"No, Tomás," he said, "that won't be necessary. We've come too late, I'm afraid."

The Rojases, father and son, met them in the hall. The older man lay a warning finger across his lips. Nodded to them to enter his apartment. His wife, a pleasant looking woman in her fifties, was sitting at the table in the living/dining room, and crying.

"¡Pobrecita!" she sobbed. "Poor little thing! She was so—sweet! And such a good neighbor! Never any men visitors. Only a girl friend or two. Never noise, bad behavior, scandal. And now we'll never see her again! Oh, the poor, poor child!"

"Mama, calm thyself!" the boy said; "This gentleman is very powerful. Perhaps he—"

"Your credentials, Sir!" Sr. Rojas said.

Jim took out his billfold. The National Security Identity Card issued him by the Costa Verdian authorities with his picture and thumbprint on it. His United States passport.

"Good!" Sr. Rojas said. "Pardon me, Your Excellency, but surely you have been in this country long enough to know that one cannot be too careful in such cases!"

"But—Trini!" Jim got out. "Where is she? What's happened to her?"

"The police took her away. The Political Activities Squad, I think, because they wore ordinary clothes. And, as usual, they were very rough, Señor! If I were you, I'd hurry down to Headquarters. She—the poor thing!—seems very frail, and—"

"Thank you, Señor Rojas!" Jim whispered. "Come on, Tomás!"

"Sir, let's look into her flat. One minute, two. The delay will count for little and we may learn something . . ."

"All right! All right! But make it fast, Tomás!" Jim said.

The door was open, because, as usual, it had been kicked in by the arresting squad. The flat was a shambles. Every stick of furniture Trini had had was in splinters. Her television set had been smashed. Her radio. Her clothes ripped to shreds. Mirrors broken. Pictures. Everything. Nothing was left. Nothing at all.

"This doesn't look like the police to me, Sir!" Tomás said.

"But we'll have to start with them, anyhow. Let's get down to Headquarters, Tomás!"

"Sir, no. They'd simply deny they had her there. And you could do nothing about it. Let's pay a call on *Don* Raoul Pérez de la Valle. At his villa, Sir. In Golden Door."

"Right. It's not too late. He'll be having supper. And I—sense—he has a certain sympathy for me. I don't believe—"

"Come on, Sir!" Tomás said.

The Director General of Security stood there. His face tightened with real concern.

"I gave no such order, Mr. Ambassador!" he said. "You seemed quite content with the young woman. And we like to keep our friends content. I can't imagine. . ."

"Your friend Fuentes Toralba? *Don* Pablo?"

"Why should *he* do a thing like that? But I'll call him if you like. Come into my study."

Jim heard the question. The explosive series of squawks that answered it. The Director General pulled the phone a little way from his ear. Fuentes Toralba's voice came over clearly.

"When have I ever gone over *your* head, Raoul? Besides, why the devil should I, in this case? The girl was exceeding expectations! Our friend was taking her openly to the best restaurants, night clubs—"

"General—García?" Jim ventured, as Pérez de la Valle hung up. "I've had the feeling that you, *mi General,* and your friend, *Don* Pablo, don't quite see eye to eye with 'The Glorious Leader'!"

"We don't," Raoul Pérez de la Valle said bluntly; "but our differences are—friendly, and manageable, so far. However, on this—item—a difference does not exist. General García approved my selection. Reluctantly, but he approved it . . ."

"Why, reluctantly?' Jim asked.

"He would have preferred a girl from the very highest stratum of society. With—a spotless reputation. So would I have. But we couldn't find one with the—requisite—physical resemblance to—the lady we'd found out you're very fond of. Our Leader, the General, wanted to waive the resemblance. I insisted it was—essential. It seems that I was right."

"You were. And one day soon, we'll have to go into what your price for the gift—the truly marvelous gift of Trini, *mi General!*—is going to be. But now there's no time. You're sure the General wouldn't, didn't—"

"The General, my dear *Don* Jaime, if he wanted the young person detained, would call *me* and tell *me* to order her arrest. He'd do that even if he knew positively that I didn't agree with the wisdom or the—timing say, of that order. He'd even allow me to argue with him about it—our relations are quite friendly, you know. Then, if I hadn't convinced him—though I must tell you that I usually do convince him; the General takes my advice much more often than he rejects it, I'm proud to say, *Don* Jaime!—he'd simply say: 'I'm sorry, Raoul, but I want it done!' And that would be that. In other words, *Don* Jaime, he would *not* circumvent me, for the very simple reason that he knows such a procedure is not necessary. Besides, you know enough about our political structures to realize that the day General García feels that he can no longer trust me to do his bidding, he will simply remove me from office and—if I'm lucky!—exile me . . ."

'That,' Jim reflected, 'is the ugly truth!'

He passed a bone dry tongue over even drier lips. Whispered:

"Then—who?"

"I'd say—the Reds. DRAP, EMMA, or ERL. And I hope for your sake it's either DRAP or EMMA—"

"Why?" Jim said.

"Because they won't harm her. They'll simply hold her for ransom— they always need money, you know, to pay for their arms and their propaganda—plus a public declaration from you denouncing *us* as Fascist swine and torturers, *Don* Jaime; which, of course, we cannot permit you to make. You understand that, don't you?"

Jim thought: 'Especially not because it's two hundred percent true. Though that doesn't make the Reds smell any better themselves, I suppose . . .' He said:

"Why not, *Don* Raoul? Or rather, how could you stop me from making such a statement, since Trini's *life* would be at stake?"

The Director General shrugged.

"We couldn't, of course. But then, neither could you, my dear *Don* Jaime, evade the consequences of having made it, which would be that we'd immediately declare you *persona non grata,* and donate you a free flight to Miami in one of our military aircraft. Result: You'd *never* see dear little Trini again. You're an experienced diplomat. So you also know that your own Government would back us up in this measure. Not to mention cashiering you from the Foreign Service—though to a man of your means, such a dismissal would probably mean little . . ."

"It wouldn't mean anything. Save me the trouble of resigning— which I'm planning to do after this tour of duty, anyhow." He looked at the Director General; said, very quietly: "But the other alternative, losing Trini, does. Though, at the moment, I don't see that you're offering me much of a choice. For, from what you've just said, to avoid making trouble for your side, I'm supposed to sit quietly by and let the Reds *kill* Trini."

"No. Why, no; of course not! You're supposed to let *us* handle the matter. Which includes placing a security officer, in civilian clothes— and female, if you like, since she could pose as a secretary translator, and hence would attract much less attention—in both the Embassy and your residence, to monitor all incoming calls. With your permission, of course. Both places are U.S. territory under International Law . . ."

"Permission granted," Jim said. "And?"

"We have ways of tracing a phone call within minutes. Our Special Squads would grab the caller before he could hang up. From him we'd quickly learn where they have dear Trini—"

"*Mi General, Don* Raoul, I will *not* consent to, or go along with, the use of—torture," Jim said. "Not even for Trini's sake. *She* wouldn't want me to."

The Director General smiled.

"*Don* Jaime, *Don* Jaime!" he said. "A *crime* has apparently been committed. A young woman who is a *citizen* of *la Republica de Costa Verde* has been—we believe—abducted. Entirely an internal matter with which *no foreigner,* however high his position, nor even, regretfully, taking into consideration the respect and esteem we hold for him personally, nor our loyal friendship for his great country, has anything whatsoever to do. You simply cannot dictate policy to us in this matter, Your Excellency!"

Jim thought: 'Peter was right. The Borgias. Machiavelli. Pontius Pilate. Judas Iscariot. *And* the Devil!' He said:

"*Don* Raoul, I *don't* apologize. I admit I'm out of line; but I don't apologize. It's a matter of personal conviction. But I might add: It won't work. Even if you kill the poor bastard by millimeters. He won't tell you. He can't. He won't know. Every subversive organization in the world knows that tactic by now. Never send a messenger who knows anything that can harm the cell. Or its variant: Send a type who has been loaded with false and misleading information. Information that he honestly believes is true, since it was fed to him by people whom— idealistic young jackass that he usually is!—he trusts implicitly."

"You seem to know an enormous amount about it, *Don* Jaime!" the Director General said.

"I," Jim said icily, "have spent most of my life in countries where respect for human dignity—and human life!—is nil."

"Still," the Director General said, "you have to leave the matter in our hands, *Don* Jaime. You have no other recourse. Now I'm going to call my youngest daughter, who is trained as a secretary, to take down and type out orders from you, in both Spanish and English, granting permission to agents of ours to enter the Embassy and your residence and to remain in both places as long as shall be necessary to effect the rescue of—*¡la Señorita* Alvarez¡—or the solution of this case in some other way—"

"Such as," Jim said bitterly, "the recovery of—her body."

"Such as the recovery of her body. Which is why I said in the beginning, *Don* Jaime, that I hoped it will not prove to be ERL that has her.

For, if it is they—" he stopped, shuddered. Jim had the sickening feeling that the shudder was unfeigned, real.

"If it is they?" he said.

"It will be delivered to you. By tomorrow morning. But it will not be—recognizable," the Director General said.

At five o'clock the next morning, at the time that the Director General of Security had said that the resolution of the case of the abduction—or the murder!—of María de la Sagrada Trinidad Alvarez Bermejo wouldn't go beyond, if either, or both, had been carried out by the *Ejercito Rojo de la Liberación,* The Red Army of the Liberation, better known as ERL from its initials, Jim Rush was sitting in an armchair beside the window of his bedroom in the residence.

From that position, he could see the entire garden, and, more importantly, the gates. He couldn't see the dozens of Security Police hidden all around the residence, but he knew they were there. He also knew that Tomás was seated by the window of one of the back bedrooms watching the rear gates, and as much as he could see of the winding mountain road which served as a service and delivery entrance to the residence. The majordomo was sure that any message, or—though he refrained from saying as much to Jim, not realizing that his employer could read what he feared in his troubled eyes—poor Trini's dead, and hideously broken, body would be delivered to the back gates, because of the much greater ease and security that approach offered the terrorists. The front gates opened out upon one of Costa Verde's major highways. Only madmen, Tomás thought, would dare use it. Captain Carasco, in charge of the Security Agents surrounding both the residence and the Embassy, agreed with him.

Jim dozed fitfully in his chair. That he could sleep seemed to him worse than shameful. But he was forty-six years old. He had been on the move practically without rest since nine o'clock of the previous morning. He had eaten practically nothing in all that time. He had engaged in a kind of nerve-draining police action for whose excitement and very real dangers he was not even remotely, either psychologically, physically, or morally, equipped to bear. 'And that,' he thought sardonically, 'was absolutely none of my—correction!—absolutely none of the United States Ambassador's goddamned business! As the next directive I'll get from the Department—possibly even from the Secretary of State, himself!— will point out to me,' he added. 'You are down there,' he quoted from the yet unreceived, but surely not imaginary letter, 'to promote the political, financial, and military interests of the United States, defend your fellow citizens residing in, or visiting Costa Verde, but *not*—surely not!—to improvise a Police Procedure Television Serial!' And when State heard, or was informed, about Trini, the directive or the letter he'd get would have to be typed on asbestos, because—

His eyes jerked open.

Trini. Oh, Jesus.

And all hell broke loose down by the front gates. Submachine gun fire. Neither Schmeissers nor Ak-47s. Something else. Slower than Schmeissers. Faster than Ak-47s. Stens likely. Brens—no. Brens were too goddamned big. They had to be tripod-mounted like BAR's. Mausers? Mauser machine *pistols,* with open-frame shoulder stocks clipped into the hand grip? Almost surely. The shots sounded lighter than the 9 mm rimfire that Stens use.

Between them, at intervals, a sodden, double-timed, belly deep roar. Shotguns. Double barreled 16 gauge, sawed off to less than thirty centimeters and loaded with buckshot. With fifty calibre, or 13.8 mm hand-poured lead balls—or nuts and bolts and pieces of scrap iron loaded on top of all that. After twenty-five years in Latin America he'd seen it all. Somebody was staging a massacre down there, an annihilation.

He heard the scream of the sirens of the police jeeps. The ripping snarl of Schmeissers.

Then all the shooting stopped. A motor—where had he heard a sound like that before?—roared, bellowed, thundered. Tires screeched, screamed in a careening, lurching turn. That motor snarled, ripping through upshifting gears at the hands of a master racing driver, double clutching, pouring it on, lead footing that accelerator, tearing the dark apart, getting out of there.

And behind it the police jeeps, hopelessly, helplessly pursuing. They'd never catch a *bolide* like that one. Not on the highway, Jim knew.

He was up and across the room now, racing for the stairs. In the hallway a blur streaked past him. Tomás. He went down the stairs, two, three at a time, almost stepping on Tomás' heels.

As they reached the porch, all the lights in the garden blazed on. Tomás raised his hand, signaling to Jim to halt.

"Wait here, Sir!" he said sharply, authoritatively. "Let me have a look first! I'll call you when it's all clear."

And Jim saw he had his Astra-Star automatic pistol in his hand.

Jim stood there, waiting. 'That motor!' he remembered now, suddenly. 'Sounded exactly like the one in Joe's Buick! But they had to tow that wreck away from the docks, so—'

Then he saw the little group of men come running, pounding, lurching up the path towards the residence. Tomás. Four others. The two Costa Verdian armed police sentries from the gates. His own two personal United States Marine guards. The two Costa Verdians were carrying something between them. A long, limp, blanket-wrapped bundle.

His heart stopped. His breath. His mind. He couldn't move. He couldn't.

They came on. Up those stairs. He couldn't move. One of the Marines, the younger one, was crying. A Marine. Crying. The one branch of the Armed Forces he, Jim Rush, would have sworn trained past and out of humanity. Crying. and now Jim could hear him. He was saying:

"The bastards. The sons of bitches. The dirty, perverted mother-fuckers. The—"

Jim bent over that bundle. Put out a hand that didn't even shake, to push aside—

"Sir!" Tomás snarled at him, his voice strangling. "I—shouldn't look—if I were you!"

He pushed aside the dirty, bloody sheet that covered her face. Looked.

And screamed like a woman in childbirth. A down and thrashing horse. A prisoner in the soundproof chambers under *la Dirección General de Seguridad* with García's interrogators at him.

He bent forward. Loosened all over. Pitched forward down the porch steps. Smashed one side of his face bloody against the gravel of the walk. Lay there, retching, sobbing, crying. Then, abruptly, nothing. Mercifully nothing. Absolutely nothing at all.

He felt the strangling splash of water on his face. Then someone was slapping him, right, and left, and right again. Hard. He could feel the slaps stinging his wet cheeks. But he didn't open his eyes. He could open them, he supposed. But he didn't want to. He didn't want consciousness back. Nor thought. Nor—least of all!—memory.

Another slap. Harder still.

"Sir!" Tomás moaned. "Wake up! Sir, you must! She needs you! Sir, she is *not* dead! She's alive, Sir! Alive!"

That did it. His eyes came open. Glared at Tomás. He said:

"She—isn't—she's not—"

"Dead? No, Sir; she's alive," Tomás said, crying, openly and unashamedly crying. "She's even—conscious. Those swine were—experts. To put her all the way out—would have been—too merciful. That's—the worst of all, Sir! To see—to watch—her suffering like this—and not even crying! Not a whimper. Not a moan. Nothing. *¡Jesus y María!* She's *all* Tluscola!"

Jim was up then, raging, wild. He bent over the sofa where they had lain her. Swept her tiny, naked, seared, cut, burned, whip-flayed, broken body up into his arms. Pressed her against him.

"Sir!" Tomás said. "You'll kill her!"

He turned her loose. Lay her gently back down onto the sofa. She smiled at him. At least he supposed it was a smile. She had three teeth missing from the front of her mouth. Both eyes were blackened, and swollen almost shut. Some especially exquisite sadist had ringed the dark areolas around the nipples of her breasts with deep cuts that bled endlessly. Some comedian, some ironist, some satirist—or more likely—how often do sadism and puritanism go together!—some moralist had fastened a dog collar around her slender neck. Her breath blew bubbles in the crimson froth her mouth was full of.

"I—love thee, *Don* Jaime," she said. Her voice was thick, drowning, unclear, but he could make that much out. Then, mercifully, she fainted.

He went absolutely blind. Shook. Sobbed. Choked. Strangled. He brought his two fists up and ground them into his eyes. The brooches of Jocasta. But in reverse.

Those swollen, flesh-embedded slits of hers fluttered open. Showed light.

"Don't—*Don* Jaime—" she gurgled, burbled, lisped. "I am—very well—now . . . For—am—I—not—with thee?"

"Oh, Jesus!" he wept. "Oh Christ, Oh God, Oh Jesus."

Then he heard the sirens screaming in. Police sirens. But the Hooooo Deeeee Haaaaahhh! of ambulances as well.

"I called the hospital, Sir!" Tomás said grimly. "And Doctor Gomez. Good thing you thought of advising him last night. He was standing by. He's on his way." Tomás stopped; smiled wryly. "I thought waking *you* up could wait!"

"Thank you, Tomás," Jim said.

Vince Gomez' dark, burgundy red Lincoln Continental came roaring through the gates long minutes before the first of the ambulances got there. Paloma was with him, sitting at his side.

He was out of the car and racing up the steps, roaring:

"Damnit, Jim, you should be deported as an undesirable alien! All you ever do is fuck up the works and—"

He stopped. Stood there. His face went livid. Turned—purple. He took a backward step. Dropped into a chair.

"Vince!" Jim said.

"Give me a minute, Jim," Vince whispered. "Feeling the way I do now—I just—might kill her. It is not—useful—to feel this way. Not—for a doctor. We're not supposed to be—quite human. We're trained to be beyond—both pity—and rage! But—"

Paloma dropped to her knees before her husband. Caught him by by the shoulders. Shook him, big as he was; screamed at him, sobbing:

"Vicente, get up from there! *¡Maldita séa!* Do something! Don't let her die!"

"Right," Vince croaked; "you're absolutely right, Paloma. I mustn't, must I?"

He got up from there. Dropped to his knees besides the sofa. Got to work.

First he took off the dog collar. Handed it to Jim. Said:

"There's an identification tube attached, Jim. If there's any threat—or message—it will be inside the tube."

It was. It was very simple. It read:

"I told you to lay off, Creep."

It was signed:

"Joe Harper."

It was then, at that moment, that James Randolph Rush voluntarily retired from the ranks of civilized men. Which was, probably, just as well. It is neither useful—nor wise—to live too far beyond the attainments of one's times.

Paloma knelt there beside her husband, working with him. Passing him his instruments, medicines, salves, ointments. Sulfa. Anti-inflammatory steroids. Penicillin pomade.

She looked at him. He sighed, said:

"I don't know, Paloma. Now, she'll at least get to the hospital alive. I'd suggest you call Padre Pío. Prayer's indicated. That's his department, not mine . . ."

"Vicente!" Paloma moaned.

"And one thing more, my Sweet!" Vince said bitingly. "Let's see you Ladies of the Liberation put your money where your mouths are, to borrow a vulgar Yanqui phrase! You're supposed to defend, help, save poor abused little bitches like this one, aren't you? Does that dedication include giving her—your blood?"

Instantly, without hesitation, Paloma stretched out her arm.

"Oh, don't be a fool, Paloma!" Vince said tiredly. "You know better than that! I can't perform a transfusion here. And besides, I don't remember what her group is. I have to check the records. In addition to which, my Dove, I need more blood than you have in your whole body. In a word, we'll need a minimum of twenty donors, and possibly even fifty. To do what I have to do, I must not merely replace the blood she's lost, and is losing, but pump *all* the blood in her body out of her, and pump an equal quantity of new blood into her. Blood that will *clot* decently, which hers doesn't. So she won't bleed to death on me if I have to operate. As I probably will have to. So she'll stop bleeding *now*, long enough for us to take X rays of her lower spine, and her pelvis, both of which may be fractured, if not smashed. Someone seems to have jumped up and down upon her down there. With both feet. Repeatedly."

"Oh, Jesus!" Jim said.

"I'm sorry, Jim," Vince said. "Was there a note?"

"Yes," Jim said. "From Harper. Joe Harper."

"You should have killed that filthy swine!" Vince said.

"I know. The next time, I will," Jim said quietly.

"Jim," Paloma said, "where's your phone?"

"In there," Jim said, and pointed.

They heard the rasp and rings and tinkles of her dialing.

"*¡Hola! ¿La residencia de Su Excelencia General García, verdad? ¡Que se pone la Señora!* What's that? I *know* it's six o'clock in the morning and that she's sleeping! Go wake her up, you cretin! This is Paloma San Ginés. Yes, yes, *la Señora de Doctor* Gomez and my call is *urgentísima*! *¡Maldita séa!* If you don't call her *now,* this instant, I'll see that you're *shot* before night, *¿comprendes?* Go call her now!"

The stretcher bearers came in. Jim stood up. Vince said:

"No, wait for Paloma, Jim. Bring her with you. I *can't* wait. You can."

"All right," Jim said.

"Luisa?" Paloma said. "Forgive me, but this really *is* an emergency Yes, yes, my dear—grave enough to wake you up at six in the morning. It's a matter of saving—a girl's life. Yes. One of those kinds of girls that I—take care of. Thank you, Luisa! The day we women arm *our* revolution, we'll make *you* Head of the State, and you can stop having to even let *Don* Manuel *believe* he is! Look, dear, this is what happened—"

She explained swiftly, succinctly, clearly.

"Yes, yes—tortured. Almost—to death. No—not almost. Actually to death, if we don't do something to save her. With appalling cruelty. The—usual—obscenities. But an unusual—inventiveness. The work of a madman. Why? Simply because she is—*la Querida* of the American Ambassador. What's that? You didn't know *Don* Jaime had a mistress? Well, yes, Luisa. This poor child. A *very* small sin for which I have already forgiven her, because she really and truly loves him. Yes, yes— very understandable. *Don* Jaime *is* a most charming man. But she will die without the blood, Luisa. Liters and liters of blood. We need—fifty donors. A hundred. What's that? You'll make the General send the police to round up all the girls in our League? Luisa! How priceless! You're the Eighth Wonder of the World!"

For the first time, Jim Rush saw the one true advantage of a Dictatorship: that it can act with a speed and dispatch that no democracy can come anywhere close to. More, because it can disregard the feelings of its citizens with a brutality that would cause the downfall of any representative form of government within a week, it often achieves a great, if totally inhuman, efficiency. Though in this case, perhaps, its inhumanity was not quite total.

By eight o'clock that morning, all the waiting rooms in the Hospital *Miguel Villalonga* were full. And with the Great, Illustrious, and Distinguished Dames of the Highest Costa Verdian Society. To give them their due, most of them were quite willing to donate their blood to this poor battered child, ex-prostitute though she was, kept mistress of the American Ambassador though she might be. They were, after all, of the twentieth century, and the whole thing had its left-handed, delightfully outrageous *chic*. It would give them something to talk about for months. Even the reluctant ones were so more out of simple physical fear of the process itself than of any scorn of Trini. Miguel Villalonga had cured Costa Verdian society of its habit of scorning the *demi-mondaine* by reducing too many of its own members—by force—to it.

Jim saw Trini for a full half hour after the total transfusions were over, while the laboratory technicians were checking the coagulation time of her entirely new blood supply. Then Vince came in, robed in pale green for surgery. With him were Dr. Guttierez, his assistant, and Doctor Moreno, Costa Verde's leading gynecologist and obstetrician.

"It clots great, Jim," Vince said. "Now we've got to go in there and patch her up for you . . ."

"Vince—" Jim got out. "What are—her chances?"

"Of survival? Good. Better than good. I'm not afraid of—losing her, Jim. But if you marry her—and it seems to me that she deserves that much from you now, after *this*—forget children. Unless you adopt them. Her pelvic girdle is smashed all to hell, Jim. The damage is major. I think I can guarantee that she'll walk again. I'd venture, almost normally. A slight limp, perhaps. But, no babies, Jim . . ."

"All right," Jim whispered; "but you tell her, later on, Vince. She's got her heart set on having a flock of kids, and—"

"One moment, Mr. Ambassador," Doctor Luis Moreno said; "if it is any comfort to you, there is no longer any special danger, should this young woman become pregnant. Her blood clots normally now. She could have a child. That is not the problem."

"Then what is?" Jim said wonderingly.

"It is my opinion," Doctor Moreno said, "that unless my good friend and colleague, Doctor Gomez here, performs a surgical miracle, she will be left with a structural malformation that will guarantee spontaneous abortion—miscarriage, if you will—within the first two months of pregnancy, ten times out of ten. In short, you need not take any special precautions to prevent pregnancy. She just won't have children, that is all."

"Jim," Vince said, "I'm not going to try for that miracle. I could do it. From what the X rays show, I'm sure I could do it. But—it's too dangerous, *Amigo.* It would take too long. I don't think she could take it. So—"

"So, to hell with a flock of kids. The world's overpopulated now. I want Trini—with me. Alive."

On the bed, Trini opened her eyes. Blinked. Stared at Jim.

"My Love," she whispered, her voice so weak, so low, he had to bend within kissing distance to hear it, "what passes with thee? Why is thy face so white?"

He stood there, wondering what to tell her. Said:

"They're going to—intervene surgically, Trini. To operate on you, and I—there's no reason for it; but I'm afraid, *Muñeca.*"

She smiled at him with grossly swollen lips. Squeezed his hand. Drew him down by tugging at it feebly to where he could hear the not-quite sounds that were all that she could make.

"Do not be—*mi Amor,*" she murmured, "I shall not die. I promise thee that I shall live. For thee. I—owe—thee—ten—babies. Remember?"

"Oh, Jesus!" Jim Rush whispered, gut crippled again, blind, and bent and kissed her battered, broken mouth.

CHAPTER

21

*B*ut, Uncle Chub—I mean Uncle Jim!" Jenny said. "I *can't* sign this! I'm scared! Joe would beat me to death!"

"Joe," Jim said, "is not even in Costa Verde, Jen. I seriously doubt he'll ever come back to this country again. He won't dare."

Jenny peered at him.

"First time *I* ever heard of anything Joe wouldn't dare do, Uncle Jim," she said. "You oughta know *that*. Look how he almost took your girl off you in that night club. By the way, how is she?"

"Better," Jim said. "No thanks to Joe. Don't change the subject, Jenny!"

"Uncle Jim, how do you know whether Joe's out of the country or not? I mean, what *proof* have you got?"

"Talked to Charlie Marriotti; you know: your father's best helicopter pilot . . ."

"Yeah," Jenny sighed. "Poor Charlie! Made the same mistake you're making, Uncle Jim; he got mixed up with the local talent. Of course, Charlie's been down here six years, but anyway you figure it, marrying one of these little monkey-chasing broads is carrying fraternizing too blamed far. So now Joe's playing around with Charlie's wife. Chick named Mariluz. With a job like Charlie's got, he's away from home a lot. 'N her and my Jo-Jo's got a *big* thing going. With hot peppers and Chili sauce on it! Enough to set the woods on fire in the middle of a rainstorm, and—"

"If so, Charlie doesn't know it," Jim said; "and, anyhow, it's just one more problem that's over, because your so-called husband paid Charlie five thousand dollars cash to fly him over the frontier into Colombia, and out of the reach—temporarily anyhow—of the local police. Which, since I have to spell everything out to you, and in words of one syllable at that, so that whatever Grass, Acid, Speed, and Horse have left you of a brain can assimilate it, means that your beloved and ever faithful Jo-Jo, the Ape-Man, won't be playing around with anybody's wife or girl friend in Costa Verde again for quite some time. Including his own, namely *you*. If he ever can, which I doubt."

"But, Uncle Jim, Colombia's nowhere from here! Joe could *walk* back across the frontier any time he wanted to, and—"

"He could, but he won't. The police found seven kilos of heroin in the black Buick of his the day of the accident, Jen. You know what they do to a man they catch with as much as five grams of hard drugs on him down here?"

Jenny licked her lips. They were neither pink, nor rose, nor red, nor even white. They were blue. 'Corpse-blue,' Jim thought.

"Yeah," Jenny whispered; "they—shoot him . . ."

"Ever see an execution? You've been down here long enough," Jim said.

"Yeah. Two of 'em. Both messy. I was s'posed to see five. Tha's how many Joe paid for us to keep the balcony for. Only I passed out after the second one. The first one was only shooting. Just like on TV. So I could take *that*. Specially after seeing so many bullfights. But they *strangled* that second poor guy. With that awful machine—"

"The *Garrote Vil.*"

"Yeah. That one. And—you know what, Uncle Jim? He—he shot off in his pants. Came. Just like he was dreaming he was making it with his best girl. Got a hard on—and when the guy they call *el Verdugo*—"

"That means 'the Executioner,' Jen. Go on."

"When the Executioner twisted that wheel that tightens up the strap around his neck, his dong kind of jumped inside his pants and the front of him got wet and—and Joe laughed like hell. Said it was a happy death. But it wasn't. That poor bastard crapped his pants, too. And pissed all over himself. Joe had paid for a balcony right over that damned machine. That was when I passed out. When that awful smell hit me. And—"

"One of the effects of strangulation, Jenny. The sphincters always loosen. But I hope Joe got a good look. Because that's what's going to happen to *him*, if he comes back here."

"Jesus!" Jenny said. "But they only *shoot* people for pushing 'shit,' Uncle Jim. And Joe's got an in with somebody *Big*. In the Government—"

276

"Big enough to get him off for the murders of a truck driver, and a Lieutenant Colonel in the Costa Verdian Security Services? Both of which call for a mandatory death sentence and precisely by means of that charming little machine you've been describing?"

"Oh, Lord!" Jenny said. "Joe—did that, Uncle Jim?"

"Yes. Before my eyes. I'd be called to testify against him. And even if I were inclined to indulge in a little perjury to save his filthy neck, there were five other witnesses, Jen; one of them the trucker's helper and best friend . . ."

"And even you wouldn't be. Inclined to try to save Joe, I mean. Not after the way he and his cute little chums messed up your girl. Ruined her—for life, eh, Uncle Jim?"

"Yes. For life. Left her so she can *never* have the baby she's longing for—that she wanted to present *me* with . . ."

Jenny grinned at him suddenly. It was a curiously wicked grin, he thought.

"Then she oughta send a substitute in. To play her position the second half, I mean. Tell her *I* volunteer. I've always been nuts about kids, anyhow. You know that, Uncle Jim. And making a baby with *you* sure Lord wouldn't call for any hardship pay! Whatcha say we start one right now? You can level with her later. You've—changed, y'know. From what I've heard you've got more'n half of these cute little local she-monkeys swinging down from the trees to grab you! You're real sexy now, y'know—"

"Only *you're* not," Jim said quietly; "that is, if you're misusing that word 'sexy' to mean desirable. Not any more, Jenny. Item one, I don't think any man in his right mind would choose a drug addict to be—or become—the mother of his child. Item two, I've always been almost excessively fastidious, a fact that you used to find as amusing as old hell. Remember the time you told that outrageously untidy little Hippy girl friend of yours that I'd probably make my bride take a bath before me on our wedding night and then inspect her strategic areas with a magnifying glass before partaking thereof?"

"Didn't say a magnifying glass, I said a microscope. And that one live germ would be grounds for divorce! And you would, too, Uncle Chub—I mean, Jim!"

"I'm glad you remember. So now I don't even have to emphasize that I have never fancied filthy sluts, and I'm using the expression in its exact physical sense, Jen. I'm sure I'd find even seriously attempting to indulge in sex with a woman who smells like a she-goat, because she hasn't had a bath in several weeks, nor cleaned her teeth, nor combed her hair, nor changed her underwear in considerably longer than that, nauseating. If you'd ever stay unstoned long enough to take a look at yourself, or, more to the point, a whiff of your various aromas, you'd discover that a heroin addict is a most unlovely object. Jenny, damnit all, you couldn't give it away, now. Hell, worse than that: You'd have a hard time even finding a stud you could *pay* to service you!"

She stared at him. Her face broke up.

"Ohhhhhhh, Uncle Jim!" she wailed.

"Look, Child," he said gently, "that's one of the main things I've been trying to tell you all this time. I'm not trying to persuade you to enter Dr. Claudio Lopez Basquez' Clinic for the hell of it. You *need* psychiatric care. Nobody ever kicked this filthy habit without it. Baby, let's get this monkey off your back, for good. And not to reconvert you into a sex object again—though there are worse things. What you are now, for instance. I'm asking you to voluntarily commit yourself. You're free, white, and six years over twenty-one. There's not a damned thing Joe Harper can do about it, because, first of all, he's a fugitive from justice, wanted for, among other things, a slight case of double murder; and secondly, here, in your actual legal place of residence, he's not your husband at all, under Costa Verdian law . . ."

He paused for breath. Went on:

"Wouldn't you like to get to be—a human being again? A normal, damned pretty young woman, the way you used to be? The girl whom—for whatever the belated compliment's worth—I *was* more than a little in love with?"

She shook her head.

"No," she said morosely. "Why should I? So I can remember they're going to—fry me—or lock me up forever for something I didn't even do?"

Jim stood there, frozen suddenly, in spite of the tropical heat. It was one of those moments that everything fell together. The instant of what creative people call inspiration. But this wasn't inspiration. It was—certainty.

"Jenny," he whispered, "it was Joe who killed Spearman, wasn't it?"

"Yeah," she said sadly. "Figured you'd tumble to that one after a while. Joe's got a thing about Black people. Can't stand 'em. He isn't even Southern, and yet—"

Jim stood there. He was thinking how to get to that next, that all important question. He said, quietly:

"I guess he found your—sleeping with a Black too hard to take. I understand that. I do, too. And I'm not especially prejudiced."

"You'd better not be! That chick of yours is practically *all* Spade!"

"No. Trini's practically all Tluscola. Though she does have some Black ancestry, I suspect. Jenny, tell me something: Did Joe kill Spearman with that gun he usually carries? I mean that big, heavy, short—"

"Three fifty-seven Magnum? I know what you call it. I've heard Joe brag about that cannon often enough. Swears it could knock a charging bull-elephant flat back on its ass at twenty feet . . ."

"Did he use—that gun, Jenny?"

"Yeah. 'N the way that big ugly thing messed up a poor little skinny fella like Ron was plain awful. But it was the only gun Joe had, then. He even had a permit to carry it, since he was working for Daddy-O as a bodyguard. Now he's got lots of guns. You don't even need permits down here . . ."

Jim stood there. Said:

"Oh, Jesus!"

"Don't see what Jesus has got to do with it. Uncle Jim—about Ron. I—I—*wasn't*—"

"You weren't *what,* Jenny?"

"Making it with him. Screwing. Balling. Fucking. I *wasn't,* Uncle Jim!"

"Jen—ny! You spent several months—"

"Shacked up with Ron. Yeah. Right. But you know *why,* Uncle Jim?"

"No. Suppose you tell me."

"Cause I was sick of always having to fight guys off. Among those California characters everybody thinks a girl's fair game. That she's always just dying to get laid. Hell, screwing isn't all *that* great. So I took up with Ron. Because he was as queer as a nine dollar bill. If a girl was to kiss him, he'd throw up, so help me. We made an agreement. We'd put on the *Big* Act. Y'know—the Great, Great Lovers—to keep the rest of those Weirdies off our necks. Necks, hell—off our asses. Don't know why, but people always think that a mixed couple are real fireballs, balling it night 'n day. So—"

"Jesus!" Jim said again.

"So when Joe stumbled up on us in that car and blasted the poor little fellow, it tore me up. But I was so scared of Joe, that—"

"Jenny, sign this damned paper!" Jim said.

"Oh, Uncle Jim don't be so *heavy.* So I'm a horse freak. So what? At least I feel good most of the time and—"

He brought his hand whistling around. It exploded across her thin face like a pistol shot. She stumbled. Fell. Lay there, looking up at him.

"You sign it, Jenny!" he said.

"Uncle Jim!" she wailed.

He bent down and dug his fingers into the long mane of her hair. It was so dirty that it looked almost brunette instead of its normal, dark honey blonde. He twisted it with slow relish. 'There's a great deal to be said for abandoning the postures and the tabus of civilization,' he thought.

Jenny moaned with pain. Whimpered:

"You're hurting me, Uncle Jim!"

"I," he said evenly, "am going to put you in the hospital, the ordinary hospital, not Lopez Basquez' Clinic, for a month if you don't get up from there. With your ass in a traction sling, at that. You heard me, Jenny! Get up!"

She stumbled to her feet. Swayed there, staring at him. She was crying.

"Gimme—your pen, Uncle Jim," she said.

After that was over, after he had signed her into Dr. Lopez' Clinic—strange how many really good medical institutions Costa Verde had; probably because it needed them! he thought—and the two grimly frowning nurses had led Jenny away, their faces reflecting their truly feminine disapproval that any woman could smell that bad, Jim stood there a moment, thinking about what he'd better do next.

He decided that he'd better pay a call on Hand Hörst, the jolly, roly-poly Bavarian who headed *Deutschesimport,* the German automobile agency that handled the imports that Volkeswagen was allowed to bring in with a certain liberality in return for licensing the manufacture of Beetles in Costa Verde: Porsche, as an affiliate of Volkswagen, with a moderate degree of official looking the other way, and Mercedes, through an eyedropper, which meant only high Government officials and/or the very, very rich could afford them.

'I,' Jim thought, 'have gone whole hog. For the first time in my life, I've done something, not because it was prudent, or wise, but because I damned well wanted to. And, Sweet Baby Jesus, how good that feels!'

What he had done was to order on Diplomatic Corps' plates—so that he didn't have to pay the absolutely ruinous import duties, until he left the country, and then only with a substantial depreciation allowance depending upon how long he'd kept the cars, or not at all, if he could push them off on his successor in the ambassadorship—a Porsche Carrera sports roadster for himself, and a Mercedes 450 SEL for the Embassy's official limousine, to replace the Cadillac which he had got rid of out of pure squeamishness, by representing it, in his report to the Department, as much more badly shot up than in fact it was. State was going to be distressed. State held that an American Ambassador should display and promote American products. But, in comparison with a Mercedes, any automobile that Detroit turned out was demonstrably so much fecal matter, if that, and the State Department could go fornicate itself in

---

280

various contorted, unsanitary, and painful positions, as far as he, Jim Rush, was concerned.

The Porsche was there, ready and waiting. He slipped under the wheel, turned the key. The flat—three and three opposed—six cylinder motor caught with a throaty roar. He put it into first, moved off. Hans waved at him. He waved back, shifted into second, gunned that air-cooled jewel of a motor, and was slammed back against the seat, the headrest, as that little bomb took off.

'This,' he reflected happily, 'is the nearest thing to sex ever invented. And for a man my age, it probably even beats it!''

But, after slamming that little mechanical miracle—'I'll bet the bastards even made *good* gas chambers!' he thought—through a series of controlled skids around ten or twelve kilometers of mountain roads, his sense of duty caught up with him. Sorrowfully, he headed back to the Embassy. He knew what he had to do next. He even—more or less!—knew how to go about doing it.

"Send that young whippersnapper into my office, Martha!" he growled, even his language chosen, down to the archaic slang, to maintain the image of the vague and somewhat testy old-timer he wanted his staff to believe he was. "You know—that so-called Cultural Attaché Washington's saddled me with. What's his name? The one who's always taking pictures?"

"Schuyler," Martha Clyde supplied. 'She,' Jim reflected wryly, 'has lived up to Tomás' description of her. Hell, no; she's exceeded it!' "First name's Van," she went on. "For Vanderbilt, I do believe!"

"Vanderbilt Schuyler. Oh, Jesus!" Jim said. "Anyhow, call him. Send him in."

"All right, Mr. Ambassador," Martha said; then: "Aren't you going to the—*hospital,* today, Sir?"

Jim looked at her. Thought: 'At the stake. With *green* faggots. Nice and slow burning!' He said:

"Yes. After I've talked with Schuyler. After office hours, in fact. Why, Martha?"

"No reason. Oh, well, I'd might as well confess my sins! You'll find out, anyhow. I—I visited the hospital yesterday. Paid a call on this—young person. I hope you'll forgive me, Mr. Ambassador; but—my feminine curiosity got the better of me!"

'No,' Jim thought, 'simmered in boiling oil. Several hours. 'Til the flesh drops off her bones!' He said, very, very quietly:

"I'll hold my forgiveness in abeyance, and reserve all judgment, until I have a first hand report—from *her*—as to how you conducted yourself, Martha. That—'young person'—as you call her, has had it rough enough from too many people now, on *my* account at that."

"Oh, I was *very* sweet to her, Mr. Ambassador! I confess I was—a little shocked, though!"

'I,' he thought, 'don't give a good goddamn. But maybe I'd better find out just what it is that shocks you. Such knowledge can come in handy, at times . . .' He said, one fair eyebrow rising towards the scar he'd got from that granite chip from the wing of the sculptured angel in the cemetery, "Shocked, Martha?"

"Yes. She—she's so *dark*, Mr. Ambassador! Almost— *mulata*, isn't she?"

He noted wryly that Martha didn't make the common North American mistake of saying "mulato" when speaking of females. Then he surrendered to an all but irresistible impulse, and grinned at her.

"No almost about it, Martha!" he said. Then he paused, trying to picture in his mind how Miguel Villalonga or Luis Sinnombre, the two half brothers, one of the two of whom, according to all reliable reports, was responsible for Trini's arrival in this vale of wrath and tears, had looked. Decided that in this case, again, as so very often in life, mere *facts* simply didn't matter, and went on recklessly: "Her father's as black as the Ace of Spades. Nice old fellow. I like him. Mother's *Mestiza:* Spanish and Tluscolan. Something to think about it, isn't it? Wonder what *our* kids—hers and mine—are going to look like?" He sauntered casually towards the door of his office. At it, he paused.

"Send me young Schuyler," he said. As he closed the door to his office behind him, he could hear her breathing in and breathing out. It was a Yoga exercise—Martha was a *chela*, pupil, of the local *Guru*, one Hriday Hanuman, that Ciudad Villalonga was fashionable enough to have!—designed for the maintenance, or the restoration, of control. Today, it wasn't working very well. She sounded like a beached whale.

Jim looked at young Schuyler. Studied that smooth, much too handsome, Hollywood Central Casting Office's idea of what a haughty-young-scion-of-great-wealth ought to look like. It was too damned good. He was an aristocrat, himself, a real one. So he knew Anglo-American aristocrats, anyhow, don't look like that. They looked—more vague. Less—forceful. More baggy, tweedy, run down, used up. Bred out.

"Sit down, Mr. Schuyler," he said.

Van Schuyler sank gracefully into his chair. Smiled his pleasant smile.

"You sent for me, Sir?" he said.

"Obviously," Jim said.

"May I ask—what for, Mr. Ambassador?"

"Maybe to send you over to Geri Pyle's boutique. To observe, Schuyler. To learn how to manage a real, honest-to-God limp wrist. And the kind of a delicate stride that Cultural Attachés usually have."

"Sir!" Van Schuyler said. "You're implying—"

"I'm not implying a damned thing. I'm *saying,* stating, that your cover's piss poor, Schuyler. Rotten. What are you, really? The Narc Bill Carter wanted to drop on me? Or—CIA?"

"Oh, Christ!" Schuyler said.

Jim grinned at him, suddenly.

"Don't worry about it, Son," he said. "My former opinion, known throughout the Department, that you types were a bunch of miserable paranoiacs who ought to be locked up in lace-trimmed straight jackets, and given blunted scissors to cut your paper dolls out with, no longer holds. After being in *this* country, I've changed my slant on a good many matters. Among them, that one. Anybody clothed and framed in his right mind wouldn't have a chance against SN-2."

"Nor against the KGB. Nor the Volkspolizei, Scipo-4. Nor Special Operations/Whitehall. Nor La Seconde Bis, Quai d'Orsay. Nor even Jerusalem's Ha Mossad L'Tafkidim Meyuhadim, who're maybe the best of all. We live in a crazy world, Mr. Ambassador. But you don't really expect me to *admit* anything, do you? I couldn't, Sir. Not even to *you.*"

"No. Of course not. What I want is something extra crazy. I want the FBI to send a man down here. Yes, you heard me right: The FBI, not the CIA. I want to give him something. A pistol. A point three five seven calibre Magnum revolver made by Smith & Wesson. I want him to take the damned ugly, oily, smelly thing back to Headquarters and run a series of ballistic tests with it. I have the strangest feeling that he'll find out, or his Department will, that the bullets will match the ones that killed a poor little Black homosexual named Ron Spearman. And that Jenny Crowley didn't do the shooting because she couldn't even *lift* a cannon like that one. Hell, I'll even bet that she doesn't know enough about firearms to get the safety off! And that the type who did ventilate Spearman had a permit for the above-mentioned sidearm and motives for using it, namely to get his hands on Jenny Crowley, and through her the Crowley millions. And I don't know how to arrange all that from down here. I'm not—cultured enough, Son . . ."

Schuyler threw back his head and laughed aloud.

"But—maybe a trifle too attached, eh, Sir?" he chuckled. "To one small example of the native population, anyhow! Sir, may I say it's a pleasure to work for and with an Ambassador who has the sense—and the taste!—that you have?"

"What d'you mean, Schuyler?"

"Oh, I drop by the hospital once in a while. To see if our mutual friend, Vince Gomez, has run across any new varieties of tropical diseases. A—cultural interest, of course. Engendered by the fact that a certain Doctor Andres Palayo Martin, whose real name happens to be Andrei Pablovitch Semanov, has been displaying the keenest interest in them. Especially the kind that can trigger major—and incurable—epidemics among the civilian populations of large temperate-zone cities. I have reason to believe, though I can't quite prove, that he stopped in a certain hotel in Philadelphia, during that sadly famous American Legion Convention in that city, some time back. Y'know, the one where a sizable number of conventioneers died—for no discernible reason?"

"Good God!" Jim said.

"Amen!" Schuyler said pleasantly. "But, Sir, in the case of *your* cultural attachment, I was *obliged* to check. Could cause no end of trouble if she were a plant, y'know. As she *was.* A fact, it seems, it took *you* exactly five minutes to find out. Which was why I started out congratulating you on your good sense. But what really pleases me is the remedial action you took. Speaking of which, could you give me lessons? I'd really like to learn how you do it!"

"How I do what?"

"Neutralization. Defusing. Then—reeducation, and conversion to *our* side, Sir! You've really crossed SN-2 up this time. Whatever reason they sent that little Voodoo Doll for, as of today, she's for real. I freely confess I tried to date her for some future occasion when she's out of the hospital, which I understand will be soon . . ."

"Tonight. Or tomorrow. I have to check with Vince," Jim said.

"One of the stickier aspects of my work: removing actual, or potential, *agents provocateurs* from the paths of important men. It's a pleasure to tell you I failed completely. That my efforts to broaden my personal culture by exploring—certain aspects of how the Tluscolan mind works, say—resulted only in an acute and painful lesson in the tribal *tabus.* And those I learned! Mainly that *anybody's* off limits, and out of line from the word 'Go!' who's not named Ambassador James Randolph Rush! I congratulate you, Sir! She's really something!"

Jim stared at him, thinking: 'All this goddamned boyish charm!'

"I thank you for that, Schuyler," he said. "But—about the other?"

"Let me, think about it. Culture's so—broadening, isn't it? My own interests are wide. They throw me into contact with all kinds of people—even collectors of antique firearms, say. And, Sir—"

"Yes, Schuyler?" Jim said.

"Do you find *me* especially *persona non grata,* as it were? You see, I'd like to hang around with you a bit, if I may. To learn your techniques, or to have some of your luck rub off on me. That's one thing—"

"And another?" Jim said.

"It could prove useful. For *both* of us, Sir. For instance, on the political level, did you know that García and Company are moving heaven and earth in Washington to promote a government to government loan? A huge one, Sir. Several billions of dollars."

"I didn't think they needed money," Jim said slowly; "what with the offshore oil discoveries . . ."

"They need it, in part, *for* the oil. To finance pipe lines, refineries, and such like. And that offshore pool won't begin to pay off for another five years. Maybe ten. Of course, it's excellent security against a loan . . ."

"Go on—" Jim said.

"Only Congress is dragging its feet. And that, I fear, is where *you* might run into trouble, Sir . . ."

"Why me?" Jim said.

"Because a strongly liberal group, spearheaded by Committeemen and Chairmen known to be good friends of yours, Sir—and of your late father—have publicly taken the position that García and Chums' total disregard for the most elementary concepts of civil rights, and ordinary human decency, their routine use of torture—incidently, Vince showed me the before and after photos of your little friend, Sir. The 'before's' almost made me toss my cookies, and I've a strong stomach. You know, the ones he took for the guidance of that Brazilian specialist in plastic surgery he called in. Dr. Sousa Dos Santos, as I recall . . ."

"García didn't do that," Jim said. "That was a Mafiosa type reprisal against me for trying to do Bill Carter a good turn by sticking my nose into the drug running trade on this end. But those thugs probably got their techniques from observing SN-2 at work. Go on, Son."

"Your friends in Congress are saying out loud that a loan to a Dictatorship that could show Hitler how to do it is inadvisable, Sir."

"I agree," Jim said. "But as long as I keep a discreet and diplomatic silence about my own opinions—which, as Ambassador to this country, I'm obliged to, Van—I fail to see why I should get into hot water about anything that Congress does, or doesn't do."

"Only that's not the angle that the danger to you is going to come from, Sir, as I see it," Van said. "Put it this way: The Glorious Leader and His Friends have changed their tactics. They want the loan—to be secured by future deliveries of crude—for refineries, pipelines, tanker docks, fertilizer plants, housing for the poor, and a public school system that will extend to the remotest village so that even the Tluscolan children will receive a free education, Sir. Noble, what?"

"Noble *mierda,*" Jim said. "What's the catch, Van?"

"Awful lot of—Frenchmen in town here of late, Sir. Last night *Les*

Ambassadeurs was full. Young, flashy types, some of them. Capable of doing a double snap roll in a Dassault Mirage F 1 B, seems to me."

"Jesus H. Christ!" Jim said.

"Wait, Sir; there's more. Other of our Gallic friends at the restaurant were older. More studious types. Heavy horn-rimmed spectacles. That special *l'Ecole Polytechnique* look . . ."

"Meaning?" Jim said.

"Sir, oil isn't the only thing that's been found down here. Costa Verde is exceedingly rich in—minerals, Sir."

"I get it. Uranium. The gift of the Old Gods . . ."

"I don't follow you there, Sir."

"Then you haven't read Peter Reynold's book. I'll lend you my copy. When Zopocomapetl erupted late in 1963, one of the things that the resulting earthquakes and landslides uncovered was the first uranium vein. And since, traditionally, the volcano's the home of the old Tlusco-lan Gods, Peter—somewhat romantically, I'll admit, but Peter's a ro-mantic at heart, for all his attempts to deny it—labeled the uranium the gift of the Old Gods . . ."

"One hell of a gift, I'd say, Sir. But you know about their attempts to buy a fast breeder reactor from the Atomic Energy Commission, don't you, Sir?"

"And also that they were turned down flat. Our Government isn't even starting to sell a reactor that turns out a huge surplus of pluto-nium every damn day to characters like García and Pals even if they swear on their mothers' graves they want it for the peaceful production of electricity. Uranium, normal uranium, can be used for peaceful pur-poses, but what the hell else can you do with plutonium and U 238 ex-cept—" He stopped, stared at young Schuyler; whispered:

"Oh, my God!"

"Right, Sir. When have you ever known the French to be especially scrupulous about what they sell and to whom? But don't worry about that detail, Sir. I'll take care of it. In the first place, that deal would never come to your attention until far too late. What worries me are the things they won't be able to keep under wraps, that will be impossible for them to hide from you as official representative of the U.S. Govern-ment down here. So you're going to be under a lot of pressure. To at least close your eyes, Sir. Look the other way when *un brave type* demon-strates a Mach two-point-five, variable geometry Mirage jet fighter. Or an *Otomat* smart missile with a built-in laser beam guidance system, say. French hardware is first rate these days, y'know. As I said before, I honestly believe your little friend's for real. But she makes you awfully vulnerable. You simply wouldn't be capable of much resistance, if some-body snatched her *again,* after all she's been through. And I wouldn't

286

blame you. Oh, I know three on a date is one too many, but I'd feel a hell of a lot better if you'd sort of discreetly let me tag along, Sir, when you take little Trini out . . ."

Jim thought about that. About how young, tall, and goddamned good-looking young Schuyler was. About how short, dried up, ugly, and middle-aged was one Ambassador James Randolph Rush. About how miserably human was human nature, after all. Then a couple of words that Van Schuyler, himself, had used popped into his not exactly un-Machiavellian head. "Neutralizing. Defusing." That was exactly what the young CIA man had said, wasn't it?

Very slowly, he smiled.

"Agreed, Van," he said; "but I'm going to provide you with some really first class cover. Three are a crowd. But *four* are two loving couples, right? Her name's Petra. Petra Stevenson—a North and South American cross. Father's a Yank, mother's Costa Verdian. Great girl. *I* call her Petra 'Culo Lindo' because the first time I saw her she was wearing a *Tanga,* but don't *you* go and call her that, at least not until she treats you to a similiar exhibition, and it *is* a treat, I assure you. She works at the boutique. And speaking of which, since time's the essence, maybe you'd better drive over there *tonight,* tell her I sent you, and bring her to the hospital with the clothes I ordered for Trini. Naturally, if she doesn't meet with your approval, you have only to let me know—"

"Sir," Van Schuyler said, "is she—anything like—*yours?*"

"No," Jim said. "Less—exotic. More conventional, I suppose. Most men would consider her far prettier than Trini is. For one thing, she's almost entirely white, a condition somewhat rare in Costa Verde, because the *Conquistadores* were few indeed, and Tluscolan strain predominates. As I told you, her father was from the States. A technician for ITT, I believe. He died some years ago, before he could arrange to take his wife and daughter to the States. But, to judge from Petra's looks, her mother must be almost pure Spanish, with only the tiniest Tluscolan mixture. I, personally, think Petra's gorgeous; but since polygamy, and, unfortunately, even a little quiet bigamy are both against the law—"

"Sir, d'you know what my next report to my superiors is going to say?"

"I can't imagine. What will it, Son?"

"That if the State Department sends out a few more Ambassadors like *you,* Sir, we've got the Cold War won!"

CHAPTER

22

When young Schuyler had left the office, Jim Rush sat there wearily thinking, or rather putting together a number of ideas in logical sequence, to wit: that, in today's world, the boundaries between peace and war were so shadowy as to be practically indistinguishable from one another; that an Embassy was roughly equivalent to a front line Command Post; and that to proceed as though the relations existing between the United States and *any* Third World nation were, or even could be, remotely normal was the act of a damned fool. Then, having restated, for clarity, these lamentable facts, he considered what he had better do about them.

'First, communications,' he thought. 'I've neglected that area on the score that, Costa Verde's being a fifth rate power, if that, it really wasn't worth the trouble or the expense. But if they're going to play for billions—and maybe even muscle their way into the Atomic Club!—I'd better do something to insure direct, unbugged connections with the States.'

He pulled his memorandum pad towards him, wrote:

"Have Carlos in."

What was next? Almost surely the threat to his own personal freedom of action—through Trini. He sat there, trying to decide not *whether,* but *how* SN-2, Security National's Second Bureau, Political Activities, was going to pull that one off. Which meant, having accepted as truthful, and even normal, Trini's contention that she, herself, didn't *know*—in the precise sense that she had not yet been given her final instructions in his regard—he, Jim Rush, must accurately divine why Pérez de la Valle had sent her to him in the first place. And all the more so because he was achingly aware that now, today, to save him even a little embarrassment, loss of face, some slight tarnishing of the luster of his fame, Trini would calmly disobey those final instructions, knowing full well that the cost of such disobedience would be—her life.

The question was—subtle. For the Director General had departed widely from the Second Bureau's norm for such operations. He had not forced some daughter of the extreme upper class to play the whore for political ends, as had been SN-2's mode of procedure since the now almost distant times of Miguel Villalonga. Instead, he had chosen a known and notorious member of the World's Oldest Profession because—

Of her resemblance to Alicia? Nonsense! In the short time he had been in Costa Verde, Jim had seen three or four Tluscolan-Spanish *Mestizas* whose resemblance to Alicia was startling. And given the known propensity of all the male Villalongas towards fun and games, the probabilities were that *Don* Raoul's choices—if duplicating Alicia's looks was what he'd wanted to do—had been wide enough to make the employment of a professional prostitute unnecessary to say the very least.

What conclusion then was to be derived from all this? Very simply that the Director General had wanted to saddle him with—a mistress who would be an embarrassment to him, in his own country, and before his superiors. So that his mere relations with her could be used as a threat to make him toe whatever line they willed. By now they knew enough about the permissiveness of North American mores to realize that his having an affair—being as he was, free and unattached!—with some daughter of the aristocracy would bring down upon his head from the State Department the mildest of reprimands, accompanied by a wry and indulgent smile.

So, therefore—Trini. Whom they *wouldn't* kidnap and threaten with torture to bring him into line! They wouldn't, because being *Latinos* and the ultimate Male Chauvinists, they, themselves, simply would not believe the threat sufficiently effective. No, they'd play upon his, Jim Rush's, fear of exposure; his aristocrat's shame at having so crass and *vulgar* a misbehavior revealed to his superiors. And their own position was all the stronger by reason of the fact that they controlled absolutely all communications, so that no information whatsoever could get back to the State Department unless they themselves released it, the one unlikely alternative being that Jim, for reasons of his own, allowed it to go out by the one medium he controlled and that they didn't, the diplomatic pouch. So now they could say, "Look, Mr. Ambassador, don't you think it would be wiser to cooperate with us in this matter? It would be most unfortunate if your superiors were to discover—oh, accidentally, of course!—some of the more interesting details of your private life. Your countrymen are not notably broadminded in such delicate matters. And while they might overlook an affair conducted on a—well—more acceptable social level, the unfortunate *facts* of this young woman's past certainly wouldn't do your good name, fame, nor reputation for sober, mature judgment any good . . ."

And there they'd have him! Because if he told them to release the story to the Stateside press and be damned, in Washington Franchot Townley or some other upper-level, delicately perfumed flunky would snort:

"We send this triple distilled jackass down there to represent—as a diplomat—the interest of the United States. And what does this impossible little idiot do? Why, fall most diplomatically into the hay—and not with some acceptably elite bit of fluff, but with some grubby, unwashed street-corner hooker!"

Thereafter, within a week, he'd be on a plane, Washington bound, in dire disgrace . . .

How to 'defuse, neutralize'—he thanked Van Schuyler again for those words!—that one? Why—marry Trini. It was as simple as that. And, what was more, it was—necessary. Whatever his own doubts, hesitations, long, long sober second thoughts, fears, it was. To save—her life. As his wife, as *¡la Señora Embajadora!* Trini would gain instant immunity from threats, force, violence. If he then defied them, beyond declaring him *persona non grata,* and sending every scandal sheet in the States a detailed history of poor Trini's past, there would be nothing they could do. Their own law permitted a foreigner to take a native born wife out of the country without any special permit whatsoever, the presentation of the marriage certificate itself serving as a valid exit visa.

Of course, the resultant scandal would be major. Yet, even to that a defense existed that would at least permit his own honorable resignation from the Department instead of the ignominy of a dismissal. And that defense? "I met and fell in love with an attractive young woman *who worked as a model at Geri Pyle's boutique.* I married her. I did not inquire into her past."

An impeccable defense. The worst he could be accused of then was impulsiveness, poor judgment. 'And not,' he thought bleakly, 'of being the utterly asinine, middle-aged damned fool I *know* I'm being! Diving headfirst into a totally inexcusable relationship that cannot possibly work out. Just as if I didn't *know* that no love whatsoever lasts, and especially not one that has everything against it, all the absolutely murderous contrasts: a man of a certain refinement of tastes, a fair degree of culture, marrying total ignorance. A New Englander with puritanism bred into his very bones takes to wife—a whore. A forty-six-year-old jackass bedding with a—child. Eighteen, nineteen, twenty at the most! A glorious girl-child who's had her body, and her life—broken, for my sake. Oh, Jesus, I—'

He put out his hand and picked up the bundle of New York and Washington papers that arrived by airmail at roughly two week intervals. These had come that very morning. He broke, tore away their mailing wrappings. As he did so, his telephone rang. He picked it up so fast that he beat Martha to it, a fact that caused him a certain malicious satisfaction. Now, she wouldn't dare listen in. An unknown female voice said:

"Ambassador Rush, please?"

He said: "Speaking."

"One moment, Sir! Dr. Gomez wishes to speak to you . . ."

There was a longish pause. During it, Jim scanned the headlines. One of the smaller ones caught his attention, probably because he and young Schuyler had been discussing that selfsame theme not half an hour before:

"State Department Denies that Vanished Indian Scientist Is in U.S.," the *Washington Post*'s lead read. Then, in smaller type: "Sir Gadahar Gorakhnath, one of the fathers of India's Atomic bomb, has not applied for political asylum in this country, a Department spokesman declares. That Sir Gadahar passed through New York several months ago, Immigrant authorities and Customs confirm; but his final destination is unknown. He remained at JFK Airport no more than an hour, then took another plane whose flight terminated in Caracas, Venezuela, after stops in Havana, Cuba, and Mexico City, Mexico. It is the State Department's and the Atomic Energy Commission's belief that he may have deplaned in Cuba, since, despite the indisputably high order of the Cambridge University-trained atomic scientist's skill, no openings for a foreign physicist currently exists in the U.S. private atomic energy industry nor in the Commission itself, not to mention the fact that the hiring of a foreign national for work in such sensitive areas would require not only State Department but Presidential approval. It seems logical, therefore, the Department spokesman continues, that the defecting Indian scientist may have offered his services to some Third World nation with ambitions to set aside the Non-Proliferating Agreements and produce that new and deadly status symbol, at least one A-bomb . . ."

Vince's voice came over the wire.

"Jim," he said, "I just examined Trini. She's okay. You can take her home tonight if you want to."

"I want to," Jim said. "Thanks, Vince."

"Don't mention it, Jim," Vince said; then: "Be—very careful of her, *Amigo*. She's going to be—awfully delicate for a while, you know."

"Don't worry about *that*, Doctor!" Jim said. "What time shall I come for her?"

"Say—eightish. After we've force-fed her, made her sleep a while. Be seeing you, Jim!"

"Likewise!" Jim said, and hung up.

He went through the other papers. The *New York Times* had a picture of Sir Gadahar Gorakhnath. The atomic scientist was a very striking man. For, not only was he remarkably handsome, but he was one of those Indians who combine perfectly Caucasian features: thin lips, aquiline nose, silkily straight hair, with a total bluish-blackness of skin, darker by far than even the deep brownish-black of the Central African races. On an impulse, Jim tore the picture out and stuck it in his billfold.

'I'll show it to young Schuyler,' he thought; 'it will serve as a conversation piece for our next encounter . . .'

Then he went back to his routine work. 'Have to give a reception or a party soon,' he thought. 'To which I *can't* invite or bring poor Trini. I simply can't. That's just one of the facts of life—her life and mine together—she'll simply have to bear with, understand.'

He was far behind in his work; the very nature of his reception in Costa Verde, the constant and unceasing 'alarums and excursions' to which he had been subjected ever since his arrival had seen to that. He worked away doggedly at the mountain of papers on his desk, until he had succeeded in reducing them considerably; but with, as well, the incidental and accidental result that by the time he finally got to the hospital that night, it was so late that Petra Stevenson and Van Schuyler had already been there, and had gone, the receptionist informed him.

'Probably itching—correction!—panting to get at each other,' he thought. The mental picture that conjured up was distinctly cheering. "Ah, youth!" he chuckled and took the lift up to the floor Trini's room was on.

When he walked into her room, he found her talking to an old woman who looked like a fugitive from Act One, Scene Three of *Macbeth*. And, to his great astonishment, they were talking in Tluscolan, of which, naturally, he understood not a single word. His surprise was fully justified, for nowadays, he was aware, even Costa Verdians and Colombians of pure Tluscolan ancestry seldom spoke that ancient and exceedingly difficult language any more, unless they were from remote mountain *pueblos* and *aldeas* where its use still persisted. Listening to what they were saying delighted him because of the sheer beauty of the sounds they made. Much of it consisted of a series of rapid clicks, made by tapping the tip of the tongue against the backs of the upper and lower teeth. He was especially pleased to note that Trini could manage these sounds, for that meant the bridgework of three false teeth in the exact upper center of her mouth—a true work of art indistinguishable from her natural teeth, and put there to replace the ones that Joe Harper's thugs had knocked out of her head—was both secure and firm. After the clicks came one or two contentious or disapproving grunts, then a staccato kettledrum roll, followed by a series of trills and runs and bird calls of a limpid loveliness that was breathtaking.

"How is it that you speak Tluscolan, Trinita?" he said.

She whirled, stared at him. Flew to him. Put her arms about his neck, said:

"*¡Por fin!* Thou hast come! I was dying from the need of thee!"

He kissed her. Said: "Who is the Witch? And, again, how is it that you speak Tluscolan, when almost nobody does nowadays, Trinita?"

She laughed gaily, said:

"I, too, am *una Bruja*! For she—Rosa—taught me sorcery and spells and enchantments from my earliest childhood. And, of course, Tluscolan, which is her native tongue. You see, *Don* Jaime, she was my nurse. For they, my fathers, were not poor, you know. And if it had not been for the great wickedness of Miguel Villalonga and Luis Sinnombre, I should have been such a one of whom thou wouldst never had need to be ashamed—"

"I'm not ashamed of you now, Trini," he said.

The old woman said something in Tluscolan. Trini answered her. The old woman said something else. Trini replied to that, as well. The old woman let fly with the sounds of a woodpecker attacking the bole of a tamarind tree. Trini dissolved into great gales of silvery laughter.

"Translation?" Jim said.

"She asked me who thou wert. I said: 'My lover!' And she: 'He is too old and too ugly to be thy lover! Is he—rich?' And I: 'Yes, very.' And she: 'Then it is all right!' "

"Doesn't she speak Spanish?" Jim said.

"Yes! Why yes, of course! Only she doesn't like to!"

"*Madre,*" Jim said to the old woman, "Would you like to come and live with Trini? And take care of her for me? She is not very strong, and has much need of care. I will pay you well."

"Of course, Son," the old woman said. "When shall I come?"

"Now," Jim said; "tonight. We will take you with us. What is your name?"

"Rosa," the old woman said.

"But, *mi Amor!*" Trini protested. "It is too small in my little flat. There is no place for Rosa to sleep, and additionally—"

"And, additionally, what?" Jim said,

"Her presence would—rob us of all—the privacy we need for—"

"For what?" he teased. "For what do we need privacy, *Trinita mía?*"

She put her arms around his neck again. Stared long and gravely into his eyes.

"For— making love," she said simply. "This night I am going to be thine, *Don* Jaime. And thou must fill my belly with thy son. Or thy daughter. This I *demand* of thee!"

"Trini—no!" he said. "It's—too dangerous! I—"

"It is *not* too dangerous. I have discussed it with Rosa and she has told me what I must do. Dost—love me, *Don* Jaime?"

"Yes," he said sadly, knowing that what he said was truth, and thinking how tragic was that truth; "with all my heart!"

"Then thou must love me with thy body, too. This night I shall be *tu novia*—thy bride. *Now* I can, *Don* Jaime. Now—I come to thee—in purity. Truly. *¡Oh, sí; con pureza, mi Amor!* Thou'rt the first man in my life. Thou shalt be—the last. And the only one. This, I promise thee."

"Trini—" he said.

"Listen! I told thee—of the ordeal of the Tluscola? I— have suffered that, *Don* Jaime. And survived it. I must tell thee—a thing. They— those animals—did *not* abuse me—that way. He, the big Blond One, would not let them. He *tried*. But he was—too hurt, too wounded. So he could not. Therefore he demanded of me a—a certain perversion. He threatened to kill me if I did not—perform it upon him. I told him: 'Kill me. It matters not. I belong to *Don* Jaime. I will die before I will betray him, even thus.' So he gave me to the others, and told them to—to ruin me. To leave my body so that it would sicken thee to see it. But when the first of them approached me to—to violate me, he, the Blond One, kicked him in his male parts, leaving him incapacitated. Then he, the big *Gringo*, drew a pistol and told them all that he would kill the man who abused of me sexually. Therefore, they did not. And the things they did do—the burning, the beating, the cuts, the—the bottle—broken—within me—were as the punishment of the Tluscola for—unchastity. I have told Rosa this, and she agrees. And Rosa is—how does one say it? *¡Ay, sí! Una Sacerdotista*—A Priestess of the Tluscola, so she *knows*. Therefore, I—come to thee—made new. Cleansed of all my sins. I could—even—marry thee now, if thou wilt—"

"I do," he said; "God, yes! Let's go find a priest!"

"No," she said. "Not now. Not here in Costa Verde. After we leave here, thou and I. To go to thy country, where my—reputation is not known, and will not be a burden to thee. *Don* Jaime, promise me a thing—"

"What thing, Trinita?"

"That thou wilt lead the life expected of thee. Go out with the Great Ladies of thy class. Attend parties, balls. *Be* the Great *Señor Embajador*! I shall expect thee—two, three nights a week—no more. I shall remain hidden in the shadows of thy life, so as not to spoil it. I shall trust thee—not—not—to fall in love with—one of them. Not to—to desert the mother of thy sons, who loves thee! And when they let you go, when thy work is finished here, I shall go with thee to *Nueva York,* and *I* shall be a great Lady and thy wife!"

"Trini—" he whispered. He had tears in his eyes. He hoped she wouldn't see them.

"Thou must teach me things. English, first! Wilt teach me English, *Don* Jaime?"

"If you will teach me Tluscolan," he said.

"But why? Of what earthly use is Tluscolan?"

"Don't know. None, perhaps. Only it sounds so beautiful!"

He picked up the smart new suitcase that Petra had brought her. She smiled at the sight; said:

"Thou hast Petra wildly happy by sending her that beautiful boy! *Don* Jaime, tell me a thing?"

"What thing, Trinita?"

"Didst do that because thou feared *I* might like him too much?"

He looked at her. Said, humbly:

"Yes, Trini."

"Ohhhhhh!" she wept. "How beautiful! That thou lovest me thus, I mean! *Don* Jaime, we cannot take Rosa home tonight! We cannot!"

"Now, Trini—just you wait and see!" he said.

She clapped her hands in delight at the sight of the Porsche. Begged him to let her drive it, which, naturally, he refused.

"It is—very fast, and a little dangerous," he said. "First I must give you lessons in driving it. Now, come on!"

They managed to squeeze into the little car by putting Rosa in first, and then having Trini sit in her lap, which seemingly pleased both of them. All the way to the new apartment building in the district next to *Puerta de Oro,* Golden Door—because in Golden Door itself, the building of apartment houses was not allowed, but only the construction of villas of great luxury—Rosa crooned lullabies in Tluscolan to Trini, holding her tenderly, like a tiny child.

But, just before they got there, Trini noticed that they were kilometers away from the *barrio* where her little flat was.

"*Don* Jaime!" she gasped. "This is not the way! Thou hast turned wrongly somewhere and—"

"I have not turned wrongly, and this is the way. I had Tomás sell your little flat and put the money in the bank for you. Then I bought thee—*us*—a new flat, Trini. With rooms for two maids, one of whom will be Rosa, and a majordomo. I have hired a couple. The woman, who is named Cecilia, is married to Pepe, who will be our butler. He is not a very good butler, but he is an excellent retired policeman who knows how to shoot and to break the arms and legs of those who might try to drag you away again . . ."

"*¡Oh, Demonios!*" she pouted. "We will have no privacy at all!"

"Yes, we will. The flat is quite big. There are two enormous bedrooms, one for thee and one for me, with a bath between them and—"

"Oh, no!" she said. "Now I am angry with thee! Now for the first time I shall be a true wife and scold thee! *One* bedroom, *Don* Jaime! For both of us! With one, little, little, narrow bed—*this* wide—" she showed him with two fingers, "so that thou canst not even roll too far apart from me! And my first orders to this Pepe will be that he *nail* the doors to the second one shut!"

"Trini—" he groaned; "I am an old man, remember? And your health is very delicate. Dr. Gomez says—"

"I care not what he says! I am a Witch, and so is Rosa, and additionally she is a midwife, and even more additionally I have sworn before the Holy Virgin to give thee *ten* babies! So do not anger at me anymore, *mi Amor!*"

"Lord!" he said. "Trini, let's settle for *one,* please? Or two, at the most. For, at my age, I cannot expect to live long enough to see even three sons not yet born grow up. Which would be a great sadness for me, and also a burden upon you and upon them . . ."

"Thou," she said firmly, "will live to have more than a hundred years. Thou wilt see not only thy sons grow up, but thy grandsons. And thou wilt know thy great-grandsons. *¡Y tus bis-bis nietos! ¡Y tus—*"

"And you, Trini?" he said. "How many will you know?"

Her face tightened. Even in the darkness of the little car he could see the grimace of pain.

"I do not know," she whispered. "Even though I am a Witch of the Tluscola, that has not been revealed to me . . ."

He decided not to go into that. He didn't believe in either Witchcraft or Prophecy; but if this old Witch had told Trini something that put a darkness upon her future—or curtailed it—he'd rather not know it. 'Where ignorance is bliss,' he thought, ' 'tis folly—'

And swept the little car up before the doorway of that imposing apartment building. The inhabitants of this *barrio* called it, a little mockingly, *Puerta de Plata,* Silver Door, by an analogy from the really splendidly luxurious Golden Door section it was next to. That wasn't its name. Originally it had been called *El Barrio Saltamontes,* The District of the Grasshopper, and had been full of very poor people who lived in shacks they had built themselves of tin cans and stolen lumber and handmade, sun-dried adobe bricks. But when an invasion of rats from this *barrio* had terrorized the great ladies—and their cooks and their maids!—in Golden Door itself, the Glorious Leader had undertaken a campaign against *Chabolismo,* a word that cannot be translated into English by another word but only by a whole phrase, since it actually means something like "The habit or the custom of living in shacks."

So he had ordered the *Chabolas*—shacks or shanties—torn down, and decent housing built in their places. At first this housing was supposed to be *viviendas sociales,* or low cost housing for the poor. And a few low cost apartment buildings actually were built in the *barrio,* as far from Golden Door as possible. But, as always in Latin America, and especially in Costa Verde, the rents for the new *viviendas sociales* proved to be far higher than the poor could afford, so they were occupied by the middle class. The poor went right on building their *chabolas* and watching the rats nibble the noses and the toes of sleeping babies farther out of town.

And land speculators and real estate promoters, seeing their opportunity, converted the *Barrio* of the Grasshopper into a district of luxury apartments not too unlike New York's Park Avenue, because the Law of Altitudes, or the Height Restrictions, which limited all construction within the Golden Door development to a maximum of two and a half stories, wouldn't permit them to build profitable apartment buildings in that most luxurious residential district in all Ciudad Villalonga. Which was why the people living in Golden Door had written, framed, and rushed the Law of Altitudes through *el Cortes Supremo* in the first place. And since these people, living in *la Colonia Puerta de Oro*'s magnificent villas, costing from several hundred thousand to more than a million North American dollars each, included the Glorious Leader and all the Ministers of the Government, for the promoters and speculators to attempt to get around the Height Restrictions within Golden Door Colony—as they dearly longed to do!—would have proved fatally unsmart, since they surely would have been jailed and probably even shot, for trying it.

But, as a place for Ambassador James Randolph Rush to keep his young mistress in, Silver Door, the ex-*Barrio* of the Grasshopper, was very nearly ideal. For one thing, practically all the movie stars lived there. And movie stars are everywhere notoriously careless of the legality and/or the sanctity of their living arrangements. Moreover, because of its proximity to Golden Door, out of sheer convenience, all the Ministers kept their *Queridas, Protegidas,* and other varieties of mistresses there; the Higher Clergy installed their "nieces" and "housekeepers" in the *barrio,* and wonder of wonders for Latin America, some of the really Great Ladies of Costa Verde's League for the Defense of Women's Rights, it was rumored, were paying the rent for a number of sleek young gigolos in studio apartments as discreet as they were smart.

All of which, in a way, distressed Jim more than a little. But in other, upper-middle-class *barrios,* he ran the serious risk of having poor Trini insulted not merely daily, but *hourly,* by the grim-faced, devoutly Catholic matrons; a fact that even his marrying her—as he fully intended to do—wouldn't remedy at all. Silver Door was the only place in Cuidad Villalonga he could live with a notorious ex-prostitute, married to her or not; so to Silver Door he bore her.

Pepe, the ex-policeman hired mainly to guard and protect Trini during Jim's absences, rather than for his practically nonexistent training as a butler, and Cecilia, his plump and pretty wife, greeted them, all bows and smiles, at the door. Rosa's presence caused the smiles to abruptly vanish; but when they learned that Rosa had been *"la Señorita's"* childhood *Niñera,* or nurse, and had been hired to take care of *la Señorita's* obviously delicate health, back came the smiles again.

As for Trini, within a scant half hour, Jim saw, she had won their total adoration. She did this by being kind to them, simply because she didn't know any better. Within minutes Cecilia was *tuteandola* and calling her *"Niña,"* a daring that would have got her fired from any house in Golden Door the first time she tried it. Jim was wearily aware that in Golden Door a real *Señorita* would have brought her up short with: "Have the goodness to address me properly, Cecilia!" And that the proper way of addressing *la Señora* or *la Señorita* would not only have banished that *"Tú"* and *"Niñ"* forever from Cecilia's mouth, but even *"Usted,"* "You," as well. In Golden Door, Cecilia would have had to say, always in the third person: "Does the *Señorita* desire that I bring *her* her breakfast?" "Does the *Señorita* wish her bath drawn?" and so forth. Which, Jim reflected, was but one of the many reasons that servants hate the Great Ladies with all their hearts and that Latin American revolutions are so frequent and ferocious.

As far as he was concerned, from the very moment they found out he was an Ambassador, they fell into the strictest habits of formality. It was always: "Does His Excellency desire this or that?" Or: *"¡Mande, Señor Embajador!"* "Command me, Mr. Ambassador!"

He occupied himself with these reflections all through supper, and with scolding Trini into eating a tiny bite from each of the various plates. After which they watched television, mostly North American programs, Westerns and astute big-city detectives solving horrible crimes, and ancient movies until bedtime.

Until that bedtime Jim Rush was dreading with all his heart.

And so, he saw now, was Trini. Her slanted Tluscolan eyes were perfectly enormous. In spite of her dark, Indian coloring, her lips were ashy white. He could see them trembling from across the room. Somehow, strangely enough, her fear—for it was that—a new bride's fear, a maiden's!—relieved and soothed his own.

"Come here, Trini," he said.

She came to him.

"Do you want me to sleep in the other room?" he said gently.

"No and no and no and no and no!" she stormed. "I want thee here with me! I—I want thee—to—to love me. To—make love to me. Only—" she wailed, "Ohhhhhh, *Don* Jaime, I am so afraid!"

"Of *me*?" he said.

"*¡Sí!* No! I have fear that thou wilt not—cannot—love me."

He laughed at her. Squeezed her slender waist; said:

"And why shan't I—can't I—love you, Trini?"

"Because I am—*torpe*—stupid. I know not what to say to thee, what to do—to make thee love me. This is the first time in my whole life I have been alone with a man I *love*. I don't even know how to make love. What I was—have been—does not teach one that, but only to—pretend it. *Don* Jaime, tell me—a thing?"

He said, as always: "What thing, Trini?"

"Wouldst thou that I be—passionate—with thee? Wild? What I mean is—that I—make much noise—and—and breathe loudly and quickly with my mouth open? Saying—things? Urging thee to—to do—things—to me?"

He didn't know which he wanted to do most: laugh—or cry. To cry, surely. This bleak, tormented misunderstanding, of everything that true manhood is, was in itself a kind of—innocence. And as such—tragic. No: pitiful.

He looked into her eyes. Said: "Would it be—true, Trini? Are you—thus?"

She bent her head. Said, miserably:

"No, *Don* Jaime. It would not be. And I am not thus. Much do I fear that I shall disappoint thee enormously for I—I am as cold as ice! I have never felt *anything* with a man. Except—disgust. Nausea, Pain."

She stopped. Looked up at him. Her eyes got very big. Took fire.

"No! That is not true! Once I did! Just once—¡Ayeee! How wonderful that was! Dost know when, *Don* Jaime? Dost recall?"

"How could I, Child?" he said.

She pouted; said:

"*Thou* shouldst. Because it was—with thee!"

He laughed; said: "Now—Trini!"

She swung back against his encircling arms, whirling around him within his embrace, with quick, sharp, *flamenco zapateo* steps, stamping a gay, wild, gypsy beat, laughing, laughing:

"*¡Ay sí! ¡Ay sí! ¡Sí, sí, sí, sí, sí y sí!* With thee! Just *dancing, mi Amor!* In the Obsidian Room. We made a hundred babies all at once!" She surged up against his ear, whispered with pure, delighted mischief: "My panties were *wet!*" Then her eyes went dark, went grave and sorrowing. She said slowly, sadly:

"But afterwards he—that *bestia*—spoiled it . . ."

He smiled at her. He felt very calm. Relaxed. Somehow, for almost the first time in his life, he was sure it would go well, that he would manage; that this night wouldn't be one of his usual disasters. He said, gently:

"Go into the dressing room and put your nightgown on. Brush your hair. One hundred strokes. That's good for the nerves, I'm told . . ."

"It's so short!" she said. "And that's *thy* fault, *mi Amor.* Because thou wert in love with *la muy zorra de mi Tía* Alicia, they made me cut it off so that I should look like her and please thee! Always before it was long. So long I could sit on it. Down to halfway the calves of my legs in the back and—"

"Let it grow out again," he said. "I love long hair."

"But the hair of *la muy zorra de mi Tía* Alicia is—"

"Trini!" he said sternly.

She stared at him a little fearfully, said:

"*¿Sí, mi Amor?*"

"I beg you to stop saying, 'that very bitchy one, my Aunt Alicia.' You are most unjust. You Aunt Alicia is one of the sweetest, kindest, best women I have ever known. That is *why* I loved her."

"Ohhhhhhhhhh!" she sobbed. "Thou *didst!* Thou dost! Thou hast admitted it! *¡Ay, pobre de mí!* How unhappy I am!"

"Come here, Trini!"

She came to him. Whispered:

"Yes, my Love. I am here, my Love. Command me, my Love. Tell me to—cut my throat, my Love! Which is what I feel like doing *now,* my Love!"

"I command you to—kiss me, Trini."

She went up on tiptoe. Kissed him. Drew back. Looked at him out of those eyes that were enormous and the black of a star blazed night and slightly slanted and misty and fearful and tender. Tluscolan eyes. Deeper than the pool they drowned the sacrificial maidens in. Promising him what they had promised the God. Her life. Even—her death, if need be. Her—forever.

"I—love thee, *Don* Jaime," she breathed. "Oh, how I love thee. I am one crazy little bird, no?"

"Like a watering pot," he said. Costa Verdians always said that: *"¡Más loca que una regadera!"* "Crazier than a watering pot!" He couldn't imagine why a watering pot was necessarily crazy, but that was what they said. And she was always crying, sprinkling tears all over like a watering pot. Which was one of the things he meant to stop, for good.

"Go put your nightdress on, Trini," he said.

When she came back, after a nerve cracking age, he was already in bed. He had on a pair of his Chinese silk pyjamas. And with sure instinct, he pretended to be fast asleep.

"Ohhhhh," she breathed. She sat down on the edge of the bed. Put out her hand. Her fingers trembled over the scar on his forehead. He caught her hand suddenly, turned it inward, kissed the palm of it with grave tenderness. She collapsed, shuddering, into his arms. He held her to him. Bent and kissed her mouth, slowly, softly. Drew back. Lay there, holding her, staring at the ceiling, rapt, unmoving, his eyes half closed and dreaming.

She raised up. Stared at him. Whispered:

"Don Jaime—what is wrong?"

He smiled at her. Said:

"Nothing. I feel—lazy. Peaceful. Besides, do we not have all night?"

She said: "Oh!" She was silent. Intensely silent. Then: *"Don* Jaime— tell me—a thing?"

"What thing, Trini?"

"Thou—canst not—love me? Do I awake—a—a revulsion in thee? A—repugnance?"

He said: "Lord!" And kissed her.

She said: "Thou art—rare."

"I know. Be quiet, will you? Be still. Rest . . ."

"No! No and no and no and no! I am not delicate! I will not break! I will be thine! Now! This minute! I will not rest—nor wait!"

She tore free of his arms. Sat up. Raked her white silk nightdress over her head, threw it to the floor.

And heard his breath stop, caught in his throat, making, momentarily, a strangling sob, the bleakest, most wintery sound she had ever heard. Saw what his eyes did, which was to dim into fjord mists, turn grey hoarfrost, congealed into purest misery, then splintering, breaking up into abrupt and jagged ice slivers of horror, revulsion, pain, as their pale irises and contracted pupils pinpointed the light, and swept it over her naked body in a hard, bright *pointillisme* that froze and burned her where it touched, like snow, like sleet, like glacial flame.

Where it touched: the long, raw-pink, ice-white scar of the self-inflicted knife slash in her left breast; the ridged scar tissue circling completely the huge, dark brown-red areolas from which the miniature phalli of her nipples stood up in visibly quivering tiny twin erections; the obscene blue-red, raw-flesh, off-white, half healed whorls and puckers where they had ground out their cigarettes against her living flesh; the fingers without nails, the livid stripes where the leaded whip had twined half way around her rib cage and bit almost to the bone . . .

Her hands flew up, cupping, hiding her breasts, then spreading into golden wings, fluttered here and here and there to cover the marks of their sick bestiality from the anguished pity of his gaze.

She saw with a pain far greater than any they had been able to inflict upon her, with a sudden, intensely destructive, crippling, suicidal self-loathing, his eyes filled up with unashamed tears, saw them brim and spill and pencil his pale, thin, tired face—aged in that one brief instant by at least a hundred years!—with distilled hurt, with a compassion that was all but castrating as far as any possibility of sex between them then, at that moment, was concerned, a *misericordia* that was a momentary—but neither small nor painless!—death.

"Oh, no!" she moaned. "Do not look! I am ugly, ugly! I will sicken thee! Awake in thee *una repugnancia* that thou canst never vanquish! A revulsion that—"

She saw his thin, wiry shoulders shake. Sensed, felt the voiceless anguish that held him.

"Oh, no, *Don* Jaime!" she sobbed, strangling, choking, weeping. "Oh no no no no no and no! *¡Por favor, Amor mío!* I am not worth even the smallest of thy tears! Do not—destroy me—thus! Do not break my heart with thy weeping! Not ever for this ugly broken—"

He put his arms up and drew her down. Bent and kissed every scar she had, wherever it was. Slowly and softly and lingeringly as if to draw out even the memory of pain, the last residue of horror in her.

Her hands came up, her fingers moved through his greying hair, softly, slowly. She clung her mouth to his, speaking against it, whispering between the adhesive renewal and break and renewal again of feverish kisses, moaning:

"Now, *Amor mío*. Please, now. I love thee. But now I need thee. I want thee. My body—wants—thine. It faints within itself with the wanting. It hurts with it. Please, my love, my own, canst thou not—even now—even yet—"

"Trini—" he murmured, "you—want—this of me—truly?"

"Please! *¡por favor!*"

But when he tried, he could not. She was—closed. Obstructed. Small. He remembered with sudden horror—the broken glass. The surgery. And realized that this—the act of love—of sex—was impossible.

"Please!" she wept. "Try! I need thee. I want thee, *mi Amor!*"

He tried once more—ever so gently. Saw her lips go absolutely white with pain. And halted. Stopped dead. Peered sorrowfully down into her small, exquisite face.

She smiled at him. Whispered: "Yes; it—hurts. But it's supposed to—the *first* time, isn't it?"

"Oh, my God!" he said.

She wrapped her two arms about his neck. Murmured:

"Let me, *Don* Jaime. That thou dost not blame thyself, or accuse thyself of brutality or—"

Then, all at once, before he could divine her intent, she arched her slim body like a bow, slammed it upward against him with terrible force. Gasped. Contorted all her face into a grimace of intolerable pain. Sighed, very softly: "Ay-yee! Ay-yeee!"

And was still, holding him softly, hotly, wetly, tremblingly, inside her body, inside her life.

He was frozen. Crippled. He could not move. All of him was paralyzed: heart, mind, body, breath. Her lips brushed against his ear. They were scalding.

"*Don* Jaime—it is gone. The pain has gone. All gone. Thou—hast made it go away . . ."

"Trini—" he moaned, breathed, whispered, sighed, or maybe didn't even say.

She surged up and found his mouth. Drew back, smiling at him.

"Make love—to me—now, please?" she said.

And then quite suddenly, it was lovely. Beautiful. Perfect. He was amazed that this was so. But it was. He, Jim Rush, who all his life had been at best a mediocre lover, and, more often than not, decidedly a bad one, was performing tender miracles with Trini, relaxed, unhurried, without anxiety, fully, peacefully in control. Because his pity had removed—completely—the whip and goad and driven haste of passion. Had stilled the beast hungers in him. Stifled them. But more—far more!—because she was Trini. Because he loved her. Because the subtle alchemy of subjectivity had entered in, performing the sacrament of transubstantiation, transforming a mere biological process, sex, into that usually unattainable glory whose name—'Take off thy shoes, this ground is Holy!'—is love, is very love!

'The options are—so limited,' he thought; 'all men have more or less the same physical equipment, all women, its complimentary opposite, so what's to do, must, perforce, be done in the same few, easily enumerated ways. What then? Since *what* we do's the same—within normalcy's broad limits!—what magic is it that, here and now, has brought soft music—lutes and viols and virginals!—murmuring through warm and flower-scented air? Has written: "Scene: A Bower with Rose Petals Strewn!" into the script? I've done this—plunged a rampant penis into a moist, receptive vagina!—with a number of women. No. I have never in my life, done this, quite *this,* before. Not if this is mere sex, a biological process whose end is reproduction. So, again, *what* is it that—no; wait. That *what*'s as wrong as all *what*'s are. As wrong as *how.* As meaningless as *why.* Leaving the only word that counts, the word that love is all about, to account for this magic, enchantment, glory! Which is—I'll stake my heart upon it!—*who.*

'And *who*—is Trini. My utterly adorable Trini. *Who* is my Lady. *Who* is—now, henceforth and forever more!—my Love.'

She tightened against him, suddenly. Shuddered. Whispered: "*¡Oh Dios mío!*" Writhed. Thrashed. Cried: "Ay-yeee! Ay-yeeeeeeee!" Clung to him, quivering, trembling, shaking. Put up her arms, dragged his face down to hers, almost breaking his mouth against hers, sobbing, sobbing, making the sounds of a whipped, heartbroken, disconsolate child.

"Trini—" he said reproachfully.

"I did not know!" she wept. "I did not even know!"

"What didn't you know, little Trini?" he said.

"That it—could be—beautiful. And I should have, that it would, that it had to be—with thee! Ohhhhh, thou! Yes, Thou! *¡Dulce asesino!* Sweet murderer! For thou hast killed me. I died. Truly. *¡Ay que buena muerte!* Oh, what a good, fine death that was!"

"Trini!" he said.

"Truly. But now I have resurrected, so that I can tell thee things!"

"What things, little Trini?"

"*Por ejemplo,* for instance, thou art not a man."

"Lord! Then what am I? A billy goat? A woman? Or a *maricon* like Geri Pyle?"

She punched him in the chest with a doubled fist, hard.

"Do not say such terrible things!" she said. "Wait! Let me think. I am very *torpe,* but I must not say this badly. Men are—animals. All haste and brutality. They hurt one. They reduce one, diminish one to—a thing. To a torn—and ravished—piece of meat. Covered with their sweat. Stinking of them. Feeling used. Shamed. Degraded. Not quite—human. Therefore, since thou didst not do any of those things, but instead all their opposites, thou—art—*not*—a man!"

He smiled at her; said, peacefully:

"Same question: What am I, then, Trini?"

"An Angel! And a Sorcerer! And—and a Musician! For thou hast played upon my body as upon a harp: made it sing and sing and sing!"

"Lord!" he said, laughing.

"*Don* Jaime—dost thou think we—did?"

"Do I think we did what, Trini?"

"Made *Jaimito*? Or *Trinita*? Or both of them at once? It *felt* like we did. Them and all their brothers and their sisters. All ten at once! Boys and girls together. And—and monsters with three heads!"

"And little green female Martians," he added gravely.

"Yes, yes! With *platillos volantes* and death ray guns as in the tele! *Don* Jaime—tell me a thing?"

"What thing, Trinita?"

"Thou must not call me *Trinita*! I am not *Trinita*. She is *Trinita*. The little one so tiny and so sweet that thou hast made inside me. I am only Trini. Though she will call me *Madrecita*! *¡Ay, que buena!* Oh, how happy I am! What was I saying?"

"As usual, you were asking me to tell you a thing."

"*¡Ay, sí!* But first thou must go to the window and look out. One can see Old Zopo from here, can one not?"

"Zopocomapetl? The volcano? No, I don't think so. Why, Trini?"

"Then, later on, thou must send Pepe to see if He is still there. Dost know why, *mi Amor?*"

"No, Trini, why?" he said.

She laughed freely, gaily, happily. Her laughter, too, was Tluscolan: silvery, pure, and right on pitch.

"Because—because I think that last little earthquake we made shook Him all down in pieces!"

"Now, Trini!" he groaned.

She looked at him, and abruptly, her face changed. A grimace of sadness, pain—he did not know which, crossed it.

"*Don* Jaime—" she whispered, "was I—good—for thee? Didst thou—enjoy me? *¿Disfrutaste de mí?*"

"Lord!" he said. "Yes. Why, yes, of course."

"And I—of thee, enormously. So much! More than I had believed a woman could of a man. But now—I am sad, because I do not think we can any more tonight. I—I hurt a little, *Don* Jaime. And I—I—seem to be—bleeding—"

He jackknifed up. Stared down at her lower body. She was. The whole of the bed beneath her was red. Soaked. Dripping.

She smiled. Said with calm conviction, perfect happiness:

"It is as the Tluscola say. I have survived the ordeal. Therefore—the

Old Gods have forgiven me. And thus thou wert the *first* man in my life. In my new life, *Don* Jaime, *mi Amor*. And thou shalt be the last. And the only one. Dost believe me?"

"Trini, for God's love!" he said. Groped for his robe. Drew it on. Raced for the phone.

"Please," she said. "Do not call Doctor Gomez. Or Doctor Moreno. Or any doctor. I will call Rosa now. And she will tell me what to do. This is a thing of the Tluscola. White men, even doctors, do not understand."

"Call her," he said. "But I'm going to call Dr. Gomez, Trini! I just don't trust Tluscola witchcraft that far!"

"Please, *mi Amor*," she wheedled; "don't. They will put me back in the hospital. And we will not be able to make little earthquakes, or shake down volcanoes—or put the right shade of blond into Jaimito's hair . . ."

"You're mad!" he howled. "Call that old Witch! But I'm going to see that you're attended to properly!" He whirled back to the phone, dialing furiously.

Rosa came. Said:

"*¡Los hombres! ¡Que brutotes y bestias sois!*"

"Do not say such things of *Don* Jaime," Trini said wrathfully, "who is an Angel and a Saint! I forbid thee to speak thus, Rosa!"

"*¡Mierda!*" Rosa said; then she crooned, tenderly: "Lie down, *Niñita*, let Rosa attend thee . . ."

She was, Jim saw, skillful enough in the conventional practice of ordinary nursing. She halted that hemorrhage quickly by applying ice cubes from the refrigerator to Trini, giving her horrible cramps in the process. Then she put an ordinary sanitary belt and pad on her, turned to Jim with an evil, witchlike cackle, and said:

"You go to the Blue Moon for next two weeks, *Don* Jaime. Leave my Baby in peace, understand?"

"Oh, Rosa!" Trini cried. "How wicked you are!"

"Not wicked, smart," Rosa said. "Men big brutes. My Baby, delicate. No more"—she used the explicit, street, gutter word—"for a while, understand?"

A half hour later—as always when it was Jim who called him—Vicente Gomez was there. He brought Luis Moreno with him. They both examined Trini carefully, while she lay there in a perfect agony of terror, not of what they might diagnose, but simply, Jim knew, that they might separate her from him.

"Seems—to have been an adhesion. From the surgery. And all that screwing broke it. But bring her in tomorrow or the day after, anyhow, Jim," Vince said.

"Of course," Jim said; "but I'd like to know why, Vince. Is she in—danger?"

"I'm going to have to run more coagulation tests. I made your old Witch—damned if she doesn't look like she circles the Cabildo's steeple on a jet propelled broomstick every night there's a full moon!—show me that sheet. Too much blood on it for comfort, Jim. There may be something in her glandular system that destroys her blood's ability to clot. She has a whole new blood supply and yet—"

"I'll bring her in, Vince," Jim said.

But that, at least, proved to be a false alarm. Trini's new blood—of the same grouping as her old, but from donors who had been selected not to have the remotest kinship with her, which hadn't been easily accomplished when the relatively high social status Trini actually came from, plus the extracurricular activities of the Dictator Miguel Villalonga and his half brother Luis Sinnombre, one of the two of whom *had* to be her father, were taken into consideration—clotted as well on the second tests as it had on the first. Maybe even a little faster and better.

"Must have been a fluke," Vince said. "You can go make bastards with my blessing, Jim. She'll need extra care, of course; but—"

"She won't retain them," Luis Moreno said. "There is not the slightest chance that she will—not with a pelvic girdle that's been smashed to splinters that way. I admit you did a magnificent job of reconstruction, Vicente; but you really shouldn't build up their hopes this way. It's definitely unkind—"

"Doctor," Jim said; "do you know anything about Tluscolan witchcraft?"

"*¿La Brujería de los Tluscola?* No, of course not! Why, Mr. Ambassador?"

"Because Rosa says Trini *will* have children. And Rosa's a Witch. And when you start putting modern science up against Rosa's witchcraft, I wouldn't bet on modern science, Doctor!"

"Nor I!" Vicente laughed. He said, in English: "All right, Jim, you can take her home now, and get on with the production of illegitimates! But take it easy for a while, will you?"

"Vince—" Jim said quietly.

"Yes, Great Swordsman? Yes, Master of the Art of Blunt Instrument Dissection?

"They—won't be bastards," Jim Rush said.

CHAPTER

23

When Peter Reynolds came out to the gate of the Old
Stuyvesant House in answer to the bell and found Jim
Rush standing there, he said:

"Well, I'll be goddamned!"

Then he grinned, and added:

"At least you didn't sneak back down to South America without giving me a chance to pin your medal on you, Jim. You know: The Order
of Unmitigated Bastards, First Class. With palms, yet. You've won it,
Boy! At least until you give me *one* good reason for that caper you pulled
off on us long suffering newspapermen down in Washington. But come
on in, will you? I see you've brought your bags. All right, I won't throw
you out on your used to be chubby little ass until I've heard what you've
got to say . . . ."

"Lord, Peter!" Jim said. "You don't mean to tell me you're pissed off
because I barred the press, including that much too inquisitive little
stringer of yours, from that session I had—involuntarily; they called *me*
in, remember?—before the Senate Committee? I *had* to. You've lived in
Costa Verde. Surely you, of all people, ought to know the kind of
reasons I had for *that*."

"Yes. It figures. You were protecting your sources. But precisely
because I know that Monkey's Paradise and those Paranoiac Throwbacks
who run it, you could have trusted *me* to handle the information intelligently and—"

308

"Peter—" Jim said quietly, "I didn't come up here to explain that to you. I came to ask a favor. A very great favor. Is Tim at his place, tonight? The favor includes him. He'll have to at least consent to it—"

"Yes, he's home. I'll call him. Give me that little bag. I can manage it in spite of my bum arm. You'll have to lug the rest in yourself. Mario's in bed by now, and has a touch of flu, so 'Licia would have both our heads off at the neck if I made him get up. Why'd you get here so late?"

"Problem finding a taxi that would bring me out this far. And the car rental desk was closed. Peter, I'm sorry. But you know I wouldn't barge in on you like this if it weren't important—"

Peter grinned at him, drawled:

"Jim, Boy, the day you feel that you can't barge in any damned time you want to, simply because the notion strikes you, you can write our friendship off. I'm damned glad to see you. And Alicia will be gladder. She's been worrying about you. Do her good to see how great you look . . ."

"Thanks, Peter," Jim said.

When they came into the house, Alicia threw her arms around Jim's neck and kissed him, fervently. Said: "Oh, Jim! I am so very happy to see you!" in a tone of voice so exactly like Trini's that Jim had to gulp a couple of times before he could reply:

"And I am even happier to see you, Alicia. Hope you're not sleepy, because I've an awful lot to tell you."

"No!" she said. "I am not sleepy at all. Have you found my double yet, Jim? If you have I shall be fearfully jealous, for as I told Peter, you get better looking every time I see you!"

" 'Licia, for God's sake; give him a chance to catch a breath before playing *la Vampiresa,* will you?" Peter said. "Suppose you go and ring up Tim and Marisol. Tell them to pop over. Jim's got talk for them, too. Ready for your first Scotch, Boy?"

"Yes, but make it light, will you? The things we've got to talk about call for a clear head . . ."

"A Speech Scrambler?" Tim O'Rourke said. "Sure, Jim; I know what a Speech Scrambler is. Or rather are. 'Cause you need at least two of the gimmicks as I recall. You hang 'em onto two telephones for security between two points. Makes the guy who's calling sound like Donald Duck on a spree backed up by a chorus of drunken dolphins, 'til you turn yours on, too; then everything comes clear, right?"

"Exactly. I want your permission—and Peter's—to put three Karl Lintz' ZD 27 Speech Scramblers, identical ones in every respect to the model I've already had put on my phones at the Embassy, the residence, and one other place I sometimes hang out at—"

"My double's house?" Alicia said.

"Ssssh! Top Secret, Alicia!" Jim said. "The point is, Tim; I want to put them on your home phone, on Peter's, and one on the phone in your newspaper's office. For round the clock unbugged and unbuggable communications with people—friends—whom I trust. I might mention I've made no such proposal to the State Department—"

"Figures. Though I *was* wondering. After you barred even our little guy in Washington from your testimony before the Senate Latin American Affairs Committee, I was beginning to think me 'n Ol' Ginger Pete here had worked our way onto your Shit List, somehow . . ."

"Tim, you know better than that! Your reporter and everybody else's. Look, both of you: I'd just as soon stay off this subject. For good and sufficient reasons, say. Won't you two Demon Reporters just take my word for it that my reasons were excellent, and let it go at that?"

Tim and Peter looked at each other. Grinned. Then they both chorused—so simultaneously that the line sounded rehearsed:

"Hell, no! Come on, Jim-Boy—give!"

"All right," Jim sighed, "I'll tell you—with the preamble that my reasons for doing that will sure as hell distress *both* your charming better halves. Alicia, Mari, please forgive me; but I've got to quiet these two Neanderthals you've married, somehow. Look Tim—and Peter—put it this way: I just don't want my girl friend—your exact double, Alicia; and, I believe, your niece—beer bottled, *again.* The first time was quite enough, thank you!"

All four of them sat there. A long time. A very long time, considering the fact that not one of them was breathing. Then Peter said, very, very softly:

"Oh, Jesus!"

"Jim!" Alicia got out, and started to cry. The way she cried was exactly like Trini, too.

"Sorry, my dear," Jim said. "Well, Peter, Tim—about those Scramblers—"

"Hell, yes!" Tim said. "I'll take an air taxi down to New York first thing tomorrow morning to buy the gimmicks. Got a specification sheet with you, Boy?"

"Yes. Only it's in Spanish."

"No matter. I'll translate it for the electronics people. Tell me: Can we publish any of what you'll tell us?"

"All of it, eventually. And specific chunks, immediately. I ask only that you take my word for what's go or no go."

"If he does not, after what you have just told us, I will *kill* him, Jim!" Marisol said fiercely, jabbing the corner of her handkerchief at the hot tears in her eyes.

"Thanks, Mari; but I'd rather that you'd let this lunkhead live. Look: The problem's the big loan that García and Chums are trying to blackmail out of our Government—"

"By threatening to go Left, and bar us from receiving any of their goddamned oil," Peter said.

"The threat's empty, as I was happy to tell the Senate Committee," Jim said. "After all the charming little tricks they've pulled on their Red captives—and their women—the Reds would receive them with open arms, and thereafter hang them. In the Plaza of the Liberation. Upside down. On fish hooks passed through certain delicate parts of their anatomies—"

"I'll bet you'd enjoy the spectacle, *now,*" Peter said.

"No, Peter; I wouldn't," Jim said soberly; "I don't find savagery—or sadism—contagious. I suppose I don't need to tell you that Catch 66 as far as the loan is concerned lies in the obvious fact that they *won't* spend the money for the reasons they say they need it. Reasons you know, since their Embassy's Press Officer leaked them to every paper north of the Rio Grande. Ciudad Villalonga has been crawling with the representatives of the French armament industry for months. My CIA man— damned good guy; we've become fast friends—is sure that the deal being cooked up includes a prefabricated atomic energy factory. For, they say, the production of cheap electricity—in a country that has more damned waterfalls than Switzerland, and could supply all of South America with current if they'd put a reasonable amount of money into hydroelectric setups: simple dams and waterpower activated turbines. But no, García and Friends must have atomic energy—by means of a fast breeder reactor, naturally—"

"One question, Jim," Peter said. "Who's their imported physicist? They've got all the uranium they need thanks to Old Zopo. Say the French sell them a breeder reactor. All that means is that they'll pile up U 238 and plutonium. But what they haven't got is the know-how. The only branch of science worth a damn in Costa Verde is medicine—out of a certain historical imperative, I'd say. But if the Butcher and his Pals have dug up some German with the training—and the Nazi inclinations—to work for them, I'm buying one way tickets for me and mine to the planet Mars. Because the day paranoiacs like that bunch get their hands on that kind of toy, you can write this whirling little chunk of rock we live on—*off*. And I say their Wizard of Oz has practically *got* to be a German. The Russians aren't going to help out a regime as far Right as Costa Verde's. Nor the late, great Mao's little slant-eyed buddies, either. Even the French won't go so far as to supply them with blueprints for the bomb. As much as they hate us, they won't. They haven't got the guts, so—"

"I don't know," Jim said. "So far, my Intelligence man hasn't been able to find anyone who fits—those essential specifications. He thinks they're dickering for some dissatisfied physicist aboard. Who *could* be a Russian with a Solzhenitsyn-type mentality, y'know. They'll offer him the moon and the stars, of course; whoever he is. Plus 'The Treatment' on a harem sized scale. By the way, my CIA boy is my *only* trustworthy means of communication out. He has a single sideband UHF transmitter-receiver with speeded-up speech modulation that only the CIA's outfit in Maryland can decode. Bounces his signals off that Geostatic satellite Ed Crowley *and* Interstat were kind enough to hang up in fixed orbit over the Caribbean for us. But since *I* don't want the CIA monitoring *all* of my incoming or outgoing information, I took advantage of being called back to the States this week by the Senate to proposition you characters. It goes without saying that what we're setting up is not a one way street. Anything either of you thinks I need to know, please call me—any hour of the day or night, at the three numbers I'm going to give you: the Embassy's for daytime, office hours. The residence's for nighttime after hours. And—one other, in case you can't reach me at either of the first two. As for the phone bills, I'll—"

"Forget 'em!" Peter said. "An *in* like this is worth a fortune to us, Jim. Anything else?"

"Not that I can think of at the moment. Lord, it's late! I had no idea—"

"Oh, no, you don't, Jim!" Alicia said. "*Now* the interesting part begins! The Women's Magazine Supplement, shall we say? Your *beeg* romance. With—my double. And—my niece. That was what you said, wasn't it?"

"Yes," Jim sighed. "That she's your double is self-evident. And she has been told—and *believes*—she is your niece. A little matter of your late—brothers—having kidnapped, for some considerable length of time, her mother . . ."

"Then, she is right," Alicia said sadly. "They did those things, my brothers. And worse. Far worse. Tell me, what is she like?"

"Very like—you," Jim said. "But more like—*this* . . ."

He put his hand in his breast pocket and came out with a thick envelope, fairly bursting with photographs. They were nearly all of Trini, except a few group shots—of Trini and Petra together; of Trini and Jim; of Trini, Petra, and Jim; of Trini, Petra, and Van; of Jim and Van; and of all four of them, these last, being, of course, automatic timer shots, taken with the camera tripod mounted. And Van Schuyler had taken them all. Van was a photographer of better than professional capabilities. It was, Jim reflected, probably the thing he did best, though the Cultural Attaché's skills were many and of an almost uniformly high order. And Van preferred Trini, because of the exquisite bone structure that she shared—Jim saw now, again—with Alicia, to even the more conventionally lovely Petra whom the young CIA man had married one month before—"To make damned sure I can take her with me, when they kick me out!" he'd said.

It took Jim some little time to find the photograph he *wanted* to show them of Trini. It was not necessarily the best among all the ones he had in that envelope. But it *was* the latest one, in point of time. Which was why—and with malice aforethought!—he selected it. As a conversational ice-breaker, he was sadly sure, as a means of getting directly to what he saw no way to escape telling them, it would have all the force of a pocket-sized A-bomb.

Having found it at last, Jim passed that photograph over to Alicia, fighting back the tremble from sheer nerves that was trying to get into his hands.

"Why, Jim!" Alicia gasped. "Now I *am* angry with you! Why did you not tell us you had got married?"

"Because—I *haven't*," Jim said.

"Oh!" Alicia said. "Forgive me, Jim. It is, of course, none of our business, but—do you *mind*, if I show this to—Peter? And to Marisol and Tim?"

"Of course not. If I hadn't wanted you to, I shouldn't have showed it to you, my dear. I have many other photos of Trini, here. Earlier ones . . ."

Peter took the photograph. Tim and Marisol crowded in, staring over his shoulder. Marisol let out an audible gasp. Tim a wry and knowing chuckle. Peter didn't say anything. He stood there, studying that picture. It was, of course, in color. Some really exquisitely toned Japanese film whose name Jim couldn't recall.

"Lord, she's beautiful!" Peter said, finally. "She looks like—"

"What, Peter?" Jim said.

"An Indian Madonna. Our Lady of the Tluscolans. Hell! Alicia's being overdelicate as usual. But I can ask you, and I will. Granted the fact that this beautiful, beautiful girl-child is close to seven months pregnant, why *haven't* you married her, Jim?"

"Because she won't marry me," Jim said. "At least not yet, not now."

"Oh!" Alicia said. "Why won't she, Jim? Isn't the—child—yours?"

"It is. That's not the problem. The problem's something else: In part, your silly Costa Verdian class complexes, Alicia. *I'm* His Excellency, the Ambassador; she's a little nobody from the wrong side of the railroad tracks. As my wife, says she, she'd ruin me socially, make my work impossible; as my mistress, says she, she can live like a cunning little mouse in a hole in the wall, somewhere on the back streets of my life, give me the ten bouncing little bastards she calmly proposes to give me, and nobody will give a damn. The latter, says she, is acceptable in Costa Verde; the former, says she, simply isn't."

Marisol and Alicia looked at each other.

"Jim," Marisol said softly; "you're going to hate me, but—she's right. Shamefully and sorrowfully, I have to say, she's right. Also, she is behaving with—great nobility. Or out of great love for you. Or both— to thus accept her own—disgrace, rather than to harm you . . ."

Jim winced at that. Sighed. Said, quietly:

"It's not quite that simple, Mari. But then, what is, in this life? The question of her disgracing herself does not apply. She'd been most thoroughly disgraced long before I met her. I know. Sounds horrible, doesn't it? Hell, it is. Any way I tell it, it comes out wrong. Slant it one way and here you have your middle-aged lecher seducing girl-children. Another, and I give you a poor, deluded, senile fool, being taken for a ride as a result of his addled, belated, but avid pursuit of folly!"

"Yet," Peter said, "knowing you, I'd stake my last red copper on my belief that neither slant is the true one. What is the truth, Jim? What actually did happen?"

"The truth in this tale, Friend Peter, follows a wildly meandering line. So build me a drink will you? And let's all sit down. Kick off your shoes, girls. Make yourselves comfy. This is going to take the rest of the night. And—I'd venture to suggest, Alicia, that a couple of gross of handkerchiefs may be necessary. This tale's that—sad. Hell, I'll probably need one or two of 'em myself. Remembering it brings tears to my eyes, though as much of rage, as of pity. So, before I begin, are you absolutely sure you want to hear it? It's—awfully rough, friends. Raw. Gamy. Filthy. Terrible. But—tragic. Truly tragic. Which is what I think redeems it. Because you can't rob tragedy of dignity, can you? At least, not entirely . . ."

"Listen to the man!" Tim snorted. "After *that* preamble he asks us if we want to hear it! How d'you propose to get us out of here, Jim-Boy: blast?"

"All right," Jim said. "And telling it *is* necessary, Tim—on the acceptable grounds of self-defense. Better that you hear it from me than have to swallow the version that the Costa Verdian Embassy's Press Secretary is going to leak to every scandal sheet in these United States, after I throw a monkey wrench into what they're planning, as I damned well am going to have to . . ."

Before he was through, both Alicia and Marisol were crying helplessly, sitting there holding each other in their arms. Because Jim Rush told them the truth, strict, unvarnished, and entire. He had to. When he openly opposed the plans of the Dictatorship, as in simple honor he had to, he knew that the *first* of their reprisals would be the attempt to rob him of both dignity and credit, through a smear campaign in the Stateside press. And for that, through a sort of extension of the theory of guilt by association, poor Trini's sad past, her late and lamentable—however involuntary!—profession, would serve admirably. As either his mistress—or his wife—it still would. But he had known from the outset that he *could* tell the Reynolds and the O'Rourkes that story. In a way, it was also *their* story. Marisol Talaveda—before, of course, her marriage to Tim—had been sent as a pawn of "The Treatment" to seduce Peter Reynolds in exactly the same fashion that Trini had been sent to him. And only Alicia's intervention, out of her own love for Peter, out of plain female jealousy among other, perhaps more noble motivations, and from her position of power as the sister of the then current Dictator Miguel Villalonga, had prevented Mari from being forced to carry out her mission, and thereby being pushed as far down the social and moral scale as the nadir poor Trini had reached by the time he had found her.

And, as for Alicia, herself, though her own personal history was an impeccable saga of almost Victorian morality, with—Jim shrewdly suspected—one carefully concealed, and entirely pardonable episode with Peter, himself, before their marriage to possibly mar it, it was most unlikely that she would dare scorn Trini for the largely involuntary practice of a profession in whose ranks her, Alicia's, own mother had been a starring—and entirely willing!—member. *Isabela de los Cienmil Amores,* Isabel of the Hundred Thousand Loves, they had called the mother of Miguel and Alicia Villalonga, and of their half brother Luis Sinnombre, Louis Without A Name, or perhaps a better translation would be Louis, the Unspeakable! as the dreaded and dreadful head of Costa Verde's Secret Police was known in those days.

He was, he saw, quite right. All of them accepted his revelations of Trini's past without comment or demurrer. Nor had he attempted to overstate matters in her defense. He'd simply told them the facts, which included Trini's attempted suicide before letting Joe Harper drag her away, the obscene extremes of torture she had suffered for his sake, her willing tossing of her life into the balance to give him the child he had so long wanted. To them—romantics one and all!—those facts clearly outweighed in the scale of things any sin Trini possibly could have committed. To him—basically colder, more cerebral—and at the aching heart of the whole matter, there remained an ugly undercurrent of doubt, and fear. The thing was done, the die was cast, his Rubicon was crossed. But could it work? Over the long, long years, could it?

'Does any love ever?' he asked himself, and gave the realist's bitter answer: 'No!'

"You may bring her *here!*" Alicia stormed. "To this *house.* You may both stay with us until you buy or build your own. And in this same neighborhood, Jim! She *is* my niece. She looks just like me—"

"Only she's a damned sight prettier!" Peter said.

"Yes. She is. Though that doesn't require much!" Alicia said. "But, more importantly, she *thinks* like me, reacts as I do. And, as my own flesh and blood, I have some claim upon her! Oh, Jim, *please* do come here to live!"

"I'll think about it," Jim said. "But tell me one more thing, Alicia; do you also have room for a Witch?"

"A Witch?" Alicia said.

"Yes. A blessed old Tluscolan Witch called Rosa. Who is entirely responsible for our child's being alive. You see, Peter and Tim, the doctors—Vince Gomez—whom both of you have to thank for your lives, as I recall—"

"Vince is the best," Tim said. "The *very* best, Jim."

"Yes," Peter said; "As a doctor—and as a human being . . ."

"True. All *three* of us are among those present and accounted for right now, because of him, remember! And—Trini. But both he and Luis Moreno—Costa Verde's number one gynecologist—swore that, after what had been done to Trini, she'd miscarry every time. Rosa didn't agree. And from the very minute wé found out Trini was pregnant, Rosa put her to bed. Kept her there three *months.* Wouldn't let her get up for anything . . ." He stopped, chuckled: "Hell, I'll bet you could hear her screaming up *here,* every time Rosa forced her to use a bedpan instead of getting up to go to the bathroom. But Rosa—who was Trini's childhood nurse, which is an indication of the kind of family Trini originally came from—is one tough old buzzard. And she won. Now Moreno says the pregnancy's perfectly normal—"

"Jim," Peter said, "beer bottling won't leave a woman incapacitated for maternity. Not if the remedial surgery is halfway decent. And you had Vince Gomez, so—"

"Not—the glass. They jumped up and down on her with both feet. Wearing boots, some of them. Her pelvic girdle was—in splinters. Hell, I might as well show you the feally filthy pictures. Look at these, will you?"

These were the *before* pictures that Vince Gomez had had taken for the guidance of Doctor Sousa Dos Santos, the great Brazilian plastic surgeon. Jim had brought those pictures with him to show to Grace Nivens when he finally got to New York. His reasons were very complicated. He was not entirely sure he understood them, himself, though they had a kind of strangely illogical logic to them. If Grace were still free and unattached, he believed himself almost honor bound to renew his courtship of her. And, since his own state was no longer exactly distinguished by its liberty or its lack of ties, he felt the need of some emotionally powerful explanations of his own conduct to offer her. Those pictures were proof that he *had* to marry Trini. But, at bottom, what real necessity had he of offering any explanations whatsoever? Hadn't Grace called it quits *first*, and—

And weren't the real reasons his *own* uncertainties, his doubts? His aching conviction that human motives were always less noble than people represent them as being for public consumption? However you explained them, the *facts* remained the same: A middle-aged New Englander, an Ambassador, the sole survivor of a distinguished family, a university graduate, a man of wide culture, was marrying—with his eyes wide open!—a nineteen-year-old girl of mixed Spanish, Tluscolan, and *Black*—'Why the hell,' he thought miserably, 'do I italicize that last word even in my mind? What difference does it make, really?'—ancestry, who, moreover, up until the moment he, himself, had taken her out of that life, had been—a whore.

'A spineless need for self-justification!' he thought, bitterly. 'I show them this poor, battered, butchered piece of meat to prove how fucking *noble* I am! What a great, great guy! And that somewhere, sometime, there was at least *one* woman—poor little bitch though she was!—who loved me enough to—'

Then he saw Alicia. Saw what was happening to her. She was sitting there holding those pictures, and staring at them through absolutely blind eyes—and shaking. Exactly the way Trini used to when she mentioned the man who—legally, anyhow—had been her father. The gestures, the motions were identical. And just as horrible. 'A family characteristic,' he thought. 'Or—a racial trait . . .'

"Oh, my God!" he said. "Alicia, I'm sorry! I didn't mean to upset you so!"

"This isn't anything," Peter growled. "You ought to have seen her the day she saw that sharpshooter blow half that solid ivory dome of yours apart on TV. Lie back, Alicia. Breathe slowly. That's it. That's it. And give me *those*. I'd better have a look at whatever variety of porn Jim's peddling these days . . ."

He took the pictures. Stared at them. Said:

"Oh, Jesus!" Passed them over to Tim. Marisol got up. Looked at them with her husband.

"People—" she whispered. "No! Not people! Animals in human form, who do things like *this,* have no right to live!"

"I'm sorry," Jim said; "that—was rotten of me. To show you these, I mean. I was being cowardly, again. Looking for self-justification, I suppose. And that she took this, suffered it almost without a whimper, being the true Tluscolan she is!—for my sake—doesn't help anything, does it? Because now I know why I brought them with me. To defend myself against the charge of being the weak-kneed fool I know I am. To show them to my friends in case any of you couldn't understand why I feel I'm very largely doing the right thing in marrying a girl who, however you try to embellish the plain facts, is, after all, an ex-hooker."

"Jesus, how you quibble!" Tim said. "You don't have to *feel* you're doing the right thing when you *are*, Jim. And not 'very largely.' Entirely. From where I sit, you're goddamned lucky to have found this one whatever she was, or may have done. Say—judging by that other snap, your plastic surgeon's a great, great man!"

"He is," Jim said. "In fact, he's the best in South America."

"And *North*," Tim said, "on the evidence of that Indian Madonna shot. Jim, may I have these? I want to publish them, with the face inked out, of course; not that it's recognizable as it is! Convince those bastards in Washington what really goes on down there . . ."

"No, Tim. It's still too dangerous. After I get her out, it will be a different story. Besides, I'm getting you better ones than these. A movie sequence filmed inside Chizenaya. Including an action closeup of a woman being raped by a trained German shepherd *dog*."

"Jesus!" Peter said. "*How* are you going to get a thing like that, Jim?"

"Through one of their own. A kid they didn't read right. As burly a looking brute as you've ever laid eyes on. But the brutishness didn't extend far enough into his interior for him to take what he was told, and had, to do. So when I met him, he was in Lopez Basquez' Psychiatric Clinic—recovering, or trying to, from an authentic emotional crackup. Or trying to fight his way back into—humanity, say. Because to be able to do the kinds of things those thugs did to Trini with impunity—by which I mean without scrambling your own guts to bloody hash, or having what's left of your mind reduced to jelly by the never ceasing echoes of your victims' screams—you have to be—special. Very special. Outside of the race of man. Beyond it. I'd like to say below it, but no animal ever displays the sheer sick cruelty that disgraces humankind. Anyhow, Jorge was trying, desperately, to fight his way back to self-forgiveness, self-respect, when I ran into him—and had, in fact, recovered sufficiently to have fallen head over heels in love with Jenny Crowley—"

"That's no evidence of sanity," Peter said. "Quite the contrary, I'd say."

"Not necessarily. Dear Jenny's much improved. Dr. Lopez says he would have her completely cured by now, if he could speak her language . . ."

"Don't tell me Jenny's having her head shrunk in Spanish!" Peter said.

"No. No, of course not. Lopez Basquez speaks perfect English. What he doesn't speak is Counter-Culture Hippy Jargon. Hence he finds communication with Jenny difficult. So do I. But at least she's off the hard stuff. Doctor Lopez dried her out gradually by the classic treatment: substituting Methadone, which is itself also addicting, but doesn't cause horrible withdrawal symptoms, for heroin, and then reducing the dosage week by week until she can do without even that. He'd let her out, allow her to come back here to the States, now that she's free to—"

"Thanks to you," Peter said. "That was one sweet job you pulled, clearing her name! Say, how'd you ever get your hands on Harper's pistol, anyhow?"

"Believe it or not, I relieved him of it, during—no, after, a shooting scrape. In which I—forgive me, Alicia!—was again, quite accidentally, I assure you, involved. And during which I didn't fire a shot, even though I was armed and could easily have eliminated Harper. A most regrettable omission I mean to remedy the very next time I meet that bastard!"

"Jim, the fire-eater!" Tim said. "Who would of thunk it!"

"*I* would," Alicia said. "I knew that Jim was something very special the first time I saw him. And if that Eiffel Tower of a girl of his had not been an utter, elongated idiot—"

"That's ancient history now, 'Licia," Peter said. "Jim, I'll bet you five bucks old Wildcat hasn't even bothered to say thank you for prying Jenny's well-used tail out of the hot seat—"

"No, but I think he means to. I've been summoned before the throne. He called me at my hotel in Washington: 'You be shore 'n come t'see me, Boy, you heah?' "

"Get back to Jenny," Peter said. "Why does Lopez Basquez think she can't be released?"

"*Yet*. He believes she needs emotional support or she'll relapse as sure as hell. One of the reasons I'm going to call on Grace. Ask her to take on Jenny's case again, up here. As well as to explain to her—if it can be explained!—about Trini . . ."

"She does not deserve explanations!" Alicia said wrathfully. "You are well rid of her, Jim!"

"Now, 'Licia—" Peter said.

"You do not believe me? Well, Jim will reach New York for this weekend, will he not? Then let him pay a call upon her—Sunday morning. Without telephoning her first!"

"'Licia," Peter said quietly, "just what the hell do you think you're doing? I'm sorry I ever told you that!"

"Told her what, Peter?" Jim said.

"Something I have no intention of repeating to you, Jim-Boy. The only intention I'm seriously entertaining right now is indulging in a little plain and fancy wife beating. Jesus! I suppose that as a Costa Verdian *and* a Villalonga, dirty fighting comes naturally to you, 'Licia. But right now, as the guy you got married to of your own free will, I'd like to know what the hell you're fighting for? Jim?"

"Unfortunately, no, Peter," Alicia said mischievously. "I am fighting for—my niece. That she be happy, finally. That she has—a chance. Jim will make her—a wonderful husband. And a marvelous father for her children. You Gringo-Pigs quite often do. I know that from my own experience with you, *mi Amor*. And if my methods displease you, I am sorry. But then, they always have, haven't they?"

"Like the time you deliberately sacrificed your own mother for my sake?" Peter said grimly.

"Or for Padre Pío's. Do not be excessively vain, Peter!"

"Oh, Lord! 'Licia—and Peter, if the two of you don't quit it, I'm going to leave. Right now. Even if I have to walk," Jim said.

"You may come stay with us!" Marisol laughed. "Leave them to have another terrible fight. They haven't had one in a long time. The proof of that is that my namesake, little Mari, is all of six years old . . .."

"Oh, no!" Alicia laughed. "You will stay here with us, Jim! And Peter and I will make peace and *not* fight, I assure you! Heaven forbid that we should!"

"Why—heaven forbid, Alicia?" Jim said.

Alicia smiled at Peter—with tender mockery, Jim thought.

"Because *every* time we fight, I end up with *another* baby!" she said.

That Sunday morning, exactly at eleven o'clock, without phoning first, Jim Rush paid a call on Grace Nivens. And he was aided in his distinctly underhanded and ungentlemanly intention to find out exactly what Alicia had been implying by the fact that, on Sundays, the condominium's imposing doorman—who looked like a motion picture version of a Field-Marshal, instead of the ratty, skinny, undersized little beggars real Field-Marshals often are—had the day off. So Jim got all the way to Grace's door, and rang the bell, without being intercepted.

Grace, herself, answered it. Stood there, staring at him. She had on a tawny silk negligee. Under which, he could clearly see, was only Grace. Her hair was tousled. Her lips were—swollen. Even slightly—bruised. She smelled of good bath salts and cologne, and cleanness, of course, being Grace. But also of—of herself. A good, big, fine, exciting smell of well used—and having damned well enjoyed it! he thought miserably—female. Her partner—her bedmate—was surely still in the apartment, he realized.

"Jim!" she whispered. "Of all the abysmally filthy tricks! Why didn't you call me, first?"

"Say—I was just checking. And now that I have—"

"Now that you have— *what,* Jim?" she said, bitterly. There were, he was startled to note, tears of pure exasperation in her eyes.

"Nothing. But that was all there ever was between us, wasn't it?"

He put out his hand to her. Smiled a slow, and secret, smile.

Said: "Good-bye, Grace."

Turned—and left her there. Forever, this time.

Or so he thought, not realizing that 'Forever' is a semantic irrelevance.

It only acquires meaning once you're dead.

CHAPTER

24

When Jim Rush deplaned at Bahía Linda Airport after an uneventful flight down from New York, he found the Embassy limousine, and his new chauffeur Wili (for Guillermo) Núñez Lobato, waiting for him. Like his predecessor, Roberto Henriques, Wili was an officer—a Captain, Jim believed—in the Costa Verdian Secret Services. But there was one great difference between *Cápitan* Núñez and the late *Teniente Colonel* Henriques: Guillermo Núñez, Tomás assured Jim, was more than a little disaffected with the current Government, and under Tomás' skillful goading, was becoming more so every day.

That the car and chauffeur were there waiting was not at all surprising: Jim had gone to a good bit of trouble to make sure they would be. First, he had phoned Martha from New York, announcing his expected time of arrival; one hour out from Ciudad Villalonga, he had requested—through the stewardess—the plane's radio operator to confirm it to the Tower, and ask the Air Traffic Control officials to reconfirm his arrival time to the Embassy by telephone.

All of which, he realized wryly, had made the pilots, flight engineer, and inflight personnel more than a little nervous; but it also served to avert the very danger they all feared: that there might be one more crazy kid hidden near the airport with a first class Chinese-made rocket launcher ready to blast any aircraft bearing Ambassador James Randolph Rush out of the sky, necessarily and inevitably taking *them* along with it when it went. Because the Tower, Jim knew perfectly well, was going to call National Security's Headquarters *first,* before even phoning the Embassy as he had requested. It was a comfort to know that every centimeter beyond *Aeropuerto Bahía Linda*'s borders was going to be swarming with armed policemen. And a vast satisfaction to realize he had procured that kind of protection for himself, his fellow passengers, and the crew of the aircraft without having had to display the prudence—or the cowardice!—of asking for it.

"Where to, Your Excellency?" Wili asked him with a knowing grin as soon as he strode through the air terminal's door. "The Embassy, the residence, or—"

"To *Or,* of course," Jim shot back at him. "I'll resume being an Ambassador tomorrow, Wili! This afternoon, and tonight, I reserve the right to function as a human being. Come on. Get this heap moving, will you?"

"Sir," Wili said as they drove off, "you got back just in time. Your—people at your apartment in Silver Door are worried sick. Especially Rosa, Sir. She—your little *Protegia,* I mean—if you will pardon the expression—hasn't eaten a mouthful since you left. Rosa says that if you don't come back soon, she'll die . . ."

"Good God!" Jim said. "Speed this thing up, will you, Wili! Break a few laws. I'll pay the fines . . ."

Pepe opened the door to the apartment. His heavy jowled face that gave him the look of a mournful bloodhound much of the time split instantly into an enormous grin.

"To God the thanks!" he said fervently. "How happy I am to see you, Mr. Ambassador! *La Niña—la* Trini, she—"

"Has been an exceedingly naughty child, I'm told. Where is she, Pepe?"

"In bed, Sir. By now she is too weak to get up. She has eaten *nothing* since you left. She cries all day long; she—"

"I," Jim said grimly, "am going to paddle her little bottom for her!"

"Unfortunately, Sir," Pepe said happily, "under the given circumstances, you can't. But you should make a note of it for the future. As much as we—Cecilia and I, Sir—love *la* Trini, this time she has been impossible!"

Jim strode towards the bedroom. But before he got there, Pepe touched his arm.

"Sir," he said, "I forgot. She—*la* Trini—has a visitor. A young fellow, Sir. Not—very good looking. Alvaro Ferrero he said he was called. He also said that he was a friend of yours. And that you, personally, once saved his life . . ."

"That last is true. That he's a friend of mine is somewhat doubtful,

Pepe. Good Lord! You haven't left him alone with Trini, have you? He once swore to kill her!"

"No, Sir. Cecilia's in there, too. And Rosa. And he especially asked to see *la* Trini. Said he wished to ask her pardon for a thing of which he'd accused her wrongly . . . My God! If it was a trick to get to her, I'll break every bone in his skinny body!"

"Wait," Jim said quietly; "here by the door, Pepe. I'll call you if I need you . . ."

But, he saw at once, he wasn't going to need Pepe's expert brutality. Alvaro sat very quietly by the bed, holding one of Trini's hands in both of his. Trini was crying. Alvaro's eyes were suspiciously moist, too. Cecilia was wiping hers. But Rosa sat there like an ancient Tluscolan idol, carved of brown granite. Possibly she was at least breathing; but even of that one couldn't really be sure, Jim thought.

"Lord!" he said in Spanish. "What this place needs is flood control!"

At once Trini flopped over. Tore at the covers, tried desperately to get out of bed.

"Hold her, Rosa!" Jim said.

Rosa held her.

"Let me go!" Trini shrieked. "Let me go, thou ugly old Witch! He hath come! My Life has come back to—and thou—"

Jim bent over the bed, kissed her. Said, reproachfully:

"Trini, you're the limit. What's this I hear about your not eating?"

"She hasn't, Sir!" Cecilia said. "Not even a crumb of bread. Nothing. I told her you would be displeased, but—"

"I was trying to get her to eat something when you came in, *Don* Jaime," Alvaro said; "but not very successfully, much do I fear . . ."

"*Hola,* Son," Jim said; "I'm surprised to see you here. Rosa, you don't mean to tell me that even you couldn't—"

"Broths," Rosa said; "soups. By squeezing her cheeks so she had to open her silly mouth. But she vomited them up again most of the time. She is one crazy little watering pot, this one!"

"Trini," Jim said, "now I *am* angry with you. Truly."

"Ohhhhhhhh!" Trini wailed. "Now I *will* die! I *will*! For if thou dost not love me, I—"

"Didn't say that. I said I was angry. And I am. For what reason do you wish to starve yourself to death? And what right have you to take Trinita with you? Answer me that, *Tonta*!"

She caught his hand, clawed it upward against her cheek. Rubbed her face against it, purring like a cat. Smiled up at him, murmured:

"I love thee, *Don* Jaime! Oh, how I love thee!"

"Fine way you've got of showing it! You'd widow me—again. Rob me of my daughter. That kind of love I can do without, Trini!"

324

"*Now* I will eat, *Don* Jaime! I will eat like a pig! For thou hast come, so now I can. Before, I could not. Truly I could not. Food choked me. I'd think: He is up there in his own country, far way, among all the tall, long-legged, lovely blonde ones, so he will forget me. He will say: 'Why should I go back to such a one? Who is little and skinny—except for her belly which is both enormous and enormously ugly! Who hath slanted eyes like a Chinese and skin as black as a *Negrita's* and—' "

"*¡Hola, Negrita!*" he said and kissed her. Turned to Rosa, said:

"Bring her some soup. Hot. And after that some cold chicken and a salad and some fresh fruit. A glass of milk, not wine. And bring *me* something to beat her with if she does not eat it."

He sat down in the chair Cecilia had vacated. Turned to Alvaro. Said with ceremonious irony:

"My house is honored! But you'd better explain what you came for, Son."

"To apologize to Trini, *Don* Jaime," Alvaro said slowly. "To ask her forgiveness. You see—I found out—the truth. I was sent here to town on a mission. To contact a friend of yours. One—Carlos. Understand?"

"Yes. Communication problems, right? You've come to the right man. He's the best."

"Yes. He is. And he has agreed to help our group. But I had been in the jungle—many months. And a man—" he shrugged ruefully, "has certain—needs . . ."

"So you went to the Blue Moon, eh, Son?" Jim said.

"Yes. I have no shame of it, *Don* Jaime! Under my circumstances, it is the simplest way. I have not the time for a prolonged courtship, you know . . ."

"Go on, Son," Jim said.

"And she—the one I selected—*refused* me. Because of my attempt upon the life of *la* Trini, of which, it seems, they *all* know. She called me imbecile, murderous swine, and a few other endearments of the same general style. Told me what really happened. That of the Nazi doctor. I have killed him, *Don* Jaime! I have killed him very slowly and very well. I have given him a miserable death!"

"Son," Jim said sorrowfully, "you don't expect me to approve of *that,* do you?"

"No. But you, *Don* Jaime, let Joe Harper go when you had him *fried.* And look at the results of your clemency to Trini!"

"I didn't mean that," Jim said. "Killing is—sometimes justified. Torture, *never.*"

"Perhaps. But in any event, *la* Trini has pardoned me. And she and I—and you, *Don* Jaime, if you will it—can be friends . . ."

"I will it," Jim said; "but don't go around messing people up again, please, Alvaro. When first I met you, I thought how fine it would be to have a son like you, so upright, and so brave, but now—"

"But now, thou hast!" Trini laughed. "Here he is!" She patted her swollen belly. Called out, gaily:

"Jaimito, art thou there? Inside me, curled up and sleeping, lazy one? Wake up; 'tis time thou met thy Papa!"

"That," Jim said solemnly, "is *not* Jaimito. That's Trinita. So help me, Trini, if it's a boy, I'm going to put him back to *cook* a little longer!"

"To boil off his poor little *thing*—and his two tiny *testiculos?* Oh no, *Don* Jaime! Thou canst not do such a thing to my Jaimito!"

"Well, maybe not," Jim said. "Have to think about it, won't we?" He turned back to Alvaro. Said, sternly:

"Promise me, Alvaro! This torture is demeaning to a man."

"I—promise, *Don* Jaime," Alvaro said.

"Then we are friends," Jim said, "and here's my hand upon it."

"And mine," Alvaro said. "Know this—you, *Don* Jaime and Trini, and all your sons, are all safe from my side—forever. There will be no more attempts upon your life. And if you need anything accomplished, such as the elimination of Joe Harper, say . . ."

"No," Jim said. "Joe—is as much *my* business, as Karl Obermüller was yours, Alvaro. If we should meet again, I'll take care of him. It is not a thing I should like to pass along to another."

"You—are small. And—seemingly—frail. But I think you are— much man, *Don* Jaime!"

"Much, no. But, perhaps enough for what I *have* to do," Jim said. "Well, Alvaro? What now?"

Alvaro smiled. Said:

"Now—I go!"

When Jim woke up that next morning, he was so tired that he picked up the telephone and called for Wili to come get him in the Mercedes. Ordinarily he would have driven to the Embassy in the Porsche which, along with Trini's little Volkswagen, he kept in the garage reserved for the owners of the condominium apartments in the basement of the building itself.

The reason he was so tired was because Trini had kept him awake until four o'clock in the morning. Shortly after he had gone to bed—in the second bedroom where he had slept whenever he came to the apartment ever since they had become sure that Trini was indeed pregnant— she appeared, climbed into bed with him, and proceeded to hug, kiss, pinch, and tickle him all the time, demanding that he tell her "a thing," which elongated and multiplied itself into hundreds of "things," mostly the details of his trip to the States, until the sky was greying into morning.

He told her all he could, editing out only those things knowledge of which might be dangerous to her, and at least two items he knew positively would make her unhappy. These were the fact that he had stayed with Peter and "that very bitchy one!" her Aunt Alicia, and his brief, sad visit to Grace. Child though she was, Trini was also all woman, and what was worse, all *Latin* woman, than which there is no more possessive and jealous breed of females on the face of the earth. Which, he soon saw, was precisely where all those "things" he had to tell her were leading. So, when she had got there, finally, saying slowly, sadly, almost with bated breath:

"*Don*—Jaime—tell me—a thing—"

He said: "*Another* thing, Trini? Good Lord!"

"Just one. A little, little thing." She said this in the English he had been teaching her with the aid of a tape recorder, and prerecorded Lingua-Phone language tapes, so it came out something like, "Joost wan. A leeetle, leeetle theeeeng—" which was so charming he had to laugh.

"All right," he said. "What thing, this time, Trini?"

"Wert—faithful—to me? Or didst—deceive me—with a blondie one?"

He said solemnly:

"Well—it's been a long time, what with Trinita occupying all your attention, so it seemed to me that tossing a grey hair or two into the air wouldn't hurt . . ."

The expression he used was another of those things that only people who *really* speak Spanish say: "It has no more importance than a grey hair tossed into the air!" "*¡No tiene más importancia que una cana tirado en aire!*" "It" being, of course, a brief indulgence, when away from home, in a little refreshing and monotony-breaking adultery.

And then he saw that teasing her *that* way, joking about *that* subject, had been a very bad idea indeed. Instantly she turned him loose. Sat up. Began to get, slowly and ponderously—she was *very* great with child by now—out of bed.

He caught her. Held her. Said:

"And just where do you think you're going, young woman?"

"To the kitchen," she whispered, "to get a knife. To—cut my throat with, *Don* Jaime!"

"Trini," he said seriously, "you'd kill—Trinita, too; remember."

She stared at him. The tears on her dark face were diamonds: blue-white and glittering.

"A girl-child *needs* the love of her father, *Don* Jaime. I know. I had it not. Only his—lust. And Trinita will be very like me. Since thou dost not—love me any longer, how canst thou love—*her?* And without thy love, we—she and *I*—are far better dead!"

He held her by both shoulders. Looked into her eyes. Said:

"I love you, Trini. With all my heart. Without you, I should die."

"Then—then why didst thou—?" she wailed.

"I didn't, *Tonta*! I was plaguing you. Teasing. Seeing how you'd react."

"Not even a beautiful blondie one like *la* Judith Lovell?"

'Peter's old girl friend,' Jim remembered suddenly. There had been a rerun of a series of her pictures on TV recently. There frequently were Judith Lovell pictures shown in Costa Verde where that actress' popularity remained remarkably high even some thirteen years after her tragic death. 'Possibly,' he mused, 'because she died here. Killed by Zopocomapetl, itself. The 1963 eruption. Funny. Peter *never* talks about that. I'll have to visit that mountain chapel where the Indians keep her body. Transformed by the volcanic ash into a statue like the ones found at Herculaneum-Pompeii. And worship her—in their macabre fashion—as a Saint. Life's ultimate irony. *The* biggest whore Hollywood ever turned out ends up as an inspiration towards piety! Lord I—'

"Ohhhhhhhhhhhhhhhhhhhh!" Trini wailed. "Thou canst not deny it! Thou canst not—"

"Trini—" he said wearily, "I have touched no other woman since I have known you." 'And not for a hell of a time *before!*' he thought with wry self-mockery. "So stop this nonsense, will you? Lie back down. But shut up, and go to sleep damnit! So you will look pretty tonight. Because tonight's *very* special. Do you know why?"

"No, *Don* Jaime. Why?" she whispered.

"Because tonight we get married, and you and I—"

"Oh, *Don* Jaime, no! It will only spoil thy life! Later on, when we go to thy country, we—"

"Later, *¡mierdas!*" he said. "*Tonight.* Trinita is going to be *born* in wedlock. Baptized in the cathedral. I will not permit her to be born a *bastard*, Trini!"

"*Don* Jaime—" she wept, "thou—thou—"

"What, Trini?"

"Art an Angel! And a Saint! And I love thee! And Trinita will adore thee! And—"

"So forth and so on. For the rest of the morning if I let you. So stop it! Shut up! Close thy chirping beak of a crazy little bird. Go to sleep like a nice little overstuffed rag doll, will you?" he said.

The first thing he did when he was ushered into the presence of Father Pío at the Episcopal Palace was to present His Grace, the Archbishop, with his personal check for fifty thousand dollars to be used for the remodeling and enlargement of the orphanage that Padre Pío sponsored. The reason he could afford so much was very simple: It was the exact sum Ed Crowley had literally forced him to take as a reward for clearing Jenny of the charge of having killed poor, Black—and additionally!—homosexual Ronald Spearman. He hadn't wanted to take the money. He'd saved Jenny from at least a long prison term by a pure fluke in which the predominating element had been luck, with all the outrageous irony that implied. And it was only this morning, when thinking of how to approach the subject of procuring through the Archbishop a young and—he hoped!—liberal priest to perform the ceremony, that it had come to him what to do with the money the old pirate of an oilman had given him. For he, Jim, had no especial love for money, as such. And this money seemed to him tainted enough to damn him.

"I thank you, Son Jim," Padre Pío wheezed. "But wait a minute, take back your check—"

"But, Father! I—"

"Oh, I'm going to take it, Son Jim! But before the *press*. With photographers present. So sterling an example will breed emulation. And I— as you see, my Son—am a most worldly old scoundrel for a fact! Especially when it comes to prying from the selfish rich a part of their ill-gotten gains for the benefit of God's poor!"

"But, Father, as I told you, this money comes from—"

"*Don* Eduardo Crowley. *¡Mierda!*" the Archbishop said. Then seeing the expression of shock on Jim's face, he laughed merrily. "And a vulgar old man, upon occasion!" he chuckled. "Especially when people talk arrant nonsense to me. I *know* Don Eduardo. He is a crook, a tightwad, a miser, and a Green Old Man who only spends money on whores. Speaking of which, I have been told that *you* are keeping one, Son Jim. A forlornly pretty child named Trinidad. Is this true?"

"Yes, Father. It is. And that's the second thing I came to see you about."

"Good. Come into my chapel. Into the Confessional. I will hear your confession, and absolve you. But I warn you from the outset you must get rid of her. I will not tolerate your living in sin, Son Jim!"

Jim stared at the old man. Grinned. Said:

"I'll be damned if I will, Father!"

Padre Pío whirled upon him like an angry old lion. Then he saw how peaceful Jim's face was, how serene. So he said evenly, softly:

"Why not, Son Jim?"

"Father, she's as big as a house. With my child."

The old priest stared at him.

"You seem proud of your sin, Son Jim!" he roared.

"I *am* proud of it, Father," Jim laughed. "At my age, making a new Christian is a thing a man has a right to be proud of. Which is the second reason I came. Would you send us a priest—a wise and tolerant priest—to our place—to marry us, Father?"

The lionlike glare in those old eyes softened.

"Son Jim, are you being—wise?" the Archbishop said slowly, thoughtfully, even—sadly. "You are—an Ambassador. From the world's richest and most powerful country. While she—"

"I am a man, Father. She is a woman. Whom *I* have got with child. Who is going to be a mother. And of *my* son or *my* daughter. I am not trying to be wise. I am trying to be—decent, Father. As I understand decency. Even—by my lights, and confessing openly that *all* religions, including *ours,* Father, seem to me childish, superstitious nonsense—a Christian. The Christian I was—brought up as. That my mother wanted me to be. Well, Father—?"

"Son, thou hast rebuked me—and I deserved it. But I will *not* send thee a priest—"

"Oh!" Jim said. "Father, you *know* there's no such thing as civil marriage in Costa Verde! You'd condemn my child to bastardy because—"

"Because of nothing. I did not say that. I said I will not send a priest. And I will not. I'll come myself. Perform the ceremony in person. Where do you live? Give me your address. And at what time shall I come over?"

"Father," Jim whispered, "now I know why all the world calls you blessed!"

"Blessed old scoundrel!" Padre Pío laughed. "Now come on! You still must confess and be shriven—or I can't marry you. And give me that address so I can send my Confessor over now to hear hers. You are a Catholic, aren't you?"

"I am—nothing. Dirt. Offal," Jim whispered. "Say—I was."

"Ha! Think you that God ever lets go of a man, Son Jim? Enough of nonsense. Come on!"

Just before he got to the Embassy, just outside the gates, in fact, Jim saw his secretary, Martha Clyde, talking to a man, and signaled to Wili to stop the car. What attracted his attention to what was an occurrence of absolutely no importance at all (Martha was far from ugly, and had, naturally, as a widow or a divorcée—he didn't know which, and cared even less—a perfect right to have all the suitors she wanted to) was the expression of rapt adoration on Martha's face. Then he looked at the man, and his breath stopped from pure astonishment. Martha Clyde, who had been shocked by his romance with a girl having some remote, far removed Black ancestry, was gazing with adoration at a man the color of triple-dipped midnight!

Then he saw that the man was not a Black by race, but only by skin color. 'One of the things that make racists seem such fools!' he snorted. 'That chap's—an Indian. Martha's Professor of Yoga, surely. And of the purest, in fact the original, Caucasian strain. Only he's black. Jet black. Blue-black. Where *have* I seen that face before? Let me see—let me see . . ."

But he couldn't remember where he had seen that strikingly handsome face before—a Brahmin god of ebony carved—so he sighed, said:

"Carry on, Wili. Time's a wasting . . ."

Once at his desk, he called young Schuyler in, said casually:

"You and your fair lady got anything special on for tonight?"

"Me and old *Culo Lindo*?" Van grinned. "By the way, Sir, I told her you called her that. She was delighted. I swear she tries to stick it out another inch or two these days . . ."

"Petra," Jim said solemnly, "has *the* most beautiful fundament in human history. Never let her wear a *Tanga* on the beach, Van, or you'll start a riot. Come on, Son—have you?"

"Nothing that can't be canceled, Sir. That new film at the Bijou, that's all. What's up?"

"A wedding. Mine and Trini's. Tonight. You're invited. Hell, you've got to be there. I need witnesses."

"Good Lord! Sir, I'm delighted! You're doing the right thing. Little Trini is so sweet and—wait 'til I tell Petra! She's going to flood the house, crying. She *adores* Trini, you know. Funny. All the girls do. And, Sir—*nobody* holds her—her past against her. She was—forced into that life . . ."

"I know. Now get out of here. And go call Petra. Call her *now*. You're a new husband so you don't know it takes a woman at least five hours to get ready for a wedding . . ."

After Van had gone, Jim sat there, staring at the phone. He was debating whether or not to invite Vince and Paloma Gomez. As far as Paloma was concerned, he had no hesitation at all, but Vince? About many things Vicente Gomez was a rockribbed conservative. Then he decided he *had* to. That Paloma would never forgive him if he didn't. Vince would just have to get over it, that was all. So he called him.

"¡*Viva la idiotez!*" "Long live idiocy!" Vicente Gomez said.

He also called Tomás and invited him and his Laura. Then, upon impulse, Carlos Suarez, the Communist leader and electronics expert.

'All the *best* people,' he thought; 'the people whom I *like*. A pity Tim and Peter and their wives can't be there. Hell!' he added happily. 'I'll have Van film the whole ceremony and tape it, too! Send them dupes. One for the books: The Middle-Aged Ambassador and his Grossly Pregnant Bride united in Holy Wedlock by His Grace, the Archbishop, no less! Jesus—another thing. I'd better call *Les Ambassadeurs* and see if their chef will consent to cater us a banquet and—'

He threw back his head and laughed aloud.

"What a wedding night *I'm* going to have! Me and my bride with a meter and a half of pregnant belly between us, getting in the way!"

The wedding went off swimmingly, the metaphor, cliché, being an understatement, if anything, considering the number of tears shed by all the women present, especially by Paloma San Ginés de Gomez, who outcried them all. And it was—punctuated? distinguished? upset? given greater verve?—all those qualifications applied, though none of them completely, Jim thought—by the presence of two unexpected and uninvited guests.

The first was one of those smooth, neatly shaggy, easy-going, ugly-handsome, casually controlled young men who are the type of the new Anglo Saxon elite. Perfectly exchangeable between New York and London; between the campuses of Oxford and Harvard. Not even by his clothes—a marvel of artful artlessness; hours spent by craftsmen tailors in the avoidance of the adverb "too"—could one distinguish his national origins. Only when he opened his mouth, and speech purred out, sparkling with supressed laughter, cultured, cultivated, precise New England American, did Jim become sure that Avery Parks was a fellow countryman.

Van Schuyler brought him, presuming—'A damned sight too much!' Jim thought acridly—upon his friendship with his boss, introducing him as: "My friend Avery Parks, one of Wildcat Ed Crowley's galley slaves. Higher echelon, though. One of the Sorcerers. Makes peanut butter, and girls' lacy scanties, out of that black gook that Ed and Company drill down to Mao-land for. Ave's at loose ends tonight, so I brought him along. Stern warning department; object lesson in the penalties for horizontal sin!"

"Translation?" Jim said to Avery Parks.

"In ordinary common-sense English, which 'Blythe Spirit' Van never talks, I'm an industrial chemist, Mr. Ambassador," Parks said. "And thanks for tolerating my presence here upon this private—this very private occasion. Ordinarily, I'd have refused to come along, but the truth is that I've been begging an introduction to you, Sir, out of Van for weeks—"

"Why?" Jim said.

"Couldn't we leave the whys 'til tomorrow, or the day after—or even next week, as you like—in your office? I'd hate putting a damper upon the festivities. And what I have to discuss with you—just might . . ."

Jim studied the young man. Decided almost instantly that he liked him very much. Part of this lay in the fact that both Grace and Trini had sharply reduced his own inferiority feelings; he no longer envied tall, handsome, self-possessed young men. By that same token, he had become free to like or dislike them as people. He considered it a stroke of luck that the first two male members of the younger generation with whom he had been thrown into contact were both extremely likable young men.

"Tomorrow, Avery. Eleven thirty, say. I'm not going anywhere. As you can see, the honeymoon's definitely over!" he said.

"Penalty for jumping the gun, Sir!" Avery said cheerfully. "Though I must say, who could blame you? In this case, any man who could and didn't should legally and medically be certified dead!"

"Thanks, Son," Jim said. He was thinking how little the expression "to jump the gun" with its implication of unseemly haste, actually applied, recalling how complicated the beginnings of his relationship with Trini had really been, how many aching months had passed before love—in its physical manifestations—had been possible between them. But he didn't say that. In fact, he didn't say anything, because, at that precise instant, Pepe, the butler, came barging into the grand salon with his mouth half open, evidently trying to pronounce words that would not come out, and the expression on his heavy face remarkably resembling that of a pole-axed steer the instant before it comes crashing down to earth.

Whatever it was that Pepe was trying to say never got said, for immediately behind him came the object of his wonder and astonishment, become, in that moment, the common feelings of all the participants and guests at Jim's highly unconventional wedding. For, beautifully coiffed, dressed, groomed, and wearing a most enchanting expression of self-congratulatory pleasure at her own daring, behind the majordomo came none other than Luisa Montenegro de García, wife of His Excellency the Glorious Leader, General of the Armies, and Head of State of the Republic of Costa Verde.

It was Paloma Gomez who recovered first.

"Why, Luisa!" she cried. "You're not the Eighth Wonder of the World; you're the Ninth!"

Jim came forward, bowed over the Most Illustrious and Most Distinguished Lady's hand.

"My house is honored," he murmured.

"Do forgive me, *Don* Jaime!" Luisa laughed. "But I literally *had* to come. When Paloma phoned and told me about it, I started getting dressed as soon as I'd hung up the phone. An occasion like this one is more than *female* strength should be expected to bear! Paloma, you're *Madrina,* aren't you? A pity. *I* should have liked to have been . . ."

"I concede you the honor, Luisa!" Paloma said at once. "I'm sure that *Don* Jaime and his bride will be most pleased to have you as their Matron of Honor. But I *won't* give up being Godmother of the child. Not even you can make me do that, Luisa!"

"I wouldn't think of it," Luisa García said. "But I'll be Godmother of the second child. Agreed, *Don* Jaime?"

"Agreed," Jim said at once. He looked around for Trini. Found her. Petra, on one side, and Laura, Tomás' wife, on the other were holding her up. Clearly, she had been on the point of fainting, or actually had, and was now coming out of it, all of which Luisa García saw.

At once she swooped down upon poor Trini, swept her into her arms and kissed her tenderly. Then the two of them were there in the center of the room—for all the others fell back as perfectly as a well choreographed ballet, and left them alone—holding each other and crying.

And *that* was a little too much for Van Schuyler's self-control. His Canon F 1 B swept up and level, his strobe made blue-white lightnings.

'Oh, Jesus! That ties it!' Jim thought.

But Luisa Garcia laughed happily.

"Young man, I want a copy of that photo!" she said. "An enlargement. As big as you can make it!"

"I shall be happy to send you one, Gracious Lady," Van murmured.

After that, of course, Jim and Trini's wedding became—and made, though each of the guests, including the wife of the Head of the State solemnly swore to keep it a secret, as for obvious reasons, chiefly Jim's official position, and Trini's horrendous past, it had to be kept—history.

Only, as in the Chinese curse, it transpired in interesting times . . .

CHAPTER

25

*F*or, in the space of a single morning—his first at the office after his return from the States—Peter Reynolds called him from Boston; Perry Winkler, the Embassy's Consular Officer who more or less kept watch over all United States citizens temporarily or permanently residing in Costa Verde, came in to complain bitterly about the behavior of one such citizen, and ask his advice about handling the problem; he received an informal note from His Excellency, the Head of the State, asking him to drop by the García Residence in Golden Door for an interesting *private* [underscored] chat; Martha barged in to announce that the plans for the first Embassy social affair, a combination dinner, reception, and ball had been completed, that the invitations had gone out, and that *Her* Excellency, the Illustrious Wife of *His* Excellency, the Head of the State, had phoned to say that she had found him a young woman of impeccable social background, grooming, looks, culture, *et al.*, who would be delighted to serve as volunteer hostess for the occasion; Avery Parks came in as promised, and dropped his— also as promised!—bombshell; and Dr. Claudio Lopez Basquez called and dropped still another, to the effect that all was *not* well with Jenny Crowley.

Not that these many manifestations of the ancient Chinese curse: "May you live in interesting times!"—based, Jim surmised, on the un-proved collateral assumption that peace and contentment are necessarily dull—occurred in the above listed order. In fact, a good many of them happened simultaneously. For instance, he was listening to Consul Perry Winkler's bitter complaints of how one Giancarlo Marriotti, a U.S. citizen of Italian descent, after years of being a model husband and a quiet, hard-working man, had suddenly taken to drunkenness and wife beating, on the last occasion overdoing the latter—and occasionally commendable! Jim thought wryly—indoor sport to the extent that his wife, a local girl named Mariluz, had had to be hospitalized, when the phone rang with Peter's incoming call.

And because the name 'Mariluz' touched a buried chord of memory somewhere in the recesses of his mind, Jim instructed Martha to put the call on hold for a few minutes while he thrashed this problem out. And very easily, and almost at once, it came to him who had first mentioned that particular name to him. Jenny. Jenny Crowley. In reference to—a supposed affair—and of an adulterous nature, naturally!—that Joe Harper was having—correction—had had with Mariluz who was the wife of—

He said:

"This Giancarlo Marriotti—a helicopter pilot, isn't he? Works for Worldwide? Better known to all and sundry, including *me*, as Charlie?"

"Right, Sir! A plain case of a man's going crazy from jealousy. Of course, the child she gave birth to three months ago *is* awfully blond for two such dark complexioned people, but—"

Jim sat there. Wispered: "Oh, Jesus!" Then: "A boy?"

"Yes, Sir! How'd you know?"

"Private sources, Perry. A boy. A blond boy complete with a double *y* chromosome, sure as hell! Let me handle this, will you? I happen to know Charlie Marriotti. He's a good type. Just get me his address. But don't warn him. I mean to pay him an unexpected visit. Now get out of here. I've got to take this call . . ."

The voice on the phone sounded exactly like Donald Duck on a spree, backed up by a chorus of drunken dolphins. Jim switched on his Speech Scrambler, turning the indicator to 'Decode' and Peter Reynolds's voice came clear:

"Jim, I'll make this fast. Their Embassy in Washington has engineered a junket. Three Congressmen, three Senators. To visit Costa Verde. To investigate social conditions, economic stability, *et al.,* in view of the requested loan. Catch?"

"Six Wrong-Go's, eh, Peter? Types who put striptease dancers on their payrolls as secretaries? Who are screwing the whole typing pool? *That* sort?"

"Plus an occasional altar boy at the Cathedral. Up to their ears in debt. Shaky tenure. Played right, this trip could convert each of them individually before their constituents as the 'Right Honorable Mister *Big,*' the guy who solved the energy crisis by tying down Costa Verde's offshore oil for the good ole Yooo Es Ayyyy. Get it?"

"Do I! And *they'll* get 'The Treatment' in all its exquisite refinements. Unless—"

"Unless what, Boy?"

"*I* foul up the deal for both parties, Guests and Hosts. Risky business. Oh hell, I can afford to be declared *non grata,* now. Thanks, Peter. Anything else?"

"No. Yes! A suggestion. Alicia's. That you put little Trini and Package on a plane. Ship her—them—to *us.* We'll rally round, take care."

"Thank her, Peter. That's very kind. But I don't think Trini and/or the Package could stand the trip. Anyhow, that danger's lessened. I've—married her, Peter. Tell 'Licia that. And spare me both comments—and congratulations, if any. It was—necessary. To forestall the very kind of pressure you're thinking of now. And since Padre Pío officiated in person, and His Nibs' own spouse attended the ceremony, any move they could make in that direction should turn out to be a Fool's Mate, don't you think?"

"Shahmat! Checkmate! Hell of a chess player you are, Boy! Jim, I'm glad. And 'Lucia will be, too, when I tell her. Only *one* thing bugs me . . ."

"Which is?" Jim said.

"Your obvious lack of enthusiasm. 'Bye now, Boy."

"Morning-after nerves, Peter! Nothing more. Good-bye—and many, many thanks," Jim said.

"There's a Mr. Parks to see you, Sir," Martha Clyde said. "A Mr. Avery Parks. He said you were expecting him."

"I am. Send him in," Jim said.

"One moment, Sir! You wouldn't want me to have a nervous breakdown, would you? The truth is, I'm worried *sick.* First you get this note from the General—"

"Inviting me to drop in for a chat. Nothing unusual about that, Martha. He's done it before . . ."

"But in connection with Mrs. García's phoning to say she's found you a hostess for our ball? Sir—she *must* know about your—your girl friend! *Everybody* does. People are always asking me for details, and refusing to believe me when I say I don't know. And when she finds out about—about the *child,* Sir, well—"

Jim grinned at his secretary. Said, peacefully:

"Luisa García knows about the child, Martha. She called me to express her disappointment that I hadn't asked her to be its Godmother, and asked to stand for the *next* kid. How d'you like that? This baby's going to have the biggest layette in history between her and Paloma Gomez. And both of 'em are spoiling hell out of Trini, who has become their *cause célèbre* and their pet. Climate of the times, Martha. Gives them a chance to demonstrate their feminism and their liberalism. So there's nothing to worry about . . ."

"Well, if their bland assumption that you plan to go on having children by a—a colored mistress doesn't worry you, Sir, I suppose I can take it," Martha sniffed.

"Martha," Jim said gently, "I *like* Trini's color. I find it nice. Warm. Comforting. Especially after years of getting chilblains from *Gringa* palefaces with frozen posteriors. Now send me Mr. Parks in, will you?"

"Mr. Ambassador, I'd still feel better if we *knew* who your hostess was going to be," Martha persisted.

Looking at her, Jim saw that she was genuinely upset. He sighed; said:

"All right. Tell Mr. Parks to wait for five minutes. Call the General's villa. Ask to speak to Mrs. García. When you've got her, put me on . . ."

That took three minutes.

"Why my niece, Patricia, of course!" Luisa Montenegro purred. "She's a lovely child. But docile. I can control *her, Don* Jaime. Otherwise the risks would be too great!"

"*What* risks, *Doña* Luisa?" Jim said.

"Of our—that is, Paloma's and my—having engineered a small tragedy. Don't tell me you don't know that you've become the *idol* of the whole younger generation, female gender, my dear *Don* Jaime!"

"Lord!" Jim said. "I've had my leg pulled before, and by experts. But you beat them all, Distinguished Lady!"

"Not a bit of it!" Luisa laughed. "Your—somewhat unconventional romance has done you no end of good among the young and rebellious, my friend. Not to mention among the older and the frustrated! You have our so very gallant French Ambassador, Rene Coutier, chewing his fingernails down to the quicks out of envy. You see, until you arrived, *he* was our star *galán*. So I had to find you a hostess I could trust not to throw herself at your head—or, perhaps, more accurately, I could prevent from doing so. Hence, my niece, Patricia. Do be a little—distant and stern with her, will you, my dear? Don't try to impress her *too* much!"

"That's a relief!" Martha said, when he told her. "Now, shall I send Mr. Parks in?"

"Yes. No, wait! Martha, honey, are *you* taking your pill every night of the month?"

"Well, I never!" Martha gasped. "Mis–ter Rush! How dare you!"

"Doesn't call for daring," Jim laughed. "You called the matter to mind just a few minutes ago, when you were objecting to my indulging in a little quiet and cosy miscegenation. Made me remember that the type *you* were embracing just outside the Embassy gates yesterday was a dead ringer for Captain Midnight. So maybe you'd better take care!"

Martha had the good grace to smile.

"Oh, *him!*" she said. "That was just my Yoga Professor, the *Guru* Hriday Hanuman—"

"And Yoga Professors *don't?*" Jim said solemnly.

"Oh, you!" Martha said. Then she added, sweetly, "Believe it or not, Sir, I really wouldn't know!" And flounced out of there.

"Sir," Avery Parks said, "I'm going to take a chance. Van told me— that your ideas have changed. That you've become more cooperative with—necessary evils like *us*. So I'm going to level with you. I'm—Bill Carter's boy. The Narc he wanted to drop on you. Any—serious objections?"

Jim thought about that. Said:

"No, Avery, none. I've never considered the Narcotics Bureau an evil. I believe some of your methods are—mistaken. Counterproductive. But your main objectives, to stamp out the drug traffic, to make narcotics addiction a thing of the past, I agree with. In fact, I agree two hundred percent."

"Good!" Avery Parks said. "So, with your permission, I'll skip the preamble and get to the point. Harper. Joe Harper, whom you, Sir, I've been told, have good reasons to love somewhat less than dearly—"

"I can bear his absence without bursting into tears," Jim said dryly. "What about him, Avery?"

"He's still active. Still flooding our East Coast with heroin. From *here*. This country. Only since that Horse Opera Walkdown you and he staged—and you *won*—he's dropped out of sight. Sir, have you any idea at all as to where he is—and how we might go about finding him?"

Jim considered that question as well. It came to him on the spur of that same instant that while he didn't know exactly where Joe Harper was, he did have an excellent idea of the general area in which that classic example of Blond Beasthood could be found; said area being the isosceles triangle whose points were the three former Tluscolan villages—now flourishing tourist resorts—called Xilchimocha, Chizenaya, and Tarascanolla, and whose legs were the now really quite good highways connecting them. That all three still had as neighbors the three Extermination-Through-Torture Camps—the only accurate way to describe them!—that Alicia's late and unlamented brother, the Dictator

Miguel Villalonga had established, and that every subsequent strongman had seen fit to maintain, augment, and make chilling use of, had not, in this case, anything to do with the matter.

But, it came to him suddenly, with a certain excitement, a notable lift and soaring of his spirit, they might be made to have!

'Not,' he thought almost gaily, 'two birds with a single stone—but five! Or the whole damned flock! That junket now—suppose a Congressman or two got lost? Stumbled by accident upon—"

He smiled at Avery Parks. Said:

"I have an idea where Harper might be found. But the area in question is too damned big. Narrowing it down is called for. So I'd suggest that you meet me outside the Lopez Basquez Clinic at ten o'clock tonight, say, and—"

The telephone on his desk buzzed. He picked it up. Martha's voice said:

"Doctor Lopez Basquez is on four, Sir. Do you wish to speak to him now, or shall I put him on hold?"

A coincidence, of course, But somehow—eerie. He said:

"Put him through to me. Mr. Parks doesn't mind waiting a moment or two . . ."

He signaled Avery for confirmation. The Narcotics agent nodded solemnly.

"Mr. Ambassador?" a woman's voice said.

"Speaking," Jim said.

"One moment, Sir! *Don* Claudio wishes to speak to you."

He waited. Then Dr. Lopez' pleasant, well modulated voice said:

"Mr. Ambassador—we've problems. With, of course, our patient, and your friend, Miss Crowley. Could you find the time to come over here this afternoon, or tonight?"

"I was planning to. Eight thirty tonight's all right?"

"Perfectly," Dr. Lopez said. "I'll be expecting your visit, Mr. Ambassador!"

"One moment, Doctor!" Jim said sharply. "Couldn't you give me a hint, *now,* of the nature of the problem?"

"Yes. Why yes, of course. A relapse. Complete—and total. Someone smuggled—the stuff into her, Mr. Rush! I confess I'm discouraged. I'd thought I was beginning to reach her, even to learn a bit of the weird jargon she employs as a substitute for English. For, if what Jenny Crowley speaks is English, then the second language *I* was taught from earliest childhood, *isn't.* And I'd prided myself upon speaking your language well . . ."

"Not my language," Jim said cheerfully; "my language is Spanish. I started in on English at age ten. And that's too late, Doctor. Your English is perfect. Far, far better than mine. The trouble is that Jenny's generation invented their own. Aquarusian, one might call it! But an idea occurs to me. Would you object to a consultation—by mail or by telephone—from Jenny's New York psychiatrist? She—a woman physician in this case—had done wonders for our patient before . . ."

"Not at all!" Dr. Lopez said. "In fact, I'd be delighted. And if she could treat herself to a short vacation down here—a *working* vacation, Mr. Ambassador—I'd be even more delighted. For God knows I need help with *this* case!"

"So much as that I can't promise," Jim said. "But I'll phone her long distance within the hour. Tonight I'll tell you what she says . . ."

The call concluded, Jim turned back to Avery.

"Has Van briefed you on the political situation here?" he said. "I mean, in its connecting ramifications with Washington?"

"Yes," Avery said; "extensively."

"And what do *you* think we ought to do?" Jim said.

"Sir—I don't know *your* political leanings!"

"Haven't any. Politics is a pain in the gut. Or in the fundament. Right, Center, and Left, governments are run not by Angels, but by men. And men regardless of their political economic, social, and/or religious beliefs always manage to vertically fornicate everything they get their hands on. Dirtily. In various unsanitary, contorted, and painful positions. A point of view you could call cynical, except that I happen to be quite pragmatic about it. I'm for what promotes the best interests of the *people* of the area in question, while at the same time not making things excessively rough for us. Which, translated into sense, means I am quite capable of supporting *opposite* political theories in two different geographical areas. Communism, Maoist style, works in China. Not well, of course; but a couple of provable degrees better than anything else that has been tried there ever has before. For the first time in that country's long history, there are no famines. Also, there is a discipline that approaches brainwashing, but that produces a degree of civic order—most of the time—that tempts me in my more irately reactionary moments to want to apply it to the North American young! Authentic social and technological progress has been made. So, I'm for it, there. I'm against it in the States and Western Europe. Undecided for most of Asia, except for India, where it might be a good thing. About Africa, I just don't know . . ."

"And—*here*, Sir?" Avery said.

"Hell, Son, we ought to throw this country to the Reds. Or to those of a Rosy Shade, such as certain university-trained idealistic Marxists I know. We might thereby lose their oil, but it's high time we stopped depending on oil as our chief energy source anyhow. We *must* make our cars and cities run on something else. Solar electricity, say. The main objection to our permitting or even giving a mild boost to a Shocking Pink take-over in Costa Verde, is that even they wouldn't respect the commercial interests of U.S. citizens such as my ex-boss, Wildcat Ed Crowley, who have sizable sums of money invested in this country. Now that's a respectable point of view, on the surface, anyhow. Only I propose to examine it a little below the surface. You don't mind my rambling on like this, do you, Son? Talking it out sort of clarifies my own thinking . . ."

"Not at all, Sir! I'm curious to see where you're going!"

"I only hope I know. Well, protecting the commercial interests of our citizens is a legitimate obligation of ours, of course. But we ought to take a long, cool look at the facts: that generally the citizens we're protecting are very, very few, the interests in questions more often than not, temporary, short-sighted to the point of myopia, frequently only apparent, since they don't necessarily coincide with those of the United States as a nation, and certainly not with those of the people of the given area, to whom they represent a ravishment of their ecological systems almost sure to make the area uninhabitable to their grandchildren—an example of which is what Worldwide's offshore drilling has done to marine life on Costa Verde's coast, and describe that in one word: extermination. So, Son, we simply cannot, for the benefit—alleged and somewhat dubious!—of the commercial interests of some very few of our citizens, continue to be guilty of the gross political immorality of supporting all over the world governments who exist upon the basis of hideous oppression of their own citizens, and operate by means of routine torture. Lord! End of sermon. Forgive me, Son!"

"Sir—I agree. So does Van. But how could we implement it? See that the milder Socialist-type Reds came to power? Types who would be independent of both Peking and Moscow, while—"

"Generally and on a worldwide scale, I don't know. I'm not God. And I'll throw in the mildly blasphemous observation that if history is to be trusted as evidence, *He* hasn't done so great, either! But here, specifically, in this one, medium-sized, assbackwards country, you may have just given me the lever: Harper. Joe Harper. Whose kickback to the existing powers that be for their gentility in looking the other way while he produces and ships out enough heroin to turn an entire generation of young Americans—with their willing and devoted cooperation!—into the witless, drooling morons they seemingly want to be, and were maybe even born, is chiefly what's keeping García and Friends more or less operating until Ed Crowley's oil can be piped in to save their wormy hides. So, tonight we pay a call on a man who has even less reason to love Jo-Jo the Blond Ape than I do. And who's eating his guts out over the type of offense no man of Latin blood is even remotely equipped to bear, and who additionally knows—goddamnit he *has* to know it!—*exactly* where Harper's heroin lab is. My guess is that persuading him to sing an operatic aria shouldn't be too hard—"

"And the offense that will persuade him is, Sir?"

"A recently—three months ago now—born blond child in a family where the husband's of Sicilian ancestry and the wife's *Mestiza,* but more Tluscolan than Spanish. The dates fit and the original accusation was made by someone who ought to know. Now get out of here. I've work to do. Stop by Van's office and round him up for tonight. Because—God bless us one and all!—another piece of this Existentialist's/Madman's puzzle just fell into place—thanks to Doctor Lopez."

"Sir, riddles *bug* me. Would you mind?"

"Jorge. Van's protegé and star photographic pupil. He's learned the essential techniques well enough, but has been reluctant to employ them. Understandably. The risks of the effects of a second descent into hell upon once shattered nerves must be great. But Jenny Crowley's relapse might provide us with a selling point—a convincing motivation if—"

"Jorge? Oh, yes! The ex-concentration camp guard. Who became detached—and impotent, which cost him his wife!—because of what he witnessed in the Women's Detention Camp near Chizenaya. From whom Van means to get—"

"Proof. Proof enough to blast García and Company from the Seats and the Corridors of Power. Has Van told you how he means to work it?"

"Yes, Sir—and it's one sweet scheme! Jorge, clad in his old uniform, and bearing expertly faked orders, is to be sent back to his old post. At the bottom of those orders will be the forged signature of an officer high enough up in National Security to be obeyed at once, a forgery so good that the local opposition who supplied Van with the artist has been transferring money from the gentleman's bank account into his wife's lover's for months on the basis of the same forger's efforts. Thereupon, of course, a cute little willing piece they set Friend Lover up with diverts most of the cash to the group's own war chest through Friend Lover's voluntary contributions to her well being. Neat, what?"

"Good Lord!" Jim said.

"Both husband and lover are citizer Costa Verde and the world could do without, Sir! If they 'waste' each other, Van's planning to send large wreaths to their funerals . . ."

"Intelligence work is basically filthy, isn't it? But I wish Van wouldn't do this kind of thing!"

"Sir, don't get Van wrong. He only borrowed a forger. It's the local DRAP urban guerrillas who're mixing love and war. All Van's doing there is cheering 'em on. But he needed a really first class penman to implement the concentration camp deal, which seems unobjectionable any way you look at it. It's like this, Sir: Jorge will show up at the Women's Detention Camp with orders from above to *film* a torture session. Said photos, stills, and motion pictures, are to be used, the orders will state, to persuade refractory types to bow to sweet reason. Only Jorge will bring all that crushing photographic evidence back to Van. That film, those photos, intelligently used will wreck these types forever, Sir! Now if you can come up with a nice, sweet, gentlemanly, clean, honest, straightforward and aboveboard method of obtaining that kind of evidence, I'll sit here like a mouse, lost in humble admiration and listen to it. So help me I will!"

"You're right, of course," Jim sighed. "Fire has to be fought with fire—and filth with filth, I suppose. I reluctantly agree to this—attempt. Though whether I agreed or not wouldn't stop Van. My control over him is nominal, which is to say it's practically nonexistent. Oh, hell—get out of here. I'll see you two lovable choirboy types tonight, Avery!"

"Yes, Sir; we'll be there!" Avery Parks said.

When Martha had put that call through to New York, and Jim heard that crisp, controlled, well known and still, despite it all, achingly beloved voice saying:

"Yes? This is she, speaking. Who's calling, please?"

He said, very, very quietly:

"Grace—"

And she, whispering:

"Jim . . . I knew it had to be you. I really don't know anyone else down there. So—"

He said again:

"Grace—"

"Yes. Speaking. But what does this *mean,* Jim Rush? Am I being graciously pardoned—for the sin of—infidelity?"

He said, quietly:

"This call's—professional, Grace. Addressed to *Doctor* Grace Nivens, Eminent Psychiatrist. I—need your help, my dear—"

"Why?" she mocked. "Have your little Hot Tamales driven you straight up the nearest wall, Jim? I was afraid they would. You're a bit too civilized for—such primitive passions, shall we say?"

"No. Sorry to disappoint you. I'm quite all right, thank you. And the native population has treated me very well indeed. The problem's Jenny. She's relapsed, Grace. At the moment, she's stoned out of her infantile skull—again. On a supply of narcotics someone smuggled into her at the local clinic. Her shrink down here, one Doctor Lopez, is beginning to despair. I suggested a consultation with you. By mail, or phone, of course. No language problems, Grace. Dr. Lopez speaks perfect English . . ."

She said, very, very softly:

"Why by mail, or phone, Jim? Do you still object to my presence in Costa Verde so violently?"

He thought about that. About the honest answer to it: that he objected to her being within reach and touch with twenty times more violence now. That, under the given circumstances, it would not only serve for nothing, but would drive him to the very borders of insanity. Or beyond them. But he couldn't tell her that. And maybe Mark Twain was right when he said that the truth was such a precious commodity that it should be used as sparingly as possible. So he said:

"No. Not at all. The situation has calmed down. There's no real danger, now. So if Wilkenson doesn't object to—some temporary loss of your company—it's entirely up to you, my dear . . ."

"Wilkenson? Oh, you mean—George. That's—ancient history, Jim . . ."

"Then I'll amend my statement to read: If your *present* companion doesn't object, I see no reason why you shouldn't—"

"*I* do," she said bitingly.

"Which is?"

"Your *total* lack of enthusiasm for the whole idea, Jim. Incidentally—there's no present companion. There hasn't been, since last Sunday morning. The one *you* so effectively spoiled, remember? You're good at that, I must admit."

"I'm good at what?" he said.

"Spoiling people's lives by remote control. Specifically, *my* life. So now I'll repeat the question, and I want an honest answer: Do *you* object to my coming to Costa Verde to assist Dr. Lopez with Jenny's case?"

He thought about that. Said:

"No, Grace. Not at all. Are you going to?"

"I don't know. I might. And then I might not. It all depends."

"It all depends upon what, Grace?" he said.

"How *serious* the opposition is."

He said:

"I don't understand. Opposition, by definition, is a transitive. Requires an object. I should need to know who's opposing whom—and why."

"The 'whom,' the person, adversary, enemy, *rival,* being opposed: *me.* 'Who'—is, or would be—doing the opposing, you should know far better than I, Jim. The—'why'? Say that—I—just might—want you back in my life again? *How* serious would the objection to such a proposition be?"

He said, quietly:

"*Very* serious, Grace."

She said:

"Oh!" Then: "Give me Dr. Lopez' number, please. I'll call him."

He gave her the number. Said:

"That's it. Good-bye, Grace—and thank you."

"Good-bye," she whispered; then: "Jim—"

"Yes, Grace?"

"To quote *you,* on another such occasion—a very similar occasion, Jim Rush!—I'm—sorry. I'm—very, very sorry," she said.

CHAPTER

26

ook at her, Jorge!" Van Schuyler shouted. "It's *their*
fault, man! They *let* this pig of a Joe Harper operate so
that they can live off their cut of the narcotics trade until such time as
the oil revenues come through! And if we let them get that far along,
there'll be no way of getting them out, ever! Are you a *man*, or aren't
you? They cost you your *wife*, and now Jenny, whom you *say* you love,
is—"

"Van," Jim said, "you're going at this all wrong. Look at him, will
you?"

Van looked. Saw the slow tears trickling down that big, square
jawed, immensely brutal face. The young CIA man sighed.

"All right. Suppose you take over then, Sir," he said.

Jim sat there by the bed they had Jenny strapped down to—the trip
had been very bad indeed, because she'd used, from the drug supply sufficient to make witless addicts of half the population of Costa Verde
they'd found stuffed between the mattresses, LSD instead of heroin. He
stared at Jorge Gonzalez, the prison guard from the Women's Concentration Camp at Chizenaya, the man whose brutal face, whose hulking,
immensely powerful body, simply didn't match his gentle soul.

Jorge, who was now in love with Jenny Crowley—if there was any
such person under that moaning, whimpering, twisting apparatus of—
vaguely!—female flesh there on that maniac-restraining bed; if she had a

mind left, or those indefinable but very real qualities we think of as raising the female human above her Simianoid ancestors, placing her 'but
little lower than the Angels,' and crowning her with glory and honor.
Jorge who had been in love with the wife, Josefina—that sexy little
piece!—who had left him when the simple biological sexual mechanism
of erection had failed him before his soul-deep accumulation of horror at
the things he had seen done to women, and had been himself forced to
do—

'Jorge,' Jim thought, 'who ironically enough has become somewhat
less than a man because essentially that is what he is: a Man. A true
man, as opposed to a beast. So—this Freudian auto-castration. This self-
imposed—punishment. For the thing *we*, Jorge, my brother!—always
punish ourselves for implacably: cowardice. The choice was simple: to
refuse to do it. To say, "I will *not* burn, flay, shock, rape, whip, freeze,
suffocate, cut, pack with broken glass—a woman, women." To say it
aloud, knowing that your refusal is going to cost you—by their slowest,
most artistic methods!—your life. And thereby by *not* saying it, by *not*
being brave enough to accept two days, three—how long *can* they keep a
man alive who has accepted the necessity of his own death?—of total
horror, you've condemned yourself to a lifetime of torture beyond their
fiendish worst: the eternal hell of self-contempt. To which—sadly!—I
welcome thee, my brother; I who have lived there all my life; I, who
long ago became the keeper of mine own prison door!'

He said:

"Jorge—"

"Sir?" Jorge said.

"Things—always cost you in this life. Choices do. And the wrong
ones come much too high."

"I don't understand you, Sir," Jorge said.

" 'S all right. I don't understand me much of the time. Take—Jenny,
now. She wanted to keep—babyhood forever. She thought growing up
was too much of a chore. When she opened her mouth, she demanded
that somebody instantly—shove in a pacifier"—he thought, shudderingly: 'Read Joe Harper's penis!'—"or else she'd howl. Now, she's paying for that . . ."

"And I, Mr. Ambassador, what am I paying for?" Jorge said.

"You know. For being alive—when your only decent choice was to
die—"

Jorge stared at him. Whispered:

"*¡Sí, Señor!*"

"A fate you share with most of humanity. With nearly every man
alive at one time or another in his life. You share it with me, Jorge.
More with me than with some others, because both of us have failed too

many times to realize or accept the simple fact that a man can't live with his own dishonor—how sorry I am that windy frauds have cheapened that word!—and stay, or function as, a man. So I'm offering you— something valuable. Precious. Of infinite worth. A thing I wish I could offer myself. Or that someone else could offer me. Redemption. Expiation. The restoral of your self-respect. And without shouting at you, browbeating you—a tactic common to young fools like my friend Van, here . . ."

"Sir!" Van said; then, very slowly: "I'm sorry. You're right and I'm sorry. Jorge I—I apologize."

"*No hay de que,*" Jorge murmured. "Go on, *Señor Embajador.*"

"Get us proof of what goes on in those camps—and we'll end them, forever. The risks are great. You may be killed. We'll do what we can to safeguard your life. But if we fail—if you die—is what you have *now* a life? Is this dull somnambulance you exist in—living? I *know*—from my own personal experience, Friend Jorge!—that a dead *man* is much, much more—than a living *thing.* Well, Son—what do you say?"

Jorge stared at him. And something like light—a far star rising!— stood and flickered in his dull and bovine eyes.

"I—will do it, *Señor Embajador!*" he said.

The other task of persuasion was easier. They found Charlie Marriotti in a waterfront tavern, already drunk, but fortunately for their mission, not yet too drunk. Mariluz had told them which *Taberna* Charlie would probably be in, speaking to them through swollen lips, whistling the words through a still bleeding toothless gap, weeping at them through puffed and blackened eyes.

"Charlie, you're a disgrace," Jim said.

Marriotti whirled; saw who the speaker was, bowed his head.

"I know that, Mr. Ambassador," he said.

"A wife beater. A drunken sot. A blot on the whole United States colony," Jim said. "Why—Charlie?"

"You *know* why, Mr. Rush! That bastard tumbled my *wife.* Left her with his kid! And—"

"And you beat on her, and pickle your brains in alcohol. Which solves *what,* Charlie?"

Marriotti bowed his head again.

"Nothing, Mr. Rush. Only every time I see that little tow-headed bastard, I go wild and—"

"Forget you're a man. *And* a Sicilian. I spent a whole summer on your home island once, Charlie. Great traditions they've got down there . . ."

Avery Parks and Van Schuyler looked at each other. Grinned. Shook their heads in envious admiration.

"Yeah. A type hangs a pair onto your forehead—you kill him. But you've seen Joe Harper in action, Mr. Rush! You *know* what that takes! And damnit all, *you* didn't kill him either! And afterwards, he—"

"Charlie—" Jim said, "didn't all the local sufferers from diarrhea of the jawbone tell you *why* I didn't kill him? Didn't they, Charlie?"

"No. Because they didn't know why. Or couldn't understand it. They all swore you had him dead to rights and let him get away!"

"That's right. He was crippled, Charlie. Had lost his sidearm. Was bleeding like a pig. And whatever it takes—courage, manhood—or want of shame, lack of pity—you name it, Charlie, it takes to perform an execution, I haven't got. And I don't think I want it. Be—uncomfortable to live with, by my lights. If there had been—and there *wasn't,* Charlie—a gun fight between him and me, I possibly—even probably— could have killed him. But to shoot down a wounded, helpless, unarmed man calls for the kind of stomach, or the kind of testicles, I haven't got. I've regretted my clemency—or my lack of will. It cost—the girl I love—much too dearly. But I'm not ashamed of it, or of myself, the way *you* are, now . . ."

Marriotti glared at him, his eyes red-streaked, rolling, wild.

"What the hell do you want me to do, Mr. Rush?" he said. "I can't even put out a contract for the bastard! None of the local hit men will touch it, not even for a G-note, and the going rate's only fifty smackeroos down here! That big blond ape can tear a regiment apart with his bare hands. So what in the name of Jesus H. Christ and Him Crucified do you want me to *do?*"

Jim Rush smiled.

"That's very simple, Charlie. Just lead *me* to him," he said.

"But, Sir!" Charlie Marriotti said. "Mr. Rush—you—you're the Ambassador! You can't—you can't afford—"

"Do you know, have you been told, what he and his simian chums did—to my girl?"

Charlie Marriotti stared at the small, slight, tired, aging man before him. Whispered:

"Yes, Mr. Rush—I know."

"Then lead me to him," Jim Rush said.

It was, he realized, the kind of an argument that a man of Marriotti's temperament would appreciate, understand. But it wasn't the true one. It was a vast oversimplification. He had no desire to kill Joe Harper. He probably wasn't capable of killing any man, even yet. He wanted sincerely to wreck that heroin lab, put it out of action, forever. He desired Joe's removal—via a long prison term—from the scene. He hoped to achieve the downfall of García and his sick, sadistic murderers by undercutting the hidden and illegal financial structure that supported them, and to do that before they had a chance to enrich themselves—and the French armament industry!—at the American taxpayer's expense, by the floating of that nefarious loan.

All that was part of it. But deep down, and essentially, his reasons lay in the nebulous borderland between thought and feeling whose nuances he had tried to explain to Jorge Gonzalez: he wanted at long last, once and for all, and finally, to get to the place where he could like, respect, even admire, himself, say at the closing curtain, meaning it, feeling it:

"You know, Jim, all in all, you've been a pretty decent sort of a guy . . ."

Others had said that of him. Peter Reynolds, for instance. But he had never said it of himself. He knew better. He had played—hell, been!—the coward all too often; on too many occasions, he had grasped at a showy counterfeit of valor instead of the rare, real, and shining thing itself. And he was far too sophisticated to equate valor with mere physical courage; he knew that bravery was quiet, interior, secret, alone—and moral—or it was nothing at all.

And—he was getting there. In the case of Trini, anyhow, he had behaved—well, and nobly. Or wasn't it wildly and foolishly? Or weren't the four qualifying adverbs synonyms, after all? Who, under high—and empty!—heaven would, or could, ever know?

When he left Giancarlo Marriotti, Avery Parks, and Vanderbilt Schuyler, the whole thing had been arranged: Three weeks from that day Worldwide Petroleum would place a Sikorsky helicopter at the disposal of His Excellency, Ambassador James Rush, at his request, and at the Embassy's expense, for an inland flight, with a party of friends to the ancient Tluscolan-Toltec ruins at Ururchizenaya, some twelve kilometers south of the modern tourist resort bearing—in part—the same name.

It wasn't too unusual a request. A helicopter was the only feasible means of reaching the celebrated ruins. For, despite their being—on the map—within what ought to have been a leisurely four or five hours hiking distance from Chizenaya, to go to the Temples and Palaces of the Serpent Gods on foot was actually beyond the physical resources of any human being who was not an expert mountain climber and a tropical badlands explorer with at least twenty-five years experience behind him. For, to do so meant a meandering trek through all but impassable jungle, inhabited by *tigres,* as the Indians called jaguars, anacondas, boa constrictors, and pythons—one example of which, shot while leisurely digesting a full grown goat, measured a little over seven meters long—

every poisonous snake known to the Americas from the tiny coral snake to the meter and a half long fer de lance, as well as an estimated fifty or sixty unknown varieties or even species in whose proximity nobody had stayed alive long enough to classify them, plus monkeys, peccaries, tapirs, three toed sloths, two toed sloths, shrews, ocelots, anteaters, iguanas, lizards without end, millions of birds, each having colors more brilliant than the next, and a hideous screech a little more ear-shattering—and last of all, those true masters, rulers and sovereign Lords of the Jungle, the insects. The Tluscola claimed with considerable justice that no city-bred white man could survive in Costa Verde's jungles for as long as two hours, for well within that space of time the insects alone would have stripped the last shred of flesh from his bones. And when to the above horrendous—and far from complete—list of the dangers of the jungle is added the incredible numbers and varieties of poisonous *plants* which also grew there, the idea of hiking from Chizenaya to the ruins became considerably less attractive.

What changed the adjective "unattractive" into the more accurate one "impossible," however, was the fact that once past the jungle, the tourist found himself confronted with the necessity of climbing a mountain chain that towered up to more than three thousand meters, with the net result that the ruins at Ururchinzenaya remained the most unvisited tourist attraction in the Western Hemisphere, if not in all the world.

Now several Costa Verdian Governments had built roads in with a view of exploiting Ururchizenaya as the matchless tourist attraction it indisputably was. But those roads, out of economic necessity, had had to be routed around the mountains, which meant a drive of one hundred fifty kilometers to achieve an actual twelve kilometers as the crow flies. And, during the rainy season, the jungle covered, grew over, and ate up those roads in weeks. The only other feasible route for building a connecting road, that is, directly over the mountains, had been estimated by competent civil engineers as realizable only at a cost of from twenty to fifty million North American dollars per *mile,* and no Costa Verdian Government to date had had that much money to invest in the project.

The García Government, therefore, had built a helicopter landing pad in the central square of the ruins. It occasionally flew distinguished visitors in—always on helicopters borrowed or rented from Worldwide. On its agenda, once the oil money came in, was the purchase of a fleet of the rotary winged aircraft to make regular tourist flights into Ururchizenaya, and other similarly inaccessible historic and scenic spots.

So Jim Rush's request had been accepted as a matter of course. The problem—and the danger—lay in the long delay before it could be accomplished. The reason for the delay was very simple: Jim, being of a philosophical bent, put it as an axiom: It is pure, mocking, malicious chance, blind and hateful accident, that more than any other factor, determines the destiny of man. He had known that a long time. Most people know it, realize it, but refuse to accept it, wanting to keep the fond and foolish illusion that they are Masters of their Fates, Captains of their Souls. To which, Jim's snorted rejoiner was: "About as much as a cockroach is!"

He had once proved the point beyond all argument by forcing a group of friends to recount *how* they had met their respective husbands or wives. In his own case he had been invited to two parties on the same night, scheduled for the same hours. He had gone to one of them, choosing it by flipping a coin, and met—Virginia. Virginia. If he had gone to the other, he might have met—Grace, say. Or someone very like her. "Hell," he was fond of saying, "I am *me* because a Liverpool tavern wench got drunkenly amorous on stout and bitter; and because on that same occasion a London cutpurse hadn't yet been hung!"

As now: a big Sikorsky freight-carrying helicopter down with a broken connecting rod in the essential cyclic-pitch control mechanism. The replacement part had already been ordered from the States by air, but had not yet arrived, which meant next week's flights at the earliest. Thereafter, there was the necessity of both reassembling and testing the most complicated section of the most intricate—and unnatural, in the sense that the helicopter has no real counterpart in nature, while the airplane does—flying machine that human ingenuity ever dreamed up. In short: three weeks. Time and to spare for the twentieth century's truest, most implacable laws to go into operation—Murphy's: "Anything that *can* go wrong will, and at the worst possible moment!" And Finagle's: *"Things* are out to get the Race of Man!"

But there was no help for that now. At best they might not encounter any serious problems, and, anyhow, the request had been made, and granted. And thereby, it had already accomplished, over Avery's and Van's loud and vehement protests, the one thing that he, Jim Rush, insisted upon: that he go along. Share the risks. Take part, in person, in the discovery, and possible ending, of Joe Harper's empire. Because—it was necessary to him. Part of the program of rehabilitation he had worked out for himself, a program far sterner than those he had traced for Jorge Gonzalez or Giancarlo Marriotti. Perhaps too stern to be accomplished by, or even asked of, any man.

On his way home, he stopped off—as requested—at General García's villa in Golden Door. He was, he noted, ushered into "The Presence" with highly suspicious speed. And those twin birds—Vultures!—of evil omen, Pérez de la Valle and Fuentes Toralba, the Glorious Leader's secret—and disloyal—opposition, were both there.

"*Don* Jaime—*Don* Jaime!" General García said. "You're the rarest—and most troublesome!—Ambassador I've ever met. You simply don't behave as a *Gringo*'s supposed to. You have the subtlest, most Machiavellian mind I've *ever* encountered in a person of your race . . ."

"For which I apologize humbly," Jim said and sipped the excellent, smoky-tasting Scotch. "But at the same time, I thank Your Excellency for the compliment. It is indeed a great one, coming from *you*."

Both *Don* Raoul and *Don* Pablo laughed heartily at that one.

"For instance, Raoul brought me *this* yesterday morning . . ."

This, Jim saw, was a photocopy of his wedding certificate, bearing, of course both his full name and Trini's, signed by His Grace, the Archbishop, and witnessed by, among others, Paloma San Ginés de Gomez *and* Luisa Montenegro de García.

Jim smiled; said:

"I seem to recall Your Excellency's labeling my state of celibacy—lamentable, not too long ago. As for—my choice, what does it reflect but my deepest appreciation for Your Excellency's—and perhaps *Don* Raoul's—most exquisite taste?"

"Touché!" Pablo Fuentes roared.

"But you needn't have carried your appreciation to such lengths," General García said crossly. "We sent dear Trini to you—to keep you amused—even happy. But you needn't have taken the matter—so seriously, say. You believe you've got her with child? A small matter. Honor would have been well—and sufficiently—served by your acknowledging, and supporting the *creatura*. That's how it's generally done, *Don* Jaime—especially when this—young woman's past might well raise questions as to the validity of her attribution—of paternity . . ."

"Except that there is no question about it, *mi General*," Jim said quietly. "I *am* the father. I know that beyond any ghost of a doubt. I know it so well that I ask to be spared the ungrateful task of having to prove it to you, and request that you take my word as a gentleman for it. Besides which—other—factors entered in."

"Such as," Raoul Pérez de la Valle put in, "Joe Harper's abduction—and torture—of poor little Trini, thus awaking in you, *Don* Jaime, a sense of obligation towards her?"

"Well—let us say that was part of it. But more, it was the so very wise provisions in your legal code, *Don* Raoul, touching upon a husband's authority over, and the protection against undue pressure thereby provided to—the young woman who has now become my wife, *la Señora Embajadora*, and from your laws' viewpoint, anyhow, automatically a citizen of my country. Say, I saw a situation arising in which I realized I should be forced—most regretfully!—to disagree with *you*, my friends. I didn't want poor Trini made a pawn in the game—the great and terrible game!—of power. Or placed in danger, or forced to suffer, for any reason whatsoever. She has, I think, already suffered far too much!"

"All right," the General said; "fair enough. You call yourself our friend. And yet, in Washington, a short time ago, you opposed the loan we need damned badly!"

"You have been misinformed, *mi General*. I did *not* oppose it. I recommended that it be granted. But, in self-defense, in defense of the legitimate interests of my country, with certain restrictive clauses written into it."

"And these were?" Fuentes Toralba said.

"That it be paid you by installments. That representatives of my government be granted—by *you*—the right to inspect the progress of the works you *say* you wanted it for. That it be immediately cancelled if convincing evidence be brought to light of its having been diverted to— other purposes, *Don* Pablo."

"And what—exactly—did you mean by your convincing evidence? Or by other purposes?" the General growled.

Jim smiled.

"A squadron of Mirage F 1 B's, newly painted in the Costa Verdian insignia, performing acrobatics in a summer sky, would be difficult to hide, no, *mi General*? And an Otomat 'Smart' missile homing in on target in a practice run, even more so, don't you think? And I'd like to add that anything—radioactive—makes me nervous. Especially a fast breeder reactor, which *can* produce ordinary electricity, of course; but which usually produces the sort of toys even the starving Indians and the teeming Chinese have proved it can produce. Beyond the fact that no one seems to have remembered that Costa Verde's thousands and thousands of waterfalls could produce the same electricity a million times more cheaply and a trillion times more safely, I must admit that a personal prejudice enters in. I am every sorry, *mi General*, but I wouldn't trust my sainted Mother whom God has with Him in Glory with a workable atomic bomb. My mother—bless her!—had a remarkably shortfused temper. And yours, begging your pardon most humbly, *mi General*, is a damned sight worse!"

The three of them sat there staring at him, absorbing his audacious— and outrageous!—brand of diplomacy.

"Besides," he went on peacefully, "the French have made a point of being as nasty to us poor *Yanquis* over the years as only they, with their gift for displaying—sneeringly—the world's worst manners—are equipped to be. I contend that their bitter memories of their miserable performance in World War II, and their resentment at the fact that we had to save their ragged *derrières* for them one more time, are their problems, not ours. But I am left with a certain reluctance to enrich their armament industry at the direct expense of the North American taxpayer, *mi General*—which includes *my* direct expense, since I happen to be one."

"You mean, *Don* Jaime, that you don't trust *us* to build the roads, schools, pipelines, refineries, infrastructures, that we need to—"

"*Mi General,* around new jet fighters, bombs, rockets, tanks, and other such insane and criminal toys, I wouldn't trust *any* military man as far as I could throw him," Jim said.

Raoul Pérez de la Valle shook his head with genuine admiration.

"And since you are not very big, *Don* Jaime, you couldn't throw him very far, could you? Very well. You have been very honest, very clear. Therefore, so shall we be. To—return to—dear little Trini. To—your wife. To this filthy little whore you have married—"

"*Don* Raoul," Jim said quietly, "the days of duelling are over. And the custom was always barbaric. Savage. But ways could be found—to make you eat those words. Chewing very, very carefully."

"I withdraw them. I don't need to offend you that way," the Director General of Security said. "Besides you have us—checkmated, have you not? By marrying her—by making dear, dear little Trini your wife—you have effectively removed any pressure we could bring to bear—through her—upon you. Is this not so?"

"I wouldn't know," Jim said. "Is it?"

"We'll let you be the judge of that, *Don* Jaime!" the General said, his voice a whipcrack. "Go on, Raoul, give him his instructions!"

"Very well, *Don* Jaime—certain august countrymen of yours, most of them reasonably well disposed towards us, inclined to grant us this very necessary loan—and *without* the restrictions you've proposed—are going to visit us within the next week. As their Ambassador, you will, of course, have to receive them. We ask only that you confirm and even reenforce their generally favorable disposition towards us, suggest to them that granting us the loan would markedly increase the stability of this part of the world . . ."

"I agree," Jim said; "it *would*. If you would really do with it what you claim you're going to . . ."

"Oh, we will! At least in part. But our need for arms in self-defense against the Red Menace is also pressing, *Don* Jaime . . ."

"There, I don't agree. And I won't recommend that the loan be granted unless the restrictions I suggested are tied to it," Jim said bluntly.

"Very well. But if you don't—a certain New York distributor of foreign films—will receive *this* one, *Don* Jaime," Raoul Pérez de la Valle purred. "The agreement's already signed. We have—for your sake!—

been deliberately vague about the date of delivery. And since no money has of yet changed hands, we could—decide not to complete the transaction, if you choose—as it seems to us you must—to be reasonable . . ."

The lights flickered out. Somebody—Pablo Fuentes, Jim guessed, drew aside a curtain. An ordinary home movie screen was bathed in an ordinary yellowish white glow. Then the titles appeared: "The Adventures of Alicia," they spelled out in Spanish. And, below that: "Starring Trini Alvarez."

It was, Jim saw, an ordinary pornographic motion picture. It was reasonably well lighted, professionally—or almost—filmed. The images were sickeningly clear. And sickening, period. It purported to show the extravagant and extensive sexual misdeeds of *Isabela de los Cienmilamores* and her instruction of her daughter Alicia Villalonga—now Peter Reynold's wife—in all the arts of vile and animalistic carnality. Again Trini's marked resemblance to Alicia had been the reason for the pornographer's having chosen her for the title role, said pornographer having been surely a propagandist for one of the far-out Leftist groups—and an utter, perverted, filthy swine.

'When you've seen one Porn-Epic, you've seen them all,' Jim thought quietly, soberly, from the dead still eye of the whirlpool he was drowning in. 'The constant use of impossibly awkward, contorted, and probably even painful positions, since the cameraman's object is to show the male and female genitalia in juxtaposition, display the actual, clinical details of penetration in order to titilate the host of paying voyeurs, thereby being forced to shoot from angles, and to produce closeups of what, in sex for sex's own sweet sake, usually can't be seen at all. The emphasis upon oral techniques that are—the so-called experts be damned!—at least semiperversions: fellatio, cunnilingus. Sodomy. The works. And this was *before,* remember. God, how pitifully *young* she was! Fourteen. Fifteen. If that. And—it doesn't matter. It doesn't matter at all. This is *not*—Trini. Not my adorable Trini. Not—the mother of my child to be. Not—anyone at all. An image—unformed—in silver salts, colored dyes, and flickering lights. Only—

'Why am I—dying?'

He was. Of sickness. Rage. Disgust. Shame. They—these heartless, soulless bastards!—had him. He'd have to—betray the best interests of his country. Bow—as men have always bowed!—before remorseless, sickening cruelty when it rides forth in overwhelming force. Or else—he could never take Trini home with him. Or else there'd be nowhere in the world where—his daughter, surely his daughter!—would not be tortured past madness by the constant reencounters with the images of her mother's—

Abysmal   Cheap   Commercial   Shame . . .

When the lights came on again they sat there staring at him with the look of greedy and waiting vultures on their slack lipped faces. But— they'd overshot their mark. They simply did not know him.

'I,' he thought miserably, the slow, held back tears running like molten lead through his revolted guts, 'will never be able to kiss—that mouth again without wanting to throw up. You—gentlemen!—have killed something very fine. My love for Trini. My belief that expiation, redemption, renewal, rebirth, are—or were, in this one rare, haunting case—even possible. And it's not her fault. She was a child. A poor, abused, endlessly violated, pitiful child. Now she is a woman. A great woman. A glorious one. Only *I* have failed her. I haven't what it takes to—forget this, which has nothing to do with *me*—with *us*—or—forgive it . . .'

Then he remembered his proposed helicopter flight into the jungle in three weeks' time. Thought about the possibilities it entailed. He'd order Charlie Marriotti down above the path to the lab. Down to less than six feet in hovering flight on some pretext or other. Then down and out— with one of the captured guns in hand. A bad, class B movie finish. But still—a finish. For Joe Harper, too, he hoped.

He turned, looked the three of them in their faces, one by one, slowly, his own unsmiling. Said:

"Deliver it and be damned!"

Turned. Walked out of there. And the silence at his going had a strangeness about it. A—rarity. As though it partook of certain qualities of his that they, like most people, were reluctant to admit he had. For how could so small, so insignificant a man be possessed of—weight, presence, dignity? They thought: *¿Señorío, hidalguez, dignidad?* Leave it like that. The two languages are as unlike as the people who speak them. There are no real equivalents.

When he came into the flat Trini was wide awake and waiting for him. She came slowly, heavily forward to greet, to kiss him. But he turned—quite involuntarily, and with a quickly suppressed shudder— his mouth away, and then she saw his eyes.

"*Don* Jaime—" she whispered; "what passes with thee. Thou'rt—as a man—*killed,* my Love! Badly—killed! Why, *Don* Jaime? *¡Oh Dios mío!* Tell me why?"

"It's nothing. A—thing, Trini. Something that happened long ago. It will—pass . . ."

"Am *I* the cause of it, my Heart?" she said soberly. "Has it to do— with me?"

"No," he said miserably. "No. It is nothing. I—"

"You lie!" she spat. "Kill me if thou wilt; but do not lie to me! For that—is to push me aside. Diminish me—force me from thee. For if I am not *thy* woman, what am I? Nothing. A thing. So tell me of this. Do not hide it from me."

He stared at her. Decided that the only way to deal with this new/old horror was to have it out. Face it. 'If it can be faced,' he thought.

He said:

"I saw—was shown—a motion picture. You were in it, Trini. You played the starring role."

She stared at him; whispered:

"*¡Las Aventuras de Alicia, verdad?*"

"Yes," he said. "The Adventures of Alicia."

She looked at him. Searched his face, his eyes. Read what was in them. Her end. Her finish.

But she didn't cry. For once, quite horribly, she didn't cry. Instead, she did a stranger thing: Slowly, softly, eerily, she began to sing. The song consisted, it seemed to him, of one sole note, endlessly held, that spiraled around, below, above the beat. It was utterly—beautiful. And just as terrible.

Before she could finish it—if it had a finish, if music that weird, unearthly, ghostly—and lovely!—could ever have either beginning or end in the world of men, Rosa tore through the door like a wild thing, and clamped one bony hand over Trini's mouth, strangling that song into abrupt silence. Then the old woman stood there holding the pregnant girl and screaming at her in Tluscolan.

Jim said:

"That chant. That song. What *is* it, Rosa?"

Rosa stared at him. Said calmly, flatly, but with complete conviction, with granitelike certainty:

"The death song of the Tluscola. When it is—needful to die—we sing that one, *Don* Jaime. Asking of the Gods—a death. Which they always grant. They have to. The song, itself, commands them."

"And, having sung it, Trini—"

"She will die soon now, *la* Trini. Now, she will die," Rosa said.

CHAPTER

27

At four o'clock of the afternoon of the same day that
Ambassador James Randolph Rush was to give his long
awaited ball, Patricia Montenegro Aguirre, the nineteen-year-old niece
of the wife of His Excellency, the Head of the State, and, since the
deaths of her parents in one of those automobile accidents that happened
with distressing frequency to highly placed Costa Verdians suspected of
secret disloyalty to The Glorious Leader, legally the adopted daughter of
Doña Luisa and the General, was visiting the studio apartment of Antonio Orozcopal, her current boy friend. She found, suddenly, to her not
very great surprise, that she wasn't especially enjoying her visit.

"Turn me loose, Tony," she said; "let me up. This is not diverting."

Tony turned her loose. Like her, he belonged to that generation to
whom "playing it cool" is the first and foremost of the commandments.
He even called his smart little apartment, "my pad."

Patricia got up. Stretched. Walked over to the huge picture window
that looked out over the street at the level of the second story. Which,
under the given circumstances, wasn't nearly high enough.

"Don't show it to all the world," Tony said; "it's mine."

Patricia stood there, looking down into the street. She said:

"Not any more, Tony. You're a Latin Lover, y'know. A lousy Latin
Lover. With you, I never get there anymore. You can't even—bring me
around, now. I—don't arrive. Not that you ever could—properly. But

you did—at first. Once in a great while. Though it was—never any-thing—much."

Tony lit a joint. Colombian marijuana. The best.

"Can—he?" he said.

"Can who?"

"The North American Ambassador."

Patricia smiled.

"I don't know," she said. "Not—yet. I'll tell you—tomorrow."

Tony sucked on the joint, noisily.

"Want a drag?" he said.

"No. Those things ruin sex. All drugs do. And I prefer sex, Tony, darling. It's—grown up. Not oral—and infantile, like those. Though with you—even sex is—infantile, isn't it?"

Tony grinned at her.

"You taste *good,* Baby!" he said.

"You don't," Patricia said. She lifted her slim arms, sniffed at her armpits. In accord with current ideas about naturality, they were un-shaven.

"Ugh!" she said. "I stink! I stink of *you.* Not a pleasant aroma. Now I'll have to shower—here. Or else Aunt Luisa might notice. And I have to go home in a hurry or else I'll catch it from her. She phoned Geri to send my new ball dress early, since she's taking me to *Don* Jaime's place before the occasion even starts . . ."

"So—it's *Don* Jaime, now," Tony said. "Turn around, Patti-Cake."

She turned languidly, saw he was pointing his camera at her. It was an expensive single-lens reflex, all black, with no chrome plating to catch an intended victim's eye and give her—usually *her*—a chance to duck, or avoid the stolen, off-beat, unflattering candid shots Tony was always taking.

Instantly Patricia pressed one arm tight across both her breasts, lifted her right leg high with the knee bent, and her lissome thigh slanted diagonally across her pelvis so that the part of her he was chiefly aiming at—as usual—the almost excessively hirsute black triangle of her mons verneris was completely hidden.

"Aw, Patti!" he said.

"No. Put that thing down. You've taken your *last* photo of me naked, Tony."

"But Patti-Cake, you're awf'l *nice,* naked."

"I know. And I don't object to being photographed nude. I simply object to what you *do* with the photos, Tony, darling."

"And what do I do with them, Pat of My Heart?"

"Show them to all your filthy friends, and boast about what you do to me—without telling them how *badly* you do it."

He put the camera down. Shoved it under the bed. Crooned:

"Come here, Patti-Cake."

She came to him slowly, stifling a yawn with the back of her hand; said:

"No funny tricks, Tony. I don't feel like it, and there's no time, any-how . . ."

"No tricks. Turn around, Pitti-Pat. Towards the window. Away from me . . ."

"Why?" she said, indifferently.

"Just—turn around. I've—a surprise for you."

She turned.

He lunged up and bit her. Hard. Sinking his teeth into the soft white flesh of the left cheek of her buttocks, growling like a bulldog, hanging on.

"¡Mierda!" she screamed; and whirling, pounded at his shaggy head with her fists until he opened his mouth, turned her loose. She scampered to the full length mirror, turned it away from the bed towards which he'd positioned it so that their reflected images would add an extra fillip to the occasion. By changing it constantly, and contorting herself considerably, she managed to observe her lovely derrière. He'd branded her, all right. A double semicircle of teeth marks showed, already blue, and rapidly turning a deep purple.

"Why'd you do that, you miserable swine?" she yelled at him.

"So it will show. So you'll have to keep your panties on, chez Don Jaime. He's got his own putita. He doesn't need mine," Tony said.

She smiled.

"I am not your littlee whor," she murmured; "nor his—nor any-one's."

"Then what are you?" he said. "You spend more time flat on your back than standing up, my Darling Pitti-Patti-Cake."

"I grant you that. Call me—Lady Bountiful. A free—and a generous soul. And—a timid, easily controlled, blushing—docile maiden. Did you know I was docile, Tony?"

"Docile? You!" Tony hooted.

"Well, I am. My Aunt Luisa says so. That's how I got the job. For—tonight. As Don Jaime's hostess for this splendid social affair. I am, Tía Luisa says, docile. I can, she says, be trusted not to hurl myself at Don Jaime's head with a famished howl. She, she also says, can control me. She said all that on the telephone—to him. Not knowing I was listening on the upstairs extension. So, Tony, dearest, you have nothing to worry about. I am not—famished, am I? You haven't left me so, have you? And being as—docile—as I am—"

"¡Mierda!" Tony said. "C'mon, let's go shower. Together."

"No. Because if we do, you'll start something. And I want to be rested for—tonight. I have to demonstrate—my docility—to *Don* Jaime, y'know . . ."

He stared at her.

"I'm beginning to think this little, old, dried up, ugly *Gringo* interests you," he said.

"He does. Want to know why?"

"Yes. Why yes, of course."

"He took a girl off the streets. *Una Puta.* A whore. A little *fulana* who's had—hundreds of men. Who knows—*has* to know—anything you *animales y bestias* can do and with what and how. Anything—and everything, *Tonito, hijo!* And this ugly, old, dried up little *Gringo* appears and drives *her*—a girl like *that*—completely around the bend. Out of her ever loving mind. So much so that when a great big gorgeous hunk of *brutote* like Joe Harper—whom *I've* been giving the eye for over a year, hoping that he'd notice and drag me off to his lair and tear *me* apart up the middle as he probably could—"

"*¡Zorra!*" Tony said. "Bitch!"

"Right. For all the good it's ever done *you, hijito;* for all *you* could ever do about it! Where was I? Oh, yes. *Don* Jaime. Cute little old *Don* Jaime. For whom his *putita* stabs herself before she'll even let Joe Harper lay a finger on her. For whom she suffers the worst tortures anyone ever thought up. For whom, it seems, she's perfectly willing to die . . ."

She stopped, grinned at him, said, in perfect American English:

"You know what, Boy? Kind o' think I'd like to try me a little bit o' that there!"

Then, with a cheerful snort of laughter, she dived into the shower.

Some hours later, she was listening, with a bored and sullen face, to a carefully thought out, well worded lecture from her adoptive mother and actual aunt. Which was a great mistake on Luisa Montenegro de García's part. A classic one. As shrewd as she normally was, *Doña* Luisa should have realized that the surest way to get the most rebellious generation in recent history to do anything, no matter how outrageous, abysmal, vile, is to tell them not to.

"Of course *Don* Jaime *is* charming, *Sobrina mía,*" she was saying, "and in odd, unusual ways. Quite *the* most charming man I've ever met. But he's dreadfully involved with that poor little creature . . ."

"Is there a child on the way?" Patricia said bluntly. "I've heard that there is."

"Well—yes. And quite soon now. So, Patricia, *Querida, do* take care!"

"Yes, Auntie," Patricia said sweetly; "I'll do that. Do not preoccupy thyself."

She was thinking:

'So it's *that* one. *La* Trini. I've seen her a couple of times at Geri Pyle's boutique. Hmmmnnn—difficult. She's—lovely. Truly lovely. Soft, sweet—and—exotic. Face like a mask of the Tluscolan Rain Goddess. And—knocked up. *Embarazada.* Most hugely and happily and disgustingly pregnant. At *his* age that'll make him feel—jaunty. Tip top. Proud. So—drastic measures are called for. Let me see . . . Let me see . . . Oh! Jolly! What a formidable idea!'

Carefully she broke open a new pack of Chesterfields. Lit one, offered another to her aunt, already lighted. Then, turning her back with elaborate casualness, she drew the bottom row of cigarettes out of the pack, crumpled them into a ball in her slim hand, dropped them into the wastepaper basket that *Doña* Luisa used for the discarded flasks, jars, and tubes of cosmetics, empty lotion bottles, used face cleansing pads, and all the other paraphernalia of female sorcery. Patricia looked at her aunt. Then, having made sure that *Doña* Luisa, totally immersed in the feminine problem of how to remove at least ten years from her age by the skillful use of makeup, would notice absolutely *nothing* from then on, she carefully replaced the missing Chesterfields with ten perfect examples of the most potent grass, weed, pot, marijuana, call it what you will, to be found in the Western Hemisphere. Thus prepared, blithely she sat down to wait until her dear *Tía* Luisa was ready.

Fortune favors the brave. And Patricia Montenegro Aguirre was your quintessential type of *la mujer latina brava.* Those four words are the perfect proof of the essential impossibility of translation. No four English words are their equivalents. Write "the quintessential type of the brave Latin woman," and they are thereby reduced to semantic irrelevancies, nonsense. For *una latina brava* is a hard, dangerous, reckless—and enormously brave in the physical sense—woman who simply doesn't give a damn for the laws, mores, customs, of the rather restrictive societies from which she springs, nor for that matter about the dictates of His Holiness, Pope of the religion which, these days, she doesn't even pretend to give lip service to, nor, one would even venture, for those of God or the Devil. She is usually *very* beautiful. And she uses that beauty as an offensive weapon. But she is never *une femme fatale* in the old fashioned sense of the French words. She isn't because she never bothers to hide her vast contempt for the whole masculine sex. She reduced the hordes of little, potbellied, cologne-drenched posturing males, talking of the *conquistas* and boasting of their *machismo—sic semper* the defense mechanisms of this world!—to lumps of quivering and terrified jelly. She is also, because sweet reason just isn't in her, and nothing inclines her to listen to any opinion that runs counter to her own, a lively pain in the ass, and may the vulgarity be pardoned for the sake of perfect exactitude! In her pure form, as Patricia, she is very, very rare. But if one has had the privilege of meeting her, and achieves the monumental feat of surviving her, one may wear one's scars like medals, for if there is any acid—and corrosive!—test of true masculinity in this world, *la mujer latina brava* is that test. She is, finally, for any man weary of this world, the perfect suicide's weapon abed.

To repeat, fortune favors the brave. And Patricia Montenegro was *Una Mujer*—or *¡por lo menos!—Una Chica Brava*. So fortune favored her: *Doña* Luisa, out of sheer nerves likely—*Don* Jaime's ball was, after all, *the* social event of the season—got her makeup all wrong. Had to wipe it all off again, and start anew. And seeing that to make her face up to the degree of perfection that the occasion demanded was going to take her much too long, she decided to take a chance, trusting as she did *Don* Jaime completely, and hoping that her lecture to dear Patti-Cake had done some little good, and sent Patricia on ahead in a chauffeur-driven limousine so that the girl could, as *Don* Jaime's official hostess, greet his guests along with him as they arrived, as protocol demanded.

When he saw her coming up the stairs of the residence, considerably before the other guests were due to arrive, Jim Rush was struck to the core of aching bitterness in his heart by the girl's serene loveliness.

'Here is—innocence,' he thought with real anguish. 'Here is purity! Oh, God, I—'

And in that moment, condemned himself to really terrible dangers, for, all unknowingly, he converted what had been no more than a lark, a prank in Patricia's mind—quite possibly involving sex, for to Patricia's generation, relieved by modern chemistry of its consequences, sex is only another among many, many amusements—to what poor Trini would have called, "A grave thing, *Don* Jaime! *¡Ay, sí, gravísimo!*"

Looking at Patti, seeing all that freshness, sweetness, purity, innocence—and she *was* fresh, sweet, pure and innocent; for one remains unmarked by that which to one is meaningless!—the bad sadness got back into his eyes. For he was actually crushed beneath the rubble of his dreams of a life with Trini, and the pain darkening his pale irises, contracting his pupils, was both a visible and a terrible thing.

Now to any woman with blood in her veins, the sight, the visible evidences of a secret—and hence romantic—sorrow, in the eyes, upon the nerve tautened face of an eligible and attractive bachelor, down-twisting his mouth in a sudden, unconscious, but not to be denied grimace of intolerable pain, is *the* most potent, and perhaps the only truly effective, aphrodisiac existing in this world of tired lust, half-hearted sin.

'Why!' she thought in sudden amazement. 'He's *not* ugly! Not at all! I—I *like* him. I could fall in love with him—if I'd let myself. Come to think of it: why not? He's not too old. He's both eligible and attractive. Very, very attractive! Time I stopped helling around anyhow. Just—the right age for—a husband. *¡Demonios!* I'm going to!' And discarded in that instant, without regrets, her diabolical plan involving the marijuana cigarettes. It would no longer do; a subtler offensive must now be mounted, a strategy designed to give more permanent results.

He said:

"I'm very glad to meet you, my dear."

She smiled at him, slowly, softly, slumberously, and with considerable histrionic skill. Whispered, her voice low, husky—she would have made a great actress, except that now, she realized with something akin to terror, the act was getting out of hand, life was imitating art:

"And I am—delighted to meet you at last, at long, long last, *Don* Jaime! Would you mind very much—would it trouble you dreadfully—if—I fell in love with you? Madly?"

He stared at her. Then he relaxed, laughed, said:

"Lord! You modern young women! And—if I did mind, my dear?"

"You'd be too late. For I already have. Now, come. Show me about the place, before the others come. Especially your bedroom. *Our* bedroom. Where we'll sleep—occasionally!—after we're married. For we're going to be married, you and I. Quite soon. What d'you say to that, *Don* Jaime?"

"That, thank God, you're joking!" he said fervently.

"Only I am *not* joking. I mean it. Seriously. Now you must kiss me—to plight our troth. *¡Carramba!* Don't just stand there! Kiss me! I—want you to, *Don* Jaime. I want you to—quite badly."

He kissed her. Not to have done so would have been more than a little ridiculous. 'And,' he thought sardonically, 'kissing girl-babies who look like this one doesn't exactly qualify a man for hardship pay, anyhow!'

"Thank you," she said solemnly; "that was nice. That was very nice, indeed. Sweet and soft and tender. So now, we are *Novios.* Engaged, no? I'll get Uncle to announce it, tonight. That is, if I can get his consent. Which may be difficult, *mi Amor.* He doesn't seem to like you very much. But since *Tía* Luisa adores you, between the two of us we ought to be able to bring him around. We usually do, about most things. Now, come on—show me about your villa. I must find a place—little and cozy and dark—where I can sneak you off to when the party becomes gay and drunken and hilarious—"

"A place?" he got out, panic fluttering his gut, because he was beginning to realize that she wasn't really joking, that this lovely and enchanting little witch very probably meant every word she said.

"Yes. Where we can be alone. To kiss and kiss and kiss for hours, as

Novios do. To kiss each other very seriously. Perhaps—after I have sounded Uncle out, if he proves too stubborn—you may have to compromise me, so that he will have no other recourse except to give in. Wouldn't you like to compromise me, *Don* Jaime? I gather from the persistence with which nearly all the boys I know attempt it, compromising a girl must be rather pleasant. Isn't it? You, I am certain, must hold *una cátedra en la materia . . .*"

"Patti," he laughed, "you flatter me! Far from holding a professorship in the art of seducing innocent young girls, I am very probably the world's worst duffer *en la materia,* as you call it. And I'd suggest we break our engagement now, at once, because for very serious reasons it couldn't possibly work out. Believe me, Child, I know . . ."

"You mean because of your *concubina?* She has no importance. You must dismiss her. You may settle a pension upon her if you like; I should not be so small-minded as to object to that. The child? Acknowledge it, provide for its support. All the world will praise you and call you gallant for having done that. Any other objections, Love of My Life?"

He stared at her, wondering how much of the truth he was going to have to tell her. Because this had to be stopped, now. Anyway you looked at it, for him, a married man, however secret his marriage had been kept—and the fact that Patricia, herself, obviously knew nothing of it, proved that it had been kept very secret indeed!—to get involved with the General's adopted daughter was surely a slow, and highly uncomfortable, form of suicide. He said slowly:

"Yes, Patricia, two. Has it never occurred to you, that I, being a *Gringo,* and hence, from the point of view of any *Latino,* mad, might not love, be in love with, very seriously—this poor, dear child whose only sin—no, not even that!—whose only madness, folly, is to love me, not wisely, but much too well?"

She cocked a merry, mocking, and incredulous eyebrow at him.

"Do you?" she said.

"Yes," he said quietly. "It so happens that I do, and with all my heart. Which brings us to my second objection, Patti, dear; which is just as serious: As a man who all his life has longed for a son, I definitely mean to keep my child."

"Very well," Patricia said crisply; "let us take up thy objections in order, *¡mi serio y adorable* Jaime! *Tu—Protegia.* You see, I am being polite, no? You will get over her, for she simply is not suitable to be thy wife. As for the child, I will adopt it. And I promise thee by all I hold dear to treat it no worse than I shall the rest of our children. Speaking of which, how many would you like?"

"Patti—" he said slowly, "there's one other problem: I don't love you. I'll admit you're lovely. *¡Que demonios!* You're breathtaking. But I don't love you. And, under the given circumstances, I'd rather not get too—"

"Involved?" she laughed merrily. "You are already too involved, *corazon mío*! For I haven't the slightest intention of letting you go! As for your not loving me, let's see what you say about that subject by—dawn tomorrow morning, shall we say? Now, come on, show me about the place. I want to see what changes in the decor and arrangements I shall want to make, and your guests will be here soon. Don't just stand there, Jaime *cariño,* come on!"

He thought, despairingly: 'I'll just have to play this one by ear!' Took her arm. Smiled at her with wry amusement. Said: "All right, my dear, come on . . .'"

He was dancing with her, for only the second time that night, since he had dutifully made the rounds of all the *Distinguidísimas e Ilustrísimas* present, when he suddenly saw the Indian Ambassador, Sir Singah Singh, standing by an archway and talking to a group of his guests.

"D'you mind, my dear?" he said, and broke off dancing. "I really must speak to the Indian Ambassador . . ."

He saw, with surprise, the expression of annoyance on her face; and perceived, with something closer to astonishment, that it was real.

"Yes," Patricia said sharply, "I most certainly *do* mind, *mi Amor*! This is only the second time you've danced with me all night!"

He smiled at her, said with cheerful resignation:

"Prime evidence that heaven protects the young and lovely! Or else by now you'd have been crippled by my clumsy treading on your toes!"

"But you're a *wonderful* dancer, *Don* Jaime!" she protested. "Quite the best I've danced with in all my life!"

He realized—his astonishment deepening into amazement, for he knew he was a poor, stiff, mechanical dancer—that she meant it. But in this case, as in quite a few others that he was not yet aware of, what he knew was no longer quite, or entirely, true. We will our personalities into being; within certain limits set by time, our innate capacities, our measurable potentialities, but above all by the strength of our wills, the intensity of our desires, we become what we want to be. Almost necessarily, if we want to bad enough, and work at it hard enough. As badly as Jim Rush wanted to be a man of action, as hard as he worked at being—charming, sophisticated, urbane . . .

But in the simple, unimportant matter of skill at dancing, he had had an unparalleled advantage: No man could have spent as many hours as he had—before pregnancy had incapacitated her—experiencing the pure sensuous delight of dancing with Trini without, unconsciously, by osmosis perhaps, absorbing at least a little of her perfect, instinctive sense of rhythm, timing, beat, even some tiny portion of her matchless grace. He had all unknowingly acquired more than a little. Relaxed, at peace, sexually fulfilled, in love with her, he had acquired a great deal. And it had stayed with him. Patricia was more right than wrong; now, at long last, he danced very well indeed.

He said:

"Then save the next one for me, will you, my dear?"

She said quietly, seriously, with a marked and audible note of sadness, even of bitterness, in her tone:

"I shall save *all* the rest for you, my dearest *Don* Jaime. In fact, I am coming with you now to make sure you don't get away—or that some of these rapacious females don't steal you from me. I have been—tormented quite enough tonight listening to their remarks as I sat there all by myself in a corner, and watched you dance by in all too many other women's arms . . ."

It came to him then with an appalled feeling of shock that he hadn't seen Patricia dancing at all, not with anyone. Which, considering the fact that she was by long odds the most stunningly lovely girl in the house, was more than strange; it was an enormity because it meant—

"Just what you're thinking. I haven't been dancing. I didn't want to. I don't want to dance with anyone but you, *mi* Jaime, ever again, as long as I live. I don't want anyone but you to touch me, to kiss me, to—to *have* me, to enjoy my body. But I musn't be indelicate, must I? Tell me, I *am* your hostess, am I not?"

"Yes, Child," he said.

"Which gives me the right—for tonight, at least—to be as jealous and possessive as I should be if I were really your hostess, *Don* Jaime— legally. Or, illegally, for that matter!"

"Lord!" he said. "You frighten me, Patricia. But then, beautiful girl-children always do."

She stared him straight in the face, said slowly, carefully, bitterly:

"How old—is Trini, *Don* Jaime?"

He sighed; said:

"You won't believe the truth, which is, I really don't know. I've resisted finding out. I'm ashamed of myself as things stand. To *know* she's—the—child—I believe she is, might hurt too much, Patricia. A poor answer, but there you have it . . ."

"Then *I* will tell you, so that you will become sufficiently ashamed of yourself to leave her. She is—almost two years younger than I. And I am nineteen."

He said, whispering the words: "Oh, Jesus!" Then: "How the devil could you know that, Patricia?"

"Because when the fact that you had become involved with her first became public knowledge, Paloma San Ginés was so enraged—at the spectacle of a man of your years, *mi Amor,* contributing to the corruption of an already well-corrupted minor—that she asked *me Tía* Luisa to find out the exact age of *la* Trini. And my Aunt Luisa sent her *Gestor*—you don't have the profession in *Gringo-Land,* d'you? It means a little man who does all the annoying routine things for you; obtains for you a passport, a driver's license, an identity card, a private detective to follow your faithless wife, y'know . . ."

"Patti," he said wearily, "I was *born* in Latin America. I have lived here three-quarters of my life. Get on with it, please?"

"Well, Aunt Luisa's *Gestor* searched the parish records. Came up with *la* Trini's baptismal certificate, which was August 4th, 1959. I cannot supply you with her birth date, but since in Costa Verde a child is always christened a little over six months of age, thy Trini should very soon now become an old woman of eighteen years, if that's any comfort to you . . ."

"Patti," he said, "I am beginning to see the one true advantage of marrying you, after all . . ."

"Oh, good! *¡Ay que buena!* Which is, *Cielo?*"

"Obtaining the legal right of beating the living hell out of you twice a day, and three times on Sundays! Now, come on!"

She caught his arm in both of hers, squeezed it, cooed, mockingly:

"How—thrilling! I should *adore* being beaten by you! *Soy muy masochista, ¿no lo sabias?*

"Oh, God!" he groaned. "Come on!"

Sir Singah said, as soon as he was near:

"*Don* Jaime, the Lady-Killer! The American Ambassador who breaks *all* the rules!"

"And which rule have I broken now, Sir Singah?" Jim said.

"Don't know. Shall have to ask dear Pat, here. Pat, darling, has he been trying to seduce you, too?"

"No," Patricia said; then she added slowly, softly, sweetly, "more's the pity!"

"Ha!" Sir Singah laughed. "Tell me, my sweet, if he were to try, would he—succeed?"

"Yes," Patricia said calmly, the half smile on her face more reenforcing than contradicting what she said; "and with—a most deplorable ease, Sir Singah!"

That brought a burst of laughter from all within earshot.

"Then, *Don* Jaime," the Indian Ambassador said solemnly, "I need only to ask your favorite flower . . ."

Jim glanced at the big white rose in Patricia's black hair.

"Roses," he said. "White roses. Why, Sir Singah?"

"To send a spray to your funeral, when His Excellency has you *shot* to-morrow morning!" Sir Singah said.

Jim grinned at him, said:

"The proper answer to that one is: *¡Ay, que buena muerte!* O, what a way to go!"

Another roar. The party, Jim saw, was definitely picking up, gaining verve.

"You're in fine form tonight, *Don* Jaime," Sir Singah said.

"I hope. But seriously, Sir Singah, I dropped by to complain of one of *your* nationals. A fellow citizen of yours who is absolutely demoralizing my secretarial staff . . ."

"And you let him beat *you* to it, *Don* Jaime?" Sir Singah said.

The laughter boomed and swelled. People—among them, Jim noted, Rene Cloutier, the French Ambassador—came rushing over to join the group.

"He," Jim said, "has certain advantages. He is a Guru. One of your famous Yoga mystics. He's called, I believe, Hriday Hanuman."

Sir Singah frowned.

"Impossible!" he snapped. "He can't be, my dear *Don* Jaime."

"What can't he be?" Jim said.

"Because, my deah fellow, no Indian *could* be called that. Hanuman's the *Monkey* God in the Hindu pantheon. This chap is obviously pulling your leg if he told you that!"

"*He* didn't. My secretary did. So maybe he's pulling *her* leg . . ."

"Or," Patricia said sweetly, "her *bragas.* Off."

The roar that went up at that made the chandeliers rattle. And with good reason. Coming from a young, well bred, upper-class—and un-married!—Latin American woman, the sally was absolutely outrageous. *Bragas* is the Spanish word for "panties."

"I wouldn't doubt it!" Jim sighed. "Then you don't know him, Sir Singah?"

"Of course not! Loathe those ruddy beggars anyhow. Give Indyah a bad name. Stuff and nonsense, every bloody bit of it. Had my way I'd have th' blinking idiots shot! Have you seen him, *Don* Jaime? Could you describe th' bounder?"

"Yes. As a matter of fact, I can. In the first place, he's *very* dark. Far darker than Indians usually are—"

Sir Singah stared at Jim.

"That means the chappie's *black,* doesn't it?"

"Yes. Blue-black. Triple dipped. Inky. But very handsome—"

Sir Singah caught Jim's arm in a powerful grip, leaned close.

"Ask your sec'rt'ry where he lives!"he hissed. "For if he's the chap I think he is, *our* Intelligence people have been looking for him for months! Dangerous fellow, *Don* Jaime. I mean to put his black arse in jail where it jolly well belongs!"

Then memory flooded all Jim's mind with light. He remembered the clipping he still had in his billfold. The one he had meant to—but had forgot—to show Van Schuyler. The last piece in the puzzle of how, even if the French sold García and Friends a fast breeder reactor, they were going to acquire the know-how to—

He turned to Rene Cloutier.

"How's the Merchants of Death business these days, M'sieur l'Ambassadeur?" he said.

"Oh, come off of it, Jim!" Rene Cloutier laughed. "Your types have sold the Shah of Iran sixteen jet fighters for every pilot he's got. More than that, if you count the ones who really know how to fly."

"Which reduces his Air Force to one man: himself," Jim said. "My spies tell me he's really a red hot pilot—a true blue-flame flyboy. But the instructors we've sent over complain that nobody could teach an Irani to get a 1916 Curtiss Jenny off the ground safely, not to mention a jet. Still, we're one up on you frugal and canny French in that regard—"

"How so?" Cloutier said pleasantly.

"The Shah has the Grisbe. Cash. Folding stuff. Money. While you've got half your sales force over here trying to sell sophisticated arms to a people who have no conceivable need for them—and who, additionally—like this gown my dearest Patricia's wearing—have no visible means of support. I say, my dear, what *does* hold it up?"

"Me," Patricia said. "Parts of me, anyhow. I'm quite nicely built, darling. Don't tell me you hadn't noticed!"

"Well," Jim said judiciously—thinking: 'That's the note! Keep it light and playful.'—"Geri's a genius. It could be—padding, y'know."

"It isn't," she said. "Later on, I'll prove that to you, Dear One. Or if you'd care to excuse yourself *now*—for a couple of *hours* say, I'll give you an immediate—and private—demonstration . . ."

"Of what, Patti?" Rene Cloutier said.

"Of the—natural padding *I* come equipped with. *I*, not the dress," Patricia said.

Rene caught her arm.

"*Zut, alors!*" he crowed. "*¡Vamos, Dulce Pastel de tiernos Golpecitos! Viens, donc, Doux Gâteau de tous les petits coups tendres! Allons nous! Profiterons nous de cette belle occasion, hein?*"

'Here's where English wins hands down,' Jim thought wryly. 'Took him four words in Spanish, and seven in French, to say—no, to express the idea of Patti-Cake, the nickname all her friends have given her in English. Probably because English is the smart, chic language these days. As chic as French used to be . . . .'

"Not—you," Patricia purred. "You've formed sufficient *ententes cordiales,* Rene, already. Him. *Don* Jaime. I'm in love with him. I am going to marry him. So—congratulate me, will you? And offer him—your condolences!"

"I do," Rene groaned. "Especially the latter. Jim, old boy, if I were you, I'd run, not walk, for the nearest exit!"

"Why?" Jim said.

"Patricia is—the original Einsteinian equation. Y'know: $E = MC^2$. Cased in cobalt. And loaded with hydrogen. Get her going, and you blow up the world!"

"How would *you* know that, Rene?" Patricia said. The challenging note in her voice came over to Jim Rush's finely tuned ear—trained by his late wife Virginia, among others!—and he recognized it. Recognized its exquisite bitchery. She was baiting Rene, daring him to say: 'You know how I know, Patti; after all, between a couple who've shared the same bee as often as we have, there can be no secrets, *n'est-ce pas?*' It was dirty, female fighting. Abysmally dirty. Because she knew that a man of Rene Cloutier's standing—he was, after all Louis le Grand, Sorbonne, *and* Saint Cyr—and the titles that he, personally, was both too modern and too sophisticated to even bother to use went back to Louis XIV—couldn't possibly say that without violating all the concepts of education, courtesy, *gentilesse,* that he had been taught all his life, without, in fact, diminishing himself in his own eyes as a man.

But the question, and more especially the tone in which it was asked, plainly nettled him. His answer to it showed a determination not to let her get off scot-free.

"I get about," he said slowly, icily. "I—hear things, Patti, dear!"

'Why do I feel—sick?' Jim thought with aching wonder. 'I should thank him! The last thing on earth I need is to get mixed up with another promiscuous little bitch.'

But Patricia was talking again, and the way her voice sounded now caused Jim to stare at her with surprise, which changed immediately and abruptly into—concern; then pity. Because what had got into her young voice, now making her clear, musical soprano rise, go reedy, shake, was not anger, but desperation. She was, Jim saw, or rather perceived, with something akin to terror, in deadly earnest. She was defending—her life. The future she meant to have. Defending it with an intensity that made him wonder how sound her psychological and emotional stability was, made him realize that he was likely to find himself, very shortly, with one hell of a problem on his hands. She said, with quiet, but unmistakable passion:

"Lies. Idle gossip. Don't try to spoil my plans—my *life,* Rene! *Don* Jaime, he is trying to—give you the wrong impression. I am a—reasonably, for these times anyhow!—good girl. Reasonably—decent. I shall make you a good—and absolutely faithful wife. Do not listen to him, please. Try—to trust me . . . ."

"*Bon petit Jesu!*" Rene said. "D'you know, she sounds as though she *means* it!"

"I *do* mean it," Patricia said. "Now stop talking about me. Go back to—serious matters. You were saying, *Amor mío*—that we are poor. That we have no visible means of support—"

"Oil," Cloutier said. "*Huile.* Petroleum. That sticky, greasy, black stuff, Jim. Found by the father of one of your *ex-petites amis.* The girl you threw into Lopez Basquez' Booby Hatch to get rid of. Effective way of clearing your decks for action, *n'est-ce pas, mon vieux?*"

"Low blow, Rene," Jim said evenly, "on the order of that kidney punch my darling Patti dealt you, when she asked you that question that you didn't want to, or didn't dare to, answer. Which was it, a fine display of *gentilesse?* Or a lack of nerve? No, don't answer that! I should prefer not knowing. The answer's sure to distress me, either way . . . ."

He could feel her eyes on his face. Coals from a brazier. A torturer's lighted cigarette ends.

"Jim, you're putting me in a deuced awkward spot, old boy," Rene said.

"Just recompense for the one you were trying to put me in. Forget it, will you? In self-defense, though, let me say that if all the little girls attributed to me these days were really mine, I'd be attending this shindig in a wheelchair. So let's just skip *les filles* for the rest of the night, shall we?"

"As long as you do not skip *me, Cielo,*" Patricia said.

"Fat chance!" Rene said. "*Don* Jaime always plucks the loveliest flowers. Still—you have to admit oil's excellent collateral, Jim."

"Except in the cases when it isn't," Jim said. "Like this one, for instance."

"Why not, *Don* Jaime?" Sir Singah boomed.

"Because it's a *national* resource. And it will belong to the Government in power when it's actually brought into the—still unbuilt—refineries, through—still unlaid—pipelines. Which requires financing that only *my* Government is in a position to grant—"

"And which *you* oppose," Rene said bitterly.

"Which I oppose. Aside from the fact that it seems to me rather a bit of a rum go, *mon cher*, to divert the American taxpayers' money to the enrichment of the French armament industry, I refused to be sucked into the mistake *you're* making. None of us—and by us, I mean the Western, largely capitalistic democracies—is going to see a drop of that oil. Because the next few Governments after this one, here in Costa Verde, are going to be Marxist. I hope mildly so; but Marxist they're going to be. Dear Patricia's Uncle has ensured that by his tactics . . ."

"Murder," Patricia whispered; "killing people—as he killed *mis papas*. Torture. Worse than Ecuador. Worse than Brazil. Worse even—than Chile. Which is—difficult, no? Uncle's a swine!"

No one answered her. They knew better. She—possibly!—could get away with remarks like those. But not even diplomatic immunity would save the man who seconded them.

"But since you oppose this celebrated loan, *Don* Jaime, why didn't you offer your Congressmen and Senators the pleasure of your company on that trip down to Ururchizenaya they undertook—yesterday, wasn't it? Perfect opportunity to sell your MP's—pardon! MC's—a bill of goods, it seems to me, Old Chap," Sir Singah said. "Even the pain of having to give up—temporarily—the rare privilege and exquisite pleasure of being able to stroke dear Pat's lovely little bum shouldn't have outweighed *that*. Why didn't you?"

"I should advise you, Sir Singah," the heavy, drumdeep bass said, "to pay a trifle less attention to my daughter's anatomy, or I shall break off diplomatic relationship with your country, and declare war. Though you might welcome that, mightn't you? One way of solving your over-population problem. As for you, *Don* Jaime, that same question's been troubling me—I mean, of course, the one Sir Singah put to you. Why *didn't* you, my friend?"

Jim looked up into the heavy, and distinctly menacing, face of the Head of the State.

"*You* know why, *mi General*," he said quietly.

"I'm not all that sure I do," General García said. "After all, you sent young Schuyler along."

"With the strictest orders to see to their comfort, not to interfere with their—pleasures, and to avoid any word or phrase that could conceivably be interpreted—as indoctrination, Your Excellency. Your—arguments, once I'd got home and thought about them, appeared to me—unassailably convincing. In short, you win. I hereby and publicly acknowledge that when a fight's conducted on *that* level, I give in. In other words, I'm a coward."

"Uncle!" Patricia gasped. "You—you threatened *her*! That poor, sweet child! Pregnant as she is! Because *Don* Jaime wouldn't bow to a personal threat. He's too brave for that, and you know it! I was at that funeral with you and Auntie. I *saw* him standing there like a rock, and bleeding to death, and refusing to move until they'd buried all those dead people!"

"Patti," the General said wearily, "you should go to the Bijou less often. Spy-thrillers are a poor basis for judging life. At least I hope you've been behaving yourself for a change . . ."

"I have—so *far*," Patricia said tartly. "But whether or not I shall continue to, depends upon *you*, Uncle Dear!"

General García stared at his niece-in-law, become his adopted daughter.

"Depends upon me—how?" he said.

"Will you—here and now—before all these people as witnesses, so you can't go back on your word, give your consent to our being married? *Don* Jaime and I? At once. Tonight. Tomorrow. The next day. Next week at the latest. More than that and I'll go crazy. Will you, *Tío*?"

"Good God!" the General exploded. "You don't mean this unprincipled little *Yanqui* blackguard has proposed to you? He can't! He has no right to!"

"No, *Tío*," Patricia said sweetly; "*I* proposed to him. I am—quite dreadfully in love with him, Uncle mine!"

The General threw back his head and roared with laughter.

"You precious little idiot!" he said. "Tell me—what did *Don* Jaime— the great *Don* Jaime—*¡Tenorio Norteamericano extraordinario!*—say to *that*?"

"He laughed at me. He pretends to believe I am joking."

"Very well, he is being wise. Let us leave it at that. You *are* joking, Pet. Agreed?"

Patricia stamped a shapely foot.

"You leave me no choice but to compromise him then, *Tío*!" she said. She whirled, caught Jim by the arm; said: "Come on!"

Jim grinned at her; said:

"You *would* look sweet in black, Patricia, dearest! Because that's what you'd be wearing if I tried to do anything serious about you. And I don't believe a dead husband—or a dead lover—would be any fun."

She smiled at him. Said, wistfully:

"But maybe you could—leave *me*—as she is. I'd like that, my love. It would be—something to remember you by . . ."

"The girl's daft!" the General snorted. "Come on, Patti; I'm sending you home. Now."

"Let her stay, Sir," Jim said. "You've my word as a gentleman that—"

"No," General García said. "Oh, I trust *you*, *Don* Jaime, largely because whatever else you may be, a fool you're not. It's this little idiot I don't—I know her too well. Besides, it's dreadfully late, anyhow. We've enjoyed your party. Good night."

And that was why the party broke up hours before it ordinarily would have. The guests trooped out like sheep, fearing the General's displeasure if they stayed.

Jim sat there in the empty grand salon, staring off into space. He hadn't the slightest desire to go to bed. Instead, he had a couple of Scotches on the rocks, light ones, but enough to relax his close to shattered nerves. They were his first drinks of the night, since, out of prudence, he had drunk nothing during the party. There were times when a man needed to be alone—as now. Needed—a breathing space—for reflection, for some long and careful thought. So he sat there, sipped his drinks, and thought, for the better part of two hours. At the end of that time, he realized that nothing he'd thought about, reflected upon, made the slightest sense. But then, what did in the very thoroughly out of joint times in which he was condemned to live?

He thought about Trini. About Patricia. About Grace. And it came to him that he had been seeking a quality nonexistent in a modern world. That even Grace didn't have, and certainly not Patricia, though her act had been masterly enough to deceive him at first. But he had seen through it before the evening was one-quarter over . . . He hadn't even needed the tart warning Tomás had given him a half hour ago:

"Sir, I see you've made another conquest. A—distinctly dangerous one, Mr. Ambassador. One that it would be—most unwise to pursue . . ."

"I have no intention of pursuing it, Tomás," Jim said dryly. "However much ill feeling exists between His Nibs and me, I should never dream of using his adopted daughter to even the score . . ."

"That's not what I mean, Sir," Tomás said. "There's no particular danger from the *General,* in the event you should decide upon a little horizontal diversion with dear Patti-Cake. He is much too occupied with the affairs of state and his own rather grandiose plans for the conquest of the entire southern half of the Western Hemisphere—and the Northern, I do believe, once he has consolidated his hold on all Central and South America—to watch her as closely as he should. The chief danger would be destroying your official effectiveness by making yourself ridiculous—as ridiculous as His Excellency himself is held to be by most people on the matters of his niece-daughter's reputation and behavior. He actually believes her to be innocent. Mischievous—but—well—untouched, shall we say? While in actual fact—"

"In actual fact, the little lady has been around, eh, Tomás? I gathered as much," Jim said.

"In actual fact," Tomás said, "it would be difficult to find a youngish man, married or single, among the rather smart circles in which she moves, of course, who has not pushed dear Patti over at one time or another. The French Ambassador for one, the—"

"Don't give me a list, Tomás," Jim said wearily. "Neither the matter, nor the young woman, herself, interests me that much . . ."

"I only hope that *she* will leave *you* in peace, Sir!" Tomás said. "She seemed quite smitten! And besides, there's a theory—a rather charitable and kindly theory it seems to me—that the young lady was deeply disturbed by the tragic deaths of her parents; in short that she's more than a little—mad, *Don* Jaime."

"I'll buy that theory, Tomás," Jim said, "and not out of charity. But because it fits a number of behavior patterns I'd observed in her that don't quite—mesh, shall we say? There's a certain—discontinuity about her mode of procedure. She doesn't move from cause to effect. She decides a thing, then seeks to cause it . . ."

"As getting her dainty little hands on you, Sir?" Tomás said.

"Oh, hell, Tomás! Don't worry about that. For Christ's sake, Man, cleaning up can wait until tomorrow! Go get some sleep, will you?"

"And you, Sir?"

"Oh, I'll be along presently," Jim Rush said.

The quality he had been looking for, and that neither Grace nor Patricia had, was—innocence. He didn't know why the hell he should have been looking for innocence in the first place, nor what earthly good it would have done him—or any man! —if he had found it; but he couldn't deny to himself that it was this rare and touching quality he—romantic fool that he was!—had been searching for in the woman who would finally share his life. And neither Grace nor Patricia had it, that was for sure!

But—Trini? Yes. God, yes! In spite of everything. She had kept it. Retained it. Regained it. Restored it. Because she, too, *believed* in that quality. Valued it.

And now she was—dying. Quite literally dying, because he—miserable little flinty-souled puritan!—could not forget a meaningless episode that had been forced upon a poor, forlorn, utterly defenseless fourteen-year-old—that's how old she had been when they had made that unspeakable obscenity of a picture! She had admitted that to him, very simply, not using it as a defense, simply stating it with the awful resignation with which she said everything these days. Fourteen. But barely pubescent. A girl-child hopeless, helpless, without recourses—years before she had even dreamed he was alive. So they had—publicly—before the cameras, under the lights, in the presence of leering spectators—

multiply fucked her, sodomized her, forced her to suck their filthy cocks, violated *everything* she was, all that basic, soul deep, essentially indestructible purity, that innocence.

They had harmed her, of course; but not destroyed her. The destruction of what a person is: mind, spirit—innocence!—soul, is always, has to be—suicide.

Nobody can do it to us. We do it to ourselves. By accepting the world's filth. By participating in the act of our own defilement. By accepting, even embracing, our own debasement. And Trini—*hadn't*. She had been violated. But there had never been the destructive element of mutuality. Of welcoming the evil forced upon her. Wallowing in it.

He caught sight of his own pale, tired, life-worn face in the mirror above the mantle. 'Look at you!' he snarled at himself. '*Don* Juan Tenorio in person! Casanova! Tall, handsome, brave, intelligent, witty— everything to offer a woman. Sitting in judgment over another's acts when you've never even managed to sin effectively, never so much as carried out a casual seduction without bumbling it, never tumbled a wench with gaiety, ease, verve, flair! Who are you that you should sit in judgment over her? I ask you, who? The All Conquering Hero, Natch! You damned little albino mouse! What does she see in you? In God's name, what?'

But the answer to that came easily enough, hurting and healing at the same time. 'My —kindness. For I *have* been kind to her. Treated her—as a human being. Even with—respect. The one thing she has wanted—needed—all her life. Because she was *never* attracted by my bonny grey eyes, or my towering height and strength. What did she call me? "Little, dried up, ugly old *Gringo*!" She was *not* deceived. And, by that same token, I can believe in her love for me, or at least for the qualities she has dreamed into me, attributed to me, sees in me, and which, goddamnit! I've got to find somewhere, ram down my stupid throat, ingest, absorb, because she *needs* them so! Needs to believe that there actually is in this world a man who is kind, gentle, humane, loving—and brave. For her to cling to. To stand as a buffer between her and all the obscene and sickening cruelty of this world. And if there is such a thing as mortal sin, I have found it, committed it, by withdrawing from this poor, forlorn—and lovely!—child the only gifts I had to give, poor and nearly worthless though they were—a little human warmth, a teaspoon full of tenderness, a drop or two—of love . . . For without them she—is—dying.'

'I'll go to her!' he thought. 'Now! Late as it is! I'll—'

Then he saw Tomás racing towards him, down the stairs. The majordomo looked as though he'd seen a troop of ghosts, or all the hosts of hell.

"Sir!" Tomás hissed. "Up there—in your bedroom! In your bed! *Her*—the General's niece! I tried to get her out of there, but she's been smoking—those cigarettes. Y'know: *pot*—and I couldn't talk any sense into her . . ."

"Oh, Jesus!" Jim said. Then: "All right, Tomás—I'll take care of it . . ."

When he came into the bedroom, she swung her long legs down from his bed, and came towards him, the acrid stinking smoke of marijuana half veiling her face. She had on his own pyjama tops. They were too short for her. And she hadn't bothered to button them. And since, under that short and gaping expanse of tawny silk, there was only Patricia, the sight was—fetching. Damned fetching.

He noted his own physiological response to it. Thought sadly:

'I, too, am only a human being. Or maybe only a conditioned reflex. Show me half covered—and truly lovely!—tits, a smooth, flat belly, nice thighs, a curly pubic bush, and I get an erection. Like any other poor bastard.'

He said, sadly:

"Your Uncle took you home. *Personally.* I saw him. And yet here you are again. In no more time than it would take to turn a car around, and drive straight back. *How,* Patricia?"

"That way. As you said, *mi Amor.* I turned a car around. Drove straight back. No. That's not true. Not quite. He would have heard me—*arrancar* the motor. I tiptoed across the back lawn—tipi—tipi—toe— *¡así!*" She put a slim finger across her lips and mimicked the motion of tiptoeing across a lawn. To see her do that clad only in his pyjama tops was a pure and unmitigated delight. "Then out the back gate—and whizzzzz over to the Boulevard Simon Bolivar where there is an all night taxi stand. So here I am—complete with all the natural equipment it took to hold up that dress—" She dropped the smoldering cigarette down upon the expensive deep pile carpeting, put both hands under her breasts, lifted them high for his inspection. "Don't you like my equipment, Jaime, *Cielo?*" she said.

"Oh, for Christ's sake!" he said disgustedly. "Patricia, it just isn't possible. The General took you home to keep you out of mischief, so he—"

"Is overconfident. And a fool. And a murderer. He killed—Papa. And Mama. I can't prove it, and Auntie refuses to believe it; but I *know* he did." Suddenly, startlingly, her eyes filled up, brimmed, spilled. "One of the reasons I *enjoy* doing things like this, Jaime. Because I *hate* him! And y—y'know what, Jaime, *Cariño?* He's proud of me! Of his chaste, innocent—*virgin*—daughter! Who is—what is it that you *Gringos* say? Oh, yes!—a pushover. A cheap little tramp. A—whore.

Not even that, really. Anybody's *Chica.* Everybody's. A Playtime girl—
who gives it away—for fun. But then, you like *Putitas,* don't you?"

He stared at her. But with—compassion now; with real and aching
pity. Said quietly:

"It so happens that I don't, Patricia. And before *you* do, let me bring
Trini into this discussion. She *isn't,* Child. If you don't know that,
you don't know anything. She wasn't even when she—was going
through the motions, say—to stay alive. Which closes that particular
subject—*forever.* Now, tell me, how the living hell did you manage to
get out of the house so fast? You surely didn't even give the General
time to fall asleep!"

"Wasn't—necessary," she said, mockingly. "As I told you, Uncle is
both overconfident and a fool. My clothes closet no longer has a back
wall. Or rather, it has a back wall that has been converted into a sliding
door. It doesn't open very wide, but sufficiently to allow someone as
thin as I am to pass through it and out upon a landing in the service
stairs, which lead down to the servants' entrance. Uncle is absolutely incapable of thinking of servants as a threat, or even as human beings, so
he has not inspected that part of the house in many years. By now I
doubt he actually remembers those stairs are actually there. A friend of
mine did the expert carpentry to provide me with my escape hatch at
my request. Uncle and Auntie were told, and believed, he was making
the closet larger. They had seen the friend—many times—but never
before in blue coveralls, and with his face most artistically dirty. The
stupidity of people who believe themselves smart is amazing, no?"

"But if your Uncle looks in your room and finds you gone, he—"

"He probably already has. Whereupon he has seen the slender figure
and the dark hair of Pura, one of the servant girls, asleep, or pretending
to be, in my bed. She resembles me—vaguely; but sufficiently in the
half light from a corridor when a door is opened into a darkened room.
She will not betray me. I have done her many favors in the past, since
her name is highly inappropriate. So stop worrying, *¡Cielo, Cariño,
Angelito mío!* And we can sweetly converse and give each other explanations in the daytime and in public. But now—"

He said:

"Why do you hate me, Patricia? You're condemning me to death, you
know!"

She said, laughingly:

"Not if we are quick, my love! No—diaphragm. No—pill. So Uncle
won't dare have you assassinated, since he will need you to remedy the
situation we are going to create, you and I! Especially if you do succeed
in pumping my belly up to a perfectly enormous size the first try! So,

get out of your things, darling. Let us commence—Operation Baby. Operation Bastard Baby, Scandal Arming, Reputation Ruining, Little Patti's Downfall! Don't you *want* to ruin me? Re-ruin me, anyhow, for the umpteenth thousand time? Ruining me is great fun, I've been told. Though I have to admit *I've* never enjoyed it very much. And a little bundle from heaven will be awf'ly good life insurance for you as far as Uncle is concerned . . ."

He said:

"No, it won't, Patricia. It won't—at all. Besides, why should I even *want* a self-confessed pushover—and a gratuitous whore—as a wife?"

She stared at him, and again those tears he had thought she was past shedding, was too hardened, too blasé, to even need any more, were there again, hot and bright and sudden in her eyes.

She said, angrily:

"*¡Oh demonios!* Why did I ever think I could tell *you* that? Only—I had to, *Jaimito mío,* you sweet little old man/baby-boy! You would have found it out, soon enough. Kissing, and telling—is the order of the day! Rene would have got around to it—delicately and with finesse!—soon enough. Among—others. Jaime, is virginity important to you? If so you shall have to marry a child, these days. Aged *eight* or thereabouts. I don't know even *one Chica* in my set who still is—"

He thought with slow, nostalgic sadness: 'Nor I, in mine.' He said:

"That's not what I'm talking about."

"Then what *are* you?" she said.

"That I should prefer that my children, if any, be *mine.* Look somewhat like me—bear my blood. Oscar Wilde once said: 'The future is only the past again, entered through another gate . . .' "

She came very close to him. So close that he could smell her. There were all the normal, civilized odors: perfume, deodorants, the dry smell of the lacquered spray the coiffeur had used to set her hair, the unpleasant stink of marijuana on her breath; but two more, breaking sharply, savagely through bath salts, cologne, cleanness, straight back to the race's essential animality: a faint, but rising now, sharp, acrid hint of sweat; a pungent, unmistakable, and wildly exciting, intoxicating odor—what it was *for,* really, he realized, its original function before our journey up the evolutionary scale had blunted all our senses—of estrus.

She said slowly, solemnly, making of her words a votive offering, an oath breakable only upon pain of death, before the high altar of the terrible goddess:

"Jaime, I should be absolutely faithful to you. I should never even be tempted not to be. I—*know* what other men are like. I am heartily sick of the lot of them. I—want you—*because* you are different. If you were mine, I shouldn't risk losing you for any reason whatsoever. Because, if you are—what I think you are—what I see in you, to lose you, would be—to lose my life. So—please! Will you be so kind?"

She stepped in closer still, leaning against him now, scalding and branding him along all his length, in spite of the layers of his clothing. Put her arms around his neck. Kissed him. She was—very expert. But her lips—and her tongue—were vile with the taste of *cannabis*. He felt sick.

She noticed his shudder. Said:

"Wait. I'll go wash my mouth out. It does taste horrible, doesn't it?"

He waited, sitting in the big chair. He wasn't even wondering how she had got back into the residence again. He knew. He had given the Marines the night off. And by now, in their sentry boxes, the ordinary guards were dead to the world. What he was thinking, or rather trying to decide, was what stratagem he could use to get her out of there in the shortest possible time. And it came to him that the *best* way was to go through with it. Briefly. Forcefully. As brutally as possible. A two minute quickie. Then: "Let's go, Girl!"

But then he thought about Trini. Remembered her eyes as she had sung that song—dying wide open of all the awful ways there are to die. And he couldn't. He literally couldn't. Not even—physically— anymore, now.

She came back and flopped down into his lap. Sprawling. Open. Kissed him. Her mouth tasted clean and fresh—and of his own mint-flavored toothpaste now.

She said, calmly:

"Play with me. Do things to me. Y'know, get me excited. I am, already, but not enough. It would hurt. I'm—too dry."

"Jesus!" he said. "Must you be so—clinical?"

"Yes. We've no time for—romance, lover! Just—plain sex. Uncle may discover I'm missing, any minute now. The possibility of pregnancy must at least exist. Or else—"

"Or else, nothing. Sorry, my dear. I just don't feel like it. A rain check, please?"

"No!" she said. Put down her hand and touched him; wailed: "¡Oh, demonios! You really aren't interested, are you? My turn, then. Let me get to work on you. A nice little *chupa-chup* job, lover? A—lollipop?"

"No, you don't!" he said. "Listen, Patricia. Nothing we could do now would change anything. I couldn't marry you even if you were to give birth to quintuplets. I couldn't, because I'm already married. And for your information, it was a Roman Catholic ceremony. It took place here in Costa Verde. And it was performed by Padre Pío, himself . . ."

She stared at him. Whispered:

"To—Trini?"

He said, harshly:

"Yes, to Trini." Waited for her to say: "You damned fool!" But she surprised him.

"That—was—gallant of you, Jaime," she said softly. "Brave. Fine. I—admire you for it. And—Trini's—so sweet. She'll make you—happy. Divinely."

Then he saw—with an awed stopping of his breath, his life, how she was crying.

"Patricia!" he said.

"I love you, you sweet damned fool!" she said brokenly. "¡Oh, demonios! I don't suppose there's any hope of your making me your mistress tonight, is there?"

He said gently:

"No, not tonight, Patricia—"

"Besides—even I don't feel up to it, now. So—I'll take that rain check, darling. Help me find my things, will you? I felt so—calorosa— in the mood—that I ripped 'em off, and threw them all over—"

She got up. He stood up as well. She pushed his pyjama top down and off. He stared at her.

"Am I—beautiful, Jim?" she said. "Am I—as beautiful as your eyes say now?"

"More," he groaned. "I told you that. You're absolutely breathtaking, Patricia."

"Then—? Please? Why—not?"

He said, harshly: "No, Patricia!"

She stepped toward him, naked and beautiful. And the night split apart in blue-white lightnings. Once, twice, three times. She paid it absolutely no attention. She came to him in the second burst of light. By the time the third went off, she was almost breaking his mouth, devouring it.

'A strobe!' he realized. 'An electronic flashgun! Oh, Jesus!'

He pushed her away from him almost brutally. Raced for the balcony. Saw the dark figure swing himself over and down, go crashing into the rose bushes. Straightened up, limping. Run off towards the back of the house. Towards the service gates. A moment later, a motor roared.

He turned back to the room Patricia lay on his bed—Salomé, Lilith, Judith of the Holfernes, Jezebel. Stretched out her arms to him. Whispered:

"That was—a photographer, Jaime. With a flashgun. Un Chantajista—a blackmailer. So—we are both dead, you and I. Because, believe me, Uncle will not let me live after having disgraced him thus. He will arrange a most convincing car smash-up just as he did for my father and mother. And have you—quietly murdered, knowing that you are powerless to save my reputation. Therefore—I propose that we—enjoy our deaths! Make them good ones—"

"No," he said; then, again, louder, strangling on the word: "No!"

"Why not—*mi* Jaime?"

He cleared his throat. Said quietly:

"There's—Trini."

"She would—never know."

He stared at her, and his eyes were very bleak.

"*I* would," he said.

She bowed her head. Looked up again. Her eyes were a star-blazed night, suddenly.

"Yes. You're right. You—must not—dirty this fine thing you have done. Nor—shame it. Now, I'll get dressed. Can you take me home?"

He said: "Yes, Patricia."

Then, for no reason at all, he repeated it.

"Yes, Patricia; I'll take you home," he said.

CHAPTER

28

Jim read the invitation. It was from the General, himself; but he knew that *Doña* Luisa had sent it. A horse show, races, and jumping competition over an Olympic regulations obstacle course. A *corrida de toros* in which the bullfighters were not going to be professional *matadores* but gentlemen amateurs. And *lady* amateurs, too; for two aristocratic misses were going to appear as *Rejoneadoras,* and kill a pair of bulls—'Bulls, hell!' he snorted; 'a pair of miserable, scrawny, scarcely weaned, and anything but dangerous calves!'—from horseback. He glanced at their names on the enclosed program. He didn't know them. The affair was scheduled for Friday of the coming week. At the *Club Hipico.* In benefit of one of Luisa Montenegro de García's favorite charities. He'd have to put in a brief appearance, he supposed.

He tossed the invitation aside. Turned back to his visitor.

"Sir," Van Schuyler laughed, "I don't know how you do it; but it really works!"

"What really works, Van?" Jim said wearily. "I've the distinct impression that nothing does, these days . . ."

"Your methods do. The French are going to pull out. The aircraft boys are packing. I understand they'll be on the next Air France flight to Paris, via Martinique and Guadalupe. How *did* you do it, Sir?"

"Dropped a flea into Reni Cloutier's ear. The French suffer from an ingrained bourgeois vice: they like to be *paid*. I pointed out to M. l'Ambassadeur that the time element made that detail unlikely, that even *oil* was piss poor collateral when it was certain to fall into the hands of a future Costa Verdian Government which will inevitably be Marxist—all the thrust of recent history *guarantees* it—and hence, by its very nature, most unlikely to honor the commitments of its predecessors—a bunch of Fascist swine!—made without its consent, and antedating its ascension to power . . ."

"But," Van said soberly, "the types with the horn-rimmed glasses are hanging on. The *Ecole Polytechnique* boys. And they're—the dangerous ones, Boss!"

"I suspect that's because, in their case, the stakes are higher. Or the game so completely insane that they're willing to accept the risk. But tell me one thing, Son: D'you think that the French, under any conceivable set of circumstances, would supply García et Cie., with an atomic physicist? Try that one on for size, Van. A 'Worst Case' hypothesis. Feed that into your computer—as part of a War Games plan. What comes out?"

Van thought about that. Said, almost instantly:

"No."

"Why not?"

"Responsibility's too direct. They sell these Neanderthals a fast breeding pile. García and Friends, through *their own* captive atomic scientist, then misuse it, producing a big, fat workable A-bomb. '*Et ça, alors?*' One gives a most expressive Gallic shrug. One says: '*Ça ce n'était pas de tout notre faute a nous!*—we sold them *cet engine-là* to make *èlectricité, Messieurs!*' "

"And if there *were* a Frenchman in the wood—correction—atomic! pile?"

Van grinned.

"He'd get cooked. And so would they. Their goose, anyhow. Because how could they deny their responsibility for what their own type helped these murderers do? My guess is that they'll provide the Wizard, all right; but that he'll be a foreigner. As un-French as possible. From as far away as possible. Procured as secretly as possible."

"Son," Jim said slowly, "you've guessed right. They have. Or somebody has—though who the guilty party was is a detail we'll never be able to prove. And that isn't even important. What is important is that he's—already here. Though the twin facts that *I* know who he is, and could locate him in three minutes flat, do have their—well, call it specific gravity in the scheme of things, don't they?"

"Good Lord, Sir! What are we waiting for then?"

"I," Jim said, "am waiting for a report from you—about your junket. It just might tie in, Van. Since I have the offbeat notion that this particular dark-complexioned gentleman in the atomic breeder pile is not necessarily an illegitimate child in the spiritual sense, and may even be quite a decent chap, if you got at least one of the things I sent you after, we just might use it to persuade him to leave. Voluntarily, and quietly. Otherwise I can always turn him over to his own country's cloak and dagger boys—who are looking for him. I'd rather not. I don't like his country's present government. They're not exactly nice people. Even the Lady—who heads it, isn't. Maybe especially that dear Lady. But since she is a Lady—or at least, female—using accurate qualifying adjectives to describe her wouldn't be diplomatic, Van. Or—gentlemanly, for that matter . . ."

"A Lady," Van mused. "A woman—Head of State. Hmmmmm. And of a state that has the possibility of producing, or has produced—Good Lord, Sir! You don't mean—"

"Exactly. But don't say it out loud. At least, not yet. Tell me, Son: How did your junket go?"

"Great, Sir. Successful on all counts. Jorge came through with his filthy movies right on schedule. Quite the filthiest I've ever seen. Made *me* toss my cookies, and I've a strong stomach. That—trained dog session—Jesus! I'd advise you not to look at them, Sir!"

"I have no intention to. But you surprise me, Van. I'd never believed that particular atrocity story. Animals of one species are *never* attracted to females of another unless the pair to be mated belong to groups so closely related as to be subspecies of one another, as in the case of mule breeding, say. I suppose you could cross a donkey with a zebra; but even within the same species, zoo keepers have found that crossing lions with tigers—both large felines—is very nearly impossible, though it has been done, on one or two occasions. But this particular atrocity story involves—female *primates,* and male quadrupeds, specifically, *canines,* and that—"

"Should be impossible. Only it—isn't. They do it. At the Women's Detention Camp at Chizenaya, they do it almost every day. It's their favorite form of amusement, Sir. Have you ever owned dogs?"

"Yes. Why, yes, of course."

"Then you know dogs are olfactory machines. Everything they do depends upon their noses. They can't see worth a damn; but they can smell—a bitch in heat from five or six *miles* away . . ."

"But a woman isn't—"

"A bitch in heat? Looking back over the—boyish exuberances of my university days—I shouldn't like to bet on that one, Sir! Forgive me—let that pass! Let's say she's—usually not. That she very seldom is. Almost—never."

"Van, I am *not* indulging in morbid curiosity! I'm flatly stating that it can't be done!"

"Then I'll just have to show you Jorge's filthy motion pictures, Sir. It can be done. And those bastards do it. Nearly every day."

"No, thank you! But—I must admit to a little morbid curiosity after all. Which, about this particular subject anyhow, I honestly didn't believe I had. But you seem to have aroused it. Since we've gone into the matter this far—a verbal explanation, please?"

"All right. A wooden device—a sort of stock. With straps that go around the wrists, the crooks of the elbows, the bend of the knees, the ankles, maintaining position. So placed that the thighs are—well-separated, Sir. With a crossbar under the abdomen at the waistline to insure the proper height—"

"Goddamnit, Van! The mere position wouldn't cause a dog—"

"Dogs. Big ones. Five or six at a time. Great Danes. Police dogs. Newfoundlanders. Mastiffs. No, it wouldn't. But when the appropriate—orifice—has been painted—or smeared with the blood of a female canine, in heat, Sir? Thus providing the precise olfactory stimulus to cause a dog to behave—most doggishly?"

"Jesus!" Jim whispered.

"Sir, d'you know what's the worst part about it? That—those women—respond. They have to. After they've been—stimulated—tormented—with an electric vibrator for the better part of an hour before the dogs are released—response—even orgasm, becomes automatic, Sir."

"Great fun!" Jim said bitterly.

"For the spectators, yes. The male spectators—the sick, voyeuristic bastards! But not all the spectators enjoy it. Some don't—"

"I'm glad of *that*!" Jim said.

"I'm not. Because the ones who don't—are prisoners, Sir. Brought over especially from the Male Detention Camp at Tarascanolla, or the one at Xilichimocha, and forced to witness the spectacle. The husbands, fathers, brothers, lovers—of the women in question . . ."

"Jesus!" Jim said again.

"They go mad. Very quickly. Most of them find ways to—kill themselves, Sir. And the women—"

"The women, what?"

"Go mad, too. Always. Think about it, Sir. It's not a—*physical* torture in the sense of being especially painful. It's—just sex, after all."

"Van, goddamnit!"

"Sir, García's experts have found a method to violate—the human *per-*

sonality. To—destroy it. To make a woman loathe, despise *herself, who* she is, her body, her own most intimate identity. When those women get a chance to kill themselves, they do it in the most horrible ways. They steal kerosene from the lamps, store it for weeks until they have enough. Then they burn themselves—alive. Or they disembowel themselves with glass from broken bottles. Not—their throats, their wrists, Sir—their bellies. Ripped open. So it will—hurt."

"Van, for the love of God!"

"I'm sorry, Sir; but you asked me. Some of the men—blind themselves. To—to punish their eyes for what they've gazed on helplessly. Sir, there's nothing that one could do to those fiends that would be enough! Nothing, Sir, above hell, and under heaven!"

"No, I suppose not," Jim whispered; "but I can think of several that would be—too much, Son."

"Too much! Why, Sir, I—"

"Yes, Van. Imitating them. Doing to them what they do to others. And thereby—joining them. Becoming their—brothers. Siamese twins—breech-birthed by the same loathesome abomination of a mother. Joined hip and thigh to them—in infamy, in shame—"

"Still—" Van whispered.

"Still, I wouldn't even kill them, Son," Jim said quietly, thoughtfully. "I'd lock them forever in cells lined floor and walls and ceiling—with mirrors. So that every way they turned, they'd have to gaze upon the ultimate horror: themselves. Upon a degradation never before equaled in this world. That ought to do it . . . ."

"It would—if they had either—intelligence or conscience, Sir. But since they have neither . . . There's a phrase I've read somewhere that fits them like a glove: 'The sheer banality of evil—' "

Jim shuddered. Said, his voice dust dry:

"Let's change this subject. Tell me: Is Jorge all right?"

"Yes. I brought him back with me. Your friend—the Communications Expert—has him in a Safe House until we—or they—can get him out of the country. In return for which I gave your friend a print of the Shaggy Dog Movie, Sir. For—propaganda purposes. I think *his* group is intelligent enough, and restrained enough, to use it—well."

"I agree. But will—*your* superiors?"

"No. And I couldn't care less. It's high time my superiors learned that Allen Dulles is dead! That the Domino Theory is nonsense. And that the only reasonable mode of procedure is *yours,* Sir. For which I thank you, most sincerely!"

"*Mine,* Son?" Jim said.

"Yes. Pragmatic flexibility. Suiting the procedure to the actual needs of the area in question, and then trying to reconcile ours with theirs as much as possible. It's intelligent, and it works. You've proven that to me, Sir—"

"Thanks, Van. What about our Sterling Lawmakers? How'd they do?"

"García's sadists could substitute them for those trained dogs, Sir. Only they probably wouldn't have the stamina. *More* filthy pictures, Chief! Stills, this time. *All* the Honorable Representatives from the States of—"

"Corruption, Venery, Drunkenness, and Confusion," Jim supplied.

"Right! Except that I'd throw in the ones of Utter Moronity and Slobbering Senility as well—"

"Thanks. Get on with it, Son!"

"All six of the gentlemen, Sir. In the hotel swimming pool. Bare-assed. With *twelve* bareassed broads. Two *each*. Some of the acrobatics was amazing, Mr. Rush. And I'm not easily amazed . . ."

"But didn't your flash gun tip them off that you were photographing them?"

"Didn't have to use it. They'd left the floodlights on. Half the time I had to stop down to f 5.6, and occasionally to even f 8 to keep from overexposing my negatives. I used a telephoto lens. Got beautiful closeups. Clear as all get out. One of the babes had a birthmark on her fanny, Sir. Came out—great!"

"Good! Now listen: The first thing we're going to do with some of that incriminating photographic evidence is to use it—if necessary—to relieve Costa Verde of its resident atomic physicist. Now. Today. Or at least by tonight. But, after that, you go get packed. You, and Petra. I'm going to fire you, Son, from your Cultural Attaché's job. Loudly and angrily and publicly—in self-defense. For disobeying orders. Which may save me from being declared *persona non grata* for a week or two longer: time that I desperately need. Or it may not. Anyhow, I've got to try. When you get to Washington, I want you to deliver prints of those delightful swimming pool shots to my good friend Senator Thomas H. Marston, from Massachusetts, with this card—"

He took out a visiting card and wrote on it:

"Use these, Tom, if you have to!" and signed it, "Jim Rush."

"Senator Marston is Chairman of the Committee that will have to rule on the proposed loan to Costa Verde. So when those rutting swine start singing the praises of this Green Hell, he'll know why, and will use your evidence to cut them down to size. Your Shaggy Dog and/or Torture Movies should be shown before the Senate's Permanent Committee on Civil Rights, and the UN's Human Rights Commission, both of which I can, and will, arrange, and see that you get due credit for your efforts, to boot. I mean to sink García and Pals. Of course, I'll probably go down with them, but, even so, it's worth it!"

"Because—of Trini, Sir?"

"Yes. You try explaining to anyone, anyone at all who doesn't know her the way we, you and I, do, all the A-Number One, Good, Fine, First Class reasons why her past doesn't count. They wouldn't believe you, Son. Hell, if I didn't know her, *I* wouldn't believe it. Took me months to become convinced that she is what she actually is: an essentially decent kid who simply wasn't allowed to follow her natural bent. That angle's—simply hopeless, Van. I'll just have to grin and bear it, and—protect her, in so far as I am able, from overt insult. But there's something else that currently worries me even more. Something that's—hanging fire. That I don't even know which group is responsible for. Someone borrowed our technique, Van. Got at least three interesting flash shots of me—being embraced by His Nibs' own niece, who is also, in case you didn't know that detail, his adopted daughter. And the young lady wasn't exactly dressed for—skiing, or ice-skating, either one . . ."

"Sir," Van said with a huge, and hugely approving, grin, "I wish you'd teach me how you do it! Truly I do! Patti-Cake, as all her friends call her, is a living doll!"

"I'd gladly teach you if I knew myself, which I don't. What burns me up is that this time I was certifiably innocent of any of the more interesting varieties of horizontal sin. The young woman deliberately invaded my privacy with—well, call it mischief, in mind. But being scared stiff is one of the best antidotes against gross and flagrant temptation ever invented. Hell, if you ever see those pictures, you'll observe I'm standing up. And clothed—if not in my right mind—at least in semiformal evening wear. A smoking jacket, a ruffled shirt, star sapphire studs, and single striped evening trousers, to be exact."

"And—Patti-Cake, Sir?"

"*My* pyjama tops. Unbuttoned down the front. No! By then, she'd taken even *that* off. She was wearing, I seem to recall, a hint of *Je Reviens* by Worth of Paris, a pearl necklace, and a rose—a *white* rose—in her raven hair . . ."

"I'd *love* to see those pictures!" Van said.

"You probably will. You and everyone else who doesn't need a Seeing-Eye dog. Whoever took them wasn't just amusing himself. What distresses me is that they'll probably turn up in some of the more unsavory segments of the public press, thus bringing them to Trini's attention, or what amounts to exactly the same thing, to your Petra's—"

"Sir, I can always ask Petra not to—"

Jim shrugged; said, wearily:

"Thus accomplishing exactly what, Van?"

"Nothing. You're right. Petra would be just as outraged as though they were pictures of *me* with another dame. More so, at the moment, thinking that you were taking advantage of Trini's helpless state. Let's hope they *don't* turn up, Sir!"

"At least not until you and your bride are safely in the States. Trini and I will be joining you shortly. Very shortly. The moment the General finds out he *isn't* going to get that loan, I'm done. *Non grata* and on a plane. Ever thought about going into newspaper work? I'm planning to buy into a small, mostly political, analysis sheet a couple of friends of mine run. So I can offer you a job. That is, of course, if you're as sick of your Combined Idiotic Assininity outfit's tattered cloaks and rusty daggers as a young man of your intelligence ought to be by now—"

"Oh, Jesus!" Van whispered. "Why didn't I think of that one, myself? I have never heard it described better! I am, Sir. Its directives are literally crawling up the back of my throat. And I'd accept *any* job you offer me without a second thought—for the privilege and the sheer pleasure of going on working with you. By the way, when are you firing me?"

"Today, Van."

"But, Sir! What about our helicopter trip to the ruins? You need me to back you up there, and—"

"I'll take Tomás with me. He's good with a gun. Quite as good as you are, Van . . . Now, sit still, and be quiet. I'm going to call Martha in—"

"*Martha,* Sir!"

"Yes. Our suspected Wizard of Oz is her current boy friend. Maybe we'd better start by testing her *bragas* with a Geiger counter for radioactivity. By now she should be reaching critical mass . . ."

Martha hit the ceiling when he repeated that remark to her. Burst into tears. Offered him her resignation, effective at once.

"I won't take it," Jim said, and grinned at her. "You're a damned good secretary even if you do suffer from radioactive pants. That's *new,* Martha! You're making history. Beats ordinary hot ones a hundred miles."

"Mis—ter Rush! Mis—terrr Rush, I—"

"Oh, come off of it, Martha! Take a look at *this.* Ever see this type before?"

He took that clipping out of his billfold and passed it over, but with the caption folded back out of sight.

"Of course!" Martha sniffed. "That's my Yoga Professor, Guru Hriday Hananum . . ."

"Unfold the clipping, Martha, dear. *Read,*" Jim said.

Martha read, stuttering over the words:

"Vanished—Indian scientist—Sir Gadahar Gorakhnath—father of India's—Atomic bomb—Ohhhhhhhhhh Jesus!"

Jim went on grinning at her.

"You've been *had,* Martha, darling," he said. "Remember all the hard times you've given me for a little alleged miscegenation? Well, my kid's likely to be on the shady side, but he sure as hell won't come out with a cobalt casing and bending the needles of every Geiger counter within five city blocks right off the scale!"

The minute he said that, he was sorry. Even Martha's lips went white. She groped blindly behind her for a chair. Van Schuyler jumped up, caught her by the arms and eased her down into it. Jim, himself, went to the water cooler and came back with a paper cup full of ice water.

Martha gulped it down, strangled on it, broke into disconsolate sobbing.

"Martha," Jim said gently; "I'm sorry. I'm a beast. An—insensitive beast. I'm very sorry. I apologize—most humbly. Do forgive me, dear . . ."

" 'S all right, Sir!" Martha wept. "You're—rrright—I—I *have* been—having an affair—with him. Even gggggot used to—to his—color. H–he was sohhhhh—ggggoood to me! Soohhh sweeet!"

"Martha, you see any rocks in my hands?" Jim said. "Hell, he may be a prince of a guy for all I know. I'm perfectly willing to do what I can to help him—if he—and *you* want me to. And he's going to need help badly, Martha. And soon."

Martha jackknifed up, her pale eyes wide.

"Sir!" she gasped. "You don't mean—"

"Yes, Martha; he very probably is in some danger. His country's Intelligence agency is definitely looking for him. And at the party a couple of nights ago, I may have unwittingly given them a lead. So I'd suggest this: Bring him over to my place tonight. I mean my place in the Silver Door. Where I live with Trini. Van and Petra will be there, too. It's safer than the residence. More private. That is, if you don't mind entering my Love Nest—Den of iniquity type pad, Martha, darling!"

"Sir—that scriptural quotation you mentioned definitely applies to me, too, doesn't it? And that other one about people who live in glass houses. Anyhow, I'm giving up rock throwing as a pastime. Or even pebble tossing. Can't—afford it. Not any more. And, Sir—he *is.* A prince of a guy. Very definitely!"

"Then marry him, Martha. Don't let stupid prejudices stand in your way . . ."

Martha's well coiffed, curly blonde head came up, proudly.

"Sir—I mean to. But can *you* afford to give me that advice?"

Jim smiled at her.

"Yes, Martha, I can. And with a clear conscience. Trini and I have been married for several weeks now," he said.

That problem was solved within minutes. Sir Gadahar gratefully accepted political asylum in the Embassy itself until Jim could query State as to the possibility of his being admitted to the States as a political refugee. They didn't even have to show him the photographs and motion pictures of the torture sessions in the prison camps. Just being in Costa Verde several months had been enough. Or, as Sir Gadahar himself put it:

"Any man who gives Manuel García an Atomic bomb is a suicidal fool!"

But after his guests had all gone home, Jim Rush was confronted, again, with the enormity of the problem facing him, its total insolubility. While the two other couples had been there, Trini had been pleasant, even mildly gay, and, to his vast relief, had eaten her supper with a mild appetite. But once his friends had departed, the frozen silence between Jim Rush and his tiny bride towered up to the glacial stars.

"Trini—" Jim groaned.

"Yes, *Don* Jaime?" she whispered.

"Why are you doing this to me?"

"But I am doing nothing to thee, *mi Amo.*"

He caught the bitter difference in pronunciation. She had cut the final "r" sound which in Spanish is trilled or rolled, "¡*mi Amorrrrr!*" converting *"mi amor,"* "my love," into that hurtful, hateful *"mi amo,"* "my master." Much more abject than *"mi dueño,"* which means "my master" too; but in the sense of guardian, guide, protector, and hence does not exclude—love. And bitterer in its groveling self-abasement than *"mi señor,"* which means "my lord" but which is quite often substituted, especially when a man is considerably older than his wife, as a token of—rather fond!—respect, for *"mi marido,"* "my husband."

"Not *tu amo,*" he said sadly; *"tu amor.* Thy love."

"But thou dost not love me," she whispered. "Not any more."

"How can you speak for me, Trini? How can you know what I feel?"

"I know. And thou hast right. I am—vile. Thou canst not love me."

"Trini—hear me. Believe me. I—love thee. Truly. I have forgot—that of the picture. It matters not."

"Thou hast not forgot it. If I saw thee—with another woman—naked—and doing—things—I should *never* forget it, ¡*mi grand Señor!* I should go—mad, *mi Amo.* I should cut my throat—and die in my blood—choking upon thy name. Thou art stronger than I; but thou hast not, canst not forget this thing. Thou canst not even—kiss me now—without—nausea—thinking that thou canst taste—on my lips—within my mouth—the vile vilenesses—of other men."

'Oh, Jesus!' he thought. 'How goddamned perceptive she is!'

"Thou'rt—an Angel. And a Saint—so thou canst try—to forgive me. But thou'rt a man, and this is beyond any man's strength, even thine. I have not—killed myself because I cannot—murder—Trinita. But—after she is born—"

"Trini!" he all but screamed.

"No, no—my Love, my Heart, my Soul—¡Amor mío, Corazon mío, Alma de mi Alma! I shall not kill myself, even then. But the Gods will take me. The Old Gods. The Angry Old Gods of the Tluscola will—stop my heart, drink my breath."

"Trini—" he moaned, or mourned. Or—both.

She took his hand, rubbed her cheek against it. But she did not kiss it. Instead she murmured, her voice a breeze rustling the chopa's leaves, soft, and sweet, and musical:

"I—love thee, Don Jaime. For a little while thou hast made my life—heaven, paradise. Thou didst not withdraw thy love from me of thy own free will. Therefore I dare give birth to Trinita, knowing that thou wilt never hate her, abuse her—shame her—as my father did me—"

"Oh, God!" he said. "God God God God!"

He dragged her into his arms, held her to him. But her hands came up, pushing against his chest.

"Let me go, Don Jaime," she said flatly, calmly; "for I am—very tired. And—lacking thy love—of this my life, itself, I think . . ."

And hearing how her voice sounded then, saying that, something in him—died.

He went down to the garage below the building and got the Porsche. For hours he slammed it around dizzy hairpin turns in rutted, gravel-surfaced mountain roads at absolutely insane speeds until some of the suicidal, death seeking rage at his own helplessness drained out of him. Then he drove it back down in the direction of Ciudad Villalonga until he came to the residence. Without even thinking about it, he drove the sleek little car through the gates, and left it parked on the drive before the door. Went up the stairs and into the hall without so much as saying good night to the Marines.

Even then, he did not go to bed. He did undress, of course; put on his pyjamas and a robe; but after having done that, he went back downstairs, dug a full quart of Scotch whiskey out of the pantry, strode into the silent empty kitchen—for the servants only stayed overnight at the residence on the rare, special occasions, such as that troublesome and trouble making party, when Jim asked them to—dragged trays of ice cubes out of the refrigerator, filled a glass with cubes and poured that excellent smoky tasting Scotch over them.

For the first time in close to twenty years—the last previous occasion being one of Virginia's long, detailed, tearful—and clinical!—confessions of one of her numerous infidelities—he deliberately tried to get drunk. But he couldn't quite do it. For although he drank for the better part of two hours he simply became—remote, detached, one bearable move away from awareness, anguish, pain. At half past the second hour of his self-defeating assault upon his own capacity for thinking, fully being, feeling pain, Patricia Montenegro came into the kitchen and stood there—or rather leaned there against the doorframe, staring at him. She swayed, drunkenly, even as she leaned there. She didn't seem quite able to stand up.

'Stoned out of her skull!' he thought contemptuously. He said:

"How the hell did you get in here, Patricia?"

"There're—" she whispered, her voice infinitely weary, infinitely sad, but completely sober, without any trace of the giddy hilariousness of marijuana, nor the blurred, slurred, unclear enunciation of drunkenness about it, "some small advantages to being the adopted daughter of the Head of the State. Your guards—know me. Even your *Yanqui* Marines. My silly face is—always in the newspapers. I told your *Yanqui* Doodle Dandies—I had a date with you. They believed *that* quite readily. Seems to me a custom of yours, Jim."

"If so—what's it to *you?*" he snarled.

"Nothing. No. That's not true. I love you—so it hurts. I am a— Latin woman. A jealous, bitchy Latin woman. If I ran into you with another woman—except Trini, whose feet I am not fit to kiss!—I'd claw out her eyes!"

"Oh, Christ!" he said.

"You've been drinking. Tell me: Are you drunk?"

"Yes," he said, "I'm drunk. I'm goddamned drunk. Why?"

"No reason. Another lie. I'm glad. Makes things easier for me—"

She walked—or rather swayed—over to the table. Swept everything off it, glasses, ice, the Scotch, so that they crashed to the floor, broke.

"Why—goddamn!" he howled.

She caught at the hem of her skirt, and swept it up around her waist. Tucked it into the broad leather belt she wore, so that it and her slip stayed up. She hadn't on any panties. She had come there with deliberate intent. She sat down on the kitchen table, then lay back across it, sprawled out, her legs and thighs agape. Contemptuously. Offensively. Obscenely. Said, wearily, flatly, calmly:

"¡Jodeme!"

He felt sick. That word is as ugly in Spanish as its equivalent is in English. As rough. Both leave all the tenderness out. Exclude—love. Involve more often than not anger. Which was what tore him now.

"That's what you want?" he grated. "All right, Bitch; you're going to get it."

He stood up. Yanked off that tawny silk robe. The pyjamas. Came to her. She smiled at him wearily, wanly. Said:

"That's what I want. And don't—play with me. I'm ready. I've been ready all night. Come on. Do it to me. Hard. Be—brutal. Hurt me. Tear me apart. Rip—"

The human male has cruelty bred into his nerves, his blood, his bone. Sadism is a very slightly surplus by-product of what the ancestral naked ape actually needed to survive in an all too hostile world. And acquired evolutionary traits are less easily discarded than we like to think they are. Gentle, civilized Jim Rush abruptly found—though one part of his mind retained, dully and bemused, enough of his ordinary sensitivity to be consciously surprised at his own reactions—that he thoroughly enjoyed what her face did in response to the deliberate savagery of his penetrating thrust, which was to twist itself into a grimace of all but mortal pain. The sounds she made—the sobbing intake of breath, the hoarse, panted "Ah, Ah, Ahhhhh!" that grated, scraped up from her throat—afforded him a marvelously evil sense of satisfaction.

But then she was silent. Raptly, intently silent, for a long, slow writhing time. Some tensely straining, sinuous moments more went by before she said:

"Jaime—" whispering his name, her voice—dying.

"*Now* what the hell?" he said.

"I—love thee. I love thee! Once—more. Like this—once more. Make me—*gozar*. Come. I—need to. I haven't—in—a longgg—Ah!—time Wait. Wait. Slowly. Slowly. Sl-low-ly—Now! Now! As hard as you can! As fast Try to *kill* me. To destroy me. Please!"

He tried. Almost succeeded. Held back by his own near drunkenness, he brought her easily and quickly to orgasm, but when he tried to race to join her, the whiskey wouldn't let him, his own anger and desperation wouldn't let him, and the anguished recognition that he was rapidly sobering up and would soon think, reflect, remember, and experience the pure hell of unrelieved, unmitigated shame wouldn't let him, so he brought her there again and again and again, one shattering climax still tearing her, not even diminished very much before she was shuddering, writhing, thrashing into the next and the next and the next and her screams were vibrating the windows with such intensity that both the Marines heard her and came racing around the house and stood there, watching through the lighted kitchen window that mortal combat, that spectacle of unrelieved ugliness, hearing that demented screaming until finally and mercifully, she fainted.

He picked her up. Stumbled up the stairs with her, elbowed the door of his bedroom open. Entered it. Lay her down across his bed. Loosened her knitted-wool sweater blouse. Tried to take it off her. Found that he couldn't. It seemed to be stuck to her. Roughly, brutally, he rolled her over face down. Tried to pull the unbuttoned blouse off her shoulders. He could have, of course, in the sense that he was strong enough; but the way it clung to her warned him not to. Bending close, he saw why it wouldn't come free. It was stuck to the flesh of her back with great clotted, dried masses of her own blood. And under the little of it he had pulled loose, her back was no longer sun-tanned olive white but mottled, blue-red, purple, cut completely to ribbons, and now in those places he had pulled the knit Jersey blouse away from beginning to bleed again sullenly.

'And I thought she was drunk—doped!' he wailed inside his mind.

He got up, went into his bathroom, came back with warm, wet towels. Soaked that knit Jersey blouse off her. Cut what was left of her slip off with a pair of scissors. Rolled her over like a limp rag doll again, unfastened the leather belt, worked it out and from under her, pulled her skirt down until she was decently covered; began to bathe her forehead, her throat, her mouth with cold water until her eyes fluttered open. She smiled at him.

"¡El Cid Campeador!" she said.

"Patti—" he husked, "I'm—sorry. You don't know how sorry—"

"I'm not," she said crisply; "it was—worth the beating to find—finally find—a *man*!"

He said:

"Your Uncle?"

"In person. He started out quite seriously to beat me to death. With his riding crop. Only he's out of condition. And I'm—tougher than I look. So he got too tired to—finish me off. Or, maybe—he couldn't quite bring himself to. He *does* love me, y'know—"

"Hell of a way to show it!" Jim said.

"For—him—a good way. Proves he—cares, Jaime. I suppose the sight of me sobbing and retching on the floor at his feet must have—at least given him pause. Then I—passed out—and that frightened him enough to make him really stop . . ."

"But why, Patti—why?" Jim said.

"*You*—darling! Somebody sent him copies of those flash photos.

Without even a note. He was so enraged I was able to steal them back from him. They're in my bag. It's downstairs in your kitchen, I suppose. I like them. I look—very nice. So do you except you've all your clothes on. A pity . . ."

"Why is that a pity?" Jim said.

"Because then he'd have had apoplexy and the revolution would be over—and won! As it is, he almost did. Incidentally, he is *not* going to do anything about you. Because, oddly enough, when I told him that you—refused me, rejected me, pushed me off, he *believed* me. Said you were smart enough to do that. Sufficiently prudent—though the word he used, mainly to taunt me, hurt my feelings, because he knows better!—was cowardly. And when I said that was nonsense, he hit back with the truth—the cruel truth—that you aren't even hungry—that way. Which got me wild. So I said I was going to jolly well awake— arouse—your carnal appetites, because I wanted—want you so terribly and precisely *that* way, that I was going out of my mind. Only I didn't put it either so chastely or so delicately. I probably screamed every *taco y palabrote y obscenidad* in the Spanish language at him. And that, of course, drove him completely around the bend, so he got his crop and started beating on me with the announced and serious intention of beating me to death. He'd locked poor *Tía* Luisa out of my room, but she could hear him beating me and me crying and yelling and screaming and him cursing me, calling me every kind of cheap *puta* on the streets, and then she was screaming louder than even I was, until she fainted, and then *I* fainted too, and all the fun and games were over in the Illustrious Mansion of the *Ilustrísimos Garcías,* First Family of the Glorious Republic of Costa Verde! Aren't you proud of yourself, *Cielo?* You do arm the nicest scandals, don't you?"

"Oh, Jesus!" he said.

"Anyhow—you're safe, darling. And that's all that matters. He *can't* take action against you unless you make a stupid mistake and do something he can accuse you of publicly . . ."

"It seems to me that I—we—already have," Jim said miserably.

"He *can't,* Jaime! Not about *this.* One doesn't call one's own women whores in public, *Amor mío!* In fact, he's gone to the country for the weekend, leaving me—he thinks!—totally incapacitated in my bed. So we have until Monday night, dearest. I—vote we make the best of it!"

"Patricia—" Jim groaned.

"Help me up. I'm going to take a nice long soak in your tub. Then— an *encore,* dearest? Please? But less—rough, this time? I don't believe I can take your slaughterhouse floor technique anymore *this* weekend . . ."

He thought bitterly, angrily, sadly:

'Why the hell not? Trini—will never know—and I have already become—a swine.'

When she came out of his bathroom finally, a full hour and a half later, she was almost her own wild plains and grasslands *pampa* creature-self, as lithe as an antelope's fawn, as graceful, her waist-length, black hair swinging about her slenderness, setting off her golden, tawny, puma's color, the singing perfection of her lines.

She saw him looking at her and stood still briefly, then shifted—'flowed' his mind supplied the accurate, the right word—from one professional model's absolutely perfect pose to another, feeling the flickering heat of his gaze as so many caresses, touching, straying, gliding—lingering, of course, where male eyes always linger, upon the thick, black, glistening wild tangles beneath her upraised arms, pluming proudly up her belly from between her thighs, upon the huge, dark cherry-red areolas, and the swelling mounds and buds within them, quivering, puckering, erecting under his insistent gaze.

"*¡Eres un Brujo!*" she laughed. "A Sorcerer! You get me all—excited—just looking at me! Go on! Look some more—it may save you—work!" Then softly, huskily, shudderingly, "Ay-yeeeee! Know what? I just *did*! A nice, lovely, soft little one! You—have—bedroom eyes . . ."

"Patricia—" he said, and his voice was very bleak, "This has to stop. It has to stop now. I was drunk before. Hurt—angry. Miserable excuses. But still, excuses. Now there'd be—none."

She came to him. Sank down beside him. Looked into his eyes. Whispered:

"Don't—think about *her*. Not now. She—can afford to—to lend me—a little happiness. She—who has a lifetime's supply of it. Whom are we hurting? She need never know . . ."

"Me," he said harshly. "My conception of myself. The very image of what I thought I was."

"And *what* did you think you were, *mi Amor? ¿Aparte, bien entendido, de un jinete de excepción de yeguas salvajes cómo yo?*"

He groaned aloud. Because what she had said meant—more or less—"Besides a champion rider of wild mares like me?"

"A little different from the run of the mill, Patricia," he said slowly. "*Not* a slave to my dangling gut . . ."

She put down a slim hand and caught hold of him, stroking, caressing, slowly, gently.

"It's not dangling *now*," she said.

"Oh, goddamn you, Patti!" he howled.

She kissed him, molding his mouth, clinging, playing absolutely maddening tactile games with her lips' soft underflesh, her tongue tip. Slid out, off, from his mouth, descending his throat kiss by slow clinging kiss, nibbled long minutes at the hard, diminutive, male nipples of his breast, slid down his lean, gold-dusted belly, poked a michievoulsy vibrating tongue tip into his umbilicus, slid further down still, her warm, wet mouth opening, engulfing him, beginning a wonderfully skillful fellatio—

He clawed his fingers into her nightblack mane, yanked her away from there, brutally; said:

"Stop it!"

She stared at him. Laughed. Said:

"*¡Eres un pudico!* Why—not? Don't you like it?"

"Yes. Very much. I just don't want *you* to do it."

Her dark eyes widened, widened. A startled, tiny leap of comprehension got into them. She whispered:

"Same question: Why not, Jim?"

"I like you. You're—a person to me. I may—even love you. I don't know. I'm sure I could if I were free to allow myself to. So I don't need—whore's tricks—from *you*."

She lay there staring at him. And it was at that very moment, almost surely, that their shared and mutual tragedy was armed. For her, the true and classic kind. Grecian, not Elizabethan, in all its enormous—Fates and Furies driven!—dimensions. Implacable. Inexorable. Inevitable—and mortal. For him, a moral one, curiously Sisyphean, because he was going to push the bruising stone of this memory—in sorrow and in anguish!—endlessly up the hill of his years until the day he died. Very slowly her eyes hazed over, filled up, went brilliant, spilled.

"I'm sorry, Patti," he said.

"Don't be. Jim—Jaime—please—*¡Por favor!* make love to me. I—I don't know how. All I know is—what any *zorra* knows: *a joder*. To—fuck. I'm sorry! You don't even like to hear me *say* it, do you?"

"Now, you're learning," he said.

"*Por favor,* Jaime! Please!"

He said: "All right." He thought: 'Forgive me, Trini. And Padre Pío's God . . .'

And—made love to her. Very well, for in this, as in the matter of his dancing, practice had brought, if not perfection, at least a notable degree of improvement. In fact, under the given circumstances, he managed rather a bit *too* well. Which wasn't a question of technique, skill, though by then he was skillful enough, and, more importantly, perfectly self-dominated, controlled. The nervous, anxiety-driven man's failing, *ejaculatio praecox,* he had definitely, and completely overcome. Instead, it was a matter of—attitudes, both his, and hers.

He rather liked Patti, but he did not love her. And it is one of life's most cruel ironies that it is far, far easier to make love—physically, sexually—granted, of course, the basic minima of normal femininity and attractiveness—to a woman one does *not* love than to the overwhelming object of all one's ardors, dreams, and desires. A certain detachment, distance—even some slight degree of indifference—all help in the maintenance of the major male obligation of self-control.

As for Patricia, for the very first time in her life she gave herself, wanting to, surrendered herself, totally, not blindly, helplessly, but willing that surrender almost blissfully. Her identity, *who* she was, she, herself, a person living, dreaming, thinking in this world, entered into what was no longer—she realized abruptly, with awe, amazement, wonder, and a flickering, icy serpent's tongue of fear!—a mere amusement, a form of play, but a—rite. A solemn ritual. The ceremony of—adoration. The self-immolation of the willing victim upon the high altar of a very cruel god.

And since a perfect act of sexual love consists basically in achieving synchronization, in adjusting the evolutionary dysfunction in the rhythms of the female and the male of the human species, so that said rhythms accord with each other in their intervals, modulation, beat, and coincide in their cresting, shattering climax, Patricia's sacrifice of—pride, identity, will, her life itself as a separate entity, as anything of her own, throwing these things and her rarely lovely body into the pyre to be consumed for, and by, her love—helped far more than his emotional detachment did in accomplishing a result he had not dreamed of achieving, that, in sober fact, he did not even want: which was to bind her, helplessly, hopelessly, and for what turned out to be the rest of her pitifully short life, into the abysmal moral slavery of unrequited love.

For 'How all occasions did inform against her'—even such simpler factors as his age, his fatigue. Because at forty-seven, the heyday in his blood *was* tamed, *was* humbled, and *did* indeed wait upon the senses; while to her now—truly, and for the first time!—flaming youth, far more important aspects of her personality, her being, than her long lost and half forgot virtue, had become as wax and melted in that fire.

For, even physically, he was tired. Not too tired, but tired enough to allow his attention to drift away from the here and now, from too close a preoccupation with the clinical details of what was going on, to forget for long minutes at a time, the physical, neural sensations, olfactory, gustatory, visual, even that most compelling, most insistent of them all, the tactile, the discernment of—pressure, texture, moisture, heat—the perception of that maddening, undulant, peristaltic cling and writhe and scald that are the female contributions to the act of love, of sex.

And thereby, he was able to prolong the act itself far beyond anything she was accustomed to, beyond, in fact, what she was—emotionally, psychologically, perhaps even physically—capable of bearing, which was a thing—a danger!—he wasn't even aware of, so how could he have guessed its consequences? How great they were going to be? How terrible?

In fact he was not concerned with these—as yet—hypothetical consequences, nor did dear Patti-Cake, herself, occupy his mind, as he went about the—to him, anyhow, since all his reflexes were too conditioned to one small being with whom, for whom, and in whom sex and love were identical, the same miracle and glory—mildly exciting routine of shared sensual pleasures. Actually, he was wondering with sad amazement why he did *not* feel the abysmal guilt he had been sure he was going to feel. Why he could think of Trini quite calmly, though with the twin determinations that she should never learn of this casual, meaningless betrayal, and that he would never repeat it. But, beyond that, it simply did not matter. It had nothing to do with Trini, nor the way he felt about her. It was a fourth-dimensional episode existing at some oblique tangent to, and without connection with what was, and always would be—his life.

Patricia moaned, suddenly, the sound dark, breath-torn, pain-rent. Which called his attention to her again. Dragged him back from his own Lotus-Eater's Land to the here and now. He contemplated that young, usually lovely face. It had become almost ugly. It was twisted, contorted, anguished, intent, surely, upon the achievement of the release, the relief of orgasm. He thought about how often, and to how great a degree, sexual love can be a form of torture. He bent and gently kissed away that ugliness, contortion, anguish. Drew back. Smiled at her.

But she surged up, rammed her face into the hollow of his throat, grinding it against him as if to erase her features by abrasion, and he felt her tears, racing like lava, searing and scalding down their conjoined, very nearly mutual flesh.

He said sadly, reproachfully, not breaking the rhythm:

"Why do—you cry?"

"Does not—the victim—cry—when *el Torturador* kills him—her!—so slowly? My life—is over, Jaime!"

"Don't say that, Patti—" he said.

"Over! *¡Y por tortura!* And I—I love *mi Atormentador*! I love thee—who art—killing me—so softly. Who—so slowly—sweetly—ends—my life!"

"Patti," he whispered. "Please!"

"I cannot live without thee, after *this*. And thy loving me—ha! This casual tip—of a few of thy leftover hours tossed—*¡Ay si!* Torment me! I *want* thee to! Like *that*—again. Please! Please! *¡Ay–Dios!*—tossed to thy—gratuitous—whore—for—poorly rendered—services—I'm not even *good* at it, am I?—is meaningless to thee. *I* am meaningless to thee. And—even to *say* it kills me!—thou'rt *hers*. Trini's. So now—"

"Patricia, for God's love!"

"So now, you will have the favor to—spoil *this*. Ruin it. Make it—ordinary. Vulgar. Or better still—bestial . . ."

"Bestial?" he said.

"*¡Ay sí!* As—before. Be *¡un brutote! ¡Una bestia!* Pound me to pieces! Tear me in halves up the middle. Brutalize me. Violate me. Make *this*—ugly. Make it—hideous . . . Make me—forget—how sweet it was! How tender!"

He said: "No. The slaughterhouse is closed, Patti. Off limits. Like that, never again, my dear . . ."

She opened her eyes. Stared at him. Said:

"Then I shall go—mad. Surely. For thee. Over thee. I shall—howl—in the street before thy door, *mi* Jaime! Until they drag me away to my cell in the *manicomio* and chain me to the wall! So—finish—*this* will you? So—that I—may go home—and finish *me*. Tell me: What's the quickest way to die? The easiest? No! What's the slowest—and the worst? I want to go out—screaming. Shrieking thy name so that all the world may—"

She stopped. Gasped. Her eyes—went out. Became opaque. Smoky. She shuddered. Said, making of the words a moaning sound. Or a mourning one. Or both.

"Jaime—no. Please, no. Oh, no. Not like—*this*! Not—killing me—so softly. No. *¡No, por favor!* Oh no no no no no no—No! Ah—Thou. Oh, Thou. James, the Cruel. Sweet—Assassin. Tender—Executioner! Thou!"

He said: "Why do you call me such things, Patti?"

She clung to him, crying; whispered:

"Art thou not thus? Hast thou not—written—*finis*—upon the last page—of my life? Men have broken women's hearts before, *Amor mío,* but who else but thee hath left one as thou art leaving me—without pride, will, mind—identity? Robbed of *what* and *who* I was? Reduced to—a *thing? Thy* thing, Jaime! Abject, without hope, bound to thee, to my need of thee, forever . . . Is this not—unpardonable? Especially since—thou canst never be wholly mine and I—*¡Ay pobre de mi!* I love thee with all my heart?"

Jim stared at her. A long time. Staring at her didn't exactly constitute hard work. Not as she was then, lying there beside him, clad only in her nightshade hair. But all he felt was sadness.

"You are free of me, Patti," he said gently. "We have no future, you and I. *This* has no future. I have a wife, who's already great with my child. In whom, not even you can find a flaw. Can you?"

"No," she whispered. "Trini is—perfect for you. She is a good child, a sweet one—who was forced into that life. It is I who am the born and perfect bitch. Only Jaime, *mi Amor*—¡*eternamente mi Amor!*—what's that got to do with—¿*can mi esclavitud?* With this—hopeless—sick —abject—slavery you've forced me into? Will facing facts free me? Indulging in sweet reason? How little you know me!"

"Patti—" he said sadly.

"So take me home. Now. I won't stay until Monday night. If I were to do that, I could never bring myself to leave you . . ." She shook her head as if to clear it; said coolly, crisply, her voice become even, calm: "Jim, lend me one of your sport shirts and a sweater, will you? You're small enough for them to fit me, thank goodness! Or else I shall have to ride through the streets of Ciudad Villalonga naked to the waist. With my breasts bare and showing. And since—they—like all the rest of me—are *yours, mi Amor;* I don't want—other men looking at them any more . . ."

"Patti, will you please, please stop it?" he said.

"Besides, my treating the shameless ones of this town to a little strip-tease through the windows of your car would surely cause you trouble. And I don't want to cause you trouble. I have finished causing you trouble, *Jaimito mío*—forever. Oh! That reminds me. Speaking of causing trouble, we'd better get rid of all the incriminating evidences before your servants come back. When do they come back, *mi Jaime?*"

"Monday." He looked at his watch. "Which is to say—tomorrow."

"Oh! Is it already Sunday? But, of course! Thou wert a devilishly long time—abusing me. Wouldst like to abuse me some more, now, *Cielo?* Thou'rt much too expert at this—abusing of girls. Who taught thee all that? Trini?"

"Various," he said. "And I wouldn't like to. I'm much too tired. What's more, *you* don't want to either."

"True," she sighed; "I am—dead. I am sore in places I did not know it was possible to become sore; I ache all over—inside and out. And—my heart is broken. I wish to die. Dost thou not have a poison to give me? Or an old fashioned straight razor with which I can cut my throat?"

"Patti, for God's sake!" he said.

"*De acuerdo.* I shall be good. Jim, my love, we now must go down into the basement, and burn the bloody rags you soaked and cut off me, in your furnace; *o séa*: my Jersey blouse, my bra, and my slip. Then we must remove the sheets from this bed and put them in the washing machine—it is an automatic one, no? Anyhow, I know how to work

them; I am a very good housewife, y'know. Could you not obtain the
ambassadorship of your country in Saudia Arabia? Then you would have
only to become a Mohammadan and then you could also marry me.
And two others. Only *I* should not permit you that!"

"Lord!" he laughed. "Speaking of the fate worse than death!"

"Thus does it seem to you? Being married to me, I mean?"

"No," he said honestly, "being married to you would be very pleasant, Patti. But being married to Trini and to you at the same time
would be just about the closest approximation to Hell any man ever
dreamed up."

"That, yes. The first day would end in a hair pulling contest. By the
end of the first week one of us would have cut the throat of the other. Of
that you can be secure. But we must not forget removing all evidences of
my having been here from your house—a detail you'd never think of,
but that comes naturally to me as the result of my lifetime practice of
sneaking around, being *la pluscumperfecta zorra!*"

He said sadly:

"Do you—mean to continue with that sort of life, Patti?"

She shook her head. Said, evenly, quietly:

"No. Nor any other. My life is—over, Jim. There's only one you, and
she's got you. So I am left—with nothing at all. Turn me loose now. Let
me up. I must go bathe again now—or at least shower. I hate to. I wish
I didn't have to . . ."

He stared at her; said:

"Why do you wish that, Patti?"

"I like your smell. You've left it all over me. I wish I could keep it;
wear it as a perfume. But Auntie has a nose like a vulture's, or an Andean condor's. She'd sniff and say: 'Pat–tee! What *have* you been doing?' "

"Lord!" Jim said.

"And I—" Patricia's voice trembled, almost broke; "I can't even tell
her—proudly!—'I've been making love, Auntie. Glorious love. With—
the *only* man in the world—with—*Don* Jaime!' "

She turned her back to him. Her shoulders shook. Then very slowly
she went into the bathroom. He didn't try to stop her.

When they drew up before the García Villa in the Porsche, she kissed
him, said:

"Jim—Jaime—"

"Yes, Patti?"

"If—something—happens to me—don't blame yourself. Don't be—
sorry—or grieve . . . Promise me?"

"Patricia!" he said.

She took his hand. Kissed the palm of it the way Trini used to do before that flickering horror in light-darkened silver salts had got between them, whispered:

"I love thee, Jaime. I shall love thee—all the rest of my life—until the day I die: Friday afternoon of this very week. At precisely five thirty P.M.!"

He said:

"You'd better explain that one, Patti!"

"No. I don't have to explain it. It will be in all the papers. A title from Hemingway: *Death in the Afternoon.* Tell me, my Jim—*mi adorado* Jaime—will you—cry?"

He said: "Oh, Jesus!"

She got out of the car. Stood there looking at him as though she meant to memorize his face. Whirled, suddenly. Plunged head down and visibly sobbing through the gateway of that magnificent villa in Golden Door.

He sighed. Thought, hoping conviction into the words: 'She's young. She'll get over this—find someone else and . . .'

He backed the Porsche up. Turned it around. Drove it back to the residence. He couldn't go back to the apartment in Silver Door. Not now. Not today. Facing Trini at that point in time, at that moral nadir of his existence, took far more courage—or more sheer gall—than he at that moment had. Again he parked the little car on the driveway, went up the stairs, ignoring the broadly grinning Marines. As he came into the hall the telephone was ringing, which meant, surely, Patti again, for who else would call him at six thirty A.M. of a Sunday morning as he saw by his watch it was? He picked it up, said, harshly:

"*¡Diga!* Speak!"

"Jim—I'm out at the airport. The plane just landed. Please come get me!" that clear, cool, crisp, well modulated—and achingly beloved!— voice said.

CHAPTER

29

When he came into the waiting room of the terminal, and saw Grace sitting there with her bags piled up around her, he stopped still, and simply stood there, recreating her anew in his mind, his heart. And, hanging there motionless, almost unbreathing, wrapped in a silence, a sadness, so deep, so all-pervading that it existed at one remove from here and now, and another from death and forever, being, maybe, equidistant from them both, what he thought—slowly and carefully, taking advantage of the fact that she had not yet seen him—in his offbeat, inconoclastic way, was that the situation between Grace Nivens and himself was the perfect demonstration of the reasons that mankind actually needs those curious games, practices, rites, and rituals, and the even more curious objects that sometimes result from them, that we call, and like to think of as—art.

For life was—so amorphous. So formless. Life didn't arrange a beginning, a swiftly rising action, a thunderous climax, a dénouement, a crashing, tremendous end. Life stirred everything into its formless, shapeless mud. Let all bright, brave beginnings peter out, all enterprises—whatever their pitch, their moment!—turn forever awry, and lose the name of action. Or else—arranged senseless confrontations, insane, purposeless ironies like—this one. Like the absolutely fiendish—and all the more so for being meaningless!—cruelty of having Grace come back into his life, surely with the intention to enter it fully, become part—the better part!—of it, round it off, complete it, too late. After he had given her up, forever. After a whole series of events, in which the inseparability of obscene farce and lofty tragedy was conclusively demonstrated, had made his doing anything remotely constructive about her, himself, their lives, an utter impossibility.

He hung there, not so much thinking as recognizing: 'I love her. *Her* and nobody else. Not Patricia, surely. And not even poor little Trini. At least, not now. I did, at first. I did until confronted with—the concrete images *I* lacked the magnitude of soul, the capacity for—forgiveness to—sustain. But I—*love*—this woman. I have from the first instant that I saw her. I love, worship, adore—this tall goddess, Diana and Pallas Athena—and perhaps even Jocasta of my deepest beginnings! I shall love her 'til—and past!—the day I die . . ."

He moved then, and suddenly her pale blue eyes—sweeping towards the door, more than a little impatiently, he was abruptly aware, with a surge of a warm and nearly total happiness, concentrated and concerned behind her heavy glasses—saw him, or rather discerned that the short, dapper figure in the doorway was actually he, and blazed with what was indisputably—joy.

She jumped up and came striding towards him. And his heart sank straight through the airport terminal's floor. For one thing, surrounded by a race of people essentially small and short, he had more or less forgot how tall she was—how immensely, terribly tall. For another, though he really had not forgot her unique, special, all her own and nobody else's beauty, he *had,* out of resignation, despair, and his own involvement—unplanned, unsought—with Trini, tried to convince himself that he had got over the way he felt about Grace, had deliberately put aside, vanquished his love for her. But thirty seconds—standing there unbreathing just inside the terminal's door, and gazing at her—had reduced that delusion to the utter nonsense he now realized it was. He loved Grace Nivens, period. And that love was unaltered and unaffected by, stood aside from, towered over the the way he felt towards other women, even towards two such rare and marvelous specimens of femininity as Trini and Patricia. He discarded within seconds the sophistries and self-torments of moral considerations; what he had done—in vain and futile attempts to fill up the echoing vacuum created by Grace's voluntary withdrawal from his life, by her absence—sank down into the utter irrelevancies that they were.

Leaving their consequences, which now rained down upon him in a series of absolutely maiming blows. The fact that he still loved Grace Nivens so much that looking at her *hurt* could, perhaps—in pain and sorrow and bitter silence!—be contained. But what under heaven and above hell could he decently do to halt, terminate, end this expression of almost rapturous delight on this countenance of Pallas Athena, beauty and intelligence combined, heliographing from a full ten meters away the news that she had finally and completely given up fighting against the way she obviously felt about him as well, and had come down here *mostly* with getting him back in mind?

He was, he realized, in one hell of a mess. Item one: He was married. And to a young, lovely, and hugely pregnant wife. Item two: After years of loftily assuming that he was distinctly superior to other men, at least as far as getting into unholy, unsavory, troublesome, and dangerous sexual *pecadillos* was concerned, he had gotten involved with a girl who, because of her ardent temperament, her exalted social position, and her iron determination, was sure to cause him more trouble than he was prepared or had even been designed to handle. The worst of it all was that it was sure to end with Grace's hating and despising him as a liar, a cheat, and a scoundrel. And that hurt. That hurt so much it brought tears to his eyes.

Which Grace saw. And misinterpreted. Misunderstood.

"Why Jim!" she whispered huskily. "Are you *that* glad to see me?"

"Yes," he groaned, dragging the truth up from the very bottom of his heart.

"Then—aren't you going to—kiss me?" she said.

He considered that from down there where he was, at one meter seventy, to up there where she was at—counting her high heels—a full one meter ninety, or for people who persist in the monumental stupidity of measuring things by the finger bones and other extremities of a long dead Anglo Saxon king, from a near dwarfish five feet six inches tall to a willowy, soaring six feet two.

The situation was so comical as to be actually sad. So with tears of pure exasperation stinging her pale blue eyes, Grace Nivens solved it. Bending forward, she put her long-fingered, immensely strong hands— the hands of the *great* female athlete she was—under Jim's armpits, lifted him effortlessly high off the floor and kissed his mouth slowly, softly, sweetly, and with aching tenderness, paying absolutely no attention to the rising galestorm of laughter, that blended into an enthusiastic explosion of handclapping throughout the waiting room, punctuated by not a few shouted *¡Bravos!* and *¡Vivas!* including that of one really excessively witty citizen who ripped out the whole phrase: "*¡Viva Blancanieves y los Siente Enanos!*" Which meant, of course, "Long Live Snow White and the Seven Dwarfs!" And Jim, of course, could have died.

Then Grace stood him back on his feet again, amid the dying titters of—Jim realized suddenly—entirely approving laughter, fished gaily and swiftly in her shoulder bag for a paper handkerchief, bent and wiped a smear of her lipstick from the corner of his mouth, smiling at him misty-eyed the while, saying:

"Jim—I'm *so* glad to see you! So *very* glad!"

And he heard, directly behind him:

"¡*Oh!*" Then: "¡*Oh, Dios mío!*"

And whirled and stared into Petra Stevenson de Schuyler's—as she herself wrote her married name, being totally Spanish in the cultural sense—truly stricken eyes.

"Petra—" he began lamely. "*Quiero presentarte—*"

But she had turned and was off, actually running, head down and shoulders visibly shaking.

'The loyalty,' he thought miserably, 'that Trini inspires in other women is astonishing. Have I *ever* known another girl to hate or even dislike her? No, never. Oh God, now—"

"Jim, I—I didn't come down here to—spoil your life. I haven't the faintest right to. And yet the minute I get here, I've started to, haven't I? So *that's* the opposition? I—congratulate you. She's—utterly lovely!"

And, at that precise moment, to his vast relief he saw Van's tall figure striding towards them.

"Hey, Boss!" Van said. "Seen my frau? She was around here a minute ago and—"

"She just ran through that door," Jim said, laughing; "and I'd deeply appreciate your dragging her back in here—by the hair, if necessary. She stumbled upon me in the act of greeting an old—and very dear—friend from New York, with considerable enthusiasm, I'll admit; but then, when one has friends like Doctor Nivens here, it's rather easy to get carried away, wouldn't you think?"

"You can say that again, Chief!" Van said fervently. "Doctor Nivens, I'm delighted to meet you! But, for the record, what sort of doctor are you? From your looks I'd guess a Ph.D. Am I right?"

"You are," Jim said, "multiplied by three. Berkeley, Vienna, and New York. Plus an M.D. Plus a Psychiatrist. Grace is my favorite *shrink*, Van. Grace, this is Van—for Vanderbilt, that is!—Schuyler, up until today my assistant. I just fired him."

"Jim, you're a swine! You should never fire such gorgeous young men!"

"That's *why* I fired him. Too gorgeous. Steals all my girls. Incidently that little creature who stormed out of here is his wife. Go get her, Van!"

When Van went rushing away towards the door, Grace turned to Jim with an honestly puzzled expression on her face, and asked:

"Jim, why was she so upset? You—you haven't been playing dirty tricks on that nice boy, have you?"

"No. God, no! Well—put it this way. She took your presence, and the fact that we were kissing each other—as a threat to *her* favorite project. A—girl friend of hers, whose cause she's actively promoting. You know how women are . . ."

He thought: 'That's just about *the* most Machiavellian example of how the exact truth can be twisted into a blackhearted, goddamned lie extant!"

"Aha!" Grace said.

"You're here now, aren't you, Grace?" he said. "So—forget it!"

Van came back with Petra, who wore a decidedly sullen face. There was even a hint of moisture about her eyes.

"I am vairee pleest to meet you, *Doctora,*" she said in her own, highly original version of English, since, like many children of bilingual households she had flatly refused to learn her father's language for the very simple reason that her schoolmates and playmates didn't speak it, and had only commenced to study it a little after marrying Van. Then curiosity, and her own basically mischievous temperament, got the better of her.

"Yoo arrre the fran of *Don* Jaime, no?" she added.

"Who is *Don* Hymie, Jim?" Grace said. "Some Jewish friend of yours?"

"No!" Jim laughed. "*I* am *Don* Hymie. That's the way the Spanish pronounce J–a–i–m–e—James. And a General is a Heneral. And Jesus Christ is Hayzoose Kreesto. It's a funny language, but you'll get used to it."

Grace turned back to Petra, and smiled.

"Yes, dear," she said. "I am a friend of *Don* Jaime's. Aren't you?"

"*¡Ay sí! Don* Jaime eees a vaireee nice man. But also a vairee naughteee wan. He used to call *me* Petra *Culo Lindo.* Tell herrr waaat that means, Van."

"Petra Pretty Tail," Van said cheerfully. "You see, the first time the Boss saw Petra she was wearing a *Tanga* . . ."

"A what?" Grace said.

"The kind of bikini bottom you call 'The String' in the States, Grace," Jim explained. "And the rest of it was a practically invisible semi-monokini, too. Which is why I never did get around to looking at her *face.* If I'd done that and seen that she's actually beautiful all over, I'd never have let this young lug steal her from me!"

"Jim," Grace laughed, "this place is good for you, so help me. Brings you out!"

"Boss, we're all set," Van said. "Tickets and all. The rough stuff's triple locked and sealed in the diplomatic pouch—which, before I get aboard the aircraft, is going to be handcuffed to my left wrist. Flight takes off at midnight—so I don't suppose we'll be seeing you any more before—"

"No, I'm afraid not," Jim said. "But in New York surely, and soon, Van. Petra! *¡Hasta pronto!* Don't I get a good-bye kiss?"

Petra kissed him. Laughed; said:

"*¡Voy a decir a Trini que estas engañandola con una Jirafa!*"

"Jim," Grace said, as they left the terminal, "just what did that last remark mean? She's full of the devil, that little girl! I'm sort of glad *she's* leaving. Tell me—what did she say?"

"I think I'd better—censor that one, Grace! Now come on," he said.

"Oh, no, you don't, Jim Rush! Let me see—let me see . . . If General is pronounced Heneral and Jesus, Hayzoose, then a Heerafa would work out in English to be—geerafa—a giraffe! *Me!*"

"Grace, dear," he sighed. "You're too damned smart for your own good. Now come on, will you, please?"

"Not until you tell me what the rest of it meant, Jim!"

"That she was going to tell her girl friend, the one whom she's promoting to—to wreck my life, since *she* can't, anymore, that I am cheating on her—with a giraffe. Satisfied, now?"

"That little Petra's going to be on a plane and out of my hair by midnight, yes, Jim! Enormously. By the way, where are you taking me?"

"I was going to ask you that. Don't you have reservations anywhere?"

She said, solemnly:

"I thought *you* were going to put me up. I don't snore, Jim. Honestly!"

He stared at her. Then he smiled.

"How I wish I could!" he said. "But that would be to arm the scandal of the century. Unfortunately, the American Ambassador is a very public figure, Grace . . ."

"I know," she said soberly. "Jim, Dr. Lopez Basquez has promised me a little suite in the clinic, itself. That's all right, isn't it? We've talked a lot by phone. He seems—nice."

"Oh, goddamn!" Jim said.

"Jim—" she said.

"Yes, Grace?"

"Don't—worry about that. Don't worry—about anything, anymore. *You* don't have to. Leave the—worrying to me. It's *I* who have to—now."

He said:

"Why, Grace?"

"Tell you tonight. At—dinner. You will take me out to dinner tonight, won't you? Or—are you otherwise—engaged?"

"I am not otherwise engaged. I am—except one or two nights I have to work—usually free to come and go as I please, Grace."

"Good. Only I won't be. Not for the rest of this week. Dr. Lopez and I are going to subject Jenny to some rough, extensive, round the clock treatment. A new kind of shock therapy, dreadfully powerful and somewhat dangerous, so she'll have to be watched every minute. So—no sleep for me this week, my love! But it's not—maiming, intelligence-reducing the way electroshock and insulin shock therapy are. By Thursday night, we should know the results. D'you have the weekend free? Friday, there's a big affair at the *Club Hipico*. Dr. Lopez told me about it yesterday by phone. Offered to take me. But I told him I'd probably be going—with you. Were you planning to go; and, if so, d'you mind taking me?"

"I wasn't planning to go. The affair's being cosponsored by the Head of the State. And he and I are—as usual!—slightly on the outs. But now I will go, and take you. There'll be bullfighting, Grace—mostly by gentlemen amateurs. And *lady* amateurs as well, come to think of it, since two veddy, veddy young ladies are going to appear as *Rejoneadoras*. Sure you can take it? It may be messy. Bloody and messy—"

"Jim, I'm a doctor. In my student days I—and all the rest of the Senior Class students—were called to the scene of a train wreck. Afterwards, we had to scissors our uniforms off each other. And that—was human blood, Jim."

"So may some of this be, Grace."

"I can take it. Jim, what are *Rejoneadoras?*"

"Bullfighters who fight from horseback. It's beautiful to watch when they're good. And it's the one branch of bullfighting that women have always been permitted to engage in. Hence *Rejoneadoras,* as opposed to *Rejoneadores,* who are men. From the *rejon,* the spear they use to kill the bull, instead of the *estoque* or sword of the conventional bullfight on foot. Of course, with these society girls they won't release anything more dangerous than a yearling calf into the ring; but, all the same, there's still a fairish amount of risk in it. Even a yearling can mess a horsewoman who's been thrown up more than somewhat . . ."

"Should be fun . . . Is this the clinic? Why, it's beautiful! Are you coming in with me, darling?"

"Yes," he said. "Why yes, of course . . ."

When he had left her there, Dr. Claudio Lopez Basquez walked out to the car with him.

"*Don* Jaime, may I ask you one or two questions that are absolutely none of my business; but that for both professional—and *personal*—reasons, I need to know?" he said.

"Fire away, Doctor!" Jim said.

"I am—most favorably impressed with *la Doctora* Nivens. I have been for several weeks now, just from our conversations over the telephone . . ."

"These are not *questions,* Doctor!" Jim said.

"I know. They are the reasons for the questions I mean to ask. But to get to the point. I had not imagined she would be so—beautiful. I am—a widower, *Don* Jaime!"

"So?" Jim said.

"Some say—you have married again. Everyone says you have—a *Protegida*—who will soon give birth to your child . . ."

"So?" Jim said, again.

"*La Doctora* Nivens has given me every reason to believe she is—strongly attached to you. Even—perhaps—in love with you . . ."

"Why don't you ask *her* that, Doctor?" Jim said.

"I mean to. But first I must ask you: Does she know of—your *Protegida*—perhaps even your second wife—or of your coming child?"

"No," Jim said. "Plan to tell her, Doctor?"

"I am not a fool! That would be the act of a *cretino, Don* Jaime. She would despise me for such tactics. So, over to you. Do *you* mean to tell her?"

"Yes," Jim said sadly. "*Don* Claudio, I shall not stand in your way. I wish you—luck. And happiness. But—allow me—a little time. Telling Grace is going to be—difficult. I was—terribly in love with her. And, by a misfortune, I thought I'd lost her. Therefore I—out of hopelessness—formed new ties. And now, when it has become impossible—Trini and I are legally married, Doctor—she comes back to me. You understand—the enormity of my problem?"

"Yes," *Don* Claudio sighed; and put out his hand to Jim. "And I pity you—much, my friend!"

That afternoon, much to his relief, Jim found Trini in a decidedly gay and laughing mood.

"Thou," she informed him through a burst of silvery giggles, "art deceiving me with—¡una Jirafa! A she-giraffe! A woman so tall that at the airport they made her wear electric lights in her hair so *los aviones* would see her and not accidentally crash into her head! ¡Una giganta so big that she carried thee off to her cave under one arm like a doll. Is all this not true, *mi Amorrrrr?*

416

"Every word of it," Jim said solemnly. "And after she got me to her lair, Trini?"

"Ay-yyi-yi-yi!" Trini cried. "There come to me—thoughts—of a certain vileness, *Cielito mío*! She—"

"What, Trini?"

"Made use of thee! As the ugly daughter of the butcher makes use of—a sausage! As the fruit vendor's old maid sister employs a—banana! As the younger nuns in the convent—utilize—tallow candles! As—"

"Trini, you're a naughty girl! But I am glad to see you so gay. Give me a kiss, will you?"

She kissed him. And all the gaiety left her, abruptly. With no transition at all.

"*Don* Jaime—" she whispered, "when I—am dead—wilt thou—marry her? *¿La Jirafa?* Petra said she—seems—kind . . ."

"Trini, for God's sake!"

"I—am not jealous of her, *Don* Jaime. I do not know why, but I am not. She is *una Doctora,* no? She must be—very intelligent . . ."

"She is," Jim said. "I asked her to come down here to take care of Jenny Crowley. She is that kind of a doctor. *Una Psiquiatra.* A Doctor of the Mind . . ."

"But is she—kind? She will not have *los prejuicios raciales* against *mi pobre* Trinita, because my baby—"

"*Our* baby," Jim corrected her.

"*Nuestra hija,*" Trini whispered, "our daughter—will be—dark . . ."

"Number one, Trinita had better be fair. Blonde—like me, or I shall believe you have put me the long, big, and twisted *horns,* Trini! Number two, Grace Nivens will *never* have anything to do with her because her own *mamacita* is going to live to be ninety-seven years and thus will be around to take care of Trinita Number Three, our granddaughter as well as Trinita Two, our daughter. So stop trying to give me away to *la Doctora* Nivens, who though she is tall and handsome and intelligent and kind will very shortly probably marry someone else—"

"Who?" Trini said. "Whom is she going to marry? *¿Con quien se va a casar?*"

"Don't know. *Don* Claudio Lopez Basquez, likely."

Trini stared at him. Those nightblack Tluscolan eyes of hers searched him at depths where he hadn't any lies left. Where only the truth remained, brutal, cruel—pure.

"Thou—must not permit her to do that, *Don* Jaime," she whispered.

"And—why not?"

"Because—thou'rt in love with her," Trini said.

"Jim—" Grace said, as she—but not he, who had barely touched the really marvelous food available at *Les Ambassadeurs*—was finishing her desert; "may I be—brazen, please?"

He smiled at her.

"Braze away, Grace!" he said.

"Do—you—love me?" she whispered. "Wait! I'm doing this badly. Let me start over. Jim—I love you. Terribly. Hopelessly. I should like to be—your wife. Or—your mistress. Or—whatever. As long—as it's forever. The forms, the concepts, don't matter. It's the actuality that counts. And I know—I've been taught—that I want you with me—for the rest of my life . . ."

He said, softly, slowly:

"I'm—very honored, Grace."

"But—back to square one. Do *you* love *me*? I've—given—given you reasons enough not to, God knows! It's important that I know . . ."

He said:

"Yes, Grace."

"How—much?"

"More—than I can bear thinking about with equanimity. To a degree that's—terrifying, terrifying, even to me."

She put her hand across the table, took his, whispered, tearfully:

"I—thank you for that, Jim."

He was silent. It was just too hard, too cruel. He didn't know how to begin. Yet, he had to. She *must* be told. It simply was too cowardly not to tell her. But she cut him off; said:

"Jim—is your love—forgiving?"

"Love that isn't—isn't love," he said quietly.

"All right. Then hear this: Jim, I have had affairs with three separate and distinct men since you left New York. Sexual affairs. The last two—even—excessively sexual—since they involved absolutely *nothing* else. No—tenderness. No—nothing. Just—carnality. Plain lust. I discovered that I can be—am!—an utter, and utterly appalling bitch. Then a little man—" she was crying angrily, frankly now, "not much more than a midget, almost a dwarf, rang my doorbell on a Sunday morning, and stood there looking at me with the face of a shopworn angel—and his heart—his clean, fine, *decent* heart—in his eyes. And said, 'Good-bye, Grace—' "

"And?" he said.

"And it was over. That affair—and all the affairs. Forever. Because I realized all I'd been trying to do was to—destroy that image. By piling filth, maybe, all over the place I had it—him—enshrined in my heart. And that it couldn't be done. That the only way to end my love for you,

Jim, was to—end me. Twenty-seven sleeping tablets—like your Virginia, maybe. A bullet through my alleged brain. A stroll through my living room window, thirty-six floors up. I've thought of—all those ways, Jim. Many times. The day you called me—suggesting that I take over Jenny's case again, you may even have—saved my life. Surely you saved my—sanity. What's left of it, anyhow. There, I've said it! Am I— forgiven, Jim?"

He said, quietly:

"No. Because there's nothing to forgive. You were—out of my life. And yours was—your own to do with it what you saw fit. To—ruin. To debase. To exalt. To make—a glory of. If you *had* broken your pledged word to me, lied to me, deceived me, then perhaps—and only per- haps!—you would have placed me in the dreadful seat of judgment, with the moral right, if not the power to—forgive—or condemn. But you did none of the three, Grace, having severed all relations with me, long before. So I ask you, most humbly, not to put upon me the burden of extraneous forgiveness. I'm not—God."

"Still—I'm glad I told you," she said sadly.

He said, his voice a whipcrack:

"I'm not!"

"Oh!" she breathed. Then: "Why not, Jim?"

"It was absolutely none of my business. And knowing it—hurts. A man *never* wants—his goddess pulled down from her high altar, Grace; not even by her own hands. Nor—the Temple he'd erected to her worship—profaned; his rites and sacrifices reduced to—heathen mumbo- jumbo—burnt vegetables, spilt wine, charred meat!"

She said: "Oh, Jesus!"

And he: "Forgive me that. Now I was being bitter. Unkind."

She said, tartly:

"Get even! Revenge yourself. Tell me—about—*your* life, down here."

He said, evenly, quietly:

"No, Grace."

"Oh. And—why not, Jim?"

"I've told you. It's—none of your business. You left me, Grace. Got out of my life. Leaving me quite equally the right to live mine any way I saw fit. And while I don't imagine that my paltry doings would ordinar- ily distress you, now that you—believe you love me, they might. I'm not—a sadist, my dear; not even mentally. I don't enjoy hurting people, not even to afford myself the luxury of unburdening a guilty conscience. I find hurting people I—love, so painful that it's destructive; and I mean to—*me*. So, let's just skip my mad career, shall we? At least for tonight. Let's just be as happy as we can, for as long as we can. I'm afraid it won't be long—"

"It will not be even five minutes if *I* can help it," that voice from the darkness said.

Jim turned in his chair. He didn't see anything. Not at first. Then that slender figure stepped out from behind one of the many, many fluted columns that make serving a meal in *Les Ambassadeurs* a damned nuisance to the waiters, but which, combined with a young jungle of green potted plants scattered about the dining room, insures each table a considerable degree of privacy.

"Patti!" Jim said.

"*¡Hola, mi Amor!*" Patricia said, and bending foward, kissed his mouth. She was very subtle about it. She didn't make the mistake of kissing him with wild and showy passion. Instead, she kissed him softly, sweetly, tenderly—and just lingeringly enough to demonstrate she meant it. Drew back, staring at him with eyes misty and aglow, exactly as if Grace Nivens didn't even exist, as though nobody existed for her except Jim Rush at that moment, nobody in all the world. She said, quietly:

"I won't ask you if you mind if I sit down, Jim, dearest, for I know you do. Only, I'm going to. Aren't you going to introduce me to the beautiful and distinguished *Doctora* Nivens? She is a psychiatrist, is she not? Very well, she can treat me. I am mad, y'know. Your fault, you swine. You've driven me completely around the bend, or—your most exquisite bedroom techniques have. He is absolutely the most marvelous lover; don't you agree, *Doctora*?"

"You've the advantage of me there, *Señorita*," Grace said tartly. "It so happens that I really do not know."

"Yet," Patricia said sweetly. "Or are you being quaintly Anglo Saxon—and mid-Victorian? If so, it's charming. Oh, quite!"

"What are *you* doing here, Patti?" Jim said. "This isn't one of your usual hangouts. In fact, I thought your set disliked it . . ."

"We do. Dreadfully dull restaurant, this. But I made your friend Avery Parks bring me here tonight, because I was sure you'd bring *la Doctora* here. I had to see what my most dangerous rival was like, no? She is—very beautiful, Jim. But isn't she a bit too tall for you? We suit each other much better, Darling. We—fit—so very nicely—in all sorts of positions, don't we?"

"Where's Avery?" Jim said.

"Oh—over there in one of the corners, sulking. He's jealous. Of you, naturally. You see, he fancies he's in love with me."

"Go call him. *Both* of you, join us," Jim said.

He glanced at Grace. Even her lips were white.

"I will *not*. I want to sit and gaze into your pale grey eyes. With or without the *Doctora's* permission. I *do* have a certain claim on you, Jim Rush. After all, I am your Number One Mistress, aren't I?"

"Jim," Grace said very, very quietly, "you're right, of course. You don't owe me any explanations whatsoever. But don't you think that under the present circumstances—"

Patricia took a chair from the next table. Turned it around, sat down, almost between them, her elbows on the table, her lovely young face cradled on the palms of her slim hands. She said, mockingly, in her very nearly perfect English:

"Permit me to introduce myself, *Doctora,* since Jim clearly has no intention to. I am Patricia Montenegro Aguirre. My only claim to fame— besides the exceedingly high honor of being *Don* Jaime's Number One Mistress—is that I am the niece, through marriage, of His Excellency, *Don* Manuel García Herredia, Chief of the State. His *only* niece—and his adopted daughter. That's why he feels free to do things like—this."

She pulled her silk shawl off her shoulders. She was wearing a short, formal cocktail dress, cut daringly low in the front, and leaving her back bare to the waist. She half turned away from Grace. Even after eight or nine hours more, her back was still a dreadful sight.

"Oh my God!" Grace said.

"My pledge—of love to *Don* Jaime here," Patricia said softly. "Can you equal it, *Doctora?*"

"You mean that your Uncle—your adoptive father beat you like this because—"

"He suspected that *Don* Jaime, the great *Don* Jaime, Lover *Extraordinario,* who has scores of women committing absolute *locuras* for his sake, had made me his mistress. Or rather, added me to the extensive list of women who swoon every time he deigns to grant them—a little smile. Yes, *Doctora.* He was wrong at the time. But since I dislike being beaten for nothing, I have since made him right . . ."

"Jim," Grace said quietly, "how much of this am I supposed to believe?"

"As little, or as much, as you like, Grace," Jim said, smiling. "It is never the act of a gentleman to contradict a lady's word. Nor—to confirm it, which, in the case of dear Patti, here, is usually even worse!"

"Jim, *Amor de mi Vida, Dueño de mi Cuerpo y mi Alma,* you are a swine, y'know. A clever, clever swine. You imply that I am lying, without even saying so. I told you that I was prepared to accept your liaison— with that dear, sweet child—oh, don't worry, I shan't distress you by naming names!—because she came first, and has literally offered up her life for you—twice. I'll accept being Number Two. But not Number Three. I overheard you confessing that you are in love with the lovely and distinguished *Doctora.* Do you confess it? Are you?"

Jim looked at her. Said calmly, evenly:

"Yes, Patricia."

Patricia stood up.

"That does it. Good-bye, *Doctora*. Good-bye, Jim. White roses are my flower. Send me—a wreath of them. And since you are both a brave and an honest man, with a note that reads: 'This death was at my hands!' "

"Jim," Grace said, watching Patti glide away from there, "she is—a little mad, you know. More than a little. I'd advise you to—keep as far from her as possible. And, not especially for my sake—though I should appreciate the favor, Great Lover!—but for your own. Is she *really* the niece and the adopted daughter of General García?"

"Yes, Grace; she is. And he did beat her like that—for exactly the reason she said. Some of the many people who would like me out of the way for political reasons finally tumbled to the fact that removing me via an engineered and nasty scandal would probably be more effective as propaganda than making me a noble martyr by shooting or blowing me up ever could be. So they chose dear Patti—without her conscious knowledge, of course; those types are devilishly clever, y'know—who is young, impressionable, and best of all for scandal arming purposes, the General's niece. Didn't work—"

"No thanks to little Patti; I'll bet she was as cooperative as all get out!" Grace said.

"Now, Grace, you aren't going to be a *jealous* female, are you?" Jim said, grinning at her.

"Jim—I love you. And love and jealousy are very nearly inseparable. But now I see I'm going to have it awfully rough down here, with absolutely gorgeous baby girls like that one hurling themselves at your head—"

"No you won't, Grace," he said quietly. "That's not the angle trouble is going to come from. I'd bet almost anything that it's going to come from another quarter altogether."

He was, of course, thinking of the effect that being told of his marriage, his rapidly approaching fatherhood, was going to have upon her, and the advantage that knowledge was going to give to so tall, handsome, cultivated, and cosmopolitan a man as Doctor Lopez Basquez. But he underestimated the Ribald Gods of Chance, whose angles—and methods—of attack approach the infinite.

He did one thing during those five days that Grace and *Don* Claudio were occupied with their round the clock and really desperate fight to save Jenny Crowley from terminal madness, restore her within acceptable limits to a normal life—and that thing was designed to cut down the angles and methods of attack of mocking, malicious fate to more reasonable proportions, or, more truly, to salve his own achingly guilty conscience: He asked Vince Gomez to examine Trini once again to determine how great a threat to her life giving birth to the child would be.

The examination was carried out not at Miguel Villalonga Hospital but at Dr. Luis Moreno's Clinic, far better equipped for this kind of exploration since Dr. Moreno's specialities were obstetrics and gynecology. Both eminent medical men concurred, were in absolute agreement: *none.* Even the delivery, they now believed, could very likely be a normal one, without the necessity of their performing a Caesarian at all.

But when he had brought her home again, Trini took—and for once, kissed his hand.

"Thou—must not grieve. But they are wrong. Of this, I shall die," she said.

He was sitting with Grace in the first row, just behind the *callejon,* which is as close to the bullring as spectators are allowed to sit, and has proved to be too close at times, since agile bulls have been known to jump over the *barrera* into the *callejon* and with a second leap get at least their horns within goring distance of the spectators' legs. They were, of course, in *sombra,* the shady side of the bullring, and just opposite the gates of *los toriles,* out of which the bulls charge, to be reduced within minutes into poor, heaving, panting, bleeding, tormented dying hulks in a spectacle which, Jim thought, despite its swirling plastic beauty you have to be a good bit of a bastard and something of a sadist to enjoy—and no apologies at all to *los aficionados* of bullfighting or even to *Don* Ernesto Hemingway's shade in Tartarus!

He was thinking again that people who enjoy blasting beautiful winged creatures down out of the sky with shotguns, pumping softnosed expansive bullets through the lungs and guts of an animal as glorious as a stag, riding and whooping behind a tiny fox and watching their hounds tear it to pieces at the end, or torturing to death a beast as noble and magnificent as a brave bull is, in short all the legions of incipient sadists and innate murderers who actually enjoy killing, should have all the bullrings, football stadiums, baseball parks, and what have you turned over to them once a year, wherein they could be equipped, at the expense of a public fund he'd gladly subscribe to, with gladiatorial swords, daggers, nets and tridents and be allowed to kill each other to their murderous little hearts' content!—when Avery Parks came up to him and whispered:

"The Whirleybird's fixed, Chief! Wednesday all right for you? To go bastard stalking, I mean?"

"Great, Avery," he said. Then he presented Avery to Grace, saying: "This handsome young fellow was Patti's escort the night she table-hopped at *Les Ambassadeurs.* By the way, Son, how are you and she making out?"

"We aren't," Avery said sadly. "Thanks to you, Chief." Then, seeing Grace's startled look, he added quickly, "Oh heck, Doctor Nivens, I didn't mean that the way it sounded. It's not the Chief's fault. Patti knows perfectly well that Mr. Rush is not interested in her. The trouble is she's both spoiled rotten, and as stubborn as a mule. In fact, I'd bet that the best way for the Chief to get her out of his hair would be to give her a wild, heavy breathing rush. Patti's one of these chicks who always want what they can't have . . ."

Grace smiled, knowingly.

"I'm not so sure I agree with you, Mr. Parks," she said. "At least in so far as the—tactics you suggest are concerned. But then, since I'm very definitely an interested party, perhaps I'm just scared. Your Patti— young and lovely as she is—isn't the kind of competition I should like to take on!"

Avery stared at her in purest astonishment. Then he mastered himself. Jim could almost hear the young Narcotics Bureau agent thinking: 'She doesn't know! She doesn't know! Jesus, what a lousy trick to play on a glorious dame like this one! But, oh hell, it's no skin off my nose . . .'

"Keep trying, Avery!" Jim laughed. "She'll come around. She knows damned well there's nothing *I* can do about her, so—"

"Yeah, I'll just have to be patient, I suppose. But being realistic about it, Mr. Rush, I still wouldn't have a ghost of a chance with Patti even if she weren't nuts over you. Item one, I'm not in her league, socially or financially, and—"

At that moment, *el Alguacil,* dressed in his sixteenth century velvet costume, cantered his heavy grey gelding out into the center of the ring. The word means "Bailiff" or "Constable" which was what an *Alguacil* originally was. Now he was a ceremonial figure that led the parade of bullfighters, *picadores, banderilleros,* and *peons* into the ring, and made the necessary verbal announcements.

He had a microphone in his hand. A long wire trailed out behind his showily prancing horse.

"Ladies and Gentlemen!" his voice came booming hollowly out of the loudspeakers. "There has been an unavoidable change in the program! Due to an injury sustained while practicing, the *Señorita* Margarita Gil Camago will be unable to appear as *Rejoneadora* this afternoon. Therefore the sixth and final bull will be killed by Her Excellency, the Most Distinguished *Señorita* Patricia Montenegro Aguirre, Niece and Adopted Daughter of His Excellency, the Head of the State!"

Jim sat there. Even his lips were white. He said: "Oh Jesus!" Then:

"Avery! Can you get anywhere close to His Nibs? This has got to be stopped, Son! This has got to be stopped, now!"

Grace stared at him; said:

"Why, Jim? Isn't she any good? And surely they'll give her an even smaller calf than they did the other girl, so—"

"Patti isn't going to fight anybody's damned calf! I'm betting it'll be a bull elephant. A rogue bull elephant! Can you, Avery?" Jim said.

"I can try, Sir. But seeing as how you're the Ambassador—"

"Avery, I couldn't get within a city block of the General! He knows perfectly damned well that I'm practically spearheading the opposition to that loan he's trying to get out of our Government. So I don't smell exactly like a rose to him these days. And you were at that party I gave, so you know what a job of gross provocation little Patti pulled off on him there. For God's sake man—get going! There's no time! Tell him to stop her! Avery, she's going to kill herself! She *told* me she was. She even told me when and where—and I, stupid fool that I am, didn't believe her! Get going, Son!"

Avery stood there. Said, very, very softly:

"Did she also tell you—why?"

"Oh, Jesus!" Jim said. "Yes. Avery, you're making me waste time! D'you want explanations, or do you want Patti *alive?*"

"Jim—" Grace said; "*tell* him."

"All right," Jim sighed. "You were at the party, so you know what she asked the General's blessing for. It appears she wasn't—joking. So, later—Sunday morning to be exact—she and I had a rather bitter fight over my contention that a forty-seven-year-old man has no business maintaining any sort of relations with a nineteen-year-old girl, even one blessed by Church and State. Or maybe especially one so blessed. Which, it may surprise you, Avery, to know, is actually how I feel about it despite all—evidences to the contrary. You and I also inhabit the same sorts of professional worlds, so you ought also to know why I couldn't—reveal to her, nor to *anyone,* Son, the first class reasons I have for being unable to grant little Patti her heart's desire—or her momentary whim. So now she considers herself the woman scorned, and actually means, I sadly fear, to shame and damn me by an outrageously public suicide. All right? Jesus, Avery, don't just stand there!"

"All right," Avery said grimly. "It's none of my business, just as you said, Chief. Patti isn't, and never has been—mine. But, Sir—'scorned' doesn't fit the impression she gave me. If we're going to use Victorianisms, 'wronged' would be more accurate, wouldn't it? I—I had—or was supposed to have—a date with her last Saturday night. She didn't show. I hunted her all over town—and couldn't find her. Until—midday, Sunday. Then *we* had *our* fight. And, for your information,

Sir—have parted company. Because I asked her whether that celebrated fight with you took place *before* or *after,* her only answer was: 'what d'*you* think?' "

Then he turned on his heels and strode away.

"Jim," Grace drawled, "the same question intrigues *me.* Up until now I'd assumed little Patti was lying about her—relations—with you, in order to bait me, say. But you're—just a bit *too* upset, lover! So, which was it? At the moment, I'm inclined to bet on—*after* . . ."

He turned, looked at her. And his eyes were very cold and still.

He said: "A girl's life—is at stake, Grace. So that question is at least uncharitable. And the motivations for my having been—most reluctantly, I assure you!—forced into a dispute with dear little Patti are—exactly the ones I said. The conditions under which the—discussion took place, the where and when, as well as the degree of intimacy preceding it, or following it, seem to me quite simply not to be anyone's concern except Patti's, and—perhaps unfortunately for me—mine, since neither Avery Park's life, fate, nor what he conceives of as his future happiness—nor even *yours,* my dear, were then involved. I ask you, for Patti's sake, not mine, to let that aspect of the question drop, will you? Not on the score that the answer to it is anything I feel I need to be excessively ashamed of, but that it would constitute a rather intolerable invasion of *her* privacy. All right?"

"The next sound you hear," Grace said sadly, "will be a dull thud! but, dearest—are you *sure?* That she's planning to do something fatal to herself, I mean? Of course *I* heard that remark about your sending white roses with a note admitting you were responsible for her death, but that's just the sort of thing that neurotics often say and seldom carry out. She wasn't nearly so precise as you've implied and—"

"Implied, hell! As I stated. It wasn't then, Grace. It was on another occasion. And she *was* precise. Chillingly so. Her exact words were: 'I shall love thee all the rest of my life until the day I die. Friday afternoon of this week. At precisely five thirty P.M.!' "

Grace looked at her watch. It was an expensive calendar model which automatically displayed the day of the week and the date, as well as hours, minutes, seconds. She said:

"Today. Now." Then, whispering the words: "When did she tell you *that,* my love? And *where?*"

He said without hesitation or taking thought:

"Sunday morning. The day you came. A little before you called me from the airport. Sitting in my car in front of the General's villa. I had taken her home, and—"

"Jim," Grace said very, very quietly, "do you realize what you just said? That you had taken this absolutely gorgeous girl-child home—

before six thirty in the morning. Because that was exactly when I called you. I remember being so—happy and excited over the thought of—seeing you, again—that I forgot even to apologize for calling you at that hour. So all my other questions transform themselves into flat statements: You had taken Patricia Montenegro home at six thirty A.M. from *your* place, lover; where—from what your friend Parks just said—she obviously had spent—the night!"

"Grace, you don't want me to confirm that, d'you?"

"No," she whispered, the tears drowning her voice, "I want you to deny it, Jim—and I'm hoping that—you can!"

He said quietly, flatly: "I'm sorry, but I can't. Grace, I love you. But you weren't here. I didn't know you were coming. I had no hopes as far as you were concerned; for what earthly reason did I have to doubt your sincerity when you, yourself, told me you were getting voluntarily—and permanently!—out of my life?"

"Jim, damn you!—I told you by phone I—I wanted you back again! I told you! And you—"

"I answered that—it was impossible, Grace. Because it was. Even then, it was—too late—"

She stared at him, and what got into her eyes then was very hard to look at. It awoke pity in him. Shame.

"Jim," she whispered, "she's—pregnant, isn't she? By—by *you* . . . And that's why—"

"I doubt it," he said wearily. "Unless her reproductive system works a hell of a lot faster than any normal human female's can, she wouldn't even *know* that yet. Anyhow, I doubt it. It's most unlikely and—Oh! Oh, my God!"

Patricia swept out into the ring at a pounding gallop. Her mount—a stallion, not a gelding—was magnificent. He was swift-blowing midnight, pluming across heaven without a star. His eyes were coals from a torturer's brazier, his breath a tearing scream of moving air. Yet Patricia controlled him effortlessly. She was, Jim realized, not only the single best *Amazona,* as the Spanish call a horsewoman, but absolutely the finest *jinete,* rider, male or female, he had ever seen.

She danced that wild black horse out to the center of the ring.

Then the gates of *los toriles,* the bullpens behind the stands, opened, and death came roaring through them. Death. The thing, itself. Six hundred kilos of midnight murder. A mountain moving. A fleshly avalanche disemboweling the earth. Horns to stop the power of breathing, to gut-rip all horses in equine history back to the first maned quadruped to loose a whinny at time's first glowing sunrise, to the last frail decorative mount to succumb to radioactive sickness at the world's own flaming end. Not a calf. Not a skinny, scrawny, tottering, half weaned not even yet a yearling. A bull. The biggest bull that Patricia Montenegro had been able to wheedle, coax, cajole, bribe, threaten out of the *granjeros;* even—he was suddenly, sickeningly sure!—stretch her lovely naked body out in some horny bastard's bed to procure. The great-grandfather of all the bulls there ever were or ever would be in this world. The *Señor Don* Lord and Master of all bulls. The Godfather of the entire taurine race.

His whistling snort tore Jim's guts apart each time he charged. His hoof thunder upended the world. And Patricia, dancing her black stallion, making that midnight horned annihilation miss her mount's tail by millimeters, doubling the horse inside the slashing arc of those horns, slapping the bull's muzzle with her gloved hand, standing up in the stirrups, laughing, laughing, a huntress, a centauress, the goddess of reckless valor, every second she remained alive, unbroken and ungored, a miracle, riding tight circles around that pounding earthquake, a golden nymph on a stormcloud mounted, riding, going on . . .

There are the same *tercios,* time divisions, the same *suertes,* the acts or feats that lend the *tercios* their names, in the art of *rejoneo,* as there are in the ordinary *corrida de toros,* but the *Rejoneador* or, in this case, *la Rejoneadora,* does them all from horseback. Most prudent *Rejoneadores,* of course, will order their *peones* to briefly run and cape the bull afoot, in order that they may observe, before cantering into the ring upon their showy and splendid mounts, whether the bull tends to hook right or left, or—God be willing!—charges straight ahead, praying that the animal has the *casta, nobleza,* stupidity, that gives the *lidiador, torero,* (but never, today, the *toreador,* since that ancient, archaic word is employed only by opera singers taking part in Bizet's *Carmen!) matador de toros, Rejoneador,* the chance to perform breath-stopping prodigies of skill and valor and stay alive.

The *torero* who fights afoot, however, is the general of a small army: His *peones* run and cape the bull to turn and tire it; his *picadores,* mounted on padded horses, perform the *suerte* of the *varas,* piercing the bull's hump with their pole lances, leaning on their twisting, cruelly punishing goads, hurting the great animal beyond belief and bearing—though Spaniards, and writers like the late, great *Don* Ernesto, and all others with a need to explain away the fact that by instinct, nature, and sheer brutish inclination, man is the cruelest of all the beasts, the most absolutely bestial, claim that the bull is so infuriated that he feels no pain; and his three *banderilleros* place the gaily festooned—and cruelly barbed!—little harpoons that have the effect of tiring the bull's neck muscles, making them ache, and reducing his tendency to put a polished horn sidewise through the *torero's* nearby and inviting guts—all this before he, the *matador de toros,* this graceful butcher in his suit of lights! performs the third and final *tercio,* that of stabbing a noble animal, already three-quarters dead of torture, to death with a sword.

But *el Rejoneador, la Rejoneadora*—for women have from earliest times been permitted to participate in this tragedy of blood and sand and sun—performs all three of the *suertes* himself, or herself. And it has become the custom, born of the Iberian's absolute need to never admit or display the slightest twinge of fear, to dispense with the precaution of having *los peones* run the bull on foot altogether, so usually the *Rejoneador* faces the at least doubled, if not tripled danger of an unknown quality from horseback from the outset. For, as every *torero* knows, it is the unexpected in bullfighting that maims or kills you. Which, it instantly became apparent, mattered to Patricia Montenegro not at all.

For after that initial exhibition of superb horsewomanship, her almost insanely reckless running of the bull, she changed horses for the *suerte* of the *varas,* or rather as it is called in the art of *rejoneo, los rejones de castigo,* the punishment spears. This mount was a white Arabian mare, and very nearly the most beautiful horse in all this world of sin. And Patti placed her spears.

Each time she plunged the spear points—made to come free from the shaft as they're placed—into the bull's hump, a flag whipped out from the shaft. And in each case, when one of these flags—designed to substitute for the *capote* or cape of the *lidiador* on foot—whipped out, to be trailed tauntingly millimeters before the bull's muzzle, the spectators could see that the device it bore was exactly the same as that of the other two: a shattered, broken, bleeding heart.

Which was not lost upon the spectators. Normally, each of the three flags automatically released, one for each *rejon de castigo* placed, snapping out just above the broken-off end of the lance shaft, bears a different device: the coat of arms of the *Rejoneador*'s distinguished house first, say; then, on placing the second spear, those of the house of his fiancée or of his wife; and last, by protocol, generally the flag of the Republic. All of which Patricia ignored. She flaunted her hurt before all the world. In the stands, people began to look around to see if they could distinguish whom she meant that bitter message for. And since quite a few of those present had also been invited guests at Ambassador James Randolph Rush's delightfully scandal-arming party, they at least thought they knew. There were also a few ladies at that bullfight who inhabited a social stratum sufficiently rarified to have already been informed—by their servants, of course, who had obtained the delicious tidbit directly from the General's own household domestic staff—that His Excellency had beaten his niece/daughter practically to death for actually having "couched herself with" *Don* Jaime, a sin that unrepentant young woman had admitted repeatedly, profanely, and at the top of her lungs. And so they all began to stare at *Don* Jaime; those who were physically close enough to him to do so, easily discerning the expression of worry and suffering upon his small pale face, and the even more pleasing fact that his guest, *la distinguida Doctora en Psiquitría* Gracia Nivens was openly crying, which news passed verbally all around the huge stadium like a train of gunpowder until, by the time Patricia placed her third and last *rejon de castigo,* the tension in the towering, circular tiers of seats was practically equal to that inside the bullring, if it did not, in fact, exceed it.

And now *los clárines,* the bugles sounded for the second *tercio,* the *suerte* of the *banderillas,* which differs from the same *suerte* in *la corrida de toros* only in the minor detail that since he must guide his mount, the *Rejoneador* usually—but not always!—places the gaily decorated little harpoons one by one instead of in pairs, as professional *banderilleros,* dashing in on their own two feet, always do. The *suertes* are first, *al cuarteo,* on the curve, a long curving run that intercepts the bull's charge at a beautifully described tangent to it, the *banderilla* or *banderillas* being thrust into his hump by the rider who is leaning from the saddle dangerously over the horns at that point; then, *al quiebro,* the feint, which consists of crowding in suicidally close, pulling the bull's head and horns aside with a faked half thrust that he hooks at, then thrusting home from a slightly different direction; and last, *poder a poder,* power to power, the most brilliant one of all, and the most dangerous, for in this case a pair of *banderillas* are always used (they can be, of course, in any of the *banderilla suertes;* but most *Rejoneadores* would rather avoid long stays in *la Clinica de los Toreros* and hence usually don't use two in *suertes* where one suffices) since the whole point of power to power is to place a pair simultaneously and perfectly side by side in the hump, which means that the *Rejoneador* must ride a thunderously galloping horse straight in on a near collision course—head-on collision at that!—with over a ton of enraged bull, using only his knees, with the reins flapping free about the horse's neck, to guide his mount. In the long history of the art, it was in failed attempts at this particular *suerte* that the majority of *Rejoneadores* who lost their lives were killed.

Patricia did her *al cuarteo* and *al quiebro* with matchless grace, with such ease and perfection that Jim Rush began to breathe almost normally again. Grace, too, had recovered her composure by then, largely because the looks of malicious delight that "all these damned little Chili Beans!" as she angrily and with unhabitual chauvinism had labeled them in her mind, had fixed her tear-streaked face, had armed all that unmatched, towering, almost Luciferian pride that *Latinas* are unaware that *Gringas* have. It was a good thing she had, because she was going to need it.

For at that moment, Patricia took the final pair of *banderillas* from the hands of one of her *peones,* and ignoring the snorting tossing bull, maddened by the pain the *rejones de castigo* and the already placed *banderillas* caused him, rode directly over to where Ambassador Rush and *la Doctora* Nivens sat.

Patti looked up at Jim. Held him with her eyes. Then slowly, ceremoniously, she leaned far out of her saddle and broke those one meter twenty centimeter long *bandilleras* over the top of the *barrera* so that the barbed ends were reduced to the lengths of a pair of lead pencils. These she kept. But she hurled the longer, paper-flower, and feather decorated shafts up to him, crying out loudly, gaily, clearly:

"For thee, my Love!"

All the people in that part of the stands gasped audibly. And Grace Nivens sent up a silent prayer to some ancient Cretan Minotaur god to lend renewed strength and fury to the bull!

Jim caught the shafts, sat there holding them. He looked exactly like a wooden Indian before a turn of the century tobacco store.

"What's she going to do now?" Grace asked dryly.

"Die," Jim groaned, "because what she's planning to do just can't be done!"

It couldn't be, but Patricia did it. At breakneck speed, galloping with the reins flapping free about the white Arabian's neck, she extended what looked like three-quarters of her sheer miracle of a body (even in the fringed leather jacket, Andalusian chaps of the type called *armitas,* tight ankle-length riding pants and calfskin boots) horizontally out from the saddle, leaned over and between those murderous horns so close that to the frozen unbreathing spectators no light showed between her body and the bull's head, and placed two broken off *banderillas,* each of them no more than twelve to fourteen centimeters long, the exact size of a schoolchild's lead pencil, *poder a poder* in the hump, precisely, exactly, perfectly to the millimeter where they should be.

When she straightened up, untouched, unhurt, the spectators split the sky.

Again she changed horses for the third and final *tercio. El Tercio de la Muerte.* The *suerte* of—Death. Of killing or being killed. This time she chose a roan gelding. A heavy, powerful mount. She worked that sweating, bleeding, tired, but still dangerous bull to where she wanted him: directly before the seats in which *el Embajador Estadounidense Don* Jaime Rush *y la Doctora* Gracia Nivens sat.

Patti took *el rejon de la muerte*—the spear of death—whose point is almost a sword, far longer and sharper than those of the punishment spears—from the hands of her faithful *peon;* turned her mount's tail towards the pawing, snorting bull as though he were not there; raised her hand and pushed her flat crowned, broad brimmed Cordovian hat far back on her head. And a gasp like a rising wind rose up from the seats before her, because from that section, the *barrera de sombra,* every man, woman, and child could see the sudden flood of tears literally pouring from her eyes. It was intensely, cripplingly moving, and when Grace looked at Jim and saw that he was crying, too, the slow pale streaks penciling his wan cheeks with light, what stabbed into her was so painful, so absolutely destructive, that she bowed her head and shuddered. But she raised it again, angrily, proudly, in time to see Patti make a quick, imperious gesture with her free hand.

One of the reporters, or some television cameraman's helper, understanding the gesture, or—more likely!—having been instructed by Patti, herself, beforehand, gave her a microphone. She took it, lifted it to that mouth that suddenly, scaldingly, in an anguish of total recall Jim Rush could both taste and feel from three meters away, and her clear sweet soprano rang out like the voices of a hundred angels from all the loudspeakers, twelve in all, above the stands, amplified tremendously by the public address system, but not distorted at all, so that every living soul in that immense stadium could hear how breath-torn it was, hear the heartbroken sobs that tore her, until she mastered herself, said slowly, clearly, her voice tear-drenched, humid, but despite that—despite the fact that it was half strangling from absolutely intolerable grief, pain, despair—perfectly intelligible:

"I dedicate—this—bull—to the man—I love. And also, because he—no longer—loves me, has—betrayed me—to him—I dedicate—my—death!"

She whirled the horse about. Dropped the microphone. Took off her hat and tossed it up and backward, her aim perfect. Grace caught it. Jim couldn't. He couldn't even breathe. Motion, even catching a flying Cordovian hat, was beyond him.

"There's—an envelope in it," Grace got out. "Oh! It—it's addressed to *me,* Jim! Shall I—?"

"Open it!" he rasped.

But it wasn't a note. It was—those pictures. Patricia's—final vengeance: Jim in evening clothes, and Patti standing before him naked and beautiful in the first one, then in the second, clinging to him and crying, the flash having illuminated her tears into jewels, and in the third one kissing him, devouring his mouth, breaking it, and in the fourth—

There was no fourth.

"For which I thank you, Dear Kind God!" Grace said.

Every living soul in the tiers was on his or her feet and all of them were screaming. A ring of burly men—those grubby, unwashed, useless scum that every Dictator in recent history has employed as a claque to "spontaneously" cheer and clap and shout his name—"Il Duce! Il Duce! Il Duce! Heil Hitler! Heil Hitler! Sieg Heil! Franco! Franco! Franco!"— were shaking their fists at Jim and roaring:

"*¡Cabron! ¡Asesino! ¡Sin Vergüenza!*"

Which aren't exactly translatable words. "Bastard, Murderer, Blackguard," will do as well as anything in English ever does for anything in Spanish, which isn't very well.

Patricia cited the bull. Held the roan gelding there, his bound and cropped tail literally pressing against the *barrera,* just across the *callejon,* not two full meters from where Jim and Grace sat in the *primera fila.* Stood up in the stirrups. She was so close to them that they could see she was sweat-soaked, trembling. She raised the *rejon.* And—instead of plunging it into that powerful hump, hurled it away from her contemptuously. Turned in her saddle. Pressed her own fingers to her mouth. Made the gesture of throwing Jim a kiss. Held him with her dark and tear-glazed eyes.

The bull got under the roan and killed him. Ripped five yards of bloody intestines out of him with every slash. Lifted him on the horns like a child's toy with the stuffing coming out, threw him completely over the wooden *burladores* and the *barrera* into the *callejon.*

Patricia leaped, jumped, fell, was thrown free—inside the ring. And black death charged that tiny, inert, pitiful figure on the ground. Lifted her, spitted clear through the muscle of her left thigh. Whirled her like a rag doll around the axis of that horn, threw her free so that she slammed sickeningly into the *barrera* just across the *callejon* from where they sat.

And Ambassador James Randolph Rush, who knew absolutely nothing about bullfighting in any practical sense, and who, additionally, was a self-confessed coward, stood up, took off his jacket, tucked it under his left arm, climbed easily and swiftly over the *barandilla* of welded iron tubing before his seat, jumped down into the *callejon*—the circular alleyway between the ring and the first row of seats, vaulted up onto the wooden *barrera* between the *callejon* and the arena, then leaped down from there into the ring, landing exactly where he meant to, a meter beyond where broken, bleeding, maybe even dying Patricia Montenegro lay. He stood one meter sixty centimeters away from the muzzle and the horns of an enraged and absolutely enormous bull, and saw that Patricia's *cuadrilla* of *peones* were already racing towards them. Since, surely by her own orders, which, she being who she was, and this being the Glorious Republic of Costa Verde, they hadn't dared disobey until far too late, they had been stationed in that section of the *callejon* next to the *toriles,* the bullpens, he also saw they were going to have to sprint across the entire ring to get anywhere close to the action. This was a matter of a full three minutes at best, time and to spare for that bull not only to finish Patricia off, if finishing her off were even necessary, but to rip the guts out of him as well, and stamp what was left of the two of them into a mingled, purplish red mess of shredded flesh, bloody tripes, and splintered bones, so thoroughly embedded into the bullring's sands that afterwards *los monosabios* would have one devil of a time scraping them up even with shovels.

So he, Jim Rush, did what he had to, in the sure and strangely comforting knowledge that getting his jackassical, idiotic, damned, and goddamned fool self killed was one thing, while living with the memory that he'd sat there in the front row and let Patti die before his very eyes was another thing altogether, and that the first would be over in minutes at the worst, but the second would go on for sick, nauseous forever—he cited that bull, and actually turned it away from Patti with a *muletazo por abajo,* using his jacket as the *muleta,* that was awkward, clumsy, inexpert, laughable, clownish, unbelievably bad, but that turned six hundred kilos of sheer murder away from Patti, and then another, to the left, this time, that was a little better, but not much, but that accomplished what he meant it to, which was to get two-horned death a little further from her still, and then capped all that, climaxed it, topped it, by bringing his jacket—accidentally? deliberately? by plain damnfool luck? a gust of wind?—up, up, up into a sculptured, plastic, superb, absolutely slow and beautiful *Ayudado por Alto* pass, which, considering the fact that he hadn't even so much as a stick, not to mention the sword that bullfighters use, to spread his improvised *muleta* properly, was roughly equivalent to piling twenty major miracles on top of one another, and proof positive that Padre Pío's God at least occasionally takes tender, considerate, and loving care of absolutely goddamned fools. Seeing his jacket soaring up like that, smoothly, steadily, slowly, bringing that huge beast's horns, head, and finally all four of his hooves off the ground, the whole tight-packed mass of humanity in those stands were brought to their feet by that same hypnotic motion, and stood there screaming their collective and almost literal guts up, as the bull went over him and almost past him, except that its left hind foot caught him full in the forehead and knocked him unconscious.

Seeing him go down, the spectators wracked sound out of existence. All except one. Except Grace Nivens who was slumped over between the lower and upper iron tubes of the *barandilla,* the protective railing between the *primera fila* of the seats and the *callejon,* in a dead faint.

By then, of course, or even some seconds before, while the last of it was still going on, the bull airborne, his hoof poised to render judgment on sheer folly, Patricia's *cuadrilla* were all there.

One of them, a retired *matador,* killed the bull with an *estocada* of really brilliant class and skill. Two *peones* picked poor Patti up. Two more Jim. Rushed them to the emergency infirmary below the stands. Two teams of doctors worked on both of them, simultaneously.

Ten minutes later, Jim Rush walked out of there on his own two feet. He had a sore belly and a headache, that was all. And, of course, an enormous aggrandizement of his legend. But it would be months before Patricia Montenegro would walk again. If she ever did. For, along with a femur smashed in seven places, she had a fractured spine.

Grace was waiting by the doors of the infirmary when he came out. She was leaning against the wall because she still wasn't all that sure that she could stand up. She was also crying helplessly.

Jim came straight towards her through the dense crowd of people waiting there, all of whom began to clap and cheer when he appeared. But, before he could reach her, a uniformed policeman stepped up to him and saluted.

"Señor Embajador," the policeman said, "His excellency, the Head of the State requests that you—and *la Doctora,* of course—join him at the Hospital *Miguel Villalonga* where they have carried *su Señorita Sobrina.* He wishes to thank you in person for your gallantry. And if it is permitted, I, too, felicitate you, Your Excellency! Do you have transportation, or shall we provide it?"

"I have the Embassy limousine and my chauffeur," Jim said, wearily. "We'll be along shortly, Officer. Now, if you'll allow me, I'd better look after my friend, *la Doctora,* who seems a bit upset . . ."

He walked over to her, took her arm. Said reproachfully:

"Come, my dear. Snap out of it, will you?"

But she didn't stop crying. She couldn't. He said: "Grace, please! Come, let's go to the car . . ."

She smiled at him then, through slowing tears; whispered:

"Darling, I've disgraced you, I'm afraid. I—I passed out. All the way. For the very first time in my life. I—couldn't take that, Jim! I couldn't! And d'you know what?"

"No, what?" he said.

"All the way down here to the infirmary, all your little Chili Beans— were staring at my middle!"

He laughed at that, freely, gaily. Said: "How I wish that they were right, and that I were the guilty party!"

"So do I," she said slowly, sadly; "but that's—become—impossible now, hasn't it? Jim—you *are* all right, aren't you?"

"Yes. Vince insists upon my reporting in for a checkup against small fractures, and internal injuries; but I feel all right. A trifle the worse for wear, but—"

"And—and she? Patti—*your* girl?"

"Lord, Grace, don't wish Patti off on me, will you? They say—she'll make it. That—she'll live. She may be paralyzed from the waist down—they don't know—"

"Oh, God!" Grace said; then: "That's going to make it awfully rough on you, isn't it? Because you've *got* to marry her now, haven't you?"

He stared at her. Said, harshly:

"For God's sake, Grace! I'm not obligated to that child. Not at all. So I—slept—or rather stayed awake with her—*one* night. Truthfully, if you'll permit me this—necessary departure from a gentleman's standards—at *her* insistence. There's a point beyond which the spectacle of a middle-aged man fighting off an absolutely stunning young creature in defense of his so-called honor becomes utterly ridiculous. One obliges—and forgets it . . . ."

"*She* didn't," Grace said.

"I'm sorry. I thought she would. I wish she had. But that doesn't alter the fact that I made her no promises and told her the exact truth—"

"Which is?"

"That I love you. *You,* not her. Nor, for that matter, which is a hell of a lot less good than it sounds, any other woman. I may not be able to do anything about—loving you, Grace. For reasons I'm going to explain to you. But not now. Now I have a devil of a headache and a sore gut. So—let's leave the deep, poignant conversations for another day, shall we?"

She whispered: "All right, darling." Stood there staring at him a little speculatively, he thought. No, almost—timidly. Even—fearfully, somehow.

He said: "What is it, Grace? What is it that you want to ask me?"

"Only—whether you've ever heard of a place called Pelicans' Island . . ."

"Well, that's an unexpected question if I ever heard one! Yes, Grace. It's down south. Just off Tarascanolla. One hotel. Fair. Miles of empty beaches. And—Pelicans, Emperor Birds, Terns, Gulls, Albatrosses, and what have you. Pretty place. I like it. Why?"

A tide of warm red color flooded her high cheeks, just below her eyes. It—erased her years. Thirty-eight? Thirty-nine? Forty? he wondered. Turned her into the schoolgirl she had been. Tall. Gawky. Timid. Shy. But wonderfully—sweet and appealing, he thought.

"I'm going down there tomorrow morning. For the weekend. To rest, I suppose you could say. Because you see, Jenny's going to make it, too. Oh, Lord! When I try to say it—it sounds horrible, even to me! Utterly—shameless. I *hate* aggressive women! Don't you?"

He said solemnly: "As long as I'm allowed to pick my aggressors, no, Grace. In your case, my dear, I'd probably let out one high-pitched boyish yelp—for form's sake, don't you know?—then lie back and enjoy it!"

"Oh, damn you, Jim Rush! You—aren't helping, you know! All right, all right! The truth—sad, humiliating truth is that I have not one, but *two* round trip plane tickets, already bought. And a reservation at the hotel. A—double, with bath. Which is surely carrying both—frankness, and aggressiveness, female gender!—far past their permissible limits. Still—*I've* been carried—or driven!—beyond mine, this week. Far beyond them. So, will you—come with me, Jim? Will you please, for God's sake come with me—before I lose my mind?"

He stood there, staring at her. A long time. A very long time. Then he said, softly, sadly.

"Yes, Grace. I owe you that much, don't I? You—and myself. Come on. Let's get out of here . . ."

CHAPTER

30

*T*he aircraft they took down to Tarascanolla was an old propeller plane, a Convair Metropolitan, much the worse for wear; but it must have been sound enough mechanically, because it got them there alive, though it took its own sweet time to do it. Jets have changed the time sense of modern man; when one goes somewhere by boat or train, the element of slowness, of leisure, is usually a matter of deliberate choice, and adds to the archaic charm of the trip. 'But the only reason,' Jim realized now, 'that you *ever* take a propeller driven aircraft is that you've stumbled onto a line that has no jets. And the damned things are unbearable!'

As this one was. It creaked, it groaned, it vibrated, and flew at such low altitudes that turbulence was a thrice a minute occurrence. He could feel airsickness creeping up on him, starting from the pit of his stomach, and crawling slowly upward towards the lower esophagus, which was one hell of a way to start what was supposed to be a romantic weekend . . .

Or—was it? Turning, he looked, unexpectedly, into Grace's eyes. Saw that she was visibly fighting back tears.

"Grace, please!" he said.

"Sorry—" she said. "I—was being morbid. Wondering—if you would have done that—risked your life like that—without a backward glance, or a second thought—for me, Jim . . ."

"For you," he said, "I'd have caught that big black bastard by the throat and *chewed* the life out of him. Now, forget it, will you? I only did that anyhow because I'm—a coward, Grace."

"A coward? Good God!"

"Yes. I was—afraid, deathly afraid that Patti—would get killed because of me; and that I'd have to remember all the rest of my life that I—because she brought that damned bull deliberately under my nose to inflict that memory on me; suicide's always a form of vengeance, isn't it?—sat there three meters away and *let* her die . . . I was also scared spitless at the risk involved. But in this world you always have to decide which set of fears to favor . . . And, maybe there was even—subconsciously—a suicidal impulse involved on my part, as well. That wouldn't surprise me either, considering what my life is now, what it's—going to be—"

She caught his hand so hard that his flesh whitened, then purpled under her grip.

"Jim, I want you to promise me something. I want your sacred oath that you *won't* tell me anything this weekend that will make me unhappy. I've—waited too long for—this. For *us* to be happy, together. I—don't think I could bear—it's being spoiled, my Dearest—"

"Nor I," he whispered.

"Oh, Jim—let's be happy! Please, let's be happy," she said.

"I'll—try. It may be a talent I haven't got; but I'll try," he said.

"Jim—" she said a little later; "General García—are you going to have trouble from him? I had the feeling that when he called you into the waiting room of the hospital to thank you for saving—Patricia— boiling you in oil was closer to what he actually had in mind!"

"It was," Jim said soberly, "but he won't dare. Because then he'd have to accuse me publicly of having had an affair with little Patti-Cake—"

"Patti-Cake!" Grace said. "Oh, Jesus! How—fitting!"

"Is it? I doubt it. Let's—in fairness—grant her that there're more depths in that little soul than were dreamt of in the philosophies of the types that hung that nickname on her. She proved that, rather conclusively, yesterday, Grace . . ."

"Jim—"Grace whispered. "Are you—*sure* you're not in love with her?"

He looked at her. Said slowly:

"You want an honest answer, or a dishonest answer to that one, my Dear?"

"An honest one, Darling. I don't want—lies between us, ever again."

"All right. I'm *not* sure. Patricia Montenegro is one of the most beautiful young women in all this world of sin. She appeals to me physically, sexually. And, truthfully, in a good many other ways as well. And down here I've had my ailing ego built up—in part by *her*—to the extent that I'm sure I could handle even the rather explosive armful that she is. In confidence, her reputation's horrendous; but well—let's say that female angels are in rather short supply these days—"

"Touché!" Grace said bitterly. "Go on, please!"

"All right. I don't think I'd even have to buy her a medieval chastity belt or chain her to the wall during my absences, since I enjoy the rather peculiar and somewhat dubious distinction of being the only man to whom she quite seriously proposed marriage and even armed a devil of a row by asking in public at a party at my house the General's permission—she's under legal age, y'know—to marry me . . . ."

"Dear God!" Grace whispered. "And he—refused?"

"Didn't have to. She admitted that I'd already declined the honor with sincere thanks. What she was trying to do was to use his consent—and he nearly always does consent to what she asks him; as Avery says, she's spoiled rotten!—to force my hand."

"But," Grace said very, very quietly, "since you *admit* you're in love with her . . . ."

"Now look, Doctor! Let's be scientific about this, shall we? The human race simply isn't monogamous by nature, though women have had to—more or less!—be, for economic reasons, and because of their physical helplessness during pregnancy. But look what's happened since the Pill, will you? In certain circles, anyhow, female promiscuity *exceeds* male, for the very simple reason that it's less tiring for the female, all right?"

"Jim, I'm going to hit you in a minute!"

"Don't," he said solemnly; "I'm delicate. I bruise easily. It would show."

"Oh Lord!" she said. "Jim—I'm scared. I'm—far from young. I'm certainly not—beautiful. I'm a little shorter than one of the World Trade Center towers, but not much, and—"

"Grace," he said, "you don't mean to sit there and tell me that you need reassurance—from *me*?"

"Yes, Jim," she whispered, "after what you've just said, I do; definitely!"

"All right. I would get seriously involved with dear little Patti-Cake only if you didn't exist, Grace. And even so, she wouldn't even be next in line. Your little receptionist, Meg, would come in rather a bit ahead of her, for one . . . ."

"I'd noticed that," Grace said tartly. "When you were getting yourself blown up and shot all over, she actually got sick. And when she found out that we'd broken up, she started studying Spanish—and checking our employment bureau for jobs available with Worldwide in this area!"

He grinned at her; said: "Thanks, Grace! I'll make a mental note of that information for future reference!"

"Jim," she said soberly, "all right—you've the upper hand. But—don't take advantage, please? That would make me *very* unhappy. Because you see, Darling, what most appeals to me about you are all the ways you *aren't* like other men . . ."

He looked at her. Said:

"Now I do thank you, my dear. Seriously. Let me end this: Straighten it out. I love—totally and completely—one woman in all the world, Grace: *You.* And that love, unfortunately—surely for me; and perhaps for both of us—has become the bedrock of my existence. I can't even imagine a world without you in it. Yet I am, being a normal human male, powerfully attracted to a number of other women, with whom I'd happily sleep—hell! happily keep busily awake with!—if that delightful pastime didn't always bring, as it damned well *always* does, so many practically unmanageable consequences in its wake. And her close to tragic feat of rather cruelly reminding me of that fact, is another thing we can both thank little Patti for . . ."

"Her. Get back to her, Jim. You said you were not sure you weren't in love with her. Put yourself in *my* place, if you can. That's a—*very* worry-making statement from where I sit!"

"I'm *not* sure. What I am sure is that I'm not enough in love with her—to risk—ruining—a relationship—Lord, what a feeble word!—to risk ruining—a miracle, a glory—that means everything to me, for her sake. For anyone's sake, for that matter. I'm—far fonder of Patti than I should be; fonder even than it's entirely safe or comfortable for me to be; but I should never have got involved with her if had not been for two factors; one of which was my belief that any possibility of my—ending my days at your side was completely over, dear."

"And the other?" Grace said.

"Grace, a little while ago, you made me promise not to tell you anything that would make you unhappy, didn't you? I'm—afraid, awfully afraid—*that* would."

She said: "Oh!" Then very quickly: "No, don't, Jim! Please, don't!"

"*Now* what shall we talk about?" he said.

"Don't know. Oh, yes! The General. You said he wouldn't do anything about you, because to do so—"

"He'd have to admit he knew I've had an affair with his adopted daughter. And he can't possibly do that, it would cost him too much 'face' in the Chinese sense. And, as a matter of fact, he *doesn't* know it. He only thinks he does. On the basis of those pictures you saw and that some blackmailer took, probably for political reasons. Only on the night that they set poor Patti up for those flashshots, and tried to set me up as well, nothing happened . . ."

"Now, Jim—" Grace said.

"God's truth. I put dear Patti the hell out of my place. But she showed up the next night, after I had had too much to drink—and was in a really low mood because of—something else—"

"Some*one* else!" Grace corrected tartly.

He stared at her. Said, the pain in his voice naked:

"Say—something else I'd—inadvertently found out about—someone else, Grace. Another case of—altar profaning, say. Look, Dear, you're skating on awfully thin ice now. I will truthfully and faithfully answer anything you ask me; but are you sure you want to know?"

"No; I don't. But I've—got to. A little more than this, anyhow. Don't worry; I'll get off the ice in time! Jim—this someone else—were you—were you in love with her?"

He said: "Yes, Grace."

And she: "How—much?"

He said, softly, slowly: "Terribly."

She said, proving again that the absolute mastery of an art or a science, superb intellectual brilliance, a really superior mind, do absolutely nothing to alter or change the *condition* of being a woman: "As much—as you do me? Or—claim to?"

He said, evenly: "Perhaps—more, Grace."

She said: "Ohhhhh, Jesus!" And started to cry.

He said, gently: "Don't, Grace. That's—over. Because of what I found out. And because I'm a coward—a moral coward, anyhow. It's much easier to face the horns of a bull, my dear—than to face up to some of the things one is. Some of the dirty, rotten, *mesquina* things one is . . .

She said: "*Mesquina,* Jim?"

"It's the right word. And there is no English equivalent. 'Petty' is close enough, I suppose. Narrow of soul. Flinty-hearted. Uncharitable. Unforgiving. A moral coward. A rockribbed New England puritan— about a good many things, anyhow."

"Jim, Dearest," she said firmly, "none of those things fit you! If they did, how could I love you so?"

"Perhaps because you're deluded. Perhaps I haven't shown you that side of me, yet. Anyway—what ended, almost surely forever, my love for—the girl in question—also terribly young, and far, far more beautiful than Patti is—was something that happened, that she did—no, not even that!—that was done to her, inflicted upon her—years before she knew I was alive. It had nothing to do with me. It has perhaps intensified the way she felt—feels—towards me. Because I don't do that sort of thing, because I've always treated her with great kindness, I have had repeated evidence from her of a certain confusion in her mind—more than evidences, proof—that she really is not quite sure that I am not the Only Begotten Son of God! Jesus, Grace, but worship's hard to take! And now—"

"You don't love her. You truly—don't, Jim?"

He looked at her, said: "If I did, I wouldn't be here now, Grace."

She said: "That's—cold comfort, Jim. In fact, it's practically deep frozen. But, I'll accept it. I have to. It's that—or give you up. And I can't do that. I—I'm not strong enough to, anymore. So if what you found out was enough to remove her from my path, you can't expect me to take the same dim view of it that you do, can you?"

He said, harshly: "It hasn't—yet. I think it's going to. I'm afraid it's going to. And I'm terrified at the prospect of the kind of life, we—you and I—could have on that basis, Grace!"

She stared at him; whispered:

"Jim, Darling—let's get off this ice, please? It's cracking . . ."

"All right," he said. "I'm sorry, my dear. I don't want to spoil your weekend. Nor—mine. I need it—need whatever little happiness I can beg, borrow, steal—even for so brief a time. So let's not only get off that rotten ice, but *stay* off it, shall we? There're quicksands beneath it, quagmire, marsh . . . Let's stay off it all the little time we can . . ."

She leaned over and kissed him, then, a long, slow, tremblingly soft and tender kiss. Straightened up, smiled at him.

"As far as you're concerned, I've hung up my skates forever," she said.

As they came in over the sea towards Tarascanolla, visible now in a shimmering wash of blue and white and gold, sea and houses and sand, and beyond that the black-green of the jungle swimming up towards them, he was thinking how lucky he had been that Trini had slept the whole of Friday afternoon, and hadn't seen that bullfight on television. He knew that because Pepe, Cecilia, and Rosa had all told him so with many, many "To God, the thanks!" thrown in. Trini slept an awful lot now. It was almost time for the child to be born, but he couldn't figure out exactly when. There had been a possible false alarm before. Trini had skipped two periods, but then—to her weeping, absolutely heart-broken disappointment—had had the third one. Except that it had been very, very light. Only two days, and a pinkish watery flow, instead of the terribly heavy menstruations she usually suffered from. So either she had become pregnant that next month, or she had remained pregnant in spite of that so-called period. A three *months'* difference in the count. And no one could be sure . . .

The plane groaned and bumped down an invisible roller coaster into Tarascanolla's airport. Bumped even more once it was on the ground, since Tarascanolla hadn't a paved flight-strip to its name. And now, to get to Pelicans' Island, they had to take a boat. He prayed to Father Pío's God that the sea wouldn't be choppy.

He was lucky. It wasn't. By the time they got to the island, he was surprised to find he was actually a little hungry. A dune buggy—*prima facie* evidence of what Pelicans' Island's roads were like—met them at the docks and carried them and their luggage up to Hotel Pelican, which sat on a high bluff, overlooking a cove. They had lunch on the terrace. The lunch was all seafoods, and close to excellent. The local white wine served with it was even better.

Grace smiled at him, and her already deeply tanned face darkened richly, especially just below her pale blue eyes.

"Shall—we go—take—a *siesta,* Darling?" she said softly.

"Yes," he said, "but—down on the beach, Grace. In swim suits. So we can have a dip, later on."

She said:

"Oh!"

He grinned at her, said:

"Why 'Oh!' Grace?"

"You just don't act like *anyone* else, Jim Rush! Or—did I sound so—well—aggressive—that I frightened you?"

He smiled at her, sadly; said:

"Do you *feel* aggressive, Grace?"

She bowed her head. Looked up again. Said:

"Yes, Jim. *Very.* So—now you're—thinking about what I told you. About the—confession you didn't even want—and wondering if I might not be—a nymphomaniac—or something—"

"I don't believe there's any such animal," he said. "I believe—know—that moods, feelings, even passions—vary. With the attendant circumstances, at times. That they're influenced by quite extraneous factors, all too often, by—bad memories—bad dreams . . ." He quoted suddenly, wryly: " 'Oh God, I could be bounded in a nutshell and count myself master of infinite space were it not—' "

" 'That I had bad dreams!' " she finished it for him. "Jim—you're sorry you came down here with me, aren't you? Let's—call the whole thing off. Take the next boat back, the next plane—"

"Which aren't until tomorrow, Grace." He smiled at her. "Let's play this by ear, shall we? So—as a prelude to the first movement, if any!—hear this: My mood is, at the moment—as our conversations on the plane coming down here should have made abundantly clear to you—all wrong. But not because of you, my Love. Rather, because of me. I feel like a bastard. For the most excellent reasons that I have been a bastard, and that I remain the Lord High Chief Commander of all Illegitimates, with all manners, kinds, and degrees of bars sinister practically blotting out my escutcheon. I am achieving a new low in bastardy by even being here with you, now. I should love to go to bed, to have glorious sex with you. I should hate—to victimize you. The problem, then, is easily stated: How to accomplish the first, without automatically causing the second. The solution—escapes me. I should like to have more time to think about it. A lazy afternoon on the beach say . . ."

"All right. Let's go change then. You go first. I'll take longer. Wait for me down there. By that cove. All right?"

He smiled, wanly; said: "All right . . ."

She got up, bent swiftly and kissed his mouth. Whispered:

"Jim—it's *not* wrong—for people in love to—to want each other. It's not. Don't be a—a rockribbed Puritan with me, please!"

When he saw her in her black, elastic bikini, he gave vent to a low, expressive wolf-whistle straight out of the nineteen forties. He was surprised—and delighted—to find that in spite of her immense height, she was very probably *the* most perfectly—and beautifully!—built woman he had ever seen. Her waist was actually smaller—in proportion to her size—than Patricia's was, or than Trini's had been, and would—maybe—get to be again; but her hips were, while still slender and shapely, broader. He remembered what Wildcat Ed Crowley had said about the size of her breasts, and throwing back his head he laughed aloud.

Her face flamed scarlet.

"Jim—I'm too *big* to wear a bikini, aren't I?" she said sadly. "I—never do. It's—new. I bought it because—because I thought you'd like it."

"I do. The only thing that could possibly improve on it would be a monokini, based upon the *Tanga*–String concept."

"Like—Petra's?" she said tartly.

"Like Petra's. And from there you could go to the original fig leaf, and from there—to nothing at all. I laughed, not at this gloriously exciting bikini, but because seeing you in it reminded me of something Ed Crowley once told me about you, and proved to me *again* that he's a fool!"

"What did he tell you, Jim?"

Jim imitated the oilman's raucous Texan's voice:

" 'That theah Grace is got th' tiniest lil' ol' titties a body ever did see. Ain't exactly flat, but they shore doan poke yore eyes out, Son!' "

"A lot *he* knows about it!" Grace sniffed. "Though he was always in there trying to paw at me, Dirty Old Man that he is!"

"Me, too," Jim said cheerfully. "I'll bet I could give Ed pointers in the Unsanitary Senior Citizens' Department!"

She laughed then. Came to him. Jackknifed down to where he was. Kissed him. Said:

"I *hope* you can, Jim. Now come on!"

They swam in the soup-warm waters, ate the sandwiches the hotel's chef had insisted they take along. Drank the whole *bote*—the leather bottle—of wine, squirting the hard red streams into their mouths. Jim, of course, taught her the trick of it, and she got it right after only two tries.

But then a silence fell between them, fathoms deep. She said, her voice, breath-torn, ragged:

"I—I'm going to swim again. To—cool off!"

He didn't follow her into the waves. He lay on the vast and empty beach and closed his eyes. Dozed a little. Then he heard her voice saying:

"Jim—"

He looked up. She was standing there before him. She was crying very quietly. The tears rolled unchecked down her tanned cheeks. And she had taken her bikini off. The two pieces of it trailed from her slim, strong, sun-browned left hand, sprinkling drops of sea water onto the sands.

He lay there, unbreathing, studying her. She was—magnificent. Glorious. Thus Aphrodite must have looked as she waded ashore through the Cyprian foam.

He smiled at her. Put up his arms. She sank down beside him. Bent and kissed his mouth. Slowly, softly, sweetly. But she didn't stop crying. She couldn't. Her mouth tasted warm and salt. Sea salt. Tear salt. He said, reproachfully:

"Why do you cry, my Love?"

She said, sobbing a little:

"Because I—I'm ashamed! You—you've forced me to be the aggressor. The—famished—bitch—begging you to—"

He grinned at her; said:

"What, Grace?"

"Oh, damn you, Jim Rush!" she said, and started to get up. But he locked his thin, wiry, surprisingly strong arms around her neck, and drew her back down again. Kissed her, with tender mockery, in a different way. Open-mouthed, deeply, with frank—and deliberately brutal—passion, playing Pan-God, Pursuing Faun, Satyr, with a wicked accumulation of skill.

She drew back, stared at him with startled—and troubled—eyes.

He laughed aloud, said:

"Now, you do look like a schoolmarm—prim, and grim! Will you please—come back from Iceland, my dear?"

"Jim—" drawling his name out, harshly, slowly.

"Yes, Dearest?"

"Don't—don't get me confused with—with your local whores!" she said angrily.

He turned her loose. Lay there looking at her. Said, evenly, flatly:

"Nor should you—try to make me—number four—that is, accepting your count as an honest one!—on your list of playboys, Grace."

She said: "Oh, Jesus!" Bent her head. Wept stormily. Looked up with streaming eyes. Whispered: "I'm—sorry, Jim. I—I've spoiled our weekend, haven't I?"

He said solemnly:

"Almost. But—not quite. Forgive me my quips, my jests, my gambols, will you? They were—my hamfisted attempts to appear light hearted, blithe, debonair. I'd say—gay, but that word's been ruined, hasn't it? Violated. As so many words, concepts, even people—have been these days. Besides, I don't feel blithe or debonair. I feel—awed. Solemn. As a man should in the presence of a miracle—"

"A—miracle?" she said.

"Yes. You. Aphrodite foam-born out of the wine-dark waters. Wading shoreward, softly, sweetly, to my waiting arms . . ."

"Jim—"

"Yes, Grace?"

"Make—love to me. Now. Please?"

He murmured: "All right." Bent to her breasts. Kissed them, cherishing the nipples. Put down his hand, searching amid her sudden fur, found her hidden quiver, gape, and scald. Her long fingers closed over his wrists, iron within velvet. She said, quietly:

"No, Jim."

He stared at her.

She said, shaking now, trembling; her voice, dark, ashudder:

"Don't—fondle me. I—don't need it. Nor any kind of—foreplay. You'll make me—spoil things. I've been—wanting this, wanting— *you*—too long."

He said: "Sorry." Entered her without preliminaries. Easily and at once. Had in that instant the answer to the one question he had wondered about, the response to a thing he had feared. Even without her shoes on she was a shade over six feet tall, and proportioned to match her height. But, as far as her—to him—immediately perceptible interior genitalia were concerned, she was no bigger than any other woman. Smaller than most. He felt a warm surge of relief, of happiness. Then he remembered. This wasn't going to go on, as he'd thought in the days when he'd wondered half fearfully whether sex between two people outwardly ill matched as they were wouldn't be—a near impossibility, a bad joke.

He moved, tentatively, slowly. She surged to meet him, the response at least quadrupling his initial thrust. Totally—ready. All peristaltic tremble, clinging, scald, engorging his rigid maleness in what seemed to him in astonishment, in anger, a deliberate attempt to end both rigidity and maleness at once, produce instant ejaculation, melt him into the undulant heat and thrash and writhe of her.

He stopped. Peered into her face. He couldn't see her eyes. She had closed them. They fluttered open. Star sapphires. No. Simply—stars.

"Jim—" she breathed.

"Yes, Grace?"

"Don't—hold back. Please."

He said: "Don't worry about me. I'm in no hurry. I can wait."

Her voice purred into his ear, cool, dry—wry. A little amused; its tone—sardonic.

"I know. I've noticed. It's—awfully unflattering, Jim Rush!"

"Lord!" he said. "Didn't mean it that way, Grace. Symptom of—old age, I suspect. Galloping senility's rapidly overtaking me, you know . . ."

She was still. All of her was still.

"No," she said quietly; "it's—evidence of—a lack of interest, isn't it? I—don't—excite you, do I?"

He shook his head, trying to clear that mirage from his eyes. That small, dark, elfin-tender face. That tiny figure, now grossly swollen. Those slanted, night-black—but night of the full moon, starry night!—Tluscolan eyes. That mouth. That mouth! Mother of his child, by him betrayed, because—

'Because I'm an utter shit,' he thought. '¡Una mierda!'

Grace said, sharply:

"Jim—what's wrong?"

"Wrong?" he whispered.

"Yes. Something is. And—terribly." She lay there beneath him, holding him, softly, sweetly, warmly, wetly, containing him, unmoving now, still, studying his face, his eyes. Said, sadly, bitterly:

"I'm—sorry! I—apologize. I shouldn't have—"

Her hands came up, pushing against his chest.

He held her; his voice sand itself, desert dry:

"Come out of the sea like Aphrodite foam-born? Attempted to—make love to—this flotsam—washed up on a far, far shore—where no life is—or ever was? This beached hulk with no joy in it? Nothing in it but bad memories, pain?"

She stopped pushing him away, stared up at him. With—real compassion, he thought. With—pity. With—something else. And that something else was—tenderness. Was—love. Then she put up those long, slender, immensely strong hands of hers, drew his head down, found his mouth. Kissed him until every nerve in his body was screaming. Until his blood matched the surf behind them, its steady beat, its sullen roar.

Then, with her eyes wide open, holding his gaze, she made love to him, powerfully, making full use of her long, strong athletic body, with no reticence, hungrily, fiercely, honestly, swiftly—'The kind of love-making,' he thought with aching wonder, 'we think of—as male. Because most women have been shamed, trained, inhibited out of it, out of this *human* directness, this acknowledged, big, fine passion—this glory!'

She surged up against him, calves and ankles stiffened, her cradling, wildly gyrating loins increasing the rhythm every second, building it up, up, up into the arching, peaking, cresting of a mountainous wave hanging there, hanging there, hanging there, impossibly, unbelievably upon the rim edges of death and forever, then downcrashing, bursting, exploding, its thunder ending the world. It was over in an incredibly brief time. Two minutes. Three. But even so—astonishingly, he had to race to join her at the end of it. Almost failed to catch up. She turned her face sidewise away from his and cried like a whipped and heart-broken child, sobbing aloud, fighting for breath, the whole magnificent length of her orgasm, for whole long minutes, longer in fact than the act of sex, of love itself had lasted, violently acquiver. Said, sometime later, when it had again become possible for her to say anything:

"God, how I needed that!"

"Sex?" he said. He hoped his voice hadn't sounded—bitter.

"Yes," she said honestly; "but—with the man I love."

He said, half jokingly, half in wonder:

"I thought women were supposed to be—slow."

"Women, yes—maybe. This outsized, overgrown, oversexed female of the canine species, no, Jim. Not with *you*. I don't believe any normal woman's ever slow with a man she's in love with. Whacked up dames with a puritanical upbringing, yes—I suppose so. But I'll make the next session last, thank you. Now that you've cooled me off so nicely, Lover! But back at the hotel, after a shower—to remove half the sand from the beach out of places where sand damned well oughtn't be!"

She drew his head down. Kissed him. Smiled at him, peacefully.

"Happy, Jim?" she said. "Was I—fun?"

"You mean," he mocked, "were you a good lay? Yes. Quite. The best I've had *this* week, anyhow!"

She gave him a two handed, stiff armed shove that sent him flying. Leaped up, caught his arms, wrestled him to the sand. Sat astride him, pinning him down, holding his arms spread out, helplessly. She was at least twice as strong as he was, he conceded.

"Jim—" she drawled. "By common consent the week begins with Sunday. So last week includes Saturday night, doesn't it? And the session that convinced your little Patti-Cake that letting a bull rip her guts out was—better, more acceptable than giving you up—to me?"

"Grace," he said quietly; "I *won't* talk about that. I refuse to, flatly. It's the—past. It even could have been—a good memory. One to be recalled, even savored, if she had let it. But she didn't. And it hadn't one good goddamned thing to do with you—except that your absence, your voluntary departure from my life—caused it. At least in part. So, forget it, will you?"

"It's forgot. I won't be presumptuous enough to say—forgiven. But one more question, Jim. The last. I won't risk spoiling the rest of our weekend—I've got far too many experiments I mean to carry out. *Kama Sutra* type experiments, Lover! I—I've never dared try them before. Because, you see, they require just that: a lover, not just a—casual bedmate. Someone—who loves me, not just my—"

"Tits, tail, and snatch," he said solemnly.

"Jim, I'm going to *hit* you!" she cried.

"Aw, g'wan, pick on somebody your size," he teased. "All right, I love you. Which *includes* tits, tail, and snatch. And I'm game. But take it easy, will you? I'm a delicate flower. Fragile. I bruise easily. I—"

"Oh, cut it out!" she said. "Jim—may I ask you that question? You—you don't have to answer it if you don't want to—"

He stared at her.

"Ask away, Grace," he said.

"Your—Patti-Cake. You said—just once. Were you—trying to salve—or save my feelings? Not—to—to hurt me?"

"No. I wasn't lying. Though I don't believe I said just once, because that wouldn't be true. I said just one night, which is true. And was quite enough, thank you! For her—too much, the poor little thing . . ."

"Oh!" Grace said. "Now, I *am* stuck."

"Why?" he said.

"I said—one question. And your answer to it—calls for, inflicts upon my badly bruised ego, at least a dozen more. All of them—absolutely none of my business—"

He smiled at her. Said:

"I'm glad you realize *that*, my dear!"

"Oh, damn!" she wailed. "Jim, you weren't hard up, the way *I* was. Nor, by the remotest stretch of the imagination, the lousy lover you accused yourself of being! So that means—Oh. Oh, my God!"

"Why, 'Oh my God!' Grace?"

"The—the *other* one!" she whispered. "The one you, yourself, said, admitted— *worships* you. And I've just remembered something *she* said. Your—Patti-Cake. That she was prepared to accept your *liaison*—with that dear, sweet child—whose name she wouldn't—distress you by saying—because she came first and has literally offered up her life for you—twice. Adds up, doesn't it? The *same* one. The—one you *claim*— you no longer love!"

"Grace," he said simply, "you're being more than a little offensive, now, my dear. I object—strongly—to that 'you *claim.'* Can you recall, or point out to me, one single occasion upon which I've lied to you? About—anything? Even when it would have been far easier to? When the truth was hurtful to you, and demeaning to me?"

"No," she whispered. "You're almost compulsively truthful, aren't you? Or—isn't it, sadistically so, my Love? Don't you tend to use truth—as a bludgeon—or a blade?"

He said wearily, sorrowfully:

"Get up. Put your bikini back on, Grace. Then, back to the hotel. To—get packed. Scratch—one weekend. One weekend—that was starting out, gloriously . . ."

"No," she said, and turned his wrists loose. Bent forward with that astonishing grace of hers. Put her mouth on his. Murmured against it. "Please, no, Jim. The subject's closed. Forever—unless *you* bring it up. I want—my weekend. Which is all I'll *ever* have from you, isn't it?" She drew her face a little way from his, stared into his eyes. Said slowly, sadly: "And I don't *want* you to tell me about her. I don't believe that now—today, I could actually bear knowing. No—not knowing, for I *do* know, don't I? I couldn't bear—hearing it—from you. So, forgive me, again, Jim. I—I should have thought this way before putting you through that—old time Country Revival Confession about my—own mad career, after we'd broken up, shouldn't I?"

"That's—all right, Grace," he said; "I've forgotten it. Let's be getting back. Come . . ."

They showered together, as lovers will, finding it, as lovers do, one of life's finest available pleasures. They did not go down to dinner. They stayed in bed, lovingly entwined, all night, and most of Sunday, with a break for lunch and a swim, and all of Sunday night as well, finding, as intelligent people usually do, that they adapted to each other easily, perfectly. For it is one of the curious facts of life that it is your intellectuals, your imaginative, creative people who are superior lovers, while your burly brutes, athletes pertaining to the heavier and more violently combative branches of sports, manual laborers, men and women heavy with muscle—and with fat!—who are your lousy ones.

Even her "experiments" had grown out of—he saw at once—her worry over the possible negative effects of the disparity between their sizes. She'd thought that the comfortable and pleasant woman superior positions were going to be impossible, that her considerable weight—though she had not a gram of fat on her long body anywhere—would be enough to crush him. They turned out not to be, her sixty-eight kilos—by the hotel's bathroom scale—easily supportable. So she tried—and enjoyed them—all. She found—as women always do—that she didn't enjoy any position that caused her to face away from him, that would not allow their eyes and mouths to meet while making love. He found—as men always do, being much further down the evolutionary scale than women are!—that he thoroughly enjoyed many of the rear entry, more animalistic positions. "Plain doggish!" she snorted; and he conceded the point, laughing, saying: "Dogs have an awful lot of fun!"

But, as that weekend slipped away, the quality of it subtly changed. The gaiety spilled out of it. What had been playful, mischievous, mocking, fun—two people refusing (or, more truthfully, trying, with a poignant, and well hidden desperation to refuse!) to take themselves, each other, or the joyous use of two really fine—if somewhat mismatched!—bodies too seriously, as though they'd agreed beforehand: "Oh, come now, let's not be solemn about a pleasant, casual weekend affair!"—became just that: solemn. Even—sad. Now they approached each other, sought each other, in a perfect agony of almost hurtful tenderness. Now seeking hands trembled almost uncontrollably as they neared each other's flesh. Now the silences between them stretched out to the rim edges of forever, and in every word they didn't say, there was a little death.

Their lovemaking became the most exquisitely agonizing of tortures conceivable: He knew, and she guessed, that this weekend was to be their all. And because they had been granted what was now, or had become, the cruelest of all miracles, that they were absolutely perfect with and for each other, his knowledge, and her belief, that they were going to have to live out the rest of their lives separately and apart, became unbearable.

She thought: 'The rest of my life? One month away from him and I'll go mad!'

And he: 'I'd do anything at all to keep her. Even—'

And suddenly death itself was between them in that bed. He no longer saw that face of Pallas Athena, all that intelligence, combined into her special, perfect, Olympian and classic beauty, did not, and could not discern that cerulean sheen barely visible beneath heavy lids and midnight lashes, drooping in exquisite languor towards love's anguished and lovely self-immolation, nor hear from the soft rounded O her lips had formed the quickening, rising, sweetsighing pulsations of her breath.

No. Instead, that elfin-tender, tawny, coppery face. Those slanted night-black—night of the full moon, starry night!—Tluscolan eyes. That mouth—that mouth—

Singing. One slow eerie note. Spiraling around, above, behind, below the beat. Utterly—beautiful. Completely terrible. Asking of the Gods—a death.

And he'd thought, formed the definite image: 'I'd do anything, anything—anything at all to keep her—to keep—Grace . . .'

And thereby—reinvoked that incantation. Reenforced that plea. Sought, all unconsciously, that way out. That unspeakable, that awful way.

'No!' he screamed, crashing the word through the vast and echoing silences of his mind; 'I didn't mean *that*! I didn't! Hear me, all ye Ancient Gods! And you, my Furies and my Fates! If she—dies giving birth to my child—if my smallness of soul, barrenness of heart, want of comprehension, compassion, pity—lack of love—condemns her—*this* will end too! By that which I hold most dear, by this very unhallowed and forbidden love for this woman who is my life, my life—I swear it! I'll accept no future based upon—'

"Jim—" Grace murmured.

"Yes?" he moaned.

"Please—"

"Please, what?" he said bitterly, absently, his mind far away and sorrowing.

"Don't hold back. Come in me—now. I'm—ready, Love. Please?"

He sighed. Said: "All right, Grace."

He moved, slowly, powerfully. She surged up to meet him, urgently, arrogantly demanding, all the tenderness gone, replaced by the whip and goad of desperation, by what was not so much passion as madness, a near suicidal seeking to use the body to blind, blot out, banish, the spector of her impending loss. There was a horror in him, a frozen hell of self-reproach, self-loathing at his heart's own core, that had the same effect, raised to the tenth power at the very least, that his drunkenness had had upon that first occasion with Patricia; in clinical terms, he remained tumescent, but could not ejaculate. The result was nightmare. Love is endlessly subjective. At what point does the cherished modern goal of becoming multiorgasmic become for a woman an incredibly cruel form of torture? At what moment does male pride at being able to outlast any sexual partner become self-defeating, an exhausting approach too near to actual death?

They lay in each other's arms, shuddering, trembling, sweat soaked, fighting for breath. And when they had come back from hell's own nearer borders, Grace kissed him gently, said:

"Jim—we're going to rest. Two hours—three. As long as it takes. Then—we're going to make love. Love—not hate. I'm going to have a bath now. A long one. Good and hot. While I'm in there—think about—me. About— *us*. About—what went wrong. So it won't again. So—*we*—won't, again. I'd like—a different ending to—to our weekend than this, my Love. A—better one. Can you—manage it?"

He said: "I don't know, Grace. I'll try . . ."

He did try. He prayed to all the Gods, including Padre Pío's, to keep remorse, guilt, sorrow, pain, a bearable remove from his anguished mind. Succeeded, well enough. The rest of it—was lovely. Only—midnight came and went. And Monday morning arrived. It was to him curiously like awaking on the morning set for his own execution. All men die. The terrible thing about capital punishment is that its victims know to the minute exactly *when* their lives are going to end.

'As mine is now,' he thought, sitting there on the balcony, outside their room, wrapped in his tawny silk robe, and watching the red dawn flaming up out of a turquoise sea. 'When she—wakes up. And I have to tell her. I—can't put it off, any longer. It's not fair to. Hell, it's not even—decent—'

He heard her voice, behind him in the room, saying sleepily, "Jim—" Then, sharply: "Jim!"

"I'm—out here, Grace . . ." he said.

He heard the springs squeak as she got up. 'The last time,' he thought sadly, 'I shall ever hear that marvelously pleasant sound—with *her*—again . . .' Then her bare feet whispering over the tiles. She came out onto the balcony just as she was, naked. He glanced quickly at the other balconies. They were all empty, the windows behind them empty. Latins are not early risers. And there were very few guests at the hotel anyhow.

She sank down on the floor beside him, pushed open his tawny robe, nuzzled and nibbled him, anywhere she wanted to. Heard suddenly, how ragged his breathing had become. Looked up and saw that he was crying.

"Oh, God!" she moaned. "Oh, my Love; what *have* I done to you?"

"You—nothing," he said brokenly. "Say—life has. And—fate, as sententious as that sounds. Plus—all three of the Eumenides, surely. I find that I have arrived at hell down that highway most marvelously paved with my own good intentions. I must—give you up. Which is roughly equivalent to saying that I must die—that's what it feels like!—and afterwards go on living. No, existing. In Tartarus, surely. In—limbo. Or—in hell."

"Jim—" she whispered, "you *have* to give me up? You *really* have to?"

"I have to," he said.

"I won't ask you why. 'Why' doesn't matter. And I—called—your Patricia—a stupid, headstrong young fool."

"Wasn't she?" he said dully.

"No. She was—a woman. A real one. I realized that—well within—the first hour of Saturday night. Jim—don't give me up. Let's—stay together. Forever."

"I can't, Grace. I simply can't."

"You can. It's very—simple—really. We go down there. Hand in hand—to our cove. Then we—swim out. Very far out, Jim. Farther than—we could possibly swim back. Like—a pair of—antique lovers. When the world—was young—and love meant something . . ."

"Grace!" he said.

"I mean it. Why—postpone what's going to happen anyhow? Without you, I shall die, Jim. Very quickly. Within the coming year. Without—doing anything overtly. I'll—just die, that's all. Of—a broken heart. The commonest cause of death there is. Anyone in my profession can tell you that. We see it, every day . . ."

"I know," he said. "That it *is* the commonest, I mean. Only I ask you—beg you—not to. I ask you to live—be happy. Or try to. For instance Lopez Basquez, a thoroughly fine and decent man, is in love with you . . ."

"Speak for yourself, John Alden!" she said bitterly.

"I can't. What I'm getting at is that I cannot kill myself. Or simply lie down and die, though both would be so easy! Easier than my life's going to be now, by far. I can't—because I can't afford to. My life is no longer my own to take. It's mortgaged to the future. It's irrevocably pledged to the redemption, support, sustenance, guidance—love—of the hostage fortune holds against my noncompliance with all life's iron rules, given in bondage through my own folly!"

"Jim—what *are* you saying?"

"Nothing, I suppose. I'm not a word-smith. Wait a minute, will you?"

He went back into the room. Took his billfold out of the night table by the bed. Switched on the bedlamp—inside the room it was still dark—and searched in it until he found what he was looking for: the color photograph of Trini that Peter Reynolds had called "An Indian Madonna," and "Our Lady of the Tluscolans."

He came back out again, and handed it to Grace without a word.

She sat there, crouched there, cringed there, studying it. Whispered, finally:

"I—never had a chance, did I, Jim? Not—from the very first. Not against—anyone—so unbelievably lovely. And—so young. So terribly—young . . . At least—two, or three, years less than Patricia, isn't she?"

He said, dully: "I don't know. I don't know how old she is. I've never—dared—ask her. But I think so, yes. Patricia says she is. And Patti occasionally tells the truth, when it suits her to . . ."

He saw the first slow tears brimming on Grace's lashes, turned away from that absolutely unbearable sight. Heard her voice, all gone, dying:

"Jim—about—about the—the child—I—I don't even need to ask, do I?"

"No," he said; "you don't need to ask, Grace."

"Are—are you—going to marry her?"

He sighed; said:

"I *have* married her, Grace. The week after I walked away—from *your* door. In New York. That Sunday morning I said: 'Good-bye—' "

She bent her head. Her shoulders shook.

"You might have spared me that, Jim Rush!" she stormed. "That's carrying cruelty—or vengefulness—to unnecessary extremes!"

"I don't mean it that way. I'm simply stating a fact. I don't think that—my disappointment, my hurt, had much to do with it. I like to think that I'm incapable of inflicting bastardy upon a child I know is mine. My—sense of obligation—"

"And your love for this gorgeous creature! Oh, Jesus! Jim, if she can look this sexy in the last stages of pregnancy, what must she be like when she's not!"

"The funny part about it is that she's not especially sexy," Jim said sadly. "She is, rather, very tender, and loving, and dutiful, operating on the principle that nothing is too good for me, that my slightest wish is her command. I find that—disturbing. Even—rather terrifying. Oh, it was amusing enough at first, when I believed she was faking it, conning me along with matchless skill. But then she proved she wasn't. On—two occasions, Grace. Proved it so thoroughly that it took all Vince Gomez' skill to save her life—both times. So now—"

"So now, knowing that—you let me engage—in a weekend—that meant everything to me, you reduce it to plain adultery. You—blithely leave me with a—memory that I shall *never* be able to bear. With—a *need* for you, that is more helpless, and more hopeless, than any main-liner's addiction! Leave me to—go mad. To die—alone. To—"

"Grace, if I had told you—before the weekend, if I had refused *your* request not to tell you until it was over, would that have been better?"

She thought about that. Said:

"No, Jim. It would have been worse. And I—thank you for the week-end. For—a good memory. For these—crumbs of your life—you've doled out to—a famished beggar!"

"Grace, please!"

"I'm sorry. Jim—one thing more: Could you—would it be possible for you to—to make love to me now? And from now—'til the boat comes? With time out to pack, of course . . . ."

He said: "Good Lord! I—I don't understand you, Grace!"

She got up—to a kneeling position. Like that she was still so tall that her head rested against the hollow of his throat.

"Don't try," she whispered; "Just—love me. One more crumb, my darling! One more glowing coal—or spark of warmth. It's going to be—a long, cold winter, you know . . . ."

He said, slowly, sadly:

"All right, Grace." He thought, as he usually did, in and through a quotation: 'Now is the Winter of Our Discontent made Glorious summer by—' absolutely no one . . .

He said: "Come inside. Come back to bed."

CHAPTER

31

*O*n Wednesday morning of that same week both Jim Rush and Grace Nivens set out upon journeys, separately, of course, and with considerable difference in the distances to be covered. Jim's was a helicopter flight over several hundred kilometers of mountain and jungle. Grace's was a taxi ride of some five or six kilometers through Ciudad Villalonga's teeming streets. But who can say, considered from the standpoint of essential meanings, which was the longer journey, the harder, or if their ultimate destinations were not the same?

Grace said in the slow, careful Berlitz Crash-Course Spanish she employed when she was alone and absolutely had to, wincing at how horrible it sounded, especially in contrast to the rippling light baritone music that came out of Jim's mouth when he talked to local people:

"Al barrio Puerta de Plata, por favor. Numero cincuenta y dos de la Avenida Jesus Pintero."

Which meant that she wanted to be taken to Jim's address in Silver Door. For Number 52, Avenue Jesus Pintero—so named in honor of Costa Verde's greatest novelist—was the apartment building in which he lived with Trini. That Jim wouldn't be there, that he had taken off that very morning on a flight down to the ruins at Ururchizenaya, Grace knew perfectly well, and was the *reason* she had chosen Wednesday itself to call. For—out of a very nearly irrational impulse, out of some obscurely masochistic need—it was Trini she wanted to see.

"¡Sí, Señora!" the taxi driver said, and opened the door for her. His eyes added *"¡Mucha Mujer!"* "Much woman!" His mind departed upon speculations that would have earned him a broken jaw from Grace had she been aware of them. But, once having given him the address, she forgot he was alive. In fact, she was not entirely sure of what she was aware of by then. The only thing she was sure of was that she hurt. She hurt physically because the body and the mind are inseparable co-components of one another, and each responds in its own way to the other's distress.

She thought with wry and bitter amusement that the popular legend of the psychiatrist madder than any of his patients was in her case becoming an appalling fact with equally appalling speed.

'I,' she thought, 'haven't what it takes to—endure this. To go to bed hurting. To hurt in my sleep. To wake up and go on hurting. Let's see—we—we, Oh God what a word!—got back here Monday night . . . Have I—eaten anything since Sunday? Sunday I was—happy. So happy! What was it I was trying to remember? Oh, yes! Whether I've eaten—even one meal since midday Sunday. I—don't think so. Come to think of it, I don't believe I have. I'll have to, soon. Why? For what? I couldn't keep it down, anyway—and starvation is as good as any other way to—'

"Here we are, Señora," the taxi driver said.

She paid him what the meter indicated. Added a tip. Walked into the building. Took the lift up to the tenth floor. She had been very well informed indeed—and by Jim's best friend in Costa Verde, Doctor Vicente Gomez Almagro, himself.

She had met the eminent surgeon her second day in Ciudad Villalonga, when, with his habitual generosity, Doctor Gomez had come himself to the clinic to check Jenny over to see whether she were up to enduring the really strenuous treatment Grace and *Don* Claudio planned to put her through, instead of sending one of his assistants as they had asked him to. Doctor Lopez Basquez—*Don* Claudio—had insisted upon their obtaining an outside opinion as a legal, rather than a medical precaution. Malpractice suits, it seemed, were far from unknown in Costa Verde. But Grace was glad he had, because she saw at once why Jim considered 'Vince' Gomez his best friend. He was the sort of person, she decided instantly, you could trust with your very life . . .

So this morning, she had gone to the Hospital *Miguel Villalonga* with that letter in her hand. That horrible, devastating, utterly shocking letter from Patricia Montenegro, mailed yesterday from the hospital itself. Of course, her professional eye had told her, from the ragged, uneven formation of the letters, the near incoherence of the—under the circumstances surprisingly grammatical and correctly spelled—English phrases, that Patti had been in great pain when she wrote, probably even delirious.

But what she had written in that letter wasn't to be dismissed, even on that score. And it had been reenforced by Claudio Lopez Basquez' flat refusal to either confirm or deny so much as a single item among all the terrible things General García's adopted daughter had either implied or stated.

"Grace," he had said, "I am—emotionally involved. You're not now interested in me. But, there is some slight chance that when you learn that the path you're following now is a *cul de sac,* an absolute blind alley, you may change towards me. I'd prefer that on that day you remembered that—I behaved as a gentleman should in this matter, my dear . . ."

She said: "Does—Doctor Gomez know? He's Jim's best friend, isn't he?"

Doctor Lopez sighed; said:

"Yes. But whether he'll tell you is another matter . . ."

But at nine o'clock this morning she had walked into Vince's office and asked him, flatly:

"Vince—is Trinidad Alvarez—a whore? Did Jim meet her at a place called The Blue Moon?"

Whereupon Vicente Gomez had exploded into such a furious defense of Trini, which included showing Grace the X rays of the self-inflicted knife wound that had been poor Trini's close to fatal defense of herself and of her love for Jim against Joe Harper's brute male aggression, as well as those hideous "before" pictures taken to guide Doctor Dos Santos' hand in the remedial plastic surgery after Joe's band of human vermin had tortured her nearly to death, that well within ten minutes he had already reduced Grace not only to absolutely helpless tears but to a state bordering upon pure hysteria.

Thereupon, seeing how really distressed she was, he had given her a tranquilizer and said:

"Forgive me, Grace. I'm a bad tempered old brute. I didn't mean to make you cry. Put it this way: I'm a convert. Y'know, like a Protestant who becomes a Catholic and then out-Popes the Pope? I did everything I could to cool off, divert, end Jim's growing interest in Maritrini, because I thought she was a cheap little tramp like all the other cheap little tramps, even though I knew she was forced into prostitution by sheer, brutal starvation as a homeless waif of thirteen. But then I *saw* how she adored him. She defied García and his swinish pals—who'd sent her to Jim. You've heard of 'The Treatment' haven't you?"

"Yes. And Patricia mentions in this letter that Trini was supposed to 'set Jim up' for political reasons . . ."

· "Only she didn't. She disobeyed her orders flatly, knowing that she'd probably die for that disobedience, Grace. And, as I *showed* you, my dear, I've had her on my hands at death's door *twice,* because she's perfectly willing to die for Jim any hour of the day or night. Jesus, Grace, I don't think I could *take* being loved the way Trini loves Jim! It would drive me straight up the nearest wall . . . ."

"From what he's told me, I gather it nearly drives him up one, too," Grace whispered. "Then, Vince—there's—there's nothing in Patricia's claim that Jim *isn't* the father of the child? That Maritrini deliberately got herself pregnant by any of two hundred old—friends—in order to—"

"Jesus!" Vicente Gomez all but screamed. "Grace, we're talking about the girl who said to me when I told her she'd *die* if she attempted to have this child: 'Swear by this, Doctor!'—this being a crucifix she'd yanked off the wall—'That *you* will attend me. And that you will save my baby so that *Don* Jaime may have his son. But that you will give no thought to me, who having done this—will no longer matter!' "

Grace bent her head. Sat there. She was crying very quietly now. Looked up. Said:

"Do you have her address, Vince? I—I want to go to see her. I want to know her. Maybe—she can teach me something. How to—live. How to live without hope, that is . . . ."

The helicopter swept on, making its rackety banging rattle. Shaking their back eye teeth out.

"Jesus!" Jim said. "What a lousy way to fly!"

"Isn't it?" Charlie Marriotti said. "You know what the difference between an airplane and a helicopter is, Mr. Ambassador?"

"Well—generally. Fixed wings versus rotary ones. Propellers or jets to drive the plane, while in these things the motor or the turbine whirl the rotary wings around, and by tilting them a little downward in the direction you want to go, you—"

"Yeah. All that. But the main difference is that an airplane *wants* to fly. And will, given half a chance. While a helicopter wants to *crash.* And will if you even blink your eye. Sir, look at—a gull. A tern. A frigate bird. An albatross. Hell, a turkey buzzard, a condor. Any decent bird is a cantilever streamlined monoplane. But *what* in nature is a helicopter, Sir? I ask you, *what?*"

"Some kinds of seed pods. Leaves. Thistle down. Hell, Charlie, I don't know—"

"Nobody does. An infuriated palm tree, drunk and staggering all over the sky. A bastard that wants to spin around its own axis. That can be knocked out of the sky by a stick or a rock thrown into its contratorque tail rotor; that—"

"Can hover," Avery Parks said. "Stand practically still in the air over one spot. Land and take off in a clearing that's got ten centimeters more length and breadth than the diameter of its rotors at zero kilometers per hour. What airplane can do that, Charlie?"

"None. Nor give its pilot ulcers inside a week, either. You know what, Ave? They took boys off Sabrejets in Korea—the first war we had jets—and tried to teach 'em to fly these damn things. Know what happened? They killed 'em. Whirleybirds killed guys who had five to fifteen Mig 15's to their credit. Real blue-flame jet jockeys. And then somebody realized that in civilian schools little old sixty-year-old blue-haired ladies in tennis shoes were learning to fly helicopters real great!"

"Why, Charlie?" Tomás said.

"Because, Tom, me friend, if you're a natural pilot, you *can't* fly a helicopter. You gotta be nuts like me, or like them little old blue-haired ladies. They was suffering from senile dementia, so flying one of these bastards was duck soup to them. Natch. Take this one. It's got controls what say you've got to pat your belly and rub your head at the same time. What makes you do everything wrong. Because in a whirleybird, wrong is right. If a guy who's a natural pilot—a real blue-flame jet jockey—does the same things his pilot's instincts tell him to do in an airplane, he'll kill his fool self in a helicopter in three minutes flat. I hate the damned things! I—"

"No, you don't!" Avery laughed. "The truth is you love 'em, Charlie. Nobody could do the things you do with a whirleybird if he didn't!"

"Yeah," Charlie said sadly. "Like I love—Mariluz. Like many another guy has loved the randiest, most no good little bitch in this world, Ave. Love, don't make sense. So you're right. I love flying these things. Fighting with 'em. Making 'em do what *I* want 'em to. And one day one of 'em's gonna kill me. Like they kill any guy who fools around with 'em too damn long . . ."

"Now, that's a cheerful thought!" Ambassador James Rush said. "But some other day, Charlie? When I'm not aboard, please?"

"*La Señora de Rush,* please?" Grace said carefully in Spanish; "the wife of—*Don* Jaime?"

Pepe stared up at her in amazement. Men *always* stared up at Grace in amazement. Except the few, the very few, who were as tall as she was.

"One moment," Pepe said. "She is—lying down, *Señora.* I do not know if she can—"

"Receive me? I know—she is with child. But tell her that *La Doctora*

Nivens is here. The friend of—*Don* Jaime. The woman, whom her friend, *Doña* Petra, calls—*la Jirafa.* The name is—fitting, no?"

"*¡Señora!*" Pepe said. "*¡Doctora!*" Then, being all man, he smiled. "If it is permitted me, I should say that—giraffes—are never beautiful, *Doctora!* And that you, *mi Señora,* are. If we grew girls like you, down here, I should enter the business of the manufacture of ladders! One moment, please!"

He was back in seconds.

"*La Señorita*—I mean *la Señora*—*Doña* Trini, the wife of His Excellency, says you are to enter the salon. She will be with you directly. In the meantime, may I offer *mi Señora, la Doctora*—a drink?"

"Thank you. A—sherry, if you have one. Very dry."

"At once, *mi Señora,*" Pepe said.

When she saw Trini coming towards her slowly, heavily, impulsively, Grace stood up, and said the exact truth, what she actually felt upon seeing this tiny, elfin—for all the great bulge of her advanced pregnancy—creature who, her mind wailed, 'has robbed me of my life!'

"My God, but you're—beautiful!"

Then she realized she had said it in English, and flounderd there trying to think how you said that in Spanish. "*¡Dios mío, que guapa es Usted!*" Or was it *linda*? No, *linda* only meant pretty. And *guapa* wasn't right either, because it meant good-looking. What was that word? Her—*her-hermosa*! That was it! Only it was far too late now. For Trini was saying, in quite remarkably good English, considering the very little time she had been studying it:

"I—thank you, *Doctora.* So—are you. Too beautiful. Petra, *mi amiga,* I mean—my fran—said that you were. You will please to sit down? I am very glad to see you."

"*Are* you?" Grace said bitterly.

"*¡Ay sí!* But yes. We 'ave much to talk, you and I. You are *la amante de mi marido, no?* The lover of my 'usband?"

"Good God!" Grace said.

Trini took her hand.

"Please to sit, *Doctora,*" she said. "Do not—how do you say it? Be afraid of me. I am not angry—with you, but only—*triste*—sad. That you—love *Don* Jaime is—natural, no? All the women do."

"There you have much right, *Señora!*" Grace said in Spanish.

"*¡Ay que buena!* That you 'ave our language to speak learned! *Mi Inglés* is very bad . . ."

"It's much better than my Spanish," Grace said humbly.

"No. I do not think so. But—if it is easier for you—I will try . . ."

"It is," Grace said quietly. "Maritrini—forgive me—for coming. But I—had to. I've heard *so* much about you . . ."

"From *Don* Jaime?" Trini said.

"No. From him—only that you were his wife, and soon would be the mother of his child. From others. Doctor Gomez. From a girl I don't— even think—you know—"

"Patricia. *La Sobrina*—how says one it? *¡Ah sí!* *La* niece of His Excellency, the Head of the State. She is also very beautiful, that one. *¡Y una fresca!* A fresh one! She almost got my poor 'usband killed! Which was *very* naughty of her, no? Because I don't think *Don* Jaime loves her very much. *¡Dios! ¡Que parlanchina soy!* What—a chatterbox, no? You were there with 'im—and saw it!"

"Dear God!" Grace breathed. "Maritrini—you—you saw that on television, didn't you?"

Trini laughed merrily at that.

"No! To God, the thanks! I was—asleep. Or—else I would have— died. Or lost my baby. But afterwards every *maliciosa, envidiosa, fresca* one in town called me up to tell me of it! You see, now I am teaching you Spanish! Tell me what those words I said mean?"

"Malicious, envious, and fresh," Grace said gently. "They're much the same in English. Which of them—do you—apply to me, Maritrini?"

"*¡Ay, no!* None of them. You are very—intelligent, *Doctora. Don* Jaime—always speaks of you with great respect. And also with much *tenura*—tenderness, no? It would not be so bad if they were all like you—all my 'usband's various loves. But most of them are like that *muy fresca* of a Patricia . . . ."

"You —take it—calmly," Grace whispered.

Trini shrugged.

"What am I—to do? He is—an Angel. *Y un Santo.* A Saint, *mi Marido. Las otras,* the women, they cannot help but love 'im. Can you?" Grace bowed her head.

"No—" she whispered; "I can't. Forgive me, Maritrini."

"There is nothing to forgive. Now, tell me a thing. Could you *suportar*—*¡Ay Dios! ¿Como se dice eso?*"

"Support?" Grace suggested. "Bear?"

"*¡Ay sí! ¡Eso es!* Could you, *Doctora, Doña* Gracia, support—bear—a little one—*una Negrita*—a leettle baby girl—who is—*Negra como yo?* Black like me?"

"You aren't black!" Grace said.

"*¡Ay sí! Soy Negra. Y India. Y Española. ¿Toda una mezcla rara, no?*"

"I find it—a beautiful mixture," Grace said. "You—are *very* beautiful, *Señora!*"

"Trini. Call me Trini. No! Call me Maritrini—as before. I like how you say it. And no one calls me that but you—and Doctor Gomez.

464

Don Vicente. He is very stern with me. He yells at me very loudly!"

"He yelled at me very loudly this morning," Grace said with a little smile.

"Then he likes you. He only yells at people he likes. What was I talking about? *¡Ay sí!* Could you *suportar mi hija? ¿Mi Trinita?* My daughter? Love—her? Be—kind to her? Or, if it is a boy, *mi Jaimito?*"

"With all my heart!" Grace said.

"I thank you. For I think you will 'ave to. I— am going to die, *Doctora.* To bring *mi hijita,* my little daughter, into this world, I must leave it."

Grace remembered suddenly what Vicente Gomez had said. And the pity that invaded her, the actual pain, was very nearly crippling.

"No!" she burst out. "You can't! You mustn't!"

"You—are—*¡Estas llorando!* You are—crying! And—for me! This is—very beautiful, *Doctora*! I thank you for it . . ."

"But Maritrini, you *must* live! He—Jim—needs you!"

"I know. But I—cannot. And since—of all the many women who love 'im, he loves only *you, Doctora*—"

"Good God!" Grace moaned.

"I ask that you—be good to 'im. *Fiel*—faithful. Loving. *Y una Madrastra buena para mi hija* . . ."

"A stepmother?" Grace translated. "*¿Una Madrastra?* No, Maritrini—if I am ever—which God forbid!—anything to your daughter, it will be a *mother.* Nothing *step* about it. Have you understood what I am trying to say?"

"*¡Ay sí! Que seras para mi hija una madre no una madrastra.* A mother who will love her—as thy own. *¿No es así, Doctora?*"

"Who will love her," Grace whispered, "and thank *you*—and God— for her—every day that I shall live!"

"*¡Ay, que buena! Doctora*—may I—kiss you? For I think I love you, too. I think I love you, very much!"

"Please!" Grace said, and put out her arms to her.

The helicopter swept down over the trees. And there that long, low building was, gleaming white in the afternoon sun.

"There it is!" Charlie Marriotti said.

"Avery, have you got the camera ready?" Jim said.

"Sure thing, Chief!" Avery said.

"Tomás—the coordinates?"

"Yes, Sir. I have marked them on the map. But Sir, do you think that General García will really—"

"Send the police? Of course. What choice has he? If he doesn't it will be tantamount to admitting that he's getting his cut from Harper, that—"

"Sir," Tomás said, "helicopters—crash. People—even Ambassadors—meet with accidents. Your Congress is going to vote on that loan this very week, no? Suppose—they deny it? While it's pending, you're valuable as a factor to be used to influence the—outcome. When it's no longer pending, when it's denied—as it's going to be, isn't it? You sent young Schuyler up there loaded for bear, didn't you?"

"Yes, Tomás," Jim said.

"You immediately become something else. The man who gave García and Friends' pretensions *un jodido real,* a really royal fucking if there ever were one—"

"Tomás, for God's sake!" Jim said.

"And when said *jodido real* includes His Excellency's niece and adopted daughter, which she herself *admits,* and tried to kill herself over, or rather over your most unkind and ungentlemanly refusal to continue the same delicate operation every night for the rest of your mutual lives, which considering how much that little creature's been around really puts you at the head of the class, Sir—"

"A real blue-flame Boy!" Charlie guffawed.

"Tomás, diarrhea of the jawbone is a most unlovely disease," Jim said, with a sidelong glance at Avery's taut young face.

"Sir," Avery said, "let him talk. Don't try to stop him to save my feelings. There's nothing he could say about little Patti that I don't already know. You see—I checked. After that justly celebrated bullfight. So now I want to say one thing: It's true, just as I told you, that *you* were responsible for my breaking off with Patti. But now I *thank* you for that. Good Lord, Sir! I might have ended up married to her! Never occurred to me that a girl in her position—socially, I mean—could be *the* worst little tramp in town . . ."

Jim looked at him. Sighed. Said:

"Son, the only relationship I've ever found between social position and tramphood has been one of an inverse order. I'm sorry to hear you've given up. A Pygmalion-Galatea relationship—and that's what any workable relationship with Patti would have to be—can be awfully rough. But worth it I think. Because the final result could have been—a work of art . . ."

"Sir," Avery said bitterly, "Pygmalion started out with—marble. Or was it ivory? Anyhow, *good* materials, Sir!"

"And God—started out with mud, Son," Jim said.

"And it shows, Sir!" Avery said. "Take a look at the human race!"

"Oh, Lord, you win!" Jim laughed. "I won't debate with you, Avery, you're too keen, and too fast for me. Now—let's see if you can get those pictures, Son . . ."

"Charlie," Avery said, "make another run, will you? Down lower. And slower, if possible. I'm not as good with a camera as Van is . . ."

"Okay. But we'll be a sitting duck if—Oh, Christ!"

They saw the people dashing out of that building. Among them the big man whose blond hair was like a beacon, as was his now heavy blond beard. And then Jim saw why Joe Harper was bearded. His right arm *still* hung limp, was visibly withered. Shaving, and many other things, Jim guessed, had become too much of a chore for him now.

He could see that Joe's bearded mouth was open, guessed that he was shouting, but the rackety battering roar of the helicopter drowned his voice. Then a slim, dark man who had competence written all over him, jerked his submachine gun, an Israeli-made *Uzi,* a murderous little marvel that can outshoot the classic Nazi Schmeisser, skyward. He didn't even aim at the cabin where they were. He aimed where any gunner who knows helicopters will always aim: at the tail rotor. At that vital, essential, set sidewise airplane-type propeller in the tail of a helicopter that, by pushing against the torque created by the main overhead rotary wings that sustain the craft, makes a helicopter more or less controllable, permits one, if one is reasonably competent, to fly the miserable violation of all the natural laws of aerodynamics in more or less a straight line.

His aim—as Jim had feared it was going to be just from looking at him, just from observing the way he handled the submachinegun—was perfect. They heard the shattering crash as the little, wooden, two-bladed propeller set horizontally and at right angles to the direction of flight went. The helicopter immediately began to gyrate, its fuselage swinging in circles counterclockwise to the one in which its main rotor blades were turning, the speed of those gyrations increasing every second.

"Charlie?" Jim said.

"We're gonna crash, Chief," Charlie said sorrowfully. "So maybe you better say your prayers!"

But he, Giancarlo Marriotti was one damned fine helicopter pilot. He went to work on the cyclic pitch control, at the same time throttling back the motor, cutting the big whirleybird down to almost hovering speed. He pulled the nose skyward, dragged her away from that building nose up like some enormous dying sea monster. The craft was still gyrating but in much, much wider circles now. On the very edge of one of those circles, Charlie saw a clearing in the jungle. He allowed, permitted, his dying bird one more powered rotation; then, directly over the clearing, he reduced the angle of attack of the forward traveling blades—which is what the cyclic pitch control essentially does—so that it was practically equal to that of the blades moving through the rearward half of the cycle, thus flattening the helicopter out, bringing its fuselage horizontal and parallel with the ground. Then in automobilistic terms, which aren't exactly correct, but do explain the general principle involved, he declutched the motor from the blades, freeing them, putting them in autorotation—freewheeling—converting his craft into an autogyro rather than a helicopter, and drifted her down into that clearing like a leaf. He didn't so much as blow out a tire in the landing gear.

"Charlie, you're an ace!" Jim Rush said.

"Yeah. But we've got three hundred 'n fifty kilometers of jungle between here and Villalonga City—"

"But only ten—or twenty—to Chizenaya," Jim said.

"Through the worst gawddamned jungle anybody ever heard of. Then up some mountains that make the Rockies look like anthills. And past the damn lab, first, before we even get started good," Charlie growled.

"There's a road around the mountains," Tomás said, "that ought to be still open, because the rainy season hasn't started yet. We get that far, we may be able to auto-stop—hitchhike is the Americanism, no?—into Chizenaya. It means going over a hundred kilometers to arrive at twelve or fifteen, but even so it's much less risky than those mountains are. . ."

"If we even get to th' damn road," Charlie said gloomily. "If we even get fifty meters without getting snakebit. But we gotta try it. We gotta get th' hell away from here, Chief. 'Cause them bastids is sure as old Ned gonna come after us. And them with machine guns. And us with pistols . . ."

"Avery?" Jim said.

"Chief, I vote we get as far from this clearing as possible, as fast as possible—watching where we put our feet down; this area is infested with poisonous snakes, you know. Charlie, can you dismount the compass? We're going to need it . . ."

"Tomás?" Jim said.

"Avery's right, Sir. But I can throw in one cheerful note. The snakes, Sir. They aren't that bad anymore. Our guerrillas have been carrying on an extermination program for the last three years. They had to: The snakes were causing ten times more casualties than García's forces. Done a good job on the insects, too. Used the residual oil from the old, played-out oil fields to spray the stagnant pools. Now the areas we're in control of—this one included—are almost comfortable—"

"But—the helicopter?" Jim said.

"We'll just have to leave it, Sir," Tomás said. "Charlie's right. We couldn't win a gun battle with those swine. Their shoulderfire arms can kill us from a range beyond that which our sidearms will carry. If we only had one Ak-47! Just one! Sir, I hope your legs are in good shape! You're going to need 'em!''

"Of course they are, Tomás! Why shouldn't they be?"

Tomás grinned at him, mockingly.

"Well, Sir, girls like little Patti-Cake generally don't leave a man feeling like the power and the glory! And *la Doctora* Nivens, whew! That's an awful lot of woman, Sir! I envy you your talents, and your ambitions, Mr. Ambassador—two such weekends in a row would leave me a stretcher case!"

"Tomás, you've a dirty mind. But I thank you for the entirely undeserved—and unearned!—flattery. Now come on!" Jim said.

They hadn't gone two full kilometers when they heard crashing in the underbrush. Avery, who was leading, signaled them to get down. They lay on their bellies in the dense, steaming growth.

'Now, if a python doesn't come slithering along,' Jim thought, 'we're fairly cosy . . .'

He raised his head then, and saw what had been making the noise: a four-wheel-drive rough terrain vehicle of the Land Rover type. Bigger than a jeep. Camouflaged—and bearing eight guerrillas in camouflaged jungle fatigues. Behind it came ten more walking. Bringing up the rear of the patrol was a jeep armed with a pole mounted Bren. The jeep carried four men, all officers, since they carried only nonstandardized side arms, as was usually the case with guerrillas, who had to use any type of arms they could get their hands on. One of them wore the P-08 Parabellum, called the 'Luger' after George Luger, who designed it; another had a Mauser M-29; the third had the World War II Nazi sidearm, the Walther P-38, and the fourth a Czech CZ—for Ceska Zbrojovka—M1924, 9 mm standard Army pistol. The troops all carried the deadly and efficient Russian Ak-47 assault rifles, with the semicircular bullet clip protruding downward and forward just ahead of the trigger guard; though two of them bore the *Uzi* submachine guns passed on to them through the worldwide Red arms-smuggling network by Palestinian Leftwingers who had captured—or stolen—them from the Israelis.

All in all the wisdom of lying on their bellies and not even breathing was indisputable. Any one of the guerrillas with his Ak-47 switched over to fire in bursts like a true submachine gun could have accounted for all four of them before they would have had time to fire a shot. And, in a situation like this one, to shoot first and ask questions later was the only intelligent choice a guerrilla patrol had. In a jungle firefight, the side that fired second usually wound up dead.

Then, abruptly, to the astonishment—and the horror—of his companions, Jim Rush stood up, exposing himself fully, but with his hands already raised high above his head in the gesture of surrender. It was this that probably saved his life. For though all those Ak-47s came level, pointed at his chest, seeing him there rock still, his hands raised, anything but threatening, the guerrillas held their fire, even glanced questioningly at their officers.

"Alvaro!" Jim called out. "Make them point their playtoys elsewhere! Guns make me nervous!"

"¡Alto! don't shoot! This Comrade is a friend of mine!" Alvaro Ferrero said.

He jumped down from his jeep. Came over to Jim. Embraced him. Said, laughing:

"There are no pretty girls in *la Selva, Don* Jaime!"

Jim motioned for the others to stand up. They did so, sheepishly.

"What's this?" Alvaro said. "An Embassy picnic? Or did you have to flee Ciudad Villalonga for your life after tossing dear little Patti-Cake to the bulls and playing *Espontaneo?*"

"Oh, Jesus!" Jim said. "Alvaro, how the devil—"

"Did I know of your latest exploit? Simple—both Tarascanolla and Chizenaya have been hooked into the national television network as of this spring, *Señor Embajador*! That farewell speech to you and to the world of *La* Patti's was most moving. It brought tears to my eyes. By the way, how is she?"

"Recovering. Alvaro, could you get us in to Chizenaya, or near it? Our helicopter had to make a forced landing and—"

"You mean, *Señor Embajador*," one of the other young officers said, "that it was shot down. One of our lookouts witnessed the action and advised us by radiotelephone. A Talkie-Walkie, no? Which was why we were searching for you. He also informed us that you'd all escaped unhurt. You were lucky. When Rafael 'Ráfagas' Ramos—who is a drug runner, a murderer, and a filthy swine—shoots at someone, he generally hits him . . ."

"He wasn't aiming at us," Jim said. "Rather he shot the tail rotor off our aircraft. Probably meant to take us alive, for their own purposes . . ."

"Ah, that would explain it. Ransom, likely. Or to persuade you to cease in your persecution of the drug traffic. Ráfagas is a most excellent marksman—which is why Joe Harper recruited him. Since you, Mr. Ambassador, crippled Harper in that gunfight down at the docks that time, he has to depend more on others . . ."

"All right, all right! I didn't cripple Harper by the docks or anywhere else, but let it pass. Could you, Alvaro?"

"To a section of the road frequented heavily enough by trucks and cars to make auto-stopping the rest of the way easy, Mr. Ambassador. Into

Chizenaya, itself, no. It would cost us the jeep, and our hides. All right?"

"Perfectly. It's a godsend, even so. Well, what are we waiting for?"

"First you and your friends must have lunch with us," Alvaro said. "Our food does not resemble that of *Les Ambassadeurs,* of course, but one—admittedly with a certain effort—can eat it. We all have the keenest desire to hear from your own lips your latest exploits. The ones the Archbishop's Board of Censorship would rate Class IV, Forbidden to the Faithful on Pain of Excommunication, as in certain motion pictures of a pornographic nature! For this, Comrades, is the great *Don* Jaime of whom I have told you. In his trophy room he keeps not the heads of slain animals, but the lace trimmed *bragas* of all the aristocratic ladies he has tumbled, along with a packing case full of *horns,* to be sent along with his visiting card to their husbands. I tell you, he should be awarded the Order of Lenin, made a Hero of the Socialist Soviet Republics, for no man has done more to confuse and demoralize bourgeois society than he!"

"Alvaro, for God's sake!" Jim groaned.

"You must tell us of *la* Patti. A blow by blow description. 'Tis said that the Glorious Leader is on the verge of a Glorious Stroke of Apoplexy!"

"I," Jim said solemnly, "don't know whether Patti's a boy or a girl, Alvaro."

"If *you* don't, *Don* Jaime," Alvaro hooted, "then neither does her mother!"

"Chief—" Charlie Marriotti said. "I'm wondering if your pals couldn't do us a little favor? I see they've got carpenter's tools in that Land Rover along with the ordinary repair job mechanic's stuff. With any kind of luck, we might be able to get the whirleybird out. Rough out a new tail-rotor prop blade. That log over there's *Ulula.* That's the Tluscolan word for ironwood, Sir. I could make a damn fine propeller outa that . . ."

"Would you lend Charlie the tools to fix our bird, Alvaro?" Jim said.

"Sí—but in return for that blow by blow account, *Don* Jaime! Speaking of your helicopter, we had better go to the place it fell, and camp there. Or else Harper and his monkey men will burn it, or worse still, steal it for their own uses . . ."

"Lieutenant," Avery said suddenly, "what is *your* feeling about the drug traffic?"

Alvaro's handsome young face darkened abruptly. He was remembering his sister Ana's death and the manner of it, Jim knew.

"That, *Señor*—"

"Parks," Avery supplied. "Avery Parks, *Teniente* . . ."

"That, *Señor* Parks, there is no filthier business in all the world!"

"Then, *Teniente!*" Avery said, excitement shaking his voice, "why don't you throw in with us? Help us destroy that lab? Put Harper and Pals completely out of business?"

Alvaro smiled.

"Because, *Señor* Parks," he said, "that would be against Party policy. I do not know if you realize it or not, but the youth of the Socialist world have escaped the decadence that is destroying corrupt bourgeois society. What is it to us if Capitalist young people persist in converting themselves into witless, will-less addicts and your great cities into asphalt jungles where no woman is safe after dark, and no affluent citizen dares take a stroll by moonlight through one of your city parks to catch a breath of air? Unwittingly, by helping you commit suicide, as a society, as a people, Harper is speeding the day when Socialist justice—which is to say *true* justice—will prevail in all the world . . ."

"Alvaro," Jim said dryly, "what is it you like better about intellectual excretia, the smell or the taste?"

Alvaro stiffened. Then he controlled himself, smiled:

"I am perfectly willing to listen to your arguments, *Don* Jaime," he said.

"You won't get any—not out of me," Jim said. "When the doctor or the midwife smacked my slimy little behind to make me bawl for the first time, I was allotted only a certain ration of breath. Don't mean to waste it, Son. I don't defend Decadent Bourgeois Capitalistic Society, which stinks so bad it's an offense in the nostrils of Padre Pío's God. But neither do I defend Advanced Progressive Socialist Society, which also stinks. In the individual human liberties department it stinks on ice. I've lived damned near half a century in this world, Alvaro, so there's at least one thing I'm sure of: No matter what system of government you invent, men, being men, will screw it up. The only choice you've got is between a Capitalist Watergate, say, or a Socialist Gulag. The only other viable alternative being the invention of a process to mass-produce Angels. By cloning, maybe. But to paraphrase Hobbes, 'Man in a state of nature is nasty, brutish, and short.' And since man, for the foreseeable future, is likely to stay in a state of nature, and that nature of the unsavory type known as human, I vote we skip political discussions, which give me a pain in the gut. I also think that you should help us destroy the lab. But not for political reasons. In defense of the young people of Ciudad Villalonga, say, who need their heads left unstoned, their minds unblown, long enough for you to convert them to Socialism, maybe. Or to Communism. Or to Catholicism, or to whatever. Believing in something is good for the alleged soul, and I've found it doesn't matter a good goddamn what you believe as long as you believe it. And—just between the two of us—in memory of a girl called Ana . . ."

Alvaro stiffened.

"Low blow, *Don* Jaime!" he said. "You are a dirty fighter!"

"I've learned to surrender to obvious imperatives. Joe Harper taught me that. Poisonous reptiles have to be eliminated not to afford me the cheap and meaningless thrill of vengeance, but in defense of society's right to exist. Come on, Alvaro; what do you say?"

Alvaro bowed his head. Looked up. Said:

"No, *Don* Jaime; I cannot."

Jim stood there.

"All right, *Amigo.* So be it then," he said.

But when they had almost got back to the clearing where Charlie Marriotti had set the crippled helicopter down without wrecking it, Alvaro halted the lead car with a raised hand. Instantly the motors of both rough-terrain vehicles were cut, and all the guerrillas deployed into the brush, silently. At once Avery Parks—probably because he needed to take the hurt little Patti had dealt him out on *somebody,* Jim realized— raced to join them.

Jim thought about what he ought to do. 'Be a hell of a thing to leave the kid without a father and—' he thought; then he said: *"¡Mierda!"* and raced after Avery. Tomás and Charlie came after them, more slowly.

They got to the clearing and lay on their bellies in the undergrowth on the edge of it.

There were men all around the helicopter. But they weren't doing anything to the crippled aircraft. Instead, they were doing something whose consequences could turn out to be a damned sight worse: They were walking all around the Sikorsky, talking in low tones, and studying it very, very carefully.

Then a big man who had been sitting on an ironwood log in the shadow of the helicopter stood up, took off his straw hat, and Jim saw his bright blond hair. Viking blond. And his considerably darker blond—as is usually the case with Nordics—beard. But his right arm dangled queerly . . . It was sadly withered now.

'If,' Jim thought, 'the net result of our expedition has been to donate Joe Harper a first class helicopter to run his stuff out to the boats in, the general maliciousness of fate has been demonstrated beyond all argument and for all time!'

Then he heard the wheeze of a man's breath beside him, and looking down, saw Charlie Marriotti sighting his long barreled thirty-eight calibre, Colt Police Special revolver at Joe Harper, holding the weapon in both hands to steady it, and already squeezing the trigger slowly, slowly—

Jim shoved his right hand under the six-inch-long barrel of Charlie's Special and slammed it skyward. The shot woke echoes, sent a shower of leaves drifting down about Joe's head. Instantly all Joe's band of brigands hit the dirt and poured a murderous volley of machinegun fire into all four perimeters of the clearing.

"Why, goddamn!" Charlie howled. "I had him! I had him dead to rights and you—"

'And I—am a fool,' Jim thought sadly. 'Or overbred, overcivilized, or something. Who can't even accept the shared responsibility of being an accessory before the fact to—murder. With his gun in his hand, shooting back, I could kill him, maybe, Charlie. Or let you do it, out of your atavistic notion that a cuckold has the right to kill the man who wronged him—a sin definitely requiring the cooperation of the wife— and always, always, Charlie!—through some failure of tenderness, love, consideration—or merely plain brute maleness!—of the cuckold's own . . . But from ambush, no. Like this, no. Living with myself is rough enough a chore as is . . .'

He pointed, said dryly:

"Bad tactics, Charlie! See what it's cost us already?"

The guerrillas were carrying a badly wounded member of their own patrol away. But now, driven by Alvaro's swift gestures, the others fanned out. Alvaro waited until they were in position. Jim crawled to the place where the wounded guerrilla had fallen. Picked up his Ak-47. Turned to the youngster next to him.

"Show me how to get the safety off this thing," he said.

Alvaro raised his hand. Let it fall. The Ak-47s barked and bucked, on individual rounds. Among Joe Harper's men, four went down in that first exchange. One of them must have been gut shot. He was screaming like a woman in childbirth.

Jim saw Tomás come slithering towards him, and an idea hit him. He said:

"Tomás, you can make a citizen's arrest, can't you, under Costa Verdian law?"

Tomás said: "Yes, Sir. But I think perforating these swine is vastly more intelligent. *Don* Jaime! For the love of God, Sir!"

For by then, Jim was halfway to his feet, clawing his brush jacket off as he straightened up, yanking his shirt over his head. For the very simple reason that the shirt had been white, and still was white enough to serve for what he had in mind, even then. Jim waved it, called out:

"Joe! I ask you to surrender! Listen to me, man! I'll get you off with a jail sentence! My friends will agree to let your men break clear, get away—if you'll come in with your hands up. Just *you*. For Christ's sake, use your head for once, you damned fool, and avoid a slaughter!"

Joe's bull bellow rocked the trees.

"You! Again! Uncle Creepie-Poo! Rafa! Kill me this lil' bastid, will you? Kill him for me right now!"

Jim saw the slim, dark man jerk his *Uzi* level, and dived, but not fast enough. Maybe nobody could have dived fast enough to get under the fire of a six hundred rounds per minute *Uzi* in the hands of Rafael 'Ráfagas' Ramos; but slight, small Jim Rush made a highly commendable try. All he took out of a burst that denuded the underbrush just above him of every leaf it had, and half the branches, showering them down upon him as one nine millimeter slug that plowed a bloody, superficial furrow straight across—from left to right, horizontally—both cheeks of his skinny buttocks.

It hurt. A grazing wound like that hurts worse—at least more immediately—than a more serious gunshot wound does, because the nerve-stunning shock of direct impact does not occur. That one hurt like hell, and in two ways: physically and morally. The moral hurt was by far the worse of the two: All day Jim Rush had been basking in a self-congratulatory glow because he had actually borne himself quite respectably in action, had dominated his nerves, held his fears in check. And now to have his display of cool nerve, of military competence, end in this humiliation!

He lay there clutching the jungle grass and weeping:

"Just like me! Goddamnit, just like me! To get shot in the ass of all places! To get shot in my stupid ass!"

Blind with rage, he rolled towards the place, sixty centimeters away, he had left his borrowed Ak-47. And by so doing, saved his life. For 'Ráfagas'—the words *means* a burst of machinegun fire, and as nickname was tailor-made for Rafael Ramos—had figured out where Jim had to be and poured a burst into the exact spot he had been three seconds or less before. Jim got to that ugly Russian assault rifle, jerked it level, then stopped. Breathed in very deeply, held that breath. Dug his elbow into the soft earth. Cradled the Ak-47 on the palm of his left hand, gripping it lightly, but firmly with his opposed thumb and all his fingers. Sighted on 'Ráfagas,' who was yanking an empty clip out of his *Uzi* and replacing it with another, through the immensely tall front sight—so made, he surmised, to clear the Ak-47's high, humped-back antirecoil mechanism—and squeezed the trigger very, very slowly and smoothly as his father had taught him to do during the days that that Teddy Roose-veltian-type gentleman-sportsman was trying—vainly!—to make a half-way decent shot out of his miserable—on all counts!—disappointment of a son.

The rifle slammed back against his shoulder, almost breaking his collarbone. He fought the rising muzzle downward again; but he didn't shoot again. He didn't have to. For Ráfagas had dropped his *Uzi,* stood up, was clutching his belly with both hands, was dancing something that looked like a really horrible caricature of the Lindy-Hop of World War II, while his blood poured out between his fingers. He was also screaming, the sound of it clear even above the gunfire, a sound that Jim Rush was never going to forget as long as he lived, a rising, metallic sound like an air-raid siren, or like the scream of a gutshot horse. The sound of utter, intolerable pain. It went on two seconds, three. Then twelve Ak-47s held on Rafael Ramos and crashed in a ragged staccato roar. The shock effect of twelve nine-millimeter full-jacketed high-powered rifle bullets—a different kind of bullet altogether from the 9 mm pistol ammunition that submachine guns generally use—knocked his cadaver, his corpse, his dead on arrival body three-quarters of the way across the clearing.

Jim Rush stared at that utter obscenity in his hands. Put it slowly and carefully down. The tears stung his eyes.

"I," he whispered, "have killed a man. I have *killed*—a man."

Then he bent his head and vomited his guts up. Noisely, terribly. Said, weeping the words, that bitter phrase of his:

"Hail the Conquering Hero Comes!"

By then it was over. Seeing their best fighter, their champion marksman, the one man in the group beside Joe Harper himself possessed of manhood, of valor—or as they themselves put it: *"¡Ráfagas tiene una pareja bien puestas!"* "Ráfagas wears his balls well hung!"—down and dead, those criminal scum Joe had recruited got out of there, or tried to. They made the classic mistake of untrained troops. They stood up to run. None of them made it to the far edge of the clearing alive.

Joe and three others were smarter. They crawled out on their bellies, widely separated from one another, and covered their retreat with brief, but well placed bursts of submachine gun fire. But that wasn't the real reason they got out of that clearing alive. The real reason was that Jim Rush raised his head and screamed at Alvaro:

"¡Dejalos ir! ¡No importa, Alvaro! ¡No los matais, por favor! ¡Dejalos vivir!"

Which phrases translate only into the fact that Jim Rush was a civilized man who, if he couldn't quite achieve the Christian ideal of loving his enemies, hadn't—as yet!—got to the place where he could kill them, or even watch them die, with impunity. The cost to him inside his nerves, his guts, inside himself, the essentially who and what he was, was terrible.

And Alvaro, who in his short life had already had his share of necessary anguish, recognized that quality in Jim's voice. Sighing, he raised his arm. Gave the signal to cease all fire.

"Look, lend me the jeep, *Teniente!*" Avery begged. "I'll bring it back to you personally! But we've got to get him out, we've got to! He's not one of your boys who've been trained and toughened up, and—he'll die, man! He's just not built to take being shot up like this!"

"Avery, will you please, for Christ's sake shut up?" Jim groaned.

"But, Sir, you're hurt! You've been shot! You—"

"Shut up, Avery. You—can't—bring the jeep back. The police will confiscate it the minute you bring me in with a gunshot wound. You know that. And I—I'm not worth—a jeep. Not now."

"Oh, Jesus!" Avery said.

"Look, Son—I've got a bullet scrape across my ass. Which hurts like old hell. And *looks* awful. But nobody ever died of a wound like this. I'll have to eat standing up, and sleep on my belly for the next two weeks— and that's about the size of it . . ."

"Sir," Avery said, "I don't want to alarm you. But in this miserable goddamned climate people have died of less than this. Far less. You've got a wound damned near thirty centimeters long, by fifteen millimeters deep. Too wide, since it was made by a bullet, not by a knife, to be sewn up. And your little Red pals haven't so much as a box of sulfanilamide powder with them, nor a tube of penicillin. I got you into this, and I want you the hell out, before that wound infects. For, among other reasons, what your girl friend, Doctor Nivens, and all the other people who heard us have words over that no good little bitch at that bullfight are going to think. They'll accuse me of setting you up, Sir! So I need that obscene profanity of a jeep of theirs!" He used, of course, one of the commonest, most popular ones.

Jim grinned at him wearily.

"Nobody's going to think any such damnfool thing, Son. Nobody who knows either of us. Besides," his grin widened, "a jeep hasn't a mother, so it *couldn't.*" He turned toward Alvaro; whispered: "*¿Porque no tienes ni sulframida ni penicilina?*"

"They captured the type who brings us our medical supplies, *Don* Jaime," Alvaro sighed. "Unfortunately for us, he knew where our clandestine laboratory in Ciudad Villalonga is—or was. Now, it no longer exists. He was very brave. He held out a whole hour before telling them. With García's trained sadists, something of a record, no? And one can no longer buy antibiotics in a *farmacia.* One needs a prescription which must be signed by one of only twelve doctors in all of the capital, or, what is even worse, one of two or three in each of the *provincias.* Doctors whom they control absolutely and who dare not write said prescriptions for anyone suspected of being even slightly Pinkish, ¿entiendes?"

"Isn't Doctor Gomez on that list? I don't see how they could keep him off. It would provoke an international scandal."

"He is," Alvaro said, "as is Dr. Moreno. But we never ask this of them, not wishing to compromise them. They have both behaved with great courage and nobility, doing us many favors in the past, as in my case, remember? Occasionally we rob a farmacia, or hold up a drug manufacturer's delivery truck at gunpoint. But the risks are too great. Generally we do without . . ."

"That boy—the one who got it right at the start—the one whose gun I used—"

"To eliminate 'Ráfagas.' A magnificent shot, Don Jaime! I felicitate you . . ."

"Oh, Jesus!" Jim said. "What about that kid, Alvaro? He was hit bad. An upper chest wound; I saw it!"

Alvaro shrugged.

"We have a well equipped field hospital, Don Jaime—and he is already in it. And the methods of the First World War—they had no wonder drugs in those days, either—managed to save a number of badly wounded men, even so. Beyond that, you may pray for him. You hold to the superstition that it helps, no?"

"No," Jim said, "but I'll pray, anyhow. Your surgeon any good?"

"First rate. And our hospital's excellent, or it was when we had supplies. Unfortunately, we dare not take you there . . ."

"Jesus H. Christ!" Avery exploded. "Nobody's going to tell SN-2 where it is, Teniente! You actually think one of us would betray you after your medics had saved the Chief's life?"

"I do not think. I know. Not out of wickedness, Señor Parks, but out of an entirely normal and understandable human weakness. El Carnecero's interrogators can obtain information from a statue of steel. Hence it is better that you do not have said information, better even for you, Señor. I, too, have a great fondness and even more respect for Don Jaime. It grieves me much to see him suffer so. I have asked the driver to bring back a medic with him. But, unfortunately, our medical corpsmen are seldom finished doctors, and rarely know very much. But whatever this one knows, I place at your disposal . . ."

"I thank you, Son," Jim said.

"Tom—" Charlie said to Tomás, "how bad off is he? I mean how much time have we got?"

"I don't know, Charlie. Depends on how long it'll take gangrene—unavoidable in gunshot wounds if you don't have what it takes to really

clean them up—to set in beyond the point it can still be reversed by antibiotics. I'd guess—two days . . ."

"Don't need two days. Give me three—four hours, and the loan of the
Teniente's carpenter tools, and I'll *make* us a new tail rotor. Put th' Chief
right down on Doc Vince Gomez' front lawn. Whatcha say, *Teniente,* can
I use the tools?"

"Of course, *Don* Carlos! To fly *Don* Jaime out is the best way. It will
procure him the aid he needs and not bring the Security Forces down
upon us. Take the tools and as many of my men to aid you as you
need . . ."

And then, of course, that one detail that proved Murphy's Law never
stops operating, that there is a basically implacable malice that governs
human fate: Charlie couldn't get his beautiful new tail rotor to balance.
He shaved away at it, calibrated and miked the dimensions until the
pitch was absolutely true, and the dimensions from hub to both tips
within a millimeter of each other at every equidistant measuring place.
But one side of that damned ironwood log he'd started out to carve what
was essentially a pusher-type airplane propeller from was simply *denser*
than the other. He could only balance the tail rotor by making one blade
too thin, and ruining the pitch. What he should have done, of course,
was to have thrown the damned thing away and started all over again
with a new piece of wood that would more or less balance over a cen-
trally placed fulcrum *before* it was carved, the precaution he had neglected to take with this one. But it *looked* so good. And the sight of
"The Chief" lying there on his belly under the shade of a tree, while
Tomás and Avery took turns fanning the flies away from the clumsy bandage around his skinny tail, through which the blood kept right on
slowly seeping, unnerved Charlie Marriotti, especially since Jim Rush,
remembering how Trini had behaved under conditions far, far—at least
a million times!—worse than this, wasn't making a sound, though the
way that ugly wound was hurting him now was really very bad.

Charlie was a tender-hearted man. He thought: 'Dead game little
fella, th' Chief. And—and decent. Married that poor little bitch when
nothing and nobody would of made him do it, simply 'cause he felt
'twas the right thing to do. And it *was,* dammit! She's been abused
enough. Came here with us. Got his poor little ass shot half off, when
he could of—ought to have!—stayed in his nice, air-cooled office and
sent us out to do this here dirty job. Jesus, maybe this sonuvabitching
whittled up stick will work anyhow! So it don't quite balance? What'll
that do? Make the whirleybird vibrate. Lots of the damn things vibrate
anyhow, 'n nothing happens, long as the vibration ain't too bad . . .

He walked over to Avery and Tomás and said, whispering the words, so as not to wake Jim up, because by then Ambassador Rush was either asleep—or more likely—had fainted from the loss of blood:

"Look, I'm gonna try it. Alone. It works, I'll set down and pick Mr. Rush up. It doesn't work, I'll bring her down on autorotation like before, and we'll just have to *carry* him out. The Chizenaya road ain't that far—and a truck or two is sure to come along before too long. Most of the stuff they use comes by boat into Tarascanolla, and then by truck into Chizenaya. So getting a lift shouldn't be that hard. All we need is for the *Teniente* to give us an escort past that Lab, just in case Jo-Jo and his monkey men feel like arguing some more. But the whirleybird's th' best bet, if th' damn thing don't shake itself to pieces . . ."

He got the helicopter off the ground with deceptive smoothness. Hovered. Backed up. Made forward and sidewise runs. But it vibrated. It vibrated like hell. He could feel the shaking through the controls.

'Take her up to a thousand. Might smooth out up higher,' he thought. He eased back on the stick, fine adjusted the cyclic pitch control. Took the big bird up, up, up.

At one thousand meters, his handmade tail rotor went. Split. Disintegrated. Threw slivers, splinters, hunks of ironwood into the main rotor, shattering one of its three blades.

Charlie sat there, his hands on the all but useless controls.

'Good-bye, Mariluz,' he thought. 'You're free now, girl. Harper'll take you back. Get a dozen bastards on you. Oh, Jesus Christ, why did *Don* Jaime hafta be such a goddamn fool? So it's me who's gotta go. Me—not a bastard like Jo-Jo Harper. Me who never screwed nobody else's Ol' Lady nor—'

He saw to his left, far to his left, the white gleam of the laboratory. He didn't think about what to do. He simply did it. He fought a broken, wildly gyrating helicopter with no tail rotor and one of its main planes gone, vibrating uncontrollably, scattering pieces of itself over ten square kilometers of jungle, disintegrating by seconds, not down but up and left, by parapsychology, maybe, by his own stubborn will until he had it directly over Joe Harper's Heroin Conversion Laboratory. Then he power-dived it. Straight down. Lit the day with flame. Brought to Jim Rush's bone dry, blistered, fevered lips the quotation from the *Rig Veda* Robert Oppenheimer had whispered at Los Alamos, the day the human race signed its own death warrant: "I am become death; shatterer of worlds!"

When they got to the laboratory, there was nothing left. Nothing at all. They buried the charred bits and pieces of what surely had been Charlie Marriotti because they were inside the helicopter's twisted frame of steel tubing, in a hole in the ground. A small, shallow hole, not needing more. They shoveled the other bits and pieces of three—or maybe four—it was absolutely impossible to tell—other men in another shallow hole, making no attempt to sort them out. Jim and Avery and Tomás speculated over whether some of those charred bone splinters, none longer than fifteen centimeters, or those curved skull fragments, none of them sufficiently intact to be fitted like a jigsaw puzzle into even one entire skull, which wouldn't have proved anything either, belonged to Joe Harper. All and all they rather hoped so, but with what was left the matter simply couldn't be proved one way or the other.

Then they started out in the jeep, with Alvaro driving, to take Ambassador Rush down to the Chizenaya Road.

Two hours after they had left the smoking embers of the laboratory, a search and destroy patrol of the Security Forces got to it. Found the wrecked helicopter, dug up the charred, splintered debris of the dead. The patrol had been attracted to the spot, because from a long distance—some seven to ten kilometers—away they had seen the helicopter start its final, fatal dive, heard the echoes of the explosion, had seen the upward broil and rush of flame. So they raised Chizenaya by mobile radio, and asked for a check from Air Traffic Control whether one of Worldwide's helicopters were missing. They knew it had to be one of Worldwide's, or else one of the Colombian Army's craft, that had blundered over into Costa Verde's airspace by error, because Costa Verde hadn't any helicopters of its own as yet, renting or borrowing them from Worldwide Petroleum for the occasionally necessary flights to places whose terrain did not permit an airplane to land.

Chizenaya called the Capital, relaying the news at the same time that there were no survivors of the crash. And since only one helicopter was missing—the one piloted by Giancarlo Marriotti, with Avery Parks, Tomás Martinez, and James Rush aboard—when the news was announced over the six o'clock newscast, Grace Nivens fainted outright for the second time in all her life. And when she regained consciousness, Claudio Lopez Basquez took one look at her face and put her back out again with an injection calculated to keep her unconscious for at least twenty-four hours.

At the Hospital *Miguel Villalonga* Vicente Gomez put Patricia Montenegro, who unfortunately had her radio on as well, under deep sedation to stop her from screaming the place down. And he placed guards before the door of a certain private room in the maternity ward of the hospital: the room in which *Doña* María de la Sagrada Trinidad Alvarez Bermejo, *Señora de Don* Jaime Rush, *Embajador Estadounidense en Costa Verde,* lay awaiting the birth of her child and weeping bitter tears because her beloved *Don* Jaime had not yet come back from Ururchizenaya.

"Anyone," Vince Gomez roared, "who tells Trini about this before her child is born, *I* will strangle personally and with my bare hands!"

Ambassador James Randolph Rush, of course, was entirely unaware of all the uproar the somewhat premature, but not all that greatly exaggerated report of his death was causing. At the moment he had enough to do to keep that quite honest error from slipping over—as it was actually doing by slow, almost imperceptible degrees—into starkly tragic fact. 'Thus earning me the unparalleled distinction of being the first human being—of whom knowledge disposeth!—whoever died of being shot in the ass. Probably because that's where my brains are located anyhow!' he thought.

Because, after Alvaro had jeeped him, Avery, and Tomás down to within three kilometers of the road—it was far too dangerous for a man with a reward of a full ten thousand Costa Verdian *pesos* on his head, alive or *dead,* the really honorable distinction Alvaro Ferrero's ceaseless attacks on the Dictatorship had earned him by then, to come in any closer—Jim Rush had to endure the jolting torture of being stretcher borne—by Avery and Tomás—the rest of the way, and after that a four hour wait, lying on his belly by the roadside while cars and trucks whined by and flatly refused to pay the slightest attention to Avery's and Tomás' increasingly desperate signals to their chauffeurs to stop. Finally, wild with rage, Tomás placed himself in the exact middle of the road and stopped a truck by putting a well aimed pistol bullet through its windshield just above the driver's head. At gunpoint the terrified driver helped Avery load Jim aboard, and afterwards turned his truck back in the direction of Chizenaya, because he had been coming *from* that city when Tomás stopped him.

By the time they got to Chizenaya finally, Jim was unconscious from fatigue, weakness, and the loss of blood. After cleaning up that bloody, but fortunately not too badly infected mess, the doctors at the hospital there gave him a shot designed to keep him in a state of pain-free limbo until at least the following noon.

So it wasn't until nearly four o'clock the next afternoon that Jim Rush learned that, officially, anyhow, he was dead. What he did then represented, he afterwards realized, a definite choice. Subconscious, perhaps, but still—a choice.

He picked up the telephone and called Grace Nivens.

CHAPTER

32

Grace," Jenny said, "what time does our plane leave?"

"At—midnight," Grace said.

"Lord, but I'm gonna be glad to get outa this Monkey's Paradise," Jenny said. "Aren't—you?"

"Yes. No. I—don't know, Jen," Grace said.

Jenny Crowley turned and peered into Grace's face. Said, whispering the words:

"Oh, no! Not *again*! And you—you never used to cry . . ."

"I know. I had to learn how. I had to be taught. And I was—by an expert. That—and a good many other things, Jenny, darling!"

"Grace—stop it. Please, stop it! It—it *scares* me!"

"Sorry. Give me—a minute, Jen. It's—difficult to—to stop. At the moment I'm—trying to convince myself that—I'll ever be able to. Ever—as long as I—live—"

"But not like that, Grace! Oh, Honey, not like *that*! Like it was *killing* you!"

"You—think—it *isn't*?" Grace said.

"But Grace!" Jenny wailed. "I can't stand seeing you this way! It breaks *me* up. You wouldn't want me to relapse *again*, would you, huh? Not when you've got me almost cured?"

"No, I shouldn't—like for you to relapse, Jenny. Only—give me a minute—will you?"

But she didn't stop crying. She couldn't.

"Oh, Jesus!" Jenny said.

The phone rang. Shrilly. Insistently. Grace picked it up.

"Yes, this is *la Doctora* Nivens speaking. Yes, yes, I'll hold the line . . ." Then: "Vince—"

"What's that? Maritrini's—in labor? And asking for *me*? Of course. I'll come over at once. No, Vince—it's *not* surprising. We've become rather good friends. I—I promised her—to take over. Both the child —and—and Jim—if anything happened to her. Say that again? But Vince, *you,* yourself, told *me* that you thought she'd die if she attempted to give birth! So why *shouldn't* she believe it? Oh! A whole blood transfusion. Because hers didn't clot before? And—she's perfectly all right? Labor is normal? Oh, Vince, I'm so glad! Truly I am! But have you —have you told her about—Jim? Oh! I agree. Afterwards. After she —has the child—as—an emotional anchor. As a reason—for—for her existence. How—lucky she is—to have that, Vince. How very, very lucky! Yes, yes—of course I'm crying! Give me *one* good reason that I shouldn't, Vince Gomez! Or better still—one even one mediocre one for—for staying alive. Good-bye! See you in ten minutes . . ."

"Grace—" Jenny said.

"Oh, for God's sake, shut up, will you? I've been tormented—quite enough for today, thank you! Oh—I'm sorry, Jen! I really should behave better, shouldn't I?"

The phone rang again. The sound of it was different. Longer. More drawn-out. That special insistence that usually marks a long distance call.

Grace picked it up again. Said:

"*¡Diga!* Speak!" Then: "Jim! Oh, Jesus! Oh, my God! Oh, you bastard! You miserable, unprincipled little bastard! To—let me—suffer —like this! A—whole damned night and—Jim, where are you? Oh, my Darling! My Dearest! My Dearest, Darling Love, I—what's that? Of course I'm hysterical! If you think going out of one's mind from sheer grief is any fun, you try it some time, Jim Rush! That is, if you ever learn to *care* that much about anybody, which I doubt. And it's a good thing you condescended to call me *today,* you sawed-off little sadist! Because by this time tomorrow, I should have been certifiably insane!"

Jenny flew across the room, yanked the earpiece a little from Grace's ear, crowding in so that they could both listen at the same time, heard Jim's voice, halting, slow, washed out, all gone, whispering:

"Grace—I *couldn't* call you. In the first place—I didn't hear the report—that somewhat but not too greatly exaggerated report—of my death. You see, I was under deep sedation; in a word, unconscious and—"

"Jim!" Grace gasped. "You—you're hurt!"

"The correct word's—shot, Grace. Grace! Are you there? Grace, listen—"

"Yeah, Uncle Jim," Jenny said, or rather sobbed into the phone, "she's here. Only she's acting kinda funny, like she's sick or something . . . Hold th' line a minute will you, huh? I—"

Grace's voice came over to him, from a little distance away, raging:

"You give me that damned phone, Jenny!" Then sharply, clearly, "Jim—"

"My dear, I'm sorry—" Jim said.

"Jim, how badly are you hurt? Don't lie to me! How—"

"Not badly at all, Grace, in one sense. I was never entirely unconscious from the wound, itself. They—the doctors down here—put me out, deliberately, because it *hurts* so damned bad. I've the world's most embarrassing wound: a bullet scrape, from left to right, clear across both cheeks of my fundament. The kind that used to get its possessor shot for cowardice in all of the less recent wars."

"Jim, stop it! You're lying—playing yourself down. If you got shot in the tail there's some other reason for it than that you were running away. You haven't that much common sense! And it doesn't matter. Where are you? How can I get there?"

"I'm in Chizenaya—in the local hospital. But don't you come here, Grace. I'll be home tomorrow. I'll have to convince the airline people to let me ride standing up, of course; but—"

"Jim—could you, convince them—today?" Grace said.

"Grace, there's no hurry. I have lost a bit of blood, you know. I don't exactly feel like the power and the glory . . ."

"Not for—me, Jim. I can—wait. For Trini. She's in—labor. With—*your* child, my Love. And—I—Oh God, how I envy her!"

They heard his voice saying, crisply:

"Thank you, my dear. I shall be there within—two hours, say. Perhaps three. There's no flight, or rather the daily one has already taken off. But there is an airtaxi service. I'll hire a small plane . . ."

"But, Jim; you're—hurt! And alone like that you—"

"I'll hire a twin-engined plane. Bring Avery and Tomás back with me. Not—poor Charlie. He was—flight testing that helicopter, Grace—after a repair. Wouldn't take us on board until he'd made sure. So—"

"So, bless him!" Grace said brokenly.

"Amen. Good-bye now, my Love . . ."

"Good-bye, Jim," Grace whispered.

Jenny stared at Grace as she hung up the phone. Said:

"I see what you mean. I'd go crazy, too!"

At that moment, another conversation was taking place; but not by phone. Even though the three men involved stood, or rather sat, on the very pinnacle of power in Costa Verde, none of them trusted their subordinates—or, for that matter, anyone, including one another, enough to talk about what they had to over the telephone. For though they controlled all telecommunications, and put wiretaps on the telephones of known enemies and supposed friends with fine impartiality, they had had the chastening experience of having had the Reds put interstation taps on their lines by simply climbing the telephone poles and patching into the connecting cables.

Another thing that had given all three of them even greater cause for caution was the ease and total success with which the United States of America's Ambassador had employed sophisticated electronic counterespionage devices to balk, frustrate, and delude them. By now General García, Head of the State, Director General of National Security Raoul Pérez de la Valle, and his assistant, *Teniente Colonel* Pablo Fuentes Toralba had been able to determine beyond a shadow of a doubt that *every* piece of information picked up by their wiretaps, and their hidden microphones in the Embassy, the residence, and Jim Rush's secondary residence in Silver Door—that clandestine love nest now converted into calm, sober, and *legal* domesticity—had been either false, misleading, or trivial; and that not one item touching on the major blows dealt them by that wily little diplomat who looked so exceedingly *Nordico, Yanqui, Gringo,* but who thought and acted in a fashion more thoroughly Latin, Machiavellian, clever, underhanded—and from their point of view, anyhow, dirtier, more crooked, more shameless than even they did—had reached them until after said blows had become *faits accomplis*—as now.

"*¡Maldita séa!*" General García exploded. "Of course I can declare him *persona non grata,* Raoul; but what good would that do?"

"*Non grata*—and release those motion pictures made by *su Señora la Embajadora* some years ago—in the exercise of her profession. That should insure both *Don* Jaime and *la* Trini a most charming welcome to the States—and even you, *mi General,* a vengeance of a sufficient intensity, no?"

"No!" García bellowed. "No and No and No and No! It is not enough! Not after all the things he has done to us! Look, Raoul, Pablo: He's wrecked our chances of obtaining that loan. He got our captive atomic physicist out of the country and even *yet* I don't know how. He bluffed or threatened or frightened off the French armament people. He has made us an outcast among the nations—worse than even Chile, and that took some doing!"

"With some—well—assistance on *our* part, *mi General!*" Pablo

Fuentes said. "If the things that actually go on in the—ah—Detention Camps *didn't*—I, personally, have always felt that this business of—the dogs is a bit—excessive, shall we say?—his spies couldn't have photographed such conclusive proofs of our—routine and habitual use of—torture and spread them before the North American Congress and the United Nations. Did you know, Your Excellency, that *only* Chile abstained from voting for the motion to censure us, passed in the Organization of American States? If it hadn't been for them, the motion would have been written into the minutes by an unanimous vote. Even Brazil and Ecuador voted against us, and that required nerve on *their* part, don't you think?"

"Yes, it did," General García said gloomily. "Which is why our motion pictures of the little Trini, obviously taken years ago, are likely to be—ineffective. In fact they could only have worked as a threat—by forcing *Don* Jaime to support us in the matter of the loan, on pain of our making them public if he didn't. But using them as a counterattack, *after* he has entirely ruined us, makes no sense at all. Everyone will realize what our motives for doing so are. Besides, after those torture pictures have been spread all over the gamier segment of the North American press, *la* Trini has but to say, 'There were men standing just outside of camera range with guns—and whips—*making* me do that!'— prettily, and with tears in her eyes, to be both forgiven and made a heroine of by the North American public! After all they *adored* Judith Lovell, who was the first and favorite daughter of the Great Whore. *¡Mierda!* We release *Las Aventuras de Alicia,* and Hollywood will offer *la* Trini a movie contract!"

"And—*Don* Jaime?" Raoul Pérez de la Valle said.

"You tell *me,* Raoul! To justify declaring this outrageously clever little blackguard *non grata,* what charges could I place against him?"

"*Estupro,*" Raoul said. "Rape. Statutory anyhow—the only kind possible with your dear adopted daughter, *mi General,* who has been *cosa facile* for any man who wanted her for years. Or—call it corrupting the morals—the quite nonexistent morals, in this case!—of a minor. After all *la* Patti-Cake, as all the world calls her—largely because all the world at one time or another has pushed her over—is still under twenty-one years of age, is she not?"

General García stared at his—up to that moment anyhow—Second in Command. When he spoke, his voice was quiet. He did not bellow, roar, or scream. He knew better. For Raoul Pérez de la Valle and Pablo Fuentes Toralba to take *this* tone with him meant that they were absolutely sure they had him. Or else they wouldn't have dared. So making threatening noises made no sense. Better to find out what it was that made them confident enough of newly acquired powers for them to take this outrageously high-handed tack with him.

"You're—baiting me!" he almost whispered.

"No—*mi General*—suggesting, mildly, that you—resign. Offering you, your lady—and *la* Patti, of course!—a safe conduct out of the country to anywhere you may care to go. We won't even block your bank account. You should be able to live quite well on—what's left of your take from your—collaboration with *Don* Joseph Harper, no, *mi General?*"

"*¡Jesus y María Santísima!*" General García said.

Raoul Pérez de la Valle sighed.

"You're getting quite the best of it, *mi General. Don* Jaime—or one of his collaborators—destroyed that heroin conversion lab. So *we* won't be able to profit from it, after you have gone. In fact, we're in for some devilish belt tightening, and a period of gloomy, straight-laced morality. To—refurbish the national image, you understand. Because we've got to get that loan, sadly reduced, I fear, and with a whole mare's nest of strings tied to it, to even do anything about the oil. Come, Manuel, *do* be a good fellow and get out, will you? It would make everything *so* much simpler for everyone, don't you think?"

Manuel García Herredia, *already* ex-Head of the State, stared at the two of them.

"And if I don't?" he said.

"You will be arrested," Pablo Fuentes said softly; "charged with malfeasance of public funds and moral corruption—dear Susana, your mistress, will be delighted to testify against you, she has already informed us, in just recompense for all the beatings you've given her over the years. And these pictures of your *daughter*—we'll forget the adjective 'adopted' for maximum effect—stark, mother naked, embracing the North American Ambassador, will be published in the *international* press, *mi General.* At the end, an outraged public opinion will force us to—well—liquidate you, Your Excellency . . ."

"Where'd you get these damned pictures from, Pablo?" General García said.

"From the young swine who took them. One Antonio Orozcopal, a former lover of your niece-daughter, *mi General.* We chose these because of the greater *international* impact. *Don* Jaime is—or has become—a famous man. Besides, these are, after a tiny bit of airbrushing at the—ah—pubic regions, at least printable. Most of the others—the dozens and dozens of others he has taken of her, aren't. Come, Sir, what do you say?"

"You win. Both of you. I'll refrain from calling you the swine you

are. But one thing, I want *Don* Jaime *dead*. And it's to *your* best interests, as well as mine, that he's killed. An—ambush, eh? Youngsters
with long hair. A few beards. Dressed like Hippies—to be labeled Red
Urban Guerrillas. Any of two dozen street corners he has to pass to get
to the Embassy, or the residence, or the place he keeps his whore in, you
know—*Avenida* Jesus Pintero—in Silver Door . . ."

"But why should we oblige you in this matter, Manuel?" Raoul said.
"It's risky. It could backfire, and—"

"Two reasons. He's got enough on both of you to hang you along
with me like the two thieves besides Our Lord. And if you don't, *I'll*
make trouble. Call out the Army units still loyal to me, personally.
Don't bother to tell me I can't win. I know I can't. But I can make the
gutters run with blood, and die happy, taking one or both of you with
me. I may be a fool, but I'm not a coward. A grand finish to a man of
my temperament is appealing, Gentlemen. Perhaps more appealing than
years of idleness, of slow dry rot. You want—a peaceful transition, *un
pronunciamiento* instead of *una revolución*? Well, I'll grant you that; but
my price is Jaime Rush's head!"

The two of them looked at each other. Thought about that. A long
time. A very long time. Then, very slowly, they nodded.

"Granted, *mi General*. And thanks for being—so reasonable," Raoul
Pérez de la Valle said.

CHAPTER

33

*T*he man with the shoulder-length Viking blond hair, and the considerably darker, almost burnt taffy colored beard scooped up his drink with a hand that looked like a vulture's claw. That hand was raw and scaly red, and strips of skin were still peeling off it. But he had to use that one. His other hand didn't work. It, nor the arm it was dangling from.

"Yeah," he said to the small, dark woman whose face looked like someone had used it for a punching bag, "Charlie won't be coming back, Mariluz. Jesus, you look like hell. Was him who beat you up like this?"

"Sí," the woman whispered; "and not once, *mi amor;* every time he gazed upon—*el niño. Our* son, Joe. Thine—and mine."

"Yours, for sure," Joe Harper laughed. "But mine? Shit, Baby! Don't hand me that one. You've had more pricks in you than a porcupine!"

"Come home with me then, and look upon him, thou as well," Mariluz said. "See his eyes like the sea and his hair like a field of ripened wheat. Then tell me, if you dare, who else could have made him thus!"

"Hell, Baby! You mean th' lil' bastard's a towhead like me? Great, Baby, great! Always did want a kid of my own, anyhow. Don't worry, I'll even acknowledge him, he looks that much like me. But since I'm already married to that cunt Jenny Crowley, ain't much I can do about you, Lucita *mía* . . ."

"She has gone. She departed for the United States of America last night—alone. Because, for some reason or another, *La Doctora* Nivens, *la Psiquiatra,* who has been curing her of her addiction to the drugs, did not go with her—"

"Who's the *Doctora* Nivens? Some dried up old witch, I'll bet. So Jen's gone? Good riddance for bad rubbish. For if there ever was a pain in th' ass, it was th' Cunt! C'mon, then. Let's split this scene. I need some sleep. And I do mean *sleep,* Baby. I'm bushed. Been on th' go since that damnfool hubby o' yours piled that damned helicopter straight through th' roof of my lab. Wiped me out, th' bastard. Gotta see His Nibs, somehow. I need a stake—enough to get me th' hell outa this Monkey's Paradise, anyhow. I've had it down here. Hell, I might even retire. Got dough enough stashed away in th' States and in Switzerland—numbered accounts, Sugar!—to live on 'til I'm two hundred years old. Only all my ready cash burnt up in that damn lab except what I had in my pockets, which ain't even enough for plane fare to Miami. But the General will stake me. He's gotta. Else I just might talk out loud in my sleep, or something . . ."

"Charlie—destroyed—your laboratory, Joe?"

"Yeah. Sure did—th' jealous jackass! With all th' free tail there is floating around he had to go off the deep end over a used-up piece like yours. Jeeez–sus! What some people won't do. So now I'm outa business. Ha! Tha's a good one! Know what I used to call the lab, Honey? *Pedro Olvidado y Hijos, S.A.* Forgotten Peter and Sons, Society Anonymous! Ain't *that* th' truth! Old Peter's sure forgot now . . ."

"Joe—" she whispered, "what am *I* going to live upon? I—and thy son?"

"Hell, Baby—don't you worry your pretty little head over that. Course we're gonna have it rough 'til I get to th' States and get my hands on th' bread. But once there, I'll send you two, three hundred—American, that is—every month for you 'n th' kid. Hell, I may even send for you when I get settled. You're kinda restful to have around, and being crippled up and burnt up on top o' that, sure as hell has took a lot outa me. Young, randy lil' bitch would probably be too much for ol' Jo-Jo, these days . . . Saaaay! You got Charlie's shaving stuff in th' house?"

"Yes, Joe."

"Could you manage to give me a halfway decent haircut, and dig me out from under all this brush without me needing a transfusion afterwards?"

"But of course, *mi Amor.* I have often cut Charlie's hair for him, and even shaved him when he was sick of the fever . . ."

"Great! And you got any shoe polish in your pad? *Black* shoe polish? Dark brown?"

"Both. Why, Joe?"

"This damn straw colored hair o' mine stands out, 'specially down here where everybody's been smeared with that old tarbrush, Mariluz. And I gotta pay a lil' visit on a guy th' night before I leave. Guy so little he hafta duck when a grasshopper shits, Baby; but from the very day I first laid my glimmers on him, damned if he ain't fucked me every time. Lil' ol' Creep. I calls him Uncle Creepie-Poo. He's th' *Gringo* Ambassador down here or something . . ."

"Not—*Don* Jaime!" Mariluz said.

"Yeah. Him. Damned if I can figger it. Tried to take his broad off him one night. Damn finest piece of mixed breed—Nigger, Indian, Spik, plus a drop o' two o' *Monkey,* like all you cunts down here! 'N I couldn't. *She* wouldn't go with me, can you beat that? 'N him needing a stepladder to tickle a rattlesnake's belly button. Dried up. Ugly. Older than God's Own Grandpappy. What hacks me right back to th' low grass, Honey, is: What can a lil' ol' Creep like that one *do* for a broad that'll drive her that nuts over him? Hell, even if he can still get it up, and shoves it into her, it oughta be so *little* she wouldn't even know it's *there!*"

He stopped, threw back his head, guffawed:

"Got it! Figgers! Ol' Uncle Creepie-Poo's just nacherly *got* to be th' greatest lil' ol' Muff-Diver in the business!"

He stopped laughing, abruptly.

"All th' same, I'm gonna take him apart. Learn him that don't nobody get away with doing a reaming job on Jo-Jo Harper's asshole. Yeah, Ol' Uncle Creep ain't gonna forget Joe Harper any time soon—"

"Joe!" Mariluz said. "You must not! *Don* Jaime is very famous, and much beloved of the people. Especially since his having saved the life of the adopted daughter of the Head of the State after she attempted to kill herself over him . . ."

"Jeeeee-sus! Not lil' Patti-Cake? I been resisting th' temptation to get into them lil' lace scanties ever since I come down here. Figger it wasn't smart for business what with th' deal I cooked up with His Nibs. You don't mean to stand there with your bare face hanging out 'n tell me Ol' Uncle Creepie-Poo knocked hisself off a lil' piece o' that there!"

"I do not understand this strange way you have of talking the English language, Joe," Mariluz said stiffly; "but if you mean to say that *Don* Jaime couched himself with *la* Patti, that yes, surely. For why else would she have got down on her knees before him—in public, at a party at his house, with her Uncle the General witnessing it—and begged *Don*

Jaime to marry her? And it was both because of his refusal to comply, and the General's to permit such a marriage, that she thereupon hurled herself bodily upon the horns of a bull in the bullring last Friday . . ."

Joe stood there, staring at her. Decided finally, from the ring of sincerity in her voice that she wasn't really lying, just exaggerating a hell of a lot, as usual.

"Jeeeee-sus, Baby!" he said again. "If even a little bit o' that yawn of yours is so, I'll let Uncle Creep off easy. Even let him live. Guess I'll just tie him up and torment him a little 'til he fesses up 'n tells me how he does it! Now, c'mon . . ."

"*Don* Jaime—" Trini whispered, "dost—like her? Art—pleased with her—thy daughter? *La Trinita?* Oh! Perhaps thou wouldst rather call— her—something else? *¿Gracia, por ejemplo? ¿O—tal vez—Patricia?*"

"Forty-seven," Jim said, "forty-eight!"

"What art thou counting, *mi Señor?*"

"The *beatings* I owe you!" Jim said. "And which, young woman, you are going to get, once you are well enough."

"Ohhhhhhhh!" Trini wailed. "Art angry with me, *mi Señor?*"

"Forty-nine! That one's for calling me *mi Señor!*"

"But—" she whispered, "what can I call thee? Since thou dost not, canst not love me, I—"

He got up, still holding that tiny, but infinitely precious little bundle in his arms. Latin American hospitals permit all sorts of liberties with newborns, such as allowing their fathers, grandfathers, grandmothers, uncles, aunts, and all manners and kinds of kissing kin to hold them and fondle them from the onset, cuddle, kiss, and rave over them as though microbes didn't exist, which is perhaps the basic reason that Latin Americans are perhaps *the* most emotionally secure people on earth, and why inferiority complexes are great rarities among them. He crossed to Trini's bed. Knelt down beside it. Said evenly, flatly:

"Look into my eyes, Trini. Look very deeply into my eyes. Do not so much as blink, or I will punish thee severely! That's it. That's it. Do not move a muscle! See if you cannot see—my soul—somewhere within them there . . ."

"¡*Don* Jaime!" she breathed. "*¡Tengo miedo!* I have much, much fear!"

"Good!" he said grimly. "Now listen to me. Hear me. I—love you, Trini. I love—the girl-child—become a woman—who is my wife, and the mother of—my daughter. I shall love her more every day that passes than I did the day before. I shall *never* cease to love, honor, and cherish her until the day I die. And if I lie in saying this—even in thought— may the Old Gods of the Tluscola drink my breath . . ."

"¡*Don* Jaime!" she gasped. "Thou must not say this! This is terrible! For now they have heard thee, *Los Dioses Viejos y*—She stopped. All of her stopped. Her breath. Her life, itself. All of her—except her eyes. They grew and grew in her tiny, elfin face, until they threatened to eclipse it. A star shone in their inky depths. Then—a galaxy. The Milky Way. The Moon. "Thou—" she whispered. "Thou—Oh, thou!"

She bent her head. Started to cry. The way she cried was—very simple. Very pure. Very beautiful. And absolutely unbearable.

"Trini—" he said reproachfully.

She lifted streaming eyes, a tear-streaked face, towards the ceiling of that hospital room, said slowly, softly, gently:

"¡*Dios Padre Quien estas en los Cielos, Te doy las Gracias!* To Thee, Oh God—for having given me back—my life. Thou knew I could not live without him, so thou hast returned his love to me. But along with—this miracle—this joy—the strength for—bearing it, please? I think that my heart is going to burst—to stop—I think that I shall—die—"

She bent forward, hiding her face against her knees, her long black ruler-straight Indian hair foaming about her shaking shoulders from the force of the sobs that tore her. He lay Trinita down beside her, caught her by the upper arms, straightened her up by main force, stared into her eyes.

"¡*Mi Amor!*" she sobbed; "Thou—thou hast spoken truly! Thou dost love me, dost thou not? Thou *dost* love me! ¡*Y yo te quiero con mi alma!* ¡*Con—mi cuerpo! Con—*"

Trinita woke up and started to cry. Trini snatched her up, cradling her in her arms, crooning:

"And—to thee, also, *Angelita mía*—I give my thanks! To thee, *mi Trinita*—who hath given me back—thy Papa. Thou hast done this too, hast thou not? Loving thee—he *must* love me. ¡*Ay que buena!* Oh, how happy I am! ¡*Mi Amor, Cielo, Corizon, Alma de mi Alma, y*—Sí, Sí, Sí—mi gran Señor! ¡Señor y Dueño y Amo de todo mi ser!* Lord and Master and Ruler of my whole being! Kiss me? Please kiss me? Oh, please, please, please!"

He kissed her, mingling their tears. They held the baby between them, in their arms.

"Is—she not sweet?" Trini whispered; "Thou sees—she is *rubia*—blonde like thee . . ."

"And yet—she's dark like thee," Jim said. "A wonderful combination, is it not? I think she will be beautiful . . ."

"Listen to him, this man! She *is* beautiful! She is *una Angelita del Cielo!* She—"

"Is a little brown wrinkled she-monkey with golden hair. Of an infinitude of ugliness like all new babies are. Still, I will be able to tolerate her, I think. At least, having fair hair, she does not make my forehead ache too much!"

"¡Ay, que barbaridad! ¡Que horror! What terrible things he says of thee, this Papa of thine, mi Vida! We must punish him, no? I tell thee what, make pipi on him!"

Almost instantly, Trinita obliged.

Jim threw back his head and laughed aloud.

And hearing that laughter, feeling it, Grace Nivens stopped just inside the doorway—and shivered. Trembled. Mastered herself at once. Came on into the room. Said softly:

"Jim—let me see her? Let—me hold her? You—you don't mind, do you, Maritrini?"

Trini stared up at her, and her dark eyes smoldered. But she managed, after one long moment of very nearly crippling anguish, a soft and tender smile.

"No, Doctora, I do not mind," she said.

"Oh Lord, but she's beautiful!" Grace whispered. "Almost—too beautiful . . ."

"Why—do—you—cry, Doctora?" Trini said.

"Pure envy, Child. I—I simply cannot help it," Grace said. "Wouldn't you, in my place? But, please don't worry about me, Maritrini. I shall take the very next plane back to New York—"

"Which is not until—two weeks," Trini said; "And Doctor Gomez— Don Vicente—says I must stay here eight whole days. Oh, how he yelled at me because I wanted to go home today! So therefore you must promise me, Doctora, not to drag my poor little 'usband off to Pelicans' Island again . . ."

They both stared at her appalled. She went on calmly.

"He is muy pequeño, mi marido. A very little one. Un chico travieso—a naughty boy, you say, no? And with you, Doctora, he has not la fuerza de voluntad, how do you say it? ¡Ay sí! He has not the will power—¿porque 'will' power, mi Amor'? Porque no 'won't' power? That would be much better in this case, I think! The will power, that he should have. Besides you are very beautiful. Will you promise me?"

"Trini, who the devil told you all this?" Jim said.

"Thy—Patti-Cake. ¡La muy fresca de tu Patricia! O, what a freshie one she is! She was here this morning, muy temprano, very early, no? In her silla de ruedas. ¿Como se dice eso, Doctora?"

"Her—wheelchair," Grace whispered.

"¡Ay sí! Wheelchair. She also talked very velozmente, with much velocity like the little machine guns of the soldiers. I must, she told me, give

thee up, my little naughty one of a 'usband! I am not, she says, suitable
for thee. She will be so kind as to adopt *mi* Trinita and bring her up as a
Lady. And she, not I, will be *tu esposa,* thy wife. So now what do you
think, my little one of a 'usband? Is not all this a very good idea?"

"I think you've been eating cold cuts, mostly sliced tongue, Trini!"
Jim laughed. "Never before have I heard you talk so much!"

"What did you tell *her,* Maritrini?" Grace ventured.

"To remove herself before I broke for her the other leg!" Trini said
wrathfully. "The very freshie one! She is—crazy, that one. *Loca, de verdad.* They should put upon her *la camisa de fuerza!*"

"The—what, Maritrini?" Grace said.

"Straightjacket," Jim supplied. "Trini, listen—"

"No. Not now. Now I will talk. And not to you, *mi Amor,* but to *tu
Querida, la Doctora.* You will please not steal 'im from me, *Doctora?*
After all, *la* Trinita needs her Papa—and I—I need him too—"

"Trini, for God's sake!" Jim groaned.

"Jim, she's quite right, so don't interfere, please!" Grace said crisply.
"Maritrini, I will not lie to you: I am quite capable of—of stealing your
husband, for I, too, love him very much. What's beyond me is
stealing—the father of your child. So please don't worry about me
anymore . . ."

"I thank you," Trini said; "I think you are a good woman, *Doctora.
Honesta.* I should like that we be—*Amigas*—frans. But I am glad you are
going away. For, if you stayed, I should be *very* afraid of you. You are—
beautiful. Intelligent. And of—*la raza*—of my 'usband. I could not
keep 'im if you wanted to take 'im from me . . ."

"Fifty!" Jim said.

"Fifty—what, Jim?" Grace said.

"That's how many back beatings I owe Trini for saying things like
that last remark," Jim said. "Grace, did you get your cable from Jenny,
yet? She should already be in New York, shouldn't she?"

"Yes. I suppose so. But naturally, being Jenny, she hasn't wired me.
My God, this child is soaked! Where are the diapers, Maritrini?"

"Over—there," Trini said, and pointed.

Deftly Grace changed Trinita, smiling tenderly at the tiny, burnt
golden mite all the time. Watching her do that, Jim found that breathing presented a certain difficulty. There were all sorts of oddly shaped,
rough edged, and pointed objects tangled in his lungs. But, at that
moment, Luisa Montenegro de García swept majestically into the room.

"*Don* Jaime," she said, "although very clearly you have betrayed my
trust, it is my duty as a Christian to forgive you. And also I thank you
for having risked your life to save that of my little *idiota* of a niece. No!

Do not speak of it. The matter is closed. Now, may I see your daughter?"

"Here she is, *Señora*," Grace said, and passed Trinita over.

Luisa stood there holding the baby, and whispering:

"How beautiful thou art, *mi pequeña*! How very beautiful! And how great the pity that *I* cannot see thee grow up!" She turned to Trini, still whispering:

"I felicitate thee, Trini! Thou hast done very well!"

"And *I* had nothing to do with it, my Lady?" Jim said.

"You! With this one and two dozen others, likely!" Luisa snorted. "You must chain him to the bedposts, Trini. For he is a very bad boy, your husband! You must watch him closely, Child!"

"This I know, my Lady," Trini said sadly.

Then they heard Patricia's voice from the hall.

"Push me in there! You heard me! I want to see her, too—this baby that should be mine!"

She was in a wheelchair, with her leg in its plaster cast thrust out before her. She put up her arms and took the baby from her aunt, sat there holding the tiny child and sobbing aloud, shamelessly.

Trinita woke up and started to howl, a high, thin, piping sound.

"She has hunger," Trini said. "Give her to me that I may feed her."

"Oh, Jesus!" Jim said.

"We—go into exile, *Don* Jaime," Luisa Montenegro de García said. "Where exactly, I do not know. Perhaps to your great State of Florida, if your country will concede us political asylum. There has been—in a rather civilized fashion this time—a *Pronunciamiento* instead of a revolt. *La Junta* of Army officers has offered the General, myself, and my niece safe conduct out of the country in return for my husband's agreement to go peacefully. I have persuaded him to accept, so that there will be no bloodshed . . ."

"Thank God for that!" Jim said. "Look *Doña* Luisa, I'll do what I can. I'll query the representatives of my home state and several others who were friends of my father's about granting you refugee status. I think I can arrange it, though the private war the General forced me into with him will make things a little difficult . . ."

"Are *you* coming back to the States, my darling Jaime?" Patricia said.

"Yes, Patti. Permanently. I'm resigning from the Diplomatic Corps. In fact, I have resigned. I only hope my resignation reaches the Secretary's desk before those videotapes of my debut as a bullfighter do. Because if those tapes get there first, he'll surely refuse my resignation in order to have the pleasure of firing me!"

"But what are you going to *do,* my love? You're far too young to retire!"

"I'm going into the newspaper business," Jim said; "buying a one-third interest in a journal two friends of mine own . . ."

"Do you need a secretary? I am a very good one. In *four* languages. And—a most excellent *mistress,* as you already know . . ."

"In how many languages?" Jim quipped.

"*¡Ay que fresca!*" Trini gasped. "Have you no shame at all, Patricia?"

"No. None. Have *you,* Trini?" Patricia said.

"Sí," Trini whispered. "Very much. An enormity of it. So much that I was—dying—of my shame, Patricia. I would be dead now, if *Don* Jaime had not been—man enough—No! *¡Angel y Santo!*—of all goodness and all honor to stand up before a priest of the Good God and in the presence of witnesses and say, 'I take unto me this woman—' To be what I am. His wife. The mother of his daughter. I say it—badly. I have not the words. But—my shame is gone, I think. For he hath taken it away. Can you say as much?"

"No. And I shouldn't even want to. Because I'd take him on any basis. And the amount of shame involved in the transaction wouldn't matter at all!" Patricia said.

"Jim," Grace drawled, "why don't you go into stock farming, instead? Raise brave bulls? With nice sharp horns?"

"*Touché!*" Patricia laughed. "Come, Auntie, let us go. There are too many of us in here, I think. And since I cannot reduce the number to what it should be: *Don* Jaime, this tiny one—or an even more beautiful duplicate of her that *I* should have made—and *me,* let us go. Jim, push me out into the hall where you can kiss me good-bye without curdling the milk in Trini's breasts, or causing this monument of a woman of yours to have a lovely, fatal stroke of apoplexy. Believe me, *Doctora,* I should weep—from joy!"

"No," Jim said, "I can kiss you good-bye here, Patti. Trini, who knows exactly what you mean to me, and more importantly, what *she* does, really won't mind—"

He bent and kissed Patricia's cheek. A light, playful, brushing kiss. Stood back, smiling.

" 'Bye now, Patti!" he said.

"*¡Oh, mierda!*" Patti said. "Get me out of here!"

"And me—" Grace sighed, after the orderly had pushed the wheelchair out of the room; "but give that crippled little witch of yours at least ten minutes lead, Jim. Because strangling a girl in a wheelchair with one's bare hands would be something less than sporting, wouldn't it?"

"*Doctora—Doña* Gracia—" Trini whispered.

"Yes, Maritrini?"

"Please to strangle her! Squeeze her by the neck like *el Garrote Vil*—until her face turns blue!"

"Believe me, Trini," Grace laughed, "it would be a pleasure!"

But, as it turned out, an unnecessary one. Four hours thirty-seven minutes counting from the very moment that Patricia swept through that door in her wheelchair, the aircraft bearing her, her Aunt Luisa, and *Don* Manuel García Herredia, ex-Head of State of *la Republica de Costa Verde,* flying at eleven thousand meters, and at nine hundred forty-seven kilometers an hour, blew up, scattering pieces of itself and the dismembered, unrecognizable bodies of its occupants and crew over some twenty square kilometers of the Caribbean.

For whatever failings one might legitimately attribute to the new Glorious Leader and Head of the State, His Excellency, General Raoul Pérez de la Valle, or his Second in Command, the newly elevated to General's rank, Pablo Fuentes Toralba, now Director General of Security, a lack of thoroughness could never be included among them.

The late General Manuel García Herredia had also been—while he lived, before pieces of his rather opulent, though somewhat charred—flesh were scattered over a vast area of the Caribbean—a very thorough man. In fact, it was he who had dinned the lessons—that in a Dictatorship, it is only by the endless exercise of the virtue of thoroughness that the Dictator stays in power, and by eternal vigilance, alive—into Pérez de la Valle's and Fuentes Toralba's willing and receptive heads.

And now he proceeded to prove that the thoroughness of a thorough man and the power of a great one—for greatness has absolutely nothing to do with morality: Adolph Hitler and Genghis Khan were great men—often extend beyond their lives.

For at four o'clock of the morning after the night in which Jim Rush had both become—at long, long last!—a father and effectuated his entirely sincere reconciliation with the coauthor of his feeble hold on immortality, his continuation in time; after the General, in just recompense for his many and hideous crimes, his wife for the lone mistake of having married him, his niece and/or adopted daughter perhaps for a slightly too frequent indulgence in horizontal sin, and the crew of the aircraft for no reason at all had collectively departed this life, Antonio Orzcopal, he of the too ready finger on a camera's shutter release, and the late Patricia Montenegro Aguirre's ex-semi-official lover, heard a knock on his door.

He was, as usual, entertaining a guest in his lazy, half-hearted, desultory fashion. Tony never lacked for little play—or more accurately bed—mates, despite the fact that Patricia's judgment of his abilities as a lover was dismally correct. One of the reasons for this somewhat contradictory state of affairs was Patricia, herself. The number of upper-class maidens who hated her was amazing and a tribute to the force of her personality. Sleeping with—the euphemism being sadly close to the truth in this case!—Tony seemed to several of them an excellent means of getting even. Another reason lay in the even sadder fact that the maidens in question didn't *know* Tony was a lousy lover, because they'd never met a good one, a man like Jim Rush say, who actually cared enough about women as people to have wanted in the first place, and to have managed in the last, to learn how. For one of the unfortunate results of rampant *machismo* is that your *macho,* your roaring, rampant male, over vast areas of this earth is only *now* beginning to learn that he is *supposed* to satisfy his mate, that women have their basic sexual needs, too, and exist as persons in their own right, not as cunning little mas-turbatory devices, awarded lordly *Him* as vehicles for his—very nearly instantaneous!—pleasure.

In any event, for Margarita Gil Camago—she whom Patricia had browbeaten, cajoled, threatened, and even bribed—a lovely and expen-sive piece of jewelry had actually changed hands—into giving up to Patti her starring role as the last *Rejoneadora* on the program that very nearly fatal Friday, the choice of that particular night to indulge in a no more than tepid whim proved most unfortunate. In fact it proved—mortal.

Tony opened the door, yawning as he did so. His friends, all members of Latin America's active Counter-Culture, Dropouts, Drug Experimenters, Mind Blowers, Rock Fans, Beards, Beads and Sandal Wearers, Kinky Sex—by their own evaluation, of course!—Experts, habitually dropped in on Tony anytime they felt like it, which was why a knock on his door, at a little after four o'clock in the morning, didn't surprise him. Then he stiffened, said:

"Who the devil are *you* types?"

That was the last thing he ever said. Shortly after that he started screaming.

Which did not trouble his assailants at all. They knew his neighbors wouldn't interfere even to the extent of telephoning the police. For by then Manuel García had taught all Costa Verdians one lesson past any possibility of its ever being unlearned again: When you hear someone screaming in the middle of the night, put sealing wax in your ears!

They, the three small, wiry, catlike men, with women's nylon stock-ings pulled down tight over their heads, had not got any further along by then than pistol whipping Tony's face into something resembling, if anything, a rather low grade of hamburger steak, when Margarita made the mistake of letting out a screech of her own. The leader turned, saw her, caught her by her long black hair, said happily:

"*¡Coño!* Cunt! Tie him up, *Chicos*. We can finish with him later."

They proceeded to rape Margarita. Taking turns. Two of them holding her while the other mounted her. Then they went on from there. One of them held a pistol pointed at her head while two of them enjoyed her simultaneously. Then after a brief discussion as to whether or not it could be done that ended in the unanimous decision to try, all three of them made use of her at the same time, which, of course, involved anal, vaginal, and buccal penetrations, and the forcing of Margarita's supple body into a position as ugly as it was painful.

Then, satisfied at last, they left her moaning and retching on the floor, and went back to work on Tony. They used their knives. Cigarette butts. A lamp cord plugged into its socket, and its two terminals disconnected from the lamp, peeled of their insulation, and passed all over Tony after his body had been anointed with warm water into which a cup of kitchen salt had been stirred. The effect of this technique, when one live wire was placed in his mouth and the other up one nostril, or in the corner of one eye, or in his ears, they found especially rewarding. Even more so was anal insertion with the free terminal lovingly caressing his testicles.

The leader looked at his watch.

"Getting late. We'd better go," he said. "Finish him off, Knuckles. No, not the throat. Just deball him. Give him time to realize that taking filthy pictures of nice girls isn't gentlemanly. *¿Eh Tonito, hijo, faltas caballerosidad, no?* Well now you're gonna *falta* something else. *¡Tus huevos, hijo!* Your cute little balls . . ."

"No!" Tony screamed. "No!"

"Cut him," the leader said.

"What about the *Chica?*" one of them said, after that. "Think she might be able to recognize us in a lineup?"

"I doubt it," the leader said; "but anyhow, why take chances? Waste her."

Margarita's final scream became a choking gurgle as that blade slipped effortlessly through her corded throat from ear to ear.

Then, leaving Margarita dead, and Tony bleeding to death very slowly, as quietly as they had come, they got out of there.

The whole thing had cost the late, great Manuel García Herredia three hundred North American dollars.

CHAPTER

34

*C*arlos Suarez parked that unmarked panel truck as high up on the mountain road as he could get it. Freed the tied-down end of that base-loaded fiberglass whip antenna, cut to half wave length. It sprang up, towering. The little man sat there before the transceiver. It was a single sideband outfit with a double conversion, F.E.T. front end. Field effect transistors, with an imput impedance of over five hundred megohms and only four point seven picofarads of stray capitance. Knife-edge sharp tuning. Twenty-seven quartz crystal controlled channels. The ability to switch back and forth between the upper and lower sidebands while dumping the carrier wave. Built-in squelch against random noises. A speech compressor that made it possible to speak ordinary everyday Spanish and still remain totally unintelligible to any listener whose outfit was not an exact duplicate of this one.

Which, naturally enough, the transmitter-receptor of *Teniente* Alvaro Ferrero, Acting Commander—since the death of the actual Commander, *Capitan* Miguel Miers, in action one month before—of the Third Regional Band of DRAP (Defensores Revolucionarios Armados del Pueblo), was.

Carlos picked up the microphone. Sat there, watching the field strength meter. When it peaked, showing that the antenna was pouring out the strongest signal possible, he began: The call signal. The identification code phrase. Then:

"*¡Alvaro! ¡Alvaro! ¿Me oyes?* Alvaro! Alvaro! Do you hear me?"

"Perfectly, Carlitos!" Alvaro Ferrero said.

"You will bring in the groups. Your band and all the others you can contact. But only to the far side of Bahía Linda, beyond the airport. Camp in the jungle there. Issue only cold rations to your men. Make no fires! Even a wisp of smoke could give you away. And wait; I repeat *wait,* until I give you the signal to attack. Let those *Idiotas* of EMMA and those murderous fanatics of ERL rush in and get themselves slaughtered. We must wait until victory is certain!"

"When will that be, Carlitos?" Alvaro said.

"When those two Birds of Evil Omen, those Vultures, Pérez de la Valle and Fuentes Toralba, make a mistake and arouse the people against them. So far, since they are only too aware of how tired the people are of *Gobiernos Personalistas* and *Dictaduras* in general, they are operating with great caution and much care—"

"And, if they do *not* make a mistake?" Alvaro said; "what then, Carlitos?"

"We will provide them with an error. But the fat one. The Great-Grandfather and Loving Grandmother of all mistakes," Carlos Suarez said.

But now, again, the overt manipulation of Fate, the uncertain and risky business of forcing events, of trying to accelerate History, proved—for the leaders of the more moderate Left, anyhow—unnecessary. His Excellency, General Raoul Pérez de la Valle, Chief of State, and his Second in Command, Director General of Security, Pablo Fuentes Toralba, conjointly and after considerable deliberation over the matter, decided that:

One, granted that they absolutely had to obtain a major loan in order to implement the development of the offshore oil fields from whose revenues the major part of Costa Verde's revenues in the future was sure to come; because,

Two, the only viable alternative to said loan, which would be to let Worldwide Petroleum and/or other similar multinational companies develop the fields themselves, construct the pipe lines, refineries, docks, tanker loading facilities, and so forth, which they would be delighted to do, of course, but only at the cost of ninety-nine year leases, guaranteed profit sharing, and the maintenance far into the future of a royalty schedule so low as to make Costa Verde the laughing stock of every other oil-producing nation in the world, was to men as constitutionally greedy as both of them were, unthinkable as an alternative at all; and

Three, their own long, close, and slavish collaboration with General García in all his megalomaniacal ambitions, plans, and what was even worse, in his oppressive procedures which had included the most prolonged, routine, and obscenely fiendish use of torture against not only his enemies but their women as well, in all of recent history, was definitely a handicap in the only country from which they had the remotest chance of obtaining a loan of the *size* they needed, that is, the United States of America; and

Four, that declaring Ambassador James Randolph Rush *persona non grata* in Costa Verde, and shipping him back to his country, where—as a known expert on Costa Verdian affairs—he was sure to be called on to testify upon the advisability of *any* loan asked by the Republic of Costa Verde, and specifically upon the personalities and the trustworthiness of the Government leaders requesting it, simply wasn't smart, especially considering all the reasons they had given the astonishingly popular—at least among female Costa Verdians!—*Don* Jaime Rush to love them somewhat less than dearly—

They reluctantly decided that the *only* place they could safely ship *Don* Jaime with the absolute certainty of his no longer being able to interfere with their plans would be to hell, itself, and, even so, they'd better keep a most vigilant watch thereafter over the subsequent doings of the Devil!

Therefore, they ordered the liquidation of Ambassador Rush and set up a minutely detailed, enormously complicated, and much too elaborate plan for carrying out his execution.

And thereby fell into the trap that Carlos Suarez had predicted they would: They made a mistake. A Gross Error. The Fat One. The Great-Grandfather and Tender Loving Grandmother of all the Political Misapprehensions that was ever misapplied in this Royally—and Vertically!—Fornicated World.

Their major error lay in the very elaborateness and complication of their plan. Any experienced conspirator knows that any plot that cannot be carried out by an escapee from an institution for mentally retarded children in five minutes flat is sure to fail. Any really elaborate plot calls for the perfect coordination of more factors than human beings, malfunctioning under stress as human beings always do, can even *remember* much less handle successfully. And it tends to leave too much incriminating evidence on view—

As, for instance, the issue of three Schmeisser Model MP–40, 9 mm rimfire submachine guns, with two additional thirty-two-round magazines to the three young Right-wing Army officers ordered to do the job, a type of weapon that was Regular Army Equipment in Costa Verde, and hence could only have come into the possession of Red guerrillas through their having been captured after a pitched battle which the Reds had won. This was a whole series of suppositions that constituted a perfect *reductio ad absurdum,* since the Reds wisely avoided pitched battles with the Regular Army, knowing that they couldn't possibly defeat crack troops, backed up both by tanks and aircraft in the field. Therefore, to a populace who had been watching—and very often cheering on!—the Reds as they staged their hit and run raids within the city itself, and the more often than not futile and fruitless pursuit of the urban guerrillas by the police and the army ever since 1963, the mere possession of the Nazi "burp guns" was sure to be a dead giveaway.

Unlike the inhabitants of an Anglo Saxon city, for instance, it would have been close to impossible to find any citizen of Ciudad Villalonga who wouldn't have known instantly that those were the wrong kinds of guns for Red political assassins, which the young officers were to be disguised as, to use to kill anybody whomsoever. To start with, even women witnesses, the class least likely to know anything about guns, would have known that much. They would *not* have known, of course, that this gun was a Schmeisser, and that that was an Ak-47, but they could see with their own eyes that these were two different kinds of guns because the two weapons simply don't look *anything* alike, and everything in their lives trains women to be visually discriminating. And any housewife, secretary, clerk, or what have you among the feminine population would have had to be certifiably moronic not to have realized that the Army and the police always used one of the two kinds and the Red urban guerrillas always used the other.

Another group of witnesses—and the whole plot turned upon its being witnessed, by people who could be deluded into attributing the authorship of, and the responsibility for, the crime to the wrong political group—was the hordes of street urchins from ten to fourteen years old, to make the matter even worse, for not only did the streetwise brats know perfectly the difference between a Schmeisser and an Ak-47, they knew that difference by name, and even staged their incessant war games with quite remarkably recognizable replicas of the two kinds of machine guns, made from old curtain rods, scrap wood, and tin cans, so the chances of Pérez de la Valle's and Fuentes Toralba's deluding them was nil.

And, as far as the adult male population of Villalonga City, it was less than even that. Military service is compulsory in Costa Verde. Ninety-seven percent of adult male citizens of the Capital could have torn down a Schmeisser into its component parts and reassembled it blindfolded, since that had been a part of their basic training while in the Armed Forces.

All of which meant that the only people who could conceivably be deluded by so-called Reds who used Schmeissers would be an occasional priest, most nuns, and all girl children under thirteen years old.

Worse even than the choice of weapons were the disguises imposed upon those not exactly voluntary executioners: blue jeans, elaborately loose and hugely flowered shirts, sandals, and—worst of all!—wigs and false beards, since being regulars in an Army whose—now Ex!—Commander in Chief, General García, had hated everything that smacked of Hippydom, and had made the peeled to the crown, short Nazi brush the regulation haircut for his soldiers, and forbade even a mustache to any officer below the rank of Captain, the chosen assassination squad hadn't had time to grow long hair and beards of its own.

Every theatergoer knows how utterly unconvincing *any* false beard is, even when applied to the actor's face by an expert makeup artist, which is why most actors, given a part requiring the character to be bearded, will, today, let their own whiskers grow out for the role. Wigs are somewhat better, but only when they fall into the three hundred to one thousand dollar price range, and are lovingly crafted by a topflight wigmaker to the wearer's contours and complexion, a matter that requires weeks of patient trial and error adjustments. It need hardly be said that the wigs issued to the men sent to kill *Don* Jaime failed utterly to meet the standards of quality implicit in such an expenditure of money and of time.

Beyond that, the whole concept of the disguises was mistaken because it simply did not take into consideration the degree of sophistication that—especially in matters relating to political double-dealing, chicanery, and fraud—the good citizens of Ciudad Villalonga had attained by then. Or rather, had had forced upon them. For the population of Costa Verde's capital, having lived under, and often been the victims of, from the late nineteen fifties to now, late in the seventies, the most unrelenting and fiendishly cruel system of political oppression ever seen in the Western Hemisphere, were, directly as a result of that terrible experience, in the political sense, very sophisticated indeed. Therefore, it was absolutely sure to occur to sizable numbers of them that while the youngsters who made up the Urban Guerrilla Attack Squads might dress like Hippies while in their natural habitat and about their normal lives and pleasures, they most certainly would *not* dress in a manner calculated to give their identities dead away when setting out to kill someone. Even if they refrained—as the assassination trio *had* to in order to make those wigs and beards visible!—from wearing a woman's stocking pulled down tightly over their faces, absolutely the best disguise ever invented, and hence by the early seventies in worldwide use by all political terrorists whatever their convictions, logically speaking they would have surely got haircuts for the occasion and worn business suits, shirts, and ties!

But beyond these simple errors there lay even graver ones: The trio were not chosen from Costa Verde's Military Intelligence Service, but rather from among those who had posted high scores as marksmen. That criterion itself was wrong: To kill someone with a submachine gun, marksmanship is scarcely called for; all that is necessary is to point the ugly obscenities in the general direction of your victim and cut loose. The volume of fire will make his death a certainty. But ordinary military service, especially among career officers, which all three of these unfortunate youngsters were, tends to penalize individual initiative, and unorthodox habits of thought. Military Intelligence personnel surely could have aimed well enough and to spare to do the actual job at hand; and conceivably, trained spies would have remembered to remove their military identification tags—worn in Costa Verde's army, by specific regulation, on a chain around one's neck—when donning their disguises. But so great is the force of habit, the rule of routine over the human mind, that not one of the three young officers even recalled that the so-called "dog-tags" were there, with the result—compounded by the fact that all three of them also wore religious medals: St. Christopher, the Holy Virgin, even one of them, the youngest, a crucifix, along with the identification tags on the same chain, a practice that would have been totally unthinkable to an authentic Red—that these flat negations and contradictions of their assumed identities were plainly visible against their bronzed and healthy young bodies, because their loose Hippy shirts were worn the way real Hippies would have worn them, that is, open to the navel. It goes without saying that a goodly number of the witnesses remarked that damning detail, and that one of them, a North American press photographer, present at the scene through absolutely no accident at all, recorded it on film forever.

Again, and most serious of all the many misapprehensions in that plot to pass themselves off as Red urban guerrillas, the would-be assassins necessarily had to be young, and thereby, as a direct result of their youth, very likely inexpert at, and unaccustomed to, murder. Men can get used to killing people, but such habituation is far from easy. Even among the S.S. and the Gestapo, a surprisingly high number of officer candidates failed, and had to be sent to rest and rehabilitation camps in order to recover from nervous breakdowns. Transferred to the regular *Wehrmacht,* these essentially decent young Germans performed splendidly. Now, of Pérez de la Valle's and Fuentes Toralba's would-be killers, not one had ever killed anyone before, nor even seen what a nine millimeter parabellum slug does to living human flesh when it tears into it at point blank range. And not having had the time, and still less the inclination, to scientifically test the aptitudes and the temperaments of their execution squad, the two conspirators simply did not know that *one* of their killers could possibly bring it off, the second, but dubiously, and the third had both a strongly developed moral sense and a basically kind heart, factors sure to crack him up when confronted with the obscene, visible, physical ugliness of murder.

Again, the complication of the plan left numerous and enormous holes in its structure for the easy entry of the one element that must be rigorously excluded from anything as serious as a political assassination: Luck. Hazard. Chance. Blind Accidentality. For in missions of this nature, there is only one kind of luck: bad. Allowed to enter in, it always fouls up the works—and dirtily.

As an example of which, take that grimy, run down, miserable little church directly across the street from the place where—marked on a street map issued them—the three submachine gunners were to station themselves. Neither *Don* Raoul or *Don* Pablo, anything but devoutly religious men, even remembered that church was there. And most certainly they did not recall that it was the church to which Padre Pío had been assigned upon his arrival in Costa Verde as a Basque refugee from Franco's Spain, nor were they aware of the simple fact that even now, despite his exalted position as Archbishop, he frequently returned there to say Mass, preach sermons, conduct the weddings, christenings, burials of his flock like any parish priest—and to bask in the total adoration of his—and God's—poor.

As—today.

Another element rung in by chance that the conspirators and their murder squad simply did not know: The spot chosen—because there Jim's Mercedes would have to make a near U turn to enter the Avenida Jesus Pintero—lay just before a low-cost housing project, occupied by relatively poor people, clinging to the lower fringes of the middle class by their fingernails as it were, and that the housewives hung their washes—forbidden though this was by law!—on the balconies overlooking the street.

Nor—last and greatest and most terrible of all!—that Jim Rush would bring the wife of his bosom and their newborn child home from the hospital on this day . . .

But there was one more factor still that was, and was not, a matter of luck. Someone telephoned Bill Jenkins, star reporter and master photographer for United Press, the man whose Viet Nam action shots are the envy and the despair of nearly every other war correspondent—photographer practicing whose difficult and dangerous twin professions in today's unquiet world, and tipped him off that something most unusual was going to happen today in *la Plaza de San Roque*, something well worth his attention, rather a bit of a "scoop" one might say . . .

The caller was none other than Pablo Fuentes Toralba himself, who, exercising that fine excess of cleverness that usually ends up by getting its possessor hanged, was preparing the perfect alibi: photographs made by a world famous reporter, a foreigner, a man of unimpeachable integrity, conclusively proving that it was the filthy, murderous Reds who had done this thing. Now there are plenty of filthy, murderous Reds in this world of sin; but one thing—and *only* that one thing—can be said in their favor: They are very seldom as stupid as most Right-wingers are. They would not, Bill Jenkins reflected later, have sent their killers in disguises far more suitable for Rio's or New Orleans' carnivals than for anything so serious as murder.

But so stood matters, and at such a peak of tension hung the plot, as Jim Rush's limousine swept towards the place and time where his conceptions of both, and himself, conceivably would end.

"Why are you sad, Trini?" he said.

"I do not know, *Cielo*. It is—a thing I feel . . ."

"Then—tell me a *thing*," Jim said, teasing her.

"No. I would not—trouble thee . . ."

"Tell me!" he said sternly.

"*Cielo, Corizon mío*, Love of my Life—I have—much fear—"

"Lord God, Trini—of what?"

"Of having to—leave thee, now that we are—happy," she whispered. "I sang the Death Song, *Don* Jaime! I asked the Gods—for death. Because thou didst not love me, because thou couldst not—"

"And they, not being crazy like watering pots, didn't listen to you," Jim said cheerfully. "Since, being Gods, they *knew* I loved you even when—being shocked and hurt—I thought I didn't . . ."

"Thou'rt not shocked *now*? Hurt now? Thou hast not even the tiniest, tiniest desire to run away with—thy *Jirafa*? With the immensely tall—and enormously beautiful—*Doctora* Nivens?"

"Trini—" he said. "Look at me."

She looked at him. Her eyes were enormous. Slanted. Night-black. Night of the full moon, silver swimming. Starry night. He bent towards her, found her mouth. The car leaned into that U turn.

And from across the street the Schmeissers opened up. Bucked. Jumped. Stuttered. The windows of the car crashed in, filling the air with the whining, white hot sleet of powdered glass.

She whispered: "*¡Dios!*"

Opened her mouth. Said "*¡Te quiero!*" Or tried to. The blood exploding out between her lips, drowned her words. Splashed and splattered all over his mouth, his throat. Thick, viscous, scalding. Turned his face into a mask. A—horror.

"Trini!" he screamed.

Wili stopped the car.

Jim rolled out of it, dragging Trini with him. Stood up. Started to walk with her in his arms straight towards those momentarily silent guns. One of them jerked level. Just one. But the youngest of the three assassins slammed his hand under it, knocking its muzzle skyward as it ripped out a long burst. On a third floor balcony *Doña* Mercedes Simonés was hanging out her wash. That burst cut her almost in half. She screamed. Went on the railing. Fell. Her dead body made, striking the street, a curiously soft and sodden sound.

Bill Jenkins raised his Leica and shot and shot and shot again. Jim Rush's face. The way his eyes were—screaming. That—rag doll—in his arms, spurting the last of her life in swift red fountain sprays down onto the pavement. The faces of the assassins. Especially that of the youngest one. The kid who was crying.

Then they, the killers, running away, diving into the getaway car, and he, Jenkins, focusing carefully on the license plate, knowing as he did so it was no good, the car surely stolen, and turning back to get the rest of that sequence that made history, that won him—for the second time—the Pulitzer Prize: Jim Rush coming on, his dead wife in his arms, crying tears of blood, moving slowly with a curious stateliness, and an enormous dignity—

And Padre Pío flying out of *la Iglesia de San Roque,* looking, in his rusty black robes, for all the world like an ancient turkey buzzard. And Jim putting Trini's body down on the sidewalk, and they, the two of them, priest and layman kneeling before it with folded hands lifting eyes equally glazed, scalded, blind, towards mercilessly uncaring, totally vacant heaven, tormenting the deaf and empty skies with the unending anguish of their silent accusations—

And the women pouring out of those houses and kneeling beside them, all around them, lifting their broad dark faces, their streaming eyes skyward—

And in the car Trinita—little Trini—lifting up a frightened howl, and a big fat woman with enormous breasts rushing to the car, tearing the door open, picking up the baby, and baring one huge brownish melon of a breast, thrusting the nipple into Trinita's tiny mouth and flopping down onto the curbstone and sitting there nursing the baby and crooning to it and crying—

And he, Bill Jenkins, getting that shot too, shooting and shooting and changing rolls of film in his Canon F 1 B single-lens reflex and his Leica M 5 without even looking and shooting again—

And suddenly stopping, caught by the expression on the face of the small man in the chauffeur's uniform who was standing there besides the riddled Mercedes and staring at his own two hands—

And moving in close, focusing on that face, on those hands, on what that face did as he, the small man in the chauffeur's uniform, stared at his hands, at the few drops splotches splatters of blood on them—

And he, Bill Jenkins, saying?

"Hers? ¿Suya?"

And Wili—Guillermo Nuñez Lobato, Captain Nuñez of the Security Police, officially and ostentatiously Ambassador Rush's chauffeur—saying, very, very quietly:

"¡Sí, Señor!"

And he, Jenkins, by some kind of interior—human, as opposed to merely reportorial—instinct, saying:

"It will wash off. Or—will it?"

"No," Wili whispered. "No. Because I was—part of it, Señor. Part of the system. An informer. Sent to—spy on the best, most decent man I ever met. As she was sent to—ruin him. But she couldn't. She decided that dying was—better—más honesta—than doing that. Now she's dead. And I—I've got her blood on my hands. On my—soul, Señor mío . . . Where it will never wash off. Because I went along with them. With people—no; not people—because things—mierdas, shits like them have resigned from the human race, haven't they?—capable of—murdering—a girl coming home from the hospital with her firstborn in her arms . . ."

He threw back his head and screamed it, then, his voice cracked, woman-shrill, the rage in it a vibrato, a scrape of steel on glass:

"¡Cabrones! ¡Matones! ¡Asesinos! You're going to pay for this! For killing—her. For the size you've cut me down to. For what you've smeared all over me. Made me eat, swallow, wallow in . . ."

And Bill Jenkins photographing his face as he screamed, said, whispered that, and the smooth, trained perfect grace of his movements as he jerked his shoulder-holstered sidearm out and raced off in the direction that car had gone—

And after that all the men in the square pouring out of it after him, roaring:

"Did you see 'em, Chauffeur? Could you recognize them? C'mon, let's go get the hijoputas!

That was but the beginning of it. One man, a lookout, the DRAP undercover man for that barrio, got to Carlos Suarez by telephone, even before the three killers had left the Square. Carlos was at his transceiver and on the air within seconds, broadcasting a general alarm, and thereafter detailed instructions to the men under his command. His urban guerrillas blocked every street leading from la Plaza de San Roque. Caught the assassins at a roadblock made by placing two Electric Light and Power Company trucks broadside across one of those streets not ten blocks from the Square.

And it was a demonstration of his quality that Carlos calmly and quietly held off the mob of would-be lynchers, led in good earnest by Wili Nuñez, at submachine-gun point, while his immediate subordinates dragged the three killers into the basement of the Power and Light Company. Then he said:

"Let us handle this, friends. These *cabrones* will get what's coming to them—but *after* we have demonstrated the proofs of their guilt—and that of those who sent them—to all the world!"

Then he went into the building behind his officers, closed the door in the faces of the still raging mob; locked it. Went down into the basement where the others were.

He stood there, looking at the three captives. Moved in close, until his face was two centimeters from their own. Spat coolly and carefully into each of their faces. Said:

"That's what I think of you. Dirt. Offal. Scum. Killers of—women. Of babies."

"Babies!" the youngest of the killers said. "Look, Sir, we didn't know—"

"That *Don* Jaime was bringing his wife home from the hospital *today* with their newborn child? And that you shits riddled both of them?"

He was not deliberately lying. In any happening like this one, rumor always outruns fact. Carlos had been told that both Trini and the child had died.

The youngest of the three killers stood there. Hung there. He tried to say something. He couldn't. No sound came out of lips turned greyish white. Then he said it, got it out, whispering the words:

"A—baby. A little—baby. Oh, Jesus! Sir—kill me. Now, this minute. I don't want to live. I can't."

Carlos didn't answer him. He went on staring into the boy's eyes, his own unblinking. Without mercy in them. With no pity at all.

The boy went to his knees. Doubled over. Clutched his middle. Vomited. Endlessly. Terribly.

Carlos sighed, then, finally, said:

"Take these two scum down into the boiler room. Make them talk. This one—we won't need to persuade . . ."

He lit a cigarette. Took it out of his mouth. Stuck it into the mouth of the weeping boy. Said to the others:

"Untie him. He won't run. This kid hasn't the granite balls you need to kill people." Then, to the boy:

"Who sent you, Son? Hell, tell the truth, and I'll get you off. A jail sentence, no more. But *not* the *Garrote Vil* . . ."

"Sir—" the boy wept; "I—I aimed high. Above the car! I—"

"And killed a poor woman hanging out her wash on her balcony!"

"Oh, Jesus!" the Boy wept. "Sir—"

"Tell me!" Carlos Suarez said.

He had it all down in writing and the boy had signed it, when his Second in Command, came in, said:

"Carlos, there's an Army Command Car outside. Full of young officers in uniform. But they've got a white flag tied to the antenna and they're saluting with their fists closed!"

"Bring one of them down here," Carlos said. "Just one. With his hands up. No sidearm. I'll dicker with them."

So it was done, and the revolution was over. From that moment, over. For the young officer said:

"Sir, we're members of the JOS, and we want to throw in with you— join you!"

"The what?" Carlos said.

"The JOS. *Jovenes Oficiales Socialistas.* Damned near *every* officer in the Army under fifty years of age, Sir! And we're with you on every count and all the way! Tell us what you want us to do."

Carlos thought about that.

"Could you take over the television and the radio broadcasting stations?" he said.

Carlos, in full uniform, with Tomás Martinez Galán, Jim's ex-butler, equally military and imposing at his side, staged that drumhead court martial of the three killers on television. Every Costa Verdian who had a TV set saw and heard it, plus everyone who could crowd into a bar or the living room of a relative or a friend. Saw the false wigs and beards exhibited and admitted as evidence. The blue jeans. The flowered shirts. The beads and sandals. Then, at last, the young killers' authentic identification tags. Two of the assassins were condemned to death. But the youngest one—that weeping, broken boy—drew life imprisonment. Everyone knew he'd be out and free in a year or two, especially since, as Carlos Suarez was careful to point out, it was extremely doubtful that even one of the bullets that killed the two women had come from his gun. The sentence was for form's sake. For the boy's confession wrecked Pérez de la Valle and Fuentes Toralba beyond any hope of recovery.

The young officers of the JOS, Young Socialist Officers, in English, stormed the Presidential Palace and the National Security Headquarters with tanks and artillery. Often, tragically enough, they were fighting against their own fathers and uncles. Because this revolution, as modern revolutions often do, involved the ideological gap between the generations. But perhaps this terrible fact contributed to the older, diehard Army men's decision to give in after three brief hours of really bloody fighting. All of history proves that Oedipus can kill Laius. But for Laius to kill Oedipus—standing tall in his pride, his youth, his manly beauty!—is quite a different matter.

The dead numbered one hundred fifty-one. The wounded, three hundred thirty.

And they garroted Raoul Pérez de la Valle and Pablo Fuentes Toralba *en la Plaza de la Liberación,* as an additional humiliation, refusing them the honor, and the comparative mercy, of a firing squad.

A *Junta* of the JOS and the leaders of the DRAP took over the Government. In the next two weeks, of course, they were forced to smash both EMMA and ERL in pitched bloody battles that cost nearly seven hundred lives. For, Marxists though they all were, they knew that any government including those two groups of insane and murderous fanatics would be totally unworkable.

All of which did Ambassador James Randolph Rush—*Don* Jaime— absolutely no good at all.

CHAPTER

35

*T*hey set up the *Capilla Ardiente,* the Lighted (or burning?) Chapel, where a formal public wake of a per-
sonage of importance is always held—and *Doña* María de la Sagrada
Trinidad Alvarez Bermejo, *Señora de* Rush, had surely achieved that distinction now that her death had sparked a revolution into flame—in the
little Church of San Roque at Jim's own request. And all Ciudad Villalonga, in endless lines, filed by to gaze upon poor Trini in her open
coffin.

All. Tens of thousands of people. All night long. And the vast majority of them were crying. Some of the women, uncontrollably, though
many a man wept too, openly and without shame. There were scenes of
pure hysteria. A psychologist interested in mob behavior patterns could
have gathered the materials for ten weighty tomes.

Doña Carolina Solis, Trinita's self-appointed wet nurse, kept the
baby, along with her own newborn son—this also with Jim's wise and
full consent—in her tiny, grubby apartment on the third floor of one of
the nearby *viviendas sociales.* And the lines coming out of the church
went across the Plaza and up the stairs to file by and gaze at the peacefully sleeping child, with two of the local policemen who lived in that
barrio voluntarily standing by to keep the lines moving. Trinita was pronounced *"¡Una Niña Sol!"* A Sun Child. And *"¡Una Angelita del Cielo,
la Pobre!"* A little Angel from Heaven, the Poor Little Thing! And "A

little Pretty Sky." Or perhaps you could render that *"¡Un Cielito Lindo!"* that they called her as "A Heavenly Little Beauty!" But both are wrong, really. Spanish simply won't go into English at all fully three-quarters of the time. But they called her all those things and as many more terms of endearment as a people as warm and loving as they are brutal and cruel can invent. Trinita would have been smothered with kisses if the policemen had not prevented that. Or very likely stolen by one of the more fanatically maternal—and sadly barren—wives.

All of which Bill Jenkins photographed. His book, *Murder In The Capital: A Photographic Essay,* became a classic. And a best seller. He sent Jim Rush a copy. Jim burned it. The memories graven on his brain, etched upon his heart, were quite enough. He didn't need this intolerably public invasion of his private grief, his quietly enshrined and very nearly sacred pain.

But what is absolutely beyond dispute is the fact that Jim Rush was not the worst sufferer on that long night that Trini's public wake dragged on. He had, at least, the consolation of knowing that his reconciliation with his child-wife, his renewed pledge of faith, of love to her, had been utterly sincere. He had known, of course, when he had made that pledge that he could not be able to halt the inclination of his vagrant heart towards Grace Nivens. But he also knew beyond the faintest shadow of a doubt that he could refrain from doing anything about that inclination. And that so long as his Fates, his Furies, the Old Gods of the Tluscola—and Father Pío's!—permitted him, Trini, and their tiny, mutual hostage to fortune a life together, he would so refrain with only an irreducible minimum of silent, sad, and well contained regrets. His absolute certainty of that fact brought a certain alleviation of the shattering shock and grief that tore him.

He also carefully refrained from giving any thought to a future that could—and almost surely would—have Grace in it. To do so at that moment seemed to him an almost blasphemous affront to Trini's memory and his grief. And because he felt that way about it, he sadly acknowledged that only a little while ago he had treated Grace Nivens very badly indeed. But again he had the consolation of knowing— believing!—he would have time to make amends, to repair the damage, the hurt he realized that he had done her.

That that consolation was hubris, that the presumption of any future at all is indefensible, that it is utter folly to count upon one's next inhaled or exhaled breath, he did not then consider. Later—and terribly—he would, almost too late.

For Grace, herself, had no consolations at all, not even the illusory one of a reasonably assured future span of time. And therefore—and through his most grievous fault!—she suffered far more than he. What she went through, sitting there in a back pew with Rosa and Cecilia and Pepe, and for a whole hour, His Excellency Tomás Martinez Galán, Captain General of the Forces of the Interior, and Vice President of the *Junta*—forever relieved of his disguise, protective cover, and rather pleasant post of head butler at the American Embassy and residence—is the perfect demonstration of the bitter fact that, once beyond the point that one hurts to such a degree of intensity that to scream would be to blaspheme against one's pain, language becomes an irrelevancy. The words to say what she, Grace Nivens, felt, watching Jim Rush's face, seeing what his eyes did when they gazed on Trini's dead body, not only don't exist but couldn't be invented, coined. For to reduce pure agony into the shaped breath-spurts of spoken sound is to rob it of the dignity that only silence gives it.

So Grace was silent as she sat there thinking not what to do, but simply *how* to do it, what method she could use to leave a world, a life, an existence she hadn't the slightest intention of even attempting to endure beyond tomorrow's sunrise, studying not which ways would be the quickest, easiest, most nearly painless, but their precise opposites: the ones great enough, terrible enough, shocking enough, sufficiently agonizing to be at least somewhat commensurate with the total horror in her.

That horror that he, Jim Rush, had inflicted upon her, dealt her with a single deadly, quietly spoken phrase.

For when she had come into the church, she had gone at once to him, her lips half opened to say—

What? What was there now to be said? She hadn't known then, didn't know now what she had tried, wanted, been about to say. For he had cut her off at once by saying evenly, quietly:

"Don't—say anything, Grace. Don't *you* say anything. Please."

She had brought her own hand up, palm outward, across her own mouth as if to ward off a visible, physical blow. Cringed. Bent. Turned. Fled to an empty pew in the back of the church. Sat there—dying.

That *"you"* emphasized ever so slightly. That utterly crushing, heart stopping *"you."* "Don't say anything, Grace. Not *you*—the woman taken in adultery. Not *you*, the woman who most in all the world have sinned against her who lies here dead."

'I didn't *know!*' she wailed inside her mind; 'And *you* did, Jim Rush! Of all the flagrant examples of unmitigated male chauvinism I've ever come up against, this—'

Then she stopped. She was utterly honest, and the defense she had been arming in her mind, that Jim had refused to confess his marriage 'before,' she was thinking wrathfully, 'dragging my elongated carcass off to bed!' simply wasn't so. Beyond the not even debatable point of who had actually dragged whom, she was immediately confronted with the fact that Jim had obviously tried to tell her upon several occasions, and had been stopped by—of this she was absolutely sure—his inability to find a way of putting it that didn't seem to him, with his dislike of giving offense, his hatred of causing pain, worse than brutal. And she—

'I *did* know,' she thought miserably. 'In my heart of hearts I knew. And I wouldn't let him tell me. I needed to pretend ignorance—of what he almost told me—by phone before I even left the States. I asked him: "How serious would the opposition to—my coming back into your life be, Jim?" And he answered me, "*Very* serious, Grace." Good God, how much of a fool does one have to be not to understand *that*? Only I—I refused to understand it. To—listen to it, even. And here, every time he tried to tell me, I wouldn't let him. Because I wasn't brave enough to hear it. And now—because of that—that cowardice, I've ruined—ended—all my life . . .'

She was sitting there, like that, not even crying, beyond even the merciful relief of tears, when the tall, dark woman who—to Grace anyhow—looked so perfectly Spanish that she might have stepped into life out of a painting by Julio Romero de Torres, that incomparable painter of *Morenas,* the word that suits dark women so much better than the weak and somehow kittenish French word *"brunettes"* ever can, slipped into the pew beside her and took her arm.

"Grace—" the dark woman said.

"I don't know you," Grace said coldly.

"I know you don't. I'm Vince's wife. Paloma. He told me to come here to look for you. He thought you'd need—help. I see he was right."

"Not the kind you—or he—can give me," Grace said.

"You're no judge of that, Grace," Paloma said evenly. "At the moment, I'd say you're no judge of anything. I'm not here to please you or to make friends. I hope we will become friends later on. But, at the moment, I don't particularly care how you feel about *me.* You can hate me if you like. As long as you'll consent to come home with me. Or to any place you want to—besides *here.*"

"No," Grace said; "I can't—leave. Not yet. And I don't hate—anybody, Paloma. Except—"

"Except you, yourself," Paloma said.

Grace said, quietly:

"Yes. And I have good reasons to."

"Tell me those reasons," Paloma said.

"No. Why should I?"

"In your profession, it's generally held that talking things out helps, isn't it?"

"But I don't want help," Grace said. "I want to die."

"The act of—a coward, Grace!"

"I *am* a coward. So?"

"*¡María Santísima!*" Paloma breathed. "I hadn't believed it would be—so difficult! Look Grace, Jim—needs you. Trinita does—even more."

"I know. I promised Maritrini—that if anything happened to her . . . She—she *knew* this was going to happen, Paloma! I don't know how she knew it; but she did!"

"She was—mostly Tluscola. The Tluscola know many things. Things we so-called civilized people don't even understand. What did you promise her, Grace?"

"That I would take—the child. Marry Jim. Take care of both of them. Only—neither she nor I had counted on Catch Ninety-Six!"

"Which is?" Paloma said.

"That—he would—come to—to hate me. To—despise me. To be reminded every time he looks into my eyes of the thing *he* feels most guilty over. For which he'll never forgive himself for now. Nor—especially not!—*me* . . ."

"Same question: Which is?"

"Adultery. With *me*. That *I* led him into. While she was—great with child. Only a little time before Trinita was born."

"*¡Niño Dios!*" Paloma said. "All right—that's rough, I'll admit. And, as a married woman who's been—well, subjected to the same sort of assaults by roving females against her home, her man—I find it particularly hard to take . . ."

"So do I," Grace said quietly; "in fact, it's—absolutely unpardonable, Paloma."

"But—it's hardly a thing to kill one's self over, Grace. If people generally did that for this particular reason, the world would have long since been depopulated, my dear!"

"But I am not people; I am *me*. And it will not be over that. It will be because he hates me. That fact, itself, is enough. The reason doesn't matter."

"But—how do you feel about *him*, Grace?"

"I love him. To an extent, and with an intensity, no *modern* woman could possibly imagine."

"And you're not—modern?"

"No. I am—Medea—to his Jason. Dido, to his Aeneas. In fact, I'm extinct. Like the Dodo Bird. Or I soon will be. This time tomorrow, surely."

"What you are is—a little crazy, I think!"

"Yes. Why yes, of course. When the pressure becomes too great, when you—hurt—too much, something—breaks, Paloma. The mind. The heart. Then—your breath. Your—life."

"*¡Niño Jesus!*" Paloma said.

"Paloma—who is that man?"

"What man, Grace?"

"The one that just came in. A big man. Tall enough for me to dance with. That's—awfully tall, Paloma."

"I still don't see—"

"*That* one. The one with the crippled arm. You know—there's something wrong about him. I'd say he's crazy, too. Crazier than I am, maybe. His hair—he's *done* something to it . . ."

"*¡María Santísima!*" Paloma said. "*¡Santa Madre de Dios!*"

"What's the matter, Paloma; you look—"

"Grace, you sit still. Don't move! I'm going outside—into the Plaza. To see if I can find a policeman . . ."

"Why, Paloma?"

"That's Joe Harper. And you're right; he's done something to his hair. Put—some grease or something into it to darken it. Ordinarily it's—very blond—"

"But *who* is Joe Harper?"

"That man. He's a swine. A drug runner. *The* worst enemy Jim has. Jim's never told you about the man Trini stabbed herself to prevent his—"

"No. Jim, no. Vince, yes. Your husband. And—showed me those—torture pictures. This Harper's the one who—?"

"Did all that? Yes. Sit still, Grace. That—laboratory! *¡Dulce Niño Jesus!* That laboratory!"

"*What* laboratory, Paloma?"

"His! Harper's! Where he made heroin, Grace! Jim—destroyed it, or helped to. Doesn't he tell you *anything,* Grace?"

"No," Grace said sadly; "he—hates me. I told you that."

"Rubbish! Anyhow, that was how and why Jim got shot this last time. So—don't move, Baby girl! *Big* Baby girl—don't move!"

Grace saw Paloma racing for the door. She thought:

'You've come to—kill Jim, haven't you, Harper? So there is—something I—can do for him. One way—I can equal her. And I—thank you for the opportunity, Joe Harper. Now, today, I thank you with all my heart . . .'

She got up. Crossed to where Joe was moving in the line of people waiting to pass Trini's bier, keeping his place in the line, so as not to attract too much attention; neither pushing, nor forcing his way ahead.

She stood before him, tall as someone out of the Norse legends:

Brunhilde, Freya, her eyes as pale as the eyes of Hel, the goddess of the Dead. Put out her slim, strong, sunburnt hand, said clearly, so that her voice crackled sudden lightnings from nave to crypt:

"Give me that!"

"Give you what, Honey?" Joe said. "Lord Jesus, but you're really somethin' ain't you? Big enough even for me! Lotta woman, Honey! I'll give you somethin' all right. Special present for Big Gals like you. Keeps it in my pants. Only this here's a *church*, Honey. Th' House o' th' *Lord*. So we *can't*. Gotta have some respect, y'know!"

"Give me that pistol, Joe. The one you've got in your pocket. The one you brought here—to kill Jim with. Only you're not going to, Joe Harper! I'm not going to let you!"

Jim turned then, slowly, dreamily, thinking: 'That was—unpardonable—what I—said to Grace. She is—less guilty than I am. *Far* less. She didn't *know*. And she surely wouldn't have—gone to bed with me—loved me—committed adultery with me—if she had known. Because it's a thing she's especially sensitive about, that she hates the very idea of—ever since that time her own husband—Nivens, Jon Nivens—let her catch him with another woman she—' Then suddenly, abruptly, he saw, recognized what was going on. Cried out:

"Grace! Get down! On the floor! Away from that maniac! Grace!"

Padre Pío turned, too. In time to see Joe yank out that automatic. A Beretta. Six point three millimeter. Practically a toy. But all the gun he could manage now with a shaking, peeling, badly burned left hand, he who had been a right hander all his life until Roberto Henriques maimed him.

The people in the lines scattered. Dived behind pews. Ran.

Joe took his own sweet time aiming. But he simply hadn't had time enough since that gunfight on the docks that had cost him his right hand forever, leaving it dangling, withered, paralyzed, to learn to use his left hand with any skill. And now, thanks to Charlie Marriotti, even that left hand looked like a vulture's claw, because Joe had had to use it to dig his way out from under the flaming ruins of that laboratory. So now, to his great disgust, Joe Harper found he simply couldn't hold on for little Old Uncle Creepie-Poo, that damned hand still trembled so.

"Joe," Jim said calmly, "put that thing down. You're in a *church*, man. At—my wife's funeral. Trini's, Joe. Haven't you done—enough to her, even yet?"

"Trini?" Joe said. "Jeeeez–zus! That sweet lil' piece o' Shady Snatch? You—you *killed* her! You jealous lil' ol' dried up Turd, you! I'm gonna—"

He yanked the trigger. The Beretta spat flame. The sound of it was not impressive. A little louder than a kid's cap pistol, but not much.

He missed Jim completely. Brought the muzzle down again. Took aim. But by then Grace was all over him. She almost broke his arm.

"Great, Girl!" he laughed happily. "Jus'—great! Big Bitch strong as you, mean as you, gonna be somethin' in th' hay, I get you to my pad! Now turn me loose, Baby. Tend to you after I gets through lettin' a lil' daylight into Ol' Uncle Creep . . ."

Grace saw, despairingly, that Jim was racing towards them down the aisle. But she had never met anyone before with half the inhuman or superhuman strength that Joe Harper had. She clenched her teeth, hung onto his arm, jerked at his wrist fiercely, trying to get the pistol away from him. And, since that Baretta was an automatic, the very force of her motions triggered it three times. One of the shots went through the loose cloth of her dress between her body and her arm. Another lodged in her left thigh. The third went into her middle, just above her navel. Which meant she was gutshot. Hit bad.

Then Jim was there. He kicked Joe in the belly, hard. Joe grunted, tore his arm loose from Grace's rapidly weakening grip. Slammed the Beretta sidewise across Jim's face, knocking him down and three-quarters of the way out. Stood there above him, aiming. At that distance he didn't need to aim very well.

And Grace Nivens knowing—as the professional clinician she was—with abysmal perfection what was happening inside her long, fine body, that she was hemorrhaging like hell into the abdominal cavity, and that if she didn't get some really first class medical help very soon, within half an hour at optimistic best, she was going to die, threw herself upon Joe Harper again. He slapped her so hard she was sure her jaw was broken, slamming her backward into a pew, turned—and heard a harsh, grating voice roar:

"¡Alto! ¡Queda Usted detenido! ¡Tira la pistola al suelo!"

But Joe didn't halt, didn't submit to being detained—or, more accurately—arrested, nor did he throw the pistol to the floor. He got off the last three shots that little seven-shot automatic had in its magazine, hitting the policeman all three times. Then, happily, he turned back to finish off Jim Rush. But the hammer slammed down on an empty chamber. He was out of ammunition. And the worst of it was that he hadn't another magazine with him. The idea that he'd have to fire that many times simply hadn't occurred to him.

He whirled then, running; leaped over the fallen policeman, slamming Paloma aside with a bone-crushing body check. Got to the church door. Out it. Paloma who was much too furious to even think of being afraid, raced after him. Stood in the doorway, screaming:

"¡Asesino! ¡Police! ¡Matalo! ¡Disparen! ¡Asesino! ¡Ha matado a Don Jaime! ¡Ha matado al Embajador!"

At her words, especially the last ones, that the assassin had killed *Don Jaime*, that he'd murdered the Ambassador, a crowd of men converged on Joe Harper. Joe was as strong as a bull. But there were more than fifty men surrounding him. And it must be recalled that now he had a paralyzed, withered, useless right arm. He had thrown the little Beretta away. With him now, he had only a switchblade knife, which he was going to have to use with a trembling, badly burned left hand.

He had, of course, the choice of raising his hands—or rather the one hand he still could raise—into the air and surrendering. But, being himself, he drew that knife and earned once more—posthumously—Jim Rush's reluctant respect, even a degree of grudging, but sincerely felt admiration. Courage is always admirable, no matter how wrongheaded it is. Joe Harper was brave. It was his only virtue, therefore let no man deny him it. So he drew that knife. At once fifty answering blades flickered out. Shone blue under the street lights.

They killed Joe Harper in *la Plaza de San Roque*. Cut him down, roaring like the great brave bull he was. And nothing so became his—miserable, bestial, swinish!—life as the manner of his leaving it.

For, even his enemies admitted, he died very, very well.

CHAPTER

36

*G*race—" Jim said ruefully; "I make one hell of a
hero, don't I? Anyhow, thanks for saving my life."

"It's all right, Jim," she said. "Don't mention it."

It was dark in the church. He couldn't see what was happening to
her. That she was bleeding very slowly and mostly internally—though
enough of it was escaping between the fingers of the hand she had
pressed to her middle for him to have seen it if that miserable grimy
little church had been illuminated by anything more than candles—but
in a way her own very exact professional knowledge told her wasn't
going to stop. That she was hurting worse than anyone who has never
experienced the brutal, miserable, unceasing, and absolutely unbearable
agony of the kind of a wound that a softnosed bullet makes as it slams
through twenty centimeters of flesh, veins, arteries, nerves, and tears
them all to hell, can possibly imagine. And when, as now, that bullet had
lodged in the abdomen, so that among the things it had ripped through
were the small intestines, that agony was increased at least by a factor of
ten, and her chances of survival decreased by something close to twenty.

But she wasn't going to tell him. She simply wasn't. She sat there
holding her middle delicately, quietly, knowing that making any one of
three or four very slight errors such as moving even a fraction of a
millimeter, or breathing faster than a rate that barely held off asphyxia
but that by slow and careful experimentation she had already determined

was all she could manage, or in that process of breathing, inhaling more air than it took to fill a very small area in her upper lungs and thus expanding them enough to crowd her diaphragm ever so slightly down into her abdominal cavity, would cause her to crash immediately and abruptly through that plateau of pain where control is just barely—and by authentic heroism!—possible to another level of intensity altogether where anything human would have to scream.

And she didn't want to scream. It would—distress Jim. It was—very important not to distress Jim. It was—terribly important not to. Not distressing Jim was one of the only two important things she had left to do.

The other one was to die.

Which would, she conceded, probably distress him a little after all. But then—maybe it wouldn't. Perhaps he would be glad not to have to see her hateful face anymore. She didn't know for sure. And, anyhow, it couldn't be helped now, one way or the other. Besides, she wouldn't be around to see his distress, which was the only forlorn comfort that she had.

Only it was taking so long. She was a big, terribly strong, overgrown horse, cow—giraffe!—of a woman and dying was going to take her a long time. Too long, maybe. She couldn't even pass out decently as any *normal* woman would have done ten minutes ago now, so maybe it was going to go on so long and get to be so bad that she wouldn't be able to manage it with dignity.

She hoped that wouldn't happen. She also hoped that Jim would go back to where he belonged, beside his dead wife's coffin and not talk to her anymore so she wouldn't have to answer him because she could taste the blood coming up the back of her throat now and talking was very shortly going to get to be more than she could manage, too, along with all the other things she already couldn't manage now.

But he did talk. He broke through her silent, prayed, implored, 'Oh shut up will you please for Christ's sake don't say anything for I—' by saying, fervently:

"God, I was scared! When that gun went off, I thought he'd killed you! And—"

"Jim—" she said slowly, softly; "would you have—cared?"

"Cared?" he grated, his voice breaking up, shudder-torn, breath-gone, pain-rent at the very thought of it, "Good God, Grace! I'd have died!"

What flooded over her, exploded inside her in that moment—was light. Glory.

"Jim—" she whispered; "go—back—to her. To—Maritrini. To—

your wife. But on the way—tell—tell Paloma—to—to come here—a—a minute, will you?"

This time he heard what was in her voice. Bent swiftly close. Saw what was coming out of both corners of her lips, penciling twin black scarlet lines down to the point of her chin.

He reeled back. Whispered, ever so quietly: "Jesus!" Whirled, his voice rattling the windows, echoing from nave to aspe to atrium to vault to crypt: "Oh, Jesus!" Then:

"Paloma! Padre Pío! Come here! For God's sake, come here!"

"Jim—" Grace said dreamily; "d'you think—she'd mind?"

"Don't talk! Please don't try to talk! Oh, Christ, how you're bleeding!"

"Trini—" Grace said; "Would—she—mind—if I—if I—"

"Grace!" Paloma cried.

"¡Santa Madre de Dios!" Padre Pío said.

"If I—kissed—you—good-bye, Jim?" Grace said.

"Grace!" he moaned.

She smiled at him with grave tenderness. Leaned forward. But she never reached his mouth. Before she got there every one of the candles in *la Iglesia de San Roque* went out at the same time. All the street lights in the city. All the stars in the sky. Through the whistling, roaring, rushing darkness, she heard people screaming, the sound of many footsteps pounding in towards them, the shriek of brakes, the dying sirens of the ambulances they had already called some time back, a couple of million years ago anyhow, to come get the wounded policeman and dead Joe Harper and that had got here finally, were just outside the door . . .

Which was what saved her. Or maybe it was because Vicente Gomez Almagro had hands that were gifts from Padre Pío's God. Or was it, perhaps, what Jim Rush said to her, whispering the words, his voice pure anguish transmuted into sound:

"Don't leave me, Grace. I need you. Trinita does. Don't end—even *her* chances—by ending mine . . ."

That was the last thing she heard for fully forty-eight hours.

When she came back, she found that she was in a hospital and that Padre Pío was praying very quietly beside her bed, and that Paloma was too, nearer the foot of it and Jim was sitting in a chair across the room looking for all the world like a recently unwrapped and badly decayed Egyptian mummy except that he was much too pale to be even a mummy, so what he looked like really was a corpse.

Then she heard Vince's deep voice yelling at Jim, and, forcing her

eyes to focus, saw him too. He was standing in the doorway and bellowing like an enraged bull, which meant he hadn't expected her to come
back quite yet from wherever it was she had been and didn't think she
could hear him.

"Jim," he was saying furiously. "You've simply got to get some sleep!
You'll crack up, man! Forty-eight straight hours and—"

He stopped abruptly. Walked over to the bed. Croaked:

"Grace—can you hear me?"

She nodded. She couldn't talk. There was a tube running up her left
nostril. Another came down from the plasma bottle suspended upside
down on its stand, and disappeared into her left arm through a huge
needle that was taped to the inside crook of her elbow to keep it from
coming out. As a doctor she knew perfectly what all those things were
for, which was to keep her more or less alive and more or less breathing
until her body recovered its natural rhythms and functions enough to
take over. She was also conscious of the miserably uncomfortable feeling
of the catheter they had rammed up her uretha, which wasn't to keep
her alive but merely to drain the urine from her bladder at a slow but
constant rate and thus prevent the uremic poisoning not infrequently oc-
curring in bedridden patients, or what was less grave but more embarrassing, to prevent them from wetting their beds in their helpless state.
Only it seemed to her they had inserted the catheter too far—'High
enough to drain the saliva from around my back teeth!' she thought
angrily. And her middle ached. Slowly, dully. But, even so, it felt so
much better than it had in that church that she smiled.

"To God, the thanks!" Padre Pío said.

Then Jim was off that chair and kneeling by that bed.

"Grace!" he said. "Grace!"

That was all he could manage. Not even that, really.

But she couldn't talk to him. She was much too weak. So she puck-
ered her mouth into the shape of a kiss. Made faintly the sound of one.
Closed her eyes again.

When she opened them again another twenty-four hours had gone by,
but she didn't know that. All she knew was they had taken the tube out
of her nose and weren't dripping plasma drop by drop into the big vein
in her arm any more, but that the catheter felt worse than ever. To make
up for that discomfort, however, the way her middle ached had descended by a couple of orders of intensity to a much more acceptable
level. And best of all, Jim had graduated from his Egyptian Mummy,
Bluish Anglo Saxon Corpse Status to his more nearly normal one of the
Wooden Indian before a Turn of the Century Cigar Store.

She said softly, clearly: "Jim—"

He metamorphosed from the Wooden Indian into a reasonable facsimile of himself, came flying across the room, flopped down on his knees beside the bed. Said:

"Grace—" Making of the very sound of her name a caress. She put up her hand, let it stray along his face. He caught it, rammed it palm upward against his mouth. She laughed, weakly, shakily, said:

"Go home. 'Til tomorrow. Get some sleep. You look awful. Then— bring Trinita—here. I want to—see her. I *need* to see her, Jim."

He said: "All right."

She closed her eyes. When she opened them, he was gone.

The next morning, she felt a great deal better. She stayed awake all morning, and even ate a little of the horrible soft foods that were all they'd let her eat on the very sound theory that solid foods would proba- bly burst the places where her small intestines had been practically knit- ted back together again by Vince Gomez' wonderfully skillful hands and leave Jim Rush widowed for the third time and Trinita an orphan.

At noon Cecilia and Pepe and Rosa all came and brought the baby. By then Trinita was definitely beginning to look human, and the fact that she was going to be her mother's image was clearly discernible. But her hair was a clear blonde, more ash than golden, and when she deigned, as she did now for whole minutes, to open her eyes, Grace could see that they were the same mist-grey that Jim's were, which made her definitely an oddity, because her skin was as dark as Trini's had been, which meant it was much, much darker than her hair and eyes.

So Grace decided that having another woman's child underfoot for practically the rest of her life wouldn't necessarily drive her completely insane and might even be rather pleasant. Then Trinita opened her grey eyes again, cooed, and made one of those involuntary gas gurgles that well fed babies do and that people mistake for laughter, with the not very surprising result that Grace fell in love with her as completely as only a woman as three hundred percent maternal as she naturally was, could.

So she kept Trinita in the bed with her, holding the child in her arms most of the time, and talking as much damned nonsense to it as though she were not a doctor and a scientist at all. She even fed it the bottled formulas that Cecilia prepared, but Rosa had to change Trinita from time to time because Grace really wasn't up to that yet.

Only, Jim didn't show up. By the time he did get there it was almost night. By which time Grace was worried sick and in an absolutely foul mood that Pepe and Cecilia made worse by trying to console her. But fi- nally they had to go home and a stiff little argument took place, compli- cated by Grace's practically nonexistent Spanish, because they wanted to take Trinita home with them, and Grace wanted to keep her. So finally a compromise was reached: Grace kept the baby, but Rosa stayed to take care of all the things that Grace couldn't do for the infant. Which meant Grace had to endure Rosa's disquieting presence, and her monumental silence, for the rest of the evening. The final result of all this was that when Jim walked into the room, Grace looked up from that tiny face she was holding against her breasts into its father's face as though she meant to compare the two, and immediately, to her own abysmal disgust, burst into tears.

"Grace!" Jim said.

Rosa, of course, didn't say anything. She just sat there like a statue of brown granite, which was all to the good, because Jim and Grace were able to talk things out just as though she weren't there, and in English, a language as incomprehensible to Rosa as Tluscolan was to them.

"Where *were* you all day, Jim Rush?" Grace said furiously. "Visiting the *rest* of them? The ones I don't even know about yet?"

He said softly, sadly:

"I was—at the cemetery, Grace."

"*All* day?" she said.

"All day," he said. And then she saw his eyes. They were red streaked. Swollen almost shut. She said:

"Oh!"

"Tomás recommended a stone cutter. I had him set up—rather than build, a little mausoleum. One of several models he keeps to show clients. I paid him a little extra so he'd set that one up and I shouldn't have to wait for him to carve a new one. It was simply a matter of assembling it, that was all. So I waited, and watched him do it. It's—nice. Black marble. There's a—seated angel—watching, listening. The angel's face is—rather like—hers. That's why I wanted it—wanted this particular one, I mean. I was afraid he might not—capture—that expression of—of brooding tenderness again . . ."

"Oh!" Grace got out, a high, tight, strangled sound.

"I also arranged—an annual payment to a local florist. Forever. Fresh flowers, daily. Which means as long as my estate lasts—and the florist stays in business, I suppose . . ."

"Jim—" Grace said.

"Yes, my dear?"

"Am I—going to have a—dead woman's ghost—between me—and my husband—in my bed—for the rest of my life?"

He looked at her; said:

"And—her child—as now, in your arms, for a good many years to come. It's—up to you, Grace. And it's—not too late. Maybe you'd better think about it. Decide—"

She said:

"You think I—have any choice in the matter, Jim? There's only one alternative to a life with you for me, now. The one I was trying to get Joe Harper to provide me—gratis. So I—wouldn't have had to—to do it—myself—"

"Grace—" he said reproachfully.

"Forgive me, Jim," she whispered. "I—I needed you here. And—and you took so long!"

He came over to her, kissed her, said:

"Sorry, my dear." Then: "But—you'll just have to let me keep this memory. It's—a good one, Grace . . ."

"I know. *She* was extraordinary. Extraordinarily good *for* you. She's left you—a far better—human being, Jim. So I have absolutely no objections, Darling. And if I did, fat lot of good they'd do me! Look at her, Jim. D'you know what: She laughed! She actually laughed! Oh, Jim, let's keep her life filled with it! With—laughter, I mean. With joy. And—"

He smiled at her. It was, she thought, *the* most peaceful smile ever seen upon a human face. He said:

"I don't know why, Grace, but I honestly believe that we're going to be all right—*really* all right, you and I—"

She laughed—for the first time in a good many weeks, now. It was a warm, soft, purring sound.

"Yes. You and I and Trinita and—and—Jim, what was that name she had reserved for the baby if it had been a boy?"

"Jaimito," Jim said.

"Hy—mee—toh! Exactly. But spelled J-a-i-m-i-t-o, right? Jaimito, little Jim. *And* Jaimito and little Grace and—"

"Grace—" he said.

"Yes, Jim?"

"I'm—an Old Party. A very Old Party. A Senior Citizen. Still a *little* unsanitary, I'll admit, but—"

"And I," she said sadly, "have—maybe five years left, or six. Before it will become impossible. Jim—please?"

"Please what, my dear?"

"Please, let's give the matter—our undivided attention, Darling, shall we? Being an only child wouldn't be good for Trinita. It isn't good for anyone. I know, because *I* was one."

"Me, too," he said. "Oh, hell, we'll just have to stay out of supermarkets, that's all!"

"Supermarkets?" she said; then she remembered. "I said that, didn't I? A big fat stupid remark about how silly you, I, and a gaggle of kids like an inverted staircase would look trooping through a supermarket. And thereby wasted a whole precious year and a half—that neither of us had to waste. No, it's actually close to two, isn't it? I'll never forgive myself for that . . ."

"You were right," he said. "We're going to look as funny as hell. You up *there,* and me down *here,* and the kids—except Trinita, of course, who simply has no possibility of growing tall—ranging from you down to me, but all of them taller than I am, you can bet on that—"

"Jim—" she drawled; "I've got that problem solved."

"Solved how?"

"I'll dress you in short pants. Hand you a lollipop. Mix you in with the bunch."

He stood there lost, rapt, contemplating that picture. Grinned, very slowly.

"Ohhhhhhhh, God! Let me out of here!" he said.